THE GOLDEN AGE
OF
FOLK AND FAIRY TALES

FROM THE BROTHERS GRIMM
TO ANDREW LANG

D1572343

THE GOLDEN AGE
OF
FOLK AND FAIRY TALES

FROM THE BROTHERS GRIMM
TO ANDREW LANG

*Edited, with Introduction
and Translations, by*

Jack Zipes

Hackett Publishing Company, Inc.
Indianapolis/Cambridge

Copyright © 2013 by Hackett Publishing Company, Inc.

16 15 14 13   1 2 3 4 5 6 7

For further information, please address
Hackett Publishing Company, Inc.
P.O. Box 44937
Indianapolis, Indiana 46244-0937

www.hackettpublishing.com

Cover design by Elizabeth L. Wilson
Cover illustration by Elena Arévalo Melville
Interior design by Elizabeth L. Wilson
Composition by Aptara, Inc.

The 1857 versions of tales from the Brothers Grimm that appear in this edition are modified translations of those that appear in *The Complete Tales of the Brothers Grimm*, translated, with an Introduction, by Jack Zipes, translation copyright © 1987 by Jack Zipes. Used by permission of Bantam Books, a Division of Random House, Inc.

Library of Congress Cataloging-in-Publication Data

The golden age of folk and fairy tales : from the Brothers Grimm to Andrew Lang / edited, with introduction and translations by Jack Zipes.
      pages cm
  Includes bibliographical references.
  ISBN 978-1-62466-032-0 (pbk.) — ISBN 978-1-62466-033-7 (cloth)
  1. Fairy tales—History and criticism. 2. Folk literature—History and criticism.
  I. Zipes, Jack, 1937–
  GR550.G58 2013
  398.209—dc23   2013015440

∞

CONTENTS

LIST OF ILLUSTRATORS

1. Brotherly Love: Anastasiya Rudaya
2. The Power of Love: Esther Cooper-Wood
3. Facing Fear: Julia Konieczna
4. Abandoned Children: Irene Bulleid
5. Dangerous Wolves and Naive Girls: Juliet Docherty
6. The Fruitful Sleep: Poppy Skelley
7. The Beast as Bridegroom: Simona Ciraolo
8. Cursed Princes and Sweet Rewards: Jin Cho Youn
9. The Fate of Spinning: Victoria Turnbull
10. The Revenge and Reward of Neglected Daughters: Dylan Giles
11. Incestuous Fathers and Sons: Josephine Birch
12. Wild and Golden Men: Melissa Castrillon
13. Extraordinary Heroes: Gemma O'Callaghan
14. Shrewd Cats and Foxes: Catherine Rowe
15. The Wishes of Fools: Jason Hibbs
16. Evil Stepmothers and Magic Mirrors: Angharad Burnard
17. The Taming of Shrews: Ania Stypulkowski
18. Bloodthirsty Husbands and Serial Killers: Elena Arévalo Melville

To Mick Gowar,
       in gratitude for his generosity and friendship,

and

To Martin Salisbury, Chris Draper, and Pam Smy,
       whose expertise and advice have been exceptional

ACKNOWLEDGMENTS

This book was born out of a chance encounter with Deborah Wilkes at a Modern Language Association Meeting some three years ago. As I strolled through the book stalls at the MLA, I began a conversation with her at the Hackett booth about my plan to publish nineteenth-century folk and fairy tales, and Deborah expressed a strong interest in my project. Before I knew it, I had signed a contract with Hackett Publishing that led to the publication of the present anthology. Throughout the process of preparing the tales for publication, Deborah has been the guiding spirit and has provided me with great advice and support. Liz Wilson has done a superb job in carefully overseeing the entire production of the book and working on all aspects of a complex undertaking. Leslie Connor has helped me enormously by correcting numerous errors and gaps in the copyediting of the book, and I am most grateful for all her suggestions.

While preparing to spend several months in Cambridge at Anglia Ruskin University on a Leverhulme Fellowship in September of 2012, I had the great fortune of encountering Martin Salisbury, Chris Draper, and Pam Smy who are the leading instructors of illustration for children's books at the School of Art. I should like to express my gratitude to the Leverhulme Trust for granting me the fellowship that brought me together with Martin, Chris, and Pam, and to Anglia Ruskin University for enabling me to collaborate with them and their students. At one point, I proposed to Martin, Pam, and Chris that I would very much like to have my forthcoming anthology of folk and fairy tales illustrated, and they offered the assistance of their talented MA and BA students and some alumni. Martin took charge of eighteen young illustrators who were assigned tale types to interpret and to illustrate under the guidance of Chris and Pam as well as Martin. I am greatly in their debt, especially to Martin, who was particularly judicious in providing advice not only to the illustrators but to me as well, and I also want to express my thanks to all the illustrators: Irene Bulleid, Josephine Birch, Angharad Burnard, Melissa Castrillon, Simona Ciraolo, Esther Cooper-Wood, Juliet Docherty, Dylan Giles, Jason Hibbs, Julia Konieczna, Elena Arévalo Melville, Gemma O'Callaghan, Catherine Rowe, Anastasiya Rudaya, Poppy Skelley, Ania Stypulkowski, Victoria Turnbull, and Jin Cho Youn. Their exceptional artwork speaks for itself.

Finally, I want to acknowledge my "debt" to several friends and colleagues who either sent me important information about the tales in this anthology or read and made corrections of parts of the manuscript. A sincere thanks to Wolfgang Mieder, David Hopkin, Hans-Jörg Uther, and Ulrich Marzolph. Finally, I want to add that certain people have rekindled my interest in folklore and fairy tales during the past three years when I thought I had retired from working in the field. Therefore, I would be amiss if I did not mention the support of Cristina Bacchilega, Don Haase, Pauline Greenhill, and Bill Gray. Lastly, I cannot thank Mick Gowar enough for his hospitality and help in Cambridge and, therefore, I am dedicating this book to him and to Martin, Chris, and Pam.

INTRODUCTION

The Golden Key to Folk and Fairy Tales: Unlocking Cultural Treasures

At the end of each of the seven editions of the Grimms' *Children's and Household Tales* (*Kinder- und Hausmärchen*), published from 1812 to 1857, the last tale was always "The Golden Key." Short and somewhat mysterious, the story concerns a poor boy who goes into the forest during a cold winter's night to search for firewood. After he collects enough wood, he discovers a small golden key and thinks to himself, 'where there's a key, there must be a casket.' Indeed, he finds a golden casket, sticks the key into the keyhole, and is about to open it when the narrator states: "Now we must wait until he unlocks the casket completely and lifts the cover. That's when we'll learn what wonderful things he found."[1]

This ending indicates just how aware the Grimms were about the never-ending process of storytelling and collecting folk tales from the very beginning of their work with folklore. They knew there was a rich abundance of stories which they had yet to discover and which other people should also seek. There would always be golden caskets of buried stories. Throughout their lives, the Grimms had encouraged friends, colleagues, and strangers to gather and share tales that emanated from an oral tradition, and by the time that they had stopped, they had fully realized the profound and prophetic quality of their simple last tale. In fact, they had opened the golden casket so wide that thousands if not hundreds of thousands of wonderful folk tales came pouring out into books throughout Europe, and they have kept coming. The Grimms had looked and found the right key.

In the centuries before the Grimms produced *Children's and Household Tales*, the literate people of Europe had generally ignored or looked down upon the stories of the common people though, ironically, these were the tales with which they had also been raised. It was not until the end of the eighteenth century and beginning of the nineteenth century when nation-states were being formed, that attitudes toward history and national identity changed and led to a "romantic" rediscovery of fairy tales and other short genres such as animal stories, legends, humorous anecdotes, riddles, witch and ghost stories, and so on. For many German romantic writers, whom the Grimms knew, there was a tendency to idealize the past. They believed, like the great poet Novalis and the fabulous writer

---

1. *The Complete Fairy Tales of the Brothers Grimm*, ed. and trans. Jack Zipes, 3rd rev. ed. (New York: Bantam, 2002), 582.

E. T. A. Hoffmann, that the essence of the golden age could only be found through the fairy tale. To a certain extent there was something utopian and romantic in the quest of pioneer European folklorists who began seeking to understand and redefine their present through collecting "common" tales of the past that became cultural treasures.

This is the reason why I consider the period from 1812 to 1912 the golden age of folk and fairy tales. It was during this period that hundreds of educated European collectors, who called themselves at first antiquarians, philologists, traditionalists, and later folklorists, began taking an intense interest in the tales of the folk that included people from all social classes, and gathering all sorts of oral stories, writing them down, and publishing them so that they would not perish. Moreover, they thought that these tales would strengthen communal and national ties.

The Grimms were not the first scholars to turn their attention to folk tales, which they considered gems of German culture, relics that needed preservation. But they played a significant part in a widespread cultural trend and set high standards for collecting folk tales that marked the work of most European and American folklorists up through the twentieth century. In fact, their long-term, scholarly investigation of narratives from all parts of Europe was a direct or indirect inspiration for philologists, collectors, and translators of tales. At one point in his foreword to the anthology *Folktales of Germany* (1966), notable American folklorist Richard Dorson remarked how the Grimms had exercised a great influence on early antiquarians and writers in Great Britain and then added:

> As with Britain, so with the countries on the continent. The brothers corresponded with, encouraged, stimulated, admired, and were admired by collectors from France to Russia and from Norway to Hungary. Their links with the giants who followed them are direct and clear. They exchanged letters with Asbjørnsen and Moe in Norway, with Emmanuel Cosquin in France, with Vuk Karadzic in Serbia, with Elias Lönnrot in Finland—all hallowed figures performing Grimm-like services for their countries. Aleksandr Nikolaevic Afanas'ev, called the "Wilhelm Grimm of Russia," lavishly praised the *Volksmärchen* of the brothers as a model for presenting the folk literature of his own country. As a result of the Grimms' prodigious and timely influence, scholars in one country after another utilized folklore as a vehicle to promote a national language, literature, history, and mythology.[2]

Of course, the Grimms' enormous productivity—they published other collections of tales and legends as well as numerous philological studies—was not

2. Richard Dorson, foreword to *Folktales of Germany*, ed. Kurt Ranke and trans. Lotte Baumann (Chicago: University of Chicago Press, 1966), xiii.

the only driving force that gave rise to the golden age of folk and fairy tales in Europe. There were such other factors as the rise of nationalism, the increase of literacy, the expansion of universities, the formation of folklore societies, and the recognition of folklore as an intellectual discipline. It is because the Grimms played such a pivotal and unusual contradictory role in the evolution of European folklore, and to a certain extent in American folklore, that I want to discuss their purpose in collecting tales before I provide an overview of the tales gathered by other European folklorists in this anthology and why and how I have framed the present collection.

The Grimm Factor

Let us begin with some observations that will place the Grimms' first edition of 1812/1815 in a sociohistorical context and that will shed light on how and why they "betrayed" their original idealistic intentions and how they, nevertheless, animated other European folklorists to fulfill them.

When Jacob (1785–1863) and Wilhelm (1786–1859) began collecting all kinds of folk tales and songs at the beginning of the nineteenth century, they were precocious students at the University of Marburg, *still in their teens.* By 1805 their entire family had moved from the small village of Hanau to the nearby provincial city of Kassel, and the Brothers were constantly plagued by money problems and concerns about their siblings. Their father had been dead for some years, and they were about to lose their mother. Their situation was further aggravated by the rampant Napoleonic Wars. Jacob interrupted his studies to serve the Hessian War Commission in 1806. Meanwhile, Wilhelm passed his law exams, enabling him to become a civil servant and to find work as a librarian in the royal library in Kassel with a meager salary. In 1807 Jacob lost his position with the War Commission, when the French occupied Kassel. Soon thereafter he was fortunate to find a position as a librarian for King Jérome, Napoleon's brother, who now ruled Westphalia. Amidst all the upheavals, their mother died in 1808, and Jacob and Wilhelm assumed full responsibility for their three younger brothers and sister. Despite the loss of their mother and difficult personal and financial circumstances from 1805 to 1812, the Brothers managed to prove themselves to be innovative scholars in the new field of German philology by publishing articles and books on medieval literature. Still in their twenties, they were about to launch the collection of tales that was to become second in popularity to the Bible throughout Germany and by the twentieth century throughout the Western world.

What fascinated or compelled the Grimms to concentrate on old German literature was a belief that the most natural and pure forms of culture—those which held communities together—were linguistic and were to be located in the past. Moreover, according to them, modern literature, even though it might be remarkably rich, was artificial and thus could not express the genuine essence of *volk* culture that emanated naturally from people's experiences and customs and bound them together. Therefore, all their energies were spent on uncovering stories from the past and understanding the meaning of words. This is why their friend, the romantic poet Clemens Brentano, asked them in 1808 to help him by collecting all types of folk tales that he needed for a book of literary fairy tales. That is, he was planning to rework and revise folk tales from an oral tradition. Accordingly, in 1810 the Brothers sent him fifty-four texts that they had fortunately copied. Fortunately, I say, because Brentano proceeded to lose the manuscript in the Ölenberg monastery in Alsace and did not use the Grimms' texts. Meanwhile the Grimms continued to collect tales from friends, acquaintances, and colleagues. When they realized that Brentano was not going to use the tales from their manuscript, they decided, on the advice of Achim von Arnim, a mutual friend and romantic author, to publish their collection, which had grown to approximately eighty-six tales, in 1812 and then another seventy tales, which they published in 1815. These two books formed the first edition of *Kinder- und Hausmärchen* and included footnotes to the tales as well as scholarly prefaces.

Although the young Grimms had not entirely formalized their concept of folklore while they worked on the publication of the first edition, and even though there were some differences between Jacob and Wilhelm, who later was to favor more drastic poetical editing of the collected tales, they basically held to their original principle: to salvage relics from the past. Broadly speaking, the Grimms sought to preserve all kinds of ancient relics as if they were sacred and precious gems that originated naturally from the soil. In their minds, the tales, myths, songs, fables, legends, epics, riddles, and other narratives that emanated from the voices of the common people contained deeper meanings than so-called educated people realized. They intended to trace and grasp the essence of cultural evolution and to demonstrate how natural language, stemming from the needs, customs, and rituals of the common people, created authentic social relations and helped forge civilized communities. This is one of the reasons why they called their collection of tales an educational manual (*Erziehungsbuch*), for the tales recalled the basic values of the Germanic peoples and also other European groups and enlightened people about their experiences through storytelling. Remarkably, the Grimms at a young age wanted to bequeath the profound oral tales of the folk to the German people not realizing that they were about to bequeath unusually striking tales to people of many different ethnic backgrounds, and that these tales assumed relevance in all cultures while also revealing particular regional belief systems. To understand the role that the tales played in their bequest to Western civilization if not the world, we must bear in mind what they stated in the preface of the first edition:

It was perhaps just the right time to record these tales since those people who should be preserving them are becoming more and more scarce. (Of course, those who still know them know a great deal, but people die away while the tales persist.) . . . Wherever tales still exist, they continue to live in a way that nobody contemplates whether they are good or bad, poetic or crude. One knows them, and one loves them because they have been absorbed in a habitual way. And one takes pleasure in them without having any reason. This is why the custom of storytelling is so splendid, and this is what this art [Poesie] has in common with everything immortal: one is disposed to like it despite the opinions of others.[3]

The Grimms celebrated and argued for the necessity of storytelling and the significance of natural poesy, which is to be understood as the authentic literature of people that springs divinely from natural existence. They believed that the tales and all their variants were distinctive and kept cultural traditions alive in every region of Europe. They respected difference and diversity, and at the same time they argued: "We wanted not merely to serve the history of Poesie [the tales] with our collection. It was our intention at the same time to bring out the living aspect in these tales so that it has an effect and can provide pleasure for whomever it could, and consequently the tales could become an actual educational manual."[4]

Although some other German collections of folk and fairy tales had preceded the Grimms' *Kinder- und Hausmärchen*, none were as diverse because the Brothers' cooperative and collective spirit spurred them to embrace all kinds of tales from German-speaking principalities. As early as 1811, Jacob even composed an appeal, "Aufforderung an die gesammten Freunde altdeutscher Poesie und Geschichte erlassen" ("Appeal to All Friends of Old German Poetry and History"), which was never sent but laid the groundwork for his later, more fully developed *Circular wegen der Aufsammlung der Volkspoesie* (*Circular-Letter Concerned with Collecting of Folk Poetry*) printed and distributed to scholars and friends in 1815. It is worth citing the initial part of this letter because it outlines the basic principles and intentions of the Grimms:

Most Honored Sir!
    A society has been founded that is intended to spread throughout all of Germany and has as its goal to save and collect all the existing songs and tales that can be found among the common German peasantry (*Landvolk*). Our fatherland is still filled with this wealth of material all over the country that our honest ancestors planted for us, and that, despite the mockery and derision heaped upon it, continues to

---

3. Brüder Grimm, "Vorrede," *Kinder- und Hausmärchen: Vergrößerter Nachdruck der zweibändigen Erstausgabe von 1812 und 1815*, ed. Heinz Rölleke (Göttingen: Vandenhoeck & Ruprecht, 1986), 1:vii.
4. Ibid., "Vorrede," 2:v.

live, unaware of its own hidden beauty and carries within it its own unquenchable source. Our literature, history, and language cannot seriously be understood in their old and true origins without doing more exact research on this material. Consequently, it is our intention to track down as diligently as possible all the following items and to write them down as faithfully as possible:

1. Folk songs and rhymes that are performed at different occasions throughout the year, at celebrations, in spinning parlors, on the dance floors, and during work in the fields; first of all, those songs and rhymes that have epic contents, that is, in which there is an event; wherever possible with their very ways, and tones.

2. Tales in prose that are told and known, in particular the numerous nursery and children's fairy tales about giants, dwarfs, monsters, enchanted and rescued royal children, devils, treasures, and magic instruments as well as local legends that help explain certain places (like mountains, rivers, lakes, swamps, ruined castles, towers, stories, and monuments of ancient times). It is important to pay special attention to animal fables, in which fox and wolf, chicken, dog, cat, frog, mouse, crow, sparrow, etc., appear for the most part.

3. Funny tales about tricks played by rogues and anecdotes; puppet plays from old times with Hanswurst[5] and the devil.

4. Folk festivals, mores, customs, and games; celebrations at births, weddings, and funerals; old legal customs, special taxes, duties, jobs, border regulations, etc.

5. Superstitions about spirits, ghosts, witches, good and bad omens, phenomena and dreams.

6. Proverbs, unusual dialects, parables, word composition.

It is extremely important that these items are to be recorded faithfully and truly, without embellishment and additions, whenever possible from the mouth of the tellers in and with their very own words in the most exact and detailed way. It would be of double value if everything could be obtained in the local live dialect. On the other hand, even fragments with gaps are not to be rejected. Indeed, all the derivations, repetitions, and copies of the same tale can be individually important. . . . Here we advise that you not be misled by the deceptive opinion that something has already been collected and recorded, and therefore that you discard a story. Many things that appear to be modern have often only been modernized and has their undamaged source beneath it. As soon as one has a great familiarity with the contents of this folk literature (*Volkspoesie*), one will gradually be able

---

5.   Hanswurst was a popular character who began appearing in books and plays of the sixteenth and seventeenth centuries. Generally considered a fool and country bumpkin, he could also be cunning and malicious. He was often featured in plays and puppet shows performed in country fairs and in vaudeville, and even today, Hanswurst is a popular cultural figure.

to evaluate the alleged simplistic, crude, and even repulsive aspects more discreetly.[6]

This circular letter along with the first edition of *Kinder- und Hausmärchen* went on to inspire numerous German, Austrian, and Swiss folklorists to begin collecting tales, and gradually the Grimms' example and translations of their editions stimulated folklorists throughout Europe and Great Britain to collect and preserve oral folk tales. If any of the editions that the Grimms published best represented their intentions and the ideals that they kept reiterating until 1857, it was their first edition because the Brothers did not hone the stories the way they refined the tales in later editions. In fact, you can hear the distinctive voices of the storytellers from whom they received the tales for their initial project, and to this extent, the tales in the first edition, some in German dialect, are more "authentic" folk tales and have more integrity to them despite the fact that they are not as aesthetically pleasing as those in later revised versions. In other words, the Grimms let the tales speak for themselves in a very blunt if not awkward manner that lends them a sense of unvarnished truth or the educational value that the Grimms sought.

In the first edition of 1812/1815 the Brothers relied on all sorts of people who either told folk tales to them or wrote them down as they themselves had heard them. All these tales were stamped by the region in which the storytellers lived, the gender of the storyteller, his or her social class, and the source of the tale that could be another storyteller or a book. For instance, there was a group of middle-class young women in Kassel consisting of Marie Hassenpflug, Jeanette Hassenpflug, Margarete Wild, Marie Wild, Dorothea Wild, and other members of these families, who provided over twenty stories. They were all well-educated and familiar with French fairy tales, and they also had nannies and servants who told them stories. Nearby, in Allendorf, Friederike Mannel, a minister's daughter, was a talented storyteller and writer, who sent several unusual tales to Wilhelm. Then there were the members of the aristocratic von Haxthausen family and the poet Jenny von Droste-Hülshof, who contributed a good number of stories, some of which they heard from peasants in the region of Münster. The consummate storyteller was Dorothea Viehmann, a tailor's wife, who lived near Kassel and told them about forty tales. The Grimms portrayed her as the exemplary peasant storyteller. Yet, she had grown up in an inn, and her family originated in the Netherlands so that her repertoire of tales was somewhat international. Another important contributor was the retired soldier Johann Friedrich Krause, who exchanged seven tales for a gift of pants leggings. Aside from collecting oral tales, the Grimms were familiar with all the major European collections of folk and fairy tales and adapted many of the narratives from other books. They knew the Ital-

---

6. Jacob Grimm, *Circular wegen Aufsammlung der Volkspoesie*, ed. Ludwig Denecke (Kassel: Brüder-Grimm Museum, 1968), 3–4.

ian works of Giovan Francesco Straparola and Giambattista Basile and the French collections of Charles Perrault, Mme Catherine d'Aulnoy, Mlle de La Force, Mme L'Héritier, and others. Moreover, they transcribed tales from such authors as Johannes Praetorius (*Der abentheurliche Glücks-Topf*, 1668), Johann August Musäus (*Volksmährchen der Deutschen*, 1782), and other authors and collectors. Even though the Grimms were comparatively young when they began collecting tales and writing annotations, they were erudite and quite knowledgeable. Consequently, the first edition of *Kinder- und Hausmärchen* is a marvelous mix of diverse voices and tales conveyed by peasants, craftsmen, middle-class women, and aristocrats. Moreover, it included important references. As Heinz Rölleke, the foremost German scholar of the Grimms' tales, has explained in a recent book, *Es war einmal . . . Die wahren Märchen der Brüder Grimm und wer sie ihnen erzählte* (2011), the tales in the first edition tend to be more raw and authentic than the tales that were published in later editions because the Grimms did not make vast changes. These tales are fascinating because they bear the imprint of their informants and are largely unknown to the general public. To grasp the historical significance of these first-edition tales, Rölleke maintains that it is important to know something about the background of the informants and sources as well as the sociocultural context in which they were gathered.[7]

Indeed, Rölleke has provided much of this information in his book, and for our purposes it is sufficient to note that the tales reveal the concerns of the informants and their wishes. For instance, many of the tales depict young protagonists in conflict with their parents, children brutally treated and abandoned, soldiers in need, young women persecuted, sibling rivalry, exploitation and oppression of young people, dangerous predators, and spiteful kings and queens abusing their power. While many of these tales were a few hundred years old before they were gathered and told by the Grimms' informants, they bear the personal and peculiar marks of the storytellers who kept them in their memory for a purpose. Despite the unusually different styles of each of the tales—and some were told and written down in dialect—they are all notable because of their terse and frank qualities. These tales were not told for children, nor can they be considered truly children's tales, though children heard or perhaps read them. The Grimms called them "children's tales" because they emitted a certain truthful innocence. They are also more folk than fairy tales and bespeak truths. Moreover, there is a wide spectrum of tale types and genres in the first edition of 1812/1815—fables, legends, jokes, farces, animal stories, and anecdotes—that are connected to events of the times and the personal experiences of the tellers. The description is bare; the dialogue, curt; and the action, swift.

---

7.   See Heinz Rölleke, ed., "Wie die Märchen zu den Brüdern Grimm gelangten," in *Es war einmal . . . Die wahren Märchen der Brüder Grimm und wer sie ihnen erzählte*, illustr. Albert Schindehütte (Frankfurt am Main: Eichborn, 2011), 31–52.

The storytellers get to the point quickly, and there is generally a fulfillment of social justice or naive morality at the end. What is justly fulfilled in all these tales was certainly lacking in the reality of the time they were told and is still lacking today.

Some of these tales continued to be printed in the following six editions of *Kinder- und Hausmärchen*, but in much different versions and often with different titles. Others were completely deleted or were relegated to the scholarly notes. There were eleven tales in different dialects, and only six remained by 1857. It is difficult to explain why the Grimms made all these deletions and changes because the reasons were different or unknown. For instance, tales like "How Some Children Played at Slaughtering" ("Wie Kinder Schlachtens mit einander spielten") and "The Children of Famine" ("Die Kinder in Hungersnoth") were omitted because they were gruesome. "Bluebeard" ("Blaubart"), "Puss in Boots" ("Der gestiefelte Kater"), and "Okerlo" ("Der Okerlo") were not reprinted because they stemmed from the French literary tradition. The same is true for "Simple Hans" ("Hans Dumm") because of its Italian origins. Some tales like "Good Bowling and Card Playing" ("Gut Kegel- und Kartenspiel"), "Herr Fix-It-Up" ("Herr Fix und Fertig,"), "Prince Swan" ("Prinz Schwann"), and "The Devil Green Coat" ("Der Teufel Grünrock") were simply replaced by other stories in later editions because the Grimms found other versions that they preferred, or they combined different versions to form a new tale. The changes made by the Grimms indicate their ideological and artistic preferences. For instance, in the 1812/1815 edition of "Snow White" ("Sneewittchen") and "Hansel and Gretel" ("Hänsel und Grethel") the wicked stepmothers were actually biological mothers, but these characters were changed in 1819 clearly because the Grimms held motherhood sacred, or because they wanted to reflect circumstances in their times when women died early due to bearing too many children and were replaced by young stepmothers, often jealous of girls almost their age. In another example, the 1812 version of "Rapunzel" is a very short provocative tale in which the young girl gets pregnant. The 1819 version is longer, much more sentimental, and without a hint of a pregnancy.

In many respects the tales in the Grimms' first edition read like startling "new" tales that are closer to traditional oral storytelling than the final collection of 210 tales in the 1857 edition. This is not to minimize or discredit the changes that the Grimms made, but to insist that the contradictory history of the Grimms' tales needs to be known fully to comprehend the influence and accomplishments of the Grimms as folklorists.

Idealistic Principles and Contradictions of the Grimm Factor

What is fascinating about the Grimms' principles of collecting and publishing folk tales is the contradictory manner in which they edited and published them. In fact, it is tempting to call the Brothers frauds because they did not live up to their own standards and to a certain extent deceived the reading public by idealizing the folk and perpetuating certain myths about their informants such as Dorothea Viehmann, pictured as the genuine peasant storyteller, and their own involvement in "tampering" with the tales that they collected. Thirty years ago, John Ellis accused the Grimms of duplicity and of purposely misleading scholars about the origins and contents of their collection,[8] while other critics, who have written about their contradictions, have explained that the Grimms' "faults" were due more to their idealism, enthusiasm, and desire to promote the study of folklore than to conceal their exaggerations or lies. After all, the folk tales, artifacts, and customs of the majority of the people had been neglected for centuries, and the Grimms often overcompensated for this neglect. At the same time they were meticulous philologists and ethical researchers who did not conceal their "questionable" methods or findings from a reading public. What became clear to them, after Jacob Grimm had sent out his 1815 Circular, was that they would have to make compromises in editing the tales of their own collection while still promulgating idealistic standards that, they believed, would benefit other folklorists. Here are some points to bear in mind:

1. After the publication of the 156 tales of the first edition in 1812 and 1815 with footnotes, the Grimms realized that they themselves would not be able to record folk tales faithfully and truly from the mouths of the tellers in the most exact and detailed way and in dialect if possible. They would have to hone and embellish the tales. They had already relied on friends and colleagues who had sought to record dialect tales, and they, too, had minimally written down tales after hearing them. But they realized that their work as librarians and later as professors and researchers would not permit them to travel and spend extensive time to do field work. The Grimms were more mediators than actual collectors of tales.

2. Some time after 1815, Wilhelm was placed in charge of editing the *Kinder- und Hausmärchen.* Up to that point the Brothers had shared the collecting and editing. This did not mean that Wilhelm single-handedly was responsible for everything, especially since Jacob was the dominant brother and since they sat at desks right across from each other their entire lives. They constantly consulted with one another. Moreover, Jacob received tales sent by friends or found them in his research. So there can be no doubt that Wilhelm continued to collaborate with Jacob while he undertook the major task of editing the six editions that followed the first. One thing is clear: their models for making revisions were the dialect tales. They favored "authentic" oral storytelling.

3. While Jacob was not happy about changing the tales that they had published or making any changes to new tales, he realized that so long as they retained

---

8.   See John Ellis, *One Fairy Story Too Many: The Brothers Grimm and Their Tales* (Chicago: University of Chicago Press, 1983).

the basics or essence of the tales they gathered, they should also be allowed to make the tales more effective by translating dialect tales, improving description, adding religious sentiments, and changing gender roles and characters to befit the realities of their day. Moreover, as both Wilhelm and Jacob began finding and receiving so many variants of the tales they published, they came to understand that they could never find a definitive folk tale, and that each tale type was mutable and called out for even more changes once it was disseminated, that is, heard or read. Likewise, they realized that, though the tales might have been collected in German-speaking regions, they could be found throughout Europe and could also be traced to Asia and Africa. Simply put, they became aware that there was no such thing as a pure Germanic tale.

4. The older and more experienced the Grimms became—we must remember that they began collecting while they were in their late teens—the more they felt confident in combining different variants of the same tale type either to strengthen a tale in their collection or to replace it with a new more appropriate version. In addition, they added essays, elaborated their footnotes with new information, and provided space for religious tales. Though they did not alter their tales to please children, they did delete some of the more ghastly tales about children and fragments that made no sense, and in 1825 they created a small edition (*Kleine Ausgabe*) of 50 tales selected from the large edition, which amounted to 210 by 1857. The small edition was intended to please bourgeois families and their tastes and went through ten printings. Altogether, there were seventeen editions of the Grimms' tales that circulated in German-speaking regions of Europe.

5. Even in the very last edition of 1857, the Grimms barely changed the claims they made in their early preface of 1819. Instead, about forty years later, in the last preface, they basically reaffirmed and clarified their claims:

> In regard to the manner in which we have collected, faithfulness and truth are what counted most of all for us. To be precise, we did not add anything from our own means and did not embellish any circumstance or feature of the story itself. Rather, we reproduced the contents just as we received them. It is self-evident that the exposition of the individual details stems from us. However, we have endeavored to retain every peculiar characteristic that we noticed in order also to allow for the diversity of nature with regard to the collection. Whoever takes on similar work will, by the way, understand that this cannot be called a careless and thoughtless approach. On the contrary, attentiveness and tact are necessary, and they can only be acquired with time in order to distinguish the simple, more pure and yet in and of itself more complete characteristics from the adulterated elements.[9]

---

9. Brüder Grimm, "Vorrede," *Kinder- und Hausmärchen: Ausgabe letzter Hand mit den Originalanmerkungen der Brüder Grimm*, ed. Heinz Rölleke (Stuttgart: Philipp Reclam, 1980), 1:21–22.

The Grimms thought that the "slight" changes they made in the tales did not make much of a difference, but rather helped to preserve the narratives because the Brothers had become such experts in the field of folklore. Due to their extensive work as philologists, they firmly believed that they could cobble variants together to bring out the profound essence of the tales and that their footnotes and essays in a separate volume provided evidence that endorsed their viewpoint. Yet, the Grimms were somewhat ingenuous in thinking that their changes did not alter the meanings of the tales, and that their high German could simulate the dialects and reinvigorate the blunt and colorful styles of diverse storytellers. One need only read and compare the 1812/1815 and 1819 versions with the 1857 versions that I have reproduced in this anthology to grasp the immense diversity of styles and contents. For example, it makes a huge difference if Snow White's biological mother, rather than a stepmother, is seeking to kill her daughter. It also makes a difference when children turn to the Christian God for help when there was no god to help them in another version of the same tale. And it is an important change when a fairy is transformed into a sorceress. In short, the Grimms could have defended their position on better grounds if they had explained that each time they retold or rewrote one of their versions, they were actually telling a "new" tale rooted in a tradition of storytelling from a specific region of Germany or Europe. That is, their major accomplishment as collectors was the rejuvenation and reinvigoration of the oral storytelling tradition through print. Each reprint or revised edition of their collection requires a close look at tales that have essentially been rewritten and retold. Moreover, the tales that have been added to the collection need to be recognized and studied.

Aside from being brilliant philologists, the Grimms were highly gifted writers—not just Wilhelm, but both brothers. For example, we must remember that the Grimms published two volumes of 585 German legends in 1816 and 1818[10] that they had collected and rewrote at the same time they were working on the *Kinder- und Hausmärchen*. Although not as famous as the folk tales, the legends evince the Grimms' great skill as writers and translators as well as their immense erudition with regard to different genres of storytelling. In 1826 they published *Irische Elfenmärchen*, a translation of Thomas Crofton Croker's *Fairy Legends and Traditions of the South of Ireland* (1825), which also attests to the Grimms' talents as writers able to grasp the Irish colloquial language and make the Irish tales accessible to German readers. The versatility and originality of the Grimms as folklorists are impressive. Indeed, their fame among folk-tale collectors spread rapidly throughout Europe and Great Britain during the nineteenth century. Although part of their fame was based on "myths" about the Grimms as intrepid folklorists who went into the fields to gather their tales

---

10.   See Brüder Grimm, eds., *Deutsche Sagen* 2 vols. (Berlin: Nicolaische Buchhandlung, 1816/1818). See also Donald Ward, ed. and trans., *The German Legends of the Brothers Grimm*, 2 vols. (Philadelphia: Institute for the Study of Human Issues, 1981).

from the lips of peasants like the allegedly authentic Dorothea Viehmann, that should not deter us from recognizing how significant the work of the Brothers was for the development of international folklore. Indeed, the partial truths about the Grimms, the numerous translations of the *Kinder- und Hausmärchen* into different European languages, the vast correspondence of the Grimms with folklorists throughout Europe, and the impact of their pioneer scholarly work contributed to the rise of the significant golden age of folk and fairy tales.

The Real and Mythic Impact of the Brothers Grimm

When Richard Dorson lauded the groundbreaking work of the Grimms in *Folktales of Germany* and discussed their prodigious influence on folklorists throughout nineteenth-century Europe, he merely touched the tip of the iceberg. The influence of the Grimms was much more profound than even he indicated, and to a certain extent, the Brothers remain highly relevant in the field of folklore to this day. Timothy Baycroft and David Hopkin present the case for the Grimms' dominant role in folklore more strongly: "It is the brothers Jacob and Wilhelm Grimm who illustrate the connection between folklore and textual criticism most powerfully, just as they demonstrate the continuing influence of Herder on romantic thought. Nationalist politics and folkloric endeavors intertwine throughout all the Grimm brothers' projects, but the Europe-wide significance of the *Kinder- und Hausmärchen* (first edition 1812) was the inspiration it provided to proto-folklorists to go out and collect 'vom Volksmund,' that is from the mouth of the people (whether or not this was the Grimms' own practice)."[11]

A good example of the breadth and depth of the Grimms' influence in the nineteenth century is the work of Johann Wilhelm Wolf (1817–1855), founder of the *Zeitschrift für Deutsche Mythologie und Sittenkunde* (*Journal for German Mythology and Customs*).[12] When and how Wolf discovered the Grimms' collections of folk tales and their philological writings on epics, folk tales, mythology, and legends is unclear. As a young boy in Cologne, he had gathered all kinds of ancient artifacts and tales. Some time during his teenage years, because of their rigid Catholicism, he fled his family and went to Belgium, where he dedicated himself to the causes of oppressed peoples and to salvaging Germanic myths and legends that derived from pagan rituals. His model for collecting and transcribing oral tales as a means to preserve community was the work of the Grimms, especially Jacob's studies of mythology and legends, and it was obvious that by the time he became a folklorist and teacher in his early thirties he had consumed

11. Timothy Baycroft and David Hopkin, eds., *Folklore and Nationalism in Europe During the Long Nineteenth Century* (Leiden: Brill, 2012), 409.

12. For more information about Wolf, see Ludig Fränkel, "Wolf, Johann Wilhelm," in *Allgemeine Deutsche Biographie (ADB)*, Vol. 43 (Leipzig: Duncker & Humboldt, 1898), 765–777.

almost every word and tale that they had written. In fact, he came to embody what the Grimms had proposed as the exemplary collector of tales: Wolf became the ideal field-worker—collecting tales, sayings, proverbs, superstitions, and artifacts directly from the mouths of the folk and writing erudite and theoretical commentaries.

Wolf's first major work, *Niederländische Sagen* (1843), was a collection of Dutch legends and tales that he had gathered while in Brussels and Ghent; it represented his endeavor to give voice to the minority Flemish people, who, he maintained, were suffering under French domination. After his return to Germany he settled first in Cologne and then Darmstadt, where he systematically collected tales from soldiers, blacksmiths, carpenters, and farmers, and published the tales in *Deutsche Märchen und Sagen* (1845) and *Deutsche Hausmärchen* (1851). Endorsing the Grimms' philosophy and approach, he believed that his collections were "educational manuals" and that the tales naturally carried within themselves moral lessons that were derived from the customs and belief systems of the common people. He was clearly a "republican" German who supported the revolutions of 1848; and he took great pleasure in meeting Jacob Grimm in Frankfurt during this period. One of his books, *Die deutsche Götterlehre. Ein Hand- und Lesebuch für Schule und Haus* (*The German Teaching of the Gods. A Handbook and Reader for the School and Home*, 1852) was intended to explain and elaborate Jacob Grimm's theories in *Deutsche Mythologie* (1835). But more important than this study was Wolf's founding of the journal *Zeitschrift für Deutsche Mythologie* in 1853. Though it lasted only four years and Wolf died after the second issue was published, this journal served briefly as one of the most central contact points for the very best German-speaking scholars in central Europe: Karl Weigand, Ignaz and Joseph Zingerle, Adalbert Kuhn, Ernst Meier, Heinrich Pröhle, Nikolaus Hocker, Wilhelm Creccelius, R. O. Waldburg, August Stöber, Karl Sinnrock, Franz Josef Vonbun, Reinhold Köhler, Wilhelm Mannhardt, Karl Ernst Hermann Krause, E. J. Reimann, Wilhelm von Ploennies, Friedrich Wöste, Heinrich Runge, and many other of the leading folklorists of this time. (Some of their tales appear in this anthology.) They contributed and commented on legends, puzzles, superstitions, nursery rhymes, children's games, folk tales, animal stories, proverbs, and myths that they had discovered in countries from France to Russia and in every region of Germany and the Hapsburg empire including Switzerland. The majority of these men did original fieldwork. Most transcribed their tales from different dialects, although some published dialect versions. What is perhaps most important is that these folklorists took great care in designating the regions in which they collected their tales. That is, their focus was on a particular region not on a nation or nation-state. Most of them also produced books and collections of stories, often with subtitles, "gathered orally from the folk" or with dedications to the Grimms.

In mid-century Europe the typical collection of tales was generally published in the standard or "high" language of the country. Therefore, any story collected orally would be transcribed or translated into a "literary" language or the dominant vernacular, and though most of the folklorists tried not to add phrases or hone their tales, they all more or less touched up the "raw" language in which they had heard the tale. Many of the tales were heard or read in one language and then written down in another. For instance, this type of transcription/translation can be seen in some of the stories in the present volume: Laura Gonzenbach's tales were told in Sicilian dialect by rural women and then written down in high German; Rachel Busk translated Roman dialect tales into English; Robert Bain and W. R. S. Ralston, Russian into English; Johann Georg von Hahn and Bernhard Schmidt, Greek into German; Wentworth Webster, Basque into English; Albert Henry Wratislaw and Jeremiah Curtin, Slavic into English. It was not until the latter part of the nineteenth century that folklorists began publishing dialect tales. Here the works of Giuseppe Pitrè, Vittorio Imbriani, François-Marie Luzel, Achille Millien, Victor Smith, and Carolina Coronedi-Berti are important. And of course, the founding and remarkable growth of folklore journals enabled folklorists to provide all kinds of source materials and essays on customs and beliefs as well as historical articles that traced the origins of the tales and their motifs. Besides Wolf's *Zeitschrift für Deutsche Mythologie und Sittenkunde*, other important journals that were founded in the latter half of the nineteenth century include *Revue Celtique* (1870), *Romania* (1872), *Alemannia* (1873), *Mélusine* (1877), *Folk-Lore Record* (1878), *Archivo per lo Studio delle Tradizioni popolari* (1882), *El Folklore Andaluz* (1882), *Revue des Traditions Populaires* (1886), *Ethnologische Mitteilungen aus Ungarn* (1887), *Journal of American Folklore* (1888), *Schweizerisches Archiv für Volkskunde* (1897).

Thanks to journals, private correspondence, and books, almost all of the leading folklorists in nineteenth-century Europe and North America were familiar with each other's works, as well as the Grimms' *Kinder- und Hausmärchen* and the Brothers' scholarly work in philology and linguistics. What is significant, however, is that most folklorists after 1850 became more precise and more thorough than the Grimms in collecting and publishing their tales; they paid more attention and respect to the tellers of the tales, the regional relevance of each tale, the linguistic peculiarities, and the significance of the tales within their sociocultural and historical contexts. It is here that the tales must be understood as part of the nationalist trends and the formation of new nation-states in the latter half of the nineteenth and early part of twentieth centuries.

Collecting folk tales was some kind of social and political act. Not only did educated middle-class collectors give voice to the lower classes, but they also spoke out in defense of their native languages and in the interests of national and regional movements that sought more autonomy for groups with very particular interests.[13] For instance, Norway separated from Denmark in 1814 and became an independent state with its own language and dialects. There was a tendency, therefore, to shake off the Danish yoke. In the 1830s and 1840s, Moe and Asbjørnsen regarded themselves as defenders of the Norwegian language and customs by collecting diverse types of folk songs, legends, and tales in dialect and transcribing them.[14] In contrast to the Grimms, Moe and Asbjørnsen traveled to different regions of Norway and inspired other collectors to write down local tales. Indeed, the collecting of such tales throughout Scandinavia had strong nationalist and regional aspects.[15] Denmark, too, manifested signs of romantic nationalism. As Reimund Kvideland points out: "The struggle against German influences in the southern boundary region created a nationalistic atmosphere in Denmark which promoted interest in folklore. Svend Grundtvig, who was working on a major publication of Danish ballads, made a public appeal for the collection of folktales."[16] In Russia, the great collector Afanas'ev also realized that his collections of tales in the 1850s and 1860s might assist the numerous ethnic groups in Russia to become more aware of the virtues of their different languages and customs.[17] Many French collectors, such as Luzel, Sébillot, Cosquin, and others, took pride in the regional traditions that they sought to keep alive, and of course, after the defeat of the French by the Prussians in 1871, there was a strong element of regionalism and nationalism that animated their collecting, whether they were liberals or conservatives.[18]

One of the more interesting examples of how politics and nationalism entered into the collecting and translating of folk tales is Walter William Strickland's work on Slavic folklore. While living in Central Europe, Strickland spent more than ten years (1896–1907) translating Karel Erben's *Sto prostonárodních pohádek a pověstí slovanských v nářečích původních* (*One Hundred Slavic Folk Tales and*

---

13. See Luisa Del Giudice and Gerald Porter, eds., *Imagined States: Nationalism, Utopia, and Longing in Oral Cultures* (Logan: Utah State University Press, 2001); Jennifer Schacker, *National Dreams: The Remaking of Fairy Tales in Nineteenth-Century England* (Philadelphia: University of Pennsylvania Press, 2003); Joep Leerssen, *National Thought in Europe: A Cultural History* (Amsterdam: Amsterdam University Press, 2006); and Baycroft and Hopkin, *Folklore and Nationalism in Europe*.

14. See Marte Hvam Hult, *Framing a National Narrative: The Legend Collections of Peter Christen Asbjørnsen* (Detroit: Wayne State University Press, 2003).

15. See Reimund Kvideland, "The Collecting and Study of Tales in Scandinavia," in *A Companion to the Fairy Tale*, eds. Hilda Ellis Davidson and Anna Chaudhri (Cambridge: D. S. Brewer, 2003), 159–68.

16. Ibid., 160.

17. See James Riordan, "Russian Fairy Tales and Their Collectors," in *A Companion to the Fairy Tale*, eds. Hilda Ellis Davidson and Anna Chaudhri (Cambridge: D. S. Brewer, 2003), 217–26. See also Tristan Landry, *La mémoire de l'oral à l'écrit: Les frères Grimm et Afanas'ev* (Saint-Nioclas: Les Presse de L'Université Laval, 2005).

18. See David Hopkin, *Voices of the People in Nineteenth-Century France* (Cambridge: Cambridge University Press, 2012).

Legends in Original Dialects, 1865). Influenced by the Grimms, Erben was one of the first Czech folklorists who studied and collected folk tales from all the oral traditions of Slavic countries, and who had strong sympathies with the Czech and Slovak peoples' resistance to Austrian domination. At the time that Strickland came across Erben's multifaceted work, he was a politically conservative British nobleman, who had a perspective that one might describe as a tourist's view of folklore and actually looked down on the Slavic people. Nevertheless, he had become so fascinated by folklore that he decided to translate the hundred Slavic tales into English and publish them in four different books from 1896 to 1907. He remained in Europe, experiencing World War I firsthand, and lived through great changes wrought by the war in central Europe. Perhaps the most important change for him was the formation of the Czechoslovak nation-state and the rise of democracies throughout Europe. Strickland became a Czech citizen, was strongly influenced by anarchism and communism, and was a vocal critic of British colonialism and imperialism. When he published all four volumes of Erben's one hundred Slavic folk tales in 1930 under the title *Panslavonic Folk-lore*, he addressed the changes he underwent and expressed different and more positive opinions about the Slavic people and their customs. At the same time, he maintained that his translations and notes, which he did not change, were vital for understanding the history, customs, and beliefs of the Slavic people because they had been gathered and presented through Erben, that is, through a man born in a Bohemian village, educated as a lawyer in Prague, who became an archivist in the city of Prague and believed that a nation could only develop and become independent if it preserved relics of the past, namely, its songs, legends, and fairy tales.

All this is not to say that European folklorists were political activists, but there was a certain mutual spirit of *romantic nationalism* that can be traced in almost every effort to collect tales from the common people in the nineteenth century. Perhaps *nationalism* is the wrong word, for the tales, the storytellers, and the collectors were more linked to regions of Europe and the peculiarities within localities. Perhaps we should be talking about and discussing romantic regionalism. What is striking is that there are strong ties and similar goals in the work of all the European folklorists that continually hark back to the Brothers Grimm, who provided the inspiration for their collecting tales and efforts to interpret them as the foundational relics of different cultural traditions.

As Johannes Bolte (1858–1937), a German folklorist and philologist, and Georg Polívka (1858–1933), a Czech folklorist and professor of Slavic literature, demonstrated in the five volumes of their meticulous reference book of the Grimms' tales, *Anmerkungen zu den Kinder- und Hausmärchen der Brüder Grimm* (1913–1932), the Grimms' "Germanic" tales were not to be defined, studied, and interpreted solely within a particular cultural heritage. Indeed, the tales that sprouted and were picked and cultivated on "German" soil could be found throughout Europe and may have come from other regions of the world. In fact, as I have mentioned, the Grimms recognized very early on in their collecting of stories that their tale types could be found in many other European countries and might not derive from Nordic myths, customs, and rituals, as much as they wanted to believe this. This awareness was one of the reasons that they never used the designation "German" in the title of their book to describe their *Kinder- und Hausmärchen* as did some other collectors and writers such as Wolf, Bechstein, and Meier. Undoubtedly, the tales revealed more about the particular conditions experienced by the storytellers and particular cultural traditions in specific regions of Europe than anything about their "national" identity. At the same time, they also reflected and continued to reflect that humans throughout the world invent and use stories in very similar ways to expose and articulate common problems and struggles as well as their wishes to overcome them.

This human urge to tell and to share experiences so that listeners might find ways to adapt to the world and improve their situation accounts for the utopian current especially in wonder and fairy tales. We tell and retell tales that become relevant in our lives, and the tales themselves form types that we use in our telling or reading to address various issues such as child abandonment, the search for immortality, sibling rivalry, incest, rape, exploitation, and so on. No tale is ever told for the first time, but every tale is memetically disseminated and retained in our memory to enable us to navigate our way through the tons of messages and stories that bombard our lives from the day we are born. The Grimms discovered how tale types evolve and change, and they put their imprint on the tales that came their way. They were not alone in their endeavors in the nineteenth century, as other collectors and folklorists reached out to preserve told tales before they changed and might evaporate. Yet, the strange thing is—as the Grimms noted—people always evaporate before tales do, and the tales have assumed different shapes and hues in the course of history.

The Elusive Categorization of Folk and Fairy Tales

In some respects folk and fairy tales appear to cry out for categorization and organization, and this may be due to the fact that they stem from real-life experiences to which they speak metaphorically. In fact, the tales are intended to have some relevance in the lives of the storytellers, listeners, collectors, and readers. There are ritual aspects to almost all folk and fairy tales; there are specific linguistic wordplays and familial and familiar references; and certainly the tales have been ordered in the minds of both speakers and listeners according to the social context in which they were told and received. But it was not until the sixteenth century, if not later, that titles were given to the tales and collectors began to print and categorize them. The more enlightened and rational people became, the more they sought to define and designate tales with specific meanings, perhaps limiting their multiple meanings but yet recognizing the power of a principle message that had valuable information. Here the Grimms' notion that their collection was an educational manual or that collecting was connected to educating provided an underlying motive in the work of most folklorists. The Grimms felt a civic responsibility that became crucial in the work of most folklorists during the golden age. As David Hopkin points out, "one could argue that the development of folklore scholarship was not fortuitous but an ideological necessity in a postrevolutionary age. Even in countries which had not gone anywhere near as far as the French in their experiments with democracy, the people now had to be courted as well as counted. . . . Whether or not actual people were consulted on their government, 'the People' mattered. One can portray this rediscovery of the culture of the people in a progressive light, as driven by the concern for, and interest in political and social needs of the many."[19]

What is fascinating about the work of collectors of folk tales is its paradoxical aspect: the more folklorists sought to grasp the nationalist or even regional qualities of the tales, the more they had to concede that the stories were transnational and transregional. They realized that "their" tales were variants or ecotypes of other tales with the same structural features. The tales and ecotypes compelled folklorists to be more scientific in their commentaries and studies, and at the same time the tales demanded that folklorists recognize unique and distinct regional features. Toward the end of the nineteenth century, European folklorists were communicating with one another about similar tales that needed classification and explanation.

Ultimately, the drive to order tale types, evinced in all the collections and studies of nineteenth-century folklorists, led to the significant work of Finnish folklorist Antti Aarne (1867–1925), namely *Verzeichnis der Märchentypen* in 1910, a massive classification system of over 2,300 tale types that enables scholars to trace and define recurring plots and motifs in diverse folk tales (largely oral) throughout the world. For instance, each tale type is labeled under a general category such as animal tales, followed by subcategories such as wild animals that are given numbers. Therefore, under wild animals there will be "The Clever Fox or Other Animals," 1–69, followed by 1 "The Theft of Fish," 2 "How the Bear Lost His Tail," 3 "Biting the Foot," and so on.

In 1928, renowned American folklorist Stith Thompson (1885–1976) translated, revised, and expanded Aarne's work as *The Types of the Folktales*, which he further revised in 1961. Folklorists referred to the tales with the initials AT plus the number so that "Little Red Riding Hood" became AT 333—"The Glutton." Finally, German folklorist Hans-Jörg Uther published

19. "Folklore Beyond Nationalism: Identity Politics and Scientific Cultures in a New Discipline," in Baycroft and Hopkin, *Folklore and Nationalism in Europe During the Long Nineteenth Century* (2012): 373.

an extensive three-volume revision, *The Types of International Folktales: A Classification and Bibliography. Based on the System of Antti Aarne and Stith Thompson*, in 2004. References to particular tale types and subcategories are now made with ATU followed by a number. In some respects the tale-type index, despite some flaws, is indispensable for anyone interested in doing research on folk tales because it facilitates the comparison of tales throughout the world and allows for a quick identification of basic structural features. What it lacks with regard to the history and deeper meanings of the tales is generally compensated for or complemented by the work of individual scholars who do more exhaustive analytical, historical, and interpretative investigations of a tale type. A case in point is Kurt Ranke's exhaustive study *Die zwei Brüder: Eine Studie zur vergleichenden Märchenforschung* (1934), which provides a good deal of the background historical information for the first section of the present volume, "Brotherly Love," and which includes several versions of the tale type ATU 300—"The Dragon Slayer" and ATU 303—"The Twins or Blood Brothers." There are now numerous books and essays dedicated to thorough studies of the more popular international tale types such as Alan Dundes' *Cinderella: A Folklore Casebook* (1982); Lutz Röhrich's *Wage es, den Frosch zu küssen: Das Grimmsche Märchen Nummer Eins in seinen Wandlungen* (1987); Ernst Philippson's *Der Märchentypus von König Drosselbart* (1923); and my *The Trials and Tribulations of Little Red Riding Hood: Versions of the Tale in Socio-Cultural Context* (1983).

In the present volume I have selected eighteen of the most popular tale types from the category Fairy Tales (ATU 300–ATU 779) to demonstrate how widespread and diverse these tales were in nineteenth-century Europe. This new book is a complement to my other anthology, *The Great Fairy Tale Tradition: From Straparola and Basile to the Brothers Grimm*, in which I published *literary* fairy tales that preceded the publication of selected fairy tales from the Grimms' *Kinder- und Hausmärchen*. In contrast, the present collection has a much different orientation and purpose. Instead of publishing *literary* tales that followed the Grimms' first edition, I have gathered fairy tales and their ecotypes from the oral tradition that were published throughout Europe and inspired more or less by the Brothers Grimm. That is, I have selected similar variants of tale types published by folklorists who gathered and published tales after the publication of the first edition of *Kinder- und Hausmärchen* in 1812/1815.

Why the focus on tales collected orally instead of literary adaptations or literary creations? What distinctions must one make when the primary way we get to know oral tales is through print? There are many answers to these questions and reasons to pay attention to orality, and the first and most obvious reason is that most readers, including folklorists, are unaware of the great treasures of the numerous nineteenth-century collections of European fairy tales that stem from oral traditions. Moreover, most people, even knowledgeable

scholars, are unaware of how different the Grimms' tales of the first edition
of the *Kinder- und Hausmärchen* are from the last edition of 1857 and how
much closer they are to the oral tradition than the latter tales. This is the
reason that I begin each of the eighteen sections in this book with a Grimm
1812/1815 tale or 1819 tale followed by an 1857 version. Storytelling and
collecting were all about change, while at the same time collectors sought
to preserve in print what was about to be changed as the tales evolved. It is
through noting changes that one can begin to distinguish regional peculiarities and begin to discuss why certain topics recur time and again in different
forms and shapes and with different emphases and outcomes throughout
Europe. At the same time, similarities can be detected. As Hopkin has noted,
"folklore was not national, or even regional, it was simultaneously more
generalised and more particular. It was this fact that late nineteenth-century
folklorists set out to explain. Consequently, rather than being, as Barry Reay
alleges, in 'absolute denial about the complexity of cultural interaction, the
hybridity of orality and literacy, tradition and modernity,'[20] folklorists were
pioneer investigators of these topics, from whom cultural historians could
still profitably learn."[21]

Almost all the collectors of oral tales in the nineteenth century were autodi-
dacts and independent scholars, mainly from middle-class backgrounds. Some
were from rural noble families, very familiar with the regions in which they were
born. There were no folklore departments at universities. Though some folklorists became professors of literature, philology, or linguistics, they were not trained
to collect and organize the tales they collected. Thus the manner in which they
recorded their tales varied greatly, and in my opinion, we should consider all the
nineteenth-century collectors as transcribers, translators, mediators, educators,
cultivators, and historians rolled into one. To collect a tale after listening to it
(or even after reading it in a manuscript or an ancient book) the collector had to
decipher and interpret what was meant before writing it down. In the case of an
oral tale, unless it was told by an educated person, it was probably told in dialect
and thus had to be translated and interpreted. Early folklorists published their
tales in books or journals to mediate between social classes, to make folk traditions known that might otherwise be ignored. Once folklorists realized the value
of their works as educators, they began cultivating tales of all kinds so that the
histories of stories would endow readers and listeners with some sense of their
social identity.

Finally, we must not forget to consider the ideological positions of the collectors and how they shared their tales with each other. As I have indicated

20.   Barry Reay, *Rural Englands: Labouring Lives in the Nineteenth Century* (Basingstroke:
Palgrave, 2004), 2.

21.   David Hopkin, "Folklore Beyond Nationalism," in *Folklore and Nationalism in Europe*,
eds. Baycroft and Hopkin, 391.

there was a spirit of national/regional romanticism that swept through the development of nineteenth-century folklore and had its conservative and progressive aspects depending on the habitus of the collector. The bottom line, I believe, is that most folklorists began with the desire to make the voices of the people heard. They wanted other people's tales to speak for themselves. This in itself is a clear ideological statement that paradoxically guarded the tales from ideology. That is, the collectors generally collected and published tales that did not adhere to their ideological positions, nor were the tales consistent or representative of a particular ideology. The voices from below, from storytellers who were sailors, fishermen, weavers, blacksmiths, cooks, servants, and so on, often resisted the categorization of upper-class collectors. There was always a tension between collector and storyteller, and collecting was filled with compromises. It was an educational process for the collector that had different results throughout Europe. Many folklorists censored or monitored the voices of the people, or shaped the voices to bespeak the ideas of the collector. Sometimes the collectors had to bow to authorities and publishers. Understanding why and understanding the contradictions that filled the tales of the Brothers Grimm and their fellow folklorists are vital aspects of the contemporary folklorist's task.

My goal in collecting the folk and fairy tales in this volume was to include as many variants of eighteen European tale types as possible that became popular in the nineteenth century. I have translated the majority of the texts from German, Italian, and French sources, unless otherwise indicated. Many of the other texts were purposely chosen from nineteenth- and early-twentieth-century English translations even though the style and language of these works are somewhat quaint and antiquated, and even though the translations are faulty. Some were even transformed and slanted to appeal to children. I believe that these oddly translated tales will provide readers with a historical sense of how remarkably different the tales read, perceived, and transmitted in the course of the nineteenth and early twentieth centuries. Since there were often errors in the texts, wording that was confusing, or anachronistic grammar, I did some light editing of the tales by other translators to provide greater clarity and to create smoother transitions. I did not make any substantial changes. My own translations are basically attempts to mediate nineteenth-century texts in a contemporary American vernacular that make the tales accessible without simulating a "folk" tone.

Fairy tales inundate our lives, and they also inundated the lives of people of all social classes in the nineteenth century. The Grimms were among the first to give these tales the recognition they deserved. My hope is that the present collection will make a modest contribution to their legacy and to the legacy of forgotten European folklorists. Moreover, I hope the tales will provide researchers with treasures that one can still find buried in golden caskets.

1. BROTHERLY LOVE

ATU 300—THE DRAGON SLAYER
AND ATU 303—THE TWINS OR BLOOD BROTHERS

It is most appropriate to begin the present collection with variants of two tale types—"The Dragon Slayer" and "The Twins or Blood Brothers"—because they may stem from the oldest stories in the world. Tales that deal with the slaying of a dragon and/or a monster, and tales about two or three brothers, who remain true to one another and rescue one another from death with the help of animals, have been disseminated on practically every continent for several thousand years. The major recognized sources are tales from Syrian mythology involving a sun god, who kills a sea monster; the myths of Perseus and Andromeda and Jason and the Golden Fleece, prominent in Ovid's *Metamorphoses* and Apollonius' *Argonautica*, that involve killing of a sea monster that threatens a damsel in distress; and the legends of St. George, which began circulating in the thirteenth century and concern a knight who kills a dragon to save a girl's chastity and to convert people to Christianity. Yet, there may have been many other related tales circulating in the oral tradition that led to fascinating variants up through the twentieth century.

The two tale types were distinct or formed distinctive narrative traditions that blended and engendered hybrid tales which retained many of the same motifs that are key to their evolution. So, in "The Dragon Slayer" tradition a young man leaves home, acquires three extraordinary dogs, learns that a seven-headed dragon is about to devour a virgin princess as sacrifice, and kills the dragon with the help of his dogs. He takes the seven tongues of the dragon as proof of his valorous deed and departs promising to return and marry the princess in one or three years. An imposter comes and pretends to have slain the dragon. This villain threatens to kill the princess if she tells the truth, but she manages to stall him one or three years until the young hero returns and exposes the imposter. Finally, the young man weds the princess. In "The Twins/Brothers" tradition, a man catches a magic fish or a woman eats a magic fish or fruit and gives birth to twins (sometimes triplets). The sons are golden and blessed with unique powers; they acquire extraordinary and grateful animals, and then set out on a journey together. At one point, they separate but leave a token of some kind (a knife in a tree, water, flower, etc.) that will decay if one of the brothers is in danger. The first brother rescues a princess from a dragon/monster and marries her. Since he is still adventurous or curious, he follows a strange beacon/light/animal to a castle where a witch/magician turns him and his animals into stone. The second brother discovers that something has happened to his twin. He travels to the kingdom where the first brother had married the princess who mistakes him for her husband. However, he places a sword between them when they go to bed. The next morning he follows the beacon, kills the witch/magician, and rescues his brother. But the first brother believes that his twin has betrayed him by sleeping with his wife. So, he chops off his head. When he learns from his wife

1

that his brother was loyal, he calls on his animals to help him obtain a magic potion so that he can revive his brother.

The plots of these two tale types were altered and transformed hundreds if not thousands of times in the oral and literary traditions of Europe before the Brothers Grimm obtained their variants. That is, it is both unusual and predictable that the Grimms themselves produced three vastly different versions of the dragon slayer/ blood brothers tale types. It is unusual because the Grimms tended not to retain more than one tale type in their collection, and here we have four. To be sure, the Grimms replaced the "Waterspring Tale," contributed by Friederike Mannel, one of their best informants, with "The Two Brothers," contributed by the von Haxthausen family, and relegated it to the footnotes in the future editions of *Kinder- und Hausmärchen*. Nevertheless, we can see that they were predictably fond of these long and complicated tales, I believe, because they dealt with twin brothers and their loyalty to one another, reflecting the Grimms' own faithful attachment to one another. Moreover, the tales emphasize the theme of collective action in which grateful animals play a role. Finally, it should be noted that, as young students, the Grimms had been very fond of courtly romances, and by the eighteenth century, the tale types of the dragon slayer and blood brothers had become very popular and adapted by publishers of so-called trivial literature or cheap books.

It is not clear to what extent the Grimms' tales may have influenced other renditions of tales about dragon slaying and brotherly love in the nineteenth century, but what is clear, as the tales that follow indicate, is that these stories were told throughout Europe and reveal how creatively the storytellers mixed motifs, added humor, and invented scenarios that were closely related to their own environments. There are touches of class struggle and familial strife, and talking animals appear to play a major role in assisting the heroes. Whatever changes were made, the theme of brotherly love dominates in these tales, while dragon slaying merely indicates the valor of the heroes.

Other interesting variants can be found in the works of Afanas'ev, Millien, Wolf, Zingerle, Widter-Wolf, Schneller, Gubernatis, Vittorio Imbriaani, Bernoni, Coronedi-Berti, Visentini, Nerucci, de Nino, and Pitrè. For the most thorough scholarly study, see Kurt Ranke's *Die zwei Brüder: Eine Studie zur vergleichenden Märchenforschung*.

******

About Johann Waterspring and Caspar Waterspring (1812)[1]
Jacob and Wilhelm Grimm

A king insisted his daughter was not to marry and had a house built for her in the most secluded part of a forest. She had to live there with her ladies-in-waiting,

---

1. "Von Johannes-Wassersprung und Caspar-Wassersprung," *Kinder- und Haus-Märchen. Gesammelt durch die Brüder Grimm*, 2 vols. (Berlin: Realschulbuchhandlung, 1812/1815).

and no other human being was allowed to see her. Near the house in the woods, however, there was a spring with marvelous qualities, and when the princess drank from it, she consequently gave birth to two princes. They were identical twins and named after the spring—Johann Waterspring and Caspar Waterspring.

Their grandfather, the old king, had them instructed in hunting, and as they grew older, they became big and handsome young men. When the day arrived for them to set out into the world, each received a silver star, a horse, and a dog to take on the journey. Once they came to a forest, they immediately saw two hares and wanted to shoot them, but the hares asked for mercy and said that they would like to serve them and that they could be useful and help them whenever they were in danger. The two brothers let themselves be persuaded and took them along as servants.

Soon after, they came upon two bears, and when they took aim at them, these animals also cried out for mercy and promised to serve them faithfully. So the retinue was increased, and now they came to a crossroad where they said, "We've got to separate here, and one of us should go to the right, and the other should head off to the left."

Before doing this, each of them stuck a knife in a tree at the crossroad so that they could determine by the rust just how the other was faring and whether he was still alive. Then they took leave from another, kissed one another, and rode off.

Johann Waterspring came to a city which was quite still and sad because the princess was to be sacrificed to a dragon that was devastating the entire country and could only be pacified by this sacrifice. It was announced that whoever wanted to risk his life and kill the dragon would receive the princess for his bride. However, nobody had volunteered. They had also tried to trick the monster by sending out the princess's chamber maid, but it realized what was happening right away and did not take the bait.

Johann Waterspring thought, 'You must try your luck. Perhaps you'll succeed.' And so he set out with his company and headed toward the dragon's nest. The battle was fierce: the dragon spewed forth fire and flames and ignited all the grass around them so that Johann Waterspring certainly would have suffocated if the hare, dog, and bear had not stamped out and subdued the fire. Finally, the dragon succumbed, and Johann Waterspring cut off its seven heads and then sliced its seven tongues, which he stuck into his sack. Now, however, he was so tired that he lay down right at that spot and fell asleep. While he was sleeping, the princess's coachman arrived, and when he saw the man lying there and the seven heads next to him, he thought, 'You've got to take advantage of this.' So he stabbed Johann Waterspring to death and took the seven heads with him. He carried everything to the king and said he had killed the monster. Indeed, he had brought the seven heads as evidence, and the princess became his bride.

In the meantime Johann Waterspring's animals had set up camp nearby after the battle. Then they slept, and when they returned to the battleground, they found their master dead. As they were looking around, they saw how the ants, whose mound had been stamped on during the battle, were spreading the sap from an oak tree on their dead ones that immediately came back to life. So, the bear went, fetched some of the sap, and spread it on Johann Waterspring. Shortly thereafter Johann was completely well and healthy and thought about the princess for whom he had fought. So he rushed to the city where her marriage to the coachman was being celebrated, and the people were saying that the coachman had killed the seven-headed dragon. Johann Waterspring's dog and bear ran into the castle where the princess tied some roast meat and wine around their necks and ordered her servants to follow the animals and to invite their owner to the wedding. So, now Johann Waterspring showed up at the wedding just as the platter with the seven dragon heads was being displayed. These were the heads that the coachman had brought with him, but now Johann Waterspring pulled out the seven tongues from his sack and placed them next to the heads. Consequently, he was declared the real dragon slayer and became the princess's husband, while the coachman was banished.

Not long thereafter Johann went out hunting and followed a deer with silver antlers. He hunted the deer for a long time but couldn't catch it. Finally, he met an old woman, who turned him, his dog, horse, and bear into stone.

Meanwhile Caspar Waterspring returned to the tree in which he and his brother had stuck their knives and saw that his brother's knife had rusted. He immediately decided to search for his twin and rode off. Soon he came to the city where his brother's wife was living. She thought he was her real husband because he looked just like him and was delighted by his return and insisted that he stay with her. But Caspar Waterspring continued traveling until he found his brother and animals, all turned into stone. Soon after he forced the old woman to break the magic spell, and then the brothers rode toward their home. Along the way, they agreed that the first one to be embraced by the princess should be her husband. Well, it turned out to be Johann Waterspring.

The Golden Children (1812)[2]
Jacob and Wilhelm Grimm

Once upon a time there was a poor man and a poor woman who had nothing but a little hut. The husband was a fisherman, and one day, as he was sitting by the water's edge and had cast out his net, he caught a golden fish, and the fish said: "If you throw me back into the water, I'll turn your little hut into a splendid castle, and in the castle there will be a cupboard. When you open it, there'll be dishes of boiled and roasted meat in them, as much as you desire.

---

2.   "Die Goldkinder," *Kinder- und Haus-Märchen. Gesammelt durch die Brüder Grimm*, 2 vols. (Berlin: Realschulbuchhandlung, 1812/1815).

But you may not tell anyone in the world how you came by your good fortune, otherwise, you will lose it all."

The fisherman threw the golden fish back into the water, and when he came home, a huge castle was standing where otherwise his hut usually stood, and his wife sat in the middle of a splendid room. The man was very pleased by this, but he also wanted to eat something.

"Wife, give me something to eat," he said. "I'm tremendously hungry."

However, his wife answered: "I don't have a thing and can't find anything in this large castle."

"Just go over there to the cupboard."

When his wife opened the cupboard, she found cake, meat, fruit, and wine.

"What more could my heart desire?" His wife was astonished, and then she said: "Tell me, where in the world has this treasure of riches come from all of a sudden?"

"I'm not allowed to tell you. If I tell you, our good fortune will vanish."

After he said this, his wife became only more curious, and she kept asking him and tormenting him and didn't allow him any peace day and night until he finally revealed to her that everything came from a golden fish. No sooner had he said this than the castle and all the rich treasures vanished, and the fisherman and his wife were sitting once again in the old fishing hut.

Now the man had to resume his work all over again, and he fished and fished until he caught the golden fish once more. The fish promised the fisherman again that, if he let it go free, the fish would give him the beautiful castle again and the cupboard full of boiled and roasted meat but only on condition that he remain silent about who granted this favor. Well, the fisherman held out for a while but eventually his wife tormented him so drastically that he revealed the secret, and in that very moment they sat once again in their shabby hut.

So the husband went fishing again, and he fished and caught the golden fish a third time.

"Listen," said the fish. "Take me home with you and cut me into six pieces. Give two to your wife to eat, two to your horse, and plant two in the ground. You'll reap a blessing by doing this. Your wife will give birth to two golden children. The horse will produce two golden foals. And two golden lilies will grow from the earth."

The fisherman obeyed, and the fish's prophesy came true. Soon the two golden children grew and became big young men. "Father," they said, "we want to set out into the world. We'll mount our golden horses, and you'll be able to see from the golden lilies how we are doing. If they are fresh, then we are healthy. If they wilt, then we're sick. If they perish, then we shall be dead."

Upon saying this they rode off and came to an inn where there were many people inside, and when the people saw the two golden children on the golden horses, they began to make fun of them. In turn, the young men became angry, and one of them became ashamed, turned around, and rode home. However, the other continued to ride on and came to a forest. But the people outside the forest told him that he shouldn't enter because it was full of robbers, and they would do some bad things to him. But the golden boy wouldn't let himself be scared by that and said: "I must and shall go through the forest!"

Then he took a bearskin and covered himself and his horse with it so that nothing more of the gold could be seen, and he then rode into the forest. Soon thereafter he heard something calling out in the bushes: "Here's one!"

Then another voice spoke: "Let him go. What should we do with a bearskin? He's as poor and empty-handed as a church mouse!"

So this is how the golden young man came away from the robbers safely and rode into a village where he saw a maiden who was so beautiful that he couldn't imagine any other maiden as beautiful as she was in the whole world. So he asked her to marry him, and the maiden said yes and she would remain true to him for the rest of her life. So they held the wedding and were happy. Then the bride's father came home, and when he saw that his daughter had married a loafer in a bearskin (for he hadn't taken off his bearskin), he became angry and wanted to murder the bridegroom. However, the bride pleaded as best she could with him: she loved him so very much, and after all, he was her husband! Finally the father calmed down, and the next morning he got up and wanted to see his son-in-law one more time, and all at once he saw a splendid, golden young man lying in bed. But the bridegroom had dreamed that he should go hunting after a magnificent stag, and when he awoke, he wanted to go into the forest to hunt this stag. His newly-wed wife implored him to stay there and was afraid that something might happen to him. However, he said: "I must and shall go off."

Upon saying this he got up and went into the forest. Soon he saw a proud stag standing before him just as in his dream. But when he took aim and was about to shoot, the stag began to flee. The golden man went after him and followed him over ditches and through bushes the entire day and wasn't tired. Yet, the deer evaded him, and the young man soon found himself in front of a witch's house. He called out and asked whether she had seen the stag. She answered, "yes," while the witch's small dog kept barking at him without stopping. So he became angry and wanted to shoot it. When the witch saw this, she changed him into a millstone. And at that very same moment the golden lily perished at the golden youth's home. When the other brother saw this, he mounted his golden steed and raced away and came upon the witch. He threatened her with death unless she restored his brother to his natural form. So the witch had to obey, and the two brothers rode home together, the first one to his bride, and the other to his father. In the meantime, the golden lily revived itself, and if the lilies haven't perished, then both of them are still standing.

The Two Brothers (1857)[3]

Jacob and Wilhelm Grimm

Once upon a time there were two brothers, one rich and the other poor. The rich brother was a goldsmith and evil-hearted. The poor brother earned a living by making brooms and was kind and honest. He had two sons who were twins, and they looked so much alike that they seemed like two peas in a pod. Every now and then the twins went to their rich uncle's house and were given the leftovers to eat.

One day the poor man happened to be in the forest gathering brushwood when he saw a bird pure as gold and more beautiful than any bird he had ever seen. So he picked up a stone, threw it at the bird, and was lucky enough to hit it. However, only a single golden feather dropped to the ground, and the bird flew off. The man took the feather and brought it to his brother, who examined it and said, "It's pure gold," and he gave him a lot of money for it.

The next day the poor man climbed a birch tree to cut a few branches. Just then the same bird flew out, and after the man searched awhile, he found a nest with an egg in it. The egg was made of gold, and he took it home with him. Afterward he showed it to his brother, who once again said, "It's pure gold," and he gave him what it was worth. Finally, the goldsmith said, "I'd like to have the bird itself."

The poor man went into the forest for a third time and saw the golden bird perched on a tree. He took a stone, knocked the bird down, and brought it to his brother, who gave him a huge amount of gold for it.

'Now I'll be able to take care of things,' the poor man thought, and went home with a happy feeling.

The goldsmith was clever and cunning and knew exactly what kind of bird it was. He called his wife and said, "Roast this golden bird for me, and make sure that none of it gets lost! I want to eat it all by myself."

Indeed, the bird was not an ordinary creature. It possessed a miraculous power, and whoever ate its heart and liver would find a gold piece under his pillow every morning. The goldsmith's wife prepared the bird, put it on a spit, and let it roast. Now it happened that, while the bird was roasting over the fire, the wife had to leave the kitchen to take care of something else. Just then the two sons of the poor broom-maker ran inside, stopped in front of the spit, and turned it a few times. When two little pieces dropped from the bird into the pan, one of the boys said, "Let's eat the two little pieces. I'm so hungry, and nobody's bound to notice it."

So they ate two pieces, but the wife returned and saw that they had eaten something.

"What did you eat?" she asked.

---

3. "Die zwei Brüder," *Kinder- und Hausmärchen gesammelt durch die Brüder Grimm*, 7th ed., 3 vols. (Göttingen: Verlag der Dieterich'schen Buchhandlung, 1857).

"A couple of pieces that fell out of the bird," they answered.

"That must have been the heart and liver," the wife said, and she was horrified. She quickly slaughtered a cock, took out its heart and liver, and put them in the golden bird so her husband would not miss them and get angry. When the golden bird was done, she carried it to the goldsmith, who consumed it all by himself until nothing remained. However, when he reached under his pillow the next morning expecting to find a gold piece, there was nothing there out of the ordinary.

In the meantime, the two boys hadn't realized how fortunate they had been. When they got up the next morning, something fell on the floor making a tingling sound. Upon looking to see what made the sound, they found two gold pieces, which they brought to their father. He was amazed and said, "How can that have happened?"

When they found another two the following morning and continued to find two every morning thereafter, the father went to his brother and told him the strange story. The goldsmith knew immediately how everything had happened and that the children had eaten the heart and liver of the golden bird. Since he was envious and hard-hearted, he sought revenge and said to the father, "Your children are in league with the devil. Don't take the gold, and don't let them stay in your house any longer. The devil's got them in his power and can also bring about your own ruin."

The father was afraid of the devil, and even though it was painful for him, he led the twins out into the forest and with a sad heart left them there. The two boys wandered about the forest and searched for the way back home, but they repeatedly lost their way and couldn't find it. Finally, they encountered a huntsman, who asked, "Where do you come from?"

"We're the poor broom-maker's sons," they answered and told him that their father no longer wanted them in his house because every morning there was a gold piece under each one of their pillows.

"Well," said the huntsman, "there's nothing really terrible about that as long as you remain good and upright and don't become lazy."

The kind man took a liking to the boys, and since he didn't have any sons himself, he took them home with him and said, "I shall be your father and raise you."

So they learned all about hunting from him, and he saved the gold pieces that they found every morning when they got up in case they were to need them in the future. One day, when they were finally grown-up, their foster father took them into the forest and said, "Today you're to be tested in shooting to determine whether I can release you from your apprenticeship and pronounce you full-fledged huntsmen."

They went with him to the raised blind and waited for a long time, but no game appeared. Then the huntsman looked above him, and when he saw some wild geese flying by in a triangle formation, he said to one of the brothers, "Now shoot one from each corner."

He did it and passed the test. Soon after, more geese came flying by in the number two formation. The huntsman told the other brother likewise to shoot one goose from each corner, and he also passed the test. Now the foster father said, "You have completed your apprenticeship, and I pronounce you both full-fledged huntsmen."

At that point the two brothers went into the forest together, discussed their situation, and decided on a plan of action. When they sat down in the evening to eat, they said to their foster father, "We're not going to touch the food or take a single bite until you grant us one request."

"What is your request?"

"Since we're now full-fledged huntsmen," they replied, "we must also prove ourselves. So we want your permission to leave and travel about the world."

"You speak like real huntsmen," said the old man joyfully. "Your desire is my very own wish. Set out on your journey. I'm sure everything will go well for you."

In a merry mood, they now ate and drank together. When the appointed day for their departure arrived, their foster father gave each of them a good gun and a dog, and since he had saved their gold pieces, he had each brother take as many of them as he desired. Then the old man accompanied them part of the way, and when they were about to take their leave, he gave them a shiny knife and said, "If you should ever separate, stick this knife into a tree at the crossroad. Then if one of you comes back, he can see how his absent brother is doing, for the side of the blade facing the direction he took will rust if he's dying but will stay bright as long as he's alive."

The two brothers set out on their journey and came to a huge forest that was impossible to cross in one day. So they spent the night there and ate what they had in their hunting pouches. On the second day they continued their journey but still were not able to reach the end of the forest. Now they had nothing more to eat, and one of them said, "We must shoot something, or we'll starve."

He loaded his gun and looked around. When he saw an old hare running nearby, he took aim, but the hare cried out:

> "Dear huntsman, if you let me live,
> two of my young to you I'll give."

Then the hare jumped into the bushes and brought back two young ones. The little creatures were so frisky and charming that the huntsmen didn't have the heart to kill them. So they kept them, and the little hares followed at their heals. Soon after, a fox came slinking by, and they were about to shoot it when the fox cried out:

> "Dear huntsmen, if you let me live,
> two of my young to you I'll give."

He also brought two young ones, and the huntsmen had no desire to kill the little foxes. They gave them to the hares for company, and the animals continued to follow the huntsmen. Soon a wolf came out of the thicket, and just as the huntsmen took aim at him, he cried out:

"Dear huntsmen, if you let me live,
two of my young to you I'll give."

The huntsmen added the two young wolf cubs to the other animals, and they all followed the two young men. Then a bear came, and he had no desire to have his days of wandering ended, so he cried out:

"Dear huntsmen, if you let me live,
two of my young to you I'll give.

Two young bear cubs joined the other animals, and now there were eight of them. Finally, who should come along shaking his mane but the lion! And he also cried out:

"Dear huntsmen, if you let me live,
two of my young to you I'll give."

He, too, fetched two of his young cubs, and now the huntsmen had two lions, two bears, two wolves, two foxes, and two hares who followed and served them. Meanwhile, however, the brothers were still starving, and they said to the foxes, "Listen, you tricky creatures, get us something to eat. After all, we know you're crafty and cunning."

"There's a village not far from here," they answered. "In the past we were able to get many a chicken there. We'll show you the way."

The brothers went to the village, bought themselves something to eat, and had their animals fed. Then they continued on their way. Since the foxes were very familiar with the region and knew exactly where the chicken yards were, they could guide the huntsmen to the right spots. For a while they traveled about, but they couldn't find jobs that would enable them all to remain together. Eventually, the brothers said, "There's no other way. We'll have to separate."

They divided the animals so that each had a lion, a bear, a wolf, a fox, and a hare. Then they said farewell, took a vow of brotherly love unto death, and stuck the knife that their foster father had given them into a tree. Then one went to the east, the other to the west.

Soon the younger brother arrived with his animals in a city that was completely draped in black crepe. He went into an inn and asked the innkeeper whether he could put up his animals there. The innkeeper gave him a stable that had a hole in the wall. The hare crawled through it and fetched himself a head of cabbage; the fox fetched a hen, and after he had eaten the hen, he went and got a cock as well. However, the wolf, the bear, and the lion were too big to slip through the hole. So the innkeeper took them to a meadow where a cow was grazing, and there they could eat their fill. After the huntsman had taken care of his animals, he asked the innkeeper why the city was draped in black crepe.

"Because our king's only daughter will perish tomorrow," said the innkeeper.

"Is she that sick?" asked the huntsman.

"No," the innkeeper replied. "She's hale and healthy, but she must die nonetheless."

"But why?" asked the huntsman.

"Outside the city there's a dragon living on a high mountain," said the innkeeper. "Every year he has demanded a pure virgin and threatened to lay waste to our entire country if he wasn't given one. Now, after many years, all the maidens have been sacrificed, and there's no one left but the king's daughter. Despite that, the dragon shows no mercy. She must be delivered to him, and that's to be done tomorrow."

"Why doesn't someone slay the dragon?" asked the huntsman.

"Ah," responded the innkeeper. "Many, many knights have tried, but they've all lost their lives. The king's promised to give his daughter's hand in marriage to the man who slays the dragon, and this man would also inherit the kingdom after the king's death."

The huntsman said nothing more, but the next morning he took his animals and climbed the dragon's mountain with them. At the top was a small church, and there were three full goblets on the altar with a piece of paper next to them that said, "Whoever drinks these goblets shall become the strongest man on earth and shall be able to wield the sword that lies buried beneath the threshold of the door." The huntsman didn't drink the goblets but went outside and searched for the sword in the ground, which he wasn't able to move. Then he went back inside, drank the goblets, and was now strong enough to pull out the sword and wield it with ease. When the hour came for the maiden to be delivered to the dragon, the king, the marshal, and the entire court accompanied her. From afar she could see the huntsman standing on top of the dragon's mountain. She thought it was the dragon standing there and waiting for her, and she didn't want to go. But finally she had to begin the painful journey; the whole kingdom would have been lost otherwise. The king and his court returned home in full mourning, but the king's marshal was assigned to stay there and watch everything from a distance.

When the king's daughter reached the top of the mountain, it was not the dragon standing there but the young huntsman, who comforted her and told her he wanted to save her. He led her into the church and locked her inside. Shortly after, with a great roar the seven-headed dragon descended on the spot. When he caught sight of the huntsman, he was astounded and said, "What do you think you're doing on this mountain?"

"I've come to fight you," replied the huntsman.

"Many a knight has lost his life here," declared the dragon. "I'll soon finish you off as well!" Then flames shot from his seven jaws.

The flames were intended to set fire to the dry grass, and the dragon hoped to smother the huntsman with the fire and smoke, but the huntsman's animals came running to his aid and stamped the fire out. The dragon then attacked the huntsman, but the man swung his sword so swiftly that it sang in the air and cut off three of the dragon's heads. Now the dragon was really furious. He rose up, began shooting flames directly at the huntsman, and got set to dive down at him. However, the huntsman once again lashed out with his sword and cut off three more heads. The monster sank to the ground and was exhausted. Nevertheless, he tried to charge the huntsman again, but the young man used his last bit of strength to cut off the dragon's tail. Then, since the huntsman couldn't continue fighting, he called his animals, who tore the dragon to pieces. When the battle was over, the huntsman opened the church and found the princess lying on the ground. She had fainted from fear and fright during the combat. So he carried her outside, where she regained consciousness and opened her eyes. When he showed her the dragon's devastated body and told her she was now free, the princess was overjoyed and said, "Now you will be my very dear husband, for my father promised my hand in marriage to the man who'd slay the dragon."

The princess then took off her coral necklace and divided it among the animals as little collars to reward them, and the lion received the golden clasp to the necklace. However, her handkerchief with her name embroidered on it went to the huntsman, who proceeded to cut out the tongues of the seven dragon's heads, wrap them in the handkerchief, and put them away carefully.

When that was done, he felt so tired and exhausted from the fire and battle that he said to the maiden, "We're both so drained and overcome with fatigue, perhaps it would be best if we slept awhile."

The princess agreed, and they lay down on the ground. Then the huntsman said to the lion, "I want you to keep watch so that no one surprises us in our sleep."

When the huntsman and the princess fell asleep, the lion lay down beside them to keep watch, but he too was tired from the battle. So he called the bear and said, "Lie down beside me. I've got to sleep a little. If anything happens, wake me up."

The bear lay down next to the lion, but he was too tired. So he called the wolf and said, "Lie down beside me. I've got to sleep a little. If anything happens, wake me up."

The wolf lay down next to the near, but he too was tired. So he called the fox and said, "Lie down beside me. I've got to sleep a little. If anything happens, wake me up."

The fox lay down beside the wolf, but he too was tired. So he called the hare and said, "Lie down beside me. I've got to sleep a little. If anything happens, wake me up."

The hare lay down next to the wolf, but he was tired. However, there was no one left whom he could call on to help him, and soon he fell asleep. Once that happened, they all remained asleep and slept soundly, the princess, the huntsman, the lion, the bear, the wolf, the fox, and the hare.

Meanwhile, the marshal, who had been assigned the task of watching everything from a distance, didn't see the dragon fly off. So, when everything was calm on the mountain, he summoned his courage and climbed the mountain, where he found the dragon lying on the ground and torn to pieces. Not far from there were the king's daughter and the huntsman with his animals. They were all sound asleep, and since the marshal was a wicked and godless man, he took his sword and cut off the huntsman's head. Next he lifted the maiden in his arms and carried her down the mountain. When she awoke, she was petrified, but the marshal said, "I've got you in my power, so you'd better say that it was I who slew the dragon."

"I can't do that," she replied. "It was a huntsman with his animals. They were the ones who did it."

Then the marshal drew out his sword and threatened to kill her if she didn't obey him. Thus he forced her to promise that she would do as he commanded. Afterward he brought her to the king, who was overcome by joy upon seeing his dear daughter alive again when he had thought she had already been torn to pieces by the dragon.

"I've slain the dragon and saved the maiden and the whole kingdom," said the marshal. "Therefore I claim your daughter for my wife as you promised."

"Is what he says true?" the king asked the maiden.

"Oh, yes," she answered. "It must probably be true, but I insist that the wedding be held in a year and a day and not before." Indeed, she hoped to hear from her dear huntsman by then.

Meanwhile, the animals were still lying asleep beside their dead master on the dragon's mountain. Then a bumble bee came and landed on the hare's nose, but the hare brushed it aside and continued to sleep. Finally, it came a second time and stung him on the nose so that he woke up. As soon as the hare was awake, he woke the fox, and the fox woke the wolf, who woke the bear, and the bear woke the lion. And when the lion saw that the maiden was gone and his master was dead, he began roaring dreadfully loud and cried out, "Who did that? Bear, why didn't you wake me?"

The bear asked the wolf, "Why didn't you wake me?"

And the wolf asked the fox, "Why didn't you wake me?"

The fox asked the hare, "Why didn't you wake me?"

The poor hare was the only one who didn't know what to answer, and the guilt fell on his shoulders. They wanted to pounce on him, but he pleaded with them and said, "Don't kill me! I'll bring our master back to life. I know a mountain where a root grows that cures and heals all kinds of sicknesses and wounds. You only have to stick the root in the sick person's mouth. But it takes two hundred hours to get to the mountain."

"Well, you've got to dash there and back and fetch the root within twenty-four hours," declared the lion.

The hare raced away, and within twenty-four hours he was back with the root. The lion put the huntsman's head back in position, and the hare stuck the root in his mouth. All at once, everything functioned again: his heart beat, and life returned to him. When the huntsman awoke, he was distressed not to find the maiden by his side. 'She must have gone away while I was asleep to get rid of me,' he thought.

In his great haste, the lion had put his master's head on backward. However, the huntsman was so preoccupied by his sad thoughts about the king's daughter that he didn't notice it. Only at noon, when he wanted to eat something, did he realize that his head was on backward. Since he was at a loss to understand how that had happened, he asked the animals. The lion told him that they had all been so tired that they had fallen asleep and that upon awakening they had found him dead with his head cut off. The hare had then fetched the root of life, but the lion in his haste had held his head the wrong way. After saying all that, the lion wanted to correct his mistake. So he tore off the head of the huntsman, turned it around, and the hare healed him again with the root. Nevertheless, the huntsman remained in a gloomy mood. He traveled about the world and made his animals dance before crowds of people. After a year had passed, he happened to return to the same city where he had rescued the king's daughter from the dragon, and this time the city was draped completely in crimson.

"What does all that mean?" he asked the innkeeper. "A year ago the city was draped in black. What's the meaning of the crimson?"

"A year ago the princess was supposed to have been delivered to the dragon," answered the innkeeper. "But the marshal fought and slew the dragon. Tomorrow his wedding with the princess will be celebrated. When the city was in mourning, it was draped in black a year ago, and now, in its joy, the city is draped in crimson."

At noon on the next day, when the wedding was to take place, the huntsman said to the innkeeper, "Do you think, innkeeper, that it might be possible for me to eat bread from the king's table right here at your place?'

"Well," said the innkeeper, "I'd be willing to bet a hundred gold pieces that you can't possibly do that."

The huntsman accepted the wager and put up a pouch with one hundred gold pieces to match the innkeeper's money. Then he called the hare and said, "Go there, my speedster, and fetch me some of the bread fit for a king."

Now, the little hare was the weakest of the animals, and it was impossible for him to pass this task on to any of the others. So, he had to perform it by himself. 'My God,' he thought, 'if I amble down the street by myself, the butchers' dogs will soon be after me!' And it happened just as he thought it would. The dogs chased after him and wanted to tear his good fur to shreds. However, you should have seen the hare run! He sped to the castle and took refuge in the sentry box without the guard noticing him. When the dogs came and tried to get him out, the soldier would take no nonsense from them and hit them with the butt of his rifle so they ran away yelping and howling. Once the hare saw the coast was clear, he ran into the palace and straight to the king's daughter. Then he sat down under her chair and scratched her foot.

"Get out of here!" she said, for she thought it was her dog. The hare scratched her foot a second time, and she repeated, "Get out of here!" for she thought it was her dog. But the hare didn't let himself be deterred and scratched a third time. Then she looked down and recognized the hare by his coral collar. So she picked him up, carried him into her chamber, and said, "My dear hare, what do you want?"

"My master, the dragon slayer, is here," he answered, "and he's sent me to fetch some bread fit for a king."

The princess was filled with joy. She summoned the baker and ordered him to bring her a loaf of bread fit for a king.

"But the baker must also carry it for me," said the hare. "Otherwise, the butchers' dogs will harm me."

The baker carried the bread up to the door of the inn for the hare. Then the hare stood up on his hind legs, took the loaf of bread in his front paws, and brought it to his master.

"You see, innkeeper," the huntsman said, "the hundred gold pieces are mine."

The innkeeper was astonished, but the huntsman continued to speak. "Well, innkeeper, I've got the bread, but now I want some of the king's roast as well."

"I'd like to see that," said the innkeeper, but he didn't want to bet anymore.

The huntsman called the fox and said, "Little fox, go there and fetch me a roast fit for a king."

The red fox knew the shortcuts better than the hare, and he went through holes and around corners without the dogs catching sight of him. Once at the castle he sat under the chair of the princess and scratched her foot. When she looked down, she recognized the fox by his coral collar, carried him into her chamber, and said, "My dear fox, what do you want?"

"My master, the dragon slayer, is here," he answered, "and he's sent me to ask for a roast fit for a king."

She summoned the cook and ordered him to prepare a roast fit for a king and to carry it for the fox up to the door of the inn. There the fox took the dish from him, wagged his tail to brush off the flies that had settled on the roast, and brought it to his master.

"You see, innkeeper," said the huntsman, "bread and meat are here, but now I want to have some vegetables fit for a king." So he called the wolf and said, "Dear wolf, go straight to the castle and fetch me some vegetables fit for a king."

So the wolf went straight to the castle, for he was afraid of no one, and when he reached the princess, he tugged at her dress from behind so that she had to turn around. She recognized him by his coral collar, took him into her chamber, and said, "My dear wolf, what do you want?"

"My master, the dragon slayer, is here," he answered, "and he's sent me to ask for some vegetables fit for a king."

She summoned the cook, who had to prepare some vegetables fit for a king, and she ordered him to carry them for the wolf to the door of the inn. There the wolf took the dish and brought it to his master.

"You see, innkeeper, now I've got some bread, meat, and vegetables, but I also want some sweets fit for a king." So he called the bear and said, "Dear bear, since you're fond of licking sweet things, go and fetch me sweets fit for a king."

So the bear trotted off to the castle, and everyone cleared out of his way. When he reached the sentry box, the guards barred his way with their guns and didn't want to let him enter the royal castle. But he stood up on his hind legs and slapped the guards left and right, forcing them to fall apart. Then he went straight to the king's daughter, stood behind her, and growled softly. She looked behind her, recognized the bear and told him to go with her into her chamber.

"My dear bear," she said, "what do you want?"

"My master, the dragon slayer, is here," he answered, "and I'm to ask for some sweets fit for a king."

She summoned the confectioner and ordered him to make sweets fit for a king and to carry them up to the door for the bear. There the bear licked the sugar plums that had rolled off, stood on his hind legs, and brought them to his master.

"You see, innkeeper," said the huntsman, "now I've got bread meat, vegetables, and sweets, but I also want to drink wine fit for a king." So he called his lion and said, "Dear lion, since you like to indulge yourself and get tipsy, go and fetch me some wine fit for a king."

When the lion strode down the street, the people fled from him, and when he came to the guards, they wanted to bar his way, but he only had to let out a roar, and they all dashed away. The lion then went to the royal chamber and knocked on the door with his tail. The king's daughter came out and recognized him by the golden clasp of her necklace. She invited him inside and said, "My dear lion, what do you want?"

"My master, the dragon slayer, is here, and I'm to ask for some wine fit for a king."

She summoned the cupbearer and ordered him to give the lion some wine fit for a king.

"I want to go with him to make sure that this is the right kind of wine," said the lion.

He went downstairs with the cupbearer, and when they were below, the cupbearer was about to draw some ordinary wine that the king's servants usually draw, but the lion said, "Stop! I want to taste the wine first." He drew half a measure for himself and drank it down. "Now," he said, "that's not the right kind."

The cupbearer glared at him and was cross. Then he went on and was about to offer him wine from another barrel reserved for the king's marshal.

"Stop!" said the lion. "I want to taste the wine first." He drew half a measure for himself and drank it down. "It's better than the first, but it's still not the right kind."

Now the cupbearer was angry and said, "How can a stupid beast understand anything about wine?"

But the lion gave him such a blow behind the ears that he fell hard on the ground. When he got up, he didn't utter a word. Instead, he led the lion into a special small cellar where the king's wine was kept solely for his private use. The lion drew half a measure for himself, tasted the wine, and said, "That's the right kind," and he ordered the cupbearer to fill six bottles with the wine. Then they climbed back upstairs, and when the lion left the cellar and stepped outside, he began to stagger back and forth. Since he was a bit drunk, the cupbearer had to carry the wine up to the door for him. There the lion took the basket in his mouth and carried it to his master.

"You see, innkeeper," the huntsman said, "I've got bread meat, vegetables, sweets, and wine fit for a king, and now I want to dine with my animals."

He sat down at the table, ate and drank, and shared his meal with the hare, the fox, the wolf, the bear, and the lion. The huntsman was in good spirits, for he realized that the king's daughter was fond of him. After the meal was over, he said, "Innkeeper, now that I've eaten and drunk just like a king, I'm going to the king's palace, where I shall marry his daughter."

"How are you going to do that?" asked the innkeeper. "She already has a bridegroom, and the wedding is to be celebrated today."

The huntsman took out the handkerchief that the king's daughter had given him on the dragon's mountain, and it still contained the seven tongues of the monster.

"All I need," he said, "is what I'm holding here in my hand."

The innkeeper looked at the handkerchief and said, "Even if I believe everything else, I can't believe this, and I'm willing to stake my house and everything I own on it."

Then the huntsman took out a pouch with a thousand gold pieces in it, put the pouch on the table, and said, "I'll match your house and property with this."

Meanwhile, the king and his daughter were sitting at the royal table, and the king asked her, "What did all those wild animals want who kept running in and out of the castle?"

"I'm not allowed to say," she answered. "But you'd do well to send for the master of those animals."

So the king sent a servant to the inn and had the stranger invited to the palace. The servant arrived just as the huntsman had concluded the bet with the innkeeper.

"You see, innkeeper," said the huntsman, "the king's sent a servant to invite me to his palace, but I refuse to go the way I am." Then he turned to the servant and said, "Please be so kind to tell the king to send me royal garments, a coach with six horses, and servants to attend me."

When the king heard the answer, he said to his daughter, "What should I do?"

"You'd do well to honor his request and send for him," she said.

So the king sent royal garments, a coach with six horses, and servants to attend him. When the huntsman saw them coming, he said, "You see, innkeeper, my request has been honored," and he dressed himself in the royal garments, took the handkerchief with the seven tongues of the dragon, and drove to the palace. When the king saw him coming, he said to his daughter, "How shall I receive him?"

"You'd do well to go and meet him," she answered.

The king went to meet him and led him up to the palace, while the animals followed behind. The king showed the young huntsman to a place next to him and his daughter. The seat on the other side was taken by the marshal, who didn't recognize the huntsman. Just then the seven heads of the dragon were carried out for display, and the king said, "Since the marshal cut off the seven heads of the dragon, I shall give him my daughter to be his wife today."

Then the huntsman stood up, opened the seven jaws, and said, "Where are the seven tongues of the dragon?"

Upon hearing that, the marshal was so frightened that he turned pale and didn't know what to reply. Finally, he said, "Dragons have no tongues."

"Liars should have no tongues," said the huntsman. "But the dragon's tongues can prove who the real dragon slayer is."

Then he unwrapped the handkerchief to reveal the seven tongues. When he stuck each tongue back into the mouth where it belonged, each fit perfectly. Next he took the handkerchief, on which the name of the king's daughter had been embroidered, showed it to the maiden, and asked her to point out which man she had given it to.

"To the man who slew the dragon," she replied.

Then he called his animals, took off their coral collars and the golden clasp from the lion, and asked the maiden to tell whose articles they were.

"The necklace and the golden clasp were mine," she answered, "but I divided the necklace among the animals who had helped in slaying the dragon."

Then the huntsman said, "After I was weary from the fight, I lay down to rest and sleep, and the marshal came and cut off my head. Then he carried off the king's daughter and pretended it was he who had slain the dragon. To prove that he's been lying, I have brought the tongues, the handkerchief, and the necklace." And then he told how his animals had healed him through a miraculous root and how he had traveled around for a year and had finally come back to the spot where he had learned about the treachery of the marshal, thanks to the innkeeper's story.

"Is it true that this man killed the dragon?" the king asked his daughter.

"Yes," she replied, "it's true. Now I may reveal the marshal's shameful crime, for it has been exposed without my speaking about it. You see, the marshal made me take a vow of silence, and that's why I had insisted upon waiting a year and a day before celebrating the wedding."

The king summoned twelve councilors and ordered them to pronounce judgment on the marshal, and they sentenced him to be torn apart by four oxen. Thus the marshal was executed, and the king gave his daughter to the huntsman and named him viceroy over the entire kingdom. The wedding was celebrated with great rejoicing, and the young king sent for his father and foster father and overwhelmed them with fine gifts. Nor did he forget the innkeeper. He, too, was sent for, and the young king said, "You see, innkeeper, I've married the king's daughter, and your house and property are mine."

"Yes," he said, "by right everything is yours."

But the young king said, "No. I intend to act with mercy, and you shall keep your house and property. Moreover, I want you to retain the one thousand gold pieces as a gift."

Now, the young king and young queen were in good spirits and had a happy life together. He often went out hunting since that gave him pleasure, and his faithful animals always accompanied him. Nearby was a forest, however, that was said to be enchanted. Whoever entered did not return very easily. But the young king had a great desire to go hunting in it, and he kept bothering the old king until he obtained permission to go there. So he rode out with a large retinue, and when he came to the forest, he saw a doe as white as snow and said to his men, "Wait here until I return. I want to hunt that beautiful doe."

He rode into the forest in pursuit of the doe, and only his animals followed him. His men stopped and waited until evening, but he didn't come back. So they rode home and said to the young queen, "The young king went hunting after a beautiful white doe in the enchanted forest and didn't return."

Upon hearing this she became very worried about him. Meanwhile, he had kept riding after the beautiful doe, never managing to overtake it. Each time he thought he had the doe within his aim, the animal would dart away and run off into the distance, until finally it vanished altogether. When the huntsman realized that he had gone deep into the forest, he took out his horn and blew it. There was no response, however, for his men couldn't hear it. After night began to fall, he saw that he couldn't get home that day. So, intending to spend the night there, he dismounted and built a fire near a tree. While he was sitting by the fire and his animals were lying beside him, he thought he heard a human voice. He looked around but didn't see anyone. Soon after, he heard a groan that sounded as though it were coming from above. When he looked up, he saw an old woman sitting in the tree moaning and groaning.

"*Oooh! Oooh!* I'm freezing," she cried.

"Climb down," he said, "and warm yourself if you're freezing."

"No, your animals will bite me," she replied.

"They won't harm you, granny," he answered. "Just come down."

However, she was a witch and said, "I'm going to throw down a switch from the tree. If you hit them on their backs with it, they won't hurt me."

Then she threw the switch to him, and when he hit them with it, they immediately lay still and were turned to stone. When the witch was safe from the animals, she jumped down, touched him with a switch, and he was turned to stone. Thereupon she laughed and dragged him and the animals to a pit where there were already many more such stones.

When the young king didn't come back at all, the young queen's worries and fears increased. Now, it happened that just at this time the other brother, who had gone to the east when the twins had separated, came to this kingdom. He had been looking for employment and had found none. Therefore, he had been traveling about and having his animals dance in front of crowds of people. Eventually, it occurred to him to take a look at the knife they had stuck into the tree upon their separation to see how his brother was doing. When he got there, his brother's side of the knife was half rusty and half bright. At once he became alarmed and thought, 'My brother must have met with a great misfortune. But perhaps I can still save him, for half the knife is bright.'

He went off to the west with his animals, and when he arrived at the city gate, the guards approached him and asked whether they should announce his arrival to his wife, for the young queen had been upset for several days about his absence and had been afraid that he had been killed in the enchanted forest. The guards, of course, believed that he was none other than the young king himself because he resembled him so much and also had the wild animals following him. The brother realized that they had mistaken him for his brother and thought, 'It's best that I pretend to be him. Then I'll be able to rescue him more easily.'

So he let himself be conducted by the guards into the palace and was jubilantly received. The young queen thought for sure he was her husband and asked him why he had stayed away so long.

"I lost my way in the forest and couldn't find the way back any sooner," he said.

In the evening he was taken to the royal bed, but he placed a double-edged sword between himself and the young queen. She didn't know what to make of it, but she didn't dare to ask.

He remained there a few days and inquired into everything concerning the enchanted forest. Finally, he said, "I must go hunting there once more."

The king and the young queen tried to talk him out of it, but he insisted and set out with a large retinue. When he reached the forest, he went through everything his brother had experienced. He saw a white doe and said to his men, "Stay here and wait until I return."

Then he rode into the forest, and his animals followed after him. But he couldn't overtake the doe and went so deep into the forest that he had to spend the night there. After he had built a fire, he heard a groan above him.

"*Oooh! Oooh!* I'm freezing!"

He looked up and saw the same witch sitting in the tree.

"If you're freezing, climb down, granny," he said, "and warm yourself."

"No, your animals will bite me," she replied.

"They won't harm you," he said.

"I'm going to throw you a switch from the tree," she said. "If you hit them with it, they won't hurt me."

When the huntsman heard that, he didn't trust the old woman and said, "I won't hit my animals. Either you come down, or I'll come get you!"

"Do you really think you can do something?" she cried. "There's no way you can harm me!"

But he answered, "If you don't come down, I'll shoot you down."

"Go ahead and shoot," she said. "I'm not afraid of your bullets."

So he took aim and fired at her, but the witch was protected against lead bullets, and she let out a shrill laugh. "You'll never hit me!" she exclaimed.

But the huntsman knew just what to do: he took off three silver buttons from his jacket and loaded his gun with them, for her witchcraft was powerless against them. When he now pulled the trigger, she fell from the tree with a scream. Then he put his foot on her and said, "You old witch, if you don't tell me right away where my brother is, I'll pick you up with both my hands and throw you into the fire."

Since she was terribly frightened, she begged for mercy and said, "He's been turned into stone along with his animals, and they're lying in a pit."

He forced her to go with him, and there he threatened her by saying, "You old monkey, now you'd better restore life to my brother and all the other creatures that are lying there, or I'll throw you into the fire!"

She took a switch and touched the stones, and his brother and the animals came back to life again, and many others as well, such as merchants, artisans, and shepherds, who rose up, thanked the huntsman for their release, and went home. Meanwhile, when the twin brothers saw each other again, they kissed each other, and their hearts were full of joy. Then they grabbed the witch, tied her up, and put her into the fire. After she was burned to death, the forest opened up all by itself and became bright and clear so that one could see the royal castle, which was about a three-hour walk from there.

Now the two brothers headed toward home together, and along the way they each told the other about their adventures. When the younger one said that he was viceroy for the whole kingdom, the other said, "I realized that right away. When I came into the city, I was mistaken for you and shown every royal honor. The young queen thought I was her husband, and I had to sleep in your bed."

When the other heard that, he became so jealous that he drew his sword and cut off his brother's head. However, when he saw his brother lying there and his red blood flowing, he was overcome by remorse.

"My brother rescued me!" he exclaimed. "And in return I've killed him!"

He uttered cries of grief, and then his hare came and offered to fetch the root of life. Soon after the hare dashed off and returned just at the right time. The dead brother was brought back to life and didn't even notice his wound. When they continued on their journey, the younger brother said, "You look like me, and your animals are like mine. Let's enter from opposite gates and go to the king's chamber at the same time from opposite directions."

So they took separate paths, and simultaneously the guards came from opposite gates to the old king and announced that the young king had returned with his animals from the hunt.

"It's not possible," the king said. "The gates are an hour's walk apart."

Just then, however, the brothers arrived at the palace courtyard from two sides and went upstairs.

"Tell me," the king said to his daughter, "which one is your husband. They look exactly alike, and I can't tell them apart."

The young queen was very upset and couldn't tell them apart either. Finally, she remembered the necklace that she had given the animals. She searched and found the golden clasp on the lion, and then she exclaimed happily, "The lion who belongs to this man and follows him is my husband!"

Then the young king laughed and said, "Yes, you've found the right one."

Now they all sat down at the table and ate and drank, and they were in a merry mood. That night, when the young king went to bed, his wife asked him, "Why did you always place a double-edged sword in our bed these last few nights? I thought you might want to slay me."

Then he realized how faithful his brother had been.

The Golden Children (1857)[4]

Jacob and Wilhelm Grimm

There was once a poor man and a poor woman who had nothing but a little hut. They supported themselves by fishing and lived hand-to-mouth. One day, however, as the husband was sitting by the water's edge and casting out his net, he happened to pull in a fish made entirely of gold. His astonishment was great, and while he was examining the fish, it began to speak and said, "Listen to me, fisherman. If you throw me back into the water, I'll turn your little hut into a splendid castle."

---

4.   "Die Goldkinder," *Kinder- und Hausmärchen gesammelt durch die Brüder Grimm*, 7th ed., 2 vols. (Göttingen: Verlag der Dieterich'schen Buchhandlung, 1857).

"What's the use of a castle," responded the fisherman, "if I don't have anything to eat?"

"I'll take care of that, too," continued the golden fish. "There'll be a cupboard in the castle. When you open it, there'll be dishes with the very best food on them and as much as you desire."

"If that's the case," said the man, "I can certainly do you a favor."

"Indeed," said the fish. "But there is a condition attached to this: You're not allowed to tell anyone in the world, no matter who it may be, how you came by your good fortune. If you so much as breathe a single word, all of it will be over."

The man threw the miraculous fish back into the water and went home. However, instead of finding his hut in its usual place, he discovered a great castle and stood gaping at it in amazement. Then he went inside and saw his wife dressed in beautiful clothes and sitting in a splendid room. She was extremely happy and asked, "Husband, how did all this happen so suddenly? I'm really pleased."

"Yes," said the man, "it pleases me too, but I'm also tremendously hungry. Give me something to eat."

"I haven't got a thing," his wife said. "And I don't know where to find anything in the new house."

"No need to worry," said the husband. "Over there's a cupboard. Just go and open it."

When she opened the cupboard, she found cake, meat, fruit, and wine. Everything looked at her enticingly. "What more could my heart desire?" she exclaimed with joy. They sat down at the table and ate and drank together. After they had finished eating, the wife asked, "Where in the world did all this come from, husband?"

"Ah," said the husband. Don't ask me about it. I'm not allowed to reveal a thing. If I tell you, then our good fortune will vanish."

"Very well," she said. "If I'm not supposed to know, then I don't want to know."

However, she was not being sincere, and she kept thinking about the matter day and night. In addition, she kept tormenting and pestering her husband until he lost his patience and declared that everything had come from a miraculous golden fish, which he had caught, and that he had given the fish back its freedom for the castle. As soon as he said that, the beautiful castle vanished instantly, cupboard and all, and once again they found themselves sitting in the old fishing hut.

Now the man had to start his work all over again, and he went fishing. As luck would have it, however, he caught the golden fish once more.

"Listen," said the fish, "if you throw me back into the water, I'll give you the castle again, and this time the cupboard will be filled with boiled and roast meats. Just be firm, and whatever you do, don't reveal who gave you all this, otherwise you'll lose everything again."

"I'll certainly be on my guard," answered the fisherman, and he threw the fish back into the water. When he returned home, everything had been restored to its former splendor, and his wife was ecstatic about their good fortune. Yet, curiosity got the better of her, and in a few days she began asking questions again about how it all had happened and how he had managed everything. Her husband kept silent for a long time, but eventually she annoyed him so much that he exploded and revealed the secret. In an instant the castle vanished, and they found themselves sitting in the hut once again.

"See what you've done!" said the husband. "Now we'll have to live in poverty again.

"Ah," said his wife. "I'd rather live in poverty than not know who's giving us all that wealth. After all, I want to keep my peace of mind."

The man went fishing again, and after a while the same thing occurred. He pulled in the golden fish for the third time.

"Listen," said the fish. "It's clear to me that I'm bound to keep falling into your hands. So take me home with you and cut me into six pieces. Give your wife two of these to eat and two to your horse. Then bury two in the ground, and you'll reap blessings from them all."

The man took the fish home with him and did as he had been told. Then it came to pass that the two pieces he had buried in the ground grew into two golden lilies, his horse had two golden foals, and his wife gave birth to two children who were all gold. The children grew up and became tall and handsome while the lilies and horses grew along with them. One day the boys said, "Father, we want to mount our golden steeds and go out into the world."

That made the old man very sad, and he replied, "How shall I bear your absence when I won't know what's happening to you?"

"The two golden lilies will stay here," they said. "So you'll be able to tell from them how we are. If they are fresh, then we're doing well. If they wilt, then we're sick. If they perish, then we shall be dead."

They rode away and came to an inn, where many people were seated inside. When the people caught sight of the two golden boys, they began to laugh at them and mock them. Hearing their mockery, one of the brothers felt ashamed and decided that he didn't want to see the world anymore. So he turned around and went back to his father. However, the other brother continued his journey and came to a great forest. Just as he was about to ride into it, some people told him, "Don't ride through the forest. It's full of robbers. They'll be rough with you, especially when they see that you're made of gold, and your horse as well. They'll kill you for sure."

But he wouldn't let himself be scared by that and said, "I've got to get through, and get through I shall."

Then he took a bearskin and covered himself and his horse with it so that nothing more of their gold could be seen. He then rode calmly into the forest.

When he had gone a little way, he heard a rustling sound in the bushes and voices talking together.

"There's one," a voice cried out from one side.

"Let him go. He's just one of those lazy vagabonds, poor as a church mouse. We won't get a thing from him," a voice said from the other side.

So the golden youth rode safely through the forest, and no harm befell him. One day he came riding into a village and saw a maiden who was so beautiful that he could not imagine any maiden more beautiful than her in the whole world. His love for her was so overwhelming that he went straight up to her and said, "I love you with all my heart. Will you be my wife?"

The maiden took such an immediate liking to him that she, in turn, gave her consent. "Yes, I'll be your wife," she said, "and remain true to you for the rest of my life."

So they held the wedding, and just as the celebration was in full swing, the bride's father came home and was very much surprised indeed to find his daughter married.

"Where's the bridegroom?" he asked.

They pointed to the golden youth, who was still wearing the bearskin, and the father was furious and said, "Never shall a daughter of mine marry a lazy vagabond!"

And he wanted to murder him. Then his daughter pleaded as hard as she could."

"But, father," she said, "he's my husband, and I love him with all my heart."

Eventually, the father calmed down, but he couldn't get over the idea that his daughter might have married a common, wretched beggar, and he woke up early the next morning to see for himself. When he looked into their room, he saw a dazzling golden man in bed, and the discarded bearskin was lying on the floor. Then he went back to his room and thought, 'It's a good thing that I kept my temper, otherwise I might have committed an awful crime.'

In the meantime, the golden youth dreamed that he was out hunting a splendid stag, and when he awoke in the morning, he said to his wife, "I want to go out hunting."

She was anxious and begged him to stay at home. "You could easily have an accident," she said.

But he answered, "I must go hunting, and hunting I shall go."

He got up and went into the forest, and before long, a proud stag stopped in front of him, just as in his dream. He took aim and was about to shoot, but the stag ran off. He chased the animal over ditches and through bushes and did not get tired all day. But in the evening the stag disappeared before his eyes, and the youth now looked around him. He saw he was standing before a small cottage and knocked. An old woman came out and asked, "What are you doing in the middle of the great forest so late?"

"Have you seen a stag?" he asked.

"Yes," she replied. "I know the stag quite well."

Now a little dog that had come outside with her began to bark viciously at the man.

"If you don't shut up, you nasty cur," he said, "I'll shoot you dead!"

"What will you do?" the witch cried angrily. "You'd shoot my little dog dead?" Immediately she turned him into a stone, and he lay flat on the ground. Meanwhile, his bride waited for him in vain and thought, 'I'm sure that my fears have come true as well as everything else that was weighing so heavily on my heart.'

At the same time, the other brother, who was standing near the golden lilies at home, saw one of the lilies suddenly droop. "Oh, God!" he said. "My brother's had a great accident. I've got to go and see if I can save him."

"Stay here," said the father. "What shall I do if I lose you as well?"

"I must go," he replied. "And go I shall."

So, he mounted his golden steed, rode off, and came to the forest where his brother was lying on the ground as a stone. The old witch came out of her house and called out to him. She wanted to trap him too, but he kept his distance from her and said,

"If you don't bring my brother back to life, I'm going to shoot you."

Unwillingly, she touched the stone with her finger, and the brother regained his human form at once. There was great rejoicing when the two brothers saw each other again: they embraced, kissed each other, and rode out of the forest together, the one to his bride, the other home to his father.

"I was positive that you had rescued your brother," said the father. "I knew when the other golden lily suddenly straightened up and began to bloom again."

From then on they lived happily, and everything went well for them until they died.

Snipp, Snapp, Snorium (1853)[5]

Benjamin Thorpe

There was once a miller who had three children, two girls and a boy. When the miller died, and the children divided the property, the daughters took the entire mill, and left their brother nothing but three sheep he tended in the forest. As he was one day wandering about, he met an old man, with whom he exchanged a sheep for a dog named Snipp. On the following day the same old man met him again, when he exchanged another sheep with him for a dog named Snapp; and on the third day his third sheep, for a dog named Snorium. The three dogs were large and strong, and obedient to their master in everything.

---

5. *Yule-Tide Stories: A Collection of Scandinavian and North German Popular Tales and Traditions from the Swedish, German, and Danish* (London: Henry G. Bohn, 1853).

When the lad found there was no good to be done at home, he resolved to go out in the world and seek his fortune. After long wandering he came to a large city, in which the houses were hung with black, and everything betokened some great and universal calamity. The youth took up his quarters with an old fisherman, of whom he inquired the cause of this mourning. The fisherman informed him that there was a huge serpent named Turenfax, which inhabited an island out in the ocean; that every year a pure maiden must be given him to be devoured; and that the lot had now fallen on the king's only daughter. When the youth had heard this, he formed the resolution of venturing a contest with the serpent, and rescuing the princess, provided fortune would befriend him. On the appointed day the youth sailed over to the island, and awaited whatever might happen. While he was sitting, he saw the young princess drawing near in a boat, accompanied by a number of people. The king's daughter stopped at the foot of the mountain and wept bitterly. The youth then approached her, greeted her courteously, and comforted her to the best of his power. When a short time had passed thus, he said: "Snipp! Go to the mountain-cave, and see whether the serpent is coming."

The dog went, but soon returned, wagged his tail, and said that the serpent had not yet made his appearance. When some time had elapsed, the youth said: "Snapp! Go to the mountain-cave, and see whether the serpent is coming."

The dog went, but soon returned without having seen the serpent. After a while the youth said: "Snorium! Go to the mountain-cave, and see whether the serpent is coming."

The dog went, but soon returned trembling violently. The youth could now easily guess that the serpent was approaching, and, consequently, made himself ready for the fight.

As Turenfax came hastening down the mountain, the youth set his dogs Snipp and Snapp on him. A desperate battle then ensued, but the serpent was so strong that the dogs were unable to master him. When the youth observed this, he set on his third dog, Snorium, and now the conflict became even fiercer; but the dogs got the mastery, and the game did not end until Turenfax received his death-wound.

When the serpent was dead, the king's daughter thanked her deliverer with many affectionate expressions for her safety, and besought him to accompany her to the royal palace. But the youth wanted to try his luck in the world for some time longer, and therefore declined her invitation. It was, however, agreed on between them that the youth should return in a year and woo the fair maiden. On parting the princess broke her gold chain in three and bound a portion round the neck of each of the dogs. To the young man she gave her ring, and they promised ever to be faithful to each other.

The young man now travelled about in the wide world, as we have said, and the king's daughter returned home. On her way she was met by a courtier, who forced her to make oath that he and no other had slain Turenfax. This courtier was thenceforward looked upon as a most doughty champion and got a promise of the princess. But the maiden would not break her faith to the youth, and deferred the marriage from day to day.

When the year had expired, the youth returned from his wandering and came to the great city. But now the houses were hung with scarlet, and all things seemed to indicate a great and general rejoicing. The youth again took up his quarters with the old fisherman and asked what might be the cause of all the joy. He was informed that a courtier had killed Turenfax, and was now about to celebrate his nuptials with the king's fair daughter. No one has heard what the miller's son said on receiving this intelligence, though it may easily be imagined that he was not greatly delighted at it.

When dinner-time came, the youth felt a longing to partake of the king's fare, and his host was at a great loss how this could be brought to pass. But the youth said: "Snipp! Go up to the palace, and bring me a piece of game from the king's table. Fondle the young princess, but strike the false courtier a blow that he may not soon forget."

Snipp did as his master had commanded him; he went up to the palace, caressed the fair princess, but struck the courtier a blow that made him black and blue. Then, seizing a piece of game, he ran off. Hereupon there arose a great uproar in the hall, and all were filled with wonder, excepting the king's daughter; for she had recognized her gold neck-chain, and thence divined who the dog's master was.

The next day a similar scene was enacted. The youth was inclined to eat some pastry from the king's own table, and the fisherman was at a loss how this could be brought about. But the youth said: "Snapp, go up to the palace, and bring me some pastry from the king's table. Fondle the young princess, but strike the false courtier a blow that he may not soon forget."

Snapp did as his master had commanded him. He went up to the palace, broke through the sentinels, caressed the fair princess, but struck the false courtier a blow that made him see the sun both in the east and west. Then, seizing a piece of pastry, he ran off. Now there was a greater uproar than on the preceding day, and every one wondered at what had taken place, excepting the king's daughter; for she again recognized her gold neck-chain, whereby she well knew who the dog's master was.

On the third day the youth wished to drink wine from the king's table and sent Snorium to fetch some. Everything now took place as before. The dog burst through the guard, entered the drinking apartment, caressed the princess, but struck the false courtier a blow that sent him tumbling head over heels on the floor. Then, seizing a flask of wine, he ran off.

The king was sorely vexed at all this and sent the courtier with a number of people to seize the stranger who owned the three dogs. The courtier went and came to where the young man dwelt with the poor fisherman. But there another game began; for the youth called to his three dogs: "Snipp! Snapp! Snorium! Clear the house."

In an instant the dogs rushed forward, and in a twinkling all the king's men lay on the ground. The youth then caused the courtier to be bound hand and foot and proceeded to the apartment where the king was sitting at table with his men. When he entered, the princess ran to meet him with great affection and began relating to her father how the courtier had deceived him. When the king heard all this and recognized his daughter's gold chain and ring, he ordered the courtier to be cast to the three dogs, while the brave youth obtained the princess, and with her half the kingdom.

The Cobbler's Two Sons (1864)[6]
Theodor Vernaleken

Once a cobbler went to fish, and caught three carps, each of ten pounds. As he went home, he lost one of the fishes, which cried out, "Stop!"

But the cobbler said, "I don't want you, because you can scream," and on he went. The same thing happened with the second fish. At last he lost the third, and when he said for the third time, "I don't want you," the fish cried out, "Take me home, it will be good luck to you."

"What good can you do me, poor fish?" asked the cobbler.

"Only take me home, and do what I now tell thee," said the fish. "Cut my belly open, and thou wilt find on the one side a lump of gold, and on the other a stone; bury these near a tree. Give the brains to thy wife, and she will present thee with two little boys with golden hair. Give the head to thy horse, and he will bring thee two colts with golden manes. Give the tail to thy dog, and he will give thee two little dogs with golden hair."

The cobbler took the fish, did as he was told, and actually received the things the fish had named. As he had now become well-to-do by means of the lump of gold, he sent his two sons to school. There he met the schoolmaster on one occasion, and the schoolmaster asked why he did not send his two sons to school. The cobbler wondered at this, and when he got home, he asked his little ones where they went to school. They answered they dare not say until they were twelve years old. They were very diligent at their books, and when they were twelve years old they confessed to their father that they had gone to school at the tree where he had buried the stone.

The two young ones now wanted to go into the wide world and asked their father to give each of them a pony and a little dog; but their father would have nothing to say to this. However, not long after, one night each boy took his pony with the golden mane and a little dog, and rode forth. When they had ridden some distance Hans said, "My dear Seppl, we must now separate, for the two of us always see alike, and that won't do. I will climb this high oak and find out two roads."

---

6. *In the Land of Marvels: Folktales from Austria and Bohemia*, trans. Edwin Johnson (London: Swan Sonnenschein, 1884).

He climbed up and saw in the distance a light, then came down again and said, "I'll go this way, you go that way; but so that we may know how each fares, let us each fasten a rose on this oak. If one comes back and finds the other's rose faded, he will know that the other is ill; but if the rose is quite dry, he will know that he is dead."

The two now separated and went upon their ways. Then Hans came to an inn, and asked the host, "What news?"

"Not much news," said the host, "only that our king is going to give a fencing-match, at which any man may fight with his daughters' suitors, and if he conquers one of them, he is to have a princess for his wife."

'Stay!' thought Hans to himself. 'Perhaps I can fight too, and take my share with the rest.'

He left horse and dog with the host, put on a ragged coat that belonged to the manservant, and betook himself to the fencing-school. The match began. All those present had already fought with the suitor of the elder daughter, and no one had gained a victory. Only Hans was left. Then the courtier laughed, and said, "Now, I shall soon have finished with this fellow."

But Hans had a quicker eye than the other and ran him through the body. Now when the king's daughter saw that this ragged young man was to be her husband, she said to her father, "I will not have him!" and then asked Hans if he would be content with 500 gulden.

"Oh, certainly, why not?" answered Hans. "There are other ladies here," and he pocketed the money.

And now the suitor of the second of the princesses went into the lists, but none could overcome him. He also looked contemptuously on Hans as he came forth; but Hans punished him by hewing his arm off. Since the younger princess would not have him, however, he got 500 gulden more, which he merrily pocketed, with the words, "There are others here!"

And now came the suitor of the youngest princess; and he had his foot cut off by his last adversary, who was none other than our Hans. But this time the same thing did not happen as before. The last princess was pleased with the golden hair and the blooming countenance of the young man, and she said to Hans that he must come up to the castle-yard, and she would look down from the window and tell him whether she would have him for her husband or not. As she had promised, the lady appeared and told Hans that he was king. And now they wanted to give Hans fine clothes, but he put them aside with thanks, begged for permission to absent himself for a short time, went to the inn, put on the fine clothes he used to wear, and rode on his pony, the little dog by his side, back into the castle.

All were astonished when they saw the young king ride up on his horse with the golden mane, and by him the little dog with golden hair, while on his neck likewise his golden locks glistened in the sunbeams. The envy of the two elder sisters increased from hour to hour. The marriage was celebrated, and the young couple lived happily for the first few weeks. But all was not at peace in the bosom of the eldest sister, for she was ever devising means to get rid of the young king. She went therefore to a witch who dwelt in a great forest outside the city, and asked her if she would not put him out of the way.

"Give me 300 gulden," said the witch, "and make ready for a hunt, in which he must pass through this forest, and I will put him out of the way, so that nobody shall see him any more."

The bargain with the witch was concluded, and the hunt arranged at the princess's desire. The witch now seated herself on a high tree in a remote part of the forest. Presently the young king came by, and seeing the little mother in this lofty height, he called to her, "What dost thou up there? Come down!"

"Ah, my lord!" answered the cunning old woman, "I dare not. The little dog might bite me. Take this rod, which I throw thee down, and switch about you, that the little dog may run away."

The young king caught the rod which she cast down, and struck over behind him, but at the same moment he vanished with his horse and his little dog. The news went like wildfire through all the city, and great was the mourning for the young king.

Let us now see what befell his brother Seppl. He came back one day to the high oak where he had separated from Hans and saw with grief that Hans' rose was withered. 'Poor Hans,' he thought to himself, 'Thou hast been even doomed to die but I will at least ascertain where thou didst die.' And he struck into the same road that Hans had taken after they had separated. When he came into the city, all the windows were hung with black, and all was in mourning. He went into the inn and asked what it meant.

"Why," said the host, "how can you ask? Don't you know that our young king has vanished? But it seems to me you only make believe, for you are yourself the king!"

This was enough for Seppl, for he suspected that the young king was his brother, because they were very much alike. So he went into the castle and was received with great joy, he alone being very sad. When the consort of the young king asked him why he was so sad, for she thought it was her husband, Seppl said he was not the young king, but his brother.

Meanwhile the eldest princess was in the wood with the witch, demanding back her 300 gulden, because the young king had come back.

"Go, fool," said the old woman, "that is his brother. Get ready for another hunt, and I will soon make away with this one also."

And in fact the envious sister contrived to bring about another hunt.

When Seppl, who now passed for the king, came to the place where his brother had vanished, he called out to the old woman sitting on the tree to come down.

She answered, "Ah, my lord! I am afraid; the little dog might bite me."

But this time the young king answered her otherwise. "If thou comest not down, old witch," he cried in a rage, "I will shoot thee. Thou hast cast a spell on my brother, and if thou dost not instantly make him alive again, thou art a dead woman."

Then the old woman was afraid, and begged that if he would only let her get down, she would then make him alive again. When she got to the ground, she struck thrice with a rod on the earth, and before her lay the king, his horse, and his little dog, but dead. Now she touched each one with the rod, and all three were restored to life. With joy the two brothers greeted each other, tore the old witch to pieces, and went back into the city. Unspeakable was the joy there. Hans again became king, and Seppl was named vice-king. And if they are not alive, probably by this time they are dead.

Translated by Edwin Johnson.

The Twins (1870)[7]
Laura Gonzenbach

Once upon a time there was a king who possessed a beautiful and large realm, but he didn't have any children. Now a war with another king happened to erupt, and the king had to contend with him and lost the battle. Consequently, all his states were taken from him, and he had to flee from his realm with his wife. They wandered about for a long time until they came to a beach near the sea where nobody was to be seen. They built a little hut there, and the king went fishing while the queen cooked the fish that he brought home, and this was the wretched way they lived with one another.

One day the king happened to catch a gold fish, which spoke to him.

"Listen to me," the fish said, "take me home with you and cut me into eight pieces. Give two to your wife, two to your horse, two to your dog, and bury two in your garden. This will bring you good fortune."

The king did just as the fish said. He brought the fish home and cut it into eight pieces. Two he gave to his queen, two to his horse, two to his dog, and two he buried in the garden. Not long thereafter, the queen appeared to be pregnant, and when her time came, she gave birth to two handsome boys, who looked so alike that one could not tell them apart from one another. On the same day, the horse brought two colts into the world, and the dog, two puppies. In the garden two swords grew, and they were made of gold and had magic powers. The two boys grew and flourished, and they became stronger and bigger with each passing day. They were so similar in appearance that their own mother and father could not tell who was who.

When they had now become big and strong young men, their father told them one day that he had once been a powerful king but that he had been defeated by a more powerful king and had been robbed of his realm.

7. *Sicilianische Märchen*, 2 vols. (Leipzig: W. Engelmann, 1870).

"Father," his sons answered him, "we want to set out into the world and regain all your states for you. Give us your blessing and let us depart."

The king and queen were very despondent and did not want to let their dear sons leave. However, the brothers answered, "If you don't want to give your blessing, we shall have to depart without it because we are determined to leave."

So their parents gave their blessing, and each one of the brothers took a magic sword from the garden, mounted one of the horses, and took one of the dogs with them. Then they rode off. After they had ridden for some time, one of them said, "Dear brother, here is the spot where we should separate. You go in that direction, and I shall go in the other, and once we have achieved something, we'll meet back here at this spot."

The other brother agreed, and they separated from one another. The one brother rode straight ahead until he came to a city which was decorated for some festival.

"Why is it that your city is decorated in such a festive way?" he asked someone on the street, and the man answered, "Our king had conquered the neighboring states of a king many years ago. Now he has a lovely daughter, and he has announced to all the knights that he is going to organize a tournament which is to last three days, and whoever is the victor on each one of these days is to marry the princess. As dowry he is going to give the victor all the neighboring states that he had one time conquered."

"What's the name of your king?" the young man asked.

The man told him the name of the king, and the youth recognized that it was the same king who had conquered his father's states. So he went first to a tavern and refreshed himself with food and drink. Then he mounted his horse, strapped on his magic sword, and rode to the tournament. Many noble knights had gathered there, but the unknown youth defeated all of them because nobody could compete with his magic sword. The next day the unknown youth reappeared at the tournament and was victorious again, and on the third day he defeated everyone once more. Then the king spoke to him, "You were victorious on all three days, and now you shall marry my daughter. But tell me, who are you?"

All at once the young man identified himself and said, "I am the son of the king whom you defeated, and whose states you want to give away as your daughter's dowry. I have regained my father's states and am satisfied. So let's us enjoy a wedding celebration."

Soon after this they held a splendid wedding, and the prince married the princess, who was more beautiful than the sun. Later he sent a carriage and beautiful clothes to his father, and he invited him to return to his realm because his son had regained his states. In the meantime the prince enjoyed living with his young wife.

One day he decided to go hunting, and he said to his wife, "I want to go hunting today, and I'll be away for three days."

He took his gold sword, mounted his horse, and called his dog. On the same day, however, his brother entered the same city from the other side, and since he looked just like his brother and had the same horse, dog, and sword, everyone thought he was the young king and greeted him in a most reverent way. He was puzzled about this and thought, 'Perhaps my brother has already been here?'

When he now came to the castle, the servants led him up into his brother's quarters, and the princess rushed toward him and said, "My dear husband, you only rode off this morning and told me that you were going to stay away for three days."

"I changed my mind," the prince answered.

So the princess led him to the table for dinner, and in the evening he had to go with her into the bedroom. When she lay down, however, he took his double-bladed sword and placed it between himself and the princess who was so frightened by this that she didn't dare ask him why he had done it. He continued to do this for two more nights.

When three days had passed, the young husband returned from the hunt, and everyone was astonished when they saw the young king again. He went straight to the castle, and when he saw his brother, who was standing in the castle courtyard, he rushed toward him, embraced him, and cried, "Dear brother, is that you? Now we can really enjoy ourselves."

Everyone was astounded, and he explained to the king and the princess, how everything had come about, and then his young wife snuggled up to him and said softly, "I've got to tell you that your brother spent three nights in your bed, but now I know why he always placed a double-edged sword between us."

After some days had passed and the parents of the two brothers arrived, they traveled once again to their states, where the prince became the king and the beautiful princess, the queen. Later, the other brother married another princess, and so they remained rich and consoled, and we just sit here and continue to get old.

The Fisherman's Two Sons (1870)[8]

François-Marie Luzel

Once upon a time, there was time,
once there will be time,
for all the tales to be told.

Once upon a time there was an old fisherman whose wife was pregnant. One evening he returned home without having caught anything. But his wife had a

---

8.   "Les deux fils du pêcheur," told by Marguerite Philippe, Commune of Pluzunet (Côtes-du-Nord) in *Contes Bretons recueillis et traduits* (Quimperlé: Clairet, 1870).

great desire to eat some fish, and so he had to return to the river right away. Once there he threw his net into the water and caught a very beautiful fish. Of course, he was extremely happy. "At least, for the present my wife will let me have a little bit of peace."

But just as he was about to take the fish from the net, it began to talk: "When I'm dead, give my flesh to your wife, my heart, covered by the water with which I shall have been washed, to your mare, and my entrails and my lungs to your dog."

The old fisherman was quite surprised to hear a fish talk like a human. Never in his life had he experienced something like this.

"I'll do it," he responded and returned to his home.

As soon as he arrived, he said to his wife. "It's me! I caught a beautiful fish! Just look at how large and beautiful it is!"

"Yes, it's true. We should cook it."

"If you had only heard what it said to me!"

"Who? The fish?"

"Yes, the fish."

"And what did he say to you?"

"That I should give you his flesh to eat, his heart covered with the water that was used to wash it to our mare, and his entrails and his lungs to our dog."

"Well then, we should do as he said."

So they cooked the fish, and the fisherman's wife ate its flesh, the horse ate its heart, and the dog its entrails. Immediately after, the fisherman's wife gave birth, and she brought forth twins into this world, two superb infants. They looked so much alike that they had to tie a ribbon on one of the arms of the twins in order to distinguish one from the other. That very same day the mare also gave birth to two foals that looked perfectly alike, and the dog likewise brought forth two puppies that were impossible to distinguish one from the other.

"A miracle!" cried the fisherman. "A foal and a pup for each one of our children."

The two boys did well. When they reached the age of fifteen or sixteen, one of them said to his parents that he was bored at home and wanted to wander about the country. His father, mother, and brother tried vainly to dissuade him and finally had to let him depart. But before he separated from his family, he told his brother that, when he got up each morning, he was to go to the trunk of a bay-tree in the garden and to stab it with his knife. If blood came out of the tree, it would mean that he was dead, but until then, his brother was not to be worried about his fate.

The brother departed and took his horse and his dog with him. He traveled quite some distance until, one day, he arrived at a long lane of old oak trees. He followed this lane, and at the far end he found himself in front of a beautiful chateau. He knocked at the door, and a doorman opened it. Then the brother asked whether they were looking to hire a servant in the chateau. He was then hired as a stable boy. Since he was a hard-working, skillful young man, and handsome to boot, he quickly pleased the lord of the chateau, and his horse and dog also pleased the lord. But more than pleasing the lord, the young man pleased the lord's daughter even more. She was a young and very beautiful lady. In short, he pleased her so much that they got married at the end of a year.

The young couple lived happily by taking walks every day in the gardens and in the woods that surrounded the chateau. One day, the fisherman's son noticed that the windows and the doors on one side of the chateau were always kept closed, and he asked his wife what the reason was for this.

"It's because," she replied, "there's a courtyard on the other side of the chateau, and it is filled with poisonous beasts, snakes, toads, salamanders, and other reptiles."

From this moment on the young man could only think about this courtyard, and he had a great desire to go and see whether he had been told the truth. One day, when he was taking a walk on the other side of the chateau with his horse and dog—his wife did not accompany him on this particular day—he passed by the door to the courtyard and said to himself, "I must absolutely see what's inside there!"

He knocked at the door, and a small old woman opened it and said to him, "Good day, my son. Have you finally come to see me?"

"Good day, grandmother."

"Quick, enter, and I'll show you the beautiful things that I have here. Take these two chains to attach your dog and horse to the posts over there."

Upon saying this, she pulled out two strands of her hair and gave them to him. Immediately the two strands of hair turned into two chains with which he attached his horse and dog to two stone posts that were on each side of the door. Upon seeing this, the horse and the dog began to struggle to protect themselves. They whined and howled, but it was all in vain. They were chained to the posts and had to remain there.

"Follow me now, my son, so that I can show you my chateau," the old woman continued talking. "Come and look at all the beautiful things that I have here. I'm sure you've never seen such things before in your life. Let's go first to see the mill of razors."

When they were in front of a large wheel completely covered with razors, the old woman said, "Look, my son, what a miracle! But get down a bit. Lean over here, and you'll see better."

And when he leaned on the railing without thinking anything bad would happen, the old devil of a woman pushed him, and he fell on a razor and was chopped into tiny pieces like sawdust!

His brother, who had stayed home, went into the garden to the bay-tree every morning when he got up to stab its trunk, and since no blood had spouted from the tree, he had not become worried and said to himself, 'God be praised! He's still alive, my dear brother!'

But, alas! On the particular morning that he stabbed the tree with his knife as he usually did, blood gushed from the trunk of the bay-tree.

"Oh, what misfortune! My poor brother's dead!" he wept out as soon as he saw the blood. And he went right away to find his father with tears streaming from his eyes.

"Alas!" he cried. "Father, my poor brother's dead!"

"How can you know that?"

"Before he left he asked me to go to the bay-tree in the garden each morning that I got up and to stab its trunk. He told me that if blood spouted from the trunk, it meant that he was dead. Alas! This morning, blood gushed from the trunk of the bay-tree. My poor brother's dead! But I want to go and search for him, and I won't stop traveling neither night nor day until I will have found him."

His father and mother begged him in vain not to go. They wept and asked him not to abandon them in their old age. But he didn't listen to them and departed with his horse and dog, just as his brother had done. Traveling full steam ahead, day and night, without stopping, he reached the same lane of oak trees just as his brother had done. He also knocked at the door of the chateau, and it opened immediately. On seeing him enter the courtyard, his brother's wife mistook him for her husband, and as she quickly descended the stairs, she ran and threw herself into his arms.

"There you are, my poor husband!" she cried. "My God! You've caused me such worry! I thought that you had gone into the courtyard behind the chateau. Nobody ever returns from there alive!"

The brother realized right away that the young woman mistook him for his brother and said, "I got lost in the woods. I don't know how, but nothing bad happened to me."

Now there was joy in the chateau once again after everyone had been greatly troubled. When dinnertime arrived, they ate at the same table. Then, together, they mounted the stairs to their bedroom. Before getting into bed, the young man placed his bare sword between his brother's wife and himself.

'Why is he doing this?' the young woman said to herself, astonished.

The fisherman's son, who was afraid of being recognized, said that he was exhausted and wanted to sleep. But the young woman did not stop asking questions and wanted to know how he had passed his time in the woods during his absence and many other things. You can imagine how embarrassed he was and frequently didn't know how to respond. In turn, he also asked why all the doors and windows in the chateau were closed.

"But I already told you that. Don't you remember?"

"Certainly not. I've forgotten."

"Well then, I'll tell you again. On that side of the chateau there's a courtyard filled with poisonous reptiles and beasts even more dangerous. And whoever enters that courtyard never returns."

Immediately he knew that his brother had entered that courtyard.

The next morning, after breakfast, he went walking on the other side of the chateau with his horse and dog.

"My brother must be inside there," he said to himself, "and no matter what, I must go and see for myself."

So, he knocked on the door. The old woman went to open it. He entered and immediately recognized his brother's horse and dog even though they were gaunt and seemed about to die from starvation.

"Good day, my son," said the old woman. "Have you also come to see me? Enter quickly so that I can show you all the beautiful things that I have here. But first take these two chains and attach your horse and dog to the stone posts over there next to the door. Then they'll stay there until you come back."

As she said this, she tore two strands of hair from her head and gave them to him. But he breathed on them, and they fell to the ground and changed immediately into two vipers.

"Hmm!" uttered the old woman when she saw this. "If you don't want to chain your horse and dog, let them run freely in the courtyard, and come with me to visit my chateau."

Now he followed her, and when they arrived at the mill of razors, she said, "Look, my son, put your head on that trough over there, and you will see something marvelous."

"Show me how to do it, grandmother."

"Well, do it like this, my son."

And she put her head on the trough. As soon as she did this, the fisherman's son grabbed her feet and threw her on the wheel covered with razors. Within seconds she fell to the ground chopped into tiny pieces like sawdust.

Then the fisherman's son walked all over the chateau to see if he could find his brother. Instead he encountered a female fox which said to him, "How did you manage to come here?"

"Can you really talk?" the astonished fisherman's son replied.

"As you see, yes, I can talk."

"I managed to get rid of the old woman."

"How did you do that?"

"How? I pushed her head first on to the wheel covered with razors, and she was chopped into tiny pieces like sawdust."

"Oh, if only this were true!"

"It's absolutely true. You can believe me."

"Well then, you've saved my life!"

As soon as the fox said this, she turned into a marvelously beautiful princess!

"There you are!" she cried out. "I spent five hundred years under the spell of that wretched witch!"

"And my poor brother? Can you tell me what has become of him?"

"Your brother was pushed by the old woman on to the wheel covered with razors, and he's been reduced to tiny pieces like sawdust. But you needn't worry. I gathered everything—his flesh, his bones, his blood. Now we need the water of life to restore him to life, and we can find it in a flask in the old witch's room."

So, they took the flesh, bones, and blood and put them into a cup. Then they spread the water of life from the flask on top. Immediately the young man's body was reassembled, and he returned to life totally fit.

"I certainly slept well!" the fisherman's son cried.

"Yes, you did, my poor brother, and without me and this beautiful princess, you wouldn't have woken up so soon!"

The two brothers threw their arms around each other and wept with joy because they were reunited. Then, accompanied by the beautiful princess whom they had saved, they returned to the other side of the chateau where the young woman was very astonished to see two husbands instead of just one. Indeed, she couldn't determine which one was her true husband because of their close resemblance!

They told her everything, and now she understood why the second brother had placed his bare sword between them during the night that he had spent with her.

Soon after, the one brother who was not married, married the beautiful princess whom he saved after having been transformed into a female fox. They sent a handsome carriage to fetch the old fisherman and his wife, and for an entire month, they celebrated with games, dances, and feasts, the likes of which you've never seen in your life.

The grandmother of my great-great-grandmother, who was somewhat related to the old fisherman, was invited to the wedding. This is why we know all about this famous wedding in our country.

The Three Brothers (1875)[9]
Domenico Comparetti

Once upon a time there were three brothers who went out into the world. Soon they found themselves in a city completely draped in black. So they asked why it was completely draped that way. The people told them that there was a magician in the vicinity, and every year they had to draw lots to see which maiden the magician would take away with him. Thereupon, the brothers asked them which maiden was chosen this time by the magician, and they said it was the king's daughter. Then the three brothers declared that they were the right

9. "I tre ragazzi," in *Novelline Popolari Italiane* (Bologna: Forni, 1875).

ones to go and set her free. In turn, the king said, "If you are the right ones to free my daughter, one of you can have her for your wife."

After they departed, they found a deep well and lowered a rope to descend. However, two of the brothers were afraid to go down. Only the third, who was a hunter, went down the well. After he arrived at the bottom, he found himself in a city in which he encountered carriages moving back and forth, and there was also a large castle. So the hunter entered the magician's castle, and there he found the princess. As soon as she saw this young man, she began to weep and told him that he had to leave immediately because the magician would soon arrive and eat him. But the hunter responded: "Easy does it! Either he'll eat me, or I'll eat him!"

Then he took out a pistol and sharpened his sword, and all of a sudden he heard a loud noise nearby. The princess said to him, "Hide before the magician gets here."

When the magician arrived in the castle, he cried out, "Who's here in my castle? I smell the blood of a Christian. He'll make for a nice bite to eat."

And the young man responded: "Come to me if you're brave enough!"

Well, the magician went into the room and took out his sword, and the two began thrashing one another. The young man cut off six of the magician's heads. So the magician asked for a moment's rest, and all six of his heads returned to him. Then they began to attack each other all over again, and once more the young man cut off six heads causing the magician to ask for another moment's rest. This time, however, the hunter didn't give it to him and cut off the other head so that the magician was really killed. Then he went to the princess and said: "You see that I've killed the magician. Now you'll be my wife."

The princess agreed because he had set her free. Then they went together to the bottom of the well where they found the rope. The brothers were above, and they pulled her up. But the hunter began thinking a bit and said to himself: 'Who's to say that they won't pull me up a little and let me fall? Then I'll be killed.' So, he tied the rope around a rock. His brothers pulled the rock up a little, and when the rock was half way up, they let it fall. Then the hunter said, "Just look at what would have been me! They would have earned a great deal from my death!"

So, he returned to the castle and walked around, here and there, until he entered a room where he saw an old woman in a corner.

"What are you doing here?" he asked her. "Tell me how to get out of here. If you don't, I'll kill you just as I killed your son."

"How am I ever supposed to tell you?" she said. "I don't know anything about that."

"Well, then I'm going to kill you."

"Let's go and look," the old woman responded. "There must be a little sack of nails here. We'll make a ladder from the nails so that you can climb up."

So they made a ladder, and the young man climbed up and out of the well. When he was above, he put his rifle on his shoulder and went back home to join his brothers. As soon as the princess saw him, she burst into tears, while he said to his brothers: "What real gentlemen you are to make me look like a fool!"

"Excuse us," they replied. "The rope tore, and we thought that you had been killed."

"Well, even if you made a fool of me a little, I forgive you," the brother replied.

Then they departed and arrived at a place where they had to cross a river. So they got into a boat, and as they were crossing, they saw the magician up in the sky. He had come flying in full fury. The two brothers said to the other one, "You're a hunter. Shoot him down."

So he shot and hit the magician who fell and landed on the boat and smashed it.

One of the brothers was a carpenter, and the others said to him: "Since you're a carpenter, repair the boat. Otherwise, we shall all drown."

So, he repaired the boat, and when they reached the head of the river, the princess began walking and noticed that she had destroyed her shoes. One of the brothers was a shoemaker. So the others said to him: "Make a pair of shoes for her."

And so he made a pair of shoes for her, and when they arrived at the king's palace, the king had the city draped in red and said, "Which one of you freed my daughter?"

The hunter said, "It was me."

But one of the other brothers said, "I repaired the boat. If I hadn't, we would have drowned."

Then the third brother said: "I made her a pair of shoes so she could walk and make it back here."

And whoever said one thing, the other said something else. The king saw that they wanted to argue and said to them: "You three want to argue, but I'm not going to give my daughter to any of you. Instead, I'm going to give you three other maidens to marry."

The brothers responded that they were content with his decision, and so they were wed and led their wives home.

The Sons of the Fisherman (1886)[10]

Emmanuel Cosquin

Once upon a time there was a fisherman, and one day, while he was fishing, he caught a large fish.

---

10. "Les fils du pêcheur," *Contes populaires de Lorraine* (Paris: Vieweg, 1886).

"Fisherman, fisherman," the fish said to him, "let me go, and you'll catch many more."

The fisherman threw the fish back into the water, and indeed, he caught many more fish. When he returned to his home, he told his wife, "I caught a large fish that said to me, 'Fisherman, fisherman, let me go, and you'll catch many more.'"

"And you didn't bring me this one?" his wife said. "I would have liked to have eaten it."

The next day, the fisherman caught the large fish once again.

"Fisherman, fisherman, let me go, and you'll catch many more."

The fisherman threw the fish back into the water, and after he finished fishing, he returned to his home.

"If you don't bring this large fish to me tomorrow," his wife said, "I'll go with you, and I'll catch it."

The following day the fisherman went off fishing, and for the third time, the large fish said, "Fisherman, fisherman, let me go, and you'll catch many more."

"No," the fisherman replied. "My wife wants to eat you."

"Very well," said the fish. "If she must eat me, give some of my bones to your dog and mare and then bury the rest of the bones in the garden behind your house. Finally, fill three vials with my blood. You will have three sons, and when they grow up, you'll give each one of them one of the vials, and if something bad happens to any one of them, the blood will immediately begin to boil."

The fisherman did what the fish told him to do, and after some time had passed, his wife gave birth to three sons. The mare dropped three colts, and the dog, three pups. At the place in the garden where he had buried the fish's bones the fisherman found three fine lances.

When the fisherman's sons had grown up, they left home to see the world and separated at a crossroad along the way. From time to time, each one looked to see if the blood began to boil in his vial.

The eldest son arrived in a village where everyone was in mourning, and he asked why. Someone told him that every year they had to deliver a young maiden to a beast with seven heads, and that the die had been cast for a princess.

Soon after he heard this, the young man went into the forest where the people had left the princess. She was on her knees and praying to God.

"What are you doing there?" the young man asked.

"Alas!" she replied. "The die has been cast, and I've been designated to be devoured by the beast with the seven heads. Quick, get out of here!"

"No," the young man said. "I'm going to wait for the beast."

And he helped the princess to mount on the rump of his horse.

Soon the beast appeared. After a long battle, the young man, assisted by his dog, cut off the seven heads of the beast with his lance. The princess thanked him a thousand times and invited him to come with her to her father's chateau. He was the king. But the young man refused, and so she gave him her kerchief marked with the initials of her name. The young man wrapped the seven tongues of the beast in the kerchief and then said good-bye to the princess who began walking along a path to her father's chateau.

When she was still in the forest, she encountered three coalmen and told them about her adventure. The coalmen threatened to kill her with their axes if she didn't take them to the place where the beast's body could be found. So the princess led them there. After they took the seven heads of the beast, they departed with the princess and made her swear that she would tell the king they were the ones who had killed the beast. They arrived together at the Louvre in Paris, and the princess said to her father that the three coalmen had saved her from the beast. The king was ecstatic and declared that he would give his daughter to one of them as his bride. But the princess refused to marry until one year and a day had passed. She was sick and sad.

Well, one year and a day went by, and the people began rejoicing about the forthcoming wedding. Just then the eldest of the fisherman's sons arrived in the city and took lodging at an inn. An old woman said to him: "A year and a day ago everyone had been sad, and now everyone is joyful. Three coalmen rescued the princess who was to be devoured by a beast with seven heads, and the king is going to have his daughter marry one of them."

So, the young man said to his dog, "Go and fetch me the best to eat in the king's palace."

The dog brought him two fine plates of food, while the king's cooks complained to their master. In turn the king sent his guards to find out where the dog had gone. The young man killed all of them with his lance except one. He let this guard live so that he could carry the news to the king. Then he told his dog to go and fetch the king's best cakes. And once again the king sent other guards, and the young man killed them just as he had done the others.

"I must go myself," the king said and went to the inn in his carriage. Then he had the young man get into the carriage and took him to his chateau where he invited him to take part in the festivities.

When the time for dessert arrived, the king said, "I would like all the people to tell a story about their adventures, and let us begin with the coalmen."

Well, they told a story of how they had saved the princess just before she was going to be devoured by the beast with the seven heads.

"Here they are," they said, "the seven heads that we have cut off."

"Sire," the young man now spoke, "look and see if there are seven tongues."

There were no tongues.

"Who is more believable," the young man continued, "the man who has the tongues or the one who has the heads?"

"The man who has the tongues," the king replied.

So the young man immediately showed the tongues, and the princess recognized the kerchief embroidered with her initials and was happier than she had ever been.

"Father," she said, "this young man is the one who rescued me."

Right after this the king ordered a gallows to be built, and the three coalmen were hanged. Then they celebrated the wedding between the fisherman's son and the princess.

That evening, after dinner, when the young man was in a room with his wife, he went to the window and noticed a chateau on fire.

"What's going on with that chateau over there?" he asked.

"I've seen that chateau on fire every evening," the princess responded, "and I can't explain what's going on."

As soon as the princess fell asleep, the young man got up and departed with his horse and dog to see what was going on. He arrived in a beautiful meadow, and in the middle of it stood a chateau. Then he met an old fairy who said to him: "My friend, would you please get off your horse and help me load this bunch of herbs onto my back?"

"Gladly," replied the young man.

But as soon as he set his foot on the ground, she waved her magic wand and changed him, his horse, and dog into clumps of grass.

Meanwhile, however, his brothers saw the blood boil in their vials and wanted to know what had become of their elder brother. The second son set out and arrived in the city. As he passed by the king's chateau, the princess happened to be at the door just at that moment and was looking for her husband to return. She believed that the young man was her husband, for the three brothers looked so much alike that they could be mistaken for one another.

"Ah!" she cried out. "There you are, my husband. Finally! You're very late."

"Excuse me," the young man responded. "I gave some orders, but they were not carried out. So, I had to do everything myself."

After dinner, the princess went to her room with the young man. When he looked out the window like his brother, he saw the chateau on fire.

"What's going on with that chateau?" he said.

"But you already asked me about it, my husband."

"Well, I don't remember what you said."

"I told you that the chateau was on fire every night and that I can't explain what is going on."

Then the young man took his horse and dog and departed. After he arrived in the meadow, he encountered the old fairy who said to him, "My friend, would you please get off your horse and help me load this bunch of herbs onto my back?"

The young man dismounted, and as soon as he did, the old fairy waved her magic wand, and he was changed into a clump of grass, along with his horse and dog.

Now, the youngest brother looked at his vial once more and saw the blood boiling, and soon he found himself in the city where the princess saw him pass by. She mistook him also for her husband, and he, too, asked her about the chateau on fire.

"I've already told you many times," she responded, "that this chateau burns every night, and I don't know anything more than just that."

So the young man departed with his horse and dog and arrived in the meadow near the chateau.

"My friend," the fairy said, "would you please get off your horse and help me load this bunch of herbs onto my back?"

"No," the young man replied. "I won't dismount. It's you who have caused my brothers to perish. If you don't return them to life, I'm going to kill you."

As he talked, he grabbed hold of her hair without setting a foot on the ground. The old lady asked for mercy, took her magic wand, and touched the clumps of grass. As soon as she did this, everything that she had transformed was returned to its original form. When she had finished, the youngest brother took his saber and cut the old fairy into a thousand pieces. Then he returned to the king's chateau with his brothers. The princess couldn't recognize which one of them was her husband.

"It's me," said the eldest.

Soon after this, his brothers married the princess's sisters, and there were grand festivities that lasted six months.

The Two Brothers (1890)[11]

J. F. Jukih

There was a man who had a wife but no sons, a female hound but no puppies, and a mare but no foal.

'What in the world shall I do?' said he to himself. 'Come, let me go away from home to seek my fortune in the world, as I haven't any at home.'

As he thought, so he did, and went out by himself into the wide world as a bee from flower to flower. One day, when it was about dinner-time, he came to a spring, took down his knapsack, took out his provisions for the journey, and began to eat his dinner. Just then a traveler appeared in front of him and sat down beside the spring to rest; he invited him to sit down by him that they might eat together. When they had inquired after each other's health and shaken hands, then the second comer asked the first on what business he was traveling about the world. He said to him: "I have no luck at home. Therefore

---

11. Albert Henry Wratislaw, *Sixty Folk-Tales from Exclusively Slavonic Sources* (Boston: Houghton, Mifflin and Company, 1890).

I am going from home; my wife has no children, my hound has no puppies, and my mare has never had a foal; I am going about the wide world as a bee from flower to flower."

When they had had a good dinner, and got up to travel further, then the one who had arrived last thanked the first for his dinner, and offered him an apple, saying: "Here is this apple for you—if I am not mistaken it was a Frederic pippin—and return home at once; peel the apple and give the peel to your hound and mare; cut the apple in two, give half to your wife to eat, and eat the other half yourself. What has hitherto been unproductive will henceforth be productive. And as for the two pips which you will find in the apple, plant them on the top of your house."

The man thanked him for the apple; they rose up and parted, the one going onwards and the other back to his house. He peeled the apple and did every-thing as the other had instructed him. As time went on, his wife became the mother of two sons, his hound of two puppies, and his mare of two foals, and, moreover, out of the house grew two apple trees. While the two brothers were growing up, the young horses grew up, and the hounds became fit for hunting. After a short time the father and mother died, and the two sons, being now left alone like a tree cut down on a hill, agreed to go out into the world to seek their fortune. Even so they did: each brother took a horse and a hound; they cut down the two apple trees, and made themselves a spear apiece, and went out into the wide world.

I can't tell you for certain how many days they traveled together; this I do know, that at the first parting of the road they separated. Here they saw it written up: "If you go by the upper road, you will not see the world for five years. If you go by the lower road, you will not see the world for three years."

Here they parted, one going by the upper and the other by the lower road. The one that went by the lower road, after three years of traveling through another world, came to a lake, beside which there was written on a post: "If you go in, you will repent it. If you don't go in, you will repent it."

'If it is so,' thought he to himself, 'let me take whatever God gives.' And so he swam across the lake. And lo! A wonder! He, his horse, and his hound were all gilded with gold. After this he speedily arrived at a very large and spa-cious city. He went up to the emperor's palace and inquired for an inn where he might pass the night. They told him, up there, yon large tower, that was an inn. In front of this tower he dismounted; servants came out and welcomed him, and conducted him into the presence of their master in the courtyard. But it was not an innkeeper, rather the king of the province himself. The king welcomed and entertained him handsomely. The next day he began to prepare to set forth on his journey. The evening before, the king's only daughter, when she saw him go in front of her apartments had observed him well, and fixed her eyes upon him. This she did because such a golden traveler had never before arrived, and consequently she was unable to close her eyes the whole night.

Her heart thumped, as it were; and it was fortunate that the summer night was brief, for if it had been a winter one, she would have hardly been able to wait for the dawn. It all seemed astonishing to her, and her brain whirled as if the king were calling her to receive a ring and an apple; the poor thing would have rushed to the door, but it was shut and there was nobody at hand. Although the night was a short one, it seemed to her that three had passed one after another. When she observed in the morning that the traveler was getting ready to go, she flew to her father, implored him not to let that traveler quit his court, but to detain him and to give her to him in marriage. The king was good-natured, and was easily won over by entreaties. Therefore, whatever his daughter begged for, she also obtained. The traveler was detained and offered marriage with the king's daughter. The traveler did not hesitate long, kissed the king's hand, presented a ring to the maiden, and she a handkerchief to him, and thus they were betrothed.

Methinks they did not wait for publication of banns. Erelong they were wedded; the wedding feast and festival were very prolonged, but came to an end in due course. One morning after all this the bridegroom was looking in somewhat melancholy fashion down on the entry through a window in the tower. His young wife asked him what ailed him? He told her that he was longing for a hunt, and she told him to take three servants and go while the dew was still on the grass. Her husband would not take a single servant, but mounting his gilded horse and calling his gilded hound, went down into the country to hunt. The hound soon found scent, and put up a stag with gilded horns. The stag began to run straight for a tower, the hound after him, and the hunter after the hound, and he overtook the stag in the courtyard, and was going to cut off its head. He had drawn his sword, when a damsel cried through the window, "Don't kill my stag, but come upstairs: let us play at draughts for a wager. If you win, take the stag; if I win, you shall give me the hound."

He was as ready for this as an old woman for a scolding match, went up into the tower, and on to the balcony, staked the hound against the stag, and began to play. The hunter was on the point of beating her, when some damsels began to sing: "A king, a king, I've gained a king!"

He looked round, she altered the position of the draughtsmen, beat him and took the hound. Again they began to play a second time, she staking the hound and he his horse. She cheated him the second time, also. The third time they began to play, he wagered himself. When the game was nearly over, and he was already on the point of beating her, the damsels began to sing this time too, just as they had done the first and second times. He looked round, she cheated and beat him, took a cord, bound him, and put him in a dungeon.

The brother, who went by the upper road, came to the lake, forded it, and came out all golden—himself, his horse, and his hound. He went for a night's lodging to the king's tower; the servants came out and welcomed him. His father-in-law asked him whether he was tired, and whether he had had any success in hunting; but the king's daughter paid special attention to him, frequently kissing him and embracing him. He was completely puzzled and wondered how it was that everybody recognized him; finally, he felt satisfied that it was his brother, who was very like him, who had been here and got married. The king's daughter was also very puzzled, and it was very distressing to her that her newly married husband was so soon tired of her, for the more affectionate she was to him, the more he repelled her.

When the morrow came, he got ready to go out to look for his brother. The king, his daughter, and all the courtiers, begged him to take a rest.

"Why," said they to him, "you only returned yesterday from hunting, and do you want to go again so soon?"

All was in vain; he refused to take the thirty servants whom they offered him, but went down into the country by himself. When he was in the midst of the country, his hound put up a stag, and he went after them on his horse, and drove it up to a tower; he raised his sword to kill the stag, but a damsel cried through a window: "Don't meddle with my stag, but come upstairs that we may have a game at draughts, then let the one that wins take away the stakes, either you my hound, or I yours."

When he went into the basement, in it was a hound and a horse—the hounds and horses recognized each other—and he felt sure that his brother had fallen into prison there. They began the game at draughts, and when the damsel saw that he was going to beat her, some damsels began to sing behind them: "A king! A king! I've gained a king!"

He took no notice, but kept his eye on the draughtsmen; then the damsel, like a she-devil, began to make eyes and wink at the young man. He gave her a flip with his coat behind the ears: "Play now!" and thus beat her.

The second game they both staked a horse. She couldn't cheat him; he took both the hound and the horse from her. The third and last time they played, he staking himself and she herself; and after giving her a slap in her face for her winking and making of eyes, he won the third game. He took possession of her, brought his brother out of the dungeon, and they went to the town.

Now the brother, who had been in prison, began to think within himself: 'He was yesterday with my wife, and who knows whether she does not prefer him to me?'

He drew his sword to kill him, but the draught-player defended himself. He darted before his brother into the courtyard, and as he stepped onto the passage from the tower, his wife threw her arms round his neck and began to scold him affectionately for having driven her from him overnight, and conversed so coldly with her. Then the first brother repented of having so foolishly suspected his brother, who had, moreover, released him from prison, and of having wanted to kill him; but his brother was a considerate person and forgave him. They kissed each other and were reconciled. He retained his wife and her kingdom with her, and his brother took the draught-player and her kingdom with her. And thus they attained to greater fortune than they could ever have even hoped for.

Translated by Albert Henry Wratislaw.

2. THE POWER OF LOVE
ATU 310—THE MAIDEN IN THE TOWER

Extremely popular throughout Europe, this tale type has an illustrious literary history with the following key works: Giambattista Basile, "Petrosinella," *Lo Cunto de li Cunti*; Charlotte-Rose de Caumont de la Force, "Persinette," *Les Contes des contes*; Friedrich Schulz, "Rapunzel," *Kleine Romane*; and Ludwig Bechstein, "Rapunzel," *Deutsches Märchenbuch*. The incarceration of a young woman in a tower (often to protect her chastity during puberty) was a common motif in various European and Asian myths and became part of the standard repertoire of medieval tales, lais, and romances throughout Europe and Asia. In addition, the motif of a pregnant woman who has a strong craving for an extravagant dish or extraordinary food is very significant. In many peasant societies people believed that it was necessary to fulfill the longings of a pregnant woman, otherwise something terrible, like a miscarriage or bad luck, might occur. Therefore, it was incumbent on the husband and other friends and relatives to use spells or charms or other means to fulfill the cravings.

In the Grimms' two versions of "Rapunzel," originally based on Schulz's story, there were some important changes made that reflect the ideological preferences of the Brothers. In the 1812 variant, the owner of the garden is a fairy; Rapunzel sleeps with the prince and becomes pregnant; he wanders about until he finds her, and her tears enable him to see again. In the final version of 1857 there is a new Christian element at the beginning; the fairy becomes a sorceress, because the Grimms believed fairies belonged to a French tradition of storytelling and generally replaced all fairies in the tales they collected with magicians or witches; Rapunzel agrees to marry the prince and no mention is made of her pregnancy; the blinded prince finds her, recovers his sight, and brings her and the twins back to his castle. In other words, the Grimms transformed the tale into a short courtly romance.

Their tendency to stylize "Rapunzel" and produce a romantic happy ending was not common in the nineteenth-century oral retellings, as can be seen in the tales gathered by Gonzenbach, Imbriani, Busk, Pitrè, Webster, Sébillot, and Lang. In their versions, the young girl who is given to a fairy, witch, or old woman, is very active and enters into a conflict during puberty with her "keeper/guardian." Sometimes the keeper/guardian is depicted as a cannibal, other times as an overbearing and strict godmother. The prince and/or a dog is a means toward liberation at a time when she has come of age to determine her own destiny. In some cases, the dog even helps her resolve her conflicts. In Sicily there is a variant from Polizzi with the title "Li Cummari," in which the old woman is an ogress. Otherwise, some other important versions can be found in the works of Bernoni, Büsching, Coronedi-Berti, Schneller, and Millien. For a comprehensive study of "Rapunzel," see Bernhard Lauer, ed., *Rapunzel: Traditionen eines euopäischen Märchenstoffes in Dichtung und Kunst*.

******

Rapunzel (1812)[12]
Jacob and Wilhelm Grimm

Once upon a time there was a husband and wife who for quite some time had been wishing in vain for a child. Finally, the woman became pregnant. Now, in the back of their house the couple had a small window that overlooked a fairy's garden filled with all kinds of flowers and herbs. But nobody ever dared to enter it.

One day, when the wife was standing at the window and looking down into the garden, she noticed a bed of wonderful rapunzel. She had a great craving to eat some of the lettuce, and yet, she knew that she couldn't get any. So, she began to waste away and look wretched. Her husband eventually became horrified and asked what was ailing her.

"If I don't get any of that rapunzel from the garden behind our house, I shall have to die."

Her husband loved her very much and thought, 'No matter what it costs, you're going to get her some rapunzel.'

So, one evening he quickly climbed over the high wall into the garden, grabbed a handful of rapunzel, and brought the lettuce to his wife. Immediately she made a salad and ate it with great zest. But the rapunzel tasted so good to her, so very good, that her craving for it became three times greater by the next day. Her husband knew that, if she was ever to be satisfied, he had to climb into the garden once more. And so, he went over the wall into the garden but was extremely terrified when he stood face-to-face with the fairy who angrily berated him for daring to come into the garden and stealing her rapunzel.

He excused himself as best he could by explaining that his wife was pregnant and that it had become too dangerous to deny her the rapunzel.

"All right," the fairy finally spoke. "I shall permit you to take as much rapunzel as you like, but only if you give me the child that your wife is carrying."

In his fear the man agreed to everything, and when his wife gave birth, the fairy appeared at once, named the baby girl Rapunzel, and took her away.

Rapunzel grew to be the most beautiful child under the sun. But when she turned twelve, the fairy locked her in a very high tower that had neither doors nor stairs, only a little window high above. Whenever the fairy wanted to enter the tower, she would stand below and call out:

> "Rapunzel, Rapunzel,
> let your hair down for me."

Rapunzel had radiant hair, as fine as spun gold. Each time she heard the fairy's voice, she unpinned her braids and wound them around a hook on the window. Then she let her hair drop twenty yards, and the fairy would climb up on it.

---

12.   *Kinder- und Haus-Märchen. Gesammelt durch die Brüder Grimm,* 2 vols. (Berlin: Real-schulbuchandlung, 1812/1815).

One day, a young prince went riding through the forest and came upon the tower. He looked up and saw beautiful Rapunzel at the window. When he heard her singing with such a sweet voice, he fell completely in love with her. However, since there were no doors in the tower and no ladder could ever reach her high window, he fell into despair. Nevertheless, he went into the forest every day until one time he saw the fairy who called out:

"Rapunzel, Rapunzel,
let your hair down."

As a result, he now knew what kind of ladder he needed to climb up into the tower. He took careful note of the words he had to say, and the next day at dusk, he went to the tower and called out:

"Rapunzel, Rapunzel,
let your hair down."

So she let her hair drop, and when her braids were at the bottom of the tower, he tied them around him, and she pulled him up. At first, Rapunzel was terribly afraid, but soon the young prince pleased her so much that she agreed to see him every day and pull him up into the tower. Thus, for a while they had a merry time and enjoyed each other's company. The fairy didn't become aware of this until, one day, Rapunzel began talking and said to her, "Tell me, Mother Gothel, my clothes are becoming too tight. They don't fit me any more."

"Oh, you godless child!" the fairy replied. "What's this I hear?"

And she immediately realized that she had been betrayed and became furious. Then she grabbed Rapunzel's beautiful hair, wrapped it around her left hand a few times, picked up a pair of scissors with her right hand, and *snip, snap*, the hair was cut off. Afterward the fairy banished Rapunzel to a desolate land where she had to live in great misery. In the course of time she gave birth to twins, a boy and a girl.

On the same day that the fairy had banished Rapunzel, she fastened the braids that she had cut off to the hook on the window, and that evening, when the prince came and called out,

"Rapunzel, Rapunzel,
let down your hair,"

she let the braids down. But when the prince climbed up into the tower, he was astonished to find the fairy instead of Rapunzel.

"Do you know what, you villain?" the angry fairy said. "Rapunzel is lost to you forever!"

In his despair the prince threw himself from the tower. He escaped with his life, but he lost both eyes. Sadly he wandered around in the forest, eating nothing but grass and roots and did nothing but weep. Some years later, he made his way to the desolate land where Rapunzel was leading a wretched existence with

her children. When he heard her voice, it sounded familiar and then he immediately recognized it. She recognized him, too, and embraced him. Two of her tears
fell upon his eyes. Then his eyes became clear again, and he could see as usual.

Rapunzel (1857)[13]
Jacob and Wilhelm Grimm

Once upon a time there was a husband and wife who for quite some time
had been wishing in vain for a child. Finally, the dear Lord gave the wife a sign
of hope that their wish would be fulfilled. Now, in the back of their house the
couple had a small window that overlooked a splendid garden filled with the
most beautiful flowers and herbs. The garden, however, was surrounded by a
high wall, and nobody dared enter it because it belonged to a sorceress who was
very powerful and feared by all.

One day when the wife was standing at the window and looking down into
the garden, she noticed a bed of the finest rapunzel lettuce. The lettuce looked so
fresh and green that her mouth watered, and she had a great craving to eat some.
Day by day this craving increased, and since she knew she couldn't get any, she
began to waste away and look pale and miserable.

Her husband became alarmed and asked, "What's wrong with you, dear
wife?"

"Ah," she responded, "I shall certainly die if I don't get any of that rapunzel
from the garden behind our house."

Her husband, who loved her, thought, 'Before I let my wife die, I'll do anything I must to make sure she gets some rapunzel.'

That day at dusk he climbed over the wall into the garden of the sorceress,
hastily grabbed a handful of rapunzel, and brought them to his wife. Immediately she made them into a salad and ate it with great zest. But the rapunzel
tasted so good to her, so very good, that her desire for them was three times
greater by the next day. If she was to have any peace, her husband knew he had
to climb into the garden once more. So at dusk he scaled the wall again, and just
as he landed on the other side, he was given a tremendous scare, for he stood
face-to-face with the sorceress.

"How dare you climb into my garden and steal my rapunzel like a thief?" she
said with an angry look. "You'll pay for this!"

"Oh!" he cried. "Please, let mercy prevail over justice. I did this only because
I was in a predicament: my wife noticed your rapunzel from our window, and
she developed such a great craving for them that she would have died if I hadn't
brought her some to eat."

Upon hearing that, the sorceress's anger subsided, and she said to him, "If it's
truly as you say, then I shall permit you to take as much rapunzel as you like,

13. *Kinder- und Hausmärchen gesammelt durch die Brüder Grimm*, 7th ed., 3 vols. (Göttingen:
Verlag der Dieterischen Buchhandlung, 1857).

but only under one condition: when your wife gives birth, I must have the child. You needn't fear about the child's well-being, for I shall take care of her like a mother."

In his fear the man agreed to everything, and when his wife had the baby, the sorceress appeared at once. She gave the child the name of Rapunzel and took her away.

Rapunzel grew to be the most beautiful child under the sun. But when she was twelve years old, the sorceress locked her in a tower located in a forest. It had neither doors nor stairs, only a little window high above. Whenever the sorceress wanted to get in, she would stand below and call out:

> "Rapunzel, Rapunzel,
> let down your hair for me."

Rapunzel's hair was long and radiant, fine as spun gold. Every time she heard the voice of the sorceress, she unpinned her braids and wound them around a hook on the window. Then she let her hair drop twenty yards, and the sorceress would climb up on it.

A few years later a king's son happened to be riding through the forest and passed by the tower. Suddenly, he heard a song so lovely that he stopped to listen. It was Rapunzel, who passed the time in her solitude by letting her sweet voice resound in the forest. The prince wanted to climb up to her, and he looked for a door but couldn't find one. So he rode home. However, the song had touched his heart so deeply that he rode out into the forest every day and listened. One time, as he was standing behind a tree, he saw the sorceress approach and heard her call out:

> "Rapunzel, Rapunzel,
> let down your hair."

Then Rapunzel let down her braids, and the sorceress climbed up to her.

"If that's the ladder one needs to get up there, I'm also going to try my luck," the prince declared.

The next day, as it began to get dark, he went to the tower and called out:

> "Rapunzel, Rapunzel,
> let down your hair."

All at once the hair dropped down, and the prince climbed up. When he entered the tower, Rapunzel was at first terribly afraid, for she had never laid eyes on a man before. However, the prince began to talk to her in a friendly way and told her that her song had touched his heart so deeply that he had not been able to rest until he had seen her. Gradually, Rapunzel overcame her fears, and when he asked her whether she would have him for her husband, she saw that he was young and handsome and thought, 'He'll certainly love me better than old Mother Gothel.' So she said yes and placed her hand in his.

"I want to go with you very much," she said, "but I don't know how I can get down. Every time you come, you must bring a skein of silk with you, and I'll weave it into a ladder. When it's finished, then I'll climb down, and you can take me away on your horse."

They agreed that until then he would come to her every evening, for the old woman came during the day. Meanwhile, the sorceress did not notice anything, until one day Rapunzel blurted out, "Mother Gothel, how is it that you are much heavier than the prince? When I pull him up, he's here in a second."

"Ah, you godless child!" exclaimed the sorceress. "What's this I hear? I thought that I had made sure you had no contact with the outside world, but you've deceived me!"

In her fury she seized Rapunzel's beautiful hair, wrapped it around her left hand several times, grabbed a pair of scissors with her right hand, and *snip, snap* the hair was cut off, and the beautiful braids lay on the ground. Then the cruel sorceress took Rapunzel to a desolate land where she had to live in great misery and grief.

On the same day that she had banished Rapunzel, the sorceress fastened the braids that she had cut off to the hook on the window, and that evening, when the prince came and called out,

"Rapunzel, Rapunzel,
let down your hair,"

she let the hair down.

The prince climbed up, but instead of finding his dearest Rapunzel on top, he found the sorceress, who gave him vicious and angry looks.

"Aha!" she exclaimed with contempt. "You want to fetch your darling wife, but the beautiful bird is no longer sitting in the nest, and she won't be singing any more. The cat has got her, and it will also scratch out your eyes. Rapunzel is lost to you, and you will never see her again!"

The prince was beside himself with grief, and in his despair he jumped off the tower. He escaped with his life, but he fell into some thorns that pierced his eyes. Consequently, he became blind and strayed about in the forest, where he ate only roots and berries and did nothing but mourn and weep about the loss of his dearest wife. Thus he wandered for many years in misery. Eventually, he made his way to the desolate land where Rapunzel was leading a wretched existence with the twins, a boy and a girl, to whom she had given birth. When he heard a voice that he thought sounded familiar, he went straight toward it, and when he reached her, Rapunzel recognized him. She embraced him and wept, and when two of her tears dropped on his eyes, they became clear, and he could see again. Then he escorted her back to his kingdom, where he was received with joy, and they lived happily and contentedly for a long time.

Beautiful Angiola (1870)[14]

Laura Gonzenbach

Once upon a time there were three neighbors, who all became pregnant at the same time. One day when they were all sitting together, one of them said, "Oh, cousins, I have such a craving for jujubes,[15] and there are none to be had."

"I'm also yearning for jujubes," said a second woman.

"Me, too. Me, too," the others cried out.

Then one woman said, "Do you know where some beautiful jujubes are growing? Over there in the garden that belongs to the witch. But we can't take any from there. If she catches us, she'll eat us. Besides, she has a donkey who guards the garden and would tell on us right away."

The first woman cried out again, "I don't care. I have such a great craving. Just come with me. The witch isn't at home right now and won't notice if we just take a few jujubes. As for the donkey, we'll throw him such juicy grass so that he won't even pay attention to us."

The other women let themselves be persuaded, and so all seven of them crawled into the witch's garden, threw some beautiful, juicy grass to the donkey, and filled their aprons with the jujubes that they picked. Fortunately, they escaped safely before the witch appeared.

The next evening the seven neighbors were sitting together again, and once again they had a great craving for the beautiful jujubes, and even though they were scared of the witch, they couldn't resist their urge and crept into the garden a second time. They threw fresh grass to the donkey, filled their aprons with jujubes, and escaped safely before the witch came back.

However, the witch had already noticed that someone had been in the garden because many jujubes were missing. She asked the donkey, but it had eaten the beautiful, juicy grass, and hadn't noticed anything. So she decided to stay in the garden on the third day. In the middle of the garden there was a ditch in which she hid herself and covered herself with leaves and branches. Only one of her long ears stuck out.

The seven neighbors were sitting with another again, and when they thought about the beautiful jujubes, their craving for them was awakened again. But one of them said, "We'd better not go there today. The witch could discover us, and then we'd be in for a terrible time."

The others laughed and said, "We succeeded twice. Why should we have bad luck today? Just come along!"

So, she let herself be persuaded, and all seven of them crawled into the garden. As they were picking the jujubes, one of them noticed the long ear of the witch that stuck out of the leaves. However, she thought it was a mushroom, went over, and wanted to pick it. All at once, the witch sprang out of the ditch,

---

14. *Sicilianische Märchen*, 2 vols. (Leipzig: W. Engelmann, 1870).

15. *Zinzuli*. In Italian, *giuggiola*.

and the seven women shrieked and fled from the garden. One of them could not, however, run so fast, and the witch caught her and wanted to eat her.

"Oh!" she cried. "Don't eat me. I had such a desire for jujubes and couldn't find some anywhere else. I promise never to enter your garden again."

"All right," the witch responded. "I'll forgive you this time but only under the condition that you promise me the baby you're carrying. Whether it's a boy or girl, you must give the child to me when it turns seven."

So the woman promised her out of great fear, and the witch let her go free. At home her six neighbors were waiting for her and asked her what had happened.

"Oh," she answered, "I had to promise her my child that I'm carrying. Otherwise, she would have eaten me."

When the time arrived, she gave birth to a lovely girl and named her Angiola. The child grew and flowered, and she became more and more beautiful with each passing day. After Angiola turned six years old, her mother sent her to school, and she learned how to sew and knit from a teacher. Whenever she went to school, she had to pass by the witch's garden, and when she was almost seven, the witch stood in front of her garden one day. Then she waved to her to come over and gave Angiola some fruit.

"Do you know, beautiful Angiola," she said. "I'm your aunt. Tell your mother that you met your aunt, and she had better not forget her promise."

Angiola went home and told her mother, who became very frightened and said, "Oh, the time's come, and I must give up my poor child. You know what, Angiola? When your aunt asks you for the answer tomorrow, tell her that you forgot to deliver the message."

When Angiola went to school the next day, the witch was there again and asked her, "Well, what did your mother say?"

"Oh, dear aunt," the child answered, "I forgot to tell her."

"All right, then tell it to her today," the witch said, "and don't forget."

Well, things went about the same the next few days. The witch waited for beautiful Angiola when she went to school and wanted to know her mother's answer. However, Angiola kept saying that she had forgotten to deliver the message. Well, one day the witch became angry and said, "If you are so forgetful, I'll have to give you a sign to take with you that will make you remember your chore."

So the witch grabbed hold of Angiola's pinky and bit it so hard that she chewed off a big chunk and said, "Now, go home and don't forget to tell your mother."

Angiola ran home weeping and showed her mother her little finger which was bleeding.

'Oh,' thought her mother, 'there's nothing I can do now. I must give my poor child to the witch. Otherwise she'll eat her out of anger.'

The next morning, as Angiola was about to go to school, her mother said, "Tell your aunt that she should do whatever she feels is good for you."

Angiola did this, and the witch said, "Good. Come with me. From now on you belong to me."

So the witch took beautiful Angiola with her and led her far away to a tower without any doors and with only one window. From then on, Angiola lived with the witch and led a good life because the witch loved her as if she were her own child. Whenever the witch came home after her excursions, she stood beneath the window and called out: "Angiola, beautiful Angiola, let down your beautiful braids and pull me up!"

Angiola had gorgeous long braids, which she let down, and then she pulled the witch up with them. Now, one day, when Angiola had grown into a beautiful maiden, the king's son happened to be hunting in the vicinity where the tower was standing. He was puzzled by a house without doors and asked himself, 'How do the people go inside?'

Just then the witch came back from one of her excursions, took her place beneath the window, and cried out: "Angiola, beautiful Angiola, let down your beautiful braids and pull me up!"

Immediately the braids fell down and the witch climbed up. This pleased the prince a great deal, and he kept himself hidden nearby until the witch went out again. Then he went over beneath the window and called out: "Angiola, beautiful Angiola, let down your beautiful braids and pull me up!"

All at once, Angiola threw her beautiful braids down and pulled the prince up to her, for she believed he was the witch. When she, however, saw the prince, she was at first frightened, but he spoke some friendly words to her and asked her to run off with him and become his wife. She let herself be persuaded, and in order to make sure that the witch would not learn where she had gone, she gave all the chairs, tables, and closets in the house something to eat because they were all living creatures and could betray her. Meanwhile, the broom stood behind the door, and Angiola could not see it and did not give it anything to eat. Then she took three magic balls from the witch's room and fled with the prince. The witch had a little dog which loved Angiola, and so the dog followed her as well.

After a short time had passed, the witch came home and cried out: "Angiola, beautiful Angiola, let down your beautiful braids and pull me up!" But the beautiful braids did not fall down no matter how often the witch called, and finally, she had to fetch a tall ladder and climb through the window. When she didn't find beautiful Angiola anywhere, she asked the chairs, tables, and closets, "Where did she go?"

"We don't know," they answered.

But the broom called from its corner, "Beautiful Angiola has fled with the prince who wants to elevate her and make her his wife."

The witch set out after them, and she had almost caught up with them when Angiola threw a magic ball behind her. A huge mountain of soap arose, and as the witch tried to climb it, she kept slipping back down. But she worked at it so long until she managed to climb over the mountain and rushed after Angiola and the prince. Then beautiful Angiola threw a second magic ball behind her, and another mountain made of large and small nails arose. Once again, the witch had to work long and hard until she climbed over it and was wiped out. When Angiola saw that the witch had almost caught up with them, she threw the third ball behind her, and a roaring river arose. The witch wanted to swim across, but the river became more and more turbulent so that she finally had to turn back. Furious, she cried out in anger and uttered a curse on beautiful Angiola: "May your beautiful face be turned into the face of a dog!" she yelled.

Within seconds Angiola's beautiful face was transformed into the face of a dog. The prince became very distressed and said, "How can I present you to my parents now? They'll never allow me to marry a maiden with a dog's face."

Consequently he took her to a small cottage in which she was to live until the evil curse was lifted from her. He himself returned to his parents and lived with them. However, whenever he went hunting, he went and visited poor Angiola. She wept bitterly over her misfortune until one day the little dog said to her, "Don't cry, beautiful Angiola. I'll go back to the witch and ask her to take away the magic curse from you."

So the little dog set out and returned to the witch. Once there, she jumped on to her lap and flattered her.

"Are you here again, you ungrateful beast?" the witch cried out and shoved the dog away.

"You left me to follow the ungrateful Angiola."

But the little dog kept flattering her until the witch became friendly and took it on her lap.

"Mother," the little dog said, "Angiola sends her greetings and kisses your hands. She is sad because she's not allowed to go to the castle with a dog's face and can't marry the prince."

"That serves her right!" the witch declared. "Why did she deceive me? As far as I'm concerned, she can keep the dog's face."

However, the little dog kept asking in such a friendly way and insisted that poor Angiola had been punished enough. Finally, the witch gave the little dog a bottle of water and said, "Bring her this, and she'll become beautiful Angiola again."

The little dog thanked the witch, jumped down from her lap with the bottle, and brought it happily to poor Angiola. When the maiden washed herself with the water, the dog's face disappeared, and she became beautiful again, more beautiful than she had been before. So now, the prince brought her to his castle full of joy, and the king and queen were so delighted by her beauty that they welcomed her with all their hearts and arranged for a splendid wedding. They remained happy and content, but we still don't even have a cent.

La Prezzemolina (1871)[16]

Vittorio Imbriani

Once upon a time there was a husband and a wife who had a window that overlooked the garden of the fairies. The wife was pregnant. One beautiful day

---

16.   *La Novellaja fiorentina* (Livorno: F. Vigo, 1871).

she looked out the window and saw a row of the most beautiful parsley! She watched and waited until the fairies had left the garden. Then she took a rope ladder and descended into the garden where she began to stuff herself with the parsley. She ate and ate and then climbed back up the ladder, closed the window, and disappeared. She did the same thing every day.

Now, one day, while the fairies were walking in the garden, the most beautiful one said, "Tell me, doesn't it seem to you that a lot of parsley is missing?"

And the others replied, "There's little left. You know what we should do? Let's all pretend to leave, and one of us will hide and wait for the person who's been eating our parsley."

So the fairies pretended to leave the garden, and the wife climbed down to eat the parsley. When she was ready to return to the window, the fairy jumped out from behind her.

"Oh, you rascal!" she cried out. "I've got you now!"

"Be gentle with me," the woman said. "I'm pregnant and crave parsley. . . ."

"Very well," the fairy said. "I shall pardon you, but look, if you give birth to a boy, you must give him the name Prezzemolino or Parsley Boy. If you have a girl, you must name her Prezzemolina or Parsley Girl. And if it is a girl, when she is older, she will belong to us. She will no longer be yours."

Just imagine the state of this woman! She burst out weeping.

"What a glutton I've been! My craving's cost me more than enough!"

And her husband constantly scolded her as well: "Glutton! See what you've done!"

When she gave birth to a baby girl, she named her Prezzemolina, and when the girl was old enough, she was sent to school. And every day that she passed the fairies, they said to her, "Little girl, tell your mother to remember what she owes us."

"Mama," Prezzemolina said, "the fairies told me that you're to remember something that you owe them."

One day, when the woman was completely exhausted, the little girl returned home and said, "The fairies told me that you're to remember something that you owe them."

"Yes, tell them they're to take it."

When the girl left for school the next day, the fairies said to her, "What did your mother say yesterday?"

"She told me you're to take whatever it is that she owes you."

"Well then, come! You're the thing that she owes us."

The girl couldn't stop howling. Indeed, that's what I believe! But let's leave the girl and turn to her mother who waited for her daughter to return. Then she remembered that she had told her to tell the fairies that they were to take what she owed them.

"Oh, I've betrayed myself! There's no way back. She won't return."

Soon afterward the fairies told the girl, "Listen, Prezzemolina, do you see this dark and gloomy room?"—It was the place where they kept their coal.—"When we return, this place must be as white as milk, and all the birds of the air must be painted on the walls. If you don't do this, we'll eat you."

How would you like to be treated like this girl? Well, the fairies left, and the girl began to weep, and she wept like I weep—sobbing. She couldn't calm down. Then there was a knock at the door. She went to see who it was and thought that the fairies had returned. She opened the door and saw Memé, who was a cousin of the fairies.

"What's wrong, Prezzemolina?" he asked. "Why are you crying?"

"You'd cry, too," she responded. "Do you see this room? When the fairies return, the black walls must be white and painted with the birds of the air. If not, they'll eat me."

"If you give me a kiss," Memé said, "I'll change this room for you in a second."

To this she responded:

> "I'd rather let those fairies eat me
> than let a man come close and kiss me."

"What you've said is very good," remarked Memé. "So I'll do you a favor and clean the room."

He waved his magic wand and the room became completely white with all the birds on the walls just as the fairies had demanded. Then Memé departed, and the fairies returned.

"You did all this?" the fairies asked.

"Yes, ladies, come and look."

The fairies looked at one another.

"So, Prezzemolina, Memé's been here!"

"I don't know this Memé, and nor was it my mamma, who gave birth to me."

Consequently, the next morning, the fairies said to one another, "What are we to do? We have to find a way to eat her . . . Prezzemolina!"

"What are your orders?"

"Tomorrow morning," they told her, "you must go to Morgan le Fay and you are to tell her to give you the Handsome Minstrel's box."

"Yes, ladies," she replied.

So, the next morning she set out. And she walked and walked until she met a lady.

"Where are you going, beautiful girl?" the lady said.

"I'm going to Morgan le Fay to get the Handsome Minstrel's box."

"Don't you know, poor girl, that she will eat you?"

"All the better for me," Prezzemolina replied. "That will put an end to everything."

"Take these two pots of grease," said the lady. "You'll find two doors that keep slamming together. Grease them, and you'll see that they'll let you pass through them."

Well then, when the girl reached the doors, she greased them from top to bottom, and they let her pass. After she walked for a while, she came across another lady, and this woman asked her the same thing: "Where are you going, little girl?"

"I'm going to Morgan le Fay for the Handsome Minstrel's box," she replied.

"Don't you know, poor girl, that she will eat you?"

"All the better for me," Prezzemolina answered. "That will put an end to everything."

"Take these two loaves of bread. You'll come across two dogs fighting and biting each other. Throw each of them a loaf, and that way you'll pass."

Well, Prezzemolina encountered these two dogs, and she threw each one of them a loaf. Then they let her pass. After she walked on for a while, she met another lady, who asked her, "Where are you going?"

"I'm going to Morgan le Fay for the Handsome Minstrel's box," she replied.

"Don't you know, poor girl, that she will eat you?"

"All the better for me," Prezzemolina answered. "That will put an end to everything."

"You're going to meet a cobbler who'll be pulling out the hair from his beard and head for thread to stitch shoes. Take this sewing thread. It's thrifty and just what he needs. Give it to him, and he'll let you pass."

Well, Prezzemolina encountered this cobbler. When she gave him all the thread, he thanked her and let her pass. Then she walked on for a while and came across the same lady who said to her, "Watch out! You know she'll eat you."

"All the better for me," Prezzemolina said. "That will put an end to everything."

"You will meet a baker who'll be cleaning the oven with her bare hands and burning them. Take these rags. They're like brushes and just what she needs. You'll see, she'll let you pass. Soon after this you'll come upon a beautiful town square where Morgan le Fay lives. You are to knock at the door of her palazzo where you'll find the Handsome Minstrel's box two flights up the stairs. When you knock, Morgan le Fay will say, 'Wait, little girl, wait a moment.' But you are to run up the two flights of stairs, take the box, and run off with it."

Well, Prezzemolina encountered the baker. And when she gave her the rags, the baker thanked her and let her pass. Then Prezzemolina knocked at Morgan le Fay's door, climbed the stairs, took the box, and ran off with it. When the fairy heard the door close, she ran to the window and saw that the girl had escaped.

"Oh, baker brushing the oven with your bare hands, stop her! Stop her!"

"Oh, do you think that I'm a fool! After so many years that I've exhausted myself cleaning the oven, she brought me what I needed. You may pass, poor girl. Run, run!"

"Oh, cobbler pulling hair from your beard and head, stop her! Stop her!"

"Oh, do you think I'm a fool. After so many years that I've exhausted myself, she brought me what I needed. Run, run, poor girl!"

"Oh, dogs who've fought and bitten so much, stop her! Stop her!"

"Oh, do you think we're fools! She gave us each a loaf of bread! Run, run, poor girl!"

"Oh, doors who've slammed so much, stop her! Stop her!"

"Oh, do you think we're fools? She greased us from top to bottom. Run, run, poor girl!"

And so they let her pass. When she was finally free, she said to herself, 'What could possibly be in this box?' After she came to a village square, she sat down and opened the box. Out jumped numerous people, and they escaped from the box singing and playing music. All of them. Just imagine the girl's desperation! She wanted to get them back into the box, and when she caught one, another ten escaped. Believe me, there was nothing she could do but burst into tears. And just then Memé appeared.

"You ninny! See what you've done?"

"Oh, I just wanted to see . . ."

"What!" Memé replied. "There's no remedy. But if you give me a kiss, I'll find the remedy."

> "I'd rather let those fairies eat me
> than let a man come close and kiss me."

"What you've said is very good," remarked Memé. "So I'll do you a favor and find the remedy."

He waved his magic wand, and all the people returned to the box, and it was closed and the same as before. So, Prezzemolina returned to the fairies' house and knocked.

"Oh god!" a fairy said. "It's Prezzemolina. How's it possible that Morgan le Fay didn't eat her?"

"Good day," Prezzemolina said. "Here's the box."

"What did Morgan le Fay say to you?" the fairies asked.

"She said to me: 'Give them my greetings.'"

"That's it," the fairies whispered. "We understand! We're the ones who are supposed to eat her. This evening, when Memé comes, we'll tell him that we're supposed to eat her."

So, in the evening, when Memé arrived, they said, "You know, Morgan le Fay didn't eat Prezzemolina. We're supposed to eat her."

"Oh, very good!" he said. "Very good!"

"Tomorrow, after she has done all the housework, we'll have her put the large kettle on the fire to boil water and wash the laundry. When the water is boiling nicely, we'll grab her and throw her into the kettle to cook."

"Excellent, excellent." he said. "We'll do it just as you say."

When the next day arrived, the fairies left the house and said nothing. They went about as they usually did. After they had departed, Memé arrived and went to Prezzemolina.

"You know," he said, "today, at a certain time, the fairies will order you to put the large kettle on the fire to wash the laundry. And, when the water begins to boil, they'll tell you to call them. Then they'll ask you to tell them when the water's ready, and they'll throw you into the water to cook."

After saying this, Memé left, and soon the fairies returned.

"Listen, Prezzemolina," they said. "After you've eaten and done all the housework, take the large kettle in which you wash the laundry and boil some water in it. When the water is boiling, call us."

So, after Prezzemolina had finished all the housework, she placed the large kettle over the fire, and they said to her: "Make a large fire."

Just imagine how great the fire was, greater than what they told her to make, and just then, Memé knocked at the door.

"Oh!" he said. "Now's the time that you are going to eat her."

And they rubbed their hands and said, "Nothing else, but!"

As the water was boiling, Prezzemolina said, "Fairies, come here and look. The water is boiling."

The fairies ran to the kettle to look at the boiling water while Memé said, "Keep up the good work!"

Then he grabbed hold of two of the fairies and stuck them in the kettle, while Prezzemolina threw the others into the water where they boiled and boiled and boiled until they fell apart and could not save their necks. They continued to boil!

"Now we are in charge of this house, my little one," Memé said. "Come with me."

He led her down into the cellar where there were numerous candles, and one was the candle of Morgan le Fay—large and grand, the largest of all the candles in the cellar and the major one of all the fairies. Her soul was a candle. If the candles were blown out, their souls died.

"You blow out those over there," Memé said, "and I'll blow out these here."

So, they blew out all the candles and they took charge of everything that had belonged to the fairies. Soon after they went to the palazzo of Morgan le Fay. Once they were settled, they made the cobbler a lord and the baker a marquise. The dogs were brought into the palazzo, and the doors were always greased.

"Now, you are to be my bride," Memé said to Prezzemolina, "and that's just right."

And so they lived happily and enjoyed their pie of life in peace while they gave me nothing, not even a slice.

Filagranata (1874)[17]

Rachel Busk

Once upon a time there was a poor woman who had a great fancy for eating parsley. To her it was the greatest luxury, and as she had no garden of her own,

---

17. *The Folk-Lore of Rome. Collected by Word of Mouth from the People* (London: Longmans, Green, 1874).

and no money to spend on anything not an absolute necessity of life, she had to go about poaching in other people's gardens to satisfy her fancy.

Near her cottage was the garden of a great palace, and in this garden grew plenty of fine parsley; but the garden was surrounded by a wall, and to get at it she had to carry a ladder with her to get up by, and, as soon as she had reached the top of the wall, to let it down on the other side to get down to the parsley-bed. There was such a quantity of parsley growing here that she thought it would never be missed, and this made her bold so that she went over every day and took as much as ever she liked.

But the garden belonged to a witch, who lived in the palace, and, though she did not often walk in this part of the garden, she knew by her supernatural powers that someone was eating her parsley; so she came near the place one day and lay in wait till the poor woman came. As soon, therefore, as she came, and began eating the parsley, the witch at once pounced down, and asked her, in her gruff voice, what she was doing there. Though dreadfully frightened, the poor woman thought it best to own the whole truth; so she confessed that she came down by the ladder, adding that she had not taken anything except the parsley and begged forgiveness.

"I know nothing about forgiveness," replied the witch. "You have eaten my parsley, and must take the consequences; and the consequences are these: I must be godmother to your first child, be it boy or girl; and as soon as it is grown to be of an age to dress itself without help, it must belong to me."

When, accordingly, the poor woman's first child was born, the witch came, as she had declared she would, to be its godmother. It was a fine little girl, and she gave it the name of Filagranata. After that she went away again, and the poor woman saw her no more till her little girl was grown up old enough to dress herself, and then she came and fetched her away inexorably; nor could the poor mother, with all her tears and entreaties, prevail on her to make any exchange for her child.

So Filagranata was taken to the witch's palace to live and was put in a room in a little tower by herself, where she had to feed the pigeons. Filagranata grew fond of her pigeons, and did not at all complain of her work, yet, without knowing why, she began to grow quite sad and melancholy as time went by; it was because she had no one to play with, no one to talk to, except the witch, who was not a very delightful companion. The witch came every day, once in the day, to see that she was attending properly to her work, and as there was no door or staircase to the tower—this was on purpose that she might not escape—the witch used to say when she came under the tower:

> Filagrannta, so fair, so fair,
> Unloose thy tresses of golden hair:
> I, thy old grandmother, am here.

and as she said these words, Filagranata had to let down her beautiful long hair through the window, and by it the witch climbed up into her chamber to her. This she did every day.

Now, it happened that about this time a king's son was travelling that way searching for a beautiful wife; for you know it is the custom for princes to go searching all over the world to find a maiden fit to be a prince's wife; at least they say so.

Well, this prince, travelling along, came by the witch's palace where Filagranata was lodged. And it happened that he came that way just as the witch was singing her ditty. If he was horrified at the sight of the witch, he was in proportion enchanted when Filagranata came to the window. So struck was he with the sight of her beauty, and modesty, and gentleness, that he stopped his horse that he might watch her as long as she stayed at the window, and thus became a spectator of the witch's wonderful way of getting into the tower.

The prince's mind was soon made up to gain a nearer view of Filagranata, and with this purpose he rode round and round the tower seeking some mode of ingress in vain, till at last, driven to desperation, he made up his mind that he must enter by the same strange means as the witch herself. Thinking that the old creature had her abode there, and that she would probably go out for some business in the morning, and return at about the same time as on the present occasion, he rode away, commanding his impatience as well as he could, and came back the next day a little earlier.

Though he could hardly hope quite to imitate the hag's rough and tremulous voice so as to deceive Filagranata into thinking it was really the witch, he yet made the attempt and repeated the words that he had heard:

> Filagranata, thou maiden fair,
> Unloose thy tresses of golden hair:
> I, thy old grandmother, am here.

Filagranata, surprised at the soft modulation of voice, such as she had never heard before, ran quickly to the window with a look of pleasure and astonishment, which gave her face a more winning expression than ever.

The prince looked up, all admiration and expectation; and the thought quickly ran through Filagranata's head: 'I have been taught to loose my hair whenever those words are said; why should not I loose it to draw up such a pleasant-looking cavalier, as well as for the ugly old hag?' And, without waiting for a second thought, she untied the ribbon that bound her tresses and let them fall upon the prince. The prince was equally quick in taking advantage of the occasion, and, pressing his knees firmly into his horse's flanks, so that it might not remain below to betray him, drew himself up, together with his steed, just as he had seen the witch do.

Filagranata, half frightened at what she had done the moment the deed was accomplished, had not a word to say, but blushed and hung her head. The prince, on the other hand, had so many words to pour out, expressive of his admiration for her, his indignation at her captivity, and his desire to be allowed to be her deliverer, that the moments flew quickly by, and it was only when Filagranata found herself drawn to the window by the power of the witch's magic words that they remembered the dangerous situation in which they stood.

Another might have increased the peril by cries of despair, or lost precious time in useless lamentations; but Filagranata showed a presence of mind worthy of a prince's wife by catching up a wand of the witch, with which she had seen her do wonderful things. With this she gave the prince a little tap, which immediately changed him into a pomegranate, and then another to the horse, which transformed him into an orange. These she set by on the shelf, and then proceeded to draw up the witch after the usual manner.

The old hag was not slow in perceiving there was something unusual in Filagranata's room.

"What a stink of Christians! What a stink of Christians!" she kept exclaiming, as she poked her nose into every hole and corner. Yet she failed to find anything to reprehend; and, as for the beautiful ripe pomegranate and golden orange on the shelf, the Devil himself could not have thought there was anything wrong with them. Thus baffled, she was obliged to finish her inspection of the state of the pigeons, and end her visit in the usual way.

As soon as she was gone Filagranata knew she was free till the next day, and so once more, with a tap of the wand, restored the horse and his rider to their natural shapes.

"And this is how your life passes every day! Is it possible?" exclaimed the prince. "No, I cannot leave you here. You may be sure my good horse will be proud to bear your little weight; you have only to mount behind, and I will take you home to my kingdom, and you shall live in the palace with my mother, and be my queen."

It is not to be supposed but that Filagranata very much preferred the idea of going with the handsome young prince who had shown so devoted an appreciation of her, and being his queen, to remaining shut up in the doorless tower and being the witch's menial; so she offered no opposition, and the prince put her onto his good horse behind him, and away they rode.

On, on, on, they rode for a long, long way, until they came at last to a wood; but for all the good horse's speed, the witch, who was not long in perceiving their escape and setting out in pursuit, was well nigh overtaking them. Just then they saw a little old woman standing by the way, making signs and calling to them to arrest their course. How great soever was their anxiety to get on, so urgent was her appeal to them to stop and listen to her that they yielded to her entreaties. Nor were they losers by their kindness, for the little old woman was a fairy, and she had stopped them, not on her own account, but to give them the means of escaping from the witch.

To the prince she said: "Take these three gifts, and when the witch comes very near, throw down first the mason's trowel; and when she nearly overtakes you again, throw down the comb; and when she nearly comes upon you again after that, throw down this jar of oil. After that she won't trouble you any more."

And to Filagranata she whispered some words, and then let them go. But the witch was now close behind, and the prince made haste to throw down the mason's trowel. Instantly there rose up a high stone wall between them, which it took the witch some time to climb over. Nevertheless, by her supernatural powers she was not long in making up for the lost time, and had soon overtaken the best speed of the good horse. Then the prince threw down the comb, and immediately there rose up between them a strong hedge of thorns, which it took the witch some time to make her way through, and that only with her body bleeding all over from the thorns. Nevertheless, by her supernatural powers she was not long in making up for the lost time, and had soon overtaken the best speed of the good horse. Then the prince threw down the jar of oil, and the oil spread and spread till it had overflowed the whole countryside; and as wherever you step in a pool of oil the foot only slides back, the witch could never get out of that, so the prince and Filagranata rode on in all safety towards the prince's palace.

"And now tell me what it was the old woman in the wood whispered to you," said the prince, as soon as they saw their safety sufficiently secured to breathe freely.

"It was this," answered Filagranata, "that I was to tell you that when you arrive at your own home you must kiss no one—no one at all, not your father, or mother, or sisters, or anyone—till after our marriage. Because if you do, you will forget all about your love for me, and all you have told me you think of me, and all the faithfulness you have promised me, and we shall become as strangers again to each other."

"How dreadful!" said the prince. "Oh, you may be sure I will kiss no one if *that* is to be the consequence. So be quite easy. It will be rather odd, to be sure, to return from such a long journey and kiss none of them at home, nor even my mother; but I suppose if I tell them how it is they won't mind. So be quite easy about that."

Thus they rode on in love and confidence, and the good horse soon brought them home.

On the steps of the palace the chancellor of the king came out to meet them, and saluted Filagranata as the chosen bride the prince was to bring home; he informed him that the king his father had died during his absence, and that he was now sovereign of the realm. Then he led him in to the queen-mother, to whom he told all his adventures, and explained why he must not kiss her until after his marriage. The queen-mother was so pleased with the beauty, and modesty, and gentleness of Filagranata that she gave up her son's kiss without repining, and before they retired to rest that night it was announced to the people that the prince had returned home to be their king, and the day was proclaimed when the feast for his marriage was to take place.

Then all in the palace went to their sleeping chambers. But the prince, as it had been his wont from his childhood upwards, went into his mother's room to kiss her after she was asleep, and when he saw her placid brow on the pillow, with the soft white hair parted on either side of it, and the eyes which were wont to gaze on him with so much love, resting in sleep, he could not forbear from pressing his lips on her forehead and giving the wonted kiss.

Instantly there passed from his mind all that had taken place since he last stood there to take leave of the queen-mother before he started on his journey. His visit to the witch's palace, his flight from it, the life-perils by the way, and, what is more, the image of Filagranata herself, all passed from his mind like a vision of the night, and when he woke up and they told him he was king, it was as if he heard it for the first time, and when they brought Filagranata to him, it was as though he knew her not nor saw her.

"But," he said, "if I am king, there must be a queen to share my throne."

Now, since a reigning sovereign could not go over the world to seek a wife, he sent and fetched him a princess suited to be the king's wife, and appointed the betrothal. The queen-mother, who loved Filagranata, was sad, and yet nothing that she could say could bring back to his mind the least remembrance of all he had promised her and felt towards her.

But Filagranata knew that the prince had kissed his mother, and this was why the spell was on him; so she said to her mother-in-law: "You get me much fine-sifted flour and a large bag of sweetmeats, and I will try if I cannot yet set this matter straight."

So the queen-mother ordered that there should be placed in her room much sifted flour and a large bag of sweetmeats. And Filagranata, when she had closed the door, set to work and made paste of the flour, and of the paste she molded two pigeons, and filled them inside with the comfits. Then at the banquet of the betrothal she asked the queen-mother to have her two pigeons placed on the table; and she did so, one at each end. But as soon as all the company were seated, before anyone was helped, the two pigeons which Fila-granata had made began to talk to each other across the whole length of the table; and everybody stood still with wonder to listen to what the pigeons of paste said to each other.

"Do you remember," said the first pigeon, "or is it possible that you have really forgotten, when I was in that doorless tower of the witch's palace, and you came under the window and imitated her voice, saying,

> 'Filagranata, thou maiden fair,
> Unloose thy tresses of golden hair:
> I, thy old grandmother, am here,'

till I drew you up?"

And the other pigeon answered,

"Si, signora, I remember it now."

And as the young king heard the second pigeon say, "Signora, I remember it now," he, too, remembered having been in a doorless tower, and having sung such a verse.

"Do you remember," continued the first pigeon, "how happy we were together after I drew you up into that little room where I was confined, and you swore if I would come with you, we should always be together and never be separated from each other any more at all?"

And the second pigeon replied, "Ah yes! I remember it now."

And as the second pigeon said, "Ah yes! I remember it now," there rose up in the young king's mind the memory of a fair sweet face on which he had once gazed with loving eyes, and of a maiden to whom he had sworn long devotion.

But the first pigeon continued: "Do you remember, or have you quite forgotten, how we fled away together, and how frightened we were when the witch pursued us, and how we clung to each other, vowed, if she overtook us to kill us, we would die in each other's arms, till a fairy met us and gave us the means to escape, and forbad you to kiss anyone, even your mother, till after our marriage?"

And the second pigeon answered, "Yes, ah yes! I remember it now."

And when the second pigeon said, "Yes, ah yes! I remember it now," the whole of the past came back to his mind, and with it all his love for Filagranata. So he rose up and would have stroked the pigeons which had brought it all to his mind, but when he touched them, they melted away, and the sweetmeats were scattered all over the table, and the guests picked them up. But the prince ran in haste to fetch Filagranata, and he brought her and placed her by his side in the banquet hall. But the second bride was sent back, with presents, to her own people.

"And so it all came right at last," pursued the narrator. "Lackaday! that there are no fairies now to make things all happen right. There are plenty of people who seem to have the devil in them for doing you a mischief, but there are no fairies to set things straight again, alas!"

Translated by Rachel Busk.

The Old Woman of the Garden (1875)[18]

Giuseppe Pitrè

Once upon a time there was a cabbage garden. The crops each year were becoming more and more scarce, and when two women began talking, one of them said:

"My friend, let's go and pick some cabbages."

"How are we to know whether anyone's there?" said the other.

"All right. I'll go and see if someone's keeping guard," the neighbor said.

She went and looked.

"There's no one. Let's go!"

They entered the garden, gathered two good batches of cabbage, and left. Then they cheerfully ate the cabbages. The next morning they returned, but one of the women was afraid that the gardener would be there. However, since they

18.   Giuseppe Pitrè, *Fiabe, novelle e racconti popolari siciliani.* 4 vols. (Palermo: Lauriel, 1875).

didn't see anybody, they entered. Once again they gathered two good batches of cabbage and ate them all.

Now let's leave them eating the cabbages and turn to the old woman who owned the garden. When she went to her garden, she cried out: "Jesus! Someone's eaten my cabbages. Well, I'm going to take care of this. . . . I'll get a dog and tie him to the gate at the entrance. When the thieves come, the dog will know what to do."

All right, let's leave the old woman who fetched a dog to guard the garden and return to the two women. One of them said to the other:

"Let's go and pick some cabbages."

"No, my friend, there's a dog there now."

"Not a problem! We'll buy some dry bread with our money and feed it to the dog. Then we can do whatever we want."

So they bought some bread, and before the dog could bark, they threw it some pieces. As soon as the dog became silent, they gathered the cabbages and left. Later on, the old woman arrived, and when she saw the damage, she cried out, "Ahh! So, you let them gather the cabbages! You're really not a good guard dog. Out you go!"

And so now the old woman took a cat to guard the garden and hid in the house, and as soon as the cat screeched *meow! meow!* she would grab the thieves by their throats.

The next day one of the women said, "Friend, let's go and pick some cabbages."

"No. There's a guard, and this means trouble for us."

"I don't think so. Let's go."

When they saw the cat, they bought some fish, and before the cat could *meow,* they threw it some fish, and the cat didn't utter a sound. The women gathered some cabbage and left. When the cat finished eating the fish, it went *meow, meow!* The old woman came running but didn't see anyone. So she picked up the cat and cut off its head. Then she said, "Now I'm going to have the cock keep guard, and when it crows, I'll come running and kill those thieves."

The next day the two women began talking with one another.

"Let's go and pick some cabbage."

"No, my friend, there's the cock."

"Doesn't matter," her friend said. "We'll take some grain with us and throw it to the cock so it won't cry out."

And this is what they did. While the cock ate the grain, they picked the cabbages and left. When the cock finished eating the grain, it crowed: "*Cock-a-doodle-do!*" So the old woman came running and saw that more cabbages had been stolen. So she picked up the cock, wrung its neck, and ate it. Then she called a peasant and said, "I want you to dig a hole in the ground just my size."

Afterward she hid herself in the large hole, but one of her ears stuck outside. The next morning the women went into the garden and didn't see a soul. The old woman had asked the peasant to dig the hole along the path that the women would have to pass, and when they came by, they didn't notice a thing. They passed the hole and collected some cabbages, and on their return, the woman who was pregnant, looked at the ground and saw a mushroom which was actually the old woman's ear.

"Friend, look at this beautiful mushroom!"

She knelt down and tugged at it. She pulled and pulled, and finally, she yanked out the old woman with all her might.

"Ahh!" the old woman said, "you're the ones who've been picking my cabbage! Just wait and see what I'm going to do to you!"

She grabbed hold of the pregnant woman, while the other scampered away as fast as her legs could carry her.

"Now I'm going to eat you alive!" the old woman said to the pregnant woman whom she had in her clutches.

"No! Listen to me! When I give birth, and my child is sixteen years old, I promise that, whether boy or girl, I'll send the child to you, and I'll keep my promise."

"All right," the old woman said. "Pick all the cabbages you want, and then leave. But remember the promise you've made."

The poor woman was more dead than alive when she returned home.

"Ah, friend," she said to her neighbor. "You managed to escape, and I'm still in trouble. I promised the old woman that I'd give her my firstborn when the child turns sixteen."

"And what do you want me to do?"

After two months, the Lord blessed the pregnant woman with a baby girl.

"Ahh, my daughter!" she said to the baby. "I'll raise you, give you my breast, but then someone is going eat you!"

And the poor mother wept. When the girl turned sixteen, she went out to buy some oil for her mother. The old woman saw her and said, "Whose daughter are you, my girl?"

"My mother's name is Sabedda," she replied.[19]

"Well, tell your mother to remember her promise. You've become a beautiful maiden. You're nice and tasty," she said as she caressed her. "Here, take some of these figs and bring them to your mother."

The maiden went to her mother and told her what had happened.

"The old woman told me to remind you of your promise."

"Why did I promise her?!" the mother began to cry.

"Why are you crying, mamma?"

But her mother said nothing. After weeping for some time, she said to her daughter, "If you meet the old woman, you're to say: 'She's still too young. . . .'"

---

19.   Here the storyteller, Elisabetta (Sabedda) Sanfratello, interjects that she has given the mother in the story her own name, as a name "for example," and then feels compelled to add that, of course, she herself was not present for the actions of the story.

The next evening the maiden went again to get some oil and met the old woman who did the same thing as she had done the day before.

Meanwhile her mother thought, "It's now or in the course of two years that I'll have to separate from my daughter." So she said to her daughter, "If you meet the old woman, tell her, 'when you see her, take her, and the promise is kept.'"

Then the old woman soon appeared and asked, "What did your mother say?"

"When you see her, take her."

"Well then, come with your grandma, for I'm going to give you many things."

She took the maiden with her, and when they arrived at the old woman's house, she locked the maiden in a closet and said, "Eat whatever's there."

After a fair amount of time had passed, the old woman said, "I want to see if you've gotten fatter."

There was a little hole in the door.

"Show me, little one. Stick out your finger."

The maiden was clever. A mouse had come by, and she had cut off its tail and showed it to the old woman.

"Ahh! How thin you are, my daughter. You've got to eat for your grandma. You're so thin, and you've got to eat."

Some more time passed.

"Come out, my daughter, so I can see you."

The maiden came out.

"Ahh! You've become nice and fat. Let's go and knead some bread."

"Yes, grandma. I know how to do it."

When they finished kneading the bread, the old woman had her heat up the oven.

"Light it for your grandma."

The maiden began to clear it out to heat the oven.

"Come on. Do it for grandma," the old woman said. "Let's put the bread in the oven."

"But, grandma, I don't know how to put the bread into the oven. I know how to do everything else, but I don't know how to put the bread into the oven."

"Well then," said the old woman, "I'll put the bread into the oven. You just have to pass it to me."

The maiden took the bread and gave it to the old woman who said, "Pull open the iron slab that closes the oven."

"But grandma, I don't have the strength to pull the slab."

"Well then, I'll pull it open."

"When the old woman kneeled down and pulled the slab open, the maiden grabbed her from behind and shoved her into the oven. Then she pushed the slab to close the oven."

"Now there's nothing more to do here. So I'll find out where my mother is."

As she went outside, a neighbor saw her.

"Well, you're alive?!"

"Why, should I be dead? Now, listen to what I'm going to tell you. I want you to look for my mother. I want to see her."

The neighbor went and called her mother, who went to the old woman's house. When her daughter told her everything that had happened, she became very happy, and they took over everything in the house.

> They remained happy and content
> While we still don't have a cent.

Told by Elisabetta (Sabedda) Sanfratello in Vallelunga.

The Fairy-Queen Godmother (1877)[20]
Wentworth Webster

There were, like many others in the world, a man and a woman over-burthened with children, and very poor. The woman did not know what to do anymore. She said she would go and beg. She goes off, far, far, far away, and she arrives at the city of the fairies. After she had told them how many children she had, all give her a great many alms—she was laden with them.

In addition, the queen of the fairies gives her twenty pounds in gold, and says to her: "If you will give me your child when you are confined—you shall bring it up in your law—I will give you a great deal of money, if you will do that."

She told her that the godmother was already decided upon, but that she would speak about it to her husband. The queen told her to go home and to return with the answer in a week.

She gets home as she best can, very much fatigued by her burthen. Her husband was astonished that she could have carried so much. She tells him what had happened with the queen of the fairies. He says to her: "Certainly, we will make her godmother."

And she returns at the end of a week to tell the queen that she accepts her. She tells her not to send the baby and to tell her when she is confined, that she will know it herself, and that she will come all right. At the end of a week she gives birth to a daughter. The queen arrives, as she had said, with a mule laden with gold. When they came back from the christening, the godmother and the child fly away; and the parents console themselves with their other children, thinking that their daughter will be happier in the house of the queen of the fairies.

The queen takes her to a corner of a mountain where her house was. She had already another goddaughter; this was a little dog, whose name was Rose,[21]

20. *Basque Legends: Collected Chiefly in the Labourd* (London: Griffith and Farran, 1877).

21. This tale, at least this version of it, with the names Rose and Bellarose, must come from the French. A little dog is mentioned in John Campbell of Islay's "The Daughter of the Skies," *Popular Tales of the West Highlands: Orally Collected Translated*, vol. 1 (Edinburgh: Edmonston and Douglas, 1860–1862).

and she named this last goddaughter Pretty-Rose. She gave her, too, a glint of diamonds in the middle of her forehead.[22] She was very pretty. She grew up in the corner of the mountain, amusing herself with this dog, and she said to her one day: "Has the queen no other houses? I am tired of being always here."

The dog said to her: "Yes, she has a very fine one by the side of the king's highway, and I will speak to my godmamma about it."

And the dog then told her how Pretty-Rose was bored, and (asked her) if she would not change her house.

She said to her, "Yes," and off they go.

While they were there one day Pretty-Rose was on the balcony, and a king's son passes, and he was astonished at the beauty of Pretty-Rose; and the king's son begged and prayed her to look at him again, and (asked her) if she would not go with him. She told him, "No, that she must tell it to her godmamma."

Then the dog said, aside : "No, without me she shall not go anywhere."

This king's son says to her: "But I will take you, too, willingly if you let me know how I shall get you?"

Rose says to him: "I give every evening to my godmother always a glass of good liqueur to make her sleep well. If, by mistake, instead of half a glass, I will give her the glass full, and she will not be able to rise any more to shut the door as usual. So, I will go and take the key to shut it. I will pretend to, and will give her back the key, leaving the door open, and you will open it when you come. She will not hear anything; she will be in a deep sleep."

The king's son said that he would come at midnight, in his flying chariot. When night came, Rose gave her godmother the good drink in a glass, brim, brim-full.

The godmother said: "What! What! Child!"

"You will sleep all the better, godmamma."

"You are right," and she drinks it all.

But she could not get up to shut the door because she had become so sleepy, and now Rose said to her: "Godmamma, I will shut the door today. Stay where you are."

The godmother gave her the key, and Rose turns and turns it back again and again in the keyhole as if she had locked it; and leaving it unlocked she gave the key to her godmother, and she puts it in her pocket. She goes to bed; but Rose and Pretty-Rose did not go to bed at all. At midnight the son of the king arrives with his flying chariot. Rose and Pretty-Rose get into it, and go to this young man's house. The next day Rose says to Pretty-Rose: "You are not so pretty as you were yesterday," and looking at her closely, "I find you very ugly to-day."

---

22.   *"Kopetaen erdian diamanteko biata batez"*—"a view of diamonds in the middle of the forehead."

Pretty-Rose said to her: "My godmamma must have taken away my diamond glint." And she said to Rose, "You must go to my godmamma, and ask her to give me back the glint that I had before."

Rose did not want to go there—she was afraid; but Pretty-Rose begged her so much that she took off the silver dress and set out.[23] When she came to the mountain, she began to call out: "Godmamma! Godmamma! Give Pretty-Rose her beautiful glint as before. I shall be angry with you for always (if you do not), and you will see what will happen to you."

The godmother said to her: "Come here, come in. I will give you breakfast."

She said, "I'm afraid you will beat me."

"No! No! Come quickly, then."

"You will give Pretty-Rose her glint?"

"Yes, yes, she has it already."

She then goes in. The queen washes her feet and wipes them, and puts her upon the velvet cushion, and gives her some chocolate and says to her that she knows where Pretty-Rose is, and that she will be married and to tell her from her not to trouble herself about her toilet, nor about anything that is necessary for the wedding and feast, and that she would come on the morning of the day.

Rose goes off then. While she is going through the city where Pretty-Rose is, she hears two ladies, who were saying to two gentlemen, "What kind of wife is it that our brother is going to take? Not like us, because he keeps her shut up so close. Let us go and see her."

The little dog said to them, "Not a bit like you, you horrible blubber-lips, as you are. You shall see her—yes."

When the young kings heard that, they were ready to run their swords through the poor little dog. When she gets to Pretty-Rose's house, she hides herself, and tells her all that has happened. Pretty-Rose gives her some good liqueur to drink, and she comes to herself. The king makes a proclamation that whoever shall (merely) spit where the little dog shall have placed her feet shall be killed, and to mind and pay attention to it.

When the marriage day had arrived, the queen came, and she brought a robe of diamonds for the wedding-day; for the next day, a robe of gold; and for the third day, a robe of silver. Judge how beautiful she was with her glint of diamonds, and her dress of diamonds, too. They could not look at her. Her godmother told her to have her sisters-in-law there, and not to be afraid of them; that they could not come near her in beauty. When Pretty-Rose went out (of her room) on the wedding-day, her sisters-in-law could not look at her because she dazzled them so much. They said to each other: "The little dog was right when she said she was beautiful, this lady."

---

23. Nothing has been said about this dress before. Something must have dropped out of the story.

And for three days Pretty-Rose walked about,[24] and every one was astounded at her beauty. When the feast was over, the godmother went home. Rose would not leave Pretty-Rose. The godmother told Pretty-Rose that she was born of poor parents, and that she had once helped them, but that what she had given them must be already exhausted. So, Pretty-Rose gave them enough for all to live grandly. She herself had four children, two boys and two girls; and if they lived well, they died well.

Told by Laurentine, who learned it from her mother.

Parsillette (1891)[25]

Paul Sébillot

There was once a man and a lady who had been married for a long time and didn't have any children. They desired very much to have one and were very sad when this didn't happen. At one point, they were told to go on a pilgrimage to have one. So, they departed on a pilgrimage. Their destination was quite far from their home. After they reached it, they set back toward home again, and the lady became pregnant. Along the way they saw a beautiful garden that had magnificent fruit.

"Oh, I want to eat some of the fruit over there, and I'll gather it myself," the lady said to her husband.

"But what if we are seen!?" the husband replied.

"Too bad!" she said to him. "I want to get some fruit, and I'm going to do so."

She went into the garden and ate some fruit, and then she loaded the carriage with some more. As she was doing this, a good little woman appeared and asked her why she had just stolen the fruit. So, the lady told her about her condition and why she had such a desire to steal the fruit. In response the good woman said to her, "Even though you've stolen my fruit, I shall say nothing. But I want to be your child's godmother. You shall have a daughter."

The lady got into her carriage and said to her husband, "I've promised the good woman that she can become our child's godmother, but I won't let her."

Finally, the day arrived when she was to give birth to her child, and she had a daughter just like the good woman had told her. And then, when the child was to be baptized, the good woman was not invited. Consequently, the good woman went to her sisters—she had two sisters, who were fairies.

"I want you to know that the lady, who stole my fruit, has given birth and didn't appoint me as the godmother," she said. "She must be punished. We must take away her child."

---

24. At a Pyrenean wedding the bride and bridegroom, with the wedding party, spend nearly the whole day in promenading through the town or village. The feast often lasts several days, and the poor bride is an object of pity, she sometimes looks so deadly tired.

25. *Revue des Traditions Populaires* 6 (1891).

The good woman departed with a large dog. When she arrived at the lady's door, she rang the bell. But they didn't want to open. So she ordered her dog to open the door, and the dog opened all the doors. Finally, they reached the door where the child was, and the good woman said to the dog, "Take away that child for me! And you, Madame, next time, keep your promises! You will never see your daughter again."

There you have it! The good woman departed with the child and arrived at her home. Immediately all the fairies of the country gathered together, and the good woman became the child's godmother. She named the girl Parsillette and gave her the gift of singing so sweetly that her voice could be heard seven miles away. The other fairies gave her all sorts of gifts such as beauty and other things. Then they gave her a nurse, and they gave her the best of upbringings. When she became older, she was so beautiful that all the gentlemen who passed by stopped to look at her. She sang so well that everybody came running to hear her sing. Upon seeing this, the good woman said to her sisters, "We must absolutely bring Parsillette to a tower, otherwise she'll be taken from us."

So the good woman took the girl to a tower three miles from the house where she had been. In this tower she had everything that was useful and pleasant for her, including a parrot that talked with her. Then the old woman said to her, "Now, whenever I come to bring something, I'll say to you, 'Parsillette, my godchild, throw down your beautiful hair!' Then you'll open the door. This is the password."

Now there was a prince who lived in this region about seven miles away, and when he heard Parsillette singing, he said, "Who's that who sings so well? I really must know who it is."

So he tried to learn about the place where the voice came from and who sang so beautifully. He was told that it was a princess who was locked in a tower.

"I've got to see her and speak to her," he said.

As he reached the tower and began prowling around it, he caught sight of the old woman, who was bringing Parsillette something to eat. Moreover, he heard what she said:

"Parsillette, my godchild, throw down your beautiful hair!"

He wrote this down in order to remember the password so that he could say it, too. Then, as soon as the good woman departed, he cried out to her:

"Parsillette, my godchild, throw down your beautiful hair."

The young woman thought that it was her godmother who had forgotten something, and so she opened the door. When she saw the young man mounting the stairs, she wanted to save herself, but where could she go? And the prince, when he saw her, he fell so much in love with her that he didn't want to leave. Indeed, he said to her that if she was willing to follow him, he would make her a queen. Well, since Parsillette was bored being alone in the tower with the parrot, she agreed and promised him that she would leave with him the next day. But once again the good woman arrived to bring her some food, and when Parsillette saw her, she hid the young man behind a curtain.

Now the parrot kept saying, "Godmother, the lover's hiding there!"

"What did your parrot say to me?" the good woman asked.

"Oh, godmother, it's just something that I taught the parrot."

Since the godmother didn't doubt her, she departed, and the young couple also departed right after her. But as the good woman was walking, she began to reflect about what the parrot had said to her.

"I think the parrot was telling me the truth. I had better check."

So she returned to the tower and cried out. But when nobody responded, she quickly climbed the stairs to the top of the tower and saw that Parsillette was fleeing in the arms of the young man. So she waved her wand, and Parsillette became just as ugly as she had been beautiful, and all the gifts that she had been given disappeared. When the prince saw that she had been changed, he didn't know what to say, and when Parsillette saw herself, she said to him, "I can't go any further because I see how angry my godmother is. I've got to return to her and ask for her pardon."

At the very moment that she said this, the young man was knocked down dead, and Parsillette returned to her godmother and asked for her pardon. Well, her godmother forgave her, and all the gifts were returned to Parsillette. And the godmother took her back to her home, not to the tower. Later the godmother married Parsillette off to a very rich prince. Parsillette never knew her parents.

Told by Joséphine Maurel, who learned this tale from her grandfather, Joseph Hubert, seventy-eight years old at Bonnétable (Sarthe).

Prunella (1900)[26]
Andrew Lang

There was once upon a time a woman who had an only daughter. When the child was about seven years old she used to pass every day, on her way to school, an orchard where there was a wild plum tree, with delicious ripe plums hanging from the branches. Each morning the child would pick one, and put it into her pocket to eat at school. For this reason she was called Prunella.

Now, the orchard belonged to a witch. One day the witch noticed the child gathering a plum, as she passed along the road. Prunella did it quite innocently, not knowing that she was doing wrong in taking the fruit that hung close to the roadside. But the witch was furious, and next day hid herself behind the hedge, and when Prunella came past, and put out her hand to pluck the fruit, she jumped out and seized her by the arm.

"Ah! you little thief!" she exclaimed. "I have caught you at last. Now you will have to pay for your misdeeds."

---

26. *The Grey Fairy Book* (London: Longmans, 1900).

The poor child, half dead with fright, implored the old woman to forgive her, assuring her that she did not know she had done wrong, and promising never to do it again. But the witch had no pity, and she dragged Prunella into her house, where she kept her till the time should come when she could have her revenge.

As the years passed Prunella grew up into a very beautiful girl. Now her beauty and goodness, instead of softening the witch's heart, aroused her hatred and jealousy. One day she called Prunella to her, and said, "Take this basket, go to the well, and bring it back to me filled with water. If you don't, I will kill you."

The girl took the basket, went and let it down into the well again and again. But her work was lost labor. Each time, as she drew up the basket, the water streamed out of it. At last, in despair, she gave it up, and leaning against the well she began to cry bitterly, when suddenly she heard a voice at her side saying, "Prunella, why are you crying?" Turning round she beheld a handsome youth, who looked kindly at her, as if he were sorry for her trouble.

"Who are you," she asked, "and how do you know my name?"

"I am the son of the witch," he replied, "and my name is Bensiabel. I know that she is determined that you shall die, but I promise you that she shall not carry out her wicked plan. Will you give me a kiss, if I fill your basket?"

"No," said Prunella, "I will not give you a kiss, because you are the son of a witch."

"Very well," replied the youth sadly. "Give me your basket and I will fill it for you." And he dipped it into the well, and the water stayed in it. Then the girl returned to the house, carrying the basket filled with water.

When the witch saw it, she became white with rage, and exclaimed, "Bensiabel must have helped you." And Prunella looked down, and said nothing.

"Well, we shall see who will win in the end," said the witch, in a great rage. The following day she called the girl to her and said, "Take this sack of wheat. I am going out for a little; by the time I return I shall expect you to have made it into bread. If you have not done it, I will kill you." Having said this she left the room, closing and locking the door behind her.

Poor Prunella did not know what to do. It was impossible for her to grind the wheat, prepare the dough, and bake the bread, all in the short time that the witch would be away. At first she set to work bravely, but when she saw how hopeless her task was, she threw herself on a chair, and began to weep bitterly.

She was roused from her despair by hearing Bensiabel's voice at her side saying. "Prunella, Prunella, do not weep like that. If you will give me a kiss, I will make the bread, and you will be saved."

"I will not kiss the son of a witch," replied Prunella. But Bensiabel took the wheat from her, and ground it, and made the dough, and when the witch returned, the bread was ready baked in the oven.

Turning to the girl, with fury in her voice, she said. "Bensiabel must have been here and helped you," and Prunella looked down, and said nothing.

"We shall see who will win in the end," said the witch, and her eyes blazed with anger.

Next day she called the girl to her and said, "Go to my sister, who lives across the mountains. She will give you a casket, which you must bring back to me." This she said knowing that her sister, who was a still more cruel and wicked witch than herself, would never allow the girl to return, but would imprison her and starve her to death. But Prunella did not suspect anything, and set out quite cheerfully. On the way she met Bensiabel.

"Where are you going, Prunella?" he asked.

"I am going to the sister of my mistress, from whom I am to fetch a casket."

"Oh poor, poor girl!" said Bensiabel. "You are being sent straight to your death. Give me a kiss, and I will save you."

But again Prunella answered as before, "I will not kiss the son of a witch."

"Nevertheless, I will save your life," said Bensiabel, "for I love you better than myself. Take this flagon of oil, this loaf of bread, this piece of rope, and this broom. When you reach the witch's house, oil the hinges of the door with the contents of the flagon, and throw the loaf of bread to the great fierce mastiff, who will come to meet you. When you have passed the dog, you will see in the courtyard a miserable woman trying in vain to let down a bucket into the well with her plaited hair. You must give her the rope. In the kitchen you will find a still more miserable woman trying to clean the hearth with her tongue; to her you must give the broom. You will see the casket on the top of a cupboard, take it as quickly as you can, and leave the house without a moment's delay. If you do all this exactly as I have told you, you will not be killed."

So Prunella, having listened carefully to his instructions, did just what he had told her. She reached the house, oiled the hinges of the door, threw the loaf to the dog, gave the poor woman at the well the rope, and the woman in the kitchen the broom, caught up the casket from the top of the cupboard, and fled with it out of the house.

But the witch heard her as she ran away, and rushing to the window called out to the woman in the kitchen, "Kill that thief, I tell you!"

But the woman replied, "I will not kill her, for she has given me a broom, whereas you forced me to clean the hearth with my tongue."

Then the witch called out in fury to the woman at the well. "Take the girl, I tell you, and fling her into the water, and drown her!"

But the woman answered, "No, I will not drown her, for she gave me this rope, whereas you forced me to use my hair to let down the bucket to draw water."

Then the witch shouted to the dog to seize the girl and hold her fast; but the dog answered, "No, I will not seize her, for she gave me a loaf of bread, whereas you let me starve with hunger."

The witch was so angry that she nearly choked, as she called out, "Door, bang upon her, and keep her a prisoner." But the door answered, "I won't, for she has oiled my hinges, so that they move quite easily, whereas you left them all rough and rusty."

And so Prunella escaped, and, with the casket under her arm, reached the house of her mistress, who, as you may believe, was as angry as she was surprised to see the girl standing before her, looking more beautiful than ever.

Her eyes flashed, as in furious tones she asked her, "Did you meet Bensiabel?"

But Prunella looked down, and said nothing.

"We shall see," said the witch, "who will win in the end. Listen, there are three cocks in the henhouse; one is yellow, one black, and the third is white. If one of them crows during the night, you must tell me which one it is. Woe to you if you make a mistake. I will gobble you up in one mouthful."

Now Bensiabel was in the room next to the one where Prunella slept. At midnight she awoke hearing a cock crow.

"Which one was that?" shouted the witch.

Then, trembling, Prunella knocked on the wall and whispered. "Bensiabel, Bensiabel, tell me, which cock crowed?"

"Will you give me a kiss if I tell you?" he whispered back through the wall.

But she answered, "No."

Then he whispered back to her. "Nevertheless, I will tell you. It was the yellow cock that crowed."

The witch, who had noticed the delay in Prunella's answer, approached her door calling angrily, "Answer at once, or I will kill you."

So Prunella answered. "It was the yellow cock that crowed."

And the witch stamped her foot and gnashed her teeth.

Soon after another cock crowed. "Tell me now which one it is," called the witch.

And, prompted by Bensiabel, Prunella answered, "That is the black cock."

A few minutes after the crowing was heard again, and the voice of the witch demanding, "Which one was that?

"And again Prunella implored Bensiabel to help her. But this time he hesitated, for he hoped that Prunella might forget that he was a witch's son and promise to give him a kiss. And as he hesitated, he heard an agonized cry from the girl. "Bensiabel, Bensiabel, save me! The witch is coming, she is close to me, I hear the gnashing of her teeth!"

With a bound Bensiabel opened his door and flung himself against the witch. He pulled her back with such force that she stumbled, and falling headlong, dropped down dead at the foot of the stairs.

Then, at last, Prunella was touched by Bensiabel's goodness and kindness to her, and she became his wife, and they lived happily ever after.

3. FACING FEAR

ATU 326—THE YOUTH WHO WANTED TO LEARN WHAT FEAR IS

This tale type is related to the numerous other European humorous tales about a country bumpkin, who is apparently so dim-witted that he is afraid of nothing, and though he remains dumb, he is also lucky and generally survives numerous trials to win a fortune or a princess, sometimes both. There tend to be two traditions to this type: one in which the protagonist seeks to learn what death is as exemplified by Chaucer's "The Pardoner's Tale" in *The Canterbury Tales* and by Giovan Francesco Straparola's "Flamminio in Seeking Death Discovers Life" in *The Pleasant Nights*, and one in which the protagonist is a misfit who sets out to learn what fear is. The more prevalent storytelling tradition is the latter that concerns the numbskull who wants to encounter fear. His most common experiences involve: mistaking a man for a ghost and harming him; spending time with dead men under a gallows; freeing a haunted castle/house; and playing cards or bowling with demons/dead people. Sometimes he never really learns what fear is, and if he does, it is through a simple incident such as exposure to water, fish, or birds that give him the creeps. Despite his stupidity, he inevitably wins a fortune.

The Brothers Grimm knew several versions of this tale type and constantly edited the variants that they published. Their first brief version of 1812 may have been influenced by a ballad written by Philippine Engelhard in her book *Spukemärchen* (1782). Their second version was first published in the magazine *Wünschelruthe* (1818) and was a combination of different variants from the oral tradition that Wilhelm cobbled together to form the printed text that became the basis of the 1857 version. Included here is also the 1856 variant from the final edition of their notes that includes references to other versions of this type tale. Interestingly the Grimms' tales have very different protagonists, such as a poor boy, a blacksmith's son, and a dumbbell. Wolf depicts a poor shoemaker's son; Zingerele, the eldest son from a large family; Gonzenbach, an ill-bred son; Luzel, a gardener; Millien, a widow's bold son. All these lower-class figures are intrepid nonconformists who refuse to be "tamed." Despite their alleged stupidity, they use their wits and courage to survive various tests and become rich. In many ways they are related to the long tradition of the thirteenth-century "Nasreddin the fool" tales that were disseminated in Turkey and were related to numerous other trickster and fool tales from the Middle East, Central Asia, the Balkans, and the Mediterranean. It is apparent that the tale type underwent major changes in Europe to articulate a lower-class antagonistic view, for neither church members, fathers, kings, nor other authority figures can tame a simple fearless "peasant." Many other variants can be found in the works of Afanas'ev, Pröhle, Schneller, Pitrè, Sébillot, de Gubernatis, Coronedi-Berti, Nerucci, Cadic, Cosquin, and Pineau.

******

Good Bowling and Card Playing (1812)[27]
Jacob and Wilhelm Grimm

Once upon a time there was an old king who had the most beautiful daughter in the world. One day he announced: "Whoever can keep watch in my old castle for three nights can have the princess for his bride."

Now, there was a young man from a poor family who thought to himself, 'Why not risk my life? I've got nothing to lose, and a lot to win. What's there to think about?'

So he appeared before the king and offered to keep watch in the castle for three nights.

"You may request three things to take with you into the castle, but they have to be lifeless objects," the king said.

"Well, I'd like to take a carpenter's bench with the knife, a lathe, and fire."

All of these things were carried into the castle for him. When it began to get dark, he himself went inside. At first everything was quiet. He built a fire, placed the carpenter's bench with the knife next to it, and sat down on the lathe. Toward midnight, however, a rumbling could be heard, first softly, then more loudly: "Bif! Baf! Hehe! Holla ho!"

It became more dreadful, and then it was somewhat quiet. Finally, a leg came down the chimney and stood right before him.

"Hey, there!" the young man cried out, "How about some more? One is too little."

The noise began once again. Another leg fell down the chimney and then another and another, until there were nine.

"That's enough now. I've got enough for bowling, but there are no balls. Out with them!"

There was a tremendous uproar, and two heads fell down the chimney. He put them in the lathe and turned them until they were smooth. "Now they'll roll much better!"

Then he did the same with the legs and set them up like bowling pins.

"Hey, now I can have some fun!"

Suddenly two large black cats appeared and strode around the fire. "Meow! Meow!" they screeched. "We're freezing! We're freezing!"

"You fools! What are you screaming about? Sit down by the fire and warm yourselves."

After the cats had warmed themselves, they said, "Good fellow, we want to play a round of cards."

"All right," he replied, "but show me your paws. You have such long claws. First I've got to give them a good clipping."

---

27. "Gut Kegel und Kartenspiel," *Kinder- und Haus-Märchen. Gesammelt durch die Brüder Grimm*, 2 vols. (Berlin: Realschulbuchhandlung, 1812/1815).

Upon saying this, he grabbed them by the scruffs of their necks and lifted them to the carpenter's bench. There he fastened them to the vise and beat them to death. Afterward he carried them outside and threw them into a pond that lay across from the castle. Just as he returned to the castle and wanted to settle down and warm himself by the fire, many black cats and dogs came out of every nook and cranny, more and more, so that he couldn't hide himself. They screamed, stamped on the fire and kicked it about, so that the fire went out. So he grabbed his carving knife and yelled, "Get out of here, you riffraff!"

And he began swinging the knife. Most of the cats and dogs ran away. The others were killed, and he carried them out and threw them into the pond. Then he went back inside to the fire and blew the sparks, so that the fire began again and he could warm himself.

After he had warmed himself, he was tired and lay down on a large bed that stood in a corner. Just when he wanted to fall asleep, the bed began to stir and raced around the entire castle.

"That's fine with me. Just keep it up!"

So the bed drove around as though six horses were pulling it over stairs and landings: "Bing bang!"

It turned upside down, from top to bottom, and he was beneath it. So he flung the blankets and pillows into the air and jumped off.

"Whoever wants to have a ride can have one!"

Then he lay down next to the fire until it was day.

In the morning the king came, and when he saw the young man lying asleep, he thought he was dead and said, "What a shame."

But when the young man heard these words, he awoke, and as soon as he saw the king, he stood up. Then the king asked him how things had gone during the night.

"Quite good. One night's gone by, the other two will go by as well."

Indeed, the other nights were just like the first. But he already knew what to do, and so on the fourth day, he was rewarded with the king's beautiful daughter.

The Young Man Who Went Out in Search of Fear (1856)[28]
Jacob and Wilhelm Grimm

There was once a young man on this earth, and his father was a blacksmith. Now this young man went to the cemetery and other dreadful places, but he

---

28. "Märchen von einem, der auszog, das Fürchten zu lernen," *Kinder- und Hausmärchen gesammelt durch die Brüder Grimm*, 7th ed., vol. 3 (Göttingen: Verlag der Dieterich'schen Buchhandlung, 1856). This version is included in the notes to the tale that were printed before the complete tales were published in 1857 in two volumes.

was never afraid. So his father said to him, "Just travel about the world for some time, and you'll soon get to know what fear is."

The young man departed, and he happened to come upon a village during the night, and since all the houses were locked, he lay down beneath the gallows. When he noticed that someone was hanging there, he asked him, "Why are you hanging there?"

"I'm innocent," answered the man who was hanged. "The schoolmaster stole the little bell from the collection bag and said that I was the thief. If you'll help me get an honest burial, I'll give you a staff with which you can beat away ghosts. The schoolmaster hid the little bell under a stone in his cellar."

When the young man heard this, he stood up, went straight to the schoolmaster's house in the village, and knocked. The schoolmaster got up but refused to open the door, because he was afraid. So the young man called out, "If you don't open up, I'll knock your door down."

So the schoolmaster opened it, and the young man grabbed him in his nightgown, just as he was, swung him over his back, and carried him to the judge's house. Then he shouted loudly, "Open up! I'm bringing you a thief!"

When the judge came out, the young man said, "Take down the poor sinner from the gallows. He's innocent. Hang this man in his place. He's the one who stole the little bell from the collection bag that's lying in his cellar under a stone."

The judge sent a servant to check the young man's story, and the little bell was discovered, so the schoolmaster was forced to confess to the theft. Consequently, the judge delivered his sentence: the innocent man was to be taken down from the gallows and buried in honor, and in his place, the thief was to be hanged.

The next night, when the innocent man was already resting in his Christian grave, the young blacksmith went to the cemetery. Then the ghost of the innocent man came and gave him the staff that he had promised.

"Now I shall go out into the world," said the blacksmith, "and search for fear."

It so happened that he soon arrived in a city where there was a haunted castle that nobody ever dared enter. When the king heard that a man had come who was afraid of nothing, he sent for him and said, "If you set this haunted castle free of the magic spell, I'll make you so rich that you'll never have to worry about money for the rest of your life."

"I'll gladly help you," the young man answered. "You only have to show me the way to the castle."

"I don't even have a key," said the king.

"I don't need one," replied the young man. "I'll find a way to get in."

The blacksmith was led to the castle, and when he came to the outer gate, he hit it with his staff, and immediately the gate sprang open. Behind it were the keys to the entire castle. So the young man unlocked the first inner door, and as soon as it was open, the ghosts came toward him. One had horns on its head, another spit fire, and they were all black as coal.

"They're really something else!" the young man said. "They must be genuine charcoal burners. I could take them home to help my father take care of the fire."

As they rushed toward him, he took his staff and walloped them six at a time. Then he grabbed the bunch of them and stuck them in a room where they were unable to move any more. After this he picked up the keys again and opened the second door. There was a coffin with a dead man inside. On the ground next to the coffin was a large black poodle with a glowing chain around its neck. The young man went up to the coffin, hit it with his staff, and said, "What are you doing in there, you old charcoal burner?"

The dead man sat up and wanted to frighten him, but the blacksmith yelled, "Get out! Right now!"

When the dead man didn't respond immediately, the blacksmith grabbed him and stuck him with the others. Then he returned to the coffin, took the glowing chain, wrapped it around himself, and yelled, "Away with you!"

But the black dog resisted and spit out fire.

"Well, if you can do that," said the young man, "then all the more reason to take you with me. You'll also help my father with the fire."

But before he could turn around, the dog disappeared—it may well have been the devil. Now he still had a small key for the last door. As he opened it, twelve black ghosts with horns on their heads and fire coming from their mouths rushed at him. But he walloped them with his staff, dragged them outside, and threw them into a barrel, which he sealed with a cover.

"Now that I've quieted them down," he said contentedly, "I feel a bit warm, and I'd like to have a drink."

So he went down to the cellar, tapped some wine from a barrel, and was in good spirits. In the meantime, the king said, "I'd like to know what's happened to him," and sent his father confessor to the haunted castle, for no one else dared to enter the place. When the father confessor, who was decrepit and hunchbacked, came to the gate and knocked, the young blacksmith opened up. However, as he caught sight of this misshapen figure in a black coat, he exclaimed, "There's one left over! What do you want, you old hunchbacked devil?"

And he locked him up as well.

Now the king waited one more day, and when the father confessor didn't return, he sent a troop of soldiers with orders to break into the castle with force. The blacksmith said, "Some people are coming. I'll let them in."

The soldiers asked him why he had locked up the king's father confessor.

"What?" he responded. "How was I to know it was the father confessor? Why did he come here in a black coat!"

"What should we tell the king?" the soldiers asked.

"Tell him to come here himself," the young man said. "I've cleaned out the castle."

When the king heard this, he became full of joy and found great treasures consisting of precious stones, silver, and old wine. All of this was once again in his possession. Then he had a suit of gold made for the young blacksmith.

"No," the young man said. "I don't want that. Only a fool would wear it," and he threw it away. "Anyway, I'm not going to leave this castle until the king helps me get to know fear. He must certainly know what it is."

Then the king had a white linen coat made for him with four gold pieces sewn inside as a reward for his efforts. But the young blacksmith said, "It's too heavy for me." And he threw it away and put on an old coat. "Anyway, before I go home to my father, I must first get to know fear."

Then he took his staff and went to the king, who led him to a cannon. The young blacksmith examined the cannon, walked around it, and asked what kind of a thing it was.

"Step aside just a little," answered the king. Then he ordered the canon to be loaded and fired.

When the canon exploded with a powerful bang, the young blacksmith cried out, "That was fear! Now I know it!"

And he went happily on his way home.

A Tale about the Boy Who Went Forth to Learn What Fear Was (1857)[29]

Jacob and Wilhelm Grimm

A father had two sons. The older was smart and sensible and could cope in any situation, while the younger was stupid and could neither learn nor understand anything. Whenever people encountered him, they said, "He'll always be a burden to his father!"

If there were things to be done, the older son was always the one who had to take care of them. Yet, if the father asked the older son to fetch something toward evening or during the night, and if that meant he would have to pass through the churchyard or some other scary place, he would answer, "Oh, no, Father, I won't go there. It gives me the creeps!"

Indeed, he was afraid.

Sometimes stories that would send shivers up anyone's spine were told by the fireside at night, and the listeners would say: "Oh, it gives me the creeps!" Often the younger son would be sitting in the corner and listening, but he never understood what they meant. "They're always saying, 'It gives me the creeps! It gives me the creeps!' But it doesn't give me the creeps. It's probably some kind of a trick that I don't understand."

---

29. *Kinder- und Hausmärchen gesammelt durch die Brüder Grimm*, 7th ed., 3 vols. (Göttingen: Verlag der Dieterich'schen Buchhandlung, 1857).

One day his father happened to say to him, "Listen, you over there in the corner, you're getting too big and strong. It's time you learned how to earn your living. Look how hard your brother works, while you're just a hopeless case."

"Oh, no, father," he responded. "I'd gladly learn something. If possible, I'd like to learn how to get the creeps. That's something I know nothing about."

When the older son heard that, he laughed and thought to himself, 'Dear Lord, my brother's really a dumbbell! He'll never amount to anything. You've got to start young to get anywhere.'

The father sighed and answered, "You're sure to learn all about getting the creeps in due time, but it won't help you earn a living."

Shortly after this, the sexton came to the house for a visit, and the father complained about his younger son, that he was incapable of doing anything, much less learning and knowing anything. "Just think, when I asked him what he wanted to do to earn a living, he actually said he wanted to learn how to get the creeps."

"If that's all he wants," the sexton replied, "he can learn it at my place. Just hand him over to me, and I'll smooth over his rough edges."

The father was pleased to do this because he thought, 'The boy needs some shaping up.' So the sexton took him to his house, where the boy was assigned the task of ringing the church bell. After a few days had passed, the sexton woke him at midnight and told him to get up, climb the church steeple, and ring the bell.

'Now you'll learn what the creeps are,' the sexton thought and secretly went up ahead of him. When the boy reached the top and turned around to grab hold of the bell rope, he saw a white figure standing on the stairs across from the sound hole.

"Who's there?" he cried out, but the figure did not answer, nor did it move an inch. "Answer me," the boy shouted, "or get out of here! You've no business being here at night."

However, the sexton didn't move, for he wanted to make the boy think he was a ghost.

The boy shouted a second time, "What do you want? If you're an honest man, say something, or I'll throw you down the stairs!"

'He really can't be as mean as that,' the sexton thought, and he kept still, standing there as if he were made of stone.

The boy shouted at him a third time, and when that didn't help, he lunged at the ghost and pushed him down the stairs. The ghost fell ten steps and lay in a corner. The boy then rang the bell, went home, got into bed without saying a word, and fell asleep. The sexton's wife waited for her husband for a long time, but he failed to return. Finally, she became anxious, woke the boy, and asked, "Do you know where my husband is? He climbed the steeple ahead of you."

"No," replied the boy. "But someone was standing across from the sound hole. When he refused to answer me or go away, I thought he was some sort of scoundrel and pushed him down the stairs. Why don't you go and see if it wasn't him? I'd feel sorry if it was."

The wife ran off and found her husband, who was lying in a corner and moaning because of a broken leg. She carried him down the stairs and then rushed off to the boy's father screaming as she went.

"Your boy has caused a terrible accident!" she cried out. "He threw my husband down the stairs and made him break a leg. Get that good-for-nothing out of our house!"

The father was mortified and ran straight to the sexton's house, where he began scolding the boy. "What kind of godless tricks have you been playing? The devil must have put you up to it!"

"Father," he replied, "just listen to me. I'm completely innocent. He was standing there in the dark like someone who had evil designs. I didn't know who he was and warned him three times to say something or go away."

"Ah," said the father, "you'll never be anything but trouble for me! Get out of my sight. I don't want to see you anymore."

"All right, father. Gladly. Just give me until daylight, and I'll go away and learn how to get the creeps. Then I'll know a trick or two and be able to earn a living."

"Learn what you want," the father said. "It's all the same to me. Here's fifty talers. Take them and go out into the wide world, but don't tell anyone where you come from or who your father is because I'm ashamed of you."

"Yes, father, as you wish. If that's all you desire, I can easily bear that in mind."

At daybreak the boy put the fifty talers in his pocket, went out on the large highway, and kept saying to himself, 'If I could only get the creeps! If I could only get the creeps!' As the boy was talking to himself a man came along and overheard him. When they had gone some distance together, they caught sight of the gallows, and the man said to him, "You see the tree over there. That's where seven men were wedded to the ropemaker's daughter. Now they're learning how to fly. Sit down beneath the tree and wait till night comes. Then you'll certainly learn how to get the creeps."

"If that's all it takes," the boy responded, "I can do it with ease. And, if I learn how to get the creeps as quickly as that, you shall have my fifty talers. Just come back here tomorrow morning."

The boy went to the gallows, sat down beneath it, and waited until evening came. Since he was cold, he made a fire. Nevertheless, at midnight the wind became colder, and he couldn't get warm in spite of the fire. When the wind knocked the hanged men against each other and they swung back and forth, he thought, 'If you're freezing down here by the fire, they must really be cold and shivering up there.' Since he felt sorry for them, he took a ladder, climbed up, untied one hanged man after the other, and hauled all seven down to the ground. Then he stirred the fire, blew on it, and set them all around it so they might warm themselves. However, they sat there without moving, and their clothes caught on fire.

"Be careful," he said, "otherwise I'll hang you all back up there."

The dead men did not hear. Indeed, they just remained silent and let their rags continue to burn. Then the boy became angry and said, "If you won't take care, I can't help you, and I surely won't let you burn me."

So he hung them up again, all in a row, sat down by his fire, and fell asleep. Next morning the man came and wanted his fifty talers.

"Well," he said, "now you know what the creeps are?"

"No," answered the boy. "How should I know? Those men up there didn't open their mouths. They're so stupid they let the few old rags they're wearing get burned."

The man realized he would never get the fifty talers that day. So he went off saying, "Never in my life have I met anyone like that!"

The boy also went his way, and once again he began talking to himself. 'Oh, if I could only get the creeps! If I could only get the creeps!'

A carter, who was walking behind him, overheard him and asked, "Who are you?"

"I don't know," answered the boy.

"Where do you come from?" the carter continued questioning him.

"I don't know."

"Who's your father?"

"I'm not allowed to tell."

"What's that you're always mumbling to yourself?"

"Oh," the boy responded, "I want to get the creeps, but nobody can teach me how."

"Stop your foolish talk," said the carter. "Come along with me, and I'll see if I can find a place for you to stay."

The boy went with the carter, and in the evening they reached an inn, where they intended to spend the night. As they entered the main room, the boy spoke loudly once more. "If I could only get the creeps! If I could only get the creeps!"

The innkeeper heard this and laughed. "If that's what you desire," he remarked, "there'll be ample opportunity for you to get it here."

"Oh, be quiet!" the innkeeper's wife said. "There have already been enough foolish fellows who've lost their lives. It would be a mighty shame if that boy with such pretty eyes never saw the light of day again."

But the boy said, "It doesn't matter how hard it may be. I want to get the creeps. That's why I left home."

He kept bothering the innkeeper until the man told him about the haunted castle nearby, where one could really learn how to get the creeps. All he had to do was to spend three nights in it. The king had promised his daughter to anyone who would undertake the venture, and she was the most beautiful maiden under the sun. There were also great treasures in the castle guarded by evil spirits. Once the treasures were set free, they would be enough to make a poor man rich. Many men had already gone into the castle, but none had ever come out again.

The next morning the boy appeared before the king and said, "If I may have your permission, I'd like to spend three nights in the haunted castle."

The king looked at him and found the boy to his liking, so he said, "You may request three things to take with you into the castle, but they must be lifeless objects."

"Well then," he answered, "I'd like to have a fire, a lathe, and a carpenter's bench with a knife."

The king had these things carried into the castle for him during the day. Just before nightfall the boy himself went up to the castle, made a bright fire in one of the rooms, set up the carpenter's bench with the knife next to it, and sat down on the lathe.

"Oh, if I could only get the creeps!" he said. "But I don't think I'll learn it here either."

Toward midnight he wanted to stir the fire again, but just as he was blowing it, he suddenly heard a scream coming from a corner. "Meow! Meow! We're freezing!"

"You fools!" he cried out. "What are you screaming for? If you're freezing, come sit down by the fire and warm yourselves."

No sooner had he said that than two big black cats ran over with a tremendous leap, sat down beside him, and glared ferociously at him with their fiery eyes. After a while, when they had warmed themselves, they said, "Comrade, let's play a round of cards."

"Why not?" he responded. "But first show me your paws." They stretched out their claws.

"My goodness!" he said. "What long nails you have! Wait, I've got to give them a good clipping."

Upon saying that, he grabbed them by the scruffs of their necks, lifted them onto the carpenter's bench, and fastened their paws in a vice.

"I was keeping a sharp eye on you two," he said, "and now I've lost my desire to play cards."

Then he beat them to death and threw them into the water. But, after he had put an end to those two and was about to sit down at his fire again, black cats and black dogs wearing some glowing chains came out of all the nooks and crannies, and they kept coming and coming so it was impossible for him to flee. They made a gruesome noise, stamped on his fire, tore it apart, and tried to put it out. He watched them calmly for a while, but when it became so awful that he could no longer stand it, he grabbed his knife and yelled, "Get out of here, you lousy creatures!" And he started swinging the knife. Some of them ran away while he killed the rest and threw them into the pond. When he returned to his place, he built up his fire again by blowing on the embers and proceeded to warm himself. As he was sitting there, his eyelids grew heavy, and he felt a strong desire to sleep. Then he looked around and saw a large bed in the corner.

"That's just what I was looking for," he said and lay down on it. But just as he was about to shut his eyes, the bed began to move by itself and raced all around the castle.

"Keep it up," he said. "But go a little faster."

The bed sped on as though it were being drawn by six horses. It rolled through doorways and up and down stairs. Then all of a sudden, *bing-bang!* it turned upside down and lay on top of him like a mountain. But he flung the blankets and pillows in the air, climbed out, and said, "Now, anyone else who wants a ride can have one." He lay down by the fire and slept until it was day.

In the morning the king came, and when he saw the boy lying on the ground, he thought that he was dead and that the ghosts had killed him.

"What a pity! He was such a handsome fellow," the king remarked. Upon hearing this, the boy sat up and said, "It's not over yet!"

The king was astonished but also glad and asked him how things had gone.

"Very well," he answered. "One night's over and done with. The other two will pass also."

Then he went to the innkeeper, who gaped at him in amazement.

"I never expected to see you alive again," he said. "Have you learned now what the creeps are?"

"No," he said. "It's no use. If only someone could tell me!"

The second night he went up to the old castle, sat down at the fire, and repeated his old refrain. "If I could only get the creeps!"

Toward midnight he heard a lot of noise and rumbling, first softly, then louder and louder. Soon it became quiet for a while until suddenly, with a loud cry, half a man came tumbling down the chimney and fell right at his feet.

"Hey there!" cried the boy. "There's a half missing. This isn't enough."

Once again the noise began. There was a roaring and howling, and the other half came tumbling down.

"Wait," the boy said. "I'll just give the fire a little stir for you."

After he had done that, he looked around and saw that the two pieces had joined together to form a gruesome-looking man who was now sitting in his place.

"That wasn't part of the bargain," said the boy. "The bench is mine."

The man tried to push him away, but the boy didn't let him. Instead, he gave the man a mighty shove and sat back down in his place. Suddenly more men came tumbling down the chimney, one after the other, and they brought nine dead men's bones and two dead men's skulls, set them up, and began to play a game of ninepins. The boy felt a desire to play as well and asked, "Hey, can I play too?"

"Yes, if you have money."

"Money enough," he answered, "but your balls aren't round." He took the skulls, put them in the lathe, and turned them until they were round.

"Now they'll roll much better," he said. "Hurray! Let's have some fun!"

He joined their game and lost some of his money, but when the clock struck twelve, everything disappeared before his eyes, and he lay down and fell asleep in peace.

The next morning the king came to inquire about him, and he asked, "How did things go for you this time?"

"I played a game of ninepins," he said, "and I lost a few talers."

"Didn't you get the creeps?"

"Not at all!" he responded. "I had a lot of fun. If I only knew what the creeps were!"

The third night he sat down on his bench again and said quite sadly, "If I could only get the creeps!"

When it grew late, six huge men came in carrying a coffin. Then he said, "Aha, that must be my cousin who died just a few days ago." He signaled to them with his finger and cried out, "Come here, little cousin, come here!"

They set the coffin on the ground, and he went over and lifted the lid. There was a dead man lying inside, and the boy felt his face, which was as cold as ice.

"Wait," he said. "I'll warm you up a bit." He went to the fire, warmed his hand, and placed it on the dead man's face, but it remained cold. So he took the dead man out and set him near the fire, then put him on his lap and rubbed his arms until his blood began circulating again. When that didn't work either, the boy recalled that two people can warm each other up when they lie in bed together. So he brought the man to the bed, covered him, and lay down beside him. After a while the dead man got warm and began to move.

"You see, cousin," said the boy. "What if I hadn't warmed you?"

But the dead man shouted, "Now I'm going to strangle you!"

"What?" the boy responded. "Is that my thanks? I'm going to put you right back into your coffin."

He lifted him up, tossed him inside, and shut the lid. Then the six men returned and carried the coffin away.

"I can't get the creeps," the boy said. "I'll never learn it here no matter how long I live."

Just then a ghastly looking man entered. He was old and larger than the others and had a long white beard.

"Oh, you scoundrel!" the man cried out. "Now you'll learn what the creeps are, for you're about to die."

"Not so fast!" said the boy. "If I'm about to die, you'll have to get me first."

"Don't worry, I'll get you," said the monster.

"Easy does it. Don't talk so big! I'm just as strong as you are if not stronger."

"We'll see about that," said the old man. "If you're stronger than I am, I'll let you go. Come, let's give it a try."

He led the boy through dark passages to a smithy, picked up an axe, and drove an anvil right into the ground with one blow.

"I can do better than that," the boy said, and he went to the other anvil. The old man, with his white beard hanging down, drew near him to watch. The boy grabbed the axe, split the anvil in two with one blow, and wedged the old man's beard in the middle.

"Now I've got you!" the boy said. "It's your turn to die!"

He seized an iron and beat the old man until he whimpered and begged the boy to stop and promised to give him great treasures. The boy pulled out the axe and let him go. The old man led him back into the castle and showed him three chests full of gold in a cellar.

"One of them," he said, "belongs to the poor, the second to the king, and the third is yours."

Just then the clock struck twelve, and the ghost vanished, leaving the boy standing in the dark.

"I'll find my way out of here all the same," he said and groped about until he found the way back to his room, where he fell asleep by the fire.

In the morning the king came and said, "Now you must have learned what the creeps are."

"No," he answered. "What are they? My dead cousin was here, and a bearded man came. He showed me a great deal of money down in the cellar, but nobody told me what the creeps are."

Then the king said, "You've saved the castle and shall marry my daughter."

"That's all fine and good," he answered, "but I still don't know what the creeps are."

Now the gold was brought up from the cellar, and the wedding was celebrated. The boy loved his wife dearly and was very happy, but he still kept saying, "If I could only get the creeps! If I could only get the creeps!"

After a while his wife became annoyed by that, but her chambermaid said, "Don't worry. I'll make sure he gets to know what the creeps are."

She went out to a brook that ran through the garden and fetched a bucket full of minnows. That night, when the young king was sleeping, his wife pulled the covers off him and poured the bucket full of cold water and minnows on him. Then the little fish began flapping all over him, causing him to wake up and exclaim, "Oh, I've got the creeps! I've got the creeps! Now I know, dear wife, just what the creeps are."

Fearless Hans (1851)[30]

Johann Wilhelm Wolf

A poor shoemaker had a son called Hans, and he was the wildest and most intrepid lad in the entire village. His father brought him to the minister to have

---

30. "Hans ohne Furcht," *Deutsche Hausmärchen* (Göttingen: Dieterich'sche Buchhandlung, 1851).

him tamed a bit, but the minister couldn't get anywhere with him. When some
good advice and warnings did not work, the minister spoke to the bell-ringer:
"He's got to be tamed even if it might cost him his life. When you go to ring
the bells tonight, take him into the church with you and lock him inside. The
ghosts, who lurk there, will trim his nails shorter."

So, that evening the bell-ringer took Hans with him, and after he rang
the bells, he sent Hans downstairs to fetch something. Meanwhile he quickly
sneaked out and locked the church doors behind him. When Hans returned
to the bell tower and saw that the bell-ringer had run off, he said, "He thinks
that I'll become afraid, but I can sleep here just as well as I can anywhere else."
And he laid himself down on a bench and fell asleep. When midnight arrived,
he suddenly heard a noise as if someone were bowling. He looked around and
saw three men dressed in black beneath him. They were using skulls of dead
people as balls to knock down nine bones set up in an alley, but they never hit
anything.

"What weaklings you are!" Hans cried out. "Give me a ball and let me roll it."

Soon after he rolled a skull, he knocked down all nine of the bones.

"Now each one of you should take a turn" he said. "I'll set up the bones."

But none of the men could knock down the bones, and Hans won nine coins
from them. At one in the morning they gathered up the bones and skulls and
slipped away under a stone.

Early the next morning the minister woke the bell-ringer and said, "Go and
see that you remove Hans's corpse from the church. I'm sure he's dead. Just leave
him lying in the churchyard. The ghosts could have just as well killed him there
as in the church."

The bell-ringer went into the church, but Hans was snoring on the bench as
he was accustomed to do, and when the bell-ringer woke him, he jumped up,
showed the bell-ringer the coins, and cried out, "Just look. I won these coins
from midnight to one in the morning. Wouldn't you like to play? If so, you'll
have to spend the night here."

"May heaven protect me!" responded the bell-ringer, and he went off to
report to the minister, who said, "Let him do what he wants. The ghosts haven't
finished with him yet."

The next evening when the bell-ringer wanted to go and ring the bells,
Hans was already standing at the church doors. Then he went inside, let
the bell-ringer lock the doors, and laid down on a bench. Toward midnight
he awoke again and saw six men dressed in black who were rolling skulls of the
dead to knock down the bowling bones, but just like the three men who had
been unsuccessful the night before, they didn't hit anything. Hans jumped up
and cried out, "Get out of the way, and let me bowl. You'll never learn how to
do it in a million years!"

And he rolled the ball and knocked down all nine pins.

"Now, I'll set the bones up, and you try again!" he said.

They played until one in the morning, and then the men gathered together all the skulls and bones. Just as they were leaving, Hans cried out, "Hey, where's my money?—Well, all right. Just go. I'll be patient until tomorrow."

The men disappeared again beneath the stone, and Hans laid himself down and slept until the light of day. Then the bell-ringer arrived. He had been sent by the minister to see how Hans was doing, and Hans called out: "Just think, I bowled better than those six guys who were here this night. Now they owe me some money, and they had better pay me, or I won't let them go. Stay the night with me. You can't believe how nice it is, and those fellows are so thin that the moon shines through their bodies. It's as if they have no flesh on their bones."

The bell-ringer shuddered when he heard this and said, "I won't stay here for all the money in the world."

Then he ran to the minister and reported everything.

"Let him be," the minister remarked. "He'll get his reward for being so rash and fresh."

During the third night Hans was lying on his bench again when there was a rattling, and he saw nine men who were bowling three balls against the bones of the dead.

"Upon my soul I can't stand to watch this!" he screamed as they kept missing. "Give me the ball!"

Then he threw the ball so hard that it broke into pieces, and all nine pins sank.

"This is how you're supposed to throw the ball, and now do just like I did! Meanwhile, I'll set up the pins."

So the game continued until one in the morning. Then the men gathered all the bones and skulls and began to leave.

"Tonight I'm not going to give away my hard-earned money!" Hans yelled and grabbed the shirt of the last man about to slip beneath the stone. However, the stone turned over, and Hans fell into a large vault where the men had disappeared.

"You lumps!" he yelled.

Just then someone tapped him on the shoulder, and as he turned around, he saw a man in white standing behind him. He was carrying numerous keys.

"I can tell from your looks that you don't belong to that group of nasty fellows who have cheated me out of my money," Hans said. "But what do you want from me?"

"I want to make you rich for the rest of your life," replied the man. "Turn and look around you for a moment. As you can see, there are three piles of money. One is for you, the next, for the bell-ringer, and the third for the minister so that he can use it for the church and distribute some of it to the poor."

Right after saying this, the man disappeared. But Hans rejoiced and was glad that he hadn't set up the bowling pins for nothing.

When the bell-ringer entered the church the next morning, Hans called out to him: "Hey, you, bring me a sack. I've got a heap of money for you."

"I thought it would come to this! The boy's gone nuts!" the bell-ringer cried and ran off.

Hans became impatient waiting for the bell-ringer to return and consequently went home. He fetched three sacks himself, filled them with money, and carried one to the bell-ringer's house. Then he threw the sack on to the table so hard that it ripped open and the sack and table fell to the ground and the shiny coins rolled all around on the floor.

"Do I have to carry all the garbage into your house for you, you lazy good-for-nothings?" Hans began scolding. "Why couldn't you come to the church yourselves and fetch the money?"

Hans did the same thing at the minister's house. Then he took his own sack, slapped it on his back, and marched out into the world. When he reached the capital city and saw the guard at the city gate, Hans was pleased so much that he said, "Hey, you, give me the sword that you're carrying on your side and the rifle on your shoulder, and I'll give you this sack of money."

"I'd gladly do this," the soldier responded, "but I'm not allowed to. Go to the captain. I'm sure he'll do it."

So Hans went to the captain and said, "Give me a sword and rifle like the other soldiers have, and I'll give you my sack of money."

"I'd gladly do this, my son, but I'm not allowed to," the captain responded. "Go to the king. I'm sure he'd be glad to do this."

So Hans went to the king and said, "Give me a sword and rifle just like your soldiers have, and I'll give you my sack full of money."

"As you will, my son," the king said, for he had plenty of room for sacks of money in his treasure chamber. Then the king arranged for Hans to be immediately dressed in a uniform and given a saber and weapon. This was a great joy for Hans, and he immediately ran to the place where the soldiers were being trained. He was supposed to drill as a recruit, but he said, "I already know all this. I've already bowled better than three men, six men, and nine men and know full well how to handle these weapons."

So the captain placed him among ranks of the older soldiers, who had already served in the army for three or four years. When Hans saw that they all had their weapons standing at their feet, he immediately cried out: "Hey, what are you lazy louts doing? Set those rifles on your shoulders!"

"At ease," the captain said. "We'll do that now. Shoulder arms!"

All the soldiers lifted their rifles to their shoulders while Hans threw his weapon onto his shoulder.

"Hans, you're not doing it right. That's next," the captain said. "Attention! Over the shoulder!"

Hans threw his rifle over his shoulder so that it caught the coat of the soldier behind him and flew about fifty feet.

"Hey, Hans what are you doing?" the captain asked.

"I'm doing everything right, and the others are nothing but lazy asses who don't know the first thing about army drills."

Hans continued to act in this way; indeed, he was so lively that the captain finally had to send a report to the king and wrote that he could no longer put up with Hans.

The king placed Hans in another regiment, but things went even worse there. When Hans went to train for the first time, the major gave him a reprimand. Then Hans cried out: "You don't know a thing, old man. Come and give me your horse and sword, and let me bark commands. I can do it better."

Then Hans threw his weapon and saber to the ground and went after the major, who shouted: "Hans, keep away from me, or I'll stab you to death!"

"We haven't reached that point yet," yelled Hans, and he tore the major from his horse lickety-split, took away his dagger and coat, and jumped on the horse. Then he rode to the front of the soldiers and continually cried out, "Shoulder arms! Present arms! March! Battalion right, left! March!"

But the soldiers couldn't follow the orders, and everything became muddled. Hans laughed himself to death and cried out: "That's right, my children. Beautiful! Now go home. You'll practice again tomorrow, and you'll be paid double as a reward for today."

The soldiers joined in the laughter because they held a grudge against the major for being so hard and severe with them.

When the king saw that nothing could be done about Hans, he thought of a way to get rid of him. There was a castle in a forest near the capitol city, and nobody ever dared to spend the night there because it was haunted. So, the king ordered Hans to appear before him and said, "Hans, if you drive the ghosts from this castle, I'll give you my daughter as bride."

Of course, the king thought that Hans would perish in the castle.

"Put that all in writing," Hans replied, "and I'll do it."

Once the king gave him a written document, Hans said, "So, now I must have tobacco and a sword."

And once he obtained all this, he set out on his way. Toward evening, after he arrived, he started a fire in the fireplace of a room. Toward midnight the door of the room flew open, and twelve men entered, sat down at the table, and began playing cards. Hans joined them and said: "It's a shame that I don't have any money, my brothers, otherwise I'd play with you. However, tomorrow the king is supposed to give me some."

The men didn't answer him and continued to play. Then Hans noticed that one of them was cheating and slapped his ear: "You swindler! I'll teach you to trick your comrades!"

Just then it turned one in the morning, and the men disappeared.

The next morning the king sent a soldier to the castle to see whether Hans was still alive. When Hans saw him, he called out to the soldier, "Hey, you! Tell the king that I need money. I can't play for nothing with nothing."

So the king sent him money and at the same time ordered the soldier to spend the night in the castle. However, the soldier shook his head anxiously and thought to himself: 'How's this going to turn out?'

Meanwhile Hans was up in the castle. In the evening he said to the soldier: "I want you to make a fire because it's cold. Meanwhile, I'll fetch some wood."

He went off, and when he returned, the soldier was lying on the floor and was dead as a doornail. Hans thought that he had fainted because of the cold and dragged him closer to the fire.

"Warm yourself, old boy," Hans said. "Then you'll come to."

Now Hans stuffed his pipe with tobacco and began to smoke. When the twelve men came again, he called out to them: "I've got money, brothers! So, let's play!"

But they didn't answer. They sat down, began to play, and didn't give him any cards. Hans let all this pass for a while, then he began to boil. He took a burning log from the fire and began beating the men while screaming, "You dirty nasty men! May the devil come and take you! What kind of manners do you have?"

However, he only beat the empty air because the clock had just struck one in the morning, and the men had vanished.

When the king saw the next morning that the castle was already somewhat brighter, as if it had been freed of the ghosts, and that Hans was still living, he became anxious and scared. He thought to himself: 'If he's already spent two nights there, he'll be able to hold out the third night.'

On the other hand, Hans was in good spirits, for he was quite happy about the cheap bargain he had made to obtain a princess and to become a prince. He hopped about and danced around the castle the entire day up and down the stairs until it was evening. At midnight the twelve men dressed in black came again, and this time there was even a thirteenth dressed in white, who motioned to Hans to go with him.

"Yes indeed," Hans said, "I'll go with you but the twelve men must go ahead of us."

And this is what happened.

So now they walked through many halls until they came to a door with many locks. The man dressed in white touched the locks, and they sprang open. As the door opened, Hans could see a large room without windows and barrels of gold standing around the room.

"The first barrels are for you," the ghost said. "Those over there are for the king, and the others are for the soldiers. And now we thank you with all our hearts, for you've redeemed us."

"You're very welcome," Hans said and returned to his room in the castle, for the ghosts had vanished. Then he laid himself down and slept like a prince.

Early the next morning he ran to the king, who was still lying in his bed, and cried out, "Hey you, give me my bride. I've got a whole row of barrels filled with gold for you."

The king sighed, got up, and went with Hans to the castle. Once there, however, he was glad to see so much money and also noticed that Hans also possessed just as much wealth as he did himself.

"Come with me, Hans," the king said. "I'll take you to the princess, and tomorrow we'll celebrate your wedding."

Up to that point things were going well, but when they came to the princess and she heard what was at stake, she became furiously angry and said she didn't want a coarse peasant for a husband.

"That's all the same to me," Hans said. "But I want you for my wife, and tomorrow you'll take me. So, don't do anything stupid."

And he left her alone and returned to the disenchanted castle.

The king was shattered to see his only daughter so miserable. Then his councilors came to him and said: "An hour away from here there's a mill where a devil has a nose seventy-seven yards long. Send Hans there to free the mill from the devil. You can be sure that he won't return from there."

So the king called for Hans right away and said, "Before you get married, you can do me one more favor and free the mill that's standing outside the city."

"Gladly," said Hans, and he went there that evening.

But there was nothing to be seen in the mill except for an old vice, a couple of stools, and an old oven. Hans put some wood on the fire, lit his pipe, and made himself comfortable. Suddenly the door flew open and in whisked a long pointed thing that had no end to it. The thing spread itself around the walls like a sail. Finally, a devil jumped into the room. The long pointed thing had grown above his mouth, and then Hans noticed that it was his nose.

"Dear brother," Hans said, "I'd like to hear you sneeze."

But the devil bellowed, "You won't be sneezing because I'm going to break your neck!"

"You can save yourself this friendly service," replied Hans, "if you value your own neck. But listen to me, you're so nimble with your nose, can you wrap it and turn it so that you can pull it quickly through the vice before I clamp it tightly? I doubt you can do that!"

"That's as easy as pie," the devil laughed and nodded his head a few times. Then he whipped the nose like lightning all around the room, first above and then under.

"Well, you're right, but everything depends on the attempt," Hans claimed. "If I succeed clamping your nose, then I'll be free. If not, I'll be yours without any protest."

"As you wish," the devil spoke and rolled his nose through the vice.

Hans turned the vice but let the devil slip through this time.

"Now do you see?" the devil laughed, and Hans made a sad face.

"Watch out! Here we go a second time!" And Hans let him roll his nose through a second time and made a more sullen face.

"And now for the third time!" the devil cried out.

But this time he wasn't successful because Hans was more nimble, and the devil screeched so loudly that people could hear him in the city.

"Now stay here nice and quiet," Hans said, but the devil swayed him with flattering words and promised him everything possible so that Hans let him go.

Now nothing in the world could help the princess. She had to take Hans as her husband. Gradually she became accustomed to him and became very fond of him because of his good heart.

One day Hans went walking with the princess in the forest. The devil with the long nose was sitting on top of a tree and grabbed the tip of the princess's hair with his claws.

"Hey, do you want me to put you back in the vice?" Hans called out.

Then the devil squealed, "No, no!" and he never let himself be seen again.

Fearless Learners (1854)[31]

Ignaz and Joseph Zingerle

1

Once upon a time there was a father who had a heap of children. In the springtime the children often climbed cherry trees, and one time the oldest boy fell off a tree. The father was standing under the tree and screamed, "Oh no, this is what I feared!"

The boy jumped to his feet right away and asked, "Father, what's fear mean?"

"What fear means," the father answered, "that's something you'll learn when you set out into the world."

As soon as his son heard this, there was no holding him back, and since he wondered a great deal about what fear was, he decided to go quickly into the world to study this art. His father let him go because he already had enough children at home and thought to himself: 'You'll learn soon enough what fear is. So I'm not worried at all.'

The boy traveled all alone straight along the country road, and when anyone addressed him and asked where he was going, he always said, "I'm going to learn about fear."

The people would then make fun of him and let him go by himself because they thought he was a fool, and nobody could do anything for him.

One evening he came to a tavern, and since it was late, he stopped to spend the night there. As he was sitting completely alone and forlorn at a table, some people took pity on him and wanted to keep him company. They talked with him about all sorts of topics and asked him among other things where he was going.

"To learn about fear," he answered.

Then they laughed at him and said, "If that's all you want, we know a good place where you can learn it."

"And where is this place," the boy asked.

"Well, you see," they said, "the tavern keeper has a castle not far from here. So you must go there, and you'll soon learn what fear means."

Immediately, the boy stood up, went to the tavern keeper, and asked him to open up the castle right away so that he could learn once and for all what fear was.

"That's something you can certainly learn over there," the tavern keeper said, and he took him to the castle and let him go inside. Then he locked the door behind the boy, but the lad didn't care, for he thought they'd let him out again in the end.

Now he went upstairs to the kitchen, gathered some wood together near the fireplace, and started a fire. Toward midnight the fire was almost burned out so that he thought he'd have to stay there in the dark. However, something started to move in the chimney, and a piece of a coffin fell down. "You couldn't have fallen down at a better time," the boy said. He took the wood and set it in the fire that began to light up again and became brighter. He hoped that, when the fire died down, something else would fall down.

Suddenly something moved again in the chimney, and a hand fell down. "I can also use this," he said. "Now I have three hands. It will help make the work easier."

Soon after there was a rumbling, and a foot fell from the chimney.

"This is also good. Three feet belong to three hands. I wonder whether anything else will come?"

There was some more rumbling, and then came another hand, and the chimney rumbled again, and another foot fell down. "Now this is good! I have four hands and four feet. When something in the middle and on top would come, then I'd have a complete person!"

All of a sudden there was much more awful rumbling, and a torso fell down into the fireplace. So the boy went over and placed the hands and feet where they belonged, and, look! everything fused tightly together as if the parts had never been separated.

"I see now that you'd probably be a guy of some kind. It's a shame that you don't also have a head."

Once again there was a rumbling, and a head rolled out of the chimney. The boy grabbed it by the hair and put it in its place. The head attached itself right away, and the boy took great pleasure with the newly made man, who lay on the fireplace.

"Good," he said. "Now you're a guy almost stronger than I am."

All at once the newly made man jumped up from the fireplace and shouted, "I'm going to tear you to pieces!"

"What! You're going to tear me to pieces when I just put you together? Shut your mouth and don't say such things, otherwise I'll show you just what tearing to pieces means!"

Now the man became somewhat more gentle and said, "Well, come with me!"

"All right, I'll certainly go with you," the boy said and followed him.

They went down into a deep cellar, where three large piles of money were on the ground. The ghost began to speak again: "One of these three piles belongs to you, another to the poor, and the third to the tavern keeper. The castle also belongs to you, and the tavern keeper, who has owned it illegally up to now, will be receiving a pile of money to compensate for the small claim that he has to the castle. So now you'll be able to live in the castle again without being disturbed, because the castle no longer belongs to an illegal owner but to one with legal claims."

Upon saying all this, the ghost disappeared, and the boy was all alone in the cellar.

In the morning the boy went upstairs and looked to see if the tavern keeper had already opened the door. As he approached, he saw that the door was already open, and the people from the tavern stood in front of the castle to see whether he had perhaps luckily succeeded to come away from the castle with his life. When he appeared fresh and healthy, they laughed and cried out: "What was it like? Do you know now what fear is?"

"No, I still don't know, but I can tell you something else if you come with me."

They were puzzled and curious to learn what he wanted to tell them and went along with him. So, he led them into the cellar, showed them the three piles, and said, "The ghost, who came in the night, gave the castle and one of the piles to me as a gift. The other pile belongs to the tavern keeper, and the third goes to the poor."

When the people from the tavern heard this, they became envious of the boy and the poor and what they were to receive. Their envy was so great that they attacked the poor boy and beat him to death. All at once, however, the three piles vanished, and the castle became just as eerie and haunted as it had always been.

Told in Meran by an anonymous storyteller.

2

Once upon a time there was a father who had three sons. One of them was called Hansel and was a real blockhead. The other two had already gone off into the world, and the father still waited for one of them to return home soon. One day Hansel decided that he, too, would like to go off into the world, for as he said, he had to learn what fear was so that he could mix with honest people. His father wanted to keep him back, but nothing helped because once Hansel had an idea in his head, nobody could drive it out of him no matter how much they might beat him.

For a long time he kept following his nose straight ahead, and one day he arrived at a tavern, where he told people why he was travelling and often mumbled under his breath: "If I could only learn what fear is so that I could return home soon and stay with my father."

In the afternoon the tavern keeper took him to the stable and showed him his horses.

"Wow!" Hansel cried out all at once. "Where did you get these two horses?"

Indeed, he recognized these horses as the ones that his brothers had ridden when they went off into the world.

"Oh," the tavern keeper said, "these horses belong to two strangers who went over to the castle and never returned. In fact, I think the castle would be the best place for you because you'd immediately learn what fear is."

When Hansel heard this, he rejoiced and went straight to the castle. As he entered to look around, he didn't find anything special and went outside again. There he saw an elder bush by the wall and amused himself by picking berries. When it became dark, he went back inside and up to the kitchen, where he started a fire to cook a pudding made of elderberries. He had just placed the pan over the fire when someone came through the door who didn't appear to be friendly. However, Hansel was not in the least afraid and blew on the fire and said to the stranger: "You've come just at the right time because I'd be bored all alone. I'm making such a large pudding of elderberries that there'll be enough for the both of us. But now you must wait a little until it's cooked."

The stranger didn't want to wait and said, "You must come with me right away!"

"I can't go with you right away," responded Hansel. "You should know that the elderberry pudding would burn if I leave, and that would be a shame."

The stranger would not be persuaded and spoke with a raspy voice: "If you don't come with me right away, I'll tear you to pieces!"

"Just look at you! I don't think you really look like a person who could tear someone to pieces!" Hans mocked him.

The stranger didn't give up and now used milder tones so that Hansel would go with him.

"Look," he said, "nothing at all will happen to your elderberry pudding if you come with me. I promise you that you'll find it in good condition when you return, and if not, you can do anything you want to me as soon as we return."

When Hansel heard that nothing would happen to his elderberry pudding, he finally let himself be persuaded and said that he'd go with the stranger.

"Aren't you afraid of anything by coming with me?" the stranger asked.

"Is that a question?" asked Hansel. "I have no idea what fear is. So, I'll do anything to find out."

Now they descended some stairs and came to a door.

"Open it," the ghost told Hansel.

"You've already heard," responded Hansel, "that I won't let anyone pull the wool over my eyes. If you don't open the door immediately, then I'm going to go back upstairs and tend to my elderberry pudding."

Now the ghost gave in and opened the door. When they entered the room, there was a monstrous dog sitting there. It had a ferocious mouth and glaring huge eyes. Hansel became furious when he saw the animal and screamed: "Just what I suspected! I knew you'd have some creature there that would gobble up my elderberry pudding. Well, now I'm going to run back upstairs and let you move on by yourself."

The ghost calmed him down by promising him again that nothing at all would happen to the elderberry pudding. Then he asked: "Do you have enough courage to chase the dog away?"

"Of course. Why shouldn't I set the beast on his way?" he replied and rammed into the side of the dog so hard that the dog ran off as quickly as the wind and sparks burst from all sides. As Hansel was looking after the dog and laughing, the ghost went a little further. Hansel saw this and yelled: "Stop right there! I don't want you to go too far ahead of me in case I have to beat you when the elderberry pudding is ruined."

The ghost waited, and Hansel caught up with him. Soon they came to a second door. The ghost told Hansel to open it, but Hansel became angry and replied. "The dog is probably eating the elderberry pudding upstairs. If you don't open the door right away, I won't get anything to eat anymore."

"The pudding's still cooking hot," the ghost said. "So he can't eat it."

But he did as Hansel said anyway and opened the door. As they entered the room, they found horrible snakes, and the ghost handed Hansel a whip and said, "There, chase the snakes away."

But Hansel didn't want to take it because he was concerned about the elderberry pudding, and he thought that the horrible snakes could eat it all up. However, the ghost encouraged him and said, "Nothing is going to happen to the elderberry pudding. Just take the whip and get rid of the reptiles!"

So Hansel took the whip and thrashed a couple of them on their backs so that they fled through the door like the wind.

Now the ghost and Hansel moved on and came to a third door.

"Open it!" said the ghost.

But Hansel didn't open it. Instead, he asked for a broom to chase away the snakes in case they were upstairs and might be consuming his elderberry pudding. So, the ghost opened the door himself and asked Hansel to enter with him into the room where three barrels were standing. In the barrels were many snakes and other horrible beasts.

"Hey, Hansel," the ghost cried out, "grab hold of those creatures and throw them out!"

"Now it doesn't matter if I obey or not," said Hansel. "The elderberry pudding is gone for sure! Tell me where to start first!"

"You can start wherever you want," the ghost answered.

"That's fine with me," replied Hansel, who rammed into a barrel and threw everything out. Then he went to the second and the third and did the same thing. When the horrible beasts were lying on the ground, they swiftly crawled through the door and were never seen again. However, the three barrels were filled with nothing but money. In the first, there were copper coins; in the second, silver coins, and in the third, gold. Hansel's eyes opened wide when he saw what was in the barrels, and the ghost said, "Now I'll explain what you have to do with the three barrels. First you're to distribute the copper coins among the poor people. Next, you're to give the silver coins to poor cloisters and churches. And the gold coins you're to keep for yourself. Now live well and thank you for redeeming me."

"Wait a second!" said Hansel. "First I must see if my elderberry pudding is still upstairs. Otherwise, you won't leave here without a beating!"

As he said this, he grabbed hold of the ghost and led him upstairs into the kitchen. The elderberry pudding was in good condition, and nothing had been burned or had been eaten. Hansel was pleased by this because he was very hungry, and he was more concerned about the elderberry pudding than anything else.

"Eat some," he said to the ghost. "You look as if you don't get much to eat."

However, the ghost didn't eat and became more and more pale.

"Eat something," Hansel said again and placed the pan before the ghost.

However, the ghost still refused to eat and finally became completely white. At that point, he said to Hansel: "Many men placed their lives at risk and perished, but you were the one who finally redeemed me. If they had had as much courage as you, I would have long since been redeemed, and I wouldn't have had to wait for you. Now, as thanks, you are to have not only the money but also the castle."

The next morning the tavern keeper went out of his house and looked up at the castle and thought: 'He's had it for sure. Now he'll certainly know what fear is.'

All of a sudden Hansel appeared, looked at the tavern keeper, and cried out: "Quick, come up here with the horses. We've got to carry the money away."

The tavern keeper was very puzzled. So, he went up to the castle and asked how the night went. Hansel told him everything but complained that he hadn't learned what fear was yet. Then the tavern keeper spoke to him and said he should now return home and tell his father about his good fortune because fear was not such an important matter.

"Yes, it would be easy to go home if I could also bring the money," Hansel said.

So the tavern keeper promised to lend him a wagon, and Hansel drove off toward home with a pile of money to his father. Once he was there, he must have also told his father about his two brothers who had perished in the castle. Whether he went marching out again to learn about fear, nobody can say.

Told by an anonymous storyteller in Schlanders.

The Fearless Young Man (1870)[32]

Laura Gonzenbach

Once upon a time there was a woman, who had enough to live on. Indeed, she didn't lack a thing, but she had a son who was fearless and was continually playing dumb pranks. So she said to herself, 'I'll bring him to my brother-in-law. He's a priest, and certainly he'll be able to make him afraid of something.'

Consequently, she went to her brother-in-law and asked him to take over her ill-bred son and fill him full of fear. The priest agreed and invited the young man to stay in his house. Soon thereafter the priest decided to call a man to help him make the boy frightened of something.

"I'll give you a nice gift," the priest said, "if you pretend to be dead this evening and let yourself be carried in a coffin into the church. My nephew will keep watch over you, and at midnight you must move about in the coffin as though you were alive."

The man promised to do this, and the priest called his nephew to him and said, "A dead man will soon be brought here, and I'd like you to help me set up the platform for the coffin in the church."

After they had set up the platform, the pallbearers came and carried the man who was pretending to be dead, and they put him into the coffin on the platform.

"Listen to me," the priest said to his nephew, "I want you to spend the night in the church and to keep watch because we cannot leave the dead alone. Are you afraid to do this?"

"Why should I be afraid?" the fellow said and locked himself with the dead man in the church.

At midnight the supposed dead man suddenly lifted an arm and let it sink quickly with a good deal of noise.

"Hey you! Be quiet!" yelled the young man. "I want to get a little sleep."

After a while the man lifted a leg and slammed it against the coffin.

'I think this dead man is coming alive again,' the young man thought, and he stood up on the frame and began beating the man with a large club so that the man jumped up, ran to the door, ripped it open, and fled.

---

32. "Von dem, der sich vor Nichts fürchtete," *Sicilianische Märchen*, 2 vols. (Leipzig: W. Engelmann, 1870).

The priest heard this racket and came running full of fear because he thought his nephew might have really killed the man.

"What's all this noise?" he asked.

"Just think, uncle," his nephew cried, "the dead man came back to life. I beat him because he became so restless and wouldn't let me sleep, and then he cleared out of here."

'Oh no,' the priest thought to himself. 'The boy was not the least afraid! I'll have to give that poor man some money to get over the beating he took.'

The next evening the priest thought up something else. He took a bunch of skulls, climbed up to the top of the church tower, and placed them along the walls. In each one of the skulls he lit a small candle so that they all looked gruesome. At the highest point of the tower he set up a skeleton and placed the cord to the bells in the skeleton's hand. Then he went downstairs, quickly called his nephew, and said, "Run up fast to the top of the tower and ring the bells!"

The young man obeyed, and when he reached the top of the tower and saw the skulls lit in such an eerie way, he thought, 'Oho, that's real neat! Now I can find my way more easily.'

When he next saw the skeleton, he called over to it, "Hey you, what are you doing up here? If you're the one who's supposed to ring the bells, then you can at least get to work, and then I'll go back down. It's either you or me."

Since the skeleton could not move and did not respond, the nephew lost his patience and said, "If you're not going to listen, you'd better take care of yourself," he threw the skeleton down the stairs. Then he began to ring the bells so that all the people came together on the street below and thought that some accident had happened. But the priest calmed them down and said, "Dear people, go back home. It's just my nephew. He plays some dumb pranks from time to time.—Come down here, nephew!"

Now the priest no longer knew what to do and thought, 'I'll try one more time, and when he doesn't become frightened, I'll have to send him away.'

So he called for another man and said, "Listen, my good friend, I'll give you a nice present if you do exactly what I tell you. Tonight you must hide yourself by that wall over there. Toward midnight I'll send my nephew to the well. When he walks by you, I want you to spring from your hiding place and scream: 'Six!' I think such a fright will scare him more than anything else because it's unexpected."

The man promised to do what the priest told him to do, and toward midnight the uncle said to his nephew, "Please go to the well and fetch me a glass of water. I'm so thirsty."

Then the young man went through the dark night to the well and held a mug in his hand. As he walked by the wall, a dark shape stood up and screamed, "Six!"

"Seven!" responded the boy completely cold-bloodedly, and he whacked the man in his face with the mug so that the mug broke into a thousand pieces and the man fell to the ground half dead.

When the priest heard the racket, he came running, and when he saw the wounded man lying on the ground, he said, "I can't stand your living with me any more. Go forth and seek your fortune in the wide world."

The nephew didn't wait for the priest to repeat himself, and off he went in the darkness of the night. He didn't take anything with him except the handle of the mug that he still held in his hand. The next morning he found himself in a desolate and wild region, and since he was thirsty and saw a well nearby, he went over and filled another mug with water and wandered off. Finally he saw a beautiful house standing in the distance, but robbers were living in it. While he headed toward the house, the mug fell from his hand, and the water ran in many little streams here and there. "Five hundred there, four hundred on the other side, six hundred over there," he said with a loud voice, and he meant the drops of water.

However, the robbers thought it was a great general who had come with his army to catch them. So they jumped up and cleared out of the house through the back door. Meanwhile, the young man entered the house and found a beautifully covered table. So he sat down and ate and drank to his heart's content. Since he had been traveling the entire night, he wanted to sleep a bit and went into the next room where he found the thirteen beds of the robbers. He took the beds apart and mounted them against the door. Then he climbed to the top of the beds and took a sword with him that had belonged to the robbers.

After a while the robbers said to one another, "Let's go back and take a look. Perhaps the soldiers have left the house."

When they arrived at the house, the captain of the robbers sent one of them inside to find out how things looked for them. The robber slipped quietly inside until he came to the door where the beds had been piled on top of one another. The young man who was lying on top of the beds saw the robber coming, drew his sword from the sheath, and called out with a loud voice: "Get out, get out!"

And then he beat the robber until he was dead. The other robbers thought he was calling all his soldiers, and therefore, they ran from there even faster than they had done the previous time. Then the young man gathered up all the treasures and valuables that were in the house and brought them to his mother, who was very delighted that her son had returned and had become such a rich man. Afterward they lived happy and content, but he never learned to fear.

Fearless Jean (1887)[33]

François-Marie Luzel

Once upon a time there was a man who boasted that he had never feared anything in his life and wasn't afraid of anything in the world. Because of this people called him Fearless Jean. He was the gardener for the parish priest. At that time there were frequent burial processions of the dead at night and even sometimes during plain day.

One night, quite late, the priest said to Jean: "Go to the church and get my glasses. I left them there on the altar and need them to prepare my Sunday sermon."

"All right," Jean responded. "I'll go."

As soon as he entered the church, the priest, who had followed him without being noticed, locked the door behind Jean, and when the young man wanted to leave, he was blocked.

'Bah!' he said to himself. 'No doubt the priest thinks I'd be afraid to spend the night in the church, but he's fooling himself.'

And he sat down in a stall of the choir counting on sleeping at his leisure. Indeed, he soon fell asleep. But toward midnight he was wakened by some loud noise from the large door caused by two claps of a bell, and he was very surprised to see the candles ignite on the altar and to hear chants and to see a procession enter. At the head of the procession there were a cross and banners as if it were the day of the great pardon at the parish. Everyone, men and women, young and old were dressed in gray. He didn't recognize anyone in the crowd. However, he thought he recognized a former priest of the parish and a rich landowner. In his childhood he had worked for the landowner as a cowherd. But both the priest and the landowner had been dead for many years. All this seemed very odd to him. A priest, whom he didn't know, climbed up on the altar and began addressing all those people in attendance.

"If there is any living person among you who wants to take the mass from me, I ask you to step forward," he spoke.

Nobody budged nor said a word. The priest repeated the same words without any success. Then he uttered them a third time with great sadness.

"I'll do it! I'll do it!" Fearless Jean finally replied.

He stepped toward and stood at the foot of the altar.

The priest said the mass from beginning to end, and Jean supplied the responses as he had been accustomed to do with his priest. After the *Ite missa est*, the unknown priest addressed Jean and said, "May the benediction of God be on you and all your close ones! For more than one hundred years I've come

---

33. "Jean-sans-peur," *Contes populaires de la Basse-Bretagne,* 3 vols. (Paris: Maisonneuve et Leclerc, 1887).

here every night to try to say the mass, and I wasn't able to do this because I couldn't find a living person to respond to me. The Lord had imposed this penitence on me—to do a mass requested and paid for by the souls of purgatory that I was never able to perform. We are three hundred souls of the parish, kept in purgatory, and you have rescued us, and now we can enter paradise together. Here is my robe, and as long as you possess it, you'll have nothing to fear, neither from the living nor from the dead, nor from anything in the world. Once again, thank you, and good-bye until those eternal joys where we shall meet once again one day."

Jean took the robe that the priest offered him, and in an instant the candles went out on the altar, and all at once the church which had been filled with faithful, peaceful, and silent followers emptied itself as if by magic.

All of this seemed very strange to Jean, and he was now convinced that the stories of the ghosts that he had often heard during the winter evening gatherings were true, and he hadn't believed them in the least until then.

At the break of day the sacristan came to ring the Angelus, and Jean was able to leave the church. When he reached the parish house, he went straight to the priest's room. The priest was still in bed, and Jean said to him in a calm voice: "Here are your glasses, father."

"Well, you must have spent the night in the church."

"You know this quite well, father."

"And you weren't afraid?"

"No, I wasn't scared, and you furnished me with the opportunity to do a good deed."

"How's that? Did you happen to see anything extraordinary?"

"Yes, I saw something extraordinary."

"What was it? Ghosts? But you don't believe in ghosts!"

"Now I do. But I'm not going to tell you what I saw. You wanted to scare me and play a trick on me. So now I'm quitting your service, and shall begin to wander around the country."

Despite the priest's efforts to keep him, Jean departed right away, and he didn't forget to take the robe with him. Later, he was overtaken by darkness in a forest, which was completely uninhabited. Then he noticed a large fire in a clearing and headed in that direction. When he reached the fire at the foot of a large oak tree, he found no one and was surprised by this because there were rocks surrounding it in the form of chairs. So, he sat down on one of them and waited.

'No doubt it's a meeting place for robbers,' he said to himself.

Upon hearing some noise above him, he raised his eyes and caught sight of two corpses, hanged men dangling above his head and knocking against each other in the wind.

"Hey, comrades," he cried out to them, "come and warm yourselves by this good fire and keep me company! It seems to be that you're not very comfortable the way you are."

And he cut them down and sat them on the rocks around the fire. Then he touched them with his robe, and they were restored to life and began speaking:

"We are two criminals who have committed all sorts of crimes during our lives, and we finished by being justly punished. We've been here a long time in the condition that you've found us, and we must remain here until someone does something for us that you've done. But there's something more to do if we are to be completely saved and if we are to be permitted to enter the paradise of God."

"All right, I'll do it," Jean responded.

And he did it. Afterward, he continued on his way. Toward sunset, he found himself beneath the walls of a beautiful chateau.

'I think I'll go and ask for lodging in this chateau,' he said to himself.

The gate was open, and he stepped into the courtyard without encountering anyone. Then he entered the chateau and went through all the rooms. He didn't see a single living soul, and this seemed strange to him. When he went to a window, he looked out and saw a house in the distance that seemed to be inhabited by people. So, he went there and asked whether he could have some food and lodging.

"Are you fearful?" the owner of the house asked.

"I don't know what fear is," Jean responded, "and I'm not afraid of anything in the world."

"Well then, if you are willing to spend the night in that chateau over there and return here tomorrow morning to tell me what you will have heard and seen, I'll reward you very well."

"Gladly," Jean replied.

He dined well, and then toward ten in the evening, he returned to the abandoned chateau.

Now, this chateau had belonged to some men who had committed every imaginable crime so that people believed that they had been damned. And ever since the men had died, people heard such a hubbub every night that no one wanted to live there, and they said that a Sabbath of the devils was held there, and among those who attended were the two men who had owned the chateau.

Jean went to sleep in a good bed with a feather mattress that was in a room on the ground floor, and he waited. Toward midnight he heard some noise in the chimney, and three people with odd features descended. They lit some candles, sat down at a table, and began to play a game of cards. In no time whatsoever they began accusing each other of cheating and started arguing. There was quite an uproar.

Jean couldn't sleep and had not gotten undressed. He stood up quietly and approached them.

"All right! Enough of this noise, comrades!" he cried. "I saw what happened, and I'll settle the matter."

The men were at first surprised, but they accepted his arbitration and proposed that he join them in their game.

"Gladly," Jean said to them, "but no cheating."

However, they continually cheated. When a card fell under the table, Jean took a candle to look for it and saw that they had cloven feet.

'I thought as much,' he said to himself. 'They're devils! Now's the time or never to make good use of my robe.'

And he took it out of his pocket and put it on the backs of the devils who began uttering frightful cries: "Mercy! Mercy! Take it off, and let us leave!"

"I'm not going to take it off, and I won't let you leave until you have promised me never to come and disturb the people who live in this chateau."

"We promise you! We'll never come again!"

"Well then, you may depart, but don't ever return or you'll not come off so cheaply the next time."

Jean took off the robe from the backs of the devils, and they returned to where they had come from, that is, from the chimney.

From that time onward, nobody heard any noise from the haunted chateau anymore, and the owners could return and live there in peace. Jean married the only daughter of the master of the chateau. She was very rich and beautiful, and they lived happily together. When they died, the robe was placed in their tomb, and it helped them again to go to paradise.

Told by Marguerite Philippe, from Pluzunet. Collected and translated into French by François-Marie Luzel in Plouaret, September 12, 1887.

Fearless William (1896)[34]

Achille Millien

Once upon a time there was a widow who lived with her two sons: one was gentle and industrious and became a shoemaker; the other, bold like a lion, who spent his time hunting. Every evening the bold son usually went out into the woods with his rifle and poached the entire night. His mother often said to him: "William, they'll catch you and put you in prison. Why can't you stay calm like your brother?"

"Mother, they call me Fearless William. I'm not afraid of anything. So, never worry about my head. Don't you fret on my account."

His brother also gave him some good advice, but that was like preaching in the desert. Therefore, one day he wanted to try to make William afraid and put an end to his habitual nocturnal adventures. He draped a sheet over himself and positioned himself on some stairs where his brother had to pass. Upon seeing this phantom blocking his way, William didn't show the slightest emotion.

"Get out of my way, so I can pass!" he cried.

---

34. "Guillaume-sans-Peur," *Étrennes Nivernais* (1896).

His brother didn't move.

"Get out of my way, or I'll kill you. . . . Ah! So you don't want to move!"

As he said this, there was a shot from his rifle. William descended the stairs and continued on his way without concerning himself with what had happened.

"Weren't you frightened?" the widow asked him when he returned home.

"Frightened? . . . Why should I have been? Frightened by that imbecile I killed on the stairs?"

"Ah! How unfortunate! You killed your brother and now you're lost. . . . You must leave quickly to escape the gendarmes!"

As she wept, the mother gave him a small bundle of clothes, and William took off on a path through the woods. He walked across the forest until evening, and when night came, he felt tired and stretched out beneath a large oak tree. All of a sudden, he noticed three hanged men above him dangling from the branches.

"Well, hello! . . . What are you all doing there? . . . Since the ground is hard, you'll make a nice bed for me."

He climbed the oak, cut down the hanged men, and placed two of them on the ground side by side.

"Good! Here's my mattress!"

He placed the third one above their heads.

"You'll be my pillow."

Then he laid down on this new kind of bed and fell asleep. Toward midnight, he was wakened by the sobbing of one of the hanged men.

"You're making too much noise for a dead man! I hope you'll soon stop this lamenting. What do you want?"

"I want to reveal a secret to you while there's still a little life in me. We were hanged because we stole some precious vases and the ornaments of the nearby church. We buried them at the foot of the big tree at the first crossroad you'll find when you take this path. I regret what I did. I want my soul to find peace. So, go and dig up the treasure and bring it to the church."

William promised to do as he said and went straight to the vicarage.

"Was something stolen from your church, father?" he asked the vicar.

"Yes, and I'll give a good reward to anyone who brings back the objects that were stolen."

"Well then, I hope that you'll have them back even today."

And William departed, and just before noon, he returned to the vicarage. He had easily found what he had gone out to search. The hanged man had not deceived him.

"Father, I've brought you the vases and the sacred ornaments."

"Thank you, my friend. I'm now going to give you the reward that I promised."

"I don't want anything but one of your robes."

"All right, take this one, but don't make bad use of it. To be sure, I wouldn't give you the robe if you hadn't proven to me that you are a good person."

William thanked him and continued on his way. That evening he arrived at an inn and asked for lodging for him and his mule—I forgot to tell you that he had a mule with him that carried his baggage.

"We don't have any room, not for you, nor for your animal."

"So we must sleep in the open air tonight?"

"There's an old uninhabited chateau near here, but I don't recommend going there because it's haunted, and you might rue the day you went there."

"Tell me the way there, and I'll go right away. I've yet to know anything that I fear. . . ."

One hour later, in plain night, he installed his mule in the stable of the chateau, and he himself entered a beautiful well-lit room, where he found a meal set for six people on a round table. There were also many well-filled casseroles steaming on a bright fire.

'Ah! Ah!' William said to himself. 'Just what I want. I'm dying of hunger, and I'm cold. Let's approach this good fire.'

After he warmed himself, he decided to sit down at the table.

"I don't like dining alone . . . but there are many settings. Perhaps the invited guests will soon arrive."

Just then there was a lot of noise in the chimney, and poof! a little man fell out.

"Well, what a droll way to make an entrance!"

A second, then another arrived from the same chimney, then three at one time.

"Good! Now we have half a dozen. . . . Now you'll get to work. You, put out the fire! You, get some water!"

One of the last to arrive was a bit larger than the others and supported his two companions while looking at Fearless William.

"What are you doing here?" he said.

"And you?"

"I'm in my own home."

"Well then, I've invited myself to dine with you. Let's go! Everyone, let's sit down at the table!"

The little man did as he was told. After dinner they began to play cards. One of the little man's cards fell under the table.

"Fetch my card," he said to William.

"Get your own card."

"I want you to fetch my card."

"And I told you I don't want to."

The little man leaned over, and instantly, William covered him with the robe that he had received from the vicar. The little man did a somersault.

"Take that off me! You're burning me!"

"No, I won't take it off you until you promise me, first, never to reappear here, neither you nor your gang."

"I promise."

"And next, you must tell me where I can find the treasure of the chateau. . . ."

"Take the robe off me, and I'll tell you everything."

"Well then, begin."

"Go down into the cellar, and at the bottom of the first stall you'll find some stairs that lead to the underground cavern of the treasure. . . . But take this robe off me! You're burning me!"

As soon as the little man was rescued, he departed by the chimney with his gang. William found the treasure and continued to dwell in the chateau, rich and tranquil.

In passing by Paris
I've finished my little tale.

Told by Anna Bernard at Beaumont-la-Ferrière.

4. ABANDONED CHILDREN
ATU 327A—HANSEL AND GRETEL

This tale type is generally categorized under the general title "the Children and the Ogre," and the diverse tales in the cycle depict ogres, giants, witches, demons, and magicians who threaten to eat children. The "Hansel and Gretel" tales are quite often combined with stories of ATU 450—"Little Brother and Sister," in which abused children run away from a nasty stepmother. The boy drinks from an enchanted stream and is turned into a doe or another animal while his beautiful sister is found by a prince who marries her. Then the stepmother discovers her happiness, tries to destroy it, and is destroyed herself. In the "Hansel and Gretel" tale type the basic motifs are woven around two children, brother and sister, who are abandoned/ abused and become lost in a forest. They seek refuge, and instead of finding a place of safety, they fall into the hands of a cannibalistic witch/ogre/giant. This villain wants to fatten the children before eating them. However, the girl finds a way to trick the witch/ogre and kills her. The children return home with a treasure, and though they had been maltreated at home, they return happily to their parents and give them the treasure. Sometimes the mother/stepmother has died, and the father benefits from his children's good fortune. Sometimes the parents are not at fault initially when the children lose themselves in the forest, and thus the happy return is more understandable.

Though there were many tales told in which children were eaten or threatened by a monster dating back to the Greek myth of Cronos, this particular tale type did not develop until the late Middle Ages. One of the first versions can be found in Martin Montanus' *Gartengesellschaft* (1590). Other important early stories that the Grimms knew are Giambattista Basile's "Ninnillo and Nenella" (1634), Charles Perrault's "Le Petit Poucet," and Mme d'Aulnoy's "Finette Cendron" (1698). The Grimms probably heard some version of "Hansel and Gretel" from Dorothea Wild, a pharmacist's daughter and future wife of Wilhelm, in 1809. Wilhelm revised the tale in each edition making it more Christian in tone, shifting the blame for abandonment from a mother to a stepmother, and placing greater blame on her by associating her with the witch. However, the most dramatic changes occurred in the fifth edition of 1843, after Wilhelm had read August Stöber's Alsatian tale "Das Eierkuchenhäuslein" ("The Little Pancake House," 1842). What is fascinating here is that Stöber collected his tale from an informant who probably had read or heard the Grimms' literary tale of "Hansel and Gretel" and had changed it for his or her purposes. Stöber himself cites the Grimms' edition as his literary source. (Interestingly, one of Stöber's changes is the transformation of the stepmother back into the biological mother, who does not die, but greets the children with her husband at the end. Both parents regret what they had done to the children.) Wilhelm, who read Stöber's collection of tales *Elsässisches Volksbüchlein* (*The Little Alsatian Folk Book*, 1842), re-appropriated certain phrases, sayings, and verses from the Alsatian dialect that he believed would lend his tale more of a quaint and folksy tone. By the time the last edition of 1857 of *Kinder- und Hausmärchen* was printed, Wilhelm had made so many changes in style and theme that the tale was twice as long as the original manuscript of 1810.

The popularity and importance of the "Hansel and Gretel" tales in the European oral and literary tradition may be attributed to the themes of child abandonment and abuse. Although it is difficult to estimate how widespread child abandonment was, it is clear that lack of birth control, famines, and poor living conditions led to the birth of many children who could not be supported and became unwanted. There was always tension when a new mother or stepmother replaced a mother who may have died from childbirth. In the Middle Ages it was common to abandon these children in front of churches, in special places of village squares, or in the forest. Sometimes the abandonment and/or abuse was due to the re-marriage of a man or woman who could not tolerate the children from a previous marriage. When children are abandoned in the fairy tales, they do not always have an encounter with a witch, but they do encounter a dangerous character who threatens their lives, and they must use their wits to find a way to return home.

Given the manner in which the tale celebrated the patriarchal home as haven, "Hansel and Gretel" became one of the most favorite of the Grimms' tales in the nineteenth century. Ludwig Bechstein wrote a similar version in his *Deutsches Märchenbuch* (1857), influenced by Stöber's and the Grimms' tales, while Engelbert Humperdinck produced his famous opera *Hänsel und Gretel* in 1893. Important folk tales of this type can be found in the collections of Pitrè, Bernoni, Imbriani, Nerucci, Luzel, Sébillot, Millien, Lambert, Afanas'ev, Panzer, and Haupt. The most thorough treatment of this tale type is Regina Böhm-Korff's *Deutung und Bedeutung von "Hänsel und Gretel"* (1991). This study traces the historical development of different versions and pays careful attention to the motif of food and famine in the tale as well as the motif of abandonment. Wolfgang Mieder's *Hänsel und Gretel: Das Märchen in Kunst, Musik, Literatur und Karikaturen* (2007) is a major source of twentieth-century adaptations in various fields of art, literature, and theater.

******

Hansel and Gretel (1812)[35]

Jacob and Wilhelm Grimm

A poor woodcutter lived on the edge of a large forest. He didn't have a bite to eat and barely provided the daily bread for his wife and two children, Hansel and

---

35. "Hänsel und Gretel," *Kinder- und Haus-Märchen. Gesammelt durch die Brüder Grimm*, 2 vols. (Berlin: Realschulbuchandlung, 1812/1815).

Gretel. It reached a point when he couldn't even provide that anymore. Indeed, he didn't know how to get out of this predicament.

One night as he was tossing and turning in bed because of his worries, his wife said to him, "Listen to me, husband, early tomorrow morning you're to take both the children and give them each a piece of bread. Then lead them into the middle of the forest where it's most dense. After you build a fire for them, then go away and leave them there. We can no longer feed them."

"No, wife," the man said. "I don't have the heart to take my own children to wild beasts that would soon come and tear them apart in the forest."

"If you don't do that," his wife responded, "we shall all have to starve to death."

She didn't give him any peace until he said yes.

The two children were still awake because of their hunger, and they had heard everything that their mother said to their father. Gretel thought, 'Now it's all over for me,' and began pitifully to weep. But Hansel spoke: "Be quiet, Gretel. Don't get upset. I'll find a way to help us."

Upon saying this, he got up, put on his little jacket, opened the bottom half of the door, and crept outside. The moon was shining very brightly, and the white pebbles glittered in front of the house like pure silver coins. Hansel stooped down to the ground and stuffed his pocket with as many pebbles as he could fit in. Then he went back into the house.

"Don't worry, Gretel. Just sleep quietly." And he lay down again in his bed and fell asleep.

Early the next morning, before the sun had even begun to rise, their mother came and woke the two children.

"Get up, children. We're going into the forest. Here's a piece of bread for each of you. But be smart and don't eat it until noon."

Gretel put the bread under her apron because Hansel had the pebbles in his pocket. Then they all set out together into the forest. After they had walked a while, Hansel stopped still and looked back at the house. He did this time and again until his father said, "Hansel, what are you looking at there and why are you dawdling? Pay attention and march along!"

"Oh, father," said Hansel, "I'm looking at my little white cat that's sitting up on the roof and wants to say good-bye to me."

"You fool," the mother said. "That's not a cat. It's the morning sun shining on the chimney."

But Hansel had not been looking at the cat. Instead, he had been looking at the shiny pebbles from his pocket that he had been dropping on the ground. When they reached the middle of the forest, the father said, "Children, I want you to gather some wood. I'm going to make a fire so you won't get cold."

Hansel and Gretel gathered together some brushwood and built quite a nice little pile. The brushwood was soon kindled, and when the fire was ablaze, the mother said, "Now, children, lie down by the fire and sleep. We're going into the forest to chop wood. When we're finished, we'll come back and get you."

Hansel and Gretel sat by the fire, and when noon came, they kept eating their pieces of bread until evening. But their mother and father did not return. Nobody came to fetch them. When it became pitch dark, Gretel began to weep, but Hansel said, "Just wait awhile until the moon has risen."

And when the full moon had risen, Hansel took Gretel by the hand. The pebbles glittered like newly minted silver coins and showed them the way. They walked the whole nightlong and arrived back at their father's house at break of day. Their father rejoiced with all his heart when he saw his children again, for he had not liked the idea of leaving them alone in the forest. Their mother also seemed to be delighted by their return, but secretly she was angry.

Not long after this, there was once again nothing to eat in the house, and one evening Gretel heard her mother say to their father: "The children found their way back one time, and I just let that go, but now there's nothing left in the house except for a half loaf of bread. Tomorrow you must take them farther into the forest so they won't find their way back home again. Otherwise, there's no hope for us."

All this saddened the father, and he thought, 'It'd be much better to share your last bite to eat with your children.' But since he had given in the first time, he also had to yield a second time.

Hansel and Gretel overheard their parents' conversation. Then Hansel got up and intended to gather pebbles once again, but they had locked the door. Nevertheless, he comforted Gretel and said, "Just sleep, dear Gretel. The dear Lord will certainly help us."

Early the next morning they each received little pieces of bread, but they were smaller than the last time. On the way into the forest Hansel crumbled the bread in his pocket and stopped as often as he could to throw the crumbs on the ground.

"Hansel, why are you always stopping and looking around?" asked the father. "Keep going!"

"Oh, I'm looking at my little pigeon that's sitting on the roof and wants to say good-bye to me," Hansel answered.

"You fool!" his mother said. "That's not your little pigeon. It's the morning sun shining on the chimney."

Now their mother led the children even deeper into the forest until they came to a spot they had never been to before in their lives. Once again they were to sleep by a large fire, and their parents were to come and fetch them in the evening.

When noon came, Gretel shared her bread with Hansel because he had scattered his along the way. Noon went by and then evening passed, but no one came for the poor children. Hansel comforted Gretel and said, "Just wait until the moon has risen, Gretel. Then I'll see the little bread crumbs that I scattered. They'll show us the way back home."

When the moon rose and Hansel looked for the bread crumbs, they were gone because the many thousands of birds that fly about the forest had found them and pecked them up. Nevertheless, Hansel believed he could find the way home and pulled Gretel along with him, but they soon lost their way in the great wilderness. They walked the entire night and all the next day as well, from morning till night, until they fell asleep from exhaustion. Then they walked for one more day, but they didn't find their way out of the forest. They were now also very hungry, for they had had nothing to eat except some berries that they had found growing on the ground.

On the third day they continued walking until noon. Then they came to a little house made of bread with cake for a roof and pure sugar for windows.

"Let's sit down and eat until we're full," said Hansel. "I want to eat a piece of the roof. Gretel, you can have part of the window since it's sweet."

Hansel had already eaten a good piece of the roof and Gretel had devoured a couple of small round windows and was about to break off a new one when they heard a shrill voice cry from inside:

> "Nibble, nibble, nibble,
> Who's that nibbling on my house?"

Hansel and Gretel were so tremendously frightened that they dropped what they had in their hands, and immediately thereafter a small ancient woman crept out of the door. She shook her head and said, "Well now, dear children, where've you come from? Come inside with me. You'll have a good time."

She took them both by the hand and led them into her little house. Then she served them a good meal of milk and pancakes with sugar and apples and nuts. Afterward she made up two beautiful beds, and when Hansel and Gretel lay down in them, they thought they were in Heaven.

The old woman, however, was really a wicked witch on the lookout for children and had built the house made of bread only to lure them to her. As soon as she had children in her power, she would kill, cook, and eat them. It would be like a feast day for her. Therefore, she was quite happy that Hansel and Gretel had come her way.

Early the next morning, before the children were awake, she got up and looked at the two of them sleeping so sweetly. She was delighted and thought, 'They'll certainly be a tasty meal for you!'

Then she grabbed Hansel and stuck him in a small coop, and when he woke up, he was behind a wire mesh used to lock up chickens, and he couldn't move about. Immediately after she shook Gretel and yelled, "Get up, you lazybones! Fetch some water, and then go into the kitchen and cook something nice. Your brother's sitting in a chicken coop. I want to fatten him up, and when he's fat enough, I'm going to eat him. But now I want you to feed him."

Gretel was frightened and wept, but she had to do what the witch demanded. So the very best food was cooked for poor Hansel so that he would become fat, while Gretel got nothing but crab shells. Every day the old woman came and called out, "Hansel, stick out your finger so I can feel whether you're fat enough."

However, Hansel stuck out a little bone, and she was continually puzzled that Hansel did not get any fatter.

One evening, after a month had passed, she said to Gretel, "Get a move on and fetch some water! I don't care whether your little brother's fat enough or not. He's going to be slaughtered and boiled tomorrow. In the meantime I want to prepare the dough so that we can also bake."

So Gretel went off with a sad heart and fetched the water in which Hansel was to be boiled. Early the next morning Gretel had to get up, light the fire, and hang up a kettle full of water.

"Make sure that it boils," said the witch. "I'm going to light the fire in the oven and shove the bread inside."

Gretel was standing in the kitchen and wept bloody tears and thought, 'It would have been better if the wild animals in the forest had eaten us. Then we would have died together and wouldn't have had to bear this sorrow, and I wouldn't have to boil the water that will be the death of my dear brother. Oh dear God, help us poor children get out of this predicament!'

Then the old woman called: "Gretel, come right away over here to the oven!"

When Gretel came, she said, "Look inside and see if the bread is already nice and brown and well-done. My eyes are weak. I can no longer see so good from a distance, and if you can't see, then sit down on the board, and I'll shove you inside. Then you can get around inside and check everything."

The witch wanted to shut the oven door once Gretel was inside, for she wanted to bake her in the hot oven and eat her, too. This is what the wicked witch had planned and why she had called the girl. But God inspired Gretel, and she said, "I don't know how to do it. First you show it to me. Sit down on the board, and I'll shove you inside."

And so the old woman sat down on the board, and since she was light, Gretel shoved her inside as far as she could, and then she quickly shut the oven door and bolted it with an iron bar. The old woman began to scream and groan in the hot oven, but Gretel ran off, and the witch was miserably burned to death.

Meanwhile, Gretel ran straight to Hansel and opened the door to the coop. After Hansel jumped out, they kissed each other and were glad. The entire house was full of jewels and pearls. So, they filled their pockets with them. Then they went off and found their way home. Their father rejoiced when he saw them again. He had not had a single happy day since his children had been away. Now he was a rich man. However, the mother had died.

Hansel and Gretel (1857)[36]

Jacob and Wilhelm Grimm

A poor woodcutter lived with his wife and his two children on the edge of a large forest. The boy was called Hansel and the girl Gretel. The woodcutter did not have much food around the house, and when a great famine devastated the

---

36.   "Hänsel und Gretel," *Kinder- und Hausmärchen gesammelt durch die Brüder Grimm*, 7th ed., 3 vols. (Göttingen: Verlag der Dieterich'schen Buchhandlung, 1857).

entire country, he could no longer provide enough for his family's daily meals. One night, as he was lying in bed and thinking about his worries, he began tossing and turning. Then he sighed and said to his wife, "What's to become of us? How can we feed our poor children when we don't even have enough for ourselves?"

"I'll tell you what," answered his wife. "Early tomorrow morning we'll take the children out into the forest where it's most dense. We'll build a fire and give them each a piece of bread. Then we'll go about our work and leave them alone. They won't find their way back home, and we'll be rid of them."

"No, wife," the man said. "I won't do this. I don't have the heart to leave my children in the forest. The wild beasts would soon come and tear them apart."

"Oh, you fool!" she said. "Then all four of us will have to starve to death. You'd better start planing the boards for our coffins!" She continued to harp on this until he finally agreed to do what she suggested.

"But still, I feel sorry for the poor children," he said.

The two children had not been able to fall asleep that night either. Their hunger kept them awake, and when they heard what their stepmother said to their father, Gretel wept bitter tears and said to Hansel, "Now it's all over for us."

"Be quiet, Gretel," Hansel said. "Don't get upset. I'll soon find a way to help us."

When their parents had fallen asleep, Hansel put on his little jacket, opened the bottom half of the door, and crept outside. The moon was shining very brightly, and the white pebbles glittered in front of the house like pure silver coins. Hansel stooped down to the ground and stuffed his pocket with as many pebbles as he could fit in. Then he went back and said to Gretel, "Don't worry, my dear little sister. Just sleep peacefully. God will not forsake us." And he lay down again in his bed.

At dawn, even before the sun began to rise, the woman came and woke the two children.

"Get up, you lazybones!" she said. "We're going into the forest to fetch some wood." Then she gave each one of them a piece of bread and said, "Now you have something for your noonday meal, but don't eat it before then because you're not getting anything else."

Gretel put the bread under her apron because Hansel had the pebbles in his pocket. Then they all set out together toward the forest. After they had walked a while, Hansel stopped and looked back at the house. He did this time and again until his father said, "Hansel, what are you looking at there? Why are you dawdling? Pay attention, and don't forget how to use your legs!"

"Oh, father," said Hansel, "I'm looking at my little white cat that's sitting up on the roof and wants to say good-bye to me."

"You fool," the mother said. "That's not a cat. It's the morning sun shining on the chimney."

But Hansel had not been looking at the cat. Instead, he had been taking the shiny pebbles from his pocket and constantly dropping them on the ground. When they reached the middle of the forest, the father said, "Children, I want you to gather some wood. I'm going to make a fire so you won't get cold."

Hansel and Gretel gathered together some brushwood and built quite a nice little pile. The brushwood was soon kindled, and when the fire was ablaze, the woman said, "Now, children, lie down by the fire, and rest yourselves. We're going into the forest to chop wood. When we're finished, we'll come back and get you."

Hansel and Gretel sat by the fire, and when noon came, they ate their pieces of bread. Since they heard the sounds of the ax, they thought their father was nearby. But it was not the ax. Rather, it was a branch that he had tied to a dead tree, and the wind was banging it back and forth. After they had been sitting there for a long time, they became so weary that their eyes closed, and they fell sound asleep. By the time they finally awoke, it was already pitch black, and Gretel began to cry and said, "How are we going to get out of the forest?"

But Hansel comforted her by saying, "Just wait awhile until the moon has risen. Then we'll find the way."

And when the full moon had risen, Hansel took his little sister by the hand and followed the pebbles that glittered like newly minted silver coins and showed them the way. They walked the whole nightlong and arrived back at their father's house at break of day. They knocked at the door, and when the woman opened it and saw it was Hansel and Gretel, she said, "You wicked children, why did you sleep so long in the forest? We thought you'd never come back again."

But the father was delighted because he had been deeply troubled by the way he had abandoned them in the forest.

Not long after that the entire country was once again ravaged by famine, and one night the children heard their mother talking to their father in bed, "Everything's been eaten up again. We only have half a loaf of bread, and after it's gone, that will be the end of our food. The children must leave. This time we'll take them even farther into the forest so they won't find their way back home again. Otherwise, there's no hope for us."

All this saddened the father, and he thought, 'It'd be much better to share your last bite to eat with your children.' But the woman would not listen to anything he said. She just scolded and reproached him. Indeed, whoever starts something, must keep going, and since he had given in the first time, he also had to yield a second time.

However, the children were still awake and had overheard their conversation. When their parents had fallen asleep, Hansel got up, intending to go out and gather pebbles as he had done before, but the woman had locked the door, and Hansel couldn't get out. Nevertheless, he comforted his little sister and said, "Don't cry, Gretel. Just sleep peacefully. The dear Lord is bound to help us."

Early the next morning the woman came and got the children out of bed. They each received little pieces of bread, but they were smaller than the last time.

On the way into the forest Hansel crumbled the bread in his pocket and stopped as often as he could to throw the crumbs on the ground.

"Hansel, why are you always stopping and looking around?" asked the father. "Keep going!"

"I'm looking at my little pigeon that's sitting on the roof and wants to say good-bye to me," Hansel answered.

"Fool!" the woman said. "That's not your little pigeon. It's the morning sun shining on the chimney."

But little by little Hansel managed to scatter all the bread crumbs on the path. The woman led the children even deeper into the forest until they came to a spot they had never in their lives seen before. Once again a large fire was made, and the mother said, "Just keep sitting here, children. If you get tired, you can sleep a little. We're going into the forest to chop wood, and in the evening, when we're done, we'll come and get you."

When noon came, Gretel shared her bread with Hansel, who had scattered his along the way. Then they fell asleep, and evening passed, but no one came for the poor children. Only when it was pitch black did they finally wake up, and Hansel comforted his little sister by saying, "Just wait until the moon has risen, Gretel. Then we'll see the little bread crumbs that I scattered. They'll show us the way back home."

When the moon rose, they set out but could not find the crumbs because the many thousands of birds that fly about the forest and fields had devoured them.

"Don't worry, we'll find the way," Hansel said to Gretel, but they couldn't find it. They walked the entire night and all the next day as well, from morning till night, but they didn't find their way out of the forest. They were now also very hungry, for they had had nothing to eat except some berries that they had found growing on the ground. Eventually they became so tired that their legs would no longer carry them, and they lay down beneath a tree and fell asleep.

It was now the third morning since they had left their father's house. They began walking again, and they kept going deeper and deeper into the forest. If help did not arrive soon, they were bound to perish of hunger and exhaustion. At noon they saw a beautiful bird as white as snow sitting on a branch. It sang with such a lovely voice that the children stood still and listened to it. When the bird finished its song, it flapped its wings and flew ahead of them. They followed it until they came to a little house that was made of bread. Moreover, it had cake for a roof and pure sugar for windows.

"What a blessed meal!" said Hansel. "Let's have a taste. I want to eat a piece of the roof. Gretel, you can have some of the window since it's sweet."

Hansel reached up high and broke off a piece of the roof to see how it tasted, and Gretel leaned against the windowpanes and nibbled on them. Then they heard a shrill voice cry from inside:

"Nibble, nibble, I hear a mouse.
Who's that nibbling at my house?"

The children answered:

"The wind, the wind; it's very mild,
blowing like the Heavenly Child."

And they didn't bother to stop eating or let themselves be distracted. Since the roof tasted so good, Hansel ripped off a large piece and pulled it down, while Gretel pushed out a round piece of the windowpane, sat down, and ate it with great relish. Suddenly the door opened, and a very old woman leaning on a crutch came slinking out of the house. Hansel and Gretel were so tremendously frightened that they dropped what they had in their hands. But the old woman wagged her head and said, "Well now, dear children, who brought you here? Just come inside and stay with me. Nobody's going to harm you."

She took them both by the hand and led them into her house. Then she served them a good meal of milk and pancakes with sugar and apples and nuts. Afterward she made up two little beds with white sheets, and Hansel and Gretel lay down in them and thought they were in Heaven.

The old woman, however, had only pretended to be friendly. She was really a wicked witch on the lookout for children and had built the house made of bread only to lure them to her. As soon as she had children in her power, she would kill, cook, and eat them. It would be like a feast day for her. Now, witches, have red eyes and cannot see very far, but they have a keen sense of smell, like animals, and can detect when human beings are near them. Therefore, when Hansel and Gretel had come into her vicinity, she had laughed wickedly and scoffed, "They're mine! They'll never get away from me!"

Early the next morning, before the children were awake, she got up and looked at the two of them sleeping so sweetly with full rosy cheeks. Then she muttered to herself, "They'll certainly make for a tasty meal!"

She seized Hansel with her scrawny hands and carried him into a small pen, where she locked him up behind a grilled door. No matter how much he screamed, it didn't help. Then she went back to Gretel, shook her until she woke up, and yelled, "Get up, you lazybones! I want you to fetch some water and cook your brother something nice. He's sitting outside in a pen, and we've got to fatten him up. Then, when he's fat enough, I'm going to eat him."

Gretel began to weep bitter tears, but they were all in vain. She had to do what the wicked witch demanded. So the very best food was cooked for poor Hansel, while Gretel got nothing but crab shells. Every morning the old woman went slinking to the little pen and called out, "Hansel, stick out your finger so I can feel how fat you are."

However, Hansel stuck out a little bone, and since the old woman had poor eyesight, she thought the bone was Hansel's finger. She was puzzled that Hansel did not get any fatter, and when a month had gone by and Hansel still seemed to be thin, she was overcome by her impatience and decided not to wait any longer.

"Hey there, Gretel!" she called to the little girl. "Get a move on and fetch some water! I don't care whether Hansel's fat or thin. He's going to be slaughtered tomorrow, and then I'll cook him."

Oh, how the poor little sister wailed as she carried the water, and how the tears streamed down her cheeks!

"Dear God, help us!" she exclaimed. "If only the wild beasts had eaten us in the forest, then we could have at least died together!"

Early the next morning Gretel had to go out, hang up a kettle fill of water, and light the fire.

"First we'll bake," the old woman said. "I've already heated the oven and kneaded the dough." She pushed poor Gretel out to the oven, where the flames were leaping from the fire. "Crawl inside," said the witch, "and see if it's properly heated so we can slide the bread in."

The witch intended to close the oven door once Gretel had climbed inside, for the witch wanted to bake her and eat her, too. But Gretel sensed what she had in mind and said, "I don't know how to do it. How do I get in?"

"You stupid goose," the old woman said. "The opening's large enough. Watch, even I can get in!"

She waddled up to the oven and stuck her head through the oven door. Then Gretel gave her a push that sent her flying inside and shut the iron door and bolted it. *Whew!* The witch began to howl dreadfully, but Gretel ran away, and the godless witch was miserably burned to death.

Meanwhile, Gretel ran straight to Hansel, opened the pen, and cried out, "Hansel, we're saved! The old witch is dead!"

Then Hansel jumped out of the pen like a bird that hops out of a cage when the door is opened. My how happy they were! They hugged each other, danced around, and kissed. Since they no longer had anything to fear, they went into the witch's house where they found chests filled with pearls and jewels all over the place. "They're certainly much better than pebbles," said Hansel, and he stuck as much as he could fit into his pockets, and Gretel said, "I'm going to carry some home, too," and she filled her apron full of jewels and pearls.

"We'd better be on our way now," said Hansel, "so we can get out of the witch's forest."

After they had walked for a few hours, they reached a large river.

"We can't get across," said Hansel. "I don't see a bridge or any way over it."

"There are no boats either," Gretel responded, "but there's a white duck swimming over there. It's bound to help us across if I ask it." Then she cried out:

> "Help us, help us, little duck!
> We're Hansel and Gretel, out of luck.
> We can't get over, try as we may.
> Please take us across right away!"

The little duck came swimming up to them, and Hansel got on top of its back and told his sister to sit down beside him.

"No," Gretel answered. "We'll be too heavy for the little duck. It should carry us across one at a time."

The kind little duck did just that, and when they were safely across and had walked on for some time, the forest became more and more familiar to them, and finally they caught sight of their father's house from afar. They began to run at once, and soon rushed into the house and threw themselves around their father's neck. The man had not had a single happy hour since he had abandoned his children in the forest, and in the meantime his wife had died. Gretel opened and shook out the apron so that the pearls and jewels bounced about the room, and Hansel added to this by tossing one handful after another from his pocket. Now all their troubles were over, and they lived together in utmost joy.

My tale is done. See the mouse run. Catch it, whoever can. Then you can make a great big cap out of its fur.

The Ogre (1854)[37]

Ignaz and Josef Zingerle

Once there was a little boy who was looking for strawberries and forgot about the time. It had already become dark, and he could no longer think about returning home. So the boy said to himself: 'Perhaps there are some people living nearby, and I can spend the night with them. I know, I'll just climb a tree and see if I can see a house somewhere.' Once he gave thought to this, it was done. He spat into his hands and climbed a pine tree like a squirrel. When he reached the peak, he looked around him on all sides and saw a cottage standing in the distance. This gave the boy great pleasure, and so he descended the tree quickly and lively and made his way to the cottage which he reached very soon. The boy wanted to enter, but the door was locked. So he knocked on the door, and it was soon opened by a small old grandma who asked him what he wanted.

"I'd like a night's lodging," said the boy. "I can't make my way out of the forest tonight, and I'm afraid of the wolves and bears."

"My good child," the grandma responded, "you've come to the wrong place because an ogre lives here, and he'd gobble you up, hair and all, if he caught sight of you."

When the boy heard this, he began to weep and pleaded to the grandmother: "Even so, please give me lodgings for the night, and hide me from the ogre."

The grandma took pity on the boy and let him enter the cottage, where she hid him in an empty little barrel, gave him a match, and said: "Duck down and

---

37. "Der Menschenfresser," *Kinder- und Hausmärchen aus Süddeutschland* (Regensburg: Pustet, 1854).

keep as still as a mouse. If the old man nevertheless gets wind of you and wants to see one of your fingers, show him this match."

Then she went off to take care of some work. However, the boy felt scared as hell in his little barrel, and he broke out into a cold sweat. So he spent a good amount of time in fear and anxiety, and then, all at once there was a crash outside, and the wild man entered the room. As he sniffed the air, he said: "The room smacks of human flesh, human flesh!"

The old grandma wanted to change his mind and said: "You smack, you smack of chicken filth."

But the ogre didn't let himself be led astray. He sniffed more and more and went over to the little barrel in which the boy was sitting. Then he spoke to the old woman with a terrible voice: "It's inside! Human flesh is inside! Stick your finger out so that I can see whether you're fat."

Immediately the boy thought of the old woman's advice and extended the match. The ogre felt it and said: "This finger's as thin as a match! It's got to be fattened up."

Then he sat down at the table, ate, drank, cursed, and went to bed as soon as he was full. The boy was, of course, grateful and thanked God for saving him. Then he, too, fell asleep.

Early the next morning the wild man went into the forest. As soon as he was away, the old grandma lifted the boy out of the little barrel and gave him breakfast. Then she said: "Now eat and still your hunger. Then I'll show you the way out of the forest."

The boy didn't let himself be asked twice. He ate like a hungry bear and then went into the forest with the old grandma. She led him threw thick and thin until they came into the open air. Then she said to the boy: "In the future don't stay so late anymore in the forest. Things could have gone much worse for you."

The boy thanked the small woman and ran over hill and dale to his home. Since then he's never been late and has always returned home at the right time.

Maria and Her Little Brother (1870)[38]
Laura Gonzenbach

Once upon a time there was a man whose wife died and left him with two children, a boy named Peppe[39] and a girl named Maria. Both children were very beautiful, and their father loved them with all his heart. He was, however, a poor man and could only support them by gathering firewood in the forest and selling the wood in the city. Since he never wanted to separate from his children, he

---

38. "Von Maria und ihrem Brüderchen," *Sicilianische Märchen*, 2 vols. (Leipzig: W. Engelmann, 1870).

39. Giuseppe or Joseph.

always took them into the forest with him, and they looked for twigs and carried small bundles to their home.

After some time had passed, the man thought about marrying again.

"Oh, father don't do it," Maria implored him. "If you bring a stepmother into our home, she'll certainly mistreat us."

"Don't worry, my child," he answered. "After all I'm here, and I'll always protect you and I'll continue to love you as much as I do now."

So he went and married a neighbor, who was a tavern keeper and had a daughter who was very ugly and one-eyed. For a while everything went well, but soon the stepmother became unfriendly toward Maria and her brother. And since Maria was so beautiful and her daughter so ugly, the stepmother could clearly not stand her and thought of ways to cause her ruin.

One day, she said to her husband, "Times are terrible. The bread has become so expensive, and your children eat so much that we'll soon become beggars. Get rid of your children because I'm not going to give them any more to eat!"

"But where should I send my children?" the father asked.

"Take them deep into the forest tomorrow, and bring them to a place so that they won't be able to find their way back," the stepmother answered.

"Oh no," said her husband, "how could I commit such a sin and leave my children in the forest all alone? I love them too much."

Well, just as it is customary that wives always get their way with husbands, this husband, too, let himself be persuaded by his wife. So he woke his two children very early the next morning and said, "Come children, I know a beautiful spot in the forest where we can find a lot of wood today."

Then they set out and took some bread with them. Along the way they met a man who was selling lupins.[40]

"Father," said Maria, "give us a senare[41] so we can buy some lupins."

The father gave them the senare, and the children bought the lupins and ate them along the way, as they walked, they threw the shells on to the ground. Finally, they reached a certain spot in the forest, and their father said, "Look, children, over there you'll find a lot of twigs. Go there and make some bundles while I chop down this old tree trunk." However, the father took a large pumpkin, tied it on to the branch of the tree so that it would swing and hit the trunk. Then he crept away and went home. The children worked the entire day, and when they stopped every now and then, they heard the pumpkin hitting the trunk and thought it was their father's ax and merrily continued gathering wood.

When evening arrived, Maria said, "Father is working very long today. Let's go and call him."

---

40. *Luppini.*
41. Two centimes.

So they went back to the spot where they had left their father. Since they couldn't find him, they began calling him, but he didn't answer. When they caught sight of the pumpkin, they realized that he had left them alone in the dark forest and began to weep bitter tears.

"Don't cry, Peppe," Maria said. "Early this morning we ate the lupins, and if we follow the path of the shells that we threw on the ground, we'll come to a place that we know, and from there we can find our way home."

So they followed the path of the shells and found their way out of the forest and arrived happily at their house. In the meantime, their father had sat down at the dinner table but had no desire to eat. He was weeping and lamenting, "Oh, my poor, dear children, I've abandoned you! Now the wild animals will eat you! Oh, my children!"

All at once the children called to him from outside the door, "Father, here we are! Open up!"

And when the father opened the door, he saw his dear children alive and well standing right before his eyes. He embraced them and told them to sit down at the table and was extremely happy that they were there again.

But the stepmother was bitter and angry that they had returned and said to her husband once more he had to take them even further into the dense forest. Her husband refused, but she screamed at him and threw a fit until he had to promise her with a heavy heart to do what she demanded.

Early the next morning he woke the children again and took them into the forest. Maria was scared that he would leave them alone once more. So she filled her pockets and her brother's pockets with beans, and along the way they ate the beans and spread the shells along the path. Their father led them to a spot in the forest where they had never been before.

"Oh, father, how strange and eerie it is here!" the children said.

"That's all the more reason we'll find much more wood here," their father answered. "Go further in the forest to a spot where you'll find a lot of twigs, and I'll start chopping this tree trunk."

The children went to the spot that their father had indicated, while he tied a pumpkin on a branch again and snuck off toward home. When it became evening, Maria said, "Peppe, I still hear father chopping down the tree, let's go and find him."

However, when they reached the tree, where the pumpkin was hanging, there was no sight of him, and they realized that he had deserted them once more.

"Don't cry, Peppe," Maria said. "We just need to follow the shells of the beans, and we'll soon find our way home."

So they followed the shells and reached home when it was pitch black. The father sat at the dinner table and moaned about his poor children.

"Father, here we are! Open up," they called outside the house, and their father joyfully opened the door and embraced his dear children.

But the wicked stepmother became more and more angry that the children had found their way home again despite everything, and she threatened her husband that if he didn't abandon his children alone in the forest again, she would chase them away. So the man woke his children early in the morning and said, "Come. Let's go into the forest and look for food."

Maria wanted to fill her pockets once more with beans, but there were no more to be found. So she took a handful of bran and stuck it into her pocket. While she walked with her father, she spread a little bran on the path. The father brought them to a very dense and dark spot in the forest and then sent them somewhat further into the woods to look for twigs. As soon as they departed, he tied a pumpkin to a branch and went home.

When it began to get dark, the children set out to look for their father, but they couldn't find him and realized that he had abandoned them.

"Don't cry, Peppe," Maria said. "I spread bran along the way. We only have to follow the trail of the bran, and we'll certainly find our way back home."

However, no matter how much they looked, they couldn't find their way because the wind had blown the bran from the path, and the children lost their way and went deeper into the dark forest. Soon they began to shed bitter tears and sat down beneath a tree to wait for sunrise. When dawn came, they wandered further, but they couldn't find their way out of the forest.

"Oh, Maria, I'm so thirsty," said Peppe. "When we come to a brook, let's get a drink of water."

Soon thereafter they came to a brook, and Peppe wanted to drink. However, Maria heard the brook murmur: "If you drink from my water, you will become a snake and your brother a little serpent."

"Oh, Peppe," Maria cried, "don't drink. Otherwise, you'll become a little serpent. We better wait a little while."

After they went further on, they came to another brook, and Peppe said, "Look, Maria, we can get a drink there."

But the brook murmured: "Whoever drinks from my water will become a rabbit."

"Peppe," Maria said, "don't drink, otherwise you'll become a rabbit. We better wait a while."

After they walked some distance, they came to another brook that murmured to Maria, "If you drink from me, you'll become more beautiful than the sun, and your brother will turn into a sheep with gold horns."

"Ah, Peppe," Maria cried out, "don't drink."

But Peppe had already bent over to drink, and no sooner did he take a few sips than he was transformed into a little sheep and had pretty gold horns. Consequently, Maria began to weep, but Peppe was and remained a sheep.

So she continued to wander with a heavy heart. But before Maria departed, she also drank some water and became even more beautiful than she had been, more beautiful than the sun. When they had traveled for some time, they came to a cave and crawled inside, and since there were no wild animals there, Maria said, "Let's live here, and during the day I'll go around and look for herbs, and we can live off them."

So Maria made a bed in the cave out of dry leaves and searched for herbs in the forest that nourished them.

Many, many years went by this way, and Maria grew to become a very beautiful maiden. Now, one day, the king happened to go hunting and came in the vicinity of the cave. All of a sudden, his dogs began to bark and crawled into the cave. So the king sent one of his hunters to see what they had found. When the hunter crept into the cave and saw the lovely maiden, he went back and reported to the king, who shouted, "Come out whoever you may be! We won't harm you."

So Maria came out, and when she stood there, she was more beautiful than the sun and moon so that the king fell madly in love with her and said, "Beautiful maiden, do you want to come to my castle and become my wife?"

"Yes," she answered, "but my little sheep must come with me."

So the king took the beautiful Maria on his horse and rode with her to his castle, and one of his hunters had to lead the little sheep. When the old queen saw her son appear with this wondrous creature, she cried out with astonishment, "Who's this girl you're bringing out of the forest?"

"Mother, this maiden is to become my wife," the king responded.

To be sure, the queen was not pleased by this, but since she loved her son so much, she let him have his way, and Maria was so beautiful that she soon won the queen's heart. So a splendid wedding was celebrated, and beautiful Maria became queen. But the little sheep still followed her everywhere she went and also had to sleep in her room.

Now that she lived in such glory and splendor, Maria no longer thought about the mistreatment that she had received from her stepmother. On the contrary. She sent her father and stepmother and her stepmother's daughter beautiful presents and made it known to them that she was now a queen. Her stepmother's heart, however, became filled with envy because her own daughter had not been so lucky, and she thought of ways to bring about the ruin of the young queen.

When she later heard that Maria was about to give birth, she set out with her daughter on a day that the king had gone off hunting. Maria received them in a friendly way, showed them around the entire castle, and finally brought them to her own room. There they saw a locked window, and the tricky stepmother said, "Why is that window closed?"

"It's right above the sea," Maria answered, "and the king doesn't want me to open it in case I might fall out."

"Oh, open it up, Maria," the stepmother requested. "I'd like to see the sea from here, and I'll hold on to you in case you're afraid of falling out."

Maria let herself be persuaded and opened the window, and as she was leaning out, her stepmother gave her a push so that she fell into the sea. Right beneath the window was a shark which held open its jaws, and when Maria fell into the water, the shark swallowed her. Then the false stepmother put the queen's nightgown on her daughter and told her to lay down in bed. She herself left the castle in a hurry.

After the king returned home and heard that the young queen was lying in bed, he went up to her. But when he looked at her and saw how ugly she was, he was shocked and said, "What happened that's made you so ugly and one-eyed?"

"I'm sick," she answered. "The wicked little sheep rammed me with his horns and knocked an eye out. That's why it's got to die."

The king became furious and had the sheep locked up in the castle dungeon and ordered the cook to sharpen his knives. The dungeon lay close to the sea. All at once the guard heard how the sheep began to moan and to speak:

> Sister, oh sister, oh curly hair,
> They're sharpening the knives and taking great care
> preparing the kettles to be nice and bright,
> then they'll cut my throat without a fight.

All at once, a voice answered from the water:

> Brother dear, I can't help you, I fear.
> The wicked shark holds me tightly in his jaw.
> I can't even give birth anymore.

So the guard went to the king and told him what he had heard. The king was astounded and went to the place where the guard usually stood. All at once he heard the little sheep lament:

> Sister, oh sister, oh curly hair,
> They're sharpening the knives and taking great care
> preparing the kettles to be nice and bright,
> then they'll cut my throat without a fight.

Immediately there was a response from a voice in the sea:

> Brother dear, I can't help you, I fear.
> The wicked shark holds me tightly in his jaw.
> I can't even give birth anymore.

The king recognized his wife's voice and had the sheep fetched from the dungeon and said, "Tell me who you were speaking with?"

"With my sister Maria," the sheep answered. "She's sitting in the jaw of a shark because the false stepmother threw her out of the window. Her ugly daughter is lying upstairs in the bed."

The king became very happy and said, "Little sheep, go to the sea, and ask your sister how I can rescue her."

The little sheep went and spoke his verse, and after Maria answered him, he continued, "Tell me, Maria, how can you be rescued?

"You'll need a strong iron hook with a large piece of bread stuck on it," she answered. "When I answer your verse, it will be a sign that the shark is sleeping on the surface of the water and his jaw is open. Then the king must stick the hook into the jaw of the shark so that I can hold onto it while he pulls me out."

And that's what they did. When Maria answered the sheep, the king stood ready with the large hook. He threw it into the shark's jaw and pulled it toward him with all his might, while Maria held on to the hook and was pulled out. No sooner was she brought into the castle than her time arrived, and she gave birth to a lovely boy. The king was very happy as was everyone in the castle. But the king had the ugly, one-eyed stepsister's head cut off. Then the head was chopped into little pieces and salted in a barrel that was sent to her mother. The servant who brought it to the woman told her: "Your daughter, the queen, has sent this beautiful tuna fish."

When the wicked woman opened the barrel, she found the blind eye of her daughter on top and recognized it right away. Then she ran to the king and demanded to have her daughter back. But the king said, "Just listen to you!" Then he ordered her to be seized and thrown into a kettle full of boiling water.

When Maria was healthy again, the king held a great feast, and they remained happy and content, and we're just empty roots without a cent.

Courtillon-Courtillette (1882)[42]

Henry Carnoy

Once upon some time ago a poor woodcutter lived in a large forest. Everything went well during those times when the peasants in the region could come and cut down the wood from the trees, but in the winter it was another story. They had to content themselves with gathering dead wood in the thickets and to make bundles of sticks and sell them for almost next to nothing in the neighboring villages.

In this case the poor woodcutter often, but not all that often, found himself without any food for himself and his family. The members of this family were his wife, two boys about twelve and thirteen, a girl called Marie, and also a female dog that the woodcutter considered part of the family. This dog was called Courtillon-Courtillette, Suivon-Suivette a name that was quite long and had been given to the dog by an old sorceress who lived in the vicinity. And the remarkable thing about this dog was that, ever since the old woman had passed by the woodcutter's hut, the dog spoke just like you and me and often mixed into the conversation.

---

42. "Courtillon-Cortillette," *Littérature orale de la Picardie* (Paris: Maisonneuve, 1883).

One winter when snow had covered the trees in the forest for six weeks, the woodcutter saw that there was no food in the hut. After having asked for charity from the people in the village in vain, he realized that he would have to die from hunger along with his poor children. So, one evening while the children had gone to bed and Courtillon-Courtillette was sleeping near the chimney, the woodcutter said to his wife:

"My poor Catherine, this morning I discovered that we don't have any more food, and I don't have any hope of finding some for a long time. Our poor children are going to die from hunger under our eyes, and I don't have the courage to let them suffer this way. I've thought about this the entire day, and this is what I intend to do: tomorrow morning we shall lead the two boys and the girl into the forest under the pretext of searching for dead wood, and when we have led them deep, very deep into the forest, we'll leave them there. They'll certainly die, but at least we won't have the sorrow of watching them die of hunger. Do you agree?"

"This is sad, all this, Pierre. But what are we to do? It's the only decision that we can make."

"All right, we've agreed. Let's go to sleep until tomorrow morning."

Pierre and Catherine went to bed, but Courtillon-Courtillette, Suivon-Suivette caught every word of the conversation. As soon as the woodcutter and his wife were asleep, she went quietly over to the bed where the children were sleeping, woke them up, and told them what she had just heard. Her report left the poor little ones in tears.

"Be quiet and don't wake your parents, or all will be lost. There's still a bag full of dried peas in the cupboard. One of you should go and take it without being seen. Tomorrow, after we've been in the forest awhile, we'll let the peas drop. This way we'll easily be able to find our path back home."

The children promised to do what the good dog had just said and then went back to sleep.

The next morning the woodcutter woke them and said, "Let's go, my children. Since there are no more bundles of wood in the house, and we've got to go and gather the wood in the thickets."

The children got up and followed their father and mother into the forest, taking care to let dried peas fall from place to place to mark out their path. Toward evening, Pierre and Catherine separated from the children and left them quite far from the house. Then the little boys and little girl began to weep.

"It's nothing," the good dog said to them. "We only have to spend the night in the forest. Tomorrow morning I'll do my best to find the way back to your parents' hut. Lay down to sleep on the moss, and I'll keep watch over you."

The children laid themselves down on the moss, and Courtillon-Courtillette, Suivon-Suivette kept guard so well that neither the wolves nor the foxes dared to approach the little sleepers. When morning came, they woke up and dutifully thanked their faithful guardian.

"Now," Courtillon-Courtillette said, "follow me, and don't get lost."

And the dog had no difficulty finding the way right back to the woodcutter's house, and they arrived there toward noon. It was the lunch time, and a peasant who had owed some money to Pierre had come and brought it to him. Catherine made use of the money to prepare a good stew.

"Our poor children!" she said as she wept. "If they were here, they'd certainly enjoy eating this good stew."

"Oh, yes!" Pierre joined in. "Our poor children! And that poor Courtillon-Courtillette, Suivon-Suivette, who went along with them! It was a bad idea of ours to let them get lost in the forest. By now the wolves have certainly eaten them."

The peasant wept as well.

"Knock, knock! Mama, papa! We've returned from the woods! We're very hungry!"

The little boys, the little girl, and Courtillon-Courtillette had found their way home. You can imagine Pierre and Catherine's joy. However, the money did not last a long time. The winter continued and had become even more terrible than before, and Pierre decided again to lose his children in the forest. And once again the good dog heard about the plot and warned her little friends.

When the next day arrived, the woodcutter, his wife, the children, and the dog departed again to gather the dead wood in the forest. The oldest of the little boys let a piece of white cheese drop from time to time. The cheese was the only thing that he had been able to find in the house. When evening came, the woodcutter and his wife disappeared, and the children slept out in the open and were guarded by Courtillon-Courtillette.

It rained the entire night, and the next day Courtillon-Courtillette could not find the path back to the hut because the water had washed away and scattered the white cheese.

"What are we going to do? What's going to become of us?" the poor children wept.

"We'll try to find a way out of the forest," said the dog.

The children endeavored to find the way, and each time they thought that they had reached the end of the forest, they had actually gone deeper. When evening arrived, they were just as lost as they had been in the morning.

"We can't stay in the forest all the time," the dog said. "Jean, climb the large fir tree, and go as high as you can. See if there is some light nearby."

Jean climbed the tree and saw nothing.

"Now it's your turn, Pierrot," Courtillon-Courtillette said.

And Pierrot also saw nothing.

"Well then, Marie, it's your turn!"

The little girl climbed as best she could until she reached the last branch of the fir tree.

"What do you see?" the dog cried out.

"I see a large frozen sea to my right."

"And to your left?"

"A frozen pond."

"And in front?"

"A large chateau that's lit up."

"All right. Get down, Marie."

The little girl descended. Courtillon-Courtillette began walking up front, and she was followed by the children. They headed in the direction of the chateau, and at the end of an hour they arrived.

"Knock, knock!"

"Who's there?" asked an old woman who came to open the door.

"We're three little children lost in the forest, and we've come to ask hospitality for the night."

"You know, don't you, that this is the devil's chateau, and he devours all those travelers he finds here in the evening?"

"It doesn't matter! We're freezing and hungry!"

"Well then, enter."

The old woman did not want to allow the dog into the house, but little Marie begged so much that she finally consented.

The children took great pleasure in eating an excellent dinner that the devil's wife served them. Then they went to sleep in a bed that the old woman showed them after she had them put straw collars around their necks. Meanwhile Courtillon-Courtillette hid herself beneath the bed. The three devil's daughters were also asleep in the same room, and they wore golden necklaces around their necks.

Soon thereafter the devil returned home and said to his wife, "I smell fresh meat."

"Not at all," she responded. "It's the cat that's just had kittens."

"You're deceiving me. I smell Christian flesh."

And he began to search the entire house until he found the children who had pretended to sleep.

"This is good! This is good! I'm going to heat my oven, and I'll roast them tonight so that I'll have an excellent breakfast for tomorrow."

The old woman went to bed while the devil heated his oven.

Courtillon-Courtillette did not lose any time. She told the children to take off their straw collars and to place them around the necks of the devil's daughters and to put their golden collars around their necks. All this was done.

Once the devil had finished heating his oven, he returned to the children's room and went to their bed. He took little Marie by her neck and was astonished to feel the golden necklace.

"What a fool I am!" he muttered. "I almost cooked my daughters. I mistook the bed."

So now he went to his daughters' bed. He felt the straw necklaces, took his children under his armpit, and carried them away to roast them.

"But we're your little daughters!" the girls cried out and wept.

"Shut up! Shut up! Do you think you can pull the wool over my eyes?!"

And he shoved them into the oven and went to bed.

When Courtillon-Courtillette heard the devil snoring, she woke the children and told them to take whatever they considered to be the most valuable things in the house, and the children didn't have to be asked twice to do this.

"Now, pay attention. I'm going to stretch out, and you three are to get on my back. Don't make a sound while doing this. We don't have much time to get out of this nasty devil's chateau."

The little girl was the first to get on the dog's back, then the two boys mounted, and Courtillon-Courtillette leapt through an open window and began running across a field.

They had been gone a long time when morning came. Upon awakening, the devil went to hug his daughters and realized his misfortune. He swore like a trooper and promised to take revenge on the two boys and the little girl. So he saddled a fast sow that was as quick as the wind and began to search for the children. It didn't take long for him to catch sight of them in the distance.

"This time I'll get them for sure! They'll pay for what they've done!" the devil screamed.

But Courtillon-Courtillette had seen the devil when she looked back. Within seconds, she said, "May the children be changed into washerwomen, and may I be changed into a large river!"

And suddenly there was a large river that ran near the field and three washerwomen at the bank of the river. Then the devil arrived.

"Have you seen Courtillon-Courtillette, Suivon-Suivette pass by here and carrying three children on her back?"

"What do you expect from us, nasty devil? We'll let you have it if you mock us!"

The devil turned around to go in another direction. Then the dog, the little girl, and the two boys started off again with renewed vigor.

When the nasty devil didn't find them on the other path, he realized that they had probably changed themselves into the river and the three washerwomen. So, he directed his sow to head back in that direction.

"Ah-ha! I see them again! Now I'll get them!" the devil cried out.

But when he arrived, he found only a large field of alfalfa, some sheep, a dog, and a shepherd.

"Shepherd, have you seen Courtillon-Courtillette pass by here with three children?"

"Courtignon-Cortignette! I think you're mocking me! Just you wait, nasty devil! Watch out for my crook!"

"I'll go off on this other path to the right. It's clear that they've probably taken this one," the devil said to himself.

As soon as he had gone off some distance, the dog took the children on her back and departed. But soon thereafter, she said:

"The devil will certainly return on his sow. May I change into a meadow, and Jeannot and Pierrot into cows, and Marie into a cowherd."

Just as this was done the devil returned and was more furious than ever before.

"Good woman, have you seen Courtillon-Courtillette, Suivon-Suivette pass by here with a girl and two boys?"

"Ah! You wicked devil! Why do you want to know?"

"To kill them! Have you seen them?"

"But of course! Of course! They've just crossed the river."

"Thank you! Thank you!" And the devil ran to the river, but his sow didn't want to cross.

"All right, wait. I'll cross some other way."

Since he had seen a large piece of cloth nearby that some peasants had hung out to whiten, he took it and threw it on the river and wanted to use it as a bridge to cross over. However, the cloth ripped, and the devil drowned.

"Now," the dog said, "let's return to our parents' home."

And she brought them back very soon. Even though the woodcutter and his wife were dying of hunger, they got on Courtillon-Courtillette's back and set out to take possession of the devil's chateau. Meanwhile the devil's wife had disappeared.

For a long time thereafter people talked about the good fortune and the wealth of the family of Pierre the woodcutter.

The Two Children and the Witch (1882)[43]

Consiglieri Pedroso

There was once a woman who had a son and a daughter. The mother one day sent her son to buy five reis' worth of beans and then said to both: "My children, go as far out on the road as you shall find shells of beans strewed on the path, and when you reach the wood, you will find me there collecting firewood."

The children did as they were told, and after the mother had gone out, they went following the track of the beans which she went strewing along the road, but they did not find her in the wood or anywhere else. As night had come on, they perceived in the darkness a light shining at a distance, easy of access. They walked on towards it, and they soon came up to an old woman who was frying cakes. The old woman was blind of one eye, and the boy went on the blind side and stole a cake, because he felt so hungry. Believing that it was her cat which had stolen the cake, she said, "You thief of a cat! Leave my cakes alone. They are not meant for you!"

The little boy now said to his sister, "You go now and take a cake."

But the little girl replied, "I cannot do so, as I am sure to laugh."

---

43. *Portuguese Folk-Tales*, trans. Henriqueta Monteiro (London: Folklore Society, 1882).

Still, as the boy persisted upon it and urged her to try, she had no other alternative but to do so. She went on the side of the old woman's blind eye and stole another of her cakes.

The old woman, again thinking that it was her cat, said, "Be off! Shoo you old pussy! These cakes are not meant for you!"

The little girl now burst out into a fit of laughter, and the old hag turning round then, noticed the two children and addressed them thus: "Ah! Is it you, my dear grandchildren? Eat, eat away, and get fat!"

She then took hold of them and thrust them into a large box full of chestnuts and shut them up. Next day she came close to the box and spoke to them thus: "Show me your little fingers, my pets, that I may be able to judge whether you have grown fat and sleek."

The children put out their little fingers as desired. But next day the old hag again asked them: "Show your little fingers, my little dears, that I may see if you have grown fat and plump!"

The children, instead of their little fingers, showed her the tail of a cat they had found inside the box. The old hag then said: "My pets, you can come out now, for you have grown nice and plump."

She took them out of the box and told them they must go with her and gather sticks. The children went into the wood searching one way while the old hag took another direction. When they had arrived at a certain spot, they met a fay[44] who said to them: "You are gathering sticks, my children, to heat the oven, but you do not know that the old hag wants to bake you in it."

She further told them that the old witch meant to order them to stand on the baker's peel, saying: "Stand on this peel, my little pets, that I may see you dance in the oven, "but that they were to ask her to sit upon it herself first so that they might learn the way to do it. The fay then went away. Shortly after they had met this good lady, they found the old witch in the wood. They gathered together in bundles all the fire-sticks they had collected and carried them home to heat the oven. When they had finished heating the oven, the old hag swept it carefully out and then said to the little ones, "Sit here, my little darlings, on this peel, that I may see how prettily you dance in the oven!"

The children replied to the witch as the good fay had instructed them: "Sit you here, little granny, that we may first see you dance in the oven."

As the hag's intention was to bake the children, she sat on the peel first so as to coax them to do the same after her, but the very moment the children saw her on the peel, they thrust the peel into the oven with the witch upon it. The old hag gave a great start and was burnt to a cinder immediately after. The children took possession of the shed and all it contained.

******

---

44. Fairy.

Another version: —There were once three brothers who went along a certain road. When night overtook them, they saw a light at a distance, and so they walked on towards it until they came to it. The light proceeded from a spot where an old woman was frying some cakes. The brothers said one to another, "Let us get upon the roof."

They made a very long hook-stick and got upon the roof. As the old hag fried her cakes, she placed them upon a dish by her. Her cat, meanwhile, sat by her side. The boys with their long hook from the top of the roof fished up the warm cakes one after the other, as the old hag placed them on the dish. Since the cat was by her side, and every time she placed a cake on the dish she found the other gone, she kept repeating and exclaiming: "Shoo, you naughty thief of a pussy! How can you manage to eat so many cakes?"

These brothers were consecrated to Saint Peter, and when they heard what the old hag said, they began to laugh, unable to suppress their merriment. The old hag, looking up towards the roof, startled, saw the boys, and told them to come down. The boys feared to do so and refused to descend, but the old witch so managed to threaten and then to cajole them that she at last induced them to come down from the roof. When she saw them down, she addressed them: "Look here, my children, stand on this baker's peel for an instant."

The boys replied, "No, no, old lady, you get upon it first, and one can then easily learn how it is done."

The old witch, believing them to be innocent and artless, stood upon the peel!

"Saint Peter, come to our help!" cried out the brothers the moment they saw her upon the peel.

Saint Peter came, pushed the old hag into the oven, stirred the fire, and shut the oven door. After this the boys continue to partake of the remaining cakes very comfortably.

The Lost Children (1887)[45]

Antoinette Bon

Once upon a time long ago in the village of Gargeac there was a man and a woman who were married. The husband was called Jacques and the woman, Toinon. Both of them were very miserly, especially the wife. She was so very, very miserly that she would have skinned a flint.

They had two children, a boy and a girl, who suffered a great deal because of the greediness of their parents. But they were so good and loved each other so much that nobody ever heard them complain. The boy was twelve and was called Jean, and the little girl, who was a bit younger, was called Jeannette.

Jacques and Toinon found that their children were costing them too much, and they decided to abandon them in the forest. The wife said to her husband:

---

45.   "Les enfants égarés," *Revue des Traditions populaires* (1887).

"I'll take them into the middle of the woods and order them to gather dead branches. When they are busily occupied, I'll leave them all alone, and we'll be rid of them because the wolves will eat them at nightfall."

As soon as it was dawn the next day the woman told Jean and Jeannette to get up. Then she led them into the forest and told them to gather dry branches. When she saw that they were busily occupied by this, she ran off. Afterward, Jean and Jeannette saw that they were alone, and they began to call their mother. However, when they realized that she was not responding, they began to weep. Then they tried to find their way back. Yet, they were not able to get out of the forest.

"Jean, climb to the top of a tree," Jeannette said to her brother. "Perhaps you'll see a house."

Jean began climbing a tree, and when he was halfway up, his little sister cried out: "Can you see anything, little brother?"

"No, my little sister, I only see the branches of the forest."

"Keep climbing higher. Perhaps you'll see a house."

Jean climbed a few branches higher.

"Do you see anything, little brother?"

"No, little sister, I only see the green branches of the forest."

Jean climbed some more, and he didn't stop until he reached the last branch.

"Do you see anything, little brother?"

"Yes, little sister, I see two houses in the distance, one white and the other red. Which one shall we go to?"

"To the red house," Jeannette responded, because it was the prettiest.

Jean climbed down the tree, and the two children went off in the direction of the red house. They knocked at the door, and a woman, as large and strong as a man, opened up to them.

"Who are you," she said to them.

"We're little children lost in the forest, and we're afraid of the wolf."

"Come in," she said. "I'm going to hide you, and you're not to make any noise because my husband is nasty, and he'll eat you."

She did her best to hide them, but the devil, who was the woman's husband, smelled the odor of Christians, and he found them and even beat his wife because she hadn't told him that she had taken in the children. He lifted Jean into his hand, and seeing that he was thin, he decided he would fatten him up, and when he was plump enough, he would kill him.

He locked Jean up in a barn-shed, and the little sister, who had become the servant of the house, brought her brother food to eat. The devil was too large to enter the shed where Jean was locked up, and after some days had passed, he ordered Jeannette to cut the end off Jean's pinky and to bring it to him so that he could see whether Jean was fat enough to be eaten. But Jeannette caught a rat, cut off its tail, brought the end of it to the devil, and told him it was her brother's finger.

"Ah," said the devil, "he's still too thin."

Some time later, he ordered Jeannette to cut another piece of the pinky to see if Jean had become fatter. So, Jeannette showed him another piece of the rat's tail, and once again he found it too thin.

When the devil asked for a piece of Jean's finger a third time, she brought him yet another piece from the rat's tail, but he realized that she was deceiving him. So he stuck his hand into the shed, pulled Jean out, and found that he was fat enough to be eaten. So he set up a sawhorse on which he wanted to bleed Jean. Then the devil put Jean back into the shed and wanted to take a walk, but before doing this, he told his wife to keep watch over Jean and especially Jeannette, whom he distrusted.

However, the devil's wife got drunk and became sleepy. So, Jeannette went to open the shed for the pigs and also let Jean out. Then she pretended not to know how Jean was to be laid out on the sawhorse.

"Are you stupid?" the devil's wife said. "Here's how you do it."

And as soon as she put herself on the sawhorse, Jean tied her on it and cut her throat. Then they took the devil's gold and silver and fled with his horses and carriage.

When the devil returned, he found his wife tied up on the sawhorse and her head cut off beside her. He went to the pigs' shed and was unable to find Jean or Jeannette, nor his horses or carriage. So he set out in search of the two children, and after some time had passed, he met a farmworker and said:

> *Have you seen Jeannette or Jean*
> *along with my carriage so fine and clean,*
> *pulled by my red and white steeds*
> *covered with gold and silver indeed?*

"What are you saying, sir? Do you mean I'm not working good enough?"
"No, you stupid ox!"

> *Have you seen Jeannette or Jean*
> *along with my carriage so fine and clean,*
> *pulled by my red and white steeds*
> *covered with gold and silver indeed?*

"No, sir."
A little further the devil encountered a shepherd who was tending his sheep.

> *Have you seen Jeannette or Jean*
> *along with my carriage so fine and clean,*
> *pulled by my red and white steeds*
> *covered with gold and silver indeed?*

"Are you saying that my dog doesn't bark good enough? Well then, bark Labri! Bark!"

And the dog began to bark at the devil as if it wanted to bite him.

"Stupid beast!" screamed the devil. "I wasn't talking about your dog."

Have you seen Jeannette or Jean
along with my carriage so fine and clean,
pulled by my red and white steeds
covered with gold and silver indeed?

"No, sir."

Now the devil entered a village just when the verger had rung the Angelus.

Have you seen Jeannette or Jean
along with my carriage so fine and clean,
pulled by my red and white steeds
covered with gold and silver indeed?

"What are you saying, sir? Do you think that I'm not ringing the bells with all my might?"

"Imbecile!" replied the devil. "Who said anything about bells?"

Have you seen Jeannette or Jean
along with my carriage so fine and clean,
pulled by my red and white steeds
covered with gold and silver indeed?

"No, sir."

The devil went still further, and he arrived at the bank of a river where some women were washing clothes.

Have you seen Jeannette or Jean
along with my carriage so fine and clean,
pulled by my red and white steeds
covered with gold and silver indeed?

"What are you saying?" asked one of the washerwomen. "That I'm not beating the clothes as I should?"

And she began to beat the clothes on a stone with all her might.

"No, you fool! I asked":

Have you seen Jeannette or Jean
along with my carriage so fine and clean,
pulled by my red and white steeds
covered with gold and silver indeed?

"Yes, sir," said one of the women. "We saw a handsome gentleman and a beautiful girl pass by here in a splendid carriage drawn by two horses."

"Which direction?"

"Toward the river."

But there wasn't a bridge, and the devil was upset because he was unable to cross the river.

Now one of the washerwomen said to the others: "We're dealing with the devil. Let's play a trick on him."

She offered to cut his hair so that he could make a bridge out of it and cross the river. The devil let her do it, and his hair was stretched out in such a way to make a bridge. But when he was in the middle of the bridge, they let the hair fall, and the devil went splash into the water and drowned.

After Jean and Jeannette had returned to their parents, the washerwoman went to them and told them that the devil had drowned. Meanwhile Jean and Jeannette made their parents rich, and everyone was happy. Even when parents have been nasty to their children, one should be good to one's parents.

> Night came.
> The cock sang.
> And the story ended.

The Story about Old Grule (1899)[46]

Marie Kosch

Once upon a time there was a father and a mother who had two children, a girl and a boy. The first was called Gretel, and the boy was called Hans. The children were disobedient, and were often given beatings. One day they would have liked to have gone into the woods to pick strawberries, but their mother said, "You're not to go out today. A storm is coming. So you have to stay at home."

But the children didn't obey. When their mother was occupied by her work, the children took their little baskets from the wall and went into the forest. There they picked strawberries, and they had hardly begun picking when it became dark. A storm arose, and it whipped the trees so violently against each other that the branches flew down. It began to thunder and lightning. Then came a good deal of hail and rain. The children were very scared and regretted that they hadn't obeyed their mother and had remained home. Fortunately they found a cave in the rocks, and they crept inside and waited until the rain had stopped.

When the thunderstorm had passed, they wanted to go home, but—what a shame!—they no longer knew the way. They walked on and on, but they only went deeper and deeper into the forest instead of finding their way out of it. Overcome with fear, they cried out, "Father! Mother!" but no one heard them. It became night, and they realized to their horror that they would have to sleep in the forest.

"You know what, Hans?" Gretel said. "Why don't you climb a tree? You usually like to climb trees. So, look around, and perhaps you'll see a light. Then we can go there." Hans did this, and he actually saw a light in the distance. So, he

---

46. "Von der alten Grule," *Deutsche Volksmärchen aus Mären* (Kremsier: Druck und Commissionsverlag Heinrich Gusek, 1899).

climbed down from the tree, took Gretel by the hand, and led her in the direction of the light he had seen. When they reached that place, they saw a little house from which the light was beaming. When they examined the house more closely, they found that it was completely made of gingerbread. The walls were of gingerbread and the roof of marzipan. They looked around for a ladder, and when they found one, they leaned it against the roof and climbed up. Once on top of the roof, they made themselves comfortable and broke off one marzipan shingle after the other and began eating them, until they had made a large hole in the roof.

A witch called Grule lived in the little house, and she liked to eat children more than anything else. She was just about to go to sleep when she heard some noise on her roof. So she ran outside and said with a deep voice, "Who's robbing my house? Who's robbing my house?"

"The wind, the wind," rang out Gretel's very soft voice.

So the witch calmed down, went back inside and laid down in the bed.

In the meantime the moon had risen, and as the witch put out her light, she noticed a large hole in the roof above her bed and a child's head peering down at her. So, she jumped up, ran outside, tore the children down from the roof, and said, "Just wait, you good-for-nothing brats. I'll teach you what it means to ruin my house. Now you'll stay inside, and I won't let you out." And with these words she stuck them in an empty chicken coop and locked the door.

For the next few days the witch brought the children good meals because she wanted to fatten them so they'd make for a good roast. She brought the children all the things they liked to eat—cake, sweets, fruit, and many other things.

When she thought that the children were fat enough, she took a knife and went with it to the coop. First she went to Gretel and said, "Girl, stick out your little finger."

But Gretel thought, 'No way,' and stuck out her apron string.

Old Grule cut it a little, and said, "Skinny, skinny."

Then she went to Hans and said again, "Boy, stick out your little finger," and Hans held out the string from his pants.

She cut into it just as she had done before and said: "Skinny, skinny," and went away.

Then she thought, 'What should I give the children so that they'll become fat? They won't become fat from good things. So I've got to try something else.' And from then on she gave them nothing but plain pap, and the children soon found all this revolting.

A little time later the witch returned to the coop with a knife and said to Gretel, "Girl, stick out your little finger," and this time Gretel held out her finger. Then Old Grule cut into it a little, and a drop of blood appeared. Then the witch said, "Fat, fat."

Next, she went to Hans and ordered him to stick out his finger as well, and he did it just as Gretel had done. She cut into it too, and when some blood came, she again said, "Fat, fat."

Now the witch went to her kitchen and made a fire in her oven. After it started to simmer, she took a wooden rake and spread the coals evenly across the entire surface of the oven. Soon after she took a wet piece of straw and swept the coals to the front of the oven and took them out. Then she went to the coop, opened it, and said, "Come, children, I have some baked plums in the oven. You can get them out for me."

So the two children ran for joy into the kitchen with Old Grule, thinking that they were finally going to get something to eat other than the eternal plain pap. Once they were there, the witch went to fetch a small oven shovel that the children were to sit on so she could push them into the oven. But while Old Grule was gone, Gretel looked into the oven and saw that there were no plums in it at all. Therefore, when Old Grule ordered her to be the first to sit on the shovel, she pretended to be so clumsy that she fell off. Then she said, "My dear Old Grule, I don't understand how to sit on it. Show me, so I can see how."

Then Old Grule pulled her skirts together, sat down on the shovel, and said, "See. This is how to do it." And as she was sitting in a firm position, Gretel gave a signal to Hans, and with a quick shove, the children pushed the witch into the oven, and Old Grule was miserably burned to death.

Gretel and Hans returned home, and although their parents were very glad that they had returned, they gave their children a good beating for their disobedience because they had already assumed their children had died somewhere.

Why Does the Cuckoo Call "Cuckoo"? The Story of the Little Boy and the Wicked Stepmother (1915)[47]

Moses Gaster

Once upon a time there was a poor man, who had a wife and two children, a boy and a girl. He was so poor that he possessed nothing in the world but the ashes on his hearth. His wife died, and after a time he married another woman, who was cantankerous and bad natured, and from morning till evening, as long as the day lasted, she gave the poor man no peace, but snarled and shouted at him. The woman said to him, "Do away with these children. You cannot even keep me. How then can you keep all these mouths?" For was she not a stepmother?

The poor man stood her nagging for a long time, but then, one night, she quarreled so much that he promised her that he would take the children into the forest and leave them there. The two children were sitting in the corner but held their peace and heard all that was going on.

---

47. *Rumanian Bird and Beast Stories* (London: Folk-Lore Society, 1915).

The next day, the man, taking his ax upon his shoulder, called to the children and said to them, "Come with me into the forest. I am going to cut wood."

The little children went with him, but before they left, the little girl filled her pocket with ashes from the hearth, and as she walked along she dropped little bits of coal the way they went. After a time they reached a very dense part of the forest, where they could not see their way any longer, and there the man said to the children, "Wait here for a while. I am only going to cut wood yonder. When I have done I will come back and fetch you home."

And leaving the children there in the thicket, he went away, heavyhearted, and returned home. The children waited for a while, and seeing that their father did not return, the girl knew what he had done. So they slept through the night in the forest, and the next morning, taking her brother by the hand, she followed the trace of the ashes which she had left on the road, and thus came home to their own house.

When the stepmother saw them, she did not know what to do with herself. She went almost out of her mind with fury. If she could, she would have swallowed them in a spoonful of water, so furious was she. The husband, who was a weakling, tried to pacify her, and to endeavor to get the children away by one means or another, but did not succeed.

When the stepmother found that she could not do anything through her husband, she made up her mind that she herself would get rid of them. So one morning, when her husband had gone away, she took the little boy, and without saying anything to anybody, she killed him and gave him to his sister to cut him up, and prepare a meal for all of them. What was she to do? If she was not to be killed like her brother, she had to do what her stepmother told her.

And so she cut him up and cooked him ready for the meal. But she took the heart, and hid it away in a hollow of a tree. When the stepmother asked her where the heart was, she said that a dog had come and taken it away.

In the evening, when the husband came home, she brought the broth with the meat for the husband to eat, and she sat down and ate of it, and so did the husband, not knowing that he was eating the flesh of his child. The little girl refused to eat it. She would not touch it. After they had finished, she gathered up all the little bones and hid them in the hollow of the tree where she had put the heart.

The next morning, out of that hollow of the tree there came a little bird with dark feathers, and sitting on the branch of a tree, began to sing, "Cuckoo! My sister has cooked me, and my father has eaten me, but I am now a cuckoo and safe from my stepmother."

When the stepmother, who happened to be near the tree, heard what that little bird was singing, in her fury and fright she took a heavy lump of salt which lay near at hand, and threw it at the cuckoo. But instead of hitting it, the lump fell down on her head and killed her on the spot. And the little boy has remained a cuckoo to this very day.

5. DANGEROUS WOLVES AND NAIVE GIRLS

ATU 333—LITTLE RED RIDING HOOD, ALSO CATEGORIZED AS THE GLUTTON

This tale type reflects the remarkable ways that the oral and literary traditions have interacted to produce conflicting versions of the same incident. The incident here is the violation or rape of a young girl who goes into the forest on an errand or to undertake some kind of initiation test. Of course, the motif of rape can be found in many Greco-Roman myths and most pagan cultures, and it is not clear when all the other significant motifs were brought together to form the basic structure of the "Red Riding Hood" tale that was disseminated in Europe. Jan Ziolkowski and Yvonne Verdier have maintained that fragments of this tale, without the red cap, can be found in late-medieval oral tales. In particular, Verdier and two other French folklorists, Paul Delarue and Charles Joisten, have argued that the tale was probably circulating among women during the early part of the seventeenth century in southern France and northern Italy and was told among women in sewing societies. These tales were never titled, and so the red cap (*chaperon*) does not play a role in them.

Delarue published a composite tale made up of several nineteenth-century versions that he called "The Grandmother" in *Le conte populaire français* (Paris: Maisonneuve et Larose, 1985). Here a young peasant woman takes some bread and milk to her grandmother. At a crossroad in the woods, she meets a werewolf, who asks her whether she is going to take the path of the pins or the path of the needles. She generally chooses the path of the needles. He rushes off to the grandmother's house and eats her, but he also puts some of her flesh in a bowl and some of her blood in a bottle before getting into the grandmother's bed. When the girl arrives, the werewolf tells her to refresh herself and eat some meat in the bowl and drink some wine. A cat or something from the fireplace condemns her for eating the flesh of her grandmother and drinking her blood. Sometimes there is a warning. All at once the werewolf asks her to take off her clothes and get into bed with him. She complies, and each time she takes off a piece of her clothing, she asks what she should do with it. The werewolf replies that she should throw it into the fireplace because she won't be needing it anymore. When the girl finally gets into bed, she asks several questions such as "my, how hairy you are, granny," until the customary "my what a big mouth you have, granny." When the wolf announces, "all the better to eat you, my dear," she declares that she has to relieve herself. He tells her to do it in bed. But she indicates that she has to have a bowel movement, and so he ties a rope around her leg and sends her into the courtyard through a window. Once there the smart girl unties the rope and ties it around a plum tree and then runs off toward home. The werewolf becomes impatient and yells, "What are you doing out there, making a load?" Then he runs to the window and realizes that the girl has escaped. He runs after her, but it is too late, and she makes it safely to her home.

It is unclear whether Charles Perrault knew some kind of oral tale like this when he wrote the first literary version in 1697. But it is clear that he must have known some version like this and transformed it into a tale in which a naive bourgeois girl pays for her stupidity and is violated in the end. Both Perrault's tale and the oral folk version became popular in the eighteenth century, and more than likely they began influencing oral and literary stories that gradually became widespread throughout Europe. Today the "Red Riding Hood" tale type is considered one of the most famous fairy tales in the world.

Perrault's tale was translated into English, German, and Russian during the eighteenth century. In 1800, Ludwig Tieck published *Leben und Tod des kleinen Rothkäppchens* (*Life and Death of Little Red Cap*), and he was the first to introduce a hunter, who saves Red Cap's life. The Grimms also felt sympathy for Little Red Cap and followed Tieck's example in their versions. In addition, they added a second didactic part to show that the grandmother and Little Red Cap learned their lesson. Their tale includes two intact segments that were sent to them by two sisters, Jeanette Hassenpflug and Marie Hassenpflug, who were familiar with the Perrault version. The first segment includes the hunter who saves granny and Little Red Riding Hood; the second is similar to a moralistic coda in which Little Red Riding Hood and her granny demonstrate that they have learned their lesson and can defeat the wolf by themselves. Wilhelm made some small but important changes to the 1812 version of the story by the 1857 edition. Basically, he made the tale more didactic and more optimistic.

Following the publication of the Grimms' more optimistic "Little Red Cap," storytellers and writers have chosen either their version or Perrault's tale to adapt in hundreds of different ways, and these two tales have also entered into the oral tradition. As we can see in the small selection of tales from the oral tradition collected by Kopf, Schneller, Sébillot, Bladé, Millien, and Marelle, storytellers have adapted the basic plot in unique ways and have either consciously or unconsciously entered into a discourse about the civilizing process that involves rape, pedophilia, and manners. For more information about the historical background to this tale type, see Jack Zipes' *The Trials and Tribulations of Little Red Riding Hood: Versions of the Tale in Socio-Cultural Context* and Alan Dundes, ed., *Little Red Riding Hood: A Casebook*.

******

Little Red Cap (1812)[48]

Jacob and Wilhelm Grimm

Once upon a time there was a sweet little maiden. Whoever laid eyes upon her couldn't help but love her. But it was her grandmother who could never give the child enough. One time she made her a present, a small, red velvet cap, and since it was so becoming and the maiden always wanted to wear it, she was only called Little Red Cap.

One day her mother said to her: "Come, Little Red Cap, take this piece of cake and bottle of wine and bring them to your grandmother. She's sick and weak, and this will strengthen her. Be nice and good and greet her from me. Go directly there and don't stray from the path, otherwise you'll fall and break the glass, and your grandmother will get nothing."

Little Red Cap promised to obey her mother. Well, the grandmother lived out in the forest, half an hour from the village, and as soon as Little Red Cap entered the forest, she encountered the wolf. However, Little Red Cap did not know what a wicked sort of an animal he was and was not afraid of him.

"Good day, Little Red Cap," he said.

"Thank you kindly, wolf."

"Where are you going so early, Little Red Cap?"

"To grandmother's."

"What are you carrying under your apron?"

"Cake and wine. My grandmother's sick and weak, and yesterday we baked this cake so it will help her get well."

"Where does your grandmother live, Little Red Cap?"

"About a quarter of an hour from here in the forest. Her house is under the three big oak trees. You can tell it by the hazel bushes," said Little Red Cap.

The wolf thought to himself, 'What a juicy morsel she'll be for me! Now, how am I going to catch her?' Then he said, "Listen, Little Red Cap, haven't you seen the beautiful flowers growing in the forest? Why don't you look around? I believe you haven't even noticed how lovely the birds are singing. You march along as if you were going straight to school in the village, and yet it's so delightful out here in the woods!"

Little Red Cap looked around and saw that the sun had broken through the trees and that the woods were full of beautiful flowers. So she thought to herself, 'If I bring grandmother a bunch of flowers, she'd certainly like that. It's still early, and I'll arrive on time.'

So she plunged into the woods to look for flowers. And each time she plucked one, she thought she saw another even prettier flower and ran after it, going

---

48. "Rotkäppchen," *Kinder- und Haus-Märchen. Gesammelt durch die Brüder Grimm*, 2 vols. (Berlin: Realschulbuchandlung, 1812/1815).

deeper and deeper into the forest. But the wolf went straight to the grandmother's house and knocked at the door.

"Who's out there?"

"Little Red Cap. I've brought you some cake and wine. Open up."

"Just lift the latch," the grandmother called. "I'm too weak and can't get up."

The wolf lifted the latch, and the door sprang open. Then he went straight to the grandmother's bed and gobbled her up. Next he took her clothes, put them on along with her nightcap, lay down in her bed, and drew the curtains.

Meanwhile, Little Red Cap had been running around and looking for flowers, and only when she had as many as she could carry did she continue on the way to her grandmother. She was puzzled when she found the door open, and as she entered the room, it seemed so strange inside that she thought, 'Oh, my God, how frightened I feel today, and usually I like to be at grandmother's.' Then she went to the bed and drew back the curtains. There lay her grandmother with her cap pulled down over her face giving her a strange appearance.

"Oh, grandmother, what big ears you have!"

"The better to hear you with."

"Oh, grandmother, what big hands you have!"

"The better to grab you with."

"Oh, grandmother, what a terribly big mouth you have!"

"The better to eat you with!"

No sooner did the wolf say that than he jumped out of bed and gobbled up poor Little Red Cap. After the wolf had the fat chunks in his body, he lay down in bed again, fell asleep, and began to snore very loudly. The huntsman happened to be passing by the house and thought to himself, 'The way the old woman's snoring, you'd better see if something's wrong.' He went into the room, and when he came to the bed, he saw the wolf lying in it. He had been searching for the wolf a long time and thought that the beast had certainly eaten the grandmother. 'Perhaps she can still be saved,' he said to himself. 'I won't shoot.' So he took some scissors and cut open the wolf's belly. After he made a couple of cuts, he saw the little red cap shining forth, and after he made a few more cuts, the girl jumped out and exclaimed, "Oh, how frightened I was! It was so dark in the wolf's body."

Soon the grandmother came out alive. Little Red Cap quickly fetched some large heavy stones, and they filled the wolf's body with them. When he awoke and tried to run away, the stones were so heavy that he fell down at once and died.

All three were delighted. The huntsman skinned the fur from the wolf. The grandmother ate the cake and drank the wine that Little Red Cap brought. And Little Red Cap thought to herself: 'Never again will you stray from the path by yourself and go into the forest when your mother has forbidden it.'

It's also been told that Little Red Cap returned to her grandmother one day to bring some baked goods. Another wolf spoke to her and tried to entice her to leave the path, but this time Little Red Cap was on her guard. She went straight ahead and told her grandmother that she had seen the wolf, that he had wished her good day, but that he had had such a mean look in his eyes that "he would have eaten me if we hadn't been on the open road."

"Come," said the grandmother. "We'll lock the door so he can't get in."

Soon after, the wolf knocked and cried out, "Open up, grandmother. It's Little Red Cap, and I've brought you some baked goods."

But they kept quiet and did not open the door. So the wicked wolf circled the house several times and finally jumped on top of the roof. He wanted to wait till evening when Little Red Cap would go home. He intended to sneak after her and eat her up in the darkness. But the grandmother realized what he had in mind. In front of the house was a big stone trough, and she said to the child, "Fetch the bucket, Little Red Cap. I cooked sausages yesterday. Get the water they were boiled in and pour it into the trough."

Little Red Cap kept carrying the water until she had filled the big, big trough. Then the smell of sausages reached the nose of the wolf. He sniffed and looked down. Finally he stretched his neck so far that he could no longer keep his balance on the roof. He began to slip from the roof and fell right into the big trough and drowned. Then Little Red Cap went happily and safely to her home.

Little Red Cap (1857)[49]
Jacob and Wilhelm Grimm

Once upon a time there was a sweet little maiden. Whoever laid eyes upon her couldn't help but love her. But it was her grandmother who loved her most. She could never give the child enough. One time she made her a present, a small, red velvet cap, and since it was so becoming and the maiden insisted on always wearing it, she was called Little Red Cap.

One day her mother said to her, "Come, Little Red Cap, take this piece of cake and bottle of wine and bring them to your grandmother. She's sick and weak, and this will strengthen her. Get an early start, before it becomes hot, and when you're out in the woods, be nice and good and don't stray from the path, otherwise you'll fall and break the glass, and your grandmother will get nothing. And when you enter her room, don't forget to say good morning, and don't go peeping into all the corners."

"I'll do just as you say," Little Red Cap promised her mother.

Well, the grandmother lived out in the forest, half an hour from the village, and as soon as Little Red Cap entered the forest, she encountered the wolf. However, Little Red Cap didn't know what a wicked sort of an animal he was and was not afraid of him.

---

49. "Rotkäppchen," *Kinder- und Hausmärchen gesammelt durch die Brüder Grimm*, 7th ed., 3 vols. (Göttingen: Verlag der Dieterich'schen Buchhandlung, 1857).

"Good day, Little Red Cap," he said.

"Thank you kindly, wolf."

"Where are you going so early, Little Red Cap?"

"To grandmother's."

"What are you carrying under your apron?"

"Cake and wine. My grandmother's sick and weak, and yesterday we baked this cake so it will help her get well."

"Where does your grandmother live, Little Red Cap?"

"About a quarter of an hour from here in the forest. Her house is under the three big oak trees. You can tell it by the hazel bushes," said Little Red Cap.

The wolf thought to himself, 'This tender young thing is a juicy morsel. She'll taste even better than the old woman. You've got to be real crafty if you want to catch them both.' Then he walked next to Little Red Cap, and after a while he said, "Little Red Cap, just look at the beautiful flowers that are growing all around you! Why don't you look around? I believe you haven't even noticed how lovely the birds are singing. You march along as if you were going straight to school, and yet it's so delightful out here in the woods!"

Little Red Cap looked around and saw how the rays of the sun were dancing through the trees back and forth and how the woods were full of beautiful flowers. So she thought to herself, 'If I bring grandmother a bunch of fresh flowers, she'd certainly like that. It's still early, and I'll arrive on time.'

So she ran off the path and plunged into the woods to look for flowers. And each time she plucked one, she thought she saw another even prettier flower and ran after it, going deeper and deeper into the forest. But the wolf went straight to the grandmother's house and knocked at the door.

"Who's out there?"

"Little Red Cap. I've brought you some cake and wine. Open up."

"Just lift the latch," the grandmother called. "I'm too weak and can't get up."

The wolf lifted the latch, and the door sprang open. Then he went straight to the grandmother's bed without saying a word and gobbled her up. Next he put on her clothes and her nightcap, lay down in her bed, and drew the curtains.

Meanwhile, Little Red Cap had been running around and looking for flowers, and only when she had as many as she could carry did she remember her grandmother and continue on the way to her house again. She was puzzled when she found the door open, and as she entered the room, it seemed so strange inside that she thought, 'Oh, my God, how frightened I feel today, and usually I like to be at grandmother's.' She called out, "Good morning!" But she received no answer. Next she went to the bed and drew back the curtains. There lay her grandmother with her cap pulled down over her face giving her a strange appearance.

"Oh, grandmother, what big ears you have!"

"The better to hear you with."

"Oh, grandmother, what big hands you have!"

"The better to grab you with."

"Oh, grandmother, what a terribly big mouth you have!"

"The better to eat you with!"

No sooner did the wolf say that than he jumped out of bed and gobbled up poor Little Red Cap. After the wolf had satisfied his desires, he lay down in bed again, fell asleep, and began to snore very loudly. The huntsman happened to be passing by the house and thought to himself, 'The way the old woman's snoring, you'd better see if something's wrong.' He went into the room, and when he came to the bed, he saw the wolf lying in it.

"So, I've found you at last, you old sinner," said the huntsman. "I've been looking for you a long time."

He took aim with his gun, and then it occurred to him that the wolf could have eaten the grandmother and that she could still be saved. So he did not shoot but took some scissors and started cutting open the sleeping wolf's belly. After he made a couple of cuts, he saw the little red cap shining forth, and after he made a few more cuts, the girl jumped out and exclaimed, "Oh, how frightened I was! It was so dark in the wolf's body."

Soon the grandmother came out. She was alive but could hardly breathe. Little Red Cap quickly fetched some large stones, and they filled the wolf's body with them. When he awoke and tried to run away, the stones were too heavy so he fell down at once and died.

All three were delighted. The huntsman skinned the fur from the wolf and went home with it. The grandmother ate the cake and drank the wine that Little Red Cap brought, and soon she regained her health. Meanwhile Little Red Cap thought to herself, 'Never again will you stray from the path by yourself and go into the forest when your mother has forbidden it.'

******

There is also another tale about how Little Red Cap returned to her grandmother one day to bring some baked goods. Another wolf spoke to her and tried to entice her to leave the path, but this time Little Red Cap was on her guard. She went straight ahead and told her grandmother that she had seen the wolf, that he had wished her good day, but that he had had such a mean look in his eyes that "he would have eaten me if we hadn't been on the open road."

"Come," said the grandmother. "We'll lock the door so he can't get in."

Soon after, the wolf knocked and cried out, "Open up, grandmother. It's Little Red Cap, and I've brought you some baked goods."

But they kept quiet and did not open the door. So Grayhead circled the house several times and finally jumped on top of the roof. He wanted to wait till evening when Little Red Cap would go home. He intended to sneak after her and eat her up in the darkness. But the grandmother realized what he had in mind.

In front of the house was a big stone trough, and she said to the child, "Fetch the bucket, Little Red Cap. I cooked sausages yesterday. Get the water they were boiled in and pour it into the trough."

Little Red Cap kept carrying the water until she had filled the big, big trough. Then the smell of sausages reached the nose of the wolf. He sniffed and looked down. Finally he stretched his neck so far that he could no longer keep his balance on the roof. He began to slip and fell right into the big trough and drowned. Then Little Red Cap went merrily on her way home, and no one harmed her.

Little Red Hood (1863)[50]

H. Kopf

Once upon a time, there was a little darling damsel, whom everybody loved that looked upon her, but her old granny loved her best of all and didn't know what to give the dear child for love. Once she made her a hood of red samite, and since it became her granddaughter so well, the girl would wear nothing else on her head. So people gave her the name of "Red Hood."

Once her mother said to Red Hood, "Go. Here is a slice of cake and a bottle of wine; carry them to old granny. She is ill and weak, and they will refresh her. But be pretty behaved, and don't peep about in all corners when you come into her room, and don't forget to say 'Good-day.' Also, walk prettily, and don't go off the road, otherwise you will fall and break the bottle, and then poor granny will have nothing."

Red Hood said, "I will observe everything well that you have told me," and gave her mother her hand upon it.

But granny lived out in a forest, half an hour's walk from the village. When Red Hood went into the forest, she met a wolf. But she did not know what a wicked beast he was, and was not afraid of him.

"God help you, Red Hood!" said he.

"God bless you, wolf!" replied she.

"Whither so early, Red Hood?"

"To granny."

"What have you there under your mantle?"

"Cake and wine. We baked yesterday; old granny must have a good meal for once, and strengthen herself therewith."

"Where does your granny live, Red Hood?"

"A good quarter of an hour's walk further in the forest, under yon three large oaks. There stands her house; further beneath are the nut trees, which you will see there," said Red Hood.

---

50. "Cerwjenawka," in Albert Henry Wratislaw, *Sixty Folk-Tales from Exclusively Slavonic Sources* (Boston: Houghton, Mifflin, 1890).

The wolf thought within himself, 'This nice young damsel is a rich morsel. She will taste better than the old woman; but you must trick her cleverly, that you may catch both.'

For a time he went by Red Hood's side. Then said he, "Red Hood! Just look! There are such pretty flowers here! Why don't you look round at them all? Methinks you don't even hear how delightfully the birds are singing! You are as dull as if you were going to school, and yet it is so cheerful in the forest!"

Little Red Hood lifted up her eyes, and when she saw how the sun's rays glistened through the tops of the trees, and every place was full of flowers, she bethought herself, 'If I bring with me a sweet smelling nosegay to granny, it will cheer her. It is still so early, that I shall come to her in plenty of time,' and therewith she skipped into the forest and looked for flowers. And when she had plucked one, she fancied that another further off was nicer, and ran there, and went always deeper and deeper into the forest.

But the wolf went by the straight road to old granny's, and knocked at the door.

"Who's there?"

"Little Red Hood, who has brought cake and wine. Open!"

"Only press the latch," cried granny. "I am so weak that I cannot stand."

The wolf pressed the latch, walked in, and went without saying a word straight to granny's bed and ate her up. Then he took her clothes, dressed himself in them, put her cap on his head, lay down in her bed, and drew the curtains.

Meanwhile little Red Hood was running after flowers, and when she had so many that she could not carry any more, she bethought her of her granny, and started on the way to her. It seemed strange to her that the door was wide open, and when she entered the room everything seemed to her so peculiar that she thought, 'Ah! My God! How strange I feel today, and yet at other times I am so glad to be with granny!'

She said, "Good-day!" but received no answer. Thereupon she went to the bed and drew back the curtains. There lay granny, with her cap drawn down to her eyes, and looking so queer!

"Ah, granny! Why have you such long ears?"

"The better to hear you."

"Ah, granny! Why have you such large eyes?"

"The better to see you."

"Ah, granny! Why have you such large hands?"

"The better to take hold of you."

"But, granny! Why have you such a terribly large mouth?"

"The better to eat you up!"

And therewith the wolf sprang out of bed at once on poor little Red Hood and ate her up. When the wolf had satisfied his appetite, he lay down again in the bed, and began to snore tremendously.

A huntsman came past and bethought himself, 'How can an old woman snore like that? I'll just have a look to see what it is.'

He went into the room and looked into the bed; there lay the wolf. "Have I found you now, old rascal?" said he. "I've long been looking for you."

He was just going to take aim with his gun, when he bethought himself, 'Perhaps the wolf has only swallowed granny, and she may yet be released.'

Therefore he did not shoot, but took a knife and began to cut open the sleeping wolf's maw. When he had made several cuts, he saw a red hood gleam, and after one or two more cuts out skipped Red Hood and cried, "Oh, how frightened I have been; it was so dark in the wolf's maw!"

Afterwards out came old granny, still alive, but scarcely able to breathe. But Red Hood made haste and fetched large stones, with which they filled the wolf's maw, and when he woke, he wanted to jump up and run away, but the stones were so heavy that he fell on the ground and beat himself to death.

Now, they were all three merry. The huntsman took off the wolf's skin; granny ate the cake and drank the wine which little Red Hood had brought, and became strong and well again; and little Red Hood thought to herself, 'As long as I live, I won't go out of the road into the forest, when mother has forbidden me.'

Translated by Henry Wratislaw.

Little Red Hat (1867)[51]
Christian Schneller

There once was an old woman who had a granddaughter by the name of Little Red Hat. One day, as they were in the field, the old woman said: "I'm going home now, and I want you to come later and bring me some soup."

After a while Little Red Hat set out for home, too, and met the ogre who said, "Oh, where are you going, my pretty Little Red Hat?"

"I'm taking this soup to my grandmother."

"Good," he responded. "I'll come along, too. But which path are you taking? The path over the stones or the path over the thorns?"

"I'm taking the path over the stones," said the maiden.

"Well, I'll take the path over the thorns," the ogre said.

They went off. But along the way Little Red Hat came to a meadow, where many beautiful and colorful flowers were blooming. The maiden began picking as many as her heart desired. Meanwhile the ogre rushed ahead and, even though he had to walk over thorns, he arrived at the grandmother's house before Little Red Hat. He went inside, struck the grandmother dead, ate her, and lay down himself in the bed. Before he did this, however, he hung the grandmother's entrails in place of the latch string on the door and put her blood, teeth, and jaws

51. "Das Rothütchen," *Märchen und Sagen aus Wälschtirol* (Innsbruck: Verlag der Wagner'schen Universitäts-Buchhandlung, 1867).

in the kitchen cupboard. No sooner was he in bed than Little Red Hat came and knocked on the door.

"Come in," the ogre called out with a muffled voice.

Little Red Hat tried to open the door, but when she noticed that she was pulling on something soft, she cried out: "Oh, how soft this thing is, grandma!"

"Just pull and keep quiet. They're the entrails of your grandmother!"

"What did you say?"

"Just pull and keep quiet!"

Little Red Hat pulled the door open, entered, and said: "Grandma, I'm hungry!"

"Just go to the cupboard," the ogre answered. "There must still be a little rice."

Little Red Hat went over to the cupboard and took out the teeth.

"Oh, how hard this thing is, grandma!"

"Eat and keep quiet. They're your grandmother's teeth!"

"What did you say?"

"Eat and keep quiet!"

After a while Little Red Hat said, "I'm still hungry, grandma!"

"Just go to the cupboard," the ogre replied. "You'll find a sandwich with chopped meat."

Little Red Hat went to the cupboard and took out the jaws.

"Oh, how red this thing is, grandma!"

"Eat and keep quiet. They're your grandmother's jaws!"

After a while Little Red Hat said again: "Grandma, I'm thirsty!"

"Just look in the cupboard," the ogre responded. "There must be a little wine there!"

Little Red Hat went and took out the blood.

"Oh, how red this wine is, grandma!"

"Drink and keep quiet! It's your grandmother's blood!"

"What did you say?"

"Just drink and keep quiet!"

After a little while Little Red Hat said, "Grandma, I'm sleepy!"

"Get undressed and get into bed with me," replied the ogre.

Little Red Hat got into bed and noticed something hairy.

"Oh, how hairy you are, grandma!"

"That's because I'm old," replied the ogre.

"Oh, what long legs you have, grandmother!"

"That comes from walking."

"Oh, what long hands you have, grandma!"

"That comes from working."

"Oh, what long ears you have, grandma!"

"That comes from listening!"

"Oh, what a large mouth you have, grandma!"

"That comes from eating children!" the ogre responded and *gulp!*—he swallowed Little Red Hat in one bite.

Mr. and Mrs. Rat (1878)[52]

Paul Sébillot

The rat and his fiancée got married, and after the wedding, the rat said to his wife: "Are you going out or are you going to remain at home?"

"I'm going to remain home to cook while you work outside."

"Very well," he said. "Call me at noon."

As she made some porridge with black wheat, Mrs. Rat fell into the saucepan and burned herself so badly that she died. When her husband heard the clock sound noon, then one, then two in the afternoon, and finally three, he returned home and was very worried. As soon as he saw that his wife was dead, he began to weep.

A good woman who encountered him asked him why he was so upset.

"It's because my wife has died," he responded.

"I'm going to start singing," the woman said, and she sang a song in a high voice.

On learning about this news, the table began to dance; the place, to sweep itself; and the door, to unhinge and hinge itself. The cart set off running down the road, and it met a good fellow who was heating his oven and asked the cart why it was so joyful.

"It's because Mrs. Rat has died," it said. "The good woman has begun to sing, the table to dance, the place to sweep itself, the door to unhinge and hinge itself, and I'm running down the road."

"Well, if that's the way it is," said the good fellow, "I'm going to throw the skin into the oven."

"And me," his good wife added, "I'm going to throw the pastry to the dogs."

"What's the matter?" asked a little girl who was passing by there.

"Haven't you heard the news? Mrs. Rat has died. The old woman is singing; the table is dancing; the place is sweeping itself; the door is unhinging and hinging itself; the cart is running down the road. The good fellow has thrown the skin into the oven, and I've thrown the pastry to the dogs."

"Ah!" said the little girl. "You should give me a tiny little pie for my grandmother Jeanette, who hasn't eaten one for seven years."

She took the tiny little pie, and came across a hare who asked her if he could eat it. She refused and said that she was carrying the pie to her grandmother Jeanette, who hadn't eaten a pie for seven years.

A little later she saw a wolf approaching who also asked permission to taste the pie. The little girl refused and told the wolf that she was keeping her tiny little pie for her grandmother Jeanette, who hadn't eaten any for seven years.

---

52.   "Le rat et la ratesse," *Littérature orale de la Haute-Bretagne* (Paris: Maisonneuve, 1881).

"Where does she live?" he asked.

"At the village over there," the child responded.

"Are you taking the path through the woods or the highway?"

"The path because the highway is too muddy."

The wolf ran and quickly arrived at the house and gobbled the good woman, took her clothes, and got into bed. When the little girl entered the house, she said: "Grandma Jeanette, I've come to bring you a tiny little pie."

"Very good," the wolf responded.

"Grandma, they've told me that I should make a soup for you."

"Very good."

"Grandma, my parents told me to see if you have lice in your head." Then the girl cried out, "Ah! You have very rough hair!"

"It's due to old age, my child."

"What big teeth you have!"

"All the better to eat you with," the wolf said, and upon saying these words, he gobbled her up."

Told by Constant Jouland (Gosmé). Translated into French by Paul Sébillot.

Little Red Riding Hood: Version of Tourangelle (1885)[53]

M. Légot

The heroine of this tale is called Little Jeanette or Fillon-Fillette, that is, a girl somewhat like a Tomboy.

Once upon a time there was a little girl living in good condition in the country, and she heard that her grandmother was sick. So, the next day she set out to see her. But when she had gone quite far and reached a crossroad, she didn't know which path to take. She encountered a very ugly man who was leading a pig, and she asked him which path she should take and told him that she was on her way to visit her sick grandmother.

"You should take the path on the left," he said to her. "It's better because it's shorter, and you'll soon get there."

The little girl went off on that path, but it was the longer one and bad. It took her a very long time for her to arrive at her grandmother's house. Indeed, she had a great deal of trouble getting there and arrived late.

In the meantime, while Jeannette had been slowed down by the mud on the longer path, the nasty man, who had just given her bad directions, took the short good path and arrived at the grandmother's house long before the girl did. He killed the poor woman and poured her blood into a bottle, stuck it in the cupboard, and got into bed.

When the little girl arrived at her grandmother's house, she knocked at the door, opened it, entered, and said: "How are you doing, grandma?"

---

53. "Le Petit Chaperon Rouge: Version Tourangelle," *Revue de L'Avranchin* 9 (1885): 90–91.

"Not well, my daughter," responded the good-for-nothing who gave the impression that he was suffering and disguised his voice. "Are you hungry?"

"Yes, grandma. What's there to eat?"

"There's some blood in the cupboard. Take the pan and fry it. Then eat it up."

The little girl obeyed.

While she was frying the blood, she heard some voices that sounded like those of angels coming from the top of the chimney, and they said: "Ah! Cursed be the little girl who's frying the blood of her grandmother!"

"What are those voices saying, grandmother, those voices that are singing from the chimney?"

"Don't listen to them, my daughter, those are just little birds singing in their own language."

And the little girl continued frying the blood of her grandmother. But the voices began once more to sing: "Ah, what a nasty scamp frying the blood of her grandmother!"

Well then, Jeannette said, "Grandmother, I'm not hungry. I don't want to eat this blood."

"All right! Come to bed, my daughter. Come to bed."

Jeannette went over to the nearby bed, and when she was there, she cried out: "What big arms you have!"

"All the better to hug you, my daughter. All the better to hug you."

"Ah! Grandmother, what long legs you have!"

"All the better to walk, my daughter. All the better to walk."

"Ah! Grandmother, what big eyes you have!"

"All the better to see you, my daughter. All the better to see you."

"Ah! Grandmother, what big teeth you have!"

"All the better to eat, my daughter. All the better to eat."

Jeannette became scared and said: "Ah! Grandmother, I've got the urge to go."

"Do it in bed, my daughter. Do it in bed."

"It would be too dirty, grandma! If you're afraid that I might run off, tie a rope around my leg. If you're bothered that I'm outside too long, just pull on the rope, and you can assure yourself that I'm still there."

"You're right, my daughter. You're right."

So the monster tied a rope around Jeannette's leg and held on to the end of the rope in his hand. When the little girl was outside, she tore the rope and ran off. A short time thereafter the false grandmother said: "Are you done, Jeannette? Are you done?"

And the same voices of the little angels that had sung from the top of the chimney responded: "Not yet, grandma! Not yet!"

After he waited a long time, the voices rang out: "I've done it."

The monster pulled the rope, but there was no one at the other end.

The wicked devil got up and was enraged. He climbed on his large pig that he had put on top of the grass roof, and he set out after the young girl to catch her. When he arrived at a river where the washerwomen were washing clothes, he said:

> "Have you seen that Tomboy girl[54]
> With a dog wagging its tail
> Tagging along on this trail?"

"Yes," the washerwomen said. "We draped a sheet on the water and spread it out so that she could cross."

"Ah," the wicked man said. "Spread out a sheet so I can cross."

The washerwomen spread out a sheet on the water, and the devil started to cross on his pig. When the pig plunged ahead, the devil cried out: "Lap, lap! Lap up the water, lap, my great pig. If you don't lap, the two of us will drown!"

But the pig wasn't able to lap up the water, and the devil drowned with his pig, and the Tomboy girl was saved.

This version was collected in Touraine by M. Légot and was first published in Revue de L'Avranchin *in 1885.*

The Wolf and the Child (1886)[55]

Jean-François Bladé

Once upon a time there was a man and a woman whose only child was a five-year-old boy. One day, this child said to his mother: "Mother, let me go all alone to my aunt's house."

"No, my friend, you're still too little to go there all alone. You'd have to go through a large forest, and the wolf would eat you."

Then the child began to cry.

"Mother, I'm telling you, I want to go there. I know all the paths in the large forest, and the wolf won't eat me."

"Very well, my friend! Since you want this so much, go, and may the Good Lord protect you from evil."

So the child departed all by himself. When he came to the middle of the large forest, he encountered the wolf dressed as a parish priest pretending to be reading his breviary.

"Good day, father."

"Good day, my friend. Where are you going?"

"I'm going to my aunt's house, father."

---

54. *Fillon fillette.*

55. "Le Loup et l'enfant," *Contes populaires de la Gascogne*, 3 vols. (Paris: Maisonneuve frères et Ch. Leclerc, 1886).

"And where does your aunt live, my friend?"

"She lives over there, father, right at the end of the large forest, where there's a small farm."

"Oh! That good woman! I know her well. She's one of my parishioners. Twice a year she brings me a pair of fat capons. Please give her my regards."

"I'll certainly do that, father."

The child continued to follow his path, and the wolf pretended to read his breviary.

'Good!' the wolf thought, 'I'll go and eat the aunt and the nephew.'

He immediately took off the priest's clothes and dashed off toward the small farm.

"Knock, knock!"

"Who's there?"

"It's your nephew, my aunt."

"Pull the little string, and the latch will lift."

So the wolf pulled the little string, pounced on the poor old woman, and devoured her without leaving anything except for a glass of blood. Once that was done he put on the dead woman's bonnet and got into bed. He was hardly in bed when the child knocked at the door.

"Knock, knock!"

"Who's there?"

"It's your nephew, my aunt."

"Pull the little string, and the latch will lift."

The child entered the room.

"Good day, my aunt."

"Good day, my friend. You must be weary. Drink some of the wine in the glass that's on the table. It's a new wine. I just opened the bottle. Now, come and get into bed with me."

The child undressed and got into bed.

"Oh, my God! How hairy your legs are, my aunt!"

"It's old age, my friend."

"Oh, my God! How shiny your eyes are, my aunt!"

"All the better to see you!"

"Oh, my God! What big teeth you have, my aunt!"

"All the better to smash you to bits, my friend."

So, the wolf strangled the child and ate him.

Little Red Riding Hood: Version 1 (1887)[56]

Achille Millien

Once upon a time there was a woman whose only child was a good and dauntless little girl. Every week, on the day that woman baked bread, she made

---

56. "Le Petit Version Rouge: Version I de Nièvre," *Mélusine* (1887).

a little loaf and said to her child: "Go and carry this little loaf of bread to your grandmother."

"Yes, mama," the little girl responded, and she would go off to her grand-mother's house located in the neighboring village.

One day, while she was on the path with the little loaf of bread in her basket, she met the wolf at a crossroad, and he asked: "Where are you going, my little one?"

At first she was frightened by the sight of the wolf, but she didn't worry because she heard some woodcutters working in the forest and responded nicely: "I'm taking this little loaf of bread to my grandmother who lives in the first house of the village over there."

"Which path are you going to take, the path of needles or the path of pins?"

"I'm taking the path of pins that I usually follow."

"Very well! Have a nice trip, my little one!"

And while the girl took the path of the pins, the wolf departed on the trail of the needles. After he arrived at the grandmother's house, he surprised her and killed her. Then he poured the pour woman's blood into some bottles on the dresser and put her flesh into a large pot in front of the fireplace. Afterward he got into the bed. Just as he was drawing the curtains and getting under the cover, he heard a knocking at the door. It was the little girl who had arrived and entered.

"Good day, grandma."

"Good day, my child."

"Is it because you're sick that you're in bed?"

"I'm a little exhausted, my child."

"I've brought you some bread. Where should I put it?"

"Put it in the arch, my child. Warm yourself. Take some of the meat that's in the pot and some of the wine in the bottle on the dresser. Eat and drink. Then come and get into my bed."

The little girl ate and drank with a hearty appetite.

The house cat, however, passed through the cat flap and said: "You're eating the flesh and drinking the blood of your grandmother, my child!"

"Did you hear what the cat said, grandma?"

"Take a stick and chase it out of the house."

But no sooner than it had disappeared the cock cried out in its turn: "You're eating the flesh and drinking the blood of your grandmother, my child!"

"Grandma, did you hear the cock?"

"Take a stick and chase it out of the house. . . . And now that you've had something to eat, come and lay down beside me."

The child began to undress and took off her apron.

"Where should I put my apron, grandma?"

"Throw it into the fire. Tomorrow we'll buy you a new one."

"Where should I put my kerchief?"

"Throw it into the fire. Tomorrow we'll buy you another one."

"Where should I put my dress?"

"Throw it into the fire . . . and come quickly to bed."

The little girl approached the bed and slipped into it.

"Ah, grandma, how hairy you are!"

"It's to keep me warm, my child."

"What large feet you have?"

"All the better to walk, my child."

"What large ears!"

"All the better to hear."

"What large eyes!"

"All the better to see."

"What a large mouth!"

"All the better to swallow you!"

And, as he said that, the wolf pounced on the poor little girl and devoured her.

Told by Marie Rougelot at Murlin in the canton of La Charité (Nièvre). Translated into French by Achille Millien.

Little Red Riding Hood: Version 2 (1887)[57]
Achille Millien

A little girl is carrying a loaf of hotly baked bread and a bottle of milk to her grandmother when she encounters bzou, the werewolf, who hurries off to the grandmother's house while the girl begins to amuse herself by gathering needles. Everything happens as in the first version. However, the cock does not play a role in this one. It is only the cat, squatting in front of the oven, who says to the little girl: "A slut is she who eats the flesh and drinks the blood of her grandmother!"

When the little girl gets undressed and gets into the bed next to the bzou, his large eyes and teeth frighten her. In order to save herself she pretends that she must leave.

"Grandma, I have to go outside."

"No, stay here, my child."

"Grandma, I'm sick. I must go outside for a moment."

The bzou takes a rope and ties it around one of the girl's feet and holds on to the other end.

"Go outside, and come back quickly."

The little girl gets out of the bed, leaves the room, and after tying the rope around the trunk of a plum tree, she runs off as fast as she can.

The bzou becomes impatient.

57. "Le Petit Chaperon Rouge: Version II de Nièvre," *Mélusine* (1887).

"Come back quickly, my child . . . come back or I'll come and get you."

He pulls the rope that resists and doesn't suspect the ruse. But, when there is no response, he jumps out of the bed and runs to the door. Furious at being duped, he rushes after the girl.

At the crossroad of the paths he sees that she is already approaching her mother's house and begins to gallop after her like a madman. With his mouth wide open, he is about to seize her when the girl places her hand on the latch and cries out: "Mama!"

And the bzou retreats without asking anything more.

Told by François Briffault at Montigny-aux-Amognes (Nièvre). Translated into French by Achille Millien.

The Little Girl and the Wolf (1887)[58]
Achille Millien

Once upon a time there was a woman who had a little girl.

"I'm going to make a loaf of bread for your grandmother," she said to her daughter, "and then I'm going to put a little cream in a small jar. I want you to carry all this to your grandmother."

When the little girl had gone some distance, she encountered the wolf who said to her: "Where are you going, my little one?"

"I'm carrying a small loaf of bread with a little cream to my grandmother."

"What path are you taking?"

"I'm going to take the path of needles, and along the way I'll gather needles with large holes for my grandmother because she doesn't see clearly anymore."

"Well, I'm going to take the path of pins."

The wolf was the first to arrive. He ate the grandmother and then put her head on a plate and poured her blood into a bottle and placed them on the chest.

When the little girl was there, he said to her: "Eat and afterward, come and lie down beside me. Eat the meat that's on the chest."

"I don't want to eat your meat. It's not cooked."

"Drink the wine."

"Your wine's no good either."

"Come and get into bed."

When she saw her grandmother in the bed, she said: "I really have to go and make pee-pee. I've got to go outside."

"Before making pee-pee, come closer to me."

When she was closer to the grandmother, she said: "Oh grandma, how hairy you are!"

"All the better to keep myself warm, my child."

---

58. "La petite fille et le loup," collected by Achille Millien in 1887.

"Oh, grandmother, what big ears you have!"

"All the better to hear, my child."

"Oh grandma, what big teeth you have!"

"All the better to eat," my child."

"Oh, my poor grandma! I've really got to go pee-pee. Tie a piece of rope around my foot if you're afraid that I'll run off and save myself."

When she was outside, she cut the rope and tied it around a piece of wood.

Then the wolf became angry that she had not returned. He got up out of the bed and ran into the courtyard. When he saw what she had done, he began running after her.

She arrived at her mother's house where there were three stairs. She was on the last one when the wolf reached the first. Then she managed to fall through the door right as it closed, and the wolf remained outside.

Told by Mme Maillot in Glux. Translated into French by Achille Millien.

The True History of Little Golden-Hood (1888)[59]
Charles Marelle

You know the tale about poor Little Red Riding-Hood, whom the wolf deceived and devoured, the girl with her cake, her little jar of butter, and her grandmother. Well, as we know today, the true story happened quite differently. First of all, the little girl was called and is still called Little Golden-Hood; secondly, she wasn't the one, nor was it her good grandmother, but the wicked wolf who was caught and devoured in the end.

Just listen.

The story begins somewhat like the tale.

There was once a little country girl, pretty and nice as a star in its season. Her real name was Blanchette, but she was more often called Little Golden-Hood because of her marvelous little cloak with a hood, gold- and fire-colored that she always wore. This little hood was given to her by her grandmother, who was so ancient that she no longer knew her age. It was supposed to bring her good luck, she said, for it was made of a ray of sunshine. And since the good old woman was considered something of a witch, everyone thought that the little hood was somewhat bewitched, too.

And so it was, as you will see.

One day the mother said to the child, "Let's see, my Little Golden-Hood, if you already know how to find your way by yourself. You're going to take this good piece of cake to your grandmother for a Sunday treat tomorrow. You're to ask her how she is, and then you're to return right away without stopping to chatter along the way with people you don't know. Do you understand?"

---

59.   "La Veritable Histoire du Petit Chaperon Rouge," *Affenschwanz. Variantes orales de contes populaires et étrangers* (Braunschweig: Westermann, 1888).

"I understand very well," replied Blanchette cheerfully. And off she went with the cake, quite proud of her errand.

But the grandmother lived in another village, and she had to cross through a large forest before arriving there. At a turning point on the path who happened to be walking there all of a sudden but the neighbor[60] wolf.

He had seen the child leave alone, and the villain had been waiting to devour her when he perceived some woodcutters right at that moment. Since they might have caught sight of him, he changed his mind. Instead of jumping on Blanchette, he came up to her wagging his tail like a good dog.

"It's you, my nice Little Golden-Hood," he said.

So the little girl stopped to talk with the wolf, and she didn't even know him.

"You know me, then?" she said to him. "And you, what's your name?"

"My name's wolf, your neighbor. And where are you going like this, my pretty one, with your little basket on your arm?"

"I'm going to my grandmother's house and am bringing her a good piece of cake for her Sunday treat tomorrow."

"And where does she live, your grandmother?"

"She lives at the other side of the forest in the first house of the village, near the windmill. I'm sure you know it well."

"Ah, yes! I know now," said the wolf. "Well, that's just where I'm going. I'll get there before you, no doubt, since you have such little legs, and I'll tell her you're coming to see her. Then she'll expect you."

Upon saying this, the wolf cut though the forest, and in five minutes he arrived at the grandmother's house where he knocked at the door: toc, toc.

No answer.

He knocked louder.

Nobody.

So, he stood up on his hind legs, put his two forepaws on the latch, and the door opened.

Not a soul in the house.

The old woman had got up early to sell herbs in the village, and she had departed in such haste that she had left her bed unmade with her large nightcap on the pillow.

'Good!' the wolf said to himself, 'I know exactly what I'll do.'

He shut the door, pulled on the grandmother's nightcap down to his eyes, lay down with his entire body in the bed, and drew the curtains.

In the meantime the good Blanchette continued to walk calmly on her way, as little girls do, amusing herself here and there by picking Easter daisies, watching the little birds making their nests, and running after the butterflies which fluttered in the sunshine.

---

60. *Compère.*

Finally she arrived at the door.

Toc, toc.

"Who's there?" said the wolf, softening his rough voice as best he could.

"It's me, grandma, your Little Golden-Hood. I've brought you a good piece of cake for your Sunday treat tomorrow."

"Press your finger on the latch, then push, my kitten."

So, Blanchette put her finger on the latch and the door opened.

"Why, you've got a cold, grandma," she said as she entered.

"Ahem! a little, a little . . ." replied the wolf, pretending to cough. "Shut the door well, my little lamb. Put your basket on the table, and then take off your dress and come and lie down beside me. You can rest a while."

The good child undressed—but keep this in mind!—she kept her little hood on her head . . .

When she saw the figure that her grandmother cut in bed, the poor little thing was very surprised.

"Oh!" she cried, "you look very much like our neighbor the wolf, grandma!"

"That's because of my bonnet, my child," replied the wolf.

"Oh! What hairy arms you've got, grandma!"

"All the better to hug you, my child."

"Oh! What a big tongue you've got, grandma!"

"All the better to respond to people, my child."

"Oh! What a mouthful of great white teeth you have, grandma!"

"That's for crunching little children!"

And the wolf opened his jaws wide to swallow Blanchette. . . .

But she lowered her head crying out "Mamma! Mamma!" and the wolf only caught her little hood.

As soon as that happened, he backed down wailing "Ow! Ow!" and shaking his jaw as if he had swallowed red-hot coals.

It was the little fire-colored hood that had burnt his tongue right down his throat.

You see, the little hood was one of those caps, one of those magic hoods, that they used to have once upon a time in the stories and were used for making oneself invisible or invulnerable.

So there was the wolf with his throat burnt. He jumped off the bed and tried to find the door, howling and howling as if all the dogs in the country were at his heels.

Just at this moment the grandmother arrived. She was returning from the village with her long sack empty on her shoulder.

"Ah, you robber!" she cried. "Just you wait!"

She quickly opened her sack across the door, and the panic-stricken wolf sprang in head first.

It was now he that was trapped and swallowed like a letter in the post. And the brave old woman tied her sack right away and ran and emptied it in the well, where the rogue, still howling, tumbled down and was drowned.

"Ah, you rascal! You thought you'd munch my little grandchild! Well, tomorrow we will make her a muff of your skin, and you yourself will be munched because we'll give your carcass to the dogs."

Upon saying this, the grandmother ran to dress poor Blanchette, who was still trembling with fear in the bed.

"Well," she said to her, "without my little hood where would you be now, my sweet?"

And, to get her back on her feet and encourage her, she had her eat a good piece of the cake and drink a good shot of wine. Then she took her by the hand and led her back to the house.

And then, who was it who gave Blanchette a good scolding when she learned what had happened? It was her mother.

But Blanchette promised over and over again that she would never again stop to listen to a wolf, so that her mother finally forgave her.

And Blanchette, the Little Golden-Hood, kept her word. And when the weather's good, she may still be seen even now in the fields with her pretty little hood, the color of the sun.

But to see her you must rise early.

6.   THE FRUITFUL SLEEP
ATU 410—SLEEPING BEAUTY

The general format of this tale type involves a childless king and queen who want to produce an heir. Unexpectedly, an animal/reptile announces that the queen will soon give birth, and when she does, she has a baby girl. Fairies/wise women are invited to the celebration/baptism, but one of them is forgotten. Out of revenge for the slight, this fairy/wise woman curses the tiny princess: she will stick herself with a spindle when she turns fifteen and then die. But one of the other fairies/ wise women softens the curse by "allowing" the girl to sleep for a hundred years and then wake up. Many valiant princes and knights try to rescue her before the time expires, but they die because they cannot break through the thorn hedge surrounding the castle in which the sleeping beauty lies. After one hundred years pass, a prince arrives to save her. The Grimms' version is the only one in which the prince kisses her so that she will awaken. In most other versions she is saved by a magic potion. Sometimes a poison girdle or splinter must be removed from her body. In addition, there is generally a second plot in which the prince's mother/king's mother tries to kill the sleeping beauty and her children. Instead, the mother is punished by her son.

Motifs of this tale can be found in the Greek myth about Thalia, the Nordic Edda, and in Marie de France's lais. There is little indication that there was an oral tradition of "sleeping beauties" in the medieval period. The first formation of the tale was probably in the fourteenth-century French prose romance *Perceforest*, which contains an episode entitled "L'histoire de Troylus et de la belle Zellandine." The romance was composed by an anonymous author, and it is in the grail tradition. In Chapter 46 of Book 3 there is an episode that deals with the birth of Princess Zellandine. She is given various gifts by three goddesses but is sentenced to eternal sleep when one of them is offended. Zellandine is destined to prick her finger while spinning and then to fall into a deep sleep. As long as a chip of flax remains in her finger, she will continue to sleep. Troylus meets her before she pricks her finger and falls in love with her. The love is mutual, but Troylus must perform some adventures before seeing her again. In the meantime Zellandine pricks her finger, and her father, King Zelland, seeks to protect her by placing her completely nude in a tower that is inaccessible except for one window. When Troylus returns to King Zelland's court, he discovers what has happened to Zellandine, and with the help of a kind spirit Zephir, who carries him up through the window, he manages to gain entrance to Zellandine's room. There, urged on by Venus, he gives way to his desire and has sexual intercourse with Zellandine. Then he exchanges rings with Zellandine and departs. Nine months later she gives birth to a child, and when the child mistakes her finger for her nipple, he sucks the flax chip out of it, and she awakes. After grieving about her lost virginity, Zellandine is comforted by her aunt. Soon after a bird-like creature comes and steals her child. Again Zellandine grieves, but since it is spring, she recovers quickly to think about Troylus. When she looks at the ring on her finger, she realizes that it was he who had slept with her. Some time later Troylus returns from his adventures to take her away with him to his kingdom. The episode between Zellandine and Troylus served as the basis for two Catalan versions, *Blandin de Cornoualha* and *Frayre de Joy e Sor de Plaser*, during the fourteenth century.

There were important literary versions in the seventeenth century that reflect the influence of *Perceforest*: Giambattista Basile's "The Sun, the Moon, and Talia" (1634), Charles Perrault's "Sleeping Beauty" (1697), and Mme d'Aulnoy's "The Doe in the Wood" (1698). Once Perrault's version circulated through the chapbooks of the Bibliothèque bleue, it began enjoying widespread oral circulation.

The Grimms were aware of both oral and literary versions. They collected their variant from Marie Hassenpflug and refined the tale by omitting sexual intercourse and the incident with the evil mother-in-law. They also gave the sleeping beauty a name that they adopted from "L'Histoire d'épine" (1731), a tale written by Count Antoine Hamilton, but Hamilton's story had nothing to do with the classic plot of the sleeping beauty. During the nineteenth century, as the versions below by Gonzenbach, Pitrè, Dardy, and Wilde demonstrate, the tale type was altered a great deal. In fact, many other unusual versions can be found in Greece, Spain, Portugal, Italy, and even in *The Arabian Nights*. "Sleeping Beauty," became one of the most popular tales of the nineteenth and twentieth centuries and was adapted for the stage and made into an opera by Engelbert Humperdinck in 1902 and Carl Reinecke in 1876. The most famous nineteenth-century musical adaptation was Peter Ilyich Tchaikovsky's ballet *The Sleeping Beauty* (1890), and the most popular filmic adaptation in the twentieth century was Walt Disney's *Sleeping Beauty* produced in 1959.

******

Briar Rose (1812)[61]

Jacob and Wilhelm Grimm

A king and a queen couldn't have children, and they wanted very much to have one. Then one day, while the queen was bathing, a crab crawled out of the water, came onshore, and said: "Your wish will soon be fulfilled, and you will give birth to a daughter."

Indeed, this is what happened, and the king was so delighted by the birth of the princess that he organized a great feast and also invited the fairies who were

---

61. "Dornröschen," *Kinder- und Haus-Märchen. Gesammelt durch die Brüder Grimm*, 2 vols. (Berlin: Realschulbuchhandlung, 1812/1815).

living in his realm. Since he only had twelve golden plates, however, one fairy had to be excluded, for there were thirteen in all.

The fairies came to the feast, and at the end of the celebration they gave the child some gifts. One gave virtue; the second, beauty, and the others gave every splendid thing that one could possibly wish for in the world. But, just after the eleventh fairy had announced her gift, the thirteenth appeared, and she was quite angry she had not been invited to the festivities.

"Since you didn't ask me to attend this celebration," she cried out, "I say to you that when your daughter turns fifteen, she will prick herself with a spindle and fall down dead!"

The parents were horrified, but the twelfth fairy hadn't made her wish yet, and she said: "The girl will not die. She will fall into a deep sleep for one hundred years."

The king still hoped to save his dear child and issued an order that all spindles in his entire kingdom were to be banned. Meanwhile, the girl grew up and became miraculously beautiful. On the day she turned fifteen, the king and queen had gone out, and she was left completely alone in the palace. So she wandered all over the place just as she pleased and eventually came to an old tower where she found a narrow staircase. Since she was curious, she climbed the stairs and came to a small door with a yellow key stuck in the lock. When she turned it, the door sprang open, and she found herself in a little room where she saw an old woman spinning flax. She took a great liking to the old woman and joked with her and said she wanted to try spinning one time. So she took the spindle from the old woman's hand, and no sooner did she touch the spindle than she pricked herself and fell down into a deep sleep.

Just at that moment the king returned to the palace with his entire courtly retinue, and everything began to fall asleep—the horses in the stable, the pigeons on the roof, the dogs in the courtyard, and the flies on the wall. Even the fire flickering in the hearth became quiet and fell asleep. The roast stopped sizzling, and the cook, who was just about to pull the kitchen boy's hair, let him go, and the maid, who was plucking the feathers of a hen, let it drop and fell asleep. And a hedge of thorns sprouted around the entire castle and grew higher and higher until it was impossible to see the castle anymore.

There were princes who heard about the beautiful Briar Rose, and they came and wanted to free her, but they couldn't penetrate the hedge. It was as though the thorns clung tightly together like hands, and the princes got stuck there and died miserable deaths. All this continued for many, many years until one day a prince came riding through the country, and an old man told him that people believed that a castle was standing behind the hedge of thorns and that a gorgeous princess was sleeping inside with her entire royal household. His grandfather had told him that many princes had come and had wanted to penetrate the hedge. However, they got stuck hanging in the thorns and had died.

"That doesn't scare me," said the prince. "I'm going to make my way through the hedge and free the beautiful princess."

So off he went, and when he came to the hedge of thorns, there was nothing but flowers that separated for him, and as he went through them, the flowers turned back into thorns. After he reached the castle, the horses were laying asleep in the courtyard, and there was an assortment of hunting dogs. The pigeons were perched on the roof and had tucked their heads beneath their wings. When he entered the palace, the flies were sleeping as was the fire in the kitchen along with the cook and the maid. When the prince continued walking, he saw the entire royal household with the king and queen lying asleep. Everything was so quiet that he could hear himself breathe.

Finally, he came to the old tower where Briar Rose was lying asleep. The prince was so astounded by her beauty that he leaned over and kissed her. Immediately after she woke up, and the king and queen and the entire royal household and the horses and the dogs and the pigeons on the roof and the flies on the walls, and the fire woke up. Indeed, the fire flared up and cooked the meat until it began to sizzle again, and the cook gave the kitchen boy a box on the ear while the maid finished plucking the chicken. Then the wedding of the prince with Briar Rose was celebrated in great splendor, and they lived happily to the end of their days.

Briar Rose (1857)[62]

Jacob and Wilhelm Grimm

In times of old there lived a king and queen, and every day they said, "Oh, if only we had a child!" Yet, they never had one.

Then one day, as the queen went out bathing, a frog happened to crawl ashore and say to her, "Your wish will be fulfilled. Before the year is out, you will give birth to a daughter."

The frog's prediction came true, and the queen gave birth to a girl who was so beautiful that the king was overjoyed and decided to hold a great feast. Not only did he invite his relatives, friends, and acquaintances, but also the wise women, in the hope that they would be generous and kind to his daughter. There were thirteen wise women in his kingdom, but he had only twelve golden plates from which they could eat. Therefore, one of them had to remain home.

The feast was celebrated with tremendous splendor, and when it drew to a close, the wise women bestowed their miraculous gifts upon the child. One gave her virtue, another beauty, the third wealth, and so on, until they had given her nearly everything one could possibly wish for in the world. When eleven of them had offered their gifts, the thirteenth suddenly entered the

---

62.   "Dornröschen," *Kinder- und Hausmärchen gesammelt durch die Brüder Grimm*, 7th ed., 3 vols. (Göttingen: Verlag der Dieterich'schen Buchhandlung, 1857).

hall. She wanted to get revenge for not having been invited, and without greeting anyone or looking around, she cried out with a loud voice, "In her fifteenth year the princess will prick herself with a spindle and fall down dead!"

That was all she said. Then she turned around and left the hall. Everyone was horrified, but the twelfth wise woman stepped forward. She still had her wish to make, and although she could not undo the evil spell, she could nevertheless soften it.

"The princess will not die," she said. "Instead, she shall fall into a deep sleep for one hundred years."

Since the king wanted to guard his dear child against such a catastrophe, he issued an order that all spindles in his kingdom were to be burned. Meanwhile, the gifts of the wise women fulfilled their promise in every way: the girl was so beautiful, polite, kind, and sensible that whoever encountered her could not help but adore her.

Now, on the day she turned fifteen, it happened that the king and queen were not at home, and she was left completely alone in the palace. So she wandered all over the place and explored as many rooms and chambers as she pleased. She eventually came to an old tower, climbed its narrow winding staircase, and came to a small door. A rusty key was stuck in the lock, and when she turned it, the door sprang open, and she saw an old woman in a little room sitting with a spindle and busily spinning flax.

"Good day, old granny," said the princess. "What are you doing there?"

"I'm spinning," said the old woman, and she nodded her head.

"What's the thing that's bobbing about in such a funny way?" asked the maiden, who took the spindle and wanted to spin too, but just as she touched the spindle, the magic spell began working, and she pricked her finger with it.

The very moment she felt the prick, she fell down on the bed that was standing there, and she was overcome by a deep sleep. This sleep soon spread throughout the entire palace. The king and queen had just returned home, and when they entered the hall, they fell asleep, as did all the people of their court. They were followed by the horses in the stable, the dogs in the courtyard, the pigeons on the roof, and the flies on the wall. Even the fire flickering in the hearth became quiet and fell asleep. The roast stopped sizzling, and the cook, who was just about to pull the kitchen boy's hair because he had done something wrong, let him go and fell asleep. Finally, the wind died down so that not a single leaf stirred on the trees outside the castle.

Soon a briar hedge began to grow all around the castle, and it grew higher each year. Eventually, it surrounded and covered the entire castle, causing it to become invisible. Not even the flag on the roof could be seen. The princess became known by the name Beautiful Sleeping Briar Rose, and a tale about her began circulating throughout the country. From time to time princes came and tried to break through the hedge and get back to the castle. However, this was impossible because the thorns clung together tightly as though they had hands, and the young men got stuck there. Indeed, they couldn't pry themselves loose and died miserable deaths.

After many, many years had gone by, a prince came to this country once more and heard an old man talking about the briar hedge. Supposedly there was a castle standing behind the hedge, and in the castle was a remarkably beautiful princess named Briar Rose, who had been sleeping for a hundred years, along with the king and queen and their entire court. The old man also knew from his grandfather that many princes had come and had tried to break through the briar hedge, but they had got stuck and had died wretched deaths.

"I'm not afraid," said the young prince. "I intend to go and see beautiful Briar Rose."

The good old man tried as best he could to dissuade him, but the prince wouldn't heed his words.

Now the hundred years had just ended, and the day on which Briar Rose was to wake up again had arrived. When the prince approached the briar hedge, he found nothing but beautiful flowers that opened of their own accord, let him through, and then closed again like a hedge. In the castle courtyard he saw the horses and the spotted hunting dogs lying asleep. The pigeons were perched on the roof and had tucked their heads beneath their wings. When he entered the palace, the flies were sleeping on the wall, the cook in the kitchen was still holding his hand as if he wanted to grab the kitchen boy, and the maid was sitting in front of the black chicken that she was about to pluck. As the prince continued walking, he saw the entire court lying asleep in the hall with the king and queen by the throne. Then he moved on, and everything was so quiet that he could hear himself breathe.

Finally, he came to the tower and opened the door to the small room in which Briar Rose was asleep. There she lay, and her beauty was so marvelous that he couldn't take his eyes off her. Then he leaned over and gave her a kiss, and when his lips touched hers, Briar Rose opened her eyes, woke up, and looked at him fondly. After that they went downstairs together, and the king and queen woke up along with the entire court, and they all looked at each other in amazement. Soon the horses in the courtyard stood up and shook themselves. The hunting dogs jumped around and wagged their tails. The pigeons on the roof lifted their heads from under their wings, looked around, and flew off into the fields. The flies on the wall continued crawling. The fire in the kitchen flared up, flickered, and cooked the meat. The roast began to sizzle again, and the cook gave the kitchen boy such a box on the ear that he let out a cry, while the maid finished plucking the chicken.

The wedding of the prince with Briar Rose was celebrated in great splendor, and they lived happily to the end of their days.

The Release from the Enchanted Sleep (1863)[63]
Theodor Vernaleken

There once lived a count who was very rich. One day he rode with his wife into their fields to take a look at the crops. To his great satisfaction everything had ripened quite well, and they both rode back home. Along the way a great storm erupted, and it drove the sand into the count's eyes so that he couldn't see anything any more. As soon as he returned home, he summoned the doctor to have him cure his eyes, but the doctor said that he couldn't help him because the sand had penetrated his eyes too deeply.

Now the count had three sons who were already quite grown up. After becoming resigned to his fate, the count learned one day that there was a spring in a neighboring country that had water which healed anyone who washed himself with it. When the oldest son heard about this, he asked permission from his father to go and search for this spring. The father immediately gave him a handsome horse, filled his pockets with money, and sent his son off with his blessings.

In the evening the prince reached a large forest in which there was an inn where men who were completely black were playing cards. They invited him to play with them. He agreed but lost all his money, and even went into debt. The black men locked him up, and he had to serve them. After half a year had passed, the second brother set out on his way, and things did not turn out any better than they had for the first son.

After a year flew by, the father waited in vain for the return of his sons. He was sad about this, and when the youngest son noticed this, he asked for permission to depart. He was much better equipped than his brothers. His father gave him his blessings, and then his son rode off. He, too, came to the inn in the forest where his brothers had stopped. The black men invited him also to play cards, but he refused to join in. He spent the night there, and early in the morning he got ready to set out again. As he went out of the door, he saw a bunch of men working. They were digging a ditch around the inn. He was about to ride off when he noticed a man among the workers who looked very much like his oldest brother. So he spoke to him and recognized him as his brother. Then, when his brother made a request, he paid off both his brothers' debts, and now all three were permitted to ride off.

They rode three days and nights one after another without resting. Along the way, they ate their food that they had brought with them on horseback. Finally they reached an abandoned hut, and they decided to spend some days there. On the third day, the youngest brother went into the forest by himself to hunt. While there he caught sight of a stag, and just as he was about to pull the trigger of his rifle, the stag stood still and said that if he didn't shoot it, the stag might help him some day. As the stag said this, it ripped out one of his hairs and gave

63. "Die Erlösung aus dem Zauberschlafe," *Kinder-und Hausmärchen in den Alpenländern* (Vienna: Braumüller, 1863).

it to him while saying: "If you are ever in danger of dying, just burn this hair, and I'll come to your help."

The prince went further into the forest and saw a large eagle sitting on a tree, and just as he was about to shoot the bird, the eagle cried out and pleaded with him to spare its life, for some day it might help him. The count was very astonished because something like this had never happened to him before. The eagle flew down from the tree and brought him a feather in its beak saying: "If you are ever in danger of dying, just burn this feather, and I'll come to your help."

He let the eagle fly away and went further into the forest, but he had barely taken ten steps when he noticed a wild boar in the bushes. He became frightened and cocked his rifle, but this animal also began to plead for its life. The boar gave him a bristle as a sign and said to him: "If you are ever in danger of dying, just burn this bristle, and I'll come to your help."

Finally the prince returned to his brothers but didn't say anything about his encounters. Nor did they ask him any questions because they didn't care about him very much, and they both only thought about taking his life.

The next morning they continued riding, and at the end of the day they came to a large castle, and in the nearby garden they saw the spring. The oldest brother wanted to enter the castle. He went to the door and found a note attached to it that said: "The spring in this garden cures all sicknesses."

He opened the door and wanted to go inside, however, he became frightened and turned around. His brothers asked him what had scared him so much, however, he couldn't answer them. Immediately thereafter the second brother went to the door and opened it, but no sooner had he taken a step inside than he became just as frightened as his brother and fell to the ground. Now the third brother also went to the door, opened it, and stepped courageously inside. He went to the first room and found a bunch of soldiers who were all asleep. He slipped into the second room and found the king sitting on the throne and the queen lying on a sofa. Both were asleep.

He didn't dare to go nearer to the king, and so he slipped into the third room where he saw a marvelously beautiful princess sleeping on a chair. Standing next to her was a table covered with diamonds and on top, a little basket with needles and thread. There was a pillow on her lap not quite finished, and next to her on another chair there was some wool. Further off there was another table with paper and pencil on it. On the other side stood a diamond inkstand. Our hero summoned his courage, sat down at the table, took a pen, and began to write. He wrote a short life history, whose son he was, and how and why he had come. Just as he was about to depart, he noticed a very small picture hanging on the wall. He took it down and saw that it was a portrait of the princess. So he went over to the sleeping princess and kissed her. Then he rushed off.

When he returned to his brothers, he told them that the castle was abandoned and totally ruined in the interior. So now they wanted to fetch water from the spring and return home. As the oldest went to fill his flask, the water vanished, and as he withdrew the flask, the water reappeared. He tried to scoop up water again, but the water vanished right away when he stuck the flask into the spring. So now he left the flask lying in the ditch and thought that when the water reappeared, the flask would fill itself with water, and then he could quickly take it out. But he had barely taken his hand away when the bubbling spring tossed the flask so high into the air that it broke. Now the second brother tried to scoop up water. However, the same thing happened to him as it did to his brother. Finally the youngest brother went to the spring, stuck his flask into the water, and filled it until it was full. Well, his brothers made a wry face, and their dislike for their rescuer grew greater. So they secretly conspired to do away with him, and when they entered the forest where they had served as slaves, they fell upon him and murdered him. In order to make sure that there would be no trace of the murder, they made a fire and threw him into it. Then they took everything away and hurried home.

However, as the fire continued to burn the brother and caught on to the hair, the feather, and the bristle, the stag, the eagle, and the boar immediately appeared. Together they pulled him out of the fire, brought all kinds of salves and herbs to him, and after half an hour he stood there whole and healthy. They also brought him some garments, and he thanked the animals and continued on his way but not to his father's castle. Instead he went to a village to work as a peasant for a farmer.

After a year had passed, the father received a letter from the princess, who, along with the entire royal court, had been released from a magic spell by his youngest son. The letter contained the request that the son who had been in her room was to come to her. At the same time she had spread the whole road to and from the father's house with diamonds, for she believed that she'd recognize the right hero by this test. Indeed, she thought he wouldn't spare the diamonds but ride right over them.

First the oldest son went to her, and she asked him what he had seen when he was in the rooms. However, he couldn't tell her anything, and she sent him home. The same thing happened to the second son. So the father wrote now that he didn't have any more sons because the third was dead. Nevertheless, the princess demanded his corpse, but he couldn't send it. The affair turned into a rumor that spread, and our young peasant also heard about it. Immediately he asked his master for permission to take a few days off from work. The farmer granted his request, and he rode off at once to the castle in his peasant clothes. Instead of sparing the diamonds he rode right over them and over the jewels as well. When he presented himself to the princess, he told her what he had seen in her room, and she greeted him as her rescuer and her bridegroom. Soon thereafter their wedding was celebrated. The father and the brothers were invited to it, and at the wedding the youngest son told the father about the faithless brothers, and the father had them executed without mercy.

Maruzzedda (1870)[64]

Laura Gonzenbach

Once upon a time there was a poor shoemaker, and he had three beautiful daughters. The youngest, however, was the most beautiful, and she was called Maruzzedda.[65] The older sisters, however, did not like Maruzzedda because she was so unusually beautiful. The shoemaker was poor and frequently had to wander about the countryside for many days in order to earn some money.

One day he said to his eldest daughter. "I want you to accompany me when I look for work. Perhaps I shall be a bit luckier. So his eldest daughter went with him, and he earned a tari. Then he said, "Listen, I'm very hungry. Let's eat ten pennies worth of food, and we'll bring just ten pennies to the others."

So they bought something to eat and brought the others half of the money. The next day the shoemaker took his middle daughter and earned three carlini. Then he said, "Let's eat fifteen pennies worth of food, and we'll bring the others just fifteen pennies."

So they bought something to eat and brought the others just half of the money. On the third day the shoemaker took Maruzzedda with him, and this time he earned two tari. "Listen, Maruzzedda," he said, "let's eat one tari worth of food, and we'll bring the others just one tari."

"No, father," she replied. "I'd prefer to go home right away, and then we can all eat with one another."

When the father returned home, he told his other two daughters what had happened, and they said, "Just look at our ill-bred sister! Shouldn't she always do what you want?"

They used these words and more to stir their father against the innocent Maruzzedda. The next morning he took her with him again and earned three tari. "Listen, Maruzzedda," he said once more, "let's eat three carlini worth of food, and we'll bring your sisters the other three."

"No, dear father," she said. "I'd prefer to go home right away. Why shouldn't we all eat together?"

When the father returned home, he told his older daughters about this once again, and they had even some harder words for their sister. "Why do you want to keep that shameless person in your house any longer? Chase her out! Get rid of her!"

---

64.   "Maruzzedda," *Sicilianische Märchen*, 2 vols. (Leipzig: W. Engelmann, 1870).

65.   Diminutive of Maria.

However, their father did not want to do this. So, the sisters proposed: "Take her with you tomorrow, and leave her behind in some desolate spot so that she won't be able to find her way back home."

The father was blinded by their jealousy and let himself be duped by the sisters. So, the next morning he took Maruzzedda with him. After they had wandered very far and had come to an unfamiliar region, he said to her, "Wait a moment, and rest a while. I'll be right back."

So Maruzzedda sat down, and the shoemaker went away. She waited and waited, but her father did not return. The sun began to set, and the father still did not return. Finally, she was very sad and thought, 'My father clearly wants to throw me out of the house. Well then, I'll set off into the wide world.'

So she wandered away and continued to wander until she was tired and it had become evening. She had no idea where she might find shelter for the night. Suddenly, however, she saw a splendid castle in the distance. She went toward it, entered, and climbed the stairs, but she encountered nobody inside. She went through the rooms that were lavishly decorated, and in one of them there was a table that had been fully set. Yet, there were no people. Finally, she reached the last room where she saw a beautiful maiden lying on top of a black frame used for coffins. She was dead.

"Well, since there is nobody here, I'm going to stay until someone comes and chases me away."

Therefore, she sat down at the table, ate, and drank to her heart's content. Then she lay down in a beautiful bed to sleep. This was the way she lived for a long time, and no one disturbed her.

One day, however, her father happened to pass this way while she was looking out the window. When he saw her, he greeted her, for he was sorry that he had abandoned her, and he asked her how she was doing.

"Oh, things are just fine," Maruzzedda responded. "I've found some work here as a servant, and they treat me well."

"May I come up for a while?" the father asked.

"No, no," she replied. "My master is very strict and has forbidden me to let anyone enter. Farewell, and greet my sisters for me."

The shoemaker went home and told his daughters that he had found Maruzzedda. And once again, they deceived him with false words so that he became angry with the innocent Maruzzedda. After some days had passed, the jealous sisters baked a cake, put some poison inside, and gave it to their father to bring to the poor maiden. However, during that very same evening, while Maruzzedda was asleep, the dead maiden appeared to her in a dream and called: "Maruzzedda! Maruzzedda!"

"What do you want?" Maruzzedda asked, half asleep, half awake.

"Tomorrow, your father will bring you a wonderful cake. But beware, and do not eat it. Give the cat a piece. The cake has poison inside."

Maruzzedda awoke and saw that she was alone. So she thought, 'I must have probably dreamed this,' and she fell back into a pleasant sleep.

The next day she saw her father coming. She allowed him to climb the stairs, but she would not let him enter.

"If my master should see you, he would discharge me from his service."

"Don't worry, my child," the shoemaker answered. "Your sisters have sent their greetings along with this cake."

"Tell my sisters that the cake is very beautiful," Maruzzedda responded, "and I thank them very much for sending it."

"Don't you want to try a little piece," the father asked.

"No, I can't right now," Maruzzedda answered. "I have work to do now. Later, when my work is finished, I'll try a piece."

Then she gave him some money and told him to go. When he was away, however, she gave the cat a piece of the cake, and the cat died right after. Then she realized how true the dead maiden's warning had been and threw the cake away.

Meanwhile, the jealous sisters became restless at home because they wanted to know what had happened to Maruzzedda. Therefore, the shoemaker traveled to the castle again the next morning. When he knocked at the door, Maruzzedda came toward him, and she was cheerful and in good health.

"How are things going, my dear child?" he asked.

"Everything is fine, dear father," she answered.

"Why won't you let me see the castle just one time?" he said.

"What are you thinking?" she replied. "That would cost me my job."

Then she gave him some money and sent him away. When the father arrived home and told his other daughters that Maruzzedda was completely healthy, they hated their poor sister even more than before. So they made a beautiful enchanted hat, and whoever put it on would become stiff and paralyzed. The father had to take this hat to Maruzzedda.

During the night, however, the dead maiden appeared to Maruzzedda in a dream once more and called out: "Maruzzedda! Maruzzedda!"

"What do you want?" she asked.

"Tomorrow morning your father will bring you a beautiful hat," the dead maiden said. "Beware, and don't put it on. Otherwise, you'll become stiff and paralyzed."

The next morning the shoemaker did indeed appear and brought his daughter a beautiful hat.

"Tell my sisters that the hat is very beautiful, and I thank them very much," she said to her father.

"Don't you even want to try it on so that I can see how it looks on you?" the father asked.

"No, no, I have to work now," she replied. "Later, when I go to mass, I'll put it on."

Upon saying this, she gave him some money and told him to go. She put the hat into a chest, but did not tear it up as she should have done. Meanwhile, her sisters were convinced that Maruzzedda had been destroyed by the hat, and they were no longer concerned about her.

About this time the dead maiden had been granted permission through God's grace to enter the heavenly paradise. Then she appeared to Maruzzedda for the last time in a dream and said, "God has permitted me to go to my final resting place, and I am leaving this castle and everything in it to you. Live a happy life, and enjoy all this splendor."

Upon saying this, she disappeared, and the black frame on which she had been lying was now empty.

Many months passed, and one day Maruzzedda decided to clean out all the chests and boxes in the castle. As she was doing this, she came upon the enchanted hat, and since she had received it so long ago, she forgot who had sent it to her and thought, 'Oh, what a pretty hat! I'm going to try it on.' No sooner did she put the hat on her head than she became stiff and paralyzed and could not move anymore. That evening the dead maiden appeared, for the Lord gave her permission to return to earth. She took poor Maruzzedda and placed her on the black frame. Then she flew back to paradise. Maruzzedda lay there as if she were dead, but she did not became pale or cold.

One day, after she had been lying like this for a long time, the king happened to go hunting, and the hunt took him into the vicinity of the castle. At one point he saw a beautiful bird, took aim, and hit it, but the bird fell right into the room where Maruzzedda was lying on the frame. The king wanted to enter the castle. However, all the doors were locked, and nobody responded to his knocking. So there was nothing else to do but climb through a window, and since the window was not very high, he ordered two of his hunters to climb through it. When they succeeded and saw the wonderful maiden, they forgot all about the bird and the king and kept staring at the dead Maruzzedda. The king became impatient and finally called out: "What are you doing inside there? Hurry up!"

The hunters went over to the window and asked the king to climb up. There was a maiden inside, and they had never seen anyone so astonishingly beautiful as she was. So the king climbed through the window into the room, and as soon as he caught sight of Maruzzedda, he could not take his eyes off of her. When he bent over her, he noticed that she was still warm and cried out, "The maiden is not dead, just unconscious! Let's bring her back to life!"

They tried to wake her. They rubbed her and loosened her clothing, but it was all in vain. Maruzzedda remained stiff. Finally, the king took off her hat in order to cool off her forehead, and all at once she opened her eyes and awoke from her slumber. Then the king announced, "You shall be my wife," and he embraced her.

However, the king had a mother, who was an evil sorceress, and consequently, he was afraid to take Maruzzedda back to the castle with him. "Stay here," he said to her, "and I'll come to you as often as I can. "From then on Maruzzedda lived in the castle and was secretly married to the king, and the king came and visited her whenever he went hunting. After one year she gave birth to their first son and called him Tamo.[66] After another year, she gave birth to a second son and called him Tamai.[67] And, when she gave birth to a third son the following year, she called him Tamero.[68]

The old queen had gradually noticed, however, that her son often went hunting and stayed away from the castle for a long time. Therefore, she investigated things, and after awhile she learned about his marriage. So, she called a loyal servant and said, "Go to the castle where the king's wife is living and say to her: 'My majesty, the queen, will grant you a pardon when you send your oldest son to her today.'"

The servant did this, and poor Maruzzedda was fooled and gave the man her eldest son. The next day the old queen had the second son fetched, and soon afterward, the third son. When she had the three children in her castle, she called her cook and said to him, "You must kill these three children and bring me their hearts and livers as proof that you have followed my orders."

The cook had children himself, and his fatherly heart took pity on the poor innocent children so that he did not kill them. Instead, he brought them to his house and hid them there. As for the queen, he brought her the heart and liver of three billy goats.

Meanwhile the king became sick and lay in his bed. Then the queen sent another messenger to Maruzzedda and told him to say: "Your husband is sick. You are to go to him and take care of him."

Maruzzedda put on three dresses, one on top of the other, and went to the castle. When she entered the courtyard, there was a huge fire burning, and the old queen was standing beside it and called out, "Throw the girl into the fire!"

"First, let me take off my clothes," Maruzzedda requested, and she took off the first dress, threw it into the fire, and cried with a loud penetrating voice, "Tamo!"

But the queen had placed a group of musicians in front of the king's door, and they had been ordered to play their instruments with all their might so that the king would not be able to hear what was happening in the courtyard. However, he heard his wife's cry, even if it was very weak.

"Stop playing your music," he said, but the musicians continued to play as loudly as they could. Then Maruzzedda threw off the second dress and cried out even louder: "Tamai!"

This time the king heard it much better and called out: "Stop your music!"

---

66. *T'amo*: "I love you."

67. *T'amai*: "I loved you."

68. *Tamerò*: "I'll love you."

But the musicians had received orders not to obey him and continued to play. Then Maruzzedda took off the third dress, and she yelled from the bottom of her anxious heart as loud as she could, "Tamero!"

The king heard the cry, jumped out of bed, and ran down into the courtyard. Just as he arrived, the servants were about to throw poor Maruzzedda into the fire. He ordered them to stop and to tie up the queen instead and to throw her into the fire. Then he embraced his wife and said, "Now you will be the queen."

"Oh," she responded, "before anything, take me to my children."

"Where are the children?" the king asked.

"What? They're not here?" the poor mother cried. "Oh my children, my dear children!"

Then she told the king how his mother had sent messengers to fetch the children, but nobody knew anything about this, and there was great sadness in the castle. However, the cook asked to see the king and said, "Your majesty and my queen, console yourselves! The old queen had ordered me to kill your children, but my heart took pity on them, and I let them live."

Then the three children were brought to them, and they embraced their parents with great joy. Finally, the king and queen celebrated with a splendid feast and gave rich gifts to the cook.

And so they lived happy and content.

But we can't even pay the rent.

Sun, Pearl, and Anna (1875)[69]
Giuseppe Pitrè

Gentlemen, there was once a king and a queen who longed to have children, either a son or daughter, because they didn't have any. At a certain point, the Lord took pity on them, and the queen became pregnant. During those times there were astrologers. So they called an astrologer, and the king said to him, "What can you tell me about the queen?"

After examining the queen, the astrologer declared, "The queen will have a daughter, but . . ."

And he stopped with "but." So the king said, "What's the meaning of this *but*?"

"Your majesty, when your daughter turns thirteen and touches a spindle, she will be cast under a spell."

Upon hearing this, the king said, "Quick! I want a house built beneath the ground."

Meanwhile the queen began preparations for giving birth, for the time had come. Indeed, she brought forth a beautiful daughter, and you can just imagine the happiness in the palace! Soon afterward they called for a wet nurse and sent

69. "Suli, Perna e Anna" *Fiabe, novelle e racconti populari siciliani*, 4 vols. (Palermo: Lauriel, 1875).

her with the baby beneath the earth so that they could see neither the sky nor the ground above. In short, the little girl grew up in another world, not seeing anything at all.

One day, when she was seven,[70] it seemed to the nurse that the girl was sleeping, and she said to herself: "I'd like to entertain myself a bit."

Thinking that the girl was in a deep sleep, she took a spindle and began spinning. But what did she do? Well, she soon had a desire to drink a glass of water in another room. So she put the spindle and the distaff on top of a chair and went off. Well, guess who woke up? The girl, of course. She got up from the bed, saw the spindle, and it seemed such a new thing that she took it into her hand, and all at once she was enchanted.

Now let's return to the nurse.

When she returned, she saw the enchanted girl, who seemed as if she were dead. "My girl! My girl! What am I going to do?" She began to cry out. Her screams were heard above the ground causing the king and queen to descend. When they saw their daughter, she seemed dead to them. The king burst into tears and immediately took the girl and had three dresses made for her, one more beautiful than the other, and then he had her dressed in them one on top of the other.

"These are the dresses that I would have made for your wedding, my daughter!"

And he ordered her to be brought to a small cottage in the country where he had a beautiful coffin built for her. Then he had her sealed in the cottage, which was not to be opened.

Now, years later, there was a prince who was out hunting, and it started to rain very hard. The poor man couldn't find any shelter and ran toward the cottage. At that time there was a ladder of silk on the side of the cottage, and once he arrived there, he had his valet climb the ladder. After the valet reached the balcony, he opened the windows to a room and saw a beautiful maiden, just as beautiful as the sun (for the girl of seven had continued to grow). The valet went back down the ladder and said to the king, "Your majesty, what a beautiful catch we've made!"

They went inside together, and the prince climbed the stairs and saw the beautiful creature just as she was—alive and breathing with a rosy complexion and the spindle in her hand. In all the confusion no one had ever thought of taking away the spindle. The prince approached her, looked at her, and said, "Oh! My daughter, I pity you. . . . What's that you have in your hands?"

As soon as he took the spindle from her hands, the maiden was revived. But she was afraid, and he said to her, "Don't be afraid. You've found a father, a brother."

---

70. The storyteller seems to have forgotten that the unlucky year is supposed to be the thirteenth year.

He gave her something to eat, restored her health and everything. Then he said to her, "I've got to go now, but you can count on my returning here tomorrow."

So he went back home with his valet, and the prince's mother said to him, "How come you're so late?"

"Mother," he said, "I really enjoyed the hunting today."

The next day they returned to the hunt, and he went to the maiden's cottage. Her name was Anna.

"How are you, Anna?"

"Very well. And you, prince?"

"I'm fine."

To be brief, by the end of nine months the maiden became very pregnant. She gave birth to a handsome baby boy and named him Sun.

Now let's turn to the old queen who worried about her son because he was rarely at the palace any more, and she wondered what he was doing. Indeed, the queen racked her brains seeking to know where her son was spending his time, and since she couldn't discover anything, she said to him, "You've got to tell me whether you're spending your time with some maiden."

And without knowing her, the queen felt a great anger toward poor Anna. The poor prince went and enjoyed his time with Sun and was crazy about him. In the meantime, as the boy grew, Anna became pregnant again. In nine months she gave birth to a baby girl and named her Pearl.

In the meantime, the old queen continued to suspect something and would say, "My son, you're doing something deceitful! What's going on in your head? . . . The entire realm is falling to pieces. . . ."

Now it so happened that the prince became sick and had to stay in bed. His mother was afraid that he might die. Clearly he became sick because he missed being with Anna! The poor prince secretly wrote a letter to her and told her not to worry about him because his sickness was nothing, and he wanted to know how the children were because he was thinking about them.

But he went from bad to worse and was overcome by fever. In his delirium he said, "Sun, Pearl, and Anna, you've taken my heart and soul."

When his mother heard this, she said, "Ahh! That whore has destroyed my son!" And after she uttered many insults, she said, "Be quiet, my son, because tonight I'm going to have you eat with Sun!"

Meanwhile, she called her son's faithful servant, the valet, and said to him, "Tell me the truth, or I'll cut off your head. What's the matter with my son?"

She was so furious with the valet that his legs trembled, and he told her everything from the beginning to the end.

"Ahh! That wicked woman!" the queen said. "Wait till I get my hands on her! Well, I want you to bring me Sun, and if his mother doesn't want to give him to you, tell her that my son wants to see him."

On official orders, the valet went to the prince's wife, and Anna asked, "How is the prince?"

"Better," the valet responded, "but today he wants to see Sun."

The mother took Sun, dressed him nicely, washed him, and gave him to the valet.

"Make sure to take care of him. Is there a risk of some treachery?"

The poor maiden's heart was speaking to her. And the valet departed, and when the old queen saw the spitting image of her son, she said to the boy, "Ahh! You're wicked, more wicked than your father!"

She took the boy by the arm and said to the cook, "Take him and slaughter him. Then I want you to cook him for me."

Instead of killing the boy, the cook took him to his home and hid him. Then he made a dish of meat to please the queen. At noon he carried it to her.

"This is Sun."

"Ahh come! Come here. I'm going to have you eat with your father who's made me suffer and almost die from the pain."

Then she went to her son with the dish and said, "Take this, my son. Eat this here. It's Sun."

The next day the vile queen said to the valet, "Now you've got to bring me Pearl so that I can have her eat with her father."

The valet went to the princess, who asked him, "How is my son doing?"

"Very well."

"And my husband?"

"Better, but he wants Pearl so that they can eat together."

The princess asked him, "Is there a risk of some treachery?"

It was as if her heart were speaking to the poor princess.

"What kind of treachery could there be?" the valet responded.

She dressed the little girl. The valet took her away in a coach, and after they arrived at the palace, the old queen said, "Ahh! You're more wicked than your father, and now I'll show you how to amuse yourself."

She called the cook and said: "Take this little girl and prepare her for me."

The cook took the little girl, hid her, and made a dish of meat that pleased the queen. She took it to her son who continued to be delirious because of the fever.

"Here," she said. "This is Pearl. Eat with Pearl, and tomorrow I'll have you eat with Anna."

The next day she said to the valet, "Tell the princess that the prince is much better and wants to see her at the palace."

The valet departed and said to the princess, "The queen wants your majesty at the palace. They are all well. The prince is almost better and would like you to be there to enjoy some peace and quiet."

The princess dressed herself with what she had. She still had the three dresses that her father had put on her, and she got into the coach. The old queen was at the window and kept looking at the road. When Anna appeared, the queen went out and approached her. As soon the queen was next to her, she grabbed Anna and dragged her by the hair, insulting her and accusing Anna of being a loose woman. Yelling and bawling, she took her into the palace and forced her into a room where there was a kettle of boiling oil. She brought her to the kettle and said, "Get undressed!"

Anna took off the first dress and cried out in distress, "Sun!" The dress clattered and sounded like church bells. The prince heard the great tumult and began to listen more attentively. Anna took off the other dress and cried out even more loudly, "Pearl," and the dress clattered again.

"Ahh!" the prince said. "That sounds like Anna crying out for our children!"

While the old queen made Anna take off the third dress, the prince got up deliriously and crawled on all fours to see what was happening. Anna took off the third dress and screamed in fright, "Anna!" The prince crawled on all fours into the room and found his mother who had grabbed hold of Anna and was about to shove her into the kettle. He could not believe his eyes, the poor prince!

He seized the queen from behind and threw her into the kettle. Then he embraced Anna and kissed her. When they searched for their children, the cook delivered them safe and sound and full of life. Little by little they made preparations for a wedding and were soon married. The cook received great compliments, and

> They remained happy and in peace
> While we sit here picking our teeth.

Told by Rosalia Varrica in Palermo.

The Enchanted Princess or The Magic Tower (1877)[71]
Bernhard Schmidt

Once and at a certain time there lived a king who was the greatest, richest, and most virtuous of all the kings in the world, and God loved him very much because of his way of life and good works. Due to his virtuousness he had also decided never to marry but to remain a bachelor. However, he would have liked to have had children. And one day he sat and wept and grieved that he didn't have a single child and that perhaps his throne would be taken over by evil hands. All of a sudden an angel appeared and told him to stop weeping. He would get a child from the calf of his leg. A short time later the king's leg began to swell, and one day, when he was out hunting, his leg was stuck by a thorn. All at once a marvelously beautiful maiden sprang out of his calf. Her entire body was armed, and she carried a lance and wore a helmet. No sooner was she born,

71. "Die verzauberte Königstochter oder der Zauberthurm," *Griechische Märchen, Sagen und Volkslieder* (Leipzig: Teubner, 1877).

however, than she was carried off by a Lámnissa[72] and brought to a large and beautiful tower. Right after she arrived she sank immediately into a deep sleep.

Now there was another king who was living during this same period, and he had an only son, whom he wanted to marry off. And this son had heard many things about the princess who was sleeping in the tower. She was supposed to be the most beautiful of all the virgins in the world but couldn't wake up until a young man released her from a magic spell. As time passed, the prince thought more and more about winning this maiden. But in order to learn how he should go about this, he went to a sorceress and asked her about this. She told him that he should take three things with him: animal meat, grain, and sea lice. He was to set out with these things and keep going straight ahead until he arrived at a gate that was close to collapsing and had the following inscription written on it:

"A calf was my mother,
A thorn bush, my midwife."

Then he was to say to the gate: "What a beautiful gate this is!" After saying this, he was to get off his horse and clean the gate. Then the gate would not collapse and kill him. Right after he was to enter, and he would come across some lions, and they would threaten to eat him. He was not to hesitate but to throw them the meat right away. Next he would encounter a huge amount of ants that would also want to eat him. But he was to throw them the grain right away, and they would spare his life. Finally, he would meet a powerful fish at the bridge that crossed a river, and it, too, would show signs of wanting to eat him. He was to throw the fish only the sacks with sea lice in them, and the fish wouldn't touch him.

After the prince had received these instructions, he prepared himself and set out on his journey the following day. When he reached the gate, he did just what the old woman had told him to do and went through without danger. Thereupon he met the lions which ate the meat that he threw to them, and they said to the prince: "Here are three hairs from our manes, and in case you come to need them, you only have to throw them into a fire, and we'll immediately be by your side."

Now the prince continued walking and came upon the ants which devoured the grain that he threw to them. They gave him one of their wings and told him exactly what the lions had told him. Now he had to cross the river, and all of a sudden a gigantic fish leapt out and wanted to swallow him. But the prince quickly threw the sea lice to the fish, which let him pass, and the fish also gave him a scale from its body and said that if the prince needed the fish, he should throw the scale into a fire.

Now the young man came to the tower and entered. All at once the princess awoke. This happened just at the time that forty days and nights had passed since she had fallen asleep. As soon as she was fully awake, she said to the prince:

72.   A kind of witch.

"Ahh, you're the one who will free me. But you still have a great deal to overcome. That old woman Lárissa will lock you in a large room, and in one half there will be four thousand cattle. The other half will be filled with a mix and variety of wheat, barley, and corn. In one single day you must cut open the cattle and order the entrails, the skins, the stomachs, the meat, and the bones. On the other side of the room you must sort the different kinds of grain on the same day. Then in the evening the old woman will throw a needle into the river that you must find within a quarter of an hour."

The next morning the prince was locked in the large room. Then he took the three hairs from the manes of the lions from his pocket and threw them into a fire. Immediately thereafter the lions appeared by his side, and they killed the cattle with their teeth and claws and completely carried out the work as prescribed. Right after this, the prince threw the wings that he had received from the ants into the fire. Immediately thereafter the ants came and sorted the different kinds of grain with their mouths.

That evening the old woman entered the room with the maiden and was astonished to see that everything had been done. Then she led the prince to the river and threw the needle into the water. But he had already thrown the scale that he had received from the fish into a fire, and just as he plunged into the water, the fish rushed to his aid, seized the needle, and brought it to him. Thereupon, the prince climbed out of the water holding the needle and gave it back to the old woman. Then he grabbed hold of his beloved princess and crossed over to the other bank where the ants and lions were waiting.

However, the Lámnissa still refused to let the prince leave and cried out to the ants and lions that they should devour the young man. But it was all in vain! So she pursued the couple herself in order to regain the princess. However, the princess threw some of her hairs behind her, and a large sea arose separating the couple from the Lámnissa. So the old woman could not continue her pursuit. Then the prince happily brought his beloved princess to his home and married her. And God, who loved the maiden very much, endowed her with a dowry that enabled her to predict the future and thereby raised her in status as though she were a goddess.

Ethna the Bride (1888)[73]
Lady Jane Francesca Elgee Wilde

The fairies, as we know, are greatly attracted by the beauty of mortal women, and Finvarra the king employs his numerous sprites to find out and carry off when possible the prettiest girls and brides in the country. These are spirited away by enchantment to his fairy palace at Knockma in Tuam, where they remain under a fairy spell, forgetting all about the earthly life and soothed to

---

73. *Ancient Legends, Mystic Charms, and Superstitions of Ireland* (Boston: Ticknor, 1888).

passive enjoyment, as in a sweet dream, by the soft low melody of the fairy music, which has the power to lull the hearer into a trance of ecstasy.

There was once a great lord in that part of the country who had a beautiful wife called Ethna, the loveliest bride in all the land. And her husband was so proud of her that day after day he had festivals in her honour; and from morning till night his castle was filled with lords and ladies, and nothing but music and dancing and feasting and hunting and pleasure was thought of.

One evening while the feast was merriest, and Ethna floated through the dance in her robe of silver gossamer clasped with jewels, more bright and beautiful than the stars in heaven, she suddenly let go the hand of her partner and sank to the floor in a faint. They carried her to her room, where she lay long quite insensible; but towards the morning she woke up and declared that she had passed the night in a beautiful palace, and was so happy that she longed to sleep again and go there in her dreams. And they watched by her all day, but when the shades of evening fell dark on the castle, low music was heard at her window, and Ethna again fell into a deep trance from which nothing could rouse her.

Then her old nurse was set to watch her; but the woman grew weary in the silence and fell asleep, and never awoke till the sun had risen. And when she looked towards the bed, she saw to her horror that the young bride had disappeared. The whole household was roused up at once, and search made everywhere, but no trace of her could be found in all the castle, nor in the gardens, nor in the park. Her husband sent messengers in every direction, but to no purpose—no one had seen her; no sign of her could be found, living or dead.

Then the young lord mounted his swiftest steed and galloped right off to Knockma, to question Finvarra, the fairy king, if he could give any tidings of the bride, or direct him where to search for her; for he and Finvarra were friends, and many a good keg of Spanish wine had been left outside the window of the castle at night for the fairies to carry away, by order of the young lord. But he little dreamed now that Finvarra himself was the traitor; so he galloped on like mad till he reached Knockma, the hill of the fairies. And as he stopped to rest his horse by the fairy rath, he heard voices in the air above him, and one said, "Right glad is Finvarra now, for he has the beautiful bride in his palace at last; and never more will she see her husband's face."

"Yet," answered another, "if he dig down through the hill to the centre of the earth, he would find his bride; but the work is hard and the way is difficult, and Finvarra has more power than any mortal man."

"That is yet to be seen," exclaimed the young lord. "Neither fairy, nor devil, nor Finvarra himself shall stand between me and my fair young wife"; and on the instant he sent word by his servants to gather together all the workmen and labourers of the country round with their spades and pickaxes, to dig through the hill till they came to the fairy palace.

And the workmen came, a great crowd of them, and they dug through the hill all that day till a great deep trench was made down to the very centre. Then at sunset they left off for the night; but next morning when they assembled again to continue their work, behold, all the clay was put back again into the trench, and the hill looked as if never a spade had touched it—for so Finvarra had ordered; and he was powerful over earth and air and sea.

But the young lord had a brave heart, and he made the men go on with the work; and the trench was dug again, wide and deep into the centre of the hill. And this went on for three days, but always with the same result, for the clay was put back again each night and the hill looked the same as before, and they were no nearer to the fairy palace. Then the young lord was ready to die for rage and grief, but suddenly he heard a voice near him like a whisper in the air, and the words it said were these: "Sprinkle the earth you have dug up with salt, and your work will be safe."

On this new life came into his heart, and he sent word through all the country to gather salt from the people; and the clay was sprinkled with it that night, when the men had left off their work at the hill.

Next morning they all rose up early in great anxiety to see what had happened, and there to their great joy was the trench all safe, just as they had left it, and all the earth round it was untouched.

Then the young lord knew he had power over Finvarra, and he bade the men work on with a good heart, for they would soon reach the fairy palace now in the centre of the hill. So by the next day a great glen was cut right through deep down to the middle of the earth, and they could hear the fairy music if they put their ear close to the ground, and voices were heard round them in the air.

"See now," said one, "Finvarra is sad, for if one of those mortal men strike a blow on the fairy palace with their spades, it will crumble to dust, and fade away like the mist." "Then let Finvarra give up the bride," said another, "and we shall be safe."

On which the voice of Finvarra himself was heard, clear like the note of a silver bugle through the hill. "Stop your work," he said. "Oh, men of earth, lay down your spades, and at sunset the bride shall be given back to her husband. I, Finvarra, have spoken."

Then the young lord bade them stop the work, and lay down their spades till the sun went down. And at sunset he mounted his great chestnut steed and rode to the head of the glen, and watched and waited; and just as the red light flushed all the sky, he saw his wife coming along the path in her robe of silver gossamer, more beautiful than ever; and he sprang from the saddle and lifted her up before him, and rode away like the storm wind back to the castle. And there they laid Ethna on her bed; but she closed her eyes and spake no word. So day after day passed, and still she never spake or smiled, but seemed like one in a trance.

And great sorrow fell upon every one, for they feared she had eaten of the fairy food, and that the enchantment would never be broken. So her husband was very miserable. But one evening as he was riding home late, he heard voices in the air, and one of them said, "It is now a year and a day since the young lord brought home his beautiful wife from Finvarra; but what good is she to him? She is speechless and like one dead; for her spirit is with the fairies, though her form is there beside him."

Then another voice answered, "And so she will remain unless the spell is broken. He must unloose the girdle from her waist that is fastened with an enchanted pin, and burn the girdle with fire, and throw the ashes before the door, and bury the enchanted pin in the earth; then will her spirit come back from Fairyland, and she will once more speak and have true life."

Hearing this the young lord at once set spurs to his horse, and on reaching the castle hastened to the room where Ethna lay on her couch silent and beautiful like a waxen figure. Then, being determined to test the truth of the spirit voices, he untied the girdle, and after much difficulty extracted the enchanted pin from the folds. But still Ethna spoke no word; then he took the girdle and burned it with fire, and strewed the ashes before the door, and he buried the enchanted pin in a deep hole in the earth, under a fairy thorn, that no hand might disturb the spot. After which he returned to his young wife, who smiled as she looked at him, and held forth her hand. Great was his joy to see the soul coming back to the beautiful form, and he raised her up and kissed her; and speech and memory came back to her at that moment, and all her former life, just as if it had never been broken or interrupted; but the year that her spirit had passed in Fairyland seemed to her but as a dream of the night, from which she had just awoke.

After this Finvarra made no further efforts to carry her off; but the deep cut in the hill remains to this day, and is called "The Fairy's Glen." So no one can doubt the truth of the story as here narrated.

The Sleeping Beauty (1891)[74]
Léopold Dardy

Once upon a time there was one of the richest and ugliest princes ever. He had crooked legs, was puffy and gummy, and had a bad odor about him. During that time there was a beautiful princess, the nicest of her epoch and country. The ugly prince once saw the maiden and loved her. He proposed and stopped at a fair nearby to see her, and indeed, they met there. But as soon as the princess saw this vile object, she said, "No. I'd prefer never to marry than to keep company with this ugly man!"

When the people at the fair saw him, they all cried out: "Ah! What an ugly person! What a dreadful prince he is! Mother of God!"

---

74. "La belle endormie," *Anthologie populaire de l'Albret* (Agen: Michel et Médan, 1891).

A wicked old fairy with wrinkled skin who was the prince's fairy godmother heard the princess's comments. She had a vindictive nature, and therefore she turned against the princess and cast a sleeping spell over the poor innocent maiden. Indeed, the beautiful girl fell asleep in a chateau at the entrance to the fair and no longer woke up.

Close to a hundred years had passed while she slept in the chateau when a nobleman who was out hunting passed this little place. Nobody had forgotten the misfortune of the princess, but no one had ever dared to enter the dilapidated country house. Bushes, nettles, and brambles were there with small holly and thick hurdles that blocked the inner courtyard. Green and gray lizards, snakes, screech owls, and small-horned owls were the only masters of the place.

The nobleman who had been out hunting had gotten lost. When he stopped at an inn, people told him the story of the chateau and the beautiful princess. In order to go the chateau he decided to sleep at the inn and to eat some rye bread, wine, salty ham, and porridge. The next day the hunter reached the bushes at an early hour and took care not to get stuck. After working his way through the bushes, he was able to reach the large room where the beautiful princess was lying on an antique bed, and she woke up right away. The maiden asked for her parents. The nobleman responded that he had not seen anyone and that the ivy covered everything up to the top of the towers.

Outside the princess didn't recognize anything. Nobody in the country remembered her or knew about her relatives. She had been asleep more than one hundred years, the poor maiden. But now the nobleman married her, and from then on, the sleeping beauty lived with him and did not have any more misfortunes.

7. THE BEAST AS BRIDEGROOM

ATU 425—THE SEARCH FOR THE LOST HUSBAND AND 425A—THE ANIMAL AS BRIDEGROOM

There are hundreds if not thousands of variants that have emanated from these two tale types. The beginnings of the tales enable us to understand what makes the types distinct and how they differ from one another. For instance, the plot of 425A generally begins with a father about to embark on a voyage. He asks his three daughters what kinds of gifts they would like him to bring back for them. The youngest daughter asks for some unusual flower/animal/object, while the other two wish for some kind of rich garment or jewel. In searching for the unusual gift for the youngest daughter, the father unknowingly enters a monster's garden and thus commits a trespass or violates a law. The monster (beast/reptile) threatens to kill him unless the father is willing to give up his youngest daughter to the monster. The plot of 425 begins with a childless royal couple, desperate to have a child even if it is an animal. Consequently, the queen gives birth to a hideous beast (pig, donkey, boar, serpent, hedgehog) who demands to marry a young woman when he grows up. In either case, once the beast weds a young woman, she is put to all sorts of tests to prove that she is worthy of him, for he is a handsome prince at night, and a ferocious beast during the day. She has no idea what he actually looks like because they sleep together in the dark. His bride must swear to keep his secret but succumbs to the questioning of her curious sisters and/or mother and divulges it. They encourage her to see what he looks like. Then she either burns his animal skin or drops wax from a candle on him as she tries to see him. The beast/bridegroom is enraged because he must continue to live a dual existence as animal and man and flies off. To prove her love for him, his "true" wife must travel the world for three or seven years to win him back. These two plots are often mixed and transformed to create unusual variants.

There is ample evidence of the early popularity of these tale types in India and the Middle East. Key works are Apuleius' "Cupid and Psyche" in *The Golden Ass* (second century), in the Sanskrit *Panchatantra* (c. third century), in the birth tale of *Vikrama's Adventures, or the Thirty Two Tales of the Throne*, and the Latin *Asinarius* (1200). By the sixteenth century the tale types had been spread in oral and literary traditions throughout Europe, the Middle East, Asia, and Africa. The most important literary versions of this tale are Giovan Francesco Straparola, "Galeotto" (*Le Piacevoli Notti*, 1550/1553); Giambattista Basile, "The Serpent" ("Lo serpe," *Lo cunto de li cunti*, 1634); Marie-Catherine d'Aulnoy, "Serpentin Vert" ("Serpentin Vert") and

"The Ram" ("Le Mouton," *Les Contes de fées*, 1697) and "The Wild Boar" ("Le Prince Marcassin," *Suite des Contes Nouveaux ou des Fées à la mode*, 1698); Henriette Julie de Murat, "The Pig King" ("Le Roy Porc," *Histoires Sublimes et Allégoriques*, 1699); Jean Paul Bignon, "Zeineb" (*Les Aventures d'Abdalla*, 1710–1714); Gabrielle-Suzanne Barbot de Villeneuve, "Beauty and the Beast" ("La Belle et la Bête," *La jeune Amériquaine et Les Contes marins*, 1740); and Jeanne-Marie Leprince de Beaumont, "Beauty and the Beast" ("La Belle et la Bête," *Magasin des enfans*, 1756).

The French writers played a significant role in popularizing the tale types, especially Mme d'Aulnoy, who was evidently familiar with different types of beast/bridegroom folk tales and was literally obsessed by the story of Psyche and Cupid, reworking or mentioning it in several fairy tales. By the time the Grimms wrote their version of "The Singing, Springing Lark," which they had heard from Henrietta Dorothea Wild in 1813, there were already numerous oral and literary versions that incorporated motifs from the oral beast bridegroom cycle and the literary tradition of "Cupid and Psyche" and "Beauty and the Beast." For instance, even before the publication of their tale, the Grimms were aware of a version in Johann Gottlieb Münch's *Mährleinbuch für meine lieben Nachbarsleute* (1799). Moreover, though they had not read it, Charles Lamb wrote the long poem *Beauty and the Beast: Or a Rough Outside with a Gentle Heart* in 1811.

There are two major related themes in these tale types: the effort by the beast to transform himself and become a civilized human being through the love of a woman, and the initiation of a young woman who must show compassion, courage, and perseverance to grasp what love means. Of course, as we can see from the versions from Norway, Russia, Germany, Italy, and Portugal that follow and from many other variants, these themes have been altered greatly, and they may also have been influenced by nineteenth-century customs of forced marriages that women were compelled to suffer with elderly men, whom they might have regarded as beasts. Whatever the case may be, tales about beauties and beasts thrived in the nineteenth and twentieth centuries, and they are still prolific throughout the world. The two most famous filmic adaptations of the tale types 425 and 425A in the twentieth century are Jean Cocteau's *Beauty and the Beast* (*La Belle et la Bête*, 1946) and Walt Disney Corporation's *Beauty and the Beast* (1991). Numerous other cinematic and television adaptations have continued to appear in the twenty-first century, not to mention stories and novels that attest to the popular appeal of this tale type.

******

The Singing, Springing Lark (1815)[75]

Jacob and Wilhelm Grimm

Once upon a time there was a man about to go on a long journey, and upon his departure he asked his three daughters what he should bring back to them. The oldest wanted pearls, the second diamonds, but the third said, "Dear father, I'd like to have a singing, springing lark."

"Yes," said the father. "If I can get one, you shall have it." So he kissed all three daughters and departed.

Now, when the time came for his return journey, he had purchased pearls and diamonds for the two oldest, but even though he had looked all over, he had not been able to find the singing, springing lark for his youngest daughter. He was particularly sorry about that because she was his favorite. In the meantime, his way took him through a forest, in the middle of which he discovered a magnificent castle. Near the castle was a tree, and way on top of this tree he saw a lark singing and springing about.

"Well, you've come just at the right time!" he said, quite pleased, and he ordered his servant to climb the tree and catch the little bird. But when the servant went over to the tree, a lion jumped out from under it, shook himself, and roared so ferociously that the leaves on the trees trembled.

"If anyone tries to steal my singing, springing lark," he cried, "I'll eat him up!"

"I didn't know the bird belonged to you," said the man. "Can I buy my way out of this?"

"No!" said the lion. "There's nothing that can save you unless you promise to give me the first thing you meet when you get home. If you agree, then I'll not only grant you your life, but I'll also give you the bird for your daughter."

However, the man refused and said, "That could be my youngest daughter. She loves me most of all and always runs to meet me when I return home."

But the servant was very frightened and remarked, "It could also be a cat or a dog."

The man let himself be persuaded, took the singing, springing lark with a sad heart, and promised the lion he would give him the first thing that met him when he got home.

When he now rode home, the first thing that met him was none other than his youngest and dearest daughter. Indeed, she came running up to him, threw her arms around him, and kissed him. When she saw that he had brought her a

---

75. "Das singende springende Löweneckerchen," *Kinder- und Haus-Märchen. Gesammelt durch die Brüder Grimm*, 2 vols. (Berlin: Realschulbuchandlung, 1812/1815).

singing, springing lark, she was even more overcome by joy. But her father could not rejoice and began to weep.

"Alas, dearest child!" he said. "I've had to pay a high price for this bird. To get it I had to promise you to a wild lion, and when he gets you, he'll tear you to pieces and eat you up."

Then he went on to tell her how everything had happened and begged her not to go there, no matter what the consequences might be. Yet, she consoled him and said, "Dearest father, since you've made a promise, you must keep it. I'll go there, and once I've made the lion nice and tame, I'll be back here safe and sound."

The next morning she had her father show her the way. Then she took leave of him and walked calmly into the forest.

Now, the lion was actually an enchanted prince. During the day he and his men were lions, and during the night they assumed their true human forms. When she arrived there, she was welcomed in a friendly way, and the wedding was celebrated. As soon as night came, the lion became a handsome man, and so they stayed awake at night and slept during the day, and they lived happily together for a long time.

One day the prince came to her and said, "Tomorrow there will be a celebration at your father's house because your oldest sister is to be married. If it would give you pleasure to attend, my lions will escort you there."

She replied that, yes, she would very much like to see her father again, and she went there accompanied by the lions. There was great rejoicing when she arrived, for they had all believed that she had been torn to pieces by the lion and had long been dead. But she told them how well off she was and stayed with them just as long as the wedding celebration lasted. Then she went back to the forest.

When the second daughter was about to be married, she was again invited to the wedding, but on this occasion she said to the lion, "This time I don't want to go without you. You must come with me."

However, the lion didn't want to attend the wedding and said it would be too dangerous for him because if a ray of light were to fall upon him, he would be changed into a dove and have to fly about with the doves for seven years.

But she didn't leave him in peace and said that she'd be sure to take good care of him and protect him from the light. So they went off together and also took their small child with them. Once there she had a hall built for him so strong and thick that not a single ray of light could penetrate it. That was the place where he was to sit when the wedding candles were lit. However, its door was made out of green wood, and it split and developed a crack that nobody saw.

Now the wedding was celebrated in splendor, but when the wedding procession with all the candles and torches came back from church and passed by the prince's hall, a very, very thin ray fell upon the prince, and he was instantly transformed into a dove. When his wife entered the hall to look for him, she could only find a white dove sitting there, and he said to her, "For seven years I shall have to fly about the world, but for every seven steps you take I shall leave a drop of red blood and a white feather to show you the way. And, if you follow the traces, you'll be able to rescue me."

Then the dove flew out the door, and she followed him. At every seventh step she took, a little drop of blood and a little white feather would fall and show her the way. Thus she went farther and farther into the wide world and never looked about or stopped until the seven years were almost up. She was looking forward to that and thought they would soon be free. But, they were still quite far from their goal.

Once, as she was moving along, she failed to find any more little feathers or little drops of blood, and when she raised her head, the dove had also vanished. 'I won't be able to get help from a mortal,' she thought, and so she climbed up to the sun and said to her, "You shine into every nook and cranny. Is there any chance that you've seen a white dove flying around?"

"No," said the sun, "I haven't, but I'll give you a little casket. Just open it when your need is greatest."

She thanked the sun and continued on her way until the moon began to shine in the evening. "You shine the whole night through and on all fields and woods. Have you seen a white dove flying around?"

"No," said the moon, "I haven't, but I'll give you an egg. Just crack it open when your need is greatest."

She thanked the moon and went farther until the Night Wind stirred and started to blow. "You blow over every tree and under every leaf. Have you seen a white dove flying around?"

"No," said the Night Wind, "I haven't, but I'll ask the three other winds. Perhaps they've seen one."

The East Wind and the West Wind came and reported they had not seen a thing, but the South Wind said, "I've seen the white dove. It's flown to the Red Sea and has become a lion again, for the seven years are over. The lion's now in the midst of a battle with a dragon that's really an enchanted princess."

Then the Night Wind said to her, "Here's what I would advise you to do: Go to the Red Sea, where you'll find some tall reeds growing along the shore. Then count them until you come to the eleventh one, which you're to cut off and use to strike the dragon. That done, the lion will be able to conquer the dragon, and both will regain their human forms. After that, look around, and you'll see the griffin sitting by the Red Sea. Get on his back with the prince, and the griffin will carry you home across the sea. Now, here's a nut for you. When you cross over the middle of the sea, let it drop. A nut tree will instantly sprout out of the water, and the griffin will be able to rest on it. If he can't rest there, he won't be strong enough to carry you both across the sea. So if you forget to drop the nut into the sea, he'll let you fall into the water."

She went there and found everything as the Night Wind had said. She counted the reeds by the sea, cut off the eleventh, and struck the dragon with it. Consequently, the lion defeated the dragon, and both immediately regained their human forms. But when the princess, who had previously been a dragon, was set free from the magic spell, she picked the prince up in her arms, got on the griffin, and carried him off with her. So the poor maiden, who had journeyed so far, stood alone and forsaken again. However, she said, "I'll keep going as far as the wind blows and so long as the cock crows until I find him."

And off she went and wandered a long, long way until she came to the castle where the two were living together. Then she heard that their wedding celebration was soon to take place. "God will come to my aid," she remarked as she opened the little casket that the sun had given her. There she found a dress as radiant as the sun itself. She took it out, put it on, and went up to the castle. Everyone at the court and the bride herself stared at her. The bride liked the dress so much she thought it would be nice to have it for her wedding and asked if she could buy it.

"Not for money or property," she answered, "but for flesh and blood."

The bride asked her what she meant by that, and she responded, "Let me sleep one night in the prince's room."

The bride didn't want to let her, but she also wanted the dress very much. Finally, she agreed, but the bridegroom's servant was ordered to give him a sleeping potion. That night when the prince was asleep, she was led into his room, sat down on his bed, and said, "I've followed you for seven years. I went to the sun, the moon, and the four winds to find out where you were. I helped you conquer the dragon. Are you going to forget me forever?"

But the prince slept so soundly that it merely seemed to him as if the wind were whispering in the firs. When morning came, she was led out of the castle again and had to give up her golden dress.

Since her ploy had not been of much use, she was quite sad and went out to a meadow, where she sat down and wept. But as she was sitting there, she remembered the egg that the moon had given her. She cracked it open, and a hen with twelve chicks jumped out, all in gold. The peeping chicks scampered about and then crawled under the mother hen's wings. There was not a lovelier sight to see in the world. Shortly after that she stood up and drove them ahead of her over the meadow until they came within sight of the bride, who saw them from her window. She liked the little chicks so much that she came right down and asked if she could buy them.

"Not for money or possessions, but for flesh and blood. Let me sleep another night in the prince's room."

The bride agreed and wanted to trick her as she had done the night before. But when the prince went to bed, he asked the servant what had caused all the murmuring and rustling during the night, and the servant told him everything:

that he had been compelled to give him a sleeping potion because a poor girl had secretly slept in his room, and that he was supposed to give him another one that night.

"Dump the drink by the side of my bed," said the prince.

At night the maiden was led into the room again, and when she began to talk about her sad plight, he immediately recognized his dear wife by her voice, jumped up, and exclaimed, "Now I'm really free from the spell! It was like a dream. The princess had cast a spell over me and made me forget you, but God has helped me just in time."

That night they left the castle in secret, for they were afraid of the princess's father, who was a sorcerer. They got on the griffin, who carried them over the Red Sea, and when they were in the middle, she let the nut drop. Immediately a big nut tree sprouted, and the griffin was able to rest there. Then he carried them home, where they found their child, who had grown tall and handsome. From then on they lived happily until their death.

The Singing, Springing Lark (1857)[76]
Jacob and Wilhelm Grimm

Once upon a time there was a man who was about to go on a long journey, and right before his departure he asked his three daughters what he should bring back to them. The oldest wanted pearls, the second diamonds, but the third said, "Dear father, I'd like to have a singing, springing lark."

"All right," said the father. "If I can get one, you shall have it."

So he kissed all three daughters good-bye and went on his way. When the time came for his return journey, he had purchased pearls and diamonds for the two oldest, but even though he had looked all over, he had not been able to find the singing, springing lark for his youngest daughter. He was particularly sorry about that because she was his favorite. In the meantime, his way took him through a forest, in the middle of which he discovered a magnificent castle. Near the castle was a tree, and way on top of this tree he saw a lark singing and springing about.

"Well, you've come just at the right time," he said, quite pleased, and he ordered his servant to climb the tree and catch the little bird. But when the servant went over to the tree, a lion jumped out from under it, shook himself, and roared so ferociously that the leaves on the trees trembled.

"If anyone tries to steal my singing, springing lark," he cried, "I'll eat him up."

"I didn't know that the bird belonged to you," said the man. "I'll make up for my trespassing and give you a great deal of gold if only you'll spare my life."

76. "Das singende springende Löweneckerchen," *Kinder- und Hausmärchen gesammelt durch die Brüder Grimm*, 7th ed., 3 vols. (Göttingen: Verlag der Dieterich'schen Buchhandlung, 1857).

"Nothing can save you," said the lion, "unless you promise to give me the first thing you meet when you get home. If you agree, then I'll not only grant you your life, but I'll also give you the bird for your daughter."

At first the man refused and said, "That could be my youngest daughter. She loves me most of all and always runs to meet me when I return home."

But the servant was very scared of the lion and said, "It doesn't always have to be your daughter. Maybe it'll be a cat or a dog."

The man let himself be persuaded and took the singing, springing lark. Then he promised the lion he would give him the first thing that met him when he got home.

Upon reaching his house, he walked inside, and the first thing that met him was none other than his youngest and dearest daughter. Indeed, she came running up to him, threw her arms around him, and kissed him. When she saw that he had brought her a singing, springing lark, she was overcome by joy. But her father couldn't rejoice and began to weep.

"My dearest child," he said. "I've had to pay a high price for this bird. In exchange I was compelled to promise you to a wild lion, and when he gets you, he'll tear you to pieces and eat you up."

Then he went on to tell her exactly how everything had happened and begged her not to go there, no matter what the consequences might be. Yet, she consoled him and said, "Dearest father, if you've made a promise, you must keep it. I'll go there, and once I've made the lion nice and tame, I'll be back here safe and sound."

The next morning she had her father show her the way. Then she took leave of him and walked calmly into the forest.

Now, it turned out that the lion was actually an enchanted prince. During the day he and his men were lions, and during the night they assumed their true human forms. When she arrived there, she was welcomed in a friendly way, and they conducted her to the castle. When night came, the lion became a handsome man, and the wedding was celebrated in splendor. They lived happily together by remaining awake at night and asleep during the day. One day he came to her and said, "Tomorrow there will be a celebration at your father's house since your oldest sister is to be married. If you wish to attend, my lions will escort you there."

She replied that, yes, she would very much like to see her father again, and she went there accompanied by the lions. There was great rejoicing when she arrived, for they all had believed that she had been torn to pieces by the lions and had long been dead. But she told them what a handsome husband she had and how well off she was. She stayed with them just as long as the wedding celebration lasted. Then she went back to the forest.

When the second daughter was about to be married, she was again invited to the wedding, but this time she said to the lion, "I don't want to go without you."

However, the lion said it would be too dangerous for him because he would be changed into a dove and have to fly about with the doves for seven years if the ray of a burning candle were to fall upon him.

"Please, come with me," she said. "I'll be sure to take good care of you and protect you from the light."

So they went off together and took their small child with them. Once there she had a hall built for him so strong and thick that not a single ray of light could penetrate it. That was the place where he was to sit when the wedding candles were lit. However, its door was made out of green wood, and it split and developed a crack that nobody saw.

The wedding was celebrated in splendor, but when the wedding procession with all the candles and torches came back from church and passed by the hall, a ray about the width of a hair fell upon the prince, and he was instantly transformed into a dove. When his wife entered the hall to look for him, she could only find a white dove sitting there, and he said to her, "For seven years I shall have to fly about the world, but for every seven steps you take I shall leave a drop of red blood and a little white feather to show you the way. And, if you follow the traces, you'll be able to set me free."

Then the dove flew out the door, and she followed him. At every seventh step she took, a drop of blood and a little white feather would fall and show her the way. Thus she went farther and farther into the wide world and never looked about or stopped until the seven years were almost up. She was looking forward to that and thought they would soon be free. But, they were still quite far from their goal.

Once, as she was moving along, she failed to find any more feathers or drops of blood, and when she raised her head, the dove had also vanished. I won't be able to get help from a mortal, she thought, and so she climbed up to the sun and said to her, "You shine into every nook and cranny. Is there any chance that you've seen a white dove flying around?"

"No," said the sun, "I haven't, but I'll give you a little casket. Just open it when your need is greatest."

She thanked the sun and continued on her way until the moon came out to shine in the evening. "You shine the whole night through and on all the fields and meadows. Is there any chance that you've seen a white dove flying around?"

"No," said the moon, "I haven't, but I'll give you an egg. Just crack it open when your need is greatest."

She thanked the moon and went farther until the Night Wind stirred and started to blow at her. "You blow over every tree and under every leaf. Is there any chance that you've seen a white dove flying around?"

"No," said the Night Wind, "I haven't, but I'll ask the three other winds. Perhaps they've seen one."

The East Wind and the West Wind came and reported they had not seen a thing, but the South Wind said, "I've seen the white dove. It's flown to the Red Sea and has become a lion again, for the seven years are over. The lion's now in the midst of a fight with a dragon that's really an enchanted princess."

Then the Night Wind said to her, "Here's what I would advise you to do: Go to the Red Sea, where you'll find some tall reeds growing along the shore. Then count them until you come to the eleventh one, which you're to cut off and use to strike the dragon. That done, the lion will be able to conquer the dragon, and both of them will regain their human forms. After that, look around, and you'll see the griffin sitting by the Red Sea. Get on his back with your beloved, and the griffin will carry you home across the sea. Now, here's a nut for you. When you cross over the middle of the sea, let it drop. A nut tree will instantly sprout out of the water, and the griffin will be able to rest on it. If he can't rest there, he won't be strong enough to carry you both across the sea. So if you forget to drop the nut into the sea, he'll let you fall into the water."

She went there and found everything as the Night Wind had said. She counted the reeds by the sea, cut off the eleventh, and struck the dragon with it. Thereupon the lion conquered the dragon, and both immediately regained their human forms. But when the princess, who had previously been a dragon, was set free from the magic spell, she picked the prince up in her arms, got on the griffin, and carried him off with her. So the poor maiden, who had journeyed so far, stood alone and forsaken again, and sat down to cry. Eventually, she took heart and said, "I'll keep going as far as the wind blows and so long as the cock crows until I find him."

And off she went and wandered a long, long way until she came to the castle where the two were living together. Then she heard that their wedding celebration was soon to take place. "God will come to my aid," she remarked as she opened the little casket that the sun had given her. There she found a dress as radiant as the sun itself. She took it out, put it on, and went up to the castle. Everyone at the court and the bride herself could not believe their eyes. The bride liked the dress so much she thought it would be nice to have it for her wedding and asked if she could buy it.

"Not for money or property," she answered, "but for flesh and blood."

The bride asked her what she meant by that, and she responded, "Let me sleep one night in the bridegroom's room."

The bride didn't want to let her, but she also wanted the dress very much. Finally, she agreed, but the bridegroom's servant was ordered to give him a sleeping potion. That night when the prince was asleep, she was led into his room, sat down on his bed, and said, "I've followed you for seven years. I went to the sun, the moon, and the four winds to find out where you were. I helped you conquer the dragon. Are you going to forget me forever?"

But the prince slept so soundly that it merely seemed to him as if the wind were whispering in the firs. When morning came, she was led out again and had to give up her golden dress.

Since her ploy had not been of much use, she was quite sad and went out to a meadow, where she sat down and wept. But as she was sitting there, she remembered the egg that the moon had given her. She cracked it open, and a hen with twelve chicks jumped out, all in gold. The peeping chicks scampered about and then crawled under the mother hen's wings. There was not a lovelier sight to see in the world. Shortly after that she stood up and drove them ahead of her over the meadow until they came within sight of the bride, who saw them from her window. She liked the little chicks so much that she came right down and asked if she could buy them.

"Not with money or possessions, but for flesh and blood. Let me sleep another night in the bridegroom's room."

The bride agreed and wanted to trick her as she had done the night before. But when the prince went to bed, he asked the servant what had caused all the murmuring and rustling during the night, and the servant told him everything: that he had been compelled to give him a sleeping potion because a poor girl had secretly slept in his room, and that he was supposed to give him another one that night.

"Dump the drink by the side of my bed," said the prince.

At night the maiden was led in again, and when she began to talk about her sad plight, he immediately recognized his dear wife by her voice, jumped up, and exclaimed, "Now I'm really free from the spell! It was like a dream. The strange princess had cast a spell over me and made me forget you, but God has delivered me from the spell just in time."

That night they left the castle in secret, for they were afraid of the princess's father, who was a sorcerer. They got on the griffin, who carried them over the Red Sea, and when they were in the middle, she let the nut drop. Immediately a big nut tree sprouted, and the griffin was able to rest there. Then he carried them home, where they found their child, who had grown tall and handsome. From then on they lived happily until their death.

The Cursed Frog (1854)[77]

Carl and Theodor Colshorn

Once upon a time there was a merchant who had three daughters. However, our dear Lord had taken away his wife. One day he decided to travel to a foreign country by sea to fetch gold and other precious things, and he consoled his weeping children by saying: "I'll bring you beautiful things when I return! What do you want?"

The eldest asked for a silk dress and added: "It must be made of three kinds silk."

The second daughter wished for a feathered hat and added: "It must have three kinds of feathers."

---

77. "Der verwunschene Frosch," *Märchen und Sagen aus Hannover* (Hannover: Carl Rümpler, 1854).

Finally the youngest said: "Dear father, bring me a rose, but it must be fresh and have three kinds of colors."

The merchant promised to do all this, kissed his daughters, and set off on his journey. After he had arrived in the foreign country, he ordered a dress made out of three kinds of silk for his eldest daughter and a hat with three kinds of feathers for his second daughter. Both were finished very soon, and they were of rare splendor. Then he also sent out messengers throughout this country to search for a three-colored rose for his youngest daughter. However, they all returned with empty hands, even though the merchant had offered them a good deal of gold, and even though there were more roses in this country than there are daisies here. So, he sailed home with a sad heart and was in a bad mood the entire voyage. Then, on this side of the ocean he traveled past a large garden in which there was nothing but roses and roses. So he went inside and searched, and lo and behold, he found a slender bush in the middle of the garden that had a three-colored rose. Overjoyed, he plucked it and wanted to continue on his way. However, he found himself bewitched and couldn't move his feet. Then a voice behind him cried out: "What do you want in my garden?"

He looked around and saw a large goggle-eyed frog sitting on the bank of a clear pond staring at him.

"You've broken off my dear rose, and therefore, you must die, unless you give me your youngest daughter to be my wife."

The merchant was horrified and begged and pleaded, but it was all in vain. So, he finally had to submit and let the ugly frog become engaged to his dearest daughter. Now his feet were set free, and he walked out of the garden. But the frog called out after him, "In seven days I shall come and fetch my wife!"

So it was with sorrow that the merchant gave his youngest daughter the fresh rose and told her what had happened. And when the terrible day arrived, she crawled beneath her bed, for she absolutely did not want to go to the frog. But about noon a splendid carriage drove up, and the frog sent his servants into the house. They went straight into her room, dragged the screaming maiden out from under the bed, and carried her into the carriage. Then the horses sped off, and in a short time they were in the blooming rose garden. In the middle of the garden right behind the clear pond, a small house was standing. The bride was brought into the house and put to rest on a soft bed. However, the frog jumped into the water.

When it became dark and the maiden awoke from her unconscious state, she heard the frog singing wonderfully sweet songs outside in the pond. And the nearer midnight approached, the sweeter he sang and the closer he came to her. At midnight the door to the room opened, and the frog hopped onto her bed. However, he had touched her heart with his sweet songs, and she took him into the bed with her and warmly covered him up. And when the next morning came, she opened her eyes, and behold, the ugliest frog had become the handsomest prince in the world. Then he thanked her with all his heart and said, "You have saved me and are now my wife!"

From then on they lived long and happily together.

East O' the Sun and West O' the Moon (1858)[78]
Peter Christen Asbjørnsen and Jørgen Moe

Once upon on a time there was a poor husbandman who had so many children that he hadn't much of either food or clothing to give them. Pretty children they all were, but the prettiest was the youngest daughter, who was so lovely there was no end to her loveliness. So one day, 'twas on a Thursday evening late at the fall of the year, the weather was so wild and rough outside, and it was so cruelly dark, and rain fell and wind blew, till the walls of the cottage shook again. There they all sat round the fire busy with this thing and that. But just then, all at once something gave three taps on the windowpane. Then the father went out to see what was the matter, and when he got out of doors, what should he see but a great big White Bear.

"Good evening to you," said the White Bear.

"The same to you," said the man.

"Will you give me your youngest daughter? If you will, I'll make you as rich as you are now poor," said the Bear.

Well, the man would not be at all sorry to be so rich, but still he thought he must have a bit of a talk with his daughter first. So he went in and told them how there was a great White Bear waiting outside, who had given his word to make them so rich if he could only have the youngest daughter.

The lassie said "No!" outright. Nothing could get her to say anything else. So, the man went out and settled it with the White Bear and asked him come again the next Thursday evening and get an answer. Meantime he talked his daughter over and kept on telling her of all the riches they would get, and how well off she would be herself, and so at last she thought better of it, and washed and mended her rags, made herself as smart as she could, and was ready to start. I can't say her packing gave her much trouble.

Next Thursday evening came the White Bear to fetch her, and she got upon his back with her bundle, and off they went. So, when they had gone a bit of the way, the White Bear said: "Are you afraid?"

"No!" she wasn't.

"Well! Mind and hold tight by my shaggy coat, and then there's nothing to fear," said the Bear.

So she rode a long, long way, till they came to a great steep hill. There, on the face of it, the White Bear gave a knock, and a door opened, and they came into a castle, where there were many rooms all lit up—rooms gleaming with silver and

---

78. *Popular Tales from the Norse*, trans. George Dasent (Edinburgh: Edmonston & Douglas, 1859).

gold. And there too was a table ready laid, and it was all as grand as grand could be. Then the White Bear gave her a silver bell, and when she wanted anything, she was only to ring it, and she would get it at once.

Well, after she had eaten and drunk, and evening wore on, she got sleepy after her journey, and thought she would like to go to bed. So, she rang the bell, and she had scarce taken hold of it before she came into a chamber, where there was a bed made, as fair and white as anyone would wish to sleep in, with silken pillows and curtains and gold fringe. All that was in the room was gold or silver, but when she had gone to bed, and put out the light, a man came and laid himself alongside her. That was the White Bear, who threw off his beast shape at night, but she never saw him, for he always came after she had put out the light, and before the day dawned, he was up and off again. So things went on happily for a while, but at last she began to get silent and sorrowful, for there she went about all day alone, and she longed to go home to see her father and mother, and brothers and sisters. So one day, when the White Bear asked what it was that she lacked, she said it was so dull and lonely there, and how she longed to go home to see her father and mother, and brothers and sisters, and that was why she was so sad and sorrowful, because she couldn't get to them.

"Well, well!" said the Bear, "perhaps there's a cure for all this, but you must promise me one thing, not to talk alone with your mother, but only when the rest are by to hear, for she'll take you by the hand and try to lead you into a room alone to talk; but you must mind and not do that, else you'll bring bad luck on both of us."

So one Sunday the White Bear came and said now they could set off to see her father and mother. Well, off they started, she sitting on his back, and they went far and long. At last they came to a grand house, and there her brothers and sisters were running about out of doors at play, and everything was so pretty, 'twas a joy to see.

"This is where your father and mother live now," said the White Bear, "but don't forget what I told you, else you'll make us both unlucky."

No! Bless her, she'd not forget, she assured him, and when she had reached the house, the White Bear turned right about and left her. Then, when she went in to see her father and mother, there was such joy, there was no end to it. None of them thought they could thank her enough for all she had done for them. Now, they had everything they wished, as good as good could be, and they all wanted to know how she got on where she lived.

Well, she said, it was very good to live where she did; she had all she wished. What she said beside, I don't know, but I don't think any of them had the right end of the stick, or that they got much out of her. But in the afternoon, after they had done dinner, all happened as the White Bear had said. Her mother wanted to talk with her alone in her bedroom, but she minded what the White Bear had said and wouldn't go upstairs.

"Oh, what we have to talk about will keep," she said and put her mother off. But somehow or other, her mother got round her at last, and she had to tell her the whole story. So she said, how every night, when she had gone to bed, a man came and lay down beside her as soon as she had put out the light, and how she never saw him, because he was always up and away before the morning dawned and how she went about woeful and sorrowing, for she thought she should so like to see him, and how all day long she walked about there alone, and how dull, dreary, and lonesome it was.

"My!" said her mother. "It may well be a troll you slept with! But now I'll teach you a lesson how to set eyes on him. I'll give you a bit of candle, which you can carry home in your bosom. Just light that while he is asleep, but take care not to drop the tallow on him."

Yes! she took the candle, and hid it in her bosom, and as night drew on, the White Bear came and fetched her away.

But when they had gone a bit of the way, the White Bear asked if all hadn't happened as he had said. Well, she couldn't say it hadn't.

"Now, mind," said he, "if you have listened to your mother's advice, you have brought bad luck on us both, and then, all that has passed between us will be as nothing."

"No," she said, she hadn't listened to her mother's advice.

So when she reached home and had gone to bed, it was the old story over again. There came a man and lay down beside her, but at dead of night, when she heard he slept, she got up and struck a light, lit the candle, and let the light shine on him, and so she saw that he was the loveliest prince one ever set eyes on, and she fell so deep in love with him on the spot that she thought she couldn't live if she didn't give him a kiss there and then. And so she did, but as she kissed him, she dropped three hot drops of tallow on his shirt, and he woke up.

"What have you done?" he cried. "Now you have made us both unlucky, for had you held out only this one year, I had been freed. For I have a step-mother who has bewitched me so that I am a White Bear by day, and a man by night. But now all ties are snapt between us. Now I must set off from you to her. She lives in a castle which stands east o' the sun and west o' the moon and there, too, is a princess, with a nose three ells long, and she's the wife I must have now."

She wept and took it ill, but there was no help for it. Go he must. Then she asked if she mightn't go with him.

No, she mightn't.

"Tell me the way, then," she said, "and I'll search you out. That surely I may get leave to do."

"Yes," she might do that, he said, but there was no way to that place. It lay east o' the sun and west o' the moon, and thither she'd never find her way.

So next morning, when she woke up, both prince and castle were gone, and then she lay on a little green patch, in the midst of the gloomy thick wood, and by her side lay the same bundle of rags she had brought with her from her old home. So when she had rubbed the sleep out of her eyes and wept till she was tired, she set out on her way, and walked many, many days, till she came to a lofty crag. Under it sat an old hag, who played with a gold apple which she tossed about. The lassie stopped and asked if she knew the way to the prince, who lived with his stepmother in the castle that lay east o' the sun and west o' the moon, and who was to marry the princess with a nose three ells long.

"How did you come to know about him?" asked the old hag. "But maybe you are the lassie who ought to have had him?"

Yes, she was.

"So, so. It's you, is it?" said the old hag. "Well, all I know about him is, that he lives in the castle that lies east o' the sun and west o' the moon, and thither you'll come, late or never; but still you may have the loan of my horse, and on him you can ride to my next neighbor. Maybe she'll be able to tell you, and when you get there, just give the horse a switch under the left ear and beg him to be off home, and, stay, this gold apple you may take with you."

So she got upon the horse, and rode a long long time, till she came to another crag, under which sat another old hag with a gold carding-comb. So now the lassie asked if she knew the way to the castle that lay east o' the sun and west o' the moon, and she answered, like the first old hag, that she knew nothing about it, except it was east o' the sun and west o' the moon.

"And thither you'll come, late or never; but you shall have the loan of my horse to my next neighbor. Maybe she'll tell you all about it, and when you get there, just switch the horse under the left ear, and beg him to be off home."

And this old hag gave her the golden carding-comb. It might be she'd find some use for it, she said. So the lassie got up on the horse and rode a far far way and a weary time. So at last she came to another great crag, under which sat another old hag, spinning with a golden spinning wheel. Her, too, she asked if she knew the way to the prince, and where the castle was that lay east o' the sun and west o' the moon. So it was the same thing over again.

"Maybe it's you who ought to have had the prince?" said the old hag.

Yes, it was.

But she, too, didn't know the way a bit better than the other two. "East o' the sun and west o' the moon it was," she knew—that was all.

"And thither you'll come, late or never; but I'll lend you my horse, and then I think you'd best ride to the East Wind and ask him. Maybe he knows those parts, and can blow you thither. But when you get to him, you need only give the horse a switch under the left ear, and he'll trot home of himself."

And so, too, she gave her the gold spinning wheel. "Maybe you'll find a use for it," said the old hag.

Then on she rode many many days, a weary time, before she got to the East Wind's house, but at last she did reach it, and then she asked the East Wind if he could tell her the way to the prince who dwelt east o' the sun and west o' the moon. Yes, the East Wind had often heard tell of it, the prince and the castle, but he couldn't tell the way, for he had never blown so far.

"But, if you will, I'll go with you to my brother the West Wind, maybe he knows, for he's much stronger. So, if you will just get on my back, I'll carry you thither."

Yes, she got on his back, and I should just think they went briskly along. So when they got there, they went into the West Wind's house, and the East Wind said the lassie he had brought was the one who ought to have had the prince who lived in the castle east o' the sun and west o' the moon, and so she had set out to seek him, and how he had come with her, and would be glad to know if the West Wind knew how to get to the castle.

"Nay," said the West Wind, "so far I've never blown, but if you will, I'll go with you to our brother the South Wind, for he's much stronger than either of us, and he has flapped his wings far and wide. Maybe he'll tell you. You can get on my back, and I'll carry you to him."

Yes! She got on his back, and so they travelled to the South Wind and weren't so very long on the way, I should think.

When they got there, the West Wind asked him if he could tell her the way to the castle that lay east o' the sun and west o' the moon, for it was she who ought to have the prince who lived there.

"You don't say so! That's she, is it?" said the South Wind.

"Well I have blustered about in most places in my time, but so far have I never blown; but if you will, I'll take you to my brother the North Wind. He is the oldest and strongest of the whole lot of us, and if he don't know where it is, you'll never find anyone in the world to tell you. You can get on my back, and I'll carry you thither."

Yes! She got on his back, and away he went from his house at a fine rate. And this time, too, she wasn't long on her way.

So, when they got to the North Wind's house, he was so wild and cross, cold puffs came from him a long way off.

"Blast you both! What do you want?" he roared out to them ever so far off so that it struck them with an icy shiver.

"Well," said the South Wind, "you needn't be so foulmouthed, for here I am, your brother, the South Wind, and here is the lassie who ought to have had the prince who dwells in the castle that lies east o' the sun and west o' the moon, and now she wants to ask you if you ever were there, and can tell her the way, for she would be so glad to find him again."

"Yes, I know well enough where it is," said the North Wind. "Once in my life I blew an aspen leaf thither, but I was so tired I couldn't blow a puff for ever so many days after. But if you really wish to go thither and aren't afraid to come along with me, I'll take you on my back and see if I can blow you thither."

Yes! With all her heart. She must and would get thither if it were possible in any way, and as for fear, however madly he went, she wouldn't be at all afraid.

"Very well, then," said the North Wind, " but you must sleep here tonight, for we must have the whole day before us, if we're to get thither at all."

Early next morning the North Wind woke her, and puffed himself up, and blew himself out, and made himself so stout and big, 'twas gruesome to look at him. And so off they went high up through the air, as if they would never stop till they got to the world's end. Down here below there was such a storm. It threw down long tracts of wood and many houses, and when it swept over the great sea, ships foundered by hundreds.

So they tore on and on—no one can believe how far they went—and all the while they still went over the sea, and the North Wind got more and more weary, and so out of breath he could scarce bring out a puff, and his wings drooped and drooped, till at last he sunk so low that the crests of the waves dashed over his heels.

"Are you afraid?" said the North Wind.

"No!" She wasn't.

But they weren't very far from land, and the North Wind had still so much strength left in him that he managed to throw her up on the shore under the windows of the castle which lay east o' the sun and west o' the moon, but then he was so weak and worn out, he had to stay there and rest many days before he could get home again.

Next morning the lassie sat down under the castle window and began to play with the gold apple. The first person she saw was the Long-nose who was to have the prince.

"What do you want for your gold apple, you lassie?" said the Long-nose and threw up the window.

"It's not for sale, for gold or money," said the lassie.

"If it's not for sale for gold or money, what is it that you will sell it for? You may name your own price," said the princess Long-nose.

"Well, if I may get to the prince, who lives here, and be with him tonight, you shall have it," said the lassie whom the North Wind had brought.

Yes! She might. That could be done. So the princess got the gold apple, but when the lassie came up to the prince's bedroom at night he was fast asleep. She called him and shook him, and between whiles she wept sore. But no matter what she did, she couldn't wake him up. Next morning as soon as day broke, came the princess with the long nose and drove her out again.

So in the daytime she sat down under the castle windows and began to card with her golden carding-comb, and the same thing happened. The princess asked what she wanted for it, and she said it wasn't for sale for gold or money, but if she might get leave to go up to the prince and be with him that night, the princess should have it. But when she went up, she found him fast asleep again, and no matter how much she called, and shook, and wept, and prayed, she couldn't get life into him. And as soon as the first gray peep of day came, then came the princess with the long nose and chased her out again.

So in the daytime the lassie sat down outside under the castle window and began to spin with her golden spinning wheel, and that, too, the princess with the long nose wanted to have. So she threw up the window and asked what she wanted for it. The lassie said, as she had said twice before, it wasn't for sale for gold or money, but if she might go up to the prince who was there and be with him alone that night, she might have it.

Yes! She might do that and welcome. But now you must know there were some Christian folk who had been carried off thither, and as they sat in their room, which was next the prince, they had heard how a woman had been in there and wept and prayed and called to him two nights running, and they told that to the prince.

That evening, when the princess came with her sleepy drink, the prince made as if he drank, but threw it over his shoulder, for he could guess it was a sleepy drink. So, when the lassie came in, she found the prince wide awake. And then she told him the whole story how she had come thither.

"Ah," said the prince, "you've just come in the very nick of time, for tomorrow is to be our wedding day. But now I won't have the Long-nose, and you are the only woman in the world who can set me free. I'll say I want to see what my wife is fit for, and beg her to wash the shirt which has the three spots of tallow on it. She'll say, yes, for she doesn't know 'tis you who put them there, but that's a work only for Christian folk, and not for such a pack of trolls, and so I'll say that I won't have any other for my bride than the woman who can wash them out, and ask you to do it."

So there was great joy and love between them all that night. But next day, when the wedding was to be, the prince said:

"First of all, I'd like to see what my bride is fit for."

"Yes!" said the stepmother, with all her heart.

"Well," said the prince, "I've got a fine shirt which I'd like for my wedding shirt, but somehow or other it has got three spots of tallow on it, which I must have washed out. And I have sworn never to take any other bride than the woman who's able to do that. If she can't, she's not worth having."

Well, that was no great thing, they said, so they agreed, and she with the long nose began to wash away as hard as she could, but the more she rubbed and scrubbed, the bigger the spots grew.

"Ah!" said the old hag, her mother, "you can't wash. Let me try."

But she hadn't long taken the shirt in hand, before it got far worse than ever, and with all her rubbing, and wringing, and scrubbing, the spots grew bigger and blacker, and the darker and uglier was the shirt.

Then all the other trolls began to wash, but the longer it lasted, the blacker and uglier the shirt grew, till at last it was as black all over as if it had been up the chimney.

"Ah!" said the prince, "You're none of you worth a straw. You can't wash. Why there, outside, sits a beggar lassie, I'll be bound she knows how to wash better than the whole lot of you. Come in, lassie!" he shouted.

Well, in she came.

"Can you wash this shirt clean, lassie?" said he.

"I don't know," she said, "but I think I can."

And almost before she had taken it and dipped it in the water, it was as white as driven snow, and whiter still.

"Yes, you are the lassie for me," said the prince.

At that the old hag flew into such a rage, she burst on the spot, and the princess with the long nose after her, and the whole pack of trolls after them—at least I've never heard a word about them since.

As for the prince and princess, they set free all the poor Christian folk, who had been carried off and shut up there, and they took with them all the silver and gold and flitted away as far as they could from the castle that lay east o' the sun and west o' the moon.

Translated by George Dasent.

The Enchanted Tsarévich (1855–1864)[79]

Alexander Afanas'ev

Once upon a time there was a merchant who had three daughters. It so happened he had one day to go to strange countries to buy wares, and so he asked his daughters, "What shall I bring you from beyond the seas?"

The eldest asked for a new coat, and the next one also asked for a new coat, but the youngest one only took a sheet of paper and sketched a flower on it.

"Bring me, Bátyushka,[80] a flower like this!"

So the merchant went and made a long journey to foreign kingdoms, but he never came across such a flower. So he returned home, and on his way he

79.   Leonard Magnus, *Russian Folk-Tales* (New York: E. P. Dutton, 1916).
80.   Father.

happened to observe a splendid lofty palace with watchtowers, turrets, and a garden. He went for a walk in the garden, and you cannot imagine how many trees he saw and flowers, every flower fairer than the other flowers.

And then he looked, and he saw a single one like the one which his daughter had sketched. "Oh," he said, "I will tear off and bring this to my beloved daughter. Evidently there is nobody here to watch me."

So he ran up and broke it off, and as soon as he had done it, in that very instant a boisterous wind arose and thunder thundered, and a fearful monster stood in front of him, a formless, winged snake with three heads.

"How dare you play the master in my garden!" cried the snake to the merchant. "Why have you broken off a blossom?"

The merchant was frightened, fell on his knees, and besought pardon.

"Very well," said the snake, "I will forgive you, but on condition that whoever meets you first, when you reach home, you must give me for all eternity. If you deceive me, do not forget, nobody can ever hide himself from me. I shall find you wherever you are."

The merchant agreed to the condition and went back home. Meanwhile, the youngest daughter saw him from the window and ran out to meet him. Then the merchant hung his head, looked at his beloved daughter, and began to shed bitter tears.

"What is the matter with you? Why are you weeping, Bátyushka?"

He gave her the blossom and told what had befallen him.

"Do not grieve, Bátyushka," said the youngest daughter. "It is God's gift. Perhaps I shall fare well. Take me to the snake."

The father took her away, set her in the palace, bade farewell, and set out for home. Then the fair maiden, the daughter of the merchant, went into the different rooms, and beheld everywhere gold and velvet; but no one was there to be seen, not a single human soul. Time went by and went by, and the fair damsel became hungry and thought, 'Oh, if I could only have something to eat!' But before she ever had thought this, in front of her stood a table, and on the table were dishes and drinks and refreshments. The only thing that was not there was birds' milk. Then she sat down to the table, drank and ate, got up, and it had all vanished.

Darkness now came on, and the merchant's daughter went into the bedroom, wishing to lie down and sleep. Then a boisterous wind rustled round and the three-headed snake appeared in front of her.

"Hail, fair maiden! Put my bed outside this door!"

So the fair maiden put the bed outside the door and herself lay on the bedstead.

She awoke in the morning, and again in the entire house there was not a single soul to be seen. And it all went well with her. Whatever she wished for appeared on the spot. In the evening the snake flew to her and ordered, "Now, fair maiden, put my bed next to your bedstead."

She then laid it next to her bedstead, and the night went by, and the maiden awoke, and again there was never a soul in the palace. And for the third time the snake came in the evening and said, "Now, fair maiden, I am going to lie with you in the bedstead."

The merchant's daughter was fearfully afraid of lying on a single bed with such a formless monster. But she could not help herself. So she strengthened her heart and lay down with him. In the morning the serpent said to her, "If you are now weary, fair maiden, go to your father and your sisters. Spend a day with them, and in the evening come back to me. But see to it that you are not late. If you are one single minute late, I shall die of grief."

"No, I shall not be late," said the maiden, the merchant's daughter, and she descended the steps. There was a barouche ready for her, and she sat down. That very instant she arrived at her father's courtyard. When the father saw her, he welcomed her, kissed her, and asked her, "How has God been dealing with you, my beloved daughter? Has it been well with you?"

"Very well, father!" And she started telling of all the wealth there was in the palace, how the snake loved her, how whatever she only thought of was in that instant fulfilled. The sisters heard and did not know what to do out of sheer envy.

Now the day was ebbing away, and the fair maiden made ready to go back, and was bidding farewell to her father and her sisters, saying, "This is the time I must go back. I was bidden to keep to my term."

But the envious sisters rubbed onions on their eyes and made as though they were weeping. "Do not go away, sister. Stay until to-morrow."

The fair maiden was very sorry for her sisters and stayed one day more. In the morning she bade farewell to them all and went to the palace. When she arrived, it was as empty as before. She went into the garden, and she saw the serpent lying dead in the pond! He had thrown himself for sheer grief into the water.

"Oh, my God, what have I done?" cried out the fair maiden, and she wept bitter tears, ran up to the pond, hauled the snake out of the water, embraced one head and kissed it with all her might. And the snake trembled, and in a minute turned into a good youth.

"I thank you, fair maiden," he said. "You have saved me from the greatest misfortune. I am no snake, but an enchanted prince."

Then they went back to the merchant's house, were betrothed, lived long, and lived for good and happy things.

The Toad (1869)[81]

François-Marie Luzel

Once upon a time there was a goodly old man who was a widower with three daughters. One day, one of his daughters said to him: "Father, would you go and

---

81.   "L'Homme-Crapeau," *Contes populaires de la Basse-Bretagne*, 3 vols. (Paris: Maisonneuve et Leclerc, 1887).

fetch a pitcher of water for me from the well? There's not a drop in the house, and I need some water for our stew."

"Very well, daughter," the old man responded.

And he took a pitcher and went to the well. Just as he leaned over the water to fill the pitcher, a toad jumped onto his face and stuck to it so tightly that all his efforts to pull the toad off were in vain.

"You won't be able to pull me off your face," the toad said, "until you promise to let me marry one of your daughters!"

The man left the pitcher near the well and ran back to the house.

"Oh, God! What's happened to you, father?" his daughters cried out when they saw what condition he was in.

"Alas, my poor children! This reptile jumped onto my face just as I was fetching water from the well, and it said right off that it won't let go of my face unless one of you consents to take him for your husband."

"Great God! What are you saying, father?" the eldest daughter responded. "Marry a toad? It's so horrible to look at!"

And she turned her head and left the house. And the second sister did just the same.

"Ah, my poor father!" the youngest daughter said. "As for me, I give my consent to marry the toad because my heart couldn't bear to see you remain in this condition."

As soon as she said this, the toad fell to the ground, and the wedding was set for the next day.

When the bride entered the church accompanied by the toad, the priest was quite astonished, and he said he would never marry a Christian with a toad. However, he ended up marrying them when the bride's father told him everything and promised him a great deal of money.

So, the toad took his wife to his chateau—for he had a beautiful chateau. When the time came to go to sleep, he led her to her room, and once there, he took off his toad skin and revealed himself to be a young and handsome prince! When the sun shone during the day he was a toad, and at night, he was a prince.

The two sisters of the newly wed bride came to visit her a few times, and they were very surprised to find her so cheerful. She continually sang and laughed.

"There's something going on there," they said to themselves. "We'll have to keep an eye on her to see what is going on."

One night, they quietly went to the chateau, looked through the keyhole, and were very astonished to see a young and handsome prince instead of a toad.

"Well, well!" they said. "A handsome prince! . . . If I had known! . . ."

They heard the prince say these words to his wife: "Tomorrow I must take a trip, and I'm going to leave my toad skin here. Please see to it that nothing bad happens to it because I still have a year and a day to remain in this shape."

"That's very good!" the two sisters said to one another as they listened at the door.

The next morning the prince departed just as he had announced he would, and his two sisters-in-law came to visit his wife.

"My God, what beautiful things you have! You must be very happy with your toad!" they said to her.

"Yes, certainly, my dear sisters. I'm very happy with him."

"Where has he gone?"

"He's on a trip."

"If you'd like, my little sister, I'll comb your beautiful hair."

"I'd like this very much, my good sister."

The young wife fell asleep while one of the sisters combed her hair with a golden comb, and once this happened, her sisters took the keys from her pocket, took the toad skin from the armoire where it had been locked up, and threw it into the fire. Upon waking, the young wife was surprised to find herself alone, and then her husband arrived a moment later, and he was red with anger.

"Ah! You unfortunate woman!" he screamed. "You've done exactly what I forbade you to do and are my misfortune as well as your own: you've burned my toad skin! Now I shall leave, and you'll never see me again."

The poor maiden began to weep and said: "I shall follow you no matter where you go."

"No, don't follow me, stay here."

And he ran off in haste. And she also ran after him.

"I told you to stay there."

"I won't stay there. I'm going to follow you!"

And he continued to run. But no matter how fast he ran, she clung to his heels. Then he threw a golden ball behind him. His wife picked it up, put it into her pocket, and continued to run after him.

"Go back to the house! Go back to the house!" he shouted at her.

"I won't ever return to the house without you!"

He threw another golden ball which she picked up like the first and put it into her pocket.

Then, he threw a third. But, seeing that she was still on his heels, he became furious and gave her a punch in her face. The blood gushed out right away, and three drops fell onto his shirt causing three stains. Well now, the poor maiden had to remain behind, and soon she lost sight of her husband. Nevertheless, she cried out: "May these three blood stains never disappear until I arrive to rub them out!"

Despite everything, she continued her pursuit. Soon she entered a large forest. A little later she followed a path beneath the trees and saw two enormous lions! But no matter! God protected her! So, she continued on her way toward them, and when she arrived near the lions, she was astonished to see that they laid down at her feet and licked her hands. As soon as they did that, she began to pet them on their heads and back. Then she resumed her journey. Further on she saw a hare sitting on its rear end on the edge of the path, and as she passed it, the hare said, "Get on my back, and I'll carry you out of the forest."

So she sat down on the hare's back, and in a short time, he carried her out of the forest.

"Now," the hare said to her before it departed, "you are near the chateau where you'll find the man you are searching for."

"Thank you, my good and divine animal," the young maiden said.

Indeed, she soon found herself on a large avenue lined with old oak trees, and not far from there she saw washerwomen washing their laundry at a pond. As she approached, she heard one of them saying, "Ah, here's a shirt that must have been bewitched! For two years now I've tried to wash out three blood stains on it. I've tried my best, but I've not succeeded!"

Upon hearing these words, the young maiden approached the washerwoman who had spoken them and said, "Please let me have that shirt for a moment. I think I know how to get rid of those three blood stains."

So the washerwoman gave her the shirt, and she spit on the three blood stains, soaked the shirt in the water, rubbed a little, and soon the three stains disappeared.

"A thousand thanks," the washerwoman said to her. "Our lord is about to marry, and he'll be happy to see that the three stains have disappeared because this is his most beautiful shirt."

"I'd like very much to find some work in your lord's chateau."

"The woman who looked after the sheep has recently left, and she hasn't been replaced yet. Come with me, and I'll recommend you."

Now the young maiden was hired as the herdswoman of the sheep. Every day she took her herd of sheep into the large forest around the chateau, and she often saw her husband who came to walk with the young princess who was to become his wife. Her heart beat very hard when she saw him. But she didn't dare to speak to him.

She still had the three golden balls, and whenever she was bored, she often amused herself by playing with the balls. One day, the young princess noticed the golden balls, and she said to her maid: "Look! Look! Those golden balls the maiden has! Go and ask her if she'll sell one of them to me."

The maid went over to the shepherdess and said: "What beautiful golden balls you have! Would you sell one of them to the princess, my mistress?"

"No, I won't sell my balls. I have nothing else to do but play with my balls to pass my time."

"Bah! You're being unreasonable. Just look at the bad condition of your clothes. Sell one of the balls to my mistress, and she'll pay you well, and you'll be able to dress yourself properly."

"I don't want any money."

"What would you like?"

"To sleep one night with your master!"

"What! You wicked girl! How dare you speak like that?"

"I won't give up one of my golden balls for anything in the world except for that."

The maid returned to her mistress, who said: "Well then, what did the shepherdess say?"

"I don't dare to tell you what she said."

"Tell me quickly."

"The wicked girl said that she won't give up one of her balls unless she can sleep one night with your husband."

"Let's see now. That doesn't matter because I want one of those balls no matter what it costs. I'll put a drug into my husband's wine at dinner, and he won't be able to be aware of anything. So, go and tell her that I accept the condition, and bring me a golden ball."

That evening, when the lord left the table, he felt such a great need to sleep that he had to rush to his bed as soon as possible. A little later, the shepherdess was allowed to enter his room. But not matter how much she called him with tender names or kissed and hugged him tightly, it was all in vain and he didn't wake up.

"Alas!" the poor maiden cried out and wept. "Have all my efforts been in vain? Have I suffered for nothing? After all it was me who married you when you were a toad and when nobody else wanted you! And I searched for you courageously two long years in the heat, in the cruelest cold, in the rain and snow, and in the middle of a storm! And now that I've found you again, you don't hear me. You sleep like a rock! Ah, I'm so unlucky!"

And she wept and sobbed, but alas! he didn't hear her.

The next morning she returned to the forest with her sheep, sad and thoughtful. In the afternoon the princess came like the day before. She was walking with her maid. When the shepherdess caught sight of her, she began playing with her two remaining golden balls. The princess desired to have another ball to make a pair, and she said to her maid again: "Go and buy a second golden ball from the shepherdess."

The maid obeyed, and to keep this story short, the bargain was concluded under the same condition as before: the shepherdess was to spend the night with the lord of the chateau in his room.

Once again the princess put a drug into the lord's wine at dinner, and like the night before, he went straight to bed after leaving the table and slept like a rock. Some time later, the shepherdess was once again allowed to enter the room, and she began complaining and sobbing once more. By chance, a valet passed by the door, heard the noise, and stopped to listen. He was very much astonished by everything that he heard, and the next morning he went to his master and said:

"My lord, there are things that are happening in the chateau about which you are unaware, and it's important that you know them."

"What do you mean? Speak quickly."

"A poor maiden, who seems to be very unfortunate and distressed, arrived at the chateau some days ago, and out of pity, she was hired as a shepherdess to replace the one who had left. One day, the princess went walking in the forest with her servant and saw her playing with some golden balls. She desired right away to have those balls and sent her maid to buy them from the shepherdess no matter what the price was. The shepherdess didn't demand money or anything except to spend a night with you in your bedroom for each one of the balls. She has already given two balls, and she has spent two nights with you in your bedroom without your knowing anything about this. It is a pity to hear her sobs and groans. I believe that she's a lost soul because she says some very strange things. For example she claims that she was your wife when you were a toad and that she's walked all over for two whole years looking for you. . . ."

"Is it possible that all this is true?"

"Yes, my lord, all this is true. And if you don't know anything about this, it's because the princess puts some drug into your wine at dinner. So, when you leave the table, you must go to sleep, and you sleep deeply until the next morning."

"Well, we'll put an end to this! I must be on my guard, and you'll soon see some new things around here."

The poor shepherdess was looked down upon and detested by the servants at the chateau because they knew that she spent nights in the lord's bedroom. The cook only gave her crusts of barley bread like she gave to the dogs.

The next morning, the shepherdess went to the forest with her sheep, and the princess bought the third golden ball at the same price of the other two so that the shepherdess was to spend the third night with the lord in his bedroom.

When the dinner hour arrived, the lord was on his guard this time. While he conversed with his neighbor, he watched the princess pour some drug into his glass of wine. He pretended not to notice, but instead of drinking the wine, he threw it beneath the table, and the princess didn't see him do this.

Upon rising from the table, the lord pretended to be sleepy like the other nights, and he went to his room. A short time thereafter the shepherdess also came. This time he didn't sleep, and as soon as he saw her, he embraced her, and they wept out of joy and happiness to have found each other again.

"For the moment, return to your room, my poor wife," he said to her after some time had passed, "and tomorrow you're to come here again."

The next day a grand dinner was held at the chateau to set the wedding day. Kings, queens, princes, princesses, and other aristocrats were present. Toward the end of the dinner, the future son-in-law stood up and said:

"My father-in-law, I would like to have your advice about a certain case. I have a small pretty casket with a small pretty golden key. I lost the key to my casket, and I had another key made. But then a short time thereafter I found the original key again. So now I have two keys instead of one. Which one, father-in-law, did you think I should use?"

"Always respect old age," the future father-in-law responded.

At that point, the prince entered a small room nearby and soon returned holding the hand of the shepherdess, dressed simply but properly, and he presented her to the company.

"Well then," he said. "Here is my original key! What I mean to say, here is my first wife whom I've found again. She is my wife, and I still love her, and I don't want anyone but her!"

And so they returned to their country where they lived together until the end of their days.

All right, there you have it, the tale of "The Toad." How did you like it?

Told by Barba Tassel, a beggar, at Plouaret in 1869. Translated by François-Marie Luzel.

The Pig King (1870)[82]

Laura Gonzenbach

Once upon a time there was a king and queen, who had no children and would have very much liked to have one. One day the queen went for a walk, and a pig ran across her way with her piglets.

"Oh, God, such a dumb beast has so many little ones, and you haven't even given me one despite all my prayers. Oh, if only I could have a child, even if it were a little pig!"

Shortly thereafter it seemed that the queen was going to have a baby, and soon her hour came. However, she gave birth to a tiny piglet. You can imagine the great astonishment and sadness in the castle and the entire land. Nevertheless, the queen declared, "This piglet is my child, and I love him just as if he were a handsome little boy that I had brought into this world."

So she suckled the piglet and loved it with all her heart. In turn the piglet thrived and grew rapidly day by day. When it had become much larger, it began to roam around the castle and grunt, "I want a wife! I want a wife!"

So the queen said to the king, "What should we do? We certainly can't give our son a princess. There is none that would take him. Let's speak to the

---

82. "Vom Re Porco," *Sicilianische Märchen*, 2 vols. (Leipzig: W. Engelmann, 1870).

washerwoman. She has three beautiful daughters. Perhaps she'll give one of them to our son for his wife."

The king was satisfied with this proposal, and the queen summoned the washerwoman.

"Listen," she said to her, "you must do me a favor. My son would like to marry, and you must give your eldest daughter to him as his wife."

"Oh, your majesty," responded the washerwoman, "should I really give my daughter to a pig?"

"Yes, you should," the queen said. "Look, your daughter will be treated like a queen, and I'll give you whatever you want."

The washerwoman was a poor old lady and let herself be persuaded to carry out the queen's will. So she went to her eldest daughter and said to her, "Just think, my daughter, the king's son wants to marry you, and you'll be treated just like a queen."

To be sure, the daughter didn't want to marry a pig. She thought, however, she would have beautiful clothes and all the money she wanted and said yes. So, a splendid wedding was celebrated, and the festivities lasted three days long. The daughter of the washerwoman was dressed in expensive clothes. While she was sitting in her beautiful dress all spread out, the pig came running up to her. He had been waddling in mud and wanted to rub the dirt off on her precious dress. However, she brusquely shoved him away and cried out, "Oh, you disgusting beast! Go away! You're dirtying my beautiful dress," and no matter how often he came close to her, she drove him away with unfriendly words.

In the evening of the third day, after the marriage had been performed, she was led into the bridal chamber and lay down on a bed. The pig waited until she had fallen asleep before he entered the room. Then he locked the door, stripped off the pigskin, and turned into a handsome, noble young man. All at once he took his sword and sliced off his wife's head, and when morning came, he slipped back into his pigskin, ran around the castle, and grunted, "I want a wife! I want a wife!"

The queen didn't have any peace of mind, for she thought, "What if he has killed the girl?"

When she went into the bridal chamber and found the dead bride in the bed, she was deeply distressed and said, "What should I tell her poor mother?"

Meanwhile, the pig ran around the castle and demanded a wife. So the queen summoned the washerwoman and tearfully told her about the unhappy fate of her daughter.

"Now you must do me a favor and bring your second daughter to me so that she will become my son's wife," she said.

"How can I send my poor child to her death," the washerwoman yammered loudly.

"You must do it," the queen said. "Just remember that if it works out, your daughter will be the first lady in the entire realm after me."

The washerwoman agreed once more and brought her second daughter to the castle, and the wedding was celebrated with great splendor for three days. The bride wore a beautiful dress and when she sat there in her gorgeous gown, the pig came running into the room. He had waddled in mud and wanted to climb on to her lap. But she cried out, "Oh, you disgusting beast! Go away! You're dirtying my beautiful dress."

On the evening of the third day she was led into the bridal chamber, and things did not go any better for her than they had gone with her older sister. When she was sound asleep, her husband entered the chamber, stripped off the pigskin, and turned into a handsome young man. Then he cut off her head. The next morning the queen came into the room and found the dead bride in the bed, while her son was running around the castle and was grunting, "I want a wife! I want a wife!"

What was she to do?

The queen had to summon the washerwoman once more to inform her about the sad fate of her daughter and to request that she send her youngest daughter to her. Then the poor woman began to weep and said, "Am I to lose all my children?"

She didn't want to give away her third daughter. But the queen continued to ask and suggested that her youngest daughter was much smarter than the other two. Perhaps she might succeed where the others failed. After a while the washerwoman let herself be persuaded and brought her youngest daughter to the castle. Indeed, she was very intelligent and more beautiful than the sun and the moon. All at once the pig came running toward her, and she bent over and called it, "My pretty little beast." Soon a splendid wedding was celebrated for three days, and the bride received the most beautiful clothes. When she was sitting down in a magnificent gown, the pig entered. It had been waddling in mud and wanted to clean itself off on her gown. So she said, "Just climb up on my lap, you dear beast. Even if you make my gown dirty, it doesn't matter. I'll put another one on later."

No matter how often she changed her gown, the pig came and dirtied her garments. However, she tolerated everything and never lost her patience. In the evening of the third day she was led into the bridal chamber, and while she was sound asleep, her husband entered, stripped off the pigskin, and lay down next to her. Before she woke up, however, he slipped back into the pigskin so that she didn't know what a handsome young man she had for a husband.

In the morning the queen entered the room with a heavy heart, and when she found the bride bright and cheery, she thanked God that everything had turned out so well.

For some days things continued like this. One evening, however, the young woman didn't fall asleep, and when her husband stripped off the pigskin, she saw him in his true shape and immediately fell in love with him with all her heart.

"Why didn't you let me know how handsome you are?" she asked.

However, he answered, "Don't tell anyone what I look like. If you do, I must go away, and you must wander for seven years, seven months, and seven days, and you must wear out seven pairs of iron shoes before you can rescue me."

So she promised him to keep quiet and not to tell a single person about him. Indeed, she kept her promise for many days. However, one day she couldn't resist an urge to tell the queen about her son.

"Oh, dear mother," she said, "if only you knew how handsome my husband is when he strips off his pigskin in the evening!"

At that very same moment the prince vanished, and no matter how much the people at the castle searched for him, he couldn't be found anywhere. So the young woman began to weep and said, "I'm responsible for his misfortune. He told me what would happen. So, now I'll wander seven years, seven months, and seven days until I find him again."

Consequently, she had seven pairs of iron shoes made for her, and even though the king and queen didn't want her to depart, she remained insistent and departed. She wandered for many many days until she came to a small cottage in which a good old woman was living.

"Oh, please," the young woman requested, "let me rest here for one night. Otherwise, I shall die of thirst."

The old woman welcomed her in a friendly way, and when she heard why the princess had left the castle, she said, "Oh, you poor girl, you must wander in the underground until you have worn out four pairs of shoes."

So she gave her a small lamp and showed her the entrance to the underworld in which she had to wander, and the poor young woman began to walk, and she traveled four years, four months, and four days beneath the earth until she had used up four pairs of shoes.

After this long time had passed, she returned to daylight and wandered on the earth once more. At one point she came to a dense forest and couldn't find a way out. Eventually she saw a light in the distance, and as she approached it, she saw a cottage and knocked on the door. A very old man opened the door. It was a hermit, who asked her what she wanted.

"Oh, father," she answered. I'm a poor maiden and have been wandering and looking for my husband," and she told him the entire story.

"Oh, you poor child," the hermit said, "you must still wander further, and I can't help you. But my older brother lives a day's journey deeper in the woods. Perhaps he can give you some counsel. You may rest here tonight. Tomorrow I'll wake you."

The next morning the hermit woke her, showed her the way, and gave her a hazel nut on her departure.

"Keep it in a safe place. It will be of use to you," he said. Then he blessed her and let her depart.

She wandered the entire day, and when it turned evening, she came to the second hermit's hut where she spent the night and told him about her troubles.

"You poor child," he answered. "I can't help you, but my older brother lives a day's journey from here deeper in the woods. Perhaps he can give you good advice."

Upon her departure the hermit gave her a chestnut and said, "Keep it in a safe place. It will be of use to you."

Then she wandered another whole day in the dark woods, and in the evening she came to the third hermit's hut where she spent the night and told him about her sorrows. But he couldn't help her. Instead, he directed her to his eldest brother who lived deeper in the forest. Upon her departure, he gave her a nut and said, "Keep it in a save place. It will be of use to you."

On the evening of the fourth day she finally came to the eldest hermit who was so ancient that she was almost frightened of him. When she told him why she was wandering about, he said, "You poor child, you must continue wandering until the seven years, seven months, and seven days are up. Then you will arrive in the city where the prince is living. Take this magic wand. That night you are to go in front of the royal castle and hit the ground with the wand. All at once a marvelous castle will rise up, and you can live in it."

Then he blessed her and let her depart.

So she continued to wander until she had used up the seven pairs of shoes, and the seven years, seven months, and seven days had flown by. Finally, one evening she came to the city where the Pig King was living. To be sure, he had his human shape, for the magic spell had finally been cast off, but he had forgotten his faithful wife, and a beautiful woman held him captive. In a few days they were to be married. When the poor young woman heard this, she felt sick in her heart. But she did what the hermit had told her to do. During the night she went before the royal castle and hit the ground with the magic wand. All at once a magnificent castle arose, and it had large rooms and halls and many servants. Of course, she went inside and began living there.

The next morning, when the Pig King went to the window, he saw the beautiful castle and was very puzzled. He called the queen so that she could see it, too. Meanwhile, the young woman had cracked the hazel nut, which the hermit had given to her, and just imagine, a beautiful gold hen with many gold chicks came out! They were very cute to see. She took the hen along with the chicks and set them on the balcony where the king and queen could see them. When the queen now saw the hen and chicks, she felt a great desire to possess them. So she called her loyal chambermaid and said to her, "Go over to the lady, and ask her whether she will sell the hen and the chicks to me. I'll give her whatever she wants for them."

The chambermaid went over to the palace and delivered the message from the queen.

"Tell your mistress," the young woman answered, "The hen and the chicks are not for sale. However, I'd gladly give them to her as a gift if she would allow me to spend one night in her bridegroom's chamber."

When the chambermaid returned with this message, the queen thought, "No, I can't let this happen. It's impossible!"

But the chambermaid said, "Why not, your majesty? We can give the king a sleeping potion tonight. Then he won't notice a thing."

So the queen agreed to the proposal, and the young woman gave the gold hen and the chicks to her and was led into the room of the king. Then she began to weep and lament: "Have you completely forgotten me? Seven years, seven months, and seven days I have wandered in rain and storm, and in the fierce heat of the sun, and I have worn out seven pairs of iron shoes in order to rescue you. And now you are going to be unfaithful to me?"

She wailed and groaned this way the entire night, but since the king had taken the sleeping potion, he could not hear her, and she had to leave the room the next morning without having wakened him.

Beneath the king's room, there was a prison, and during that night the prisoners had heard everything that the poor woman had lamented, and they were astounded by all this. Meanwhile, she went home, cracked open the chestnut, and found a little teacher made of gold with her little pupils who were knitting and sewing. They were very pretty to see, and they were all made of gold. So she took the toys and set them on the balcony, and when the queen saw the figures, she had a craving to posses them and sent her chambermaid over to the young woman to see if they were for sale.

"Tell your mistress," the young woman said, "I shall gladly give them to her as a gift if she will let me spend a night in her bridegroom's room."

The queen resisted, but the chambermaid said, "Why not? We'll give the king another sleeping potion so that he won't notice a thing."

When evening arrived, and the king was sitting at the table, the queen mixed a sleeping potion in his wine so that he fell sound asleep. Later when his real wife came, he couldn't hear how she wept and wailed the entire night. But the prisoners heard it, and when the king awoke, they requested that he come to them for a few moments. They had something to say to him. So the king went to the prisoners, who said, "Your majesty, for two nights we've been hearing moans and groans from a lady's voice in your room."

"How can it be that I haven't heard a thing?" responded the king. "Tonight I won't drink any wine."

Meanwhile his poor wife was very sad and had already gone home. When she arrived, she cracked the nut, and found a beautiful gold eagle which shone in the sun with great splendor. She took the eagle and placed it on the balcony as she had done with the other figures, and no sooner did the queen catch sight of it than she wished to possess it and sent her chambermaid over to buy the eagle at any price. But the young woman continued to give the same answer: "Tell your mistress I'll be delighted to give it to her as a gift if she lets me spend a night in her bridegroom's room."

"All right," thought the queen, "I'll just give the king another sleeping potion."

When evening came and the king was sitting at the table, he took great care not to drink any of the wine which the queen offered him, instead he poured it out beneath the table. However, he pretended that he had been overwhelmed by sleep and went to bed where he began to snore as though he were sound asleep. All at once the door opened, and his real wife entered, sat down on the bed, and began to lament: "Have you completely forgotten me? Seven years, seven months, and seven days I wandered. In storms and rain, and in the glowing furious heat of the sun, and I wore out seven pairs of iron shoes to save you, and now you want to be unfaithful to me?"

When the king heard all this, he remembered his faithful wife, jumped up, embraced her, and kissed her.

"Yes," he said, "you are my dear wife. Don't worry. We shall flee this place tomorrow."

The next morning, after his wife had left him, he stood up, freed all the prisoners as a gesture of thanks for warning him, and secretly equipped a ship in the harbor without the queen noticing it. That night he went on board the ship with his wife and sailed home to his parents. You can imagine how they rejoiced when they saw their son and their dear daughter-in-law again! They celebrated with a beautiful party, and they remained rich and consoled, and we're just sitting here and getting old.

The Little Feather of Fenist the Bright Falcon (1874)[83]

Peter Polevoi

Once upon a time there was an old widower who lived with his three daughters. The elder and the middle one were fond of show and finery, but the youngest only troubled herself about household affairs, although she was of a loveliness which no pen can describe and no tale can tell. One day the old man got ready

---

83.   Peter Polevoi, *Narodnuiya Russkiya Skazki* (St. Petersburg: 1874). Translation in R. Nisbet Bain, *Russian Fairy Tales: From the Skazki of Polevoi* (London: Lawrence and Bullen, 1893).

to go to market in the town and said: "Now, my dear daughters, say! What shall I buy for you at the fair?"

The eldest daughter said: "Buy me, dear dad, a new dress!"

The middle daughter said: "Buy me, dear dad, a silk kerchief!"

But the youngest daughter said: "Buy me, dear dad, a little scarlet flower!"

The old man went to the fair where he bought for his eldest daughter a new dress, for his middle daughter a silk kerchief, but, though he searched the whole town through, he could not find a little scarlet flower. He was already on his way back when there met him a little old man, whom he knew not, and this little old man was carrying a little scarlet flower. Our old man was delighted, and he asked the stranger: "Sell me thy little scarlet flower, thou dear little old man!"

The old man answered him: "My little scarlet flower is not for sale, 'tis mine by will, it has no price and cannot be priced, but I'll let thee have it as a gift if thou wilt marry thy youngest daughter to my son!"

"And who then is thy son, dear old man?"

"My son is the good and valiant warrior-youth Fenist the bright falcon. By day he dwells in the sky beneath the high clouds, by night he descends to the earth as a lovely youth."

Our old man fell a-thinking. If he did not take the little scarlet flower, he would grieve his daughter, and if he did take it, there was no knowing what sort of a match he would be making. He thought and thought, and at last he took the little scarlet flower, for it occurred to him that if this Fenist the bright falcon, who was thus to be wedded to his daughter, did not please him, it would be possible to break the match off. But no sooner had the strange old man given him the little scarlet flower than he vanished from before his eyes just as if he had never met him at all. The old man scratched his head and began to ponder still more earnestly: "I don't like the look of it at all!" he said, and when he got home, he gave his elder daughters their things, and his youngest daughter her little scarlet flower, and said to her: "I don't like thy little scarlet flower a bit, my daughter. I don't like it at all!"

"Wherefore so vexed at it, dear father?" quoth she.

Then he stooped down and whispered in her ear: "The little scarlet flower of thine is willed away. It has no price, and money could not buy it for me. I have married thee beforehand for it to the son of the strange old man whom I met in the way, to Fenist the bright falcon." And he told her everything that the old man had told him of his son.

"Grieve not, dear father!" said the daughter. "Judge not of my intended by the sight of thine eyes, for though he come a-flying, we shall love him all the same."

And the lovely daughter shut herself up in her little gabled chamber, put her little scarlet flower in water, opened her window, and looked forth into the blue distance.

Scarcely had the sun settled down behind the forest when, whence he came who knows, Fenist the bright falcon darted up in front of her little window. He had feathers like flowers, he lit upon the balustrade, fluttered into the little window, flopped down upon the floor, and turned into a goodly young warrior. The damsel was so terrified, she very nearly screamed, but the good youth took her tenderly by the hand, looked tenderly into her eyes, and said: "Fear me not, my destined bride! Every evening until our marriage I will come flying to thee. Whenever thou placest in the window the little scarlet flower, I'll appear before thee. And here is a little feather out of my little wing, and whatever thou mayst desire, go but out on the balcony, wave this little feather, and immediately I will appear before thee."

Then Fenist the bright falcon kissed his bride and fluttered out of the window again. And he found great favor in her eyes, and henceforth she placed the little scarlet flower in the window every evening, and so it was that whenever she placed it there, the goodly warrior-youth, Fenist the bright falcon, came down to her.

Thus a whole week passed by, and Sunday came round. The elder sisters decked themselves out to go to church, attired themselves in their new things, and began to laugh at their younger sister.

"What art thou going to wear?" said they. "Thou hast no new things at all."

And she answered: "No, I have nothing, so I'll stay at home."

But she bided her time, went out on the balcony, waved her flowery feather in the right direction, and, whence I know not, there appeared before her a crystal carriage and horses and servants in gold galloon, and they brought for her a splendid dress embroidered with precious stones. The lovely damsel sat in the carriage, and went to church. When she entered the church, every one looked at her and marvelled at her beauty and her priceless splendor.

"Some Tsarevna or other has come to our church, depend upon it!" the good people whispered among themselves. When the service was over, our beauty got into her carriage and rolled home, got into the balcony, waved her flowery feather over her left shoulder, and in an instant the carriage and the servants and the rich garments had disappeared. The sisters came home and saw her sitting beneath the little window as before.

"Oh, sister!" cried they. "Thou hast no idea what a lovely lady was at mass this morning. 'Twas a thing marvelous to behold, but not to be described by pen or told in tales."

Two more weeks passed by, and two more Sundays, and the lovely damsel threw dust in the eyes of the people as before, and took in her sisters, her father, and all the other orthodox people. But on the last occasion when she was taking off her finery, she forgot to take out of her hair her diamond pin. The elder sisters came from church and began to tell her about the lovely Tsarevna, and as their eyes fell upon her hair, they one with one voice: "Little sister, what is that thou hast got?"

The lovely damsel cried also and ran off into her little room beneath the gables. And from that time forth the sisters began to watch the damsel and to listen of a night at her little room and discovered and perceived how at dawn Fenist the bright falcon fluttered out of her little window and disappeared behind the dark woods. And the sisters thought evil of their younger sister. And they strewed pieces of broken glass on the window-sill of their sister's little dormer chamber, and stuck sharp knives and needles there, that Fenist the bright falcon, when he lit down upon the window, might wound himself on the knives. And at night Fenist the bright falcon flew down and beat vainly with his wings and beat again, but could not get through the little window. He only wounded himself on the knives and cut and tore his wings. And the bright falcon lamented and fluttered upward and cried to the fair damsel: "Farewell, lovely damsel! Farewell, my betrothed! Thou shalt see me no more in thy little dormer chamber! Seek me in the land of Thrice-nine in the empire of Thrice-ten. The way thither is far. Thou must wear out slippers of iron. Thou must break to pieces a staff of steel. Thou must fret away reins of stone, before thou canst find me, good maiden!"

And at the self-same hour a heavy sleep fell upon the damsel, and through her sleep she heard these words yet could not awaken. In the morning she awoke, and lo! knives and needles were planted on the window-sill, and blood was trickling from them. All pale and distraught, she wrung her hands and cried: "Lo! My distresses have destroyed my darling beloved!" And the same hour she packed up and started from the house and went to seek her bright-white love, Fenist the shining falcon.

The damsel went on and on through many gloomy forests. She went through many dreary morasses. She went through many barren wildernesses, and at last she came to a certain wretched little hut. She tapped at the window and cried: "Host and hostess, shelter me, a poor damsel, from the dark night!"

An old woman came out upon the threshold: "We crave thy pardon, lovely damsel! Whither art thou going, lovey-dovey?"

"Alas, granny! I seek my beloved Fenist the bright falcon. Wilt thou not tell me where to find him?"

"Nay, I know not, but pray go to my middle sister, she will show thee the right way. And lest thou shouldst stray from the path, take this little ball. Whithersoever it rolls, thither will be thy way!"

The lovely damsel passed the night with the old woman, and on the morrow, when she was departing, the old woman gave her a little gift. "Here," said she, "is a silver spinning-board and a golden spindle. Thou wilt spin a spindleful of flax and draw out threads of gold. The time will come when my gift will be of service to thee."

The damsel thanked her and followed the rolling ball. Whether 'twere a long time or a short matters not, but the ball rolled all the way to another little hut. The damsel knocked at the door, and the second old woman opened it. The old woman asked her questions and said to her: "Thou hast still a long way to go, damsel, and it will be no light matter to find thy betrothed. But look now! When thou comest to my elder sister, she will be able to tell thee better than I can. But take this gift from me for thy journey—a silver saucer and a golden apple. The time will come when they will be of use to thee."

The damsel passed the night in the hut and then went on farther after the rolling ball. She went through the woods farther and farther, and at every step the woods grew blacker and denser, and the tops of the trees reached to the very sky. The ball rolled right up to the last, but an old woman came out upon the threshold and invited the lovely damsel to take shelter from the dark night. The damsel told the old woman whither she was going and what she sought.

"Thine is a bad business, my child!" said the old woman. "Thy Fenist the bright falcon is betrothed to the Tsarevna over the sea and will shortly be married to her. When thou gettest out of the wood on to the shores of the blue sea, sit on a little stone, take out thy silver spinning-board and thy golden spindle, and sit down and spin, and the bride of Fenist the bright falcon will come out to thee and will buy thy spindle from thee. But thou must take no money for it, only ask to see the flowery feathers of Fenist the bright falcon!"

The damsel went on farther, and the road grew lighter and lighter, and behold! there was the blue sea. Free and boundless it lay before her, and there, far, far away above the surface of the sea, bright as a burning fire, gleamed the golden summits of the marble palace halls. 'Surely that is the realm of my betrothed which is visible from afar!' thought the lovely damsel, and she sat upon the little stone, took out her silver spinning-board and her golden spindle, and began spinning flax and drawing golden thread out of it. And all at once, she saw coming to her along the sea-shore, a certain Tsarevna, with her nurses and her guards and her faithful servants, and she came up to her and watched her working, and began to bargain with her for her silver spinning-board and her golden spindle.

"I will give them to thee for nothing, Tsarevna, only let me look on Fenist the bright falcon!"

For a long time the Tsarevna would not consent, but at last she said: "Very well, come and look at him when he is lying down to rest after dinner, and drive the flies away from him!"

And she took from the damsel the silver spinning-board and the golden spindle and went to her terem. She made Fenist the bright falcon drunk after dinner with a drink of magic venom, and then admitted the damsel when an unwakable slumber had overpowered him.

The damsel sat behind his pillow, and her tears flowed over him in streams. "Awake, arise, Fenist the bright falcon!" said she to her love. "I, thy lovely damsel, have come to thee from afar. I have worn out slippers of iron. I have ground down a staff of steel. I have fretted away reins of stone. Everywhere and all times have I been seeking thee, my love."

But Fenist the bright falcon slept on, nor knew nor felt that the lovely damsel was weeping and mourning over him. Then the Tsarevna also came in and bade them lead out the lovely damsel, and awoke Fenist the bright falcon.

"I have slept for long," said he to his bride, "and yet it seemed to me as if someone had been here and wept and lamented over me."

"Surely thou hast dreamt it in thy dreams?" said the Tsarevna. "I myself was sitting here all the time and suffered not the flies to light on thee."

The next day the damsel again sat by the sea and held in her hands the silver saucer and rolled the little golden apple about on it. The Tsarevna came out walking again, went up to her, looked on and said, "Sell me thy toy!"

"My toy is not merchandise, but an inheritance. Let me but look once more on Fenist the bright falcon, and thou shalt have it as a gift."

"Very well, come again in the evening, and drive the flies away from my bridegroom!"

And again she gave Fenist the bright falcon a drink of magic sleeping venom and admitted the lovely damsel to his pillow. And the lovely damsel began to weep over her love, and at last one of the burning tears fell from her eyes upon his cheeks.

Then Fenist the bright falcon awoke from his heavy slumbers and cried, "Alas! Who was it who burned me?"

"Oh, darling of my desires!" said the lovely damsel, "I, thy maiden, have come to thee from afar. I have worn out shoes of iron. I have worn down staves of steel. I have gnawed away wafers of stone. I have sought thee everywhere, my beloved! This is the second day that I, thy damsel, have sorrowed over thee, and thou wakedst not from thy slumber, nor made answer to my words!"

Then only did Fenist the bright falcon know his beloved again and was so overjoyed that words cannot tell of it. And the damsel told him all that had happened, how her wicked sisters had envied her, how she had wandered from land to land, and how the Tsarevna had bartered him for toys. Fenist fell in love with her more than ever, kissed her on her sugary mouth, and bade them set the bells a-ringing without delay, and assemble the boyars and the princes and the men of every degree in the market-place. And he began to ask them, "Tell me, good people, and answer me according to good sense, which bride ought I to take to wife and shorten the sorrow of life: her who sold me, or her who bought me back again?"

And the people declared with one voice: "Her who bought thee back again!"

And Fenist the bright falcon did so. They crowned him at the altar the same day in wedlock with the lovely damsel. The wedding was joyous and boisterous and magnificent. I also was at this wedding and drank wine and mead, and the bumpers overflowed, and every one had his fill, and the beard was wet when the mouth was dry.

Translated by R. Nisbet Bain.

The Emperor Scursuni (1875)[84]

Giuseppe Pitrè

Once there were two friends, and one of them had a son while the other had no children at all. They both loved this son very much. The two friends were important merchants who sailed the seas and visited many kingdoms. One day the friend who didn't have a son had to depart on a voyage, and the young man asked him and his father whether he could embark with him and learn something about sailing and trading. But both the father and godfather refused to give their permission. However, the son insisted so much that both men finally had to yield and agreed to let him depart.

While they were on the high seas in two different ships, a fierce storm erupted, and it was so violent that the two ships lost contact with each other. The young man was on one of them, and his godfather on the other. The godfather's ship managed to get through the storm, but the young man's ship hit a reef, and the entire crew drowned. Fortunately, the young man managed to grab hold of a plank and began to maneuver it so that he eventually reached land. Once there, he began to wander about and felt discouraged. When he entered a forest filled with wild animals, he climbed a tree at night to protect himself from them. The next day he looked around to make sure that there were no more wild animals so he could continue on his way. As he was walking, he came upon some walls surrounding the forest, and he began climbing them to see what was on the other side. Once he reached the top of one of the walls, he saw a large city, for the walls had been built to protect the people from the animals so they wouldn't be eaten.

Upon realizing this, the young man looked around to see how he could climb down from the walls and head toward the city to save himself. Finally, after he found a way, he climbed down and began walking toward the city. Once he was there, he went looking about for something to eat. Soon he found a few shops and entered, but wherever he went to ask for food, nobody would give him anything to eat or any information. Finally, he went to ask for food at the royal palace, but the guard remained silent. Driven by hunger and desperation because nobody would talk to him, he began to walk

---

84. "Lu 'Mperaturi Scursuni," *Fiabe, novelle e racconti popolari siciliani,* 4 vols. (Palermo: Lauriel, 1875).

through all the rooms of the palace because it was a matter of life and death. When he entered the very best room filled with royal beds and many other things, he decided to rest there. But all at once he saw some beautiful young ladies, who set the table for him to eat. So he sat down, and once he finished eating, he lay down to sleep.

This way of life continued for another two weeks. Then one night, while he was sleeping, an extremely beautiful young woman accompanied by two maidens appeared before him.

"Are you courageous and steadfast?" she asked him.

"Yes, I am," he responded.

"Well, if you are courageous and reliable, I shall tell you my secret. I am the daughter of the Emperor Scursuni, and before my father died, he cast a spell on this city and on all the people, servants, soldiers, and also on me. This spell continues to hold its sway over us because a sorcerer maintains it. But if you promise to stay by my bedside for one year without looking at me and telling anyone about my secret, the spell over this city will be broken, and I'll be empress and you'll be acclaimed emperor by all the people."

He responded by saying that he was ready to withstand anything that might occur. Well, after a few days the young man asked the princess to let him go and see his father, mother, and godfather, and he would return as soon as possible. She was undecided as to whether she should let him go, but he kept on asking until she gave in. However, she told him not to speak to anyone about her secret and immediately commanded a ship that was to transport him and gave him a wand.

"All you have to do is tell this wand where you want to go, and you'll immediately find yourself in your father's realm."

She also gave him some of her treasures, and as soon he arrived at the port of his father's city, he ordered that all the treasures be carried to the best inn. When he went there himself, he asked the innkeeper whether there were any sea merchants in the city. The innkeeper responded that there were two very important merchants, but they had been reduced to poverty because the son of one of these friends had drowned at sea. The other merchant, the father of the son, did not believe him and accused his friend in a lawsuit of being guilty of his son's death. In the process both of them lost everything they had.

When the son heard this story, he immediately sent for his father and said, "I would like to do some business with you and your friend because I've heard that you are experienced sea merchants."

His father responded that it was impossible to do business with the other merchant because both he and his friend had gone bankrupt due to a lawsuit concerning his son who had been lost at sea.

"None of this matters to me," the young merchant said, "because I'll provide all the capital that you'll need."

Upon saying this, he ordered a great meal to be prepared and sent for the other merchant and the wives of the two men. When they began to eat, the two merchants scowled at each other and couldn't eat a thing. As soon as the young man noticed this, he picked up a forkful of food from his plate and offered it to his father.

"Dear father," he said, "please accept this morsel because your son is right by your side, safe and sound."

Upon hearing this, they all jumped for joy, hugged and kissed each other, and shed tears of joy. Afterward the young man brought out the treasures and divided them between his father and his godfather so that they could continue trading as merchants. At the same time, however, he told them he had to make a return voyage without telling them where. His mother wanted to know where he was going and began to plead with him to tell them where, and she pleaded so much that her son told her everything that had happened and about the splendid princess whom he met and was not allowed to gaze at her beautiful body.

"Take this Holy Week candle," his mother responded, "and when she is asleep, you can light the candle and look at her beautiful body."

Her son departed, and when he arrived at the Emperor Scursuni's city, he went to the royal palace, where he met the princess, who was waiting for him. When she went to bed that night and fell asleep—and it seemed to him that he had to wait a hundred years to see her body—he took the candle, lit it, and held it over her body to see her beauty. By accident a drop of wax fell on her flesh so that she awoke and cried out, "You traitor! You've revealed my secret! Because of you I shall have to remain under the magic spell, and so will everyone else! The only way you can save me is by going into the wild forest, where you must fight the sorcerer and kill him."

"Oh, woe is me!" the young man responded. "Tell me, what do I have to do after I've killed him?"

"I'm going to give you a magic wand to do battle with the sorcerer," she said. "After he's dead, you're to slit open his stomach, and you'll find a rabbit. Then you're to slit open the rabbit, and you'll find a dove. Cut open the dove, and you'll find three eggs. Guard them as though they were your own eyes and carry them to me safe and sound. This is what you must do to free the city and all of us who are in it. Otherwise, you'll be brought under the spell just like everyone else."

The young man departed and headed toward the forest, armed with the magic wand that was given to him by the princess. When he arrived at the edge of the forest, he found a herd of cows, and all the cowherds and the padrone who owned the cows were with them. He approached them and told them that he had lost his way and would like a piece of bread. Not only did the padrone give him something to eat, but he kept him on as a cowherd. After some days passed, the padrone told him to take the cows out to pasture but not to allow them to enter the forest because there was a sorcerer, who killed both cows and humans. The young man said he would do as he said. However, he took the cows and drove them right into the forest. When the owner saw this, he became desperate and began to weep because none of the cowherds would go into the forest to bring the cows back. The young man, however, entered the forest with another boy, and they were both frightened. Meanwhile, the sorcerer saw the cows, flew into a rage, and picked up an iron club with six bronze spikes. As soon as the boy saw the sorcerer approach, he shit in his pants out of fear and hid behind a bush. However, the young man was steadfast and held his ground.

"Traitor!" cried the sorcerer when he arrived. "Why have you come and caused all this damage to my forest?"

"I've not only come to damage your forest but to destroy your life."

Immediately they began to fight, and they fought the entire day until they were finally exhausted. Yet, neither one of them was wounded, and while they were fighting, the magician said, "If I had a good soup of bread and wine, I'd slaughter you just like a swine!"

And the young man responded,

> "If I had a good soup of milk and bread,
> I'd slaughter you and slice off your head!"

After saying this, they said farewell and agreed to meet the next day to continue their battle. The young man herded the cows, and together with the boy, he drove them back to the barn. When they arrived, everyone was astounded because they had come back safe and sound. The boy told the owner and everyone else all about the great battle between the sorcerer and the young man that he had watched, and he mentioned that the young man had asked for bread and milk. So the owner ordered bread and milk to be prepared for the next day and had the bread and milk put into a pail. Then he gave the pail to the young boy and told him to have it ready the following day.

When daylight arrived, the young man took the cows into the forest once again, and the battle began. As they fought, the sorcerer demanded bread and wine to cut the young man to the ground. But he couldn't get any. The young man demanded bread and milk to kill the sorcerer, and all at once the bread and milk appeared. The young man scooped up a handful of bread and milk, and after he munched on it, he dealt a blow to the head of the sorcerer causing him to fall to the ground dead. Immediately he sliced open the sorcerer's stomach and found the rabbit. Then he sliced open the rabbit and found the dove. Finally, he sliced open the dove and found the three eggs that he guarded carefully as he returned the cows to the barn. Everyone welcomed him in triumph, and the owner wanted him to remain on the farm where he would be well treated. But he responded that he couldn't stay, and after presenting the forest to the owner as a gift, he departed. When he arrived at the city, he went straight into the royal palace, and the princess came to greet him. She took him by the hand and led him into secret cabinet of the Emperor Scursuni, her father, and she took the emperor's crown and put it on his head.

"You are now the emperor," she said, "and I'm the empress."

Once he was crowned, she led him to the balcony, took out the three eggs, and said, "Throw one to the right, one to the left, and the last one, straight ahead."

As soon as he did this, all the people began to speak, shout, and proclaim their freedom. The carriages started to roll. The troops began their exercises, and the guards changed posts. Everyone began to thank the man who had liberated them and cried out, "Long live our emperor! Long live our empress!"

> And so they remained emperor and empress
> While we are still poor and live in distress.

Collected by Antonio Rasti at Palazzo-Adriano.

The Great Beast (1880)[85]
James Bruyn Andrews

A merchant, who had three daughters, being about to set forth on a long voyage, asked each of them what present she would like him to bring back for her. The eldest wished a bonnet, the second a gown, and the youngest only a rose. He went on his journey, and, his business done, he started on his way home. Passing one night through a wood, he lost his way, and after wandering for a long while his horse became so jaded that he could go no further. Seeing a garden hard by, he went near and found the gate wide open, but he could find no living being.

He entered and beheld within a beautiful palace. Having put his horse in the stable, which seemed to have been made ready for him, he then turned his steps towards the palace. It was open and entirely deserted, though a bed was ready made, and a splendid dinner set out. He began to dine and was deftly served by unseen hands. Immediately after eating, overcome by fatigue, he went at once to bed and soon fell soundly asleep until the morning, in spite of his uneasiness at his strange surroundings.

When he had arisen, his breakfast was given him, and his horse cared for in the same mysterious way. The morning being fine, he started early on his journey, and he crossed the garden without seeing a soul and marvelling greatly at what had befallen him. Just before reaching the gate his eye was caught by the sight of a rose of singular beauty. Recalling his daughter's wish he picked it,

---

85.   *Stories from Mentone* (London: The Folk-Lore Record, 1880).

when at once sprung up before him a dreadful monster, who, in great wrath, threatened him with death for having stolen the loveliest and rarest ornament of his garden.

"I never dreamt I was doing so much harm," said the frightened merchant, and he recounted to him the wish of his daughter.

The beast seemed interested, asked many questions about her, and at last said that though he had been robbed of what was most dear to him, he would pardon him if the daughter was given to him.

"Begone," said he, "but return within three days or you shall all die."

The father felt forced to promise, but when he reached home, he had not the least heart to tell her the wretched lot that awaited her. Seeing him always sad, she questioned him and ended by knowing all. And, as two days were already gone, and the palace far away, she unselfishly begged him to start at once. Hastening, with all speed, they reached the palace of the beast when but a few minutes were left of the third day, and found him in a pitiable state, half dead. They set to work to nurse him, and when he had rallied, the merchant tore himself away from his daughter with sad forebodings.

Two years passed, during which she lived in the palace, seeing the beast daily, when one day, after much urging, she besought the beast to give her leave to pay a short visit to her family, whom she had not since seen.

"Remain but three days," said the beast, "or you will find me dead."

She came back the third day, but by ill luck so late that she found the beast dying. So good had he been to her that she had become very fond of him, and she was overwhelmed with remorse at the evil she had unwillingly done him.

She tended him lovingly, and when he had come to himself, spoke tender words to him, promising never again to leave him, and even to become his wife. No sooner had she said this than the beast turned into a young and handsome prince, for it was this promise that he had to await. They were married at once and ever after lived happily together.

The Maiden and the Beast (1882)[86]

Consiglieri Pedroso

There was once a man who had three daughters; he loved them all, but there was one he loved more than the others. As he was going to the fair one day, he inquired what they would like him to bring them. One said she would like to have a hat and some boots, the other one asked for a dress and a shawl, the one he loved most did not ask for anything. The man, in surprise, said, "Oh! my child, do you not want anything?"

"No, I want nothing. I only wish that my dear father may enjoy health."

---

86. *Portuguese Folk-Tales*, trans. Henriqueta Monteiro (London: Folklore Society, 1882).

"You must ask for something. It matters not what it is. I shall bring it to you," replied the father.

But, in order that the father should not continue to importune her, she said, "I wish my father to bring me a slice of roach off a green meadow."

The good man set off to the fair, bought all the things that his daughters had asked him, and searched everywhere for the "slice of roach off a green meadow," but could not find it, for it was something that was not to be had. He therefore started for home in great distress of mind, because she was the daughter he loved most and wished most to please. As he was walking along, he happened to see a light shining on the road, and as it was already night, he walked on and on until he reached the light that came from a hut in which lived a shepherd. So, the man went in and inquired of him, "Can you tell me what palace is that yonder, and do you think they would give me shelter there?"

The shepherd replied, in great astonishment, "Oh! sir, but . . . in that palace no one resides. Something is seen there which terrifies people from living in it."

"What does it matter? It will not eat me up; and, as there is no one living in it, I shall go and sleep there to-night."

He went up to the building, found it all lit up very splendidly, and, on entering into the palace, he found a table ready laid. As he approached the table, he heard a voice which said, "Eat and lie down on the bed which you see there, and in the morning rise and take with you what you will find on that table, which is what your daughter asked you for. But at the end of three days you must bring her here."

The man was very pleased to be able to take home what his daughter had asked him for, but at the same time was distressed at what the voice had said it required him to do. He threw himself on the bed, and on the following morning he arose, went straight to the table, and found upon it the slice of roach off a green meadow. He took it up and went home. The moment he arrived his daughters surrounded him: "Father, what have you brought us? Let us see what it is?"

The father gave them what he had brought them. The third daughter, the one he loved most, did not ask him for anything, but simply if he was well. The father answered her, "My daughter, I come back both happy and sad! Here you have what you asked me for."

"Oh! Father, I asked you for this because it was a thing which did not exist. But why do you come back sad?"

"Because I must take you at the end of three days to the place where this was given to me."

He recounted all that had occurred to him in the place, and what the voice had told him to do. When the daughter heard all, she replied, "Do not distress yourself, father, for I shall go, and whatever God wills, will happen."

And so it happened that at the end of three days the father took her to the enchanted palace. It was all illuminated and in a blaze of light. The table was laid, and two beds had been prepared. As they entered, they heard a voice saying, "Eat and remain with your daughter three days that she may not feel frightened."

The man remained the three days in the palace, and at the end went away leaving the daughter alone! The voice spoke to her every day, but no form was seen. At the end of a few days the girl heard a bird singing in the garden. The voice said to her, "Do you hear that bird sing?"

"Yes, I hear him," replied the girl. "Does it bring any news?"

"It is your eldest sister who is going to be married, would you like to be present?" asked the voice.

The girl in great delight said, "Yes, I should like to go very much,—will you let me go?"

"I will allow you," rejoined the voice, "but you will not return!"

"Yes, I shall come back," said the girl.

The voice gave her then a ring so that she should not forget her promise, saying, "Now mind that at the end of three days a white horse will come for you. It will give three knocks—the first is for you to dress and get ready; the second for you to take leave of your family; and the third for you to mount it. If at the third knock you are not on the horse, it will go away and leave you there."

The girl went home. A great feast had been prepared, and the sister was married. At the end of three days the white horse came to give the three knocks. At the first the girl commenced to get ready; at the second knock she took leave of her family; and at the third she mounted on the horse. The voice had given the girl a box with money to take to her father and her sisters. On that account they did not wish her to return to the enchanted palace, because she was now very rich. But the girl remembered what she had promised, and the moment she found herself on the horse, she darted off. After a certain time the bird returned and began to sing very contentedly in the garden. The voice said to her, "Do you hear the bird sing?"

"Yes I hear it," replied the girl, "Does it bring any news?"

"It is that another of your sisters is about to marry,[87] and do you wish to go?"

"Yes, I wish to go. And would you allow me to go?"

"I will let you go," replied the voice, "but you will not return!"

"Yes, I shall return," said the girl.

The voice then said, "Remember that if at the end of three days you do not come back, you shall remain there, and you will be the most hapless girl there is in the world!"

---

87. There are different versions of this story, viz.: "It is that your sister has given birth to a girl. I would like you to be her godmother. And do you wish to go?"

The girl started off. A great feast was given, and the sister was married. At the end of three days the white horse came. It gave the first knock, and the girl dressed herself to go. It gave the second knock, and the girl took leave of her friends. It gave the third knock, and the girl mounted the horse and returned to the palace. After some time the bird again sang in the garden, but in melancholy tones—very dull tones indeed. The voice said to her, "Do you hear the bird sing?"

"Yes, I hear it," replied the girl. "Is there any news?"

"Yes, there is. Your father is dying and does not wish to die without taking leave of you."

"And will you allow me to go and see him?" asked the girl, indeed much distressed.

"Yes, I will let you go; but I know you will not return this time."

"Oh yes, I shall come back," replied the girl.

The voice then said to her, "No, you will not return—you will not! Your sisters will not let you come, but you and they will be the most unhappy girls in this world if you do not come back at the end of three days."

The girl went home. The father was very ill, yet he could not die until he saw her, and he had hardly taken leave of his daughter when he died. The sisters gave the girl a sleeping draught as she had requested them and left her to sleep. The girl had begged them most particularly to awaken her before the white horse should come. What did the sisters do? They did not awaken her, and they took off the ring she wore. At the end of three days the horse came. It gave the first knock; it knocked the second time; it knocked the third time, and went away, and the girl remained at home. As the sisters had taken away the ring, she forgot everything of the past and lived very happily with her sisters. A few days after this, fortune began to leave her and her sisters, until one day the two said to her, "Sister, do you remember the white horse?"

The girl then recollected everything and began to cry, saying, "Oh! What misfortune is mine! Oh, you have made me very wretched! What has become of my ring?"

The sisters gave her the ring, and the girl took her departure in great affliction. She reached the enchanted palace and found everything about it looking very dull, very dark, and the palace shut up. She went straight into the garden, and she there found a huge beast lying on the ground.

The beast had barely seen her when he cried out, "Go away, you tyrant, for you have broken my spell! Now you will be the most wretched girl in the world, you and your sisters."

As the beast finished saying this, it died. The girl returned to her sisters in great distress, weeping very bitterly, and she remained in the house without eating or drinking, and after a few days died also. The sisters became poorer by degrees for having been the cause of all this trouble.

The Small-Tooth Dog (1895)[88]

Sidney Oldall Addy

Once upon a time there was a merchant who travelled about the world a great deal. On one of his journeys thieves attacked him, and they would have taken both his life and his money if a large dog had not come to his rescue and driven the thieves away.

When the dog had driven the thieves away he took the merchant to his house, which was a very handsome one, and dressed his wounds and nursed him until he was well.

As soon as he was able to travel the merchant began his journey home, but before starting he told the dog how grateful he was for his kindness, and asked him what reward he could offer in return, and he said he would not refuse to give him the most precious thing that he had.

And so the merchant said to the dog, "Will you accept a fish that I have that can speak twelve languages?"

"No," said the dog, "I will not."

"Or a goose that lays golden eggs?"

"No," said the dog, "I will not."

"Or a mirror in which you can see what anybody is thinking about?"

"No," said the dog, "I will not."

"Then what will you have?" said the merchant.

"I will have none of such presents," said the dog, "but let me fetch your daughter and take her to my house."

When the merchant heard this, he was grieved, but what he had promised had to be done, so he said to the dog, "You can come and fetch my daughter after I have been at home for a week."

So at the end of the week the dog came to the merchant's house to fetch his daughter, but when he got there, he stayed outside the door and would not go in. But the merchant's daughter did as her father told her, and came out of the house dressed for a journey and ready to go with the dog.

When the dog saw her, he looked pleased, and said: "Jump on my back, and I will take you away to my house."

So she mounted on the dog's back, and away they went at a great pace until they reached the dog's house, which was many miles off.

But after she had been a month at the dog's house, she began to mope and cry.

---

88.   *Household Tales with Other Traditional Remains: Collected in the Counties of York, Lincoln, Derby, and Nottingham* (London: David Nutt, 1895).

"What are you crying for?" said the dog.

"Because I want to go back to my father," she said.

The dog said, "If you will promise me that you will not stay at home more than three days I will take you there. But, first of all," said he, "what do you call me?"

"A great, foul, small-tooth dog," said she.

"Then," said he, "I will not let you go."

But she cried so pitifully that he promised again to take her home. "But before we start," said he, "tell me what you call me."

"Oh," she said, "your name is Sweet-as-a-honeycomb."

"Jump on my back," said he, "and I'll take you home."

So he trotted away with her on his back for forty miles, when they came to a stile.

"And what do you call me?" said he, before they got over the stile.

Thinking that she was safe on her way, the girl said, "A great, foul, small-tooth dog."

But when she said this, he did not jump over the stile, but turned right round about at once, and galloped back to his house with the girl on his back.

Another week went by, and again the girl wept so bitterly the dog promised her again to take her to her father's house.

So the girl got on the dog's back again, and they reached the first stile as before, and then the dog stopped and said, "And what do you call me?"

"Sweet-as-a-honeycomb," she replied.

So the dog leaped over the stile, and they went on for twenty miles until they came to another stile.

"And what do you call me?" said the dog, with a wag of his tail.

She was thinking more of her father and her own home than of the dog, so she answered, "A great, foul, small-tooth dog."

Then the dog was in a great rage, and he turned round about and galloped back to his own house as before.

After she had cried for another week, the dog promised again to take her back to her father's house. So she mounted upon his back once more, and when they got to the first stile the dog said, "And what do you call me?"

"Sweet-as-a-honeycomb," she said.

So the dog jumped over the stile, and away they went—for now the girl made up her mind to say the most loving things she could think of—until they reached her father's house.

When they got to the door of the merchant's house, the dog said, "And what do you call me?"

Just at that moment the girl forgot the loving things that she meant to say, and began, "A great—" but the dog began to turn, and she got fast hold of the door latch, and was going to say "foul," when she saw how grieved the dog looked and remembered how good and patient he had been with her, so she said, "Sweeter-as-a-honeycomb."

When she had said this, she thought the dog would have been content and have galloped away, but instead of that he suddenly stood up on his hind legs, and with his fore legs he pulled off his dog's head and tossed it high in the air. His hairy coat dropped off, and there stood the handsomest young man in the world, with the finest and smallest teeth you ever saw.

Of course they were married and lived together happily.

8. CURSED PRINCES AND SWEET REWARDS

ATU 440—THE FROG KING OR IRON HENRY

This tale type could also be called "Lost and Found." It concerns a young maiden/princess, who goes to a well for water or is near water in a well or fountain. She loses a valuable object such as a ball or bracelet or cannot fetch water because she is prevented from doing this by a reptile. A frog/toad/snake agrees to retrieve the object or to fetch water, providing that the young woman promises him three wishes. Once she returns home, she tries to renege but under pressure from her father/mother, she agrees to keep her promise to the reptile who follows her home. For the third wish, the reptile wants to sleep in her bed. The maiden, a virgin, accepts reluctantly and then discovers that the reptile is a handsome prince. In some variants, she throws him against the wall or is requested to chop off his head. The story generally ends in marriage with the prince who regains his human form. In tales based on the Grimms' final edited version, there is a short incident that reveals the loyalty of the prince's faithful servant Iron Henry. In other versions that reflect this tale type's close connection to beast/bridegroom stories, the maiden is tested after she takes off the reptile's skin and must search for him all over the world.

It is not clear how old this tale type is, but it is clearly related to ancient beast/bridegroom stories and initiation rituals that involve a young maiden overcoming her fear of sexual intercourse. One of the first written versions in Latin appeared in Berthold von Regensburg's thirteenth-century *Rusticanus de sanctis*. The Grimms thought that this tale type was one of the oldest and most beautiful in the world, and it was therefore placed as number one in their collection from the first edition of 1812 to the seventh and final edition of 1857. Their interest in the tale was so great that they published a second variant in 1815 in the second volume of their first edition.

The original draft for the Grimms' versions of the "Frog King" tales was probably provided by a member of the Wild family in 1810. By 1810 the Grimms were well aware of other late-medieval versions, especially the Scottish one published in John Bellenden's *The Complaynt of Scotlande* (1548) as well as tales contributed by Marie Hassenpflug and the family von Haxthausen. The editing changes made by Wilhelm Grimm from 1819 to 1857 indicate that he was anxious to de-eroticize the tale and to emphasize the moral of listening to the father and keeping one's promises. In the versions by Halliwell-Phillipps, Pitrè, Luzel, Jones, Knopf, Kulish, Jacobs, and Jahn, there is greater experimentation and indications that the maiden, often a lower-class figure, is much more emancipated than she is in the Grimms' versions. In a major study of the tale, *Wage es den Frosch zu küssen! Das Grimmsche Märchen Nummer Eins in seinen Wandlungen* (1987), Lutz Röhrich demonstrates that the maiden is much more independent in making her choices than in the Grimms' versions and also that the sexual innuendoes are stronger in most variants. Interestingly, there are no known versions in which the maiden kisses the frog to release him from the spell until very late in the nineteenth century. Perhaps the first interesting variant is Ulrich Jahn's dialect tale, "The Queen and the Frog" (1891), which he followed with a more traditional version, "The Princess and the Scabby Toad" (1891). However, even before the publication of Jahn's versions, the great German caricaturist, Wilhelm Busch had published the illustrated tale, "The Two Sisters" (1881). In his mock fairy tale, a good sister meets a frog and kisses him three times out of kindness, and he turns into a prince, while the lazy sister meets a male water sprite, whom she kisses, and then he drags her into his underwater realm.

******

The Frog King or Iron Henry (1812)[89]
Jacob and Wilhelm Grimm

Once upon a time there was a princess who went out into the forest and sat down at the edge of a cool well. She had a golden ball that was her most favorite plaything. She threw it up high and caught it in the air and was delighted by all this. One time the ball flew up quite high, and as she stretched out her hand and bent her fingers to catch it again, the ball hit the ground near her and rolled and rolled until it fell right into the water.

The princess was horrified as she looked after it, but the well was so deep that she couldn't see the bottom. Then she began to weep miserably and to grieve: "Oh, if only I had my ball again! I'd give anything—my clothes, my jewels, my pearls, and anything else in the world—to get my ball back!"

As she sat there groaning, a frog stuck its head out of the water and said: "Why are you weeping so miserably?"

"Oh," she said, "you nasty frog, you can't help me! My gold ball has fallen into the water."

"Well, I won't demand your pearls, your jewels, and your clothes," the frog responded. "But if you will accept me as your companion and let me sit next to you and let me eat from your little golden plate and sleep in your little bed and love and cherish me, I'll retrieve your ball for you."

The princess thought, 'What nonsense the simpleminded frog is blabbering. He's got to remain in his water. But perhaps he can get me my ball. So I'll say yes to him.' And she said, "Yes, fair enough, but first fetch me the golden ball. I promise you everything."

The frog dipped his head under the water and dived down. It didn't take long before he came back to the surface with the ball in his mouth. He threw it on the ground, and when the princess caught sight of the ball again, she quickly ran

89.   "Der Froschkönig oder der eiserne Heinrich," *Kinder- und Haus-Märchen. Gesammelt durch die Brüder Grimm*, 2 vols. (Berlin: Realschulbuchhandlung, 1812/1815).

over to it, picked it up, and was so delighted to have the ball in her hand again that she thought of nothing else but to rush back home with it. The frog called after her: "Wait, princess, take me with you the way you promised!"

But she didn't pay any attention to him.

The next day the princess sat at the table and heard something coming up the marble steps, *splish, splash! splish, splash!* Soon thereafter it knocked at the door and cried out: "Princess, youngest daughter, open up!"

She ran to the door and opened it, and there was the frog whom she had forgotten. Horrified, she quickly slammed the door shut and sat down back at the table. But the king saw that her heart was thumping and said, "Why are you afraid?"

"There's a nasty frog outside," she said. "He retrieved my golden ball from the water, and I promised him that he could be my companion. But I never believed at all he could get out of the water. Now he's standing outside in front of the door and wants to come inside."

As she said this, there was a knock at the door, and the frog cried out:

> "Princess, youngest daughter,
> Open up!
> Don't you remember, what you said
> down by the well's cool water?
> Princess, youngest daughter,
> Open up!"

The king said: "You must keep whatever you've promised. Go and open the door for the frog."

She obeyed, and the frog hopped inside and followed her at her feet until they came to her chair, and when she sat down again, he cried out: "Lift me up to a chair beside you."

The princess didn't want to do this, but the king ordered her to do it. When the frog was up at the table, he said: "Now push your little golden plate nearer to me so we can eat together."

The princess had to do this as well, and after he had eaten until he was full, he said: "Now I'm tired and want to sleep. Bring me upstairs to your little room. Get your little bed ready so that we can lay down in it."

The princess became terrified when she heard this. She was afraid of the cold frog. She didn't dare to touch him, and now he was to lay in her bed next to her. She began to weep and didn't want to comply with his wishes at all. But the king became angry and ordered her to do what she had promised, or she'd be held in disgrace. Nothing helped. She had to do what her father wanted, but she was bitterly angry in her heart. So she picked up the frog with two fingers, carried him upstairs into her room, laid herself down in her bed, and instead of setting him down next to her, she threw him *crash!* against the wall. "Now you'll leave me in peace, you nasty frog!"

But the frog didn't fall down dead. Instead, when he fell down on the bed, he was a handsome young prince. So, now he was her dear companion, and she cherished him as she had promised, and in their delight they fell asleep together.

The next morning a splendid coach arrived that was drawn by eight horses with feathers and glistening gold harnesses. The prince's Faithful Henry was with them. He had been so distressed when he had learned his master had been turned into a frog that he had ordered three iron bands to be wrapped around his heart to keep it from bursting from sadness. The prince got into the coach with the princess, and his faithful servant took his place at the back so they could travel to the prince's realm. And after they had traveled some distance, the prince heard a loud cracking noise behind him. So, he turned around and cried out:

> "Henry, the coach is breaking!"
> "No, my lord, it's really nothing
> but the band around my heart,
> which nearly came apart
> when you turned into a frog and your fortune fell
> and you were made to live in that dreary well."

Two more times the prince heard the cracking noise and thought the coach was breaking, but the noise was only the sound of the bands springing from Faithful Henry's heart because his master had been released from the spell and was happy.

The Frog Prince (1815)[90]
Jacob and Wilhelm Grimm

Once upon a time there was a king who had three daughters, and in his courtyard there was a well with beautiful clear water. On a hot summer's day the eldest daughter went down to the well and scooped out a glass full of water. However, when she looked at it and held it up to the sun, she saw that the water was murky. She found this very unusual and wanted to scoop out another glass when a frog stirred in the water, stuck its head up high, and finally jumped on to the edge of the well, where he spoke:

> "If you'll be my sweetheart, my dear,
> I'll give you water clearer than clear."

"Oh, who'd ever want to be a nasty frog's sweetheart?" she cried out and ran away.

Then she told her sisters that there was an odd frog down at the well that made the water murky. The second sister became curious, and so she went down to the well and scooped a glass of water for herself, but it was just as murky as

---

90. "Der Froschkönig," *Kinder- und Haus-Märchen. Gesammelt durch die Brüder Grimm,* 2 vols. (Berlin: Realschulbuchandlung, 1812/1815).

her sister's glass so that she wasn't able to drink it. Once again, however, the frog was on the edge of the well and said:

> "If you'll be my sweetheart, my dear,
> I'll give you water clearer than clear."

"Do you think that would suit me?" the princess replied and ran away.

Finally, the third sister went, and things were no better. But when the frog spoke,

> "If you'll be my sweetheart, my dear,
> I'll give you water clearer than clear,"

she replied, "Yes, why not? I'll be your sweetheart. Get me some clean water."

However, she thought, 'That won't do you any harm. You can speak to him just as you please. A dumb frog can never become my sweetheart.'

Meanwhile the frog had jumped back into the water, and when she scooped up some water a second time, it was so clear that the sun gleamed nicely with joy in the glass. Then she drank and quenched her thirst and also brought her sisters some of the water.

"Why were you so simpleminded and afraid of the frog," she said to them, and afterward the princess didn't think anything more about it and went happily to bed. However, after she had been lying there for a while and couldn't fall asleep, she suddenly heard some scratching on the door and then some singing:

> "Open up! Open Up!
> Princess, youngest daughter,
> don't you remember, what you said
> when I sat on the well on the water's edge?
> You wanted to be my sweetheart, my dear,
> and I gave you water more clear than clear."

"Oh, that's my sweetheart, the frog," the princess said, "and since I gave him my word, I'll open the door."

So she got out of bed, opened the door a little, and then lay back down in the bed. The frog hopped after her and hopped on the bed down by her feet and remained there. When the night was over and morning dawned, the frog sprang off the bed and went out through the door. The next evening when the princess was once again lying in bed, there was some scratching and singing at the door once more. The princess opened the door, and the frog laid in the bed at her feet until it turned day. On the third evening the frog came just like he had done the previous evenings.

"This is the last time that I'll open the door to you," the princess said to him. "In the future there will be no more of this."

Then the frog jumped and crawled under her pillow, and the princess fell asleep. When she woke up the next morning, she thought the frog would hop off again. Instead, she saw a handsome young prince standing before her, and he told her that he had been the bewitched frog and that she had saved him because she had promised to be his sweetheart. Then the two of them went to the king, who gave them his blessing, and a wedding was held. Meanwhile, the two other sisters were angry with themselves because they had not taken the frog to be their sweetheart.

The Frog King or Iron Henry (1857)[91]

Jacob and Wilhelm Grimm

In olden times, when wishing still helped, there lived a king whose daughters were all beautiful, but the youngest was so beautiful that the sun itself, which had seen so many things, was always filled with amazement each time it cast its rays upon her face. Now, there was a great dark forest near the king's castle, and in this forest, beneath an old linden tree, was a well. Whenever the days were very hot, the king's daughter would go into this forest and sit down by the edge of the cool well. If she became bored, she would take her golden ball, throw it into the air, and catch it. More than anything else she loved playing with this ball.

One day it so happened that the ball did not fall back into the princess's little hand as she reached out to catch it. Instead, it bounced right by her and rolled straight into the water. The princess followed it with her eyes, but the ball disappeared, and the well was deep, so very deep that she couldn't see the bottom. She began to cry, and she cried louder and louder, for there was nothing that could comfort her. As she sat there grieving over her loss, a voice called out to her, "What's the matter, Princess? Your tears could move even a stone to pity."

She looked around to see where the voice was coming from and saw a frog sticking his thick, ugly head out of the water. "Oh, it's you, you old water-splasher," she said. "I'm crying because my golden ball has fallen into the well."

"Be quiet and stop crying," the frog responded. "I'm sure I can help you. But what will you give me if I fetch your plaything?"

"Whatever you like, dear frog," she said. "My clothes, my pearls and jewels, even the golden crown I'm wearing on my head."

"I don't want your clothes, your pearls and jewels, or your golden crown," the frog replied. "But if you will love me and let me be your companion and playmate, and let me sit beside you at the table, eat from your little golden plate, drink out of your little cup, and sleep in your little bed—if you promise me all that, I'll dive down and retrieve your golden ball."

<hr>

91.   "Der Froschkönig oder der eiserne Heinrich," *Kinder- und Hausmärchen gesammelt durch die Brüder Grimm*, 7th ed., 3 vols. (Göttingen: Verlag der Dieterich'schen Buchhandlung, 1857).

"Oh, yes," she said. "I'll promise you anything you want if only you'll bring back the ball!" However, she thought, 'What nonsense that stupid frog talks! He just sits in the water croaking with the rest of the frogs. How can he expect a human being to accept him as a companion?'

Once the frog had her promise, he dipped his head under the water, dived downward, and soon came paddling back to the surface with the ball in his mouth. When he threw it onto the grass, the princess was so delighted to see her beautiful plaything again that she picked it up and ran off with it.

"Wait, wait!" cried the frog. "Take me with you. I can't run like you."

He croaked as loudly as he could, but what good did it do? She paid no attention to him. Instead, she rushed home and soon forgot about the poor frog, who had to climb back down into his well.

The next day, as she sat at the table with the king and his courtiers and ate from her little golden plate, something came crawling *splish, splash, splish, splash* up the marble steps. When it reached the top, it knocked at the door and cried out, "Princess, youngest daughter, open up!"

She ran to see who was outside. But when she opened the door and saw the frog, she quickly slammed the door shut and went back to the table in a state of fright. The king could clearly see her heart was thumping and said, "My child, what are you afraid of? Has a giant come to get you?"

"Oh, no," she answered. "It's not a giant, but a nasty frog."

"What does a frog want from you?"

"Oh, dear father, yesterday when I was sitting and playing near the well in the forest, my golden ball fell into the water, and because I cried so much, the frog fetched it for me, and because he insisted, I had to promise he could be my companion. But I never thought he'd get out of the water. Now he's outside and wants to come in and be with me."

Just then there was a second knock at the door, and a voice cried out: "Princess, Princess, youngest daughter, open up and let me in. Have you forgotten what you promised down by the well's cool water? Princess, Princess, youngest daughter, open up and let me in."

Then the king said, "If you've made a promise, you must keep it. Go and let him in."

After she went and opened the door, the frog hopped into the room and followed her right to her chair, where he plopped himself down and cried out, "Lift me up beside you!"

She refused until the king finally ordered her to do so. Once the frog was on the chair, he wanted to climb onto the table, and when he made it to the table, he said, "Now push your little golden plate nearer to me so we can eat together."

To be sure, she did this, but it was quite clear that she didn't like it. The frog enjoyed his meal, while each bite the princess took got stuck in her throat.

Finally he said, "I've had enough, and now I'm tired. Carry me upstairs to your room and get your silken bed ready so we can go to sleep."

The princess began to cry because the cold frog frightened her. She didn't even have enough courage to touch him, and yet, now she was supposed to let him sleep in her beautiful, clean bed. But the king gave her an angry look and said, "It's not proper to scorn someone who helped you when you were in trouble!"

So she picked up the frog with her two fingers, carried him upstairs, and set him down in a corner. Soon after she had got into bed, he came crawling over to her and said, "I'm tired and want to sleep as much as you do. Lift me up, or I'll tell your father!"

These words made the princess extremely angry, and after she picked him up, she threw him against the wall with all her might. "Now you can have your rest, you nasty frog!"

However, when he fell to the ground, he was no longer a frog but a prince with kind and beautiful eyes. So, in keeping with her father's wishes, she accepted him as her dear companion and husband, whereupon the prince told her that a wicked witch had cast a spell over him, and no one could have got him out of the well except her. Now he intended to take her to his kingdom the next day. Then they fell asleep, and in the morning, when the sun woke them, a coach drawn by eight white horses came driving up. The horses had ostrich plumes on their heads and harnesses with golden chains. At the back of the coach stood Faithful Henry, the young king's servant. He had been so distressed when he had learned his master had been turned into a frog that he had ordered three iron bands be wrapped around his heart to keep it from bursting from grief and sadness. But now the coach had come to bring the young king back to his kingdom, and Faithful Henry helped the prince and princess into it and then took his place at the back again. He was overcome by joy because his master had been saved.

When they had traveled some distance, the prince heard a cracking noise behind him, as if something had broken. He turned around and cried out:

> "Henry, the coach is breaking!"
> "No, my lord, it's really nothing
> but the band around my heart,
> which nearly fell apart
> when the wicked witch, she cast her spell
> and made you live as a frog in a well."

The cracking noise was heard two more times along the way, and the prince thought each time that the coach was breaking, but the noise was only the sound of the bands snapping from Faithful Henry's heart, for he knew his master was safe and happy.

The Maiden and the Frog (1849)[92]

James Orchard Halliwell-Phillipps

Many years ago there lived on the brow of a mountain, in the north of England, an old woman and her daughter. They were very poor, and obliged to work very hard for their living, and the old woman's temper was not very good, so that the maiden, who was very beautiful, led but an ill life with her. The girl, indeed, was compelled to do the hardest work, for her mother got their principal means of subsistence by travelling to places in the neighbourhood with small articles for sale, and when she came home in the afternoon, she was not able to do much more work. Nearly the whole domestic labour of the cottage devolved therefore on the daughter, the most wearisome part of which consisted in the necessity of fetching all the water they required from a well on the other side of the hill, there being no river or spring near their own cottage.

It happened one morning that the daughter had the misfortune, in going to the well, to break the only pitcher they possessed, and having no other utensil she could use for the purpose, she was obliged to go home without bringing any water. When her mother returned, she was unfortunately troubled with excessive thirst, and the girl, though trembling for the consequences of her misfortune, told her exactly the circumstance that had occurred. The old woman was furiously angry, and so far from making any allowances for her daughter, pointed to a sieve which happened to be on the table and told her to go at once to the well and bring her some water in that, or never venture to appear again in her sight.

The young maiden, frightened almost out of her wits by her mother's fury, speedily took the sieve, and though she considered the task a hopeless one to accomplish, almost unconsciously hastened to the well.

When she arrived there, beginning to reflect on the painful situation in which she was placed, and the utter impossibility of her obtaining a living by herself, she threw herself down on the brink of the well in an agony of despair. Whilst she was in this condition, a large frog came up to the top of the water and asked her for what she was crying so bitterly.

She was somewhat surprised at this, but not being the least frightened, told him the whole story, and that she was crying because she could not carry away water in the sieve.

"Is that all?" said the frog. "Cheer up, my hinny! for if you will only let me sleep with you for two nights, and then chop off my head, I will tell you how to do it."

The young maiden thought that the frog could not be in earnest, but she was too impatient to consider much about it, and at once made the required promise. The frog then instructed her in the following words, —

---

92. *Popular Rhymes & Nursery Tales of England* (London: John Russell Smith, 1849).

Stop with fog (moss).
And daub with clay;
And that will carry
The water away.

Having said this, he dived immediately under the water, and the girl, having followed his advice, got the sieve full of water, and returned home with it, not thinking much of her promise to the frog. By the time she reached home, the old woman's wrath was appeased, but as they were eating their frugal supper very quietly, what should they hear but the splashing and croaking of a frog near the door, and shortly afterwards the daughter recognised the voice of the frog of the well saying, —

Open the door, my hinny, my heart,
Open the door, my own darling;
Remember the words you spoke to me.
In the meadow by the well-spring.

She was now dreadfully frightened, and hurriedly explained the matter to her mother, who was also so much alarmed at the circumstance that she dared not refuse admittance to the frog, who, when the door was opened, leapt into the room explaining:

Go wi' me to bed, my hinny, my heart,
Go wi' me to bed, my own darling;
Remember the words you spoke to me,
In the meadow by the well-spring.

This command was also obeyed, although as may be readily supposed, she did not much relish such a bedfellow. The next day, the frog was very quiet, and evidently enjoyed the fare they placed before him—the purest milk and finest bread they could procure. In fact, neither the old woman nor her daughter spared any pains to render the frog comfortable. That night, immediately after supper was finished, the frog again exclaimed:

Go wi' me to bed, my hinny, my heart,
Go wi' me to bed, my own darling;
Remember the words you spoke to me,
In the meadow by the well-spring.

She again allowed the frog to share her couch, and in the morning, as soon as she was dressed, he jumped towards her, saying:

Chop off my head, my hinny, my heart,
Chop off my head, my own darling;
Remember the words you spoke to me,
In the meadow by the well-spring.

The maiden had no sooner accomplished this last request than in the stead of the frog there stood by her side the handsomest prince in the world, who had long been transformed by a magician, and who could never have recovered his natural shape until a beautiful virgin had consented of her own accord to make him her bedfellow for two nights. The joy of all parties was complete; the girl and the prince were shortly afterwards married, and lived for many years in the enjoyment of every happiness.

The Little Mouse with the Stinky Tail (1875)[93]

Giuseppe Pitrè

They say that once upon a time there was a king, who had a beautiful daughter, more beautiful than words can say. She received marriage proposals from many monarchs and emperors, but her father was unwilling to give her to anyone because every night he heard a voice that told him:

"Do not allow your daughter to marry!"

Each and every day this maiden looked at herself in the mirror and said, "How can it be that I am so very beautiful and yet cannot marry?"—and she continued to be bothered by this.

One day, when they all were dining, the princess said to her father:

"Father, how is it that I am so very beautiful and yet cannot marry? Let me speak my mind clearly: I *want* to get married!"

"My daughter, do you think I can simply *order* people to marry you?"

"Well, father, let me say this: I'll give you two days to find me a husband. If you can't do it within two days, I'll kill myself."

"Since it's come to this," the king said, "listen to what you must do. Dress yourself today in your finest outfit and sit at the window. The first person who passes by and looks at you will be the one you marry."

The princess did exactly what he said. And while she was seated at the window, along came a little mouse with a tail that was very long and very stinky. As he passed by, he looked at her. When the girl saw this, she ran inside the house screaming.

"Father, do you know what happened? Just now a mouse passed by and looked at me. Is this the one I must marry?"

"Yes, my daughter, isn't that what I told you? The first one who passes by is the one you must marry."

Well, back and forth they went, she saying "no" and he saying "yes," until it was dawn. Then the king wrote to all the princes and people of nobility inviting them to a great wedding feast to celebrate his daughter's marriage. Soon the

---

93. "Lu surciteddu cu la cuda fitusa," *Fiabe, novelle e racconti popolari siciliani*, 4 vols. (Palermo: Lauriel, 1875).

guests arrived and took seats at the table. At the height of the festivities they heard a tapping at the door, and who do you think it was?

The mouse with the stinky tail.

A servant went to open the door, and when he saw a mouse, he said, "What do *you* want here?"

"Go and tell the king that the mouse has come to marry his daughter."

The servant went to tell the king, laughing scornfully, but the king ordered him to admit the creature. Once inside, the mouse ran and took a seat right next to the princess.

Poor girl! When she saw him next to her, she shrank away from him in disgust, but the little mouse just pressed himself closer and closer to her, as if he didn't have a seat of his own. The king explained to his guests why the mouse was there, and they all laughed and said, "You're right! That's right! The little mouse should marry the princess!"

The next day there was another great banquet, and at the height of things, *presto!* The mouse appeared again and took his seat next to the princess. At this point the guests all began laughing up their sleeves. When the little mouse saw this, he went up to the king and gave him a warning: everyone at the table had better stop their laughing, otherwise there was going to be trouble.

The little mouse was so short that he couldn't reach the table from his chair. So, in order to eat, he had to get up onto the middle of the table, and no one dared to say anything. But at this banquet there was one rather fastidious lady. When the first course came, the mouse began to run around to all the plates, and this lady suffered in silence. The same thing happened with the second course. When it happened with the third course, she lost control and attacked the mouse with all kinds of abuse. The mouse was furious at being treated so harshly and began leaping at the faces of all the guests. At the height of this turmoil, the table vanished, along with the guests and the palace and everything else, and they all found themselves scattered here and there in the valley.

Now let's leave them and return to the princess. Finding herself alone in the valley, she began to cry, saying over and over,

"Oh my little mouse, at first I didn't want you, but now I long for you!"

Then she set out walking, trusting to God and to fortune, and eventually she met a hermit, who asked her,

"What are you doing here, my fine young lady, alone amongst all these animals? You should be careful, lest you meet up with Mamma-draga the ogress or with a lion, and then poor you!"

"That's not what I'm worried about. What I need is to find my little mouse. At first I didn't want him, but now I long for him. Oh my dear little mouse, where did you go?"

"Do you want my advice?" the hermit asked. "Turn around and go back, otherwise your life will be in danger."

"What choice do I have? Whether I live or die, I have to find the little mouse."

"Oh my child, in order to find him you'll have to make a long journey. Here's what to do. Go further, and you'll come upon another hermit, older than me. He will be able to tell you where to search."

So she said good-bye to him and went forward, singing the same song over and over:

"Oh my little mouse, where in the world can you be?"

As she walked along, she met an old man with a white beard, so long that it reached his feet. She was afraid, but he said, "Don't be afraid, my child. I am baptized flesh, the same as you. Tell me, where are you going?"

"I am looking for the little mouse with the stinky tail."

"Then here's what you must do. Dig a hole in the ground as big as yourself, go down the hole, and then it's up to you to see what happens."

The poor girl had no way of digging such a hole. Then she thought of taking out her hairpin and using that, and so she began to dig. Eventually she had dug a very large hole, and she disappeared down into it. She found a large underground chamber and began to walk along in the dark.

"Here's to luck and good fortune!" she said to herself.

She had to pass through so many spiderwebs that they clung to her pretty face and made it dark as smoke. For every cobweb she pulled from her face, a hundred others clung there. After she had walked for an entire day, she heard the rustling sound of water. Drawing closer, she saw a pond full of water. She wanted to cross it, but the pond was too deep. So she began to cry and to repeat,

> "Oh my little mouse, how I long for you!
> Oh my little mouse, where in the world can you be?"

There was no way she could go forward, and there was no turning back because the hole had closed up again. All she could do was to cry.

At this moment, a shower of water began pouring down on her from above. "What can I do now?" she asked. "If I haven't died by this time, surely I'm going to die now."

As she said this, she heard a voice that said, "Why all this whimpering? You're hurting my ears! Just throw yourself into this pond, and see what happens."

The girl had no choice but to throw herself into the water. All at once she found herself inside a huge palace, a marvel to behold. She entered the first room, and it was all made of glass. She entered the second room, and it was all velvet. She entered the third, and it was all gold and sequins with great couches and lamps, such as she had never seen before. She walked so far that she couldn't find the spot where she had entered, and now she was lost—that's how huge the palace was. Feeling completely lost, she cried out,

"Oh my little mouse, what should I do?"

And a voice answered, "Just make a command."

"My command," she said, "is for something to eat."

Suddenly a beautiful table appeared before her, and it was completely set with a big plate of pasta and so many other dishes that even someone with no appetite would have wanted to eat. The poor girl began eating with gusto. But the strange thing was, she didn't see anybody, and the dishes came and went of their own accord with no one carrying them.

Next she found herself inside a carriage in the middle of a garden. She saw many lovely things there, but couldn't figure out where they were coming from. When evening came, she found a beautiful bed and lay down in it.

Midnight came, and she heard a rustling noise. When she looked, she saw a little mouse approaching her bed. The poor girl was terrified and trembling like a leaf because she didn't know who he was. She prayed to God for help, reciting a string of Our Fathers and Hail Marys.

Morning came, and she didn't see a soul. 'What strange things happened last night!' she said to herself, as she went on with her day. Evening came, she went to bed, and again she heard the rustling noise. "Who could it possibly be?" She had no way of knowing. The third night came, and precisely at midnight the mouse appeared. "*Pi-ti-pi-ti, pi-ti-pi-ti*," the mouse was dancing.

"Oh blessed Mary, all this commotion again?" she said. "Tell me, who in the world are you to be making such a racket?"

"Who am I? Just light the lamp and you'll see who I am."

She got down from her bed and lit the lamp, and what did she see? A handsome young man!

"I was the little mouse with the stinky tail because of a wicked spell that turned me into a mouse. The only way I could be set free from the spell was if a maiden would fall in love with me and suffer all the terrible things you have suffered. Once you came all the way here without feeling disgusted by me, I was able to turn back into a man."

Well, you can imagine the joy that girl felt! The two of them made their way out of the underground place, and at once were engaged and married.

And so they lived on, in contentment and peace,
While we just sit here, cleaning our teeth.

Told by a young girl named Maria Giuliano in Palermo.

Penny Jack (1888)[94]

François-Marie Luzel

A poor orphan lived on alms which he daily collected from door to door. One day a gentleman, passing along the highway, gave him a penny (*deux sous*).

94. "Jannac aux Deux Sous," *Mélusine* (September, 1888). Also published in *Folklore* and translated by W. A. Clouston.

Laughing and dancing with joy at the possession of so much money, he rushed to the town, shouting through the streets, "I've a penny! I've a penny!"

As his clothes were in rags, he went to a draper's and ordered coat, vest, and trousers. "Have you the money, my boy?" asked the merchant.

"O yes," showing his cash.

"Get you gone, Penny Jack!" said the draper, pushing him out of the door.

The name "Penny Jack" stuck to him. At play with some youngsters he lost his money, wept like a calf, and set off for the country. On the way he drinks at a fountain, lies down, and passes the night. In the morning, as he is about to drink again, he perceives an enormous frog in the basin, and shrinks back in horror.

"Don't be alarmed, my boy; come, kiss me."

And the frog leaps up on the edge of the basin. After some persuasion and the promise of his finding money in abundance, Jack kissed the frog. He is directed to look behind a moss-grown stone for money, and is told he will get as much more there tomorrow at the same hour. Jack finds money enough, which he takes, and then runs back to town. "Look! look!" cries he, showing his money; "my pockets full of gold and silver."

The street boys and swindlers get round him, and he is soon left without a coin. The next night he spends at the fountain, and tells of his loss in the morning.

"Never mind," says the frog, "kiss me again, and you'll get plenty."

But the frog is now larger and more hideous, and Jack has scruples which poverty overcomes. Money is got and lost as before, and for the third time Jack goes to the fountain. The frog is now so large as to fill the basin, and hideously swollen up with poison; but, when kissed a third time, a spell is broken, and the frog becomes a beautiful princess, who thanks Jack, and tells him that a charm had kept her in the ugly form he had seen in the fountain, until a "virgin" young man of twenty years should kiss her thrice. She was going to her father, a powerful king of the east, but she intended to marry Jack, who would succeed her father. Meanwhile, he was to return to town, and after a year and a day he must come to the fountain, at eight in the morning, alone and fasting. She would be there, and would take him to her father. He must kiss no other woman, and take care to come fasting, else he should not see her.

He takes a new supply of money, and this time puts it in the keeping of the mistress of an inn where he stays. One of the servant girls took a fancy for him, in spite of his silliness, but he would have nothing to do with her, telling her how he must marry a princess, and stating the precautions he must observe. The girl clasped him round the neck, and kissed him, thus trying to make him break his promise; but Jack still kept to it, and would go on the day appointed to the fountain. She tries in vain to get him misled as to the exact date; and, as he sets out, she slips a pea into his pocket.

Jack arrives too early at the fountain, and, while waiting, finds the pea in his pocket, and thoughtlessly eats it and falls asleep. The princess comes presently, discovers him asleep, and exclaims: "Alas, he has either eaten, or embraced another!" She places in his hands a paper, on which she had written: "Alas, Jack, you have eaten, or perhaps kissed a woman before coming here, and you are asleep. I shall be back at ten o'clock to-morrow at this fountain. Be careful to come fasting, and without having kissed either woman or girl."

Jack awakes, and cries when he sees not the princess; and, finding the paper, he takes it to the inn, where the girl reads it to him. Next morning he sets out again, but the girl has slipped a bean into his vest, which he eats, and then falls asleep, as before. The princess comes, and leaves a paper with him: she will give him one more chance; to-morrow, at noon. He awakes, and is full of sorrow, and, returning to the inn, gets the girl to read the paper for him as before. The girl puts a fig into his pocket before he starts a third time for the fountain. Jack eats the fig and falls asleep. When he awakes he discovers a paper in his hand, and half of the princess's gold ring. This time Jack gets the schoolmaster to read the paper: The princess will return no more; she has gone to her Castle of Gold, held by four chains over the Red Sea. If he loves her he may see her there, but only after many trials and much hardship. She adds that, as soon as he returns to the inn, he must pull off all the buttons of his clothes, and, as each came off, someone in the house would die. So he goes back to the inn, pulls off his buttons, and all die, the girl first. Then he takes his staff and the half-ring, and sets out in quest of the Golden Castle.

After long travel and vain inquiries, he meets with an old hermit, who refers him to an elder brother-hermit, who commands all the beasts, from whom he receives an ointment that can heal any wound, and a ball which rolls before him when the anchorite says: "Go, my ball; go straight to my brother, the hermit to his hermitage two hundred leagues hence."

Jack follows. When the ball strikes against the door, out comes the elder hermit, who recognises the ball, but knows nothing of the Golden Castle, nor do the beasts, whom he summons, and who come, from the mouse to the lion, from the goat to the camel. Jack is sent by him three hundred leagues off to his brother-hermit, who commands all the feathered tribes. He follows a conducting-ball, as before, and feels very tired when it raps at the door of the third hermit. Out comes a man of great age, who is so wise that he knows all Jack's history and his mission, but confesses he knows not the Golden Castle. He summons his birds, from the wren to the eagle. It is only after two calls that the eagle appears, last of all, and, when questioned as to the cause of his delay, he says that he was far away at the Golden Castle of the Red Sea, where the princess was next day to be married; oxen, calves, sheep, and so on, were being slaughtered in great numbers, and he had been getting his share.

The eagle undertakes to carry Jack to the Castle, on condition of having a supply of fresh meat all the way. Twelve sheep are killed, and the quarters and Jack are fastened on the eagle's back. Whenever the bird cries "Oak!" Jack gives him a quarter of a sheep. The provision is all consumed as the Red Sea appears. "Oak! oak!" cries the eagle.

"You've eaten the whole," says Jack.

"Give me meat," rejoins the eagle, "or my strength is gone."

Jack has to give the bird four more successive supplies, taken from the calves of his legs and his thighs. He is at length set down on the castle wall, nearly dead from the loss of blood, but the ointment restores him, and he is as well as ever.

As the bridal procession goes to church, Jack puts himself in the way, and he is recognised by the bride. She pretends sudden sickness, and the ceremony is postponed till next day. In like manner she delays it for three days more. On the third day the wedding-dinner takes place, but they had not yet been to church. Jack is invited as a foreign prince, the princess having sent him splendid robes and jewels. At the end of the feast, stories were told, and the princess, when asked, rose and related her story: "I had, your majesty, a key for my wardrobe, which I lost. I got a new key instead. I have now found the old one. Which would your majesty advise me to use?"

The king said: "Honour is ever due to the eldest."

Replied the princess: "That is also my opinion," and, pointing to Jack, she told how he had freed her from the spell, and so forth. So Jack was married to the princess, and in course of time became king.

Translated by W. A. Clouston.

The Wonderful Frog (1889)[95]

W. Henry Jones and Lewis L. Knopf

There was once, I don't know where, a man who had three daughters. One day the father thus spoke to the eldest girl: "Go, my daughter, and fetch me some fresh water from the well."

The girl went, but when she came to the well a huge frog called out to her from the bottom that he would not allow her to draw water in her jug until she threw him down the gold ring on her finger.

"Nothing else? Is that all you want?" replied the girl. "I won't give away my rings to such an ugly creature as you," and she returned as she came with the empty pitchers.

So the father sent the second girl, and she fared as the first; the frog would not let her have any water, as she refused to throw down her gold ring. Her father gave his two elder daughters a good scolding, and then thus addressed the youngest: "You go, Betsie, my dear, you have always been a clever girl. I'm sure you will be able to get some water, and will not allow your father to suffer thirst; go, shame your sisters!"

---

95. *The Folk-Tales of the Magyars: Collected by Kriza, Erdélyi, and Others* (London: Elliot Stock, 1889).

Betsie picked up the pitchers and went, but the frog again refused the water unless she threw her ring down; but she, as she was very fond of her father, threw the ring in as demanded, and returned home with full pitchers to her father's great delight.

In the evening, as soon as darkness set in, the frog crawled out of the well, and thus commenced to shout in front of Betsie's father's door: "Father-in-law! Father-in-law! I should like something to eat."

The man got angry and called out to his daughters: "Give something in a broken plate to that ugly frog to gnaw."

"Father-in-law! Father-in-law! This won't do for me; I want some roast meat on a tin plate," retorted the frog.

"Give him something on a tin plate then, or else he will cast a spell on us," said the father. The frog began to eat heartily, and, having had enough, again commenced to croak: "Father-in-law! Father-in-law! I want something to drink."

"Give him some slops in a broken pot," said the father.

"Father-in-law! Father-in-law! I won't have this; I want some wine in a nice tumbler."

"Give him some wine then," angrily called out the father.

The frog guzzled up his wine and began again: "Father-in-law! Father-in-law! I would like to go to sleep."

"Throw him some rags in a corner," was the reply.

"Father-in-law! Father-in-law! I won't have that. I want a silk bed," croaked the frog.

This was also given to him, but no sooner had he gone to bed than again he began to croak, "Father-in-law! Father-in-law! I want a girl, indeed."

"Go, my daughter, and lie by the side of him," said the father to the eldest. "Father-in-law! Father-in law! I don't want her, I want another."

The father sent the second girl, but the frog again croaked: "Father-in-law! Father-in-law! I don't want her. Betsie is the girl I want."

"Go, my Betsie," said the father, quite disheartened, "else this confounded monster will cast a spell on us."

So Betsie went to bed with the frog, but her father thoughtfully left a lamp burning on the top of the oven. When the frog noticed this, he crawled out of bed and blew the lamp out. The father lighted it again, but the frog put it out as before, and so it happened a third time. The father saw that the frog would not yield and was therefore obliged to leave his dear little Betsie in the dark by the side of the ugly frog, and felt great anxiety about her. In the morning, when the father and the two elder girls got up, they opened their eyes and mouths wide in astonishment, because the frog had disappeared, and by the side of Betsie they found a handsome Magyar lad, with auburn locks, in a beautiful costume, with gold braid and buttons and gold spurs on his boots. The handsome lad asked for Betsie's hand, and, having received the father's consent, they hastened to celebrate the wedding, so that christening might not follow the wedding too soon.

The two elder sisters looked with invidious eyes on Betsie, as they also were very much smitten with the handsome lad. Betsie was very happy thereafter, so happy that if anyone doubt it he can satisfy himself with his own eyes. If she is still alive, let him go and look for her, and try to find her in this big world.

The Snake and the Princess (1890)[96]
P. Kulish

There was an emperor and empress who had three daughters. The emperor fell ill and sent his eldest daughter for water. She went to fetch it, when a snake said, "Come! Will you marry me?"

The princess replied: "No, I won't."

"Then," said he, "I won't give you any water."

Then the second daughter said: "I'll go. He'll give me some."

She went, and the snake said to her: "Come! Will you marry me?"

"No," she said, "I won't."

He gave her no water. She returned and said: "He gave me no water. He said: If you will marry me, I will give it."

The youngest said: "I will go. He will give me some."

She went, and the snake said to her: "Come! Will you marry me?"

"I will," she said.

Then he drew her water from the very bottom, cold and fresh. She brought it home, gave it her father to drink, and her father recovered. Then on Sunday a carriage came, and those with it said:

> "Open the door,
>   Princess!
> Why did the dear one love?
> Why draw water from the ford,
>   Princess?"

She was terrified, wept, and went and opened the door. Then they said again:

> "Open the rooms,
>   Princess!
> Why did the dear one love?
> Why draw water from the ford,
>   Princess?"

---

96. Albert Wratislaw, *Sixty Folk-Tales from Exclusively Slavonic Sources* (Boston: Houghton, Mifflin, 1889)

Then they came into the house and placed the snake in a plate on the table. There he lay, just as if he were of gold! They went out of the house and said:

"Sit in the carriage.
    Princess!
Why did the dear one love?
Why draw water from the ford, Princess?"

They drove off with her to the snake's abode. There they lived and had a daughter born to them. They also took a godmother to live with them, but she was a wicked woman. The child soon died, and the mother died soon after it. The godmother went in the night to the place where she was buried and cut off her hands. Then she came home, and heated water-gruel, scalded the hands, and took off the gold rings. Then the princess—such was the ordinance of God— came to her for the hands, and said:

"The fowls are asleep, the geese are asleep,
Only my godmother does not sleep.
She scalds white hands in water-gruel,
She takes off golden rings."

The godmother concealed herself under the stove.
The Princess said again:

"The fowls are asleep, the geese are asleep,
Only my godmother does not sleep.
She scalds white hands in water-gruel,
She takes off golden rings."

The next day they came and found the godmother dead under the stove. They didn't give her proper burial, but threw her into a hole.

The Well of the World's End (1890)[97]

Joseph Jacobs

Once upon a time, and a very good time it was, though it wasn't in my time, nor in your time, nor anyone else's time, there was a girl whose mother had died, and her father had married again. And her stepmother hated her because she was more beautiful than herself, and she was very cruel to her. She used to make her do all the servant's work, and never let her have any peace. At last, one day, the stepmother thought to get rid of her altogether; so she handed her a sieve and said to her: "Go, fill it at the Well of the World's End and bring it home to me full, or woe betide you." For she thought she would never be able to find the Well of the World's End, and, if she did, how could she bring home a sieve full of water?

---

97.   *English Fairy Tales* (London: David Nutt, 1890).

Well, the girl started off, and asked everyone she met to tell her where was the Well of the World's End. But nobody knew, and she didn't know what to do, when a queer little old woman, all bent double, told her where it was, and how she could get to it. So she did what the old woman told her, and at last arrived at the Well of the World's End. But when she dipped the sieve in the cold, cold water, it all ran out again. She tried and she tried again, but every time it was the same; and at last she sat down and cried as if her heart would break.

Suddenly she heard a croaking voice, and she looked up and saw a great frog with goggle eyes looking at her and speaking to her.

"What's the matter, dearie?" it said.

"Oh, dear, oh dear," she said, "my stepmother has sent me all this long way to fill this sieve with water from the Well of the World's End, and I can't fill it no how at all."

"Well," said the frog, "if you promise me to do whatever I bid you for a whole night long, I'll tell you how to fill it."

So the girl agreed, and then the frog said:

"Stop it with moss and daub it with clay,

And then it will carry the water away," and then it gave a hop, skip, and jump, and went flop into the Well of the World's End.

So the girl looked about for some moss, and lined the bottom of the sieve with it, and over that she put some clay, and then she dipped it once again into the Well of the World's End; and this time, the water didn't run out, and she turned to go away. Just then the frog popped up its head out of the Well of the World's End, and said: "Remember your promise."

"All right," said the girl; for thought she, 'what harm can a frog do me?'

So she went back to her stepmother, and brought the sieve full of water from the Well of the World's End. The stepmother was fine and angry, but she said nothing at all. That very evening they heard something tap tapping at the door low down, and a voice cried out:

"Open the door, my hinny, my heart,
Open the door, my own darling;
Mind you the words that you and I spoke,
Down in the meadow, at the World's End Well."

"Whatever can that be?" cried out the stepmother, and the girl had to tell her all about it, and what she had promised the frog.

"Girls must keep their promises," said the stepmother. "Go and open the door this instant." For she was glad the girl would have to obey a nasty frog.

So the girl went and opened the door, and there was the frog from the Well of the World's End. And it hopped, and it skipped, and it jumped, till it reached the girl, and then it said:

> "Lift me to your knee, my hinny, my heart;
> Lift me to your knee, my own darling;
> Remember the words you and I spoke,
> Down in the meadow by the World's End Well."

But the girl didn't like to, till her stepmother said: "Lift it up this instant, you hussy! Girls must keep their promises!"

So at last she lifted the frog up on to her lap, and it lay there for a time, till at last it said:

> "Give me some supper, my hinny, my heart,
> Give me some supper, my darling;
> Remember the words you and I spake,
> In the meadow, by the Well of the World's End."

Well, she didn't mind doing that, so she got it a bowl of milk and bread, and fed it well. And when the frog had finished, it said:

> "Go with me to bed, my hinny, my heart,
> Go with me to bed, my own darling;
> Mind you the words you spake to me,
> Down by the cold well, so weary."

But that the girl wouldn't do, till her stepmother said: "Do what you promised, girl; girls must keep their promises. Do what you're bid, or out you go, you and your froggie."

So the girl took the frog with her to bed, and kept it as far away from her as she could. Well, just as the day was beginning to break what should the frog say but:

> "Chop off my head, my own darling;
> Remember the promise you made to me,
> Down by the cold well so weary."

At first the girl wouldn't, for she thought of what the frog had done for her at the Well of the World's End. But when the frog said the words over again, she went and took an axe and chopped off its head, and lo! and behold, there stood before her a handsome young prince, who told her that he had been enchanted by a wicked magician, and he could never be unspelled till some girl would do his bidding for a whole night, and chop off his head at the end of it.

The stepmother was that surprised when she found the young prince instead of the nasty frog, and she wasn't best pleased, you may be sure, when the prince told her that he was going to marry her stepdaughter because she had unspelled him. So they were married and went away to live in the castle of the king, his father, and all the stepmother had to console her was, that it was all through her that her stepdaughter was married to a prince.

The Queen and the Frog (1891)[98]

Ulrich Jahn

Once there was a king and a queen who loved each other very much. At one point the king had to go to war, and the queen remained completely alone in the castle with her faithful maid. Every day the queen climbed up to the tower and looked out to see if her husband might soon be returning home, but there was nothing to see. Then she would always weep, and her maid consoled her. She frequently went into the garden and sat down beneath a plum tree next to a brook. When the plums became ripe, she shook them from the tree and ate them. In the process, however, her hands became dirty. So she went to the brook to wash them, and her ring fell into the water. She was deeply horrified and sat down on the bank of the brook where she burst out crying, for she thought her husband was now dead.

All at once a large frog appeared, looked at her, and said: "My princess, why are you weeping?"

But the princess didn't listen to him. So, he crawled to her feet and asked once more: "My princess, why are you weeping?"

Then she looked at him and said: "You hideous old frog. Why should I tell you? You won't be able to help me anyway."

"Is that so? Do you know that for sure?" said the frog. "I already know why you are crying. You've lost your ring."

Immediately the princess looked at him and said: "Oh, dear frog, if you know something about it and have found it, can you bring it to me?"

"Yes," said the frog. "It's something I can do, but you must promise me something if I do it."

"Whatever you want. Just get me the ring," the princess replied.

"But I won't be asking for some little thing. You must marry me."

Upon hearing this the queen laughed and thought: 'You dumb frog! You should have wished for something else.' And then she said: "All right, I'll gladly do it. —Now get me the ring!"

Immediately thereafter the frog plunged into the water and swam away. It took a good while, and the princess thought already that the frog had lied to her, but then it came crawling out of the water and actually had the ring in its mouth.

"Children! People!" the princess cried out as she took the ring and quickly ran into the castle. Meanwhile the frog called after her that he'd soon be coming to her.

Some days later the princess was sitting in her room and sewing a silk shirt for her husband. All at once she heard a soft knock on the lower part of the door, and a voice began to sing: "Open up the door for me, beautiful princess!"

---

98. "Die Koenigin un de Pogg," *Volksmärchen aus Pommern und Rügen* (Leipzig: Diederich Soltau's Verlag, 1891).

"Oh," the princess said, "maid, come here quickly. That's certainly the frog I told you about. Go and open up the door for him."

In response the frog began to sing again:

> "Not the maid, beautiful princess!
> Don't you recall what you said at the brook,
> When you lost your ring in that very same brook,
> and gave your word to wed me, oh beautiful princess?"

So the princess stood up and opened the door.

When the frog hopped into the room, he sang again: "Set me down on your little chair, beautiful princess!"

"Maid," responded the princess, "listen to what the frog demands. Since he brought the ring back to me, we shall do as he wishes, Put him on the chair!"

> "Not the maid, beautiful princess!
> Don't you recall what you said at the brook,
> When you lost your ring in that very same brook,
> and gave your word to wed me, oh beautiful princess?"

Now the princess put on silk gloves and lifted him onto the chair. But the frog began to sing once more: "Give me something to eat, beautiful princess!"

"Maid, go and fetch milk and some buns for the frog," she said, but the frog sang out:

> "Not the maid, beautiful princess!
> Don't you recall what you said at the brook,
> When you lost your ring in that very same brook,
> and gave your word to wed me, oh beautiful princess?"

So the princess went to the kitchen and fetched milk and some white bread. And after the frog had eaten a great deal, he sang: "Wipe my mouth, beautiful princess!"

"Well, what a nerve!" said the princess. "Maid, take the napkin, and wipe his mouth!"

Then the frog sang once more:

> "Not the maid, beautiful princess!
> Don't you recall what you said at the brook,
> When you lost your ring in that very same brook,
> and gave your word to wed me, oh beautiful princess?"

So, once again, the princess had to do everything herself. Meanwhile the frog began to sing once more: "Give me a little kiss, beautiful princess!"

And now the princess almost fainted out of horror, and she said: "Maid, you must do this. I can't."

But the frog gazed at her with such a distressed look and had two large tears in its eyes and sang softly:

"Not the maid, beautiful princess!
Don't you recall what you said at the brook,
When you lost your ring in that very same brook,
and gave your word to wed me, oh beautiful princess?"

Then the princess thought about her promise and said: "I hadn't expected this. Maid, go and fetch me a kerchief and bind my eyes with it so that at least I won't see the frog."

The maid did this, and the princess stretched out her hands to find the frog, and it was very slippery in her hands. She puckered and sprayed her lips, immediately there was a tremendous noise. She became so frightened that she tore off the kerchief and she saw her own husband standing right before her eyes—cheerful and healthy!

All this had happened like this: While he was away in the war, a wicked witch had cast a magic spell on him and turned him into a frog. She said that he was to remain a frog until a princess gave him a kiss. After this had happened, the king was very depressed and swam through rivers and streams until he had arrived at the brook where his wife was sitting. Indeed, he had immediately thought that no other person but his wife would ever give him a kiss.

The Princess and the Scabby Toad (1891)[99]
Ulrich Jahn

Once upon a time there was a king who had only one daughter. She was a real tomboy. She loved to spend time with young boys most of all and run all over the place from morning until evening. When she turned ten years old, she used to lay in her boat on the water the entire day, and one time as she was doing this, the golden bracelet, which the old king had given to her for her birthday, slipped from her arm and fell into the water. Now she was in great trouble, for the bracelet was immensely valuable, and the king didn't like to lose money. Consequently, he ordered all the fishermen of his realm to come to the sea, and they had to spend an entire week fishing for the bracelet. But, although they worked day and night and churned up the bottom of the sea, they couldn't find the bracelet. It had vanished and remained vanished.

One day the princess stood on the beach and looked out into the distance with a sad face. All of a sudden something splashed in the water, and a large and fat scabby toad crawled onto the sand, gaped at the princess, and said: "What will you give me if I bring back the bracelet to you?"

---

99. "Die Königstochter und die Schorfkröte," *Volksmärchen aus Pommern und Rügen* (Leipzig: Diederich Soltau's Verlag, 1891).

"A gold coin as big as a taler!" the princess quickly answered. Indeed, she desired nothing more in the entire world than to regain the bracelet.

But the scabby toad replied: "I won't bring back the bracelet to you for gold and silver. But if you grant me three wishes, I'll dive down and bring it to you from the bottom of the sea."

"Well, I must quickly go and ask my father," the princess said, and *whoosh!* she ran to the castle to the old king's room and told him about the toad's request.

'What could an old, fat scabby toad possibly wish for himself?' the king thought. 'Anyway, in the final analysis the bracelet is worth three wishes.' So, he allowed his daughter to make a promise to the toad. Of course the plump reptile was very happy when the princess give her word to him. Within seconds the toad was in the water again, and after a few moments he splashed his way out of the sea and carried the bracelet around his neck. The princess quickly took off the bracelet and asked the toad about his three wishes.

"I'll demand them when it suits me," the toad replied and crawled back into the water.

In the meantime the princess ran to the castle with her bracelet and was totally overwhelmed by joy. As time passed and she turned eighteen years old, she had completely forgotten the story about the bracelet. Then one day, when she was sitting at the table with her mother and father, there was a knock at the door. A servant ran and opened the door. *Splish, splash*, the fat scabby toad came crawling inside and said: "Princess, I've come today to solve your puzzle. My first wish is to dine three weeks in a row with you at the king's table."

"Nothing doing!" said the princess.

"But you promised to give me three wishes for getting you the bracelet," the toad answered.

"Promises are meant to be kept," said the old king, and as soon as he said this, the case was closed. The servant was ordered to set the toad on a chair next to the princess. A little plate stood right in front of him, and the princess put all the food on the table onto his plate.

When the three weeks had passed, the scabby toad said: "Now I'm going to make my second wish. You are to make my little bed every morning, and I want to sleep three weeks straight in the castle."

"Will you just take a look at this foolish toad!" the princess said and didn't want to hear anything about this.

Now even though the old king tended to be more concerned about money, he also had an honest heart, and therefore, he said: "That's to no avail. You made a promise, and a person who makes a promise must keep it, especially a king and his children."

And so the toad's second wish was fulfilled. He slept three straight weeks in the castle, and the princess made the little bed every morning.

After some time had passed, the princess had even greater worries when it came to the outrageous toad's third wish. Indeed, she had a right to be concerned, for everything had already been bad enough!

"My little princess," the toad began saying, "I have one more free wish, and so I wish to spend three straight weeks next to you in your little bed."

To be sure, the princess had already become accustomed to the reptile, and the toad had long since stopped seeming so ugly and nasty as in the beginning. But when she heard these words, she closed her ears, ran to the old king, and said: "Father, I can't grant the third wish! The cold, slimy, filthy thing wants to sleep in my bed!"

At first the king didn't know what his daughter was talking about. But when he learned that it all concerned the toad's third request, he said, "My dear child, that doesn't help things. Whoever says A must also say B. You gave your promise, and now you must keep it."

"All right then, I'll place my little skirt between us," the princess cried out, and that's what she in fact did so that the reptile couldn't come too close. She also counted the days on her ten fingers because she yearned so much for the day when she'd be rid of the ugly guest.

When the last night had finally passed and morning dawned, the princess turned around and wanted to throw the toad out of the bed. However, she was astonished to see that the toad wasn't there anymore. Instead, there was a marvelously handsome prince with a gold star on his chest. He told her that he had been bewitched and turned into a toad. Now she had released him from the spell, and if she wouldn't mind, he'd like to marry her.

Of course, he was quite different from the nasty toad, and she immediately said yes. So, right after they got dressed, they went to the old king and asked for his blessing. Indeed, he had the engagement and the wedding take place that very same day, and when he died, the prince became his successor to the realm. And so he lived there with his young queen in peace and happiness, and if they haven't died, then they are still living today.

9. THE FATE OF SPINNING

ATU 500/501—THE NAME OF THE SUPERNATURAL HELPER AND THE THREE OLD SPINNING WOMEN

These tale types have been categorized under the wrong name, for almost all the tales in this category focus on the significance of spinning, especially on its significance for women. Moreover, the major protagonist is a young woman from the lower classes, who is generally exploited by her father/mother/grandmother; the king who marries her; and the little demonic man/predator, who tries to take advantage of her. The initial situation varies. A father falsely boasts about his daughter's ability to spin straw into gold; a mother berates her for being lazy and not knowing how to spin and gives her to a queen or prince while claiming that her daughter is a superb worker who loves spinning; a grandmother/mother chases her away because she has eaten up all her food, and the girl must find work somewhere. Once the maiden is in a castle, she must produce something that she normally can't do such as spinning straw into gold or spinning an extraordinary amount of flax. A small man suddenly appears, or three elderly women come by. They help her on condition that she give up her firstborn baby or that she recognizes them as relatives. Sometimes the demonic man wants her for a wife. In many variants she must guess the name of the little man. Once the maiden is successful, no matter what the version of the tale type is, she never has to spin again, which seems to be her major goal.

The importance of spinning in the economy of Europe from the medieval period to the end of the nineteenth century can be documented in the thousands of folk and fairy tales that were disseminated by word of mouth and through print. The most popular "spinning" tale is, of course, "Rumpelstiltskin," and like many tales about spinning, it reveals how important spinning could be for women: a good spinner could rise in social status and find a husband through her diligent efforts. And there are also thousands of tales that depict how a young woman wins a man by demonstrating her industriousness as a spinner. Yet by the nineteenth century, with the rise of manufacturing, attitudes began to change, and most of the tales dealing with "Rumpelstiltskin" and "The Three Old Spinning Women" demonstrate a shift in attitude. That is, spinning was regarded as hard labor, and once a man was won, the young woman sought to abandon this craft.

The major literary sources for this tale type are Giambattista Basile, "The Seven Bits of Bacon Rind," *Lo cunto de li cunti* (1634), and Marie-Jeanne L'Héritier, "Ricdin-Ricdon," *La Tour ténébreuse et les jours lumineux* (1705). The Grimms were well aware of these tales, but they also knew many others that had an influence on their various spinning tales. Johannes Praetorius (a pseudonym for Hans Schultze) published a humorous version in his book *Abentheurlichen Glücks-Topf*

(1669), and Sophie Albrecht's *Graumännchen oder die Burg Rabenbühl* ("*The Little Gray Man or the Castle Rabenbühl*," 1799) was strongly influenced by Mlle L'Héritier's "Ricdin-Ricdon." The oral versions for the 1812 version of "Rumpelstiltskin" were provided by the Hassenpflug family and Henriette Dorothea Wild, while the oral version for "About Nasty Flax Spinning" was obtained from Jeanette Hassenpflug. From 1819 onward, Wilhelm kept changing both tales due to other variants that he received. The name "Rumpelstilzchen" (Rumpelstiltskin) does not have any particular meaning. The Grimms took it from Johann Fischart's index of children's games in his book *Geschichtklitterung* (1575) in which a ghost by the name of Rumpele is mentioned.

In the tales that follow there are different perspectives about the value of spinning for the women of these stories, and many of them, probably told by women in spinning huts or rooms, reveal how the spinners would actually like *not* to spin anymore, but use their spinning to entangle a man and to weave the threads and narrative strands of their own lives. These stories were widely known throughout nineteenth-century Europe. In the English tradition, Rumpelstiltskin generally goes by the name of Tom-Tit-Tot, and there are hundreds of different versions of this tale in Great Britain, as the English folklorist Edward Clodd has shown in his book *Tom Tit Tot: An Essay of Savage Philosophy* (1898). For the most part the name of the little man with the magic touch is comical and bizarre, and it functions mainly as a riddle that the young maiden must solve to protect herself and her child.

******

Rumpelstiltskin (1812)[100]
Jacob and Wilhelm Grimm

Once upon a time there was a miller who was poor, but he had a beautiful daughter. Now it happened that he came to talk with the king one time and said, "I have a daughter who knows the art of transforming straw into gold."

So the king had the miller's daughter summoned to him right away and ordered her to change an entire room of straw into gold in one night, and if she couldn't do this, she would die. She was locked in the room where she sat and wept. For the life of her, she didn't have the slightest inkling of how to change straw into gold. All of a sudden a little man entered the room and said, "What will you give me if I change everything into gold?"

She took off her necklace and gave it to the little man, and he did what he promised. The next morning the king found the entire room filled with gold, but because of this, his heart grew even greedier, and he locked the miller's daughter in another room full of straw that was even larger than the first, and she was to change it all into gold. Then the little man came again, and she gave him a ring from her hand, and everything was changed into gold.

---

100. "Rumpelstilzchen," *Kinder- und Haus-Märchen. Gesammelt durch die Brüder Grimm*, 2 vols. (Berlin: Realschulbuchhandlung, 1812/1815).

However, on the third night the king had her locked again in another room that was larger than the other two and filled with straw.

"If you succeed, you shall become my wife," he said.

Then the little man came again and spoke: "I'll do everything for you one more time, but you must promise me your firstborn child that you have with the king."

In her desperate situation she gave him her promise, and when the king saw once again how the straw had been changed into gold, he took the beautiful miller's daughter for his wife.

Soon thereafter the queen gave birth, and the little man appeared before her and demanded the promised child. However, the queen offered the little man all that she could and all the treasures of the kingdom if he would let her keep her child, but everything was in vain. Then the little man said, "In three days I'll come again to fetch the child. But if you know my name by then, you shall keep your child."

During the first and second nights the queen tried to think of the little man's name, but she wasn't able to come up with a name and became completely depressed. On the third day, however, the king returned home from hunting and told her, "I was out hunting the day before yesterday, and when I went deep into the dark forest, I came upon a small cottage, and in front of the house there was a ridiculous little man, hopping around as if he had only one leg and screeching:

"Today I'll brew, tomorrow I'll bake.
Soon I'll have the queen's namesake.
Oh, how hard it is to play my game,
for Rumpelstiltskin is my name!"

When the queen heard this, she rejoiced, and when the dangerous little man came, he asked, "What's my name, your Highness?" she responded first by guessing,

"Is your name Conrad?"

"No."

"Is your name Henry?"

"No."

"Is your name Rumpelstiltskin?"

"The devil told you that!" the little man screamed, and he ran angrily away and never returned.

Rumpelstiltskin (1857)[101]

Jacob and Wilhelm Grimm

Once upon a time there was a miller who was poor, but he had a beautiful daughter. Now it happened that he was talking with the king one time, and in

---

101.   "Rumpelstilzchen," *Kinder- und Hausmärchen gesammelt durch die Brüder Grimm*, 7th ed., 3 vols. (Göttingen: Verlag der Dieterich'schen Buchhandlung, 1857).

order to make himself seem important, he said to the king, "I have a daughter who can spin straw into gold."

"That is an art that pleases me!" the king replied. "If your daughter is as talented as you say, then bring her to my castle tomorrow, and I'll put her to a test."

When the maiden was brought to him, he led her into a room that was filled with straw. There he gave her a spinning wheel and spindle and said, "Now get to work! If you don't spin this straw into gold by morning, you must die." Then he locked the door himself, and she remained inside all alone.

The miller's poor daughter sat there feeling close to her wits' end, for she knew nothing about spinning straw into gold, and her fear grew greater and greater. When she began to weep, the door suddenly opened, <u>and a little man entered.</u>

"Good evening, mistress miller, why are you weeping so?"

"Oh," answered the maiden, "I'm supposed to spin straw into gold, and I don't know how."

The little man then asked, "What will you give me if I spin it for you?"

"My necklace," the maiden said.

The little man took the necklace and saw down at the wheel, and *whizz, whizz, whizz,* three times round, the spool was full. Then he inserted another one, and *whizz, whizz, whizz,* the second was full. And so it went until morning, when all the straw was spun, and all the spools were filled with gold. The king appeared right at sunrise, and when he saw the gold, he was surprised and pleased, but his heart grew even greedier. He locked the miller's daughter in another room that was even larger than the first and ordered her to spin all the straw into gold if she valued her life. The maiden didn't know what to do and began to weep. Once again the door opened, and the little man appeared and asked, "What will you give me if I spin the straw into gold for you?"

"The ring from my finger," answered the maiden.

The little man took the ring, began to work away at the wheel again, and by morning he had spun all the straw into shining gold. The king was extremely pleased by the sight, but his lust for gold was still not satisfied. So he had the miller's daughter brought into an even larger room filled with straw and said to her, "You must spin all this into gold tonight. If you succeed, you shall become my wife." To himself he thought, 'Even though she's just a miller's daughter, I'll never find a richer woman anywhere in the world.'

When the maiden was alone, the little man came again for a third time and asked, "What will you give me if I spin the straw into gold once more?"

"I have nothing left to give," answered the maiden.

"Then promise me your first child when you become queen."

'Who knows whether it will ever come to that?' thought the miller's daughter. And since she knew of no other way out of her predicament, she promised the little man what he had demanded. In return the little man spun the straw into gold once again. When the king came in the morning and found everything as he had wished, he married her, and the beautiful miller's daughter became a queen.

After a year she gave birth to a beautiful child. The little man had disappeared from her mind, but he suddenly appeared in her room and said, "Now give me what you promised."

The queen was horrified and offered the little man all the treasures of the kingdom if he would let her keep her child, but the little man replied, "No, something living is more important to me than all the treasures in the world."

Then the queen began to grieve and weep so much that the little man felt sorry for her. "I'll give you three days' time," he said. "If you can guess my name by the third day, you shall keep your child."

The queen spent the entire night trying to recall all the names she had ever heard. She also sent a messenger out into the country to inquire high and low what other names there were. On the following day, when the little man appeared, she began with Kaspar, Melchior, Balzer, and then repeated all the names she knew, one after the other. But to all of them, the little man said, "That's not my name."

The second day she had her servants ask around in the neighboring area what names people used, and she came up with the most unusual and strangest names when the little man appeared.

"Is your name Ribsofbeef or Muttonchops or Lacedleg?"

But he always replied, "That's not my name."

On the third day the messenger returned and reported, "I couldn't find a single new name, but as I was climbing a high mountain at the edge of the forest, where the fox and the hare say good night to each other, I saw a small cottage, and in front of the cottage was a fire, and around the fire danced a ridiculous little man who was hopping on one leg and screeching:

> "Today I'll brew, tomorrow I'll bake.
> Soon I'll have the queen's namesake.
> Oh, how hard it is to play my game,
> for Rumpelstiltskin is my name!"

You can imagine how happy the queen was when she heard the name. And as soon as the little man entered and asked, "What's my name, your Highness?" she responded first by guessing,

"Is your name Kunz?"

"No."

"Is your name Heinz?"

"No."

"Can your name be Rumpelstiltskin?"

"The devil told you! The devil told you!" the little man screamed, and he stamped so ferociously with his right foot that his leg went deep into the ground up to his waist. Then he grabbed the other foot angrily with both hands and ripped himself in two.

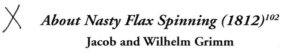

About Nasty Flax Spinning (1812)[102]
Jacob and Wilhelm Grimm

In olden times there lived a king who loved flax spinning more than anything in the world, and the queen and his daughters had to spin the entire day. If he didn't hear wheels humming, he became angry.

One time he had to take a trip, and before he departed, he gave the queen a large box with flax and said: "All this must be spun before I return home."

The princesses became distressed and wept.

"If we have to spin all of that, we'll have to sit the entire day and won't be able to stand up even one time."

However, the queen said, "Console yourselves. I'll certainly help you."

Now, there were three especially ugly spinsters in this country. The first had such a large lower lip that it hung down below her chin. The second had an index finger on her right hand that was so thick and wide that one could have made three fingers out of it. The third had a thick and wide flat foot that was as wide as half a baking board. The queen summoned these women to her on the day that the king was to come home. She sat them down in a row in her room, gave each one of them a spinning wheel, and told them what they were to say when the king questioned them.

When the king arrived, he heard the humming of the wheels in the distance and was delighted and thought of praising his daughters. However, as he entered the room and saw the three horrible spinsters sitting there, he was at first terrified and then stepped toward them and asked the first one how she got that terrible large lower lip.

"From licking, from licking."

Then he asked the second one how she got such a thick finger.

"From turning the thread, from turning and twining the thread."

As she said this, she let the thread wind around her finger a couple of times.

Finally, he asked the third one where she got such a thick foot.

"From treading, from treading."

When the king heard all this, he ordered the queen and the princesses never to touch a spinning wheel again, and consequently, they were able to put an end to their agony.

---

102.   "Von dem bösen Flachspinnen," *Kinder- und Haus-Märchen. Gesammelt durch die Brüder Grimm*, 2 vols. (Berlin: Realschulbuchhandlung, 1812/1815).

X **The Three Spinners (1857)**[103]
Jacob and Wilhelm Grimm

There was once a lazy maiden who didn't want to spin, and no matter what her mother said, she refused to spin. Finally, her mother became so angry and impatient that she beat her, and her daughter began to cry loudly. Just then the queen happened to be driving by, and when she heard the crying, she ordered the carriage to stop, went into the house, and asked the mother why she was beating her daughter, for her screams could be heard out on the street. The woman was too ashamed to tell the queen that her daughter was lazy and said, "I can't get her to stop spinning. She does nothing but spin and spin, and I'm so poor that I can't provide enough flax."

"Well," the queen replied, "there's nothing I like to hear better than the sound of spinning, and I'm even happier when I hear the constant humming of the wheels. Let me take your daughter with me to my castle. I've got plenty of flax, and she can spin as much as she likes."

The mother was delighted to give her consent, and the queen took the maiden with her. After they reached the castle, she led the maiden upstairs to three rooms that were filled with the finest flax from floor to ceiling.

"Now, spin this flax for me," she said. "And if you finish all this, you shall have my oldest son for your husband. It doesn't matter to me that you're poor. Since you work industriously and you never stop, that in itself is dowry enough."

The maiden was deeply frightened, for she couldn't have spun the flax even if she were to live three hundred years and sit there every day from morning till night. Therefore, when she was left alone, she began to weep and sat there for three days without lifting a finger. On the third day the queen came back to the room, and when she saw that nothing had been spun, she was puzzled. But the maiden made up an excuse and said she had been so tremendously upset about leaving her mother's house that she had been unable to begin working. The queen accepted this excuse, but upon leaving she said, "Tomorrow you must begin your work for me."

When the maiden was alone again, she didn't know what to do or where to turn. In her distress she went over to the window and saw three women coming in her direction: the first had a broad flat foot, the second had such a large lower lip that it hung down over her chin, and the third had an immense thumb. They stopped in front of her window, looked up, and asked the maiden what the matter was. She told them about her predicament, and they offered to help her.

"We'll spin your flax for you in no time at all," they said. "But only if you invite us to your wedding and are not ashamed of us. Moreover, you must call us your cousins, and let us eat at your table."

103. "Die drei Spinnerinnen," *Kinder- und Hausmärchen gesammelt durch die Brüder Grimm*, 7th ed., 2 vols. (Göttingen: Verlag der Dieterich'schen Buchhandlung, 1857).

"With all my heart," she responded. "Just come in and get to work right away."

She let the three odd women in and cleared a place for them in the first room where they could sit down and begin their spinning. One drew out the thread and began treading the treadle, the other wet the thread, and the third twisted it and struck the table with her finger. Whenever she struck it, a reel of yarn dropped to the ground, and it was always most delicately spun. The maiden concealed the three spinners from the queen, and every time the queen came, the maiden showed her such a large amount of spun yarn that there was no end to the queen's praise for her. When the first room was empty of flax, they moved on to the second and then the third until it, too, was cleared of flax. Now the three women took their leave and said to the maiden, "Don't forget what you've promised us. Your good fortune will depend on it."

When the maiden showed the queen the empty rooms and the large piles of yarn, the queen arranged for the wedding, and the bridegroom was happy to get such a skilled and industrious wife and gave her tremendous praise.

"I have three cousins," said the maiden, "and since they've done many good things for me, I'd like to invite them to the wedding. Please allow me to do this and let them sit at our table."

The queen and the bridegroom said, "Why, of course, we'll allow this."

When the feast was just about to begin, the three women entered in bizarre costumes, and the bride said, "Welcome, dear cousins."

"Ahh!" said the bridegroom. "How did you ever come by such ghastly-looking friends?"

Then he went to the one with a broad flat foot and asked, "How did you get such a flat foot?"

"From treading," she answered. "From treading."

Next the bridegroom went to the second and asked, "How did you get such a drooping lip?"

"From licking," she answered. "From licking."

Then he asked the third one, "How did you get such an immense thumb?"

"From twisting thread," she answered. "From twisting thread."

Upon hearing this the prince was alarmed and said, "Never ever shall my beautiful wife touch a spinning wheel again."

Thus she was able to rid herself of the terrible task of spinning flax.

The Three Aunts (1852)[104]
Peter Christen Asbjørnsen and Jørgen Moe

Once on a time there was a poor man who lived in a hut far away in the wood and got his living by shooting. He had an only daughter, who was very pretty,

104. *Popular Tales from the Norse*, trans. George Dasent (Edinburgh: Edmonston & Douglas, 1859).

and as she had lost her mother when she was a child and was now half grown up, she said she would go out into the world and earn her bread.

"Well, lassie!" said the father, "true enough you have learnt nothing here but how to pluck birds and roast them, but still you may as well try to earn your bread."

So the girl went off to seek a place, and when she had gone a little while, she came to a palace. There she stayed and got a place, and the queen liked her so well that all the other maids got envious of her. So they made up their minds to tell the queen how the lassie said she was good to spin a pound of flax in four-and-twenty hours, for you must know the queen was a great housewife, and thought much of good work.

"Have you said this? Then you shall do it," said the queen. "But you may have a little longer time if you choose."

Now, the poor lassie dared not say she had never spun in all her life, but she only begged for a room to herself. That she got, and the wheel and the flax were brought up to her. There she sat sad and weeping, and knew not how to help herself. She pulled the wheel this way and that, and twisted and turned it about, but she made a poor hand of it, for she had never even seen a spinning wheel in her life.

But all at once, as she sat there, in came an old woman to her.

"What ails you, child?" she said.

"Ah!" said the lassie, with a deep sigh, "it's no good to tell you, for you'll never be able to help me."

"Who knows?" said the old wife. "Maybe I know how to help you after all."

'Well,' thought the lassie to herself, 'I may as well tell her,' and so she told her how her fellow-servants had given out that she was good to spin a pound of flax in four-and-twenty hours.

"And here am I, wretch that I am, shut up to spin all that heap in a day and a night, when I have never even seen a spinning wheel in all my born days."

"Well, never mind, child," said the old woman. "If you'll call me Aunt on the happiest day of your life, I'll spin this flax for you, and so you may just go away and lie down to sleep."

Yes, the lassie was willing enough, and off she went and lay down to sleep. Next morning when she awoke, there lay all the flax spun on the table, and that so clean and fine, no one had ever seen such even and pretty yarn.

The queen was very glad to get such nice yarn, and she set greater store by the lassie than ever. But the rest were still more envious, and agreed to tell the queen how the lassie had said she was good to weave the yarn she had spun in four-and-twenty hours. So the queen said again, as she had said it she must do it; but if she couldn't quite finish it in four-and-twenty hours, she wouldn't be too hard upon her, she might have a little more time. This time, too, the lassie dared not say, no, but begged for a room to herself, and then she would try. There she sat again, sobbing and crying, and not knowing which way to turn, when another old woman came in and asked, "What ails you, child?"

At first the lassie wouldn't say, but at last she told her the whole story of her grief.

"Well, well!" said the old wife, "never mind. If you'll call me Aunt on the happiest day of your life, I'll weave this yarn for you, and so you may just be off and lie down to sleep."

Yes, the lassie was willing enough. So, she went away and lay down to sleep. When she awoke, there lay the piece of linen on the table, woven so neat and close, no woof could be better. So the lassie took the piece and ran down to the queen, who was very glad to get such beautiful linen, and set greater store than ever by the lassie. But as for the others, they grew still more bitter against her, and thought of nothing but how to find out something to tell about her.

At last they told the queen the lassie had said she was good to make up the piece of linen into shirts in four-and-twenty hours. Well, all happened as before; the lassie dared not say she couldn't sew. So she was shut up again in a room by herself, and there she sat in tears and grief. But then another old wife came, who said she would sew the shirts for her if she would call her Aunt on the happiest day of her life. The lassie was only too glad to do this, and then she did as the old wife told her, and went and lay down to sleep.

Next morning when she woke she found the piece of linen made up into shirts, which lay on the table—and such beautiful work no one had ever set eyes on. And more than that, the shirts were all marked and ready for wear. So, when the queen saw the work, she was so glad at the way in which it was sewn, that she clapped her hands, and said, "Such sewing I never had, nor even saw, in all my born days."

And after that she was as fond of the lassie as of her own children, and she said to her, "Now, if you like to have the Prince for your husband, you shall have him, for you will never need to hire work-women. You can sew, and spin, and weave all yourself."

So as the lassie was pretty, and the Prince was glad to have her, the wedding soon came on. But just as the prince was going to sit down with the bride to the bridal feast, in came an ugly old hag with a long nose—I'm sure it was three ells long. So up got the bride and made a curtsey, and said, "Good-day, Auntie."

"*That* Auntie to my bride?" said the prince.

"Yes, she was!"

"Well, then, she'd better sit down with us to the feast," said the prince, but to tell you the truth, both he and the rest thought she was a loathsome woman to have next you.

Just then in came another ugly old hag. She had a back so humped and broad, she had hard work to get through the door. Up jumped the bride in a trice, and greeted her with "Good-day, Auntie!"

And the prince asked again if that were his bride's aunt. They both said, "Yes."

So the prince said, if that were so, she, too, had better sit down with them to the feast. But they had scarce taken their seats before another ugly old hag came in, with eyes as large as saucers, and so red and bleared, 'twas gruesome to look at her. But up jumped the bride again, with her "Good-day, Auntie," and her, too, the prince asked to sit down; but I can't say he was very glad, for he thought to himself, 'Heaven shield me from such Aunties as my bride has!'

So when he had sat a while, he could not keep his thoughts to himself any longer, but asked, "But how, in all the world can my bride, who is such a lovely lassie, have such loathsome misshapen Aunts?"

"I'll soon tell you how it is," said the first. "I was just as good-looking when I was her age, but the reason why I've got this long nose is, because I was always kept sitting, and poking, and nodding over my spinning, and so my nose got stretched and stretched, until it got as long as you now see it."

"And I," said the second, "ever since I was young, I have sat and scuttled backwards and forwards over my loom, and that's how my back has got so broad and humped as you now see it."

"And I," said the third, "ever since I was little, I have sat, and stared and sewn, and sewn and stared, night and day; and that's why my eyes have got so ugly and red, and now there's no help for them."

"So, so!" said the prince, "'twas lucky I came to know this, for if folk can get so ugly and loathsome by all this, then my bride shall neither spin, nor weave, nor sew all her life long."

Translated by George Webb Dasent.

The Girl Who Could Spin Gold from Clay and Long Straw (1853)[105]
Benjamin Thorpe

There was once an old woman who had an only daughter. The lass was good and amiable, and also extremely beautiful; but, at the same time, so indolent, that she would hardly turn her hand to any work. This was a cause of great grief to the mother, who tried all sorts of ways to cure her daughter of so lamentable a failing; but there was no help. The old woman then thought no better plan could be devised than to set her daughter to spin on the roof of their cot in order that all the world might be witness of her sloth. But her plan brought her no nearer the mark. The girl continued as useless as before.

One day, as the king's son was going to the chase, he rode by the cot, where the old woman dwelt with her daughter. On seeing the fair spinner on the roof,

---

105. *Yule-Tide Stories: A Collection of Scandinavian and North German Popular Tales and Traditions from the Swedish, German, and Danish* (London: Henry G. Bohn, 1853).

he stopped and inquired why she sat spinning in such an unusual place. The old woman answered: "Aye, she sits there to let all the world see how clever she is. She is so clever that she can spin gold out of clay and long straw."

At these words the prince was struck with wonder; for it never occurred to him that the old woman was ironically alluding to her daughter's sloth. He therefore said: "If what you say is true, that the young maiden can spin gold from clay and long straw, she shall no longer sit there, but shall accompany me to my palace and be my consort."

The daughter thereupon descended from the roof and accompanied the prince to the royal residence, where, seated in her maiden-bower, she received a pail full of clay and a bundle of straw, by way of trial, whether she were so skillful as her mother had said.

The poor girl now found herself in a very uncomfortable state, knowing but too well that she could not spin flax, much less gold. So, sitting in her chamber, with her head resting on her hand, she wept bitterly. While she was thus sitting, the door was opened, and in walked a very little old man, who was both ugly and deformed. The old man greeted her in a friendly tone, and asked why she sat so lonely and afflicted. "I may well be sorrowful," answered the girl. "The king's son has commanded me to spin gold from clay and long straw, and if it be not done before tomorrow's dawn, my life is at stake."

The old man then said: "Fair maiden, weep not, I will help thee. Here is a pair of gloves, when thou hast them on, thou wilt be able to spin gold. Tomorrow night I will return, when if thou hast not found out my name, thou shalt accompany me home and be my wife."

In her despair she agreed to the old man's condition, who then went his way. The maiden now sat and spun, and by dawn she had already spun up all the clay and straw, which had become the finest gold it was possible to see.

Great was the joy throughout the whole palace that the king's son had got a bride who was so skillful and, at the same time, so fair. But the young maiden did nothing but weep, and the more the time advanced the more she wept, for she thought of the frightful dwarf, who was to come and fetch her.

When evening drew nigh, the king's son returned from the chase and went to converse with his bride. Observing that she appeared sorrowful, he strove to divert her in all sorts of ways and said he would tell her of a curious adventure, provided only she would be cheerful. The girl entreated him to let her hear it. Then said the prince: "While rambling about in the forest today, I witnessed an odd sort of thing. I saw a very, very little old man dancing round a juniper bush and singing a singular song."

"What did he sing?" asked the maiden inquisitively, for she felt sure that the prince had met with the dwarf.

"He sang these words," answered the prince:

> "Today I the malt shall grind.
> Tomorrow my wedding shall be.
> And the maiden sits in her bower and weeps.
> She knows not what I am called.
> I am called *Titteli Ture*.
> I am called *Titteli Ture*."

Was not the maiden now glad? She begged the prince to tell her over and over again what the dwarf had sung. He then repeated the wonderful song until she had imprinted the old man's name firmly in her memory. She then conversed lovingly with her betrothed, and the prince could not sufficiently praise his young bride's beauty and understanding. But he wondered why she was so overjoyed, being, like every one else, ignorant of the cause of her past sorrow.

When it was night, and the maiden was sitting alone in her chamber, the door was opened, and the hideous dwarf again entered. On beholding him the girl sprang up and said: "Titteli Ture! Titteli Ture! Here are the gloves."

When the dwarf heard his name pronounced, he was furiously angry and hastened away through the air, taking with him the whole roof of the house.

The fair maiden now laughed to herself and was joyful beyond measure. She then lay down to sleep and slept till the sun shone. The following day her marriage with the young prince was solemnized, and nothing more was ever heard of Titteli Ture.

Kruzimügeli (1863)[106]

Theodor Vernaleken

Once there was a king who wished to marry, but he had determined to take none other to wife than one who had jet black hair and eyes. Whether she were high or low born did not matter to him. So he caused a proclamation to be made through the land that all maidens with the above-named qualifications should appear before him.

Many announced themselves, but some had not the degree of blackness desired by the king, and others wore false hair; in short, there was something deficient in every one.

A charcoal-burner now came with his daughter, and as she noticed the throng before the king's palace, she asked her father what it meant. He answered that the king desired to wed a maiden with black hair and black eyes, but that none could be found possessing these according to the king's desire.

---

106. "Kruzimügeli," *Kinder-und Hausmärchen in den Alpenländern* (Vienna: Braumüller, 1863). Translation in *In the Land of Marvels: Folktales from Austria and Bohemia*, with preface and trans. Edwin Johnson (London: Swan Sonnenschein, 1884).

The charcoal-burner's daughter had both. So she said to her father, "May I go?"

But he replied, "It seems to me thou art stupid indeed to think the king will take thee to wife."

But she said that she only wanted to go that she might see a little of the castle. Her father gave her leave to go, and she went. On the way she met a little man who called to her, "Ho, maiden! What wilt thou give me if thou becomest queen?"

"Why, my little man, what can I give thee? I have nothing," she replied.

Then the dwarf began again, "Thou wilt be queen, but thou must know at the end of three years that my name is Kruzimügeli. If not, thou art mine."

"Well, if that is all, I will attend to it," she said, and ran to the castle without thinking any more of the dwarf, who rubbed his hands with glee and looked after her.

When the king looked upon the maiden, he resolved at once to make her his queen, for her hair shone and her eyes sparkled with blackness. So the wedding took place, and they lived very happily. She had almost forgotten that the three years were drawing to a close, and oh! horror! she had forgotten the name of the dwarf! She became melancholy and wept the whole day. The king, who loved her dearly, caused fetes to be held for her amusement, but all in vain. If he asked why she was so sad, she always answered that she could not tell him.

One day the king's forester went into the forest for game for the royal table. Deep in the forest he saw a dwarf, who had made a fire, and who was leaping about it with malicious joy, and singing:

"*She knows not—oh, what jollity!*
My name is Kruzimügeli!"

The huntsman heard this and went home. He met the queen in the castle garden, where she was walking, plunged in grief. He at once told her of the adventure in the forest, and when she heard the name Kruzimügeli, she was almost beside herself for joy, for next day was the last of the third year, and the dwarf would come to ask the queen his name.

Next day, in fact, he came and asked the queen, "Now, lady queen, dost thou know my name? Thou hast only three guesses, and if thou dost not guess right, thou belongest to me."

The queen answered, "It seems to me it is Steffel."

When the dwarf heard this, he leaped for joy, and cried with all his might, "Missed!"

Then the queen said, "Then it is Beitle."

Again he made a bound, and cried again, "Missed!"

Then the queen said quite carelessly, "Then it is Kruzimügeli."

When he heard this, he burst, without a word, through the wall into the open air. All endeavors to close up the hole made in the wall proved fruitless. The queen lived with her consort long and happily.

Translated by Edwin Johnson.

Lignu di Scupa (1870)[107]
Laura Gonzenbach

Once upon a time, a woman had a daughter, who was just as beautiful as the sun and the moon. However, the woman was poor and, therefore, sent her little daughter to her own mother, who kindly took her in and kept her in her home. Now the grandmother had a pan, which she usually lent to her neighbors when they wanted to bake something. In turn, they had to give her part of whatever they baked when they brought back the pan.

Now one day it so happened that the old woman had to go out, and she left her granddaughter alone at home. A neighbor came by and said, "Some fish were just brought to me, and I'd like to bake them. Do me a favor and give me the pan."

The maiden gave her the pan, and the neighbor baked the fish, and when she brought back the pan, she also carried along four baked fish on a plate. When the maiden saw the beautifully baked fish that smelled so deliciously, she could not resist the temptation and ate a small piece. Then, because it tasted so good, she gradually ate all four fish. When her grandmother came home, she asked the girl right away, "Did our neighbor bring some fish?"

"I lent her the pan," the maiden said, "but she didn't bring any fish in return."

So the grandmother became angry, went over to the neighbor, and cried out, "What's the meaning of this? You took my pan and didn't give me any of your baked fish in return!"

But the neighbor answered, "What are you saying? I laid aside four fish for you and gave them to your granddaughter!"

The grandmother ran quickly back home and scolded and beat her granddaughter so that the maiden screamed and cried. Just at that moment the prince rode by. He had been out hunting. When he heard the terrible noise, he stopped his horse and asked the old woman why she was beating the maiden. The grandmother was ashamed to tell him that her granddaughter had eaten the fish, and therefore she answered, "Your majesty, my granddaughter does nothing all day but spin, and she spins three rolls of flax each day. It's only for her good that I beat her because I want her to put down the spindle awhile and rest."

When the prince heard that and looked at the beautiful maiden, he said, "If your granddaughter is so diligent, I shall take her to my castle where she will become my wife."

---

107. "Die Geschichte von Lignu di scupa," *Sicilianische Märchen*. 2 vols. (Leipzig: W. Engelmann, 1870). The meaning of the Sicilian name "*Lignu di scupa*" is "broomstick."

So he took her with him and brought her to his father in the castle, where he told the old king everything that had happened.

"Good," said the king. "If she can spin three rolls of flax every day, she must be able to spin ninety rolls in one month. If she does that, she will become your wife."

The prince led her to a large room in which there was a mass of straw for her to spin ninety rolls of flax. She was locked in this room, and only in the evening did the king have her fetched so she could participate in the evening conversation. However, the poor maiden wept day and night because it was impossible for her to spin all the straw.

One day as she sat there and wept, a fine gentleman suddenly stood before her. It was no one else but Master Paul.[108]

"Why are you weeping?" he asked.

Then she told him everything, and the devil answered, "Good, I'll spin all this straw, and on the last day of the month everything will be finished. But, when I bring back the flax on the last day and you cannot tell me what my name is, you will belong to me and must follow me."

The maiden gave her promise, and Master Paul took the straw and disappeared. Now the poor maiden thought about the stranger's name day and night, and since nothing occurred to her, she kept weeping and became skinnier and sadder with each day that passed. When she was led to the king in the evening, she sat there silently, said nothing, and didn't laugh. The king was sorry to see her so sad and issued a proclamation throughout the entire country that whoever could get his son's bride to laugh would receive a royal gift.

People came from all over, rich and poor, and they told her funny stories every evening, but she didn't laugh. Instead, she became even more silent because there were only three days left before the end of the month.

On the last evening an old peasant came to the castle and wanted to walk up the stairs.

"What do you want in the king's palace," the guards asked him.

"I know a funny story that I want to tell the prince's bride so that I can perhaps get her to laugh."

"Oh, come on, you dumb peasant. It's almost a month since people have come here every evening to try to get the young queen to laugh, and nobody has succeeded yet. Do you think your foolish story can work?"

The peasant began to scream loudly, "I want to go up and try. Maybe my story is not so foolish!"

When the king heard all the noise, he asked what was happening. His ministers told him that there was a peasant below who wanted to tell the young queen a story, and the guards didn't want to let him pass.

---

108.   Mastru Paulu, the devil.

"Why not?" asked the king. "Tell them to let him come up."

The peasant came up the stairs, went before the maiden, and said, "Excellency, let me tell you what happened to me. Today I went into the forest to fetch some wood. All of a sudden, I heard a strange song, and this is the way it went:

> "Spin, spin, let's spin our game,
> the lady's expected all the same.
> Spin, spin, let's spin our game.
> Lignu di Scupa is my name."[109]

When the maiden heard this song, she realized immediately who had sung it and began to laugh out of joy. Indeed, all at once she became well and cheerful. So the king gave the peasant a beautiful gift and dismissed him with great pleasure.

When the maiden was led back to her room, the king said to her, "Tomorrow you must have the flax finished, and then we shall celebrate your wedding to my son."

Then she sat down in her room and waited for Master Paul. At midnight he appeared on time and brought the flax with him that had been marvelously spun and finished.

"Here is the flax," Master Paul said. "Now, do you know my name?"

"Your name's Lignu di Scupa!" she merrily exclaimed.

So he no longer had any power over her and left her in great anger. The maiden slept peacefully the rest of the night, and when the king entered her room the next morning and saw all the beautifully spun flax, he became very happy and said, "Now you will become my son's wife."

They held three days of festivities, and at the end of this time, the prince married the beautiful maiden. Indeed, they remained happy and content, and we were left without a cent.

The Aunts (1882)[110]

Consiglieri Pedroso

There was an old woman who had a granddaughter, and whilst one day the girl was looking out the window, the king happened to pass by the house at the time and was immediately struck by her beauty. He knocked at the door, and the old woman came to open the door and asked his majesty what might be his pleasure. The king replied that he wanted to see the maiden. The old woman then told him that the maiden he had seen at the window would make him a

---

109. *Filati, filati, filamu,*
Sta sira a Signura aspettamu,
Filati, filati, filamu,
Lignu di scupa iu mi chiamu.
110. *Portuguese Folk-Tales*, trans. Henriqueta Monteiro (London: Folklore Society, 1882).

shirt that could be drawn through the eye of a needle. Upon hearing this, the king said that he would marry the maiden if she succeeded in doing such a wonderful thing, but that in the event of her not succeeding, he would have her put to death.

When the king departed, the girl, who had not said or thought of doing such a thing, began to weep. An old woman, however, appeared to her and told her not to be troubled, for she would make the shirt for her. But she must promise her to call her "aunt" before every one present at the wedding banquet on her marriage day. The maiden readily promised her to do so, and soon after the shirt appeared all at once ready made, and it was given to the king.

On receiving the shirt the king said that he was not yet satisfied, and that the girl must prove herself more clever still. Therefore, the grandmother told him that her granddaughter could hear anything that was said three leagues off. When the maiden knew of this, she commenced to cry again, but the woman returned and informed her that if she promised to call her "aunt" on the day of the marriage, before every one, she would tell her what the king would say at the hunt he had gone to three leagues away. The girl promised to comply; and the woman shortly after came and informed her of what the king had said at the hunt. The grandmother then went to the king to tell him. But, as his majesty required yet more proofs of the maiden's extraordinary cleverness, the granny told him that her daughter was so quick at her work that she could wind in half an hour a whole skein of thread. When the girl heard of this, she began to weep because she knew she was not able to do so. The woman, however, who always came to her help, returned once more and offered to do it for her if she complied with the usual promise. The maiden readily agreed to this, and immediately the skein appeared ready wound. The day of the marriage was at last fixed upon, and the king married the maiden. Whilst they were sitting at the banquet, which was given on the occasion, a knock was suddenly heard at the door of the hall, and a woman entered who was exceedingly ugly and had very large prominent eyes. The maiden, now a queen, rose at once from the table, and addressed her in this way: "Good afternoon, aunt, give me your blessing!"

Every one present was much surprised at what they saw and heard, but the ugly woman, turning towards the king, explained to him that the reason of her having such very large eyes came from straining them to make a shirt that could pass through the eye of a needle. After a while another knock was heard at the door, and in came another woman with exceedingly large ears. The queen rose and saluted her thus, "Good afternoon, aunt, bestow me your blessing!"

Every one present was much surprised, but the woman went up to the king and explained that her ears had become so exceedingly large from her constantly listening to what was said at the distance of three leagues. Not long after this a third knock was heard, and another woman entered who was very, very ugly, and had very long arms. The queen rose from the table and said to her, saluting her, "Good afternoon, aunt, bestow your blessing upon me!"

All the people were much astonished, but the woman told the king that she had such long arms because she had been obliged to wind a whole skein in half an hour. The king then rose and said to the queen that he did not require her to make the shirt, nor to hear what was said at the distance of three leagues, nor did he expect her to wind a whole skein of thread in half an hour. And thus it was that the maiden was saved from having to accomplish what her grandmother had told the king she was capable of doing.

Translated by Henriqueta Monteiro.

The Lazy Spinning-Girl Who Became a Queen (1889)[111]

W. Henry Jones

A common woman had a daughter who was a very good worker, but she did not like spinning; for this her mother very often scolded her, and one day got so vexed that she chased her down the road with the distaff. As they were running, a prince passed by in his carriage. As the girl was very pretty, the prince was very much struck with her and asked her mother, "What is the matter?"

"How can I help it?" said the mother. "After she has spun everything that I had, she asked for more flax to spin."

"Let her alone, my good woman," said the prince. "Don't beat her. Give her to me, and let me take her with me. I will give her plenty to spin. My mother has plenty of work that needs to be done, so she can enjoy herself spinning as much as she likes."

The woman gave her daughter away with the greatest pleasure, thinking that what she was unwilling to do at home she might be ashamed to shirk in a strange place, and get used to it, and perhaps even become a good spinster after all. The prince took the girl with him and put her into a large shed full of flax, and said, "If you spin all you find here during the month, you shall be my wife."

Upon seeing the great place full of flax, the girl nearly had a fit, as there was enough to have employed all the girls in the village for the whole of the winter; nor did she begin to work, but sat down and fretted over it, and thus three weeks of the month passed by. In the meantime she always asked the person who brought her food, "What news is there?"

Each one told her something or other. One night, at the end of the third week, as she was terribly downcast, suddenly a little man half an ell long, with a beard one and a half ells long, slipped in and said, "Why are you worrying yourself, you good, pretty spinning-girl?"

"That's just what's the matter with me," replied the girl. "I am not a good spinster, and still they will believe that I am a good spinster, and that's the reason why I am locked up here."

---

111. *The Folk-Tales of the Magyars: Collected by Kriza, Erdélyi, and Others* (London: Elliot Stock, 1889).

"Don't trouble about that," said the little man. "I can help you and will spin all the flax during the next week if you agree to my proposal and promise to come with me if you don't find out my name by the time that I finish my spinning."

"That's all right," said the girl, "I will go with you," thinking that then the matter would be all right.

The little dwarf set to work. It happened during the fourth week that one of the men-servants, who brought the girl's food, went out hunting with the prince. One day he was out rather late, and so was very late when he brought the food. The girl said, "What's the news?"

The servant told her that that evening as he was coming home very late he saw, in the forest, in a dark ditch, a little man half an ell high, with a beard one and a half ells long, who was jumping from bough to bough, and spinning a thread, and humming to himself: "My name is Dancing Vargaluska. My wife will be good spinster Sue."

Sue, the pretty spinning-girl, knew very well what the little man was doing, but she merely said to the servant, "It was all imagination that made you think you saw it in the dark."

But she brightened up, for she knew that all the stuff would be spun, and that he would not be able to carry her off, as she knew his name. In the evening the little man returned with one-third of the work done and said to her, "Well, do you know my name yet?"

"Perhaps, perhaps," said she, but she would not have told his real name for all the treasures in the world, fearing that he might cease working if she did. Nor did she tell him when he came the next night. On the third night the little man brought the last load; but this time he brought a wheelbarrow with him, with three wheels, to take the girl away with him. When he asked the girl his name, she said, "If I'm not mistaken your name is Dancing Vargaluska."

On hearing this the little man rushed off as if somebody had pulled his nose. The month being up, the prince sent to see if the girl had completed her work; and when the messenger brought back word that all was finished, the king was greatly astonished how it could possibly have happened that so much work had been done in so short a time, and went himself, accompanied by a great suite of gentlemen and court-dames, and gazed with great admiration upon the vast amount of fine yarn they saw. Nor could they praise the girl enough, and all found her worthy to be queen of the land.

Next day the wedding was celebrated, and the girl became queen. After the grand wedding-dinner the poor came, and the king distributed alms to them. Amongst them were three deformed beggars, who struck the king very much: one was an old woman whose eyelids were so long that they covered her whole face; the second was an old woman whose lower lip was so long that the end of it reached to her knee; the third old woman's posterior was so flat that it was like a pancake.

These three were called into the reception-room and asked to explain why they were so deformed. The first said, "In my younger days I was such a good spinster that I had no rival in the whole neighborhood. I spun till I got so addicted to it that I even used to spin at night. The effect of all this was that my eyelids became so long that the doctors could not get them back to their places."

The second said, "I have spun so much during my life and for such a length of time that with continually biting off the end of the yarn my lips got so soft that one reached my knees."

The third said, "I have sat so much at my spinning that my posterior became flat as it is now."

Hereupon the king, knowing how passionately fond his wife was of spinning, got so frightened that he strictly prohibited her ever spinning again. The news of the story went out over the whole world, into every royal court and every town; and the women were so frightened at what had happened to the beggars that they broke every distaff, spinning wheel, and spindle, and threw them into the fire!

Translated by W. Henry Jones.

Tom Tit Tot (1890)[112]
Joseph Jacobs

Once upon a time there was a woman, and she baked five pies. And when they came out of the oven, they were that overbaked the crusts were too hard to eat. So she says to her daughter:

"Darter," says she, "put you them there pies on the shelf, and leave 'em there a little, and they'll come again."—She meant, you know, the crust would get soft.

But the girl, she says to herself: "Well, if they'll come again, I'll eat 'em now." And she set to work and ate 'em all, first and last.

Well, come supper-time the woman said: "Go you, and get one o' them there pies. I dare say they've come again now."

The girl went and she looked, and there was nothing but the dishes. So back she came and says she: "Noo, they ain't come again."

"Not one of 'em?" says the mother.

"Not one of 'em," says she.

"Well, come again, or not come again," said the woman, "I'll have one for supper."

"But you can't, if they ain't come," said the girl.

"But I can," says she. "Go you, and bring the best of 'em."

"Best or worst," says the girl, "I've ate 'em all, and you can't have one till that's come again."

112. *English Fairy Tales* (London: David Nutt, 1890).

Well, the woman she was done, and she took her spinning to the door to spin, and as she span she sang:

> "My darter ha' ate five, five pies to-day.
> My darter ha' ate five, five pies to-day."

The king was coming down the street, and he heard her sing, but what she sang he couldn't hear, so he stopped and said:

"What was that you were singing, my good woman?"

The woman was ashamed to let him hear what her daughter had been doing, so she sang, instead of that:

> "My darter ha' spun five, five skeins to-day.
> My darter ha' spun five, five skeins to-day."

"Stars o' mine!" said the king. "I never heard tell of anyone that could do that."

Then he said: "Look you here, I want a wife, and I'll marry your daughter. But look you here," says he, "eleven months out of the year she shall have all she likes to eat, and all the gowns she likes to get, and all the company she likes to keep; but the last month of the year she'll have to spin five skeins every day, and if she don't, I shall kill her."

"All right," says the woman; for she thought what a grand marriage that was. And as for the five skeins, when the time came, there'd be plenty of ways of getting out of it, and likeliest, he'd have forgotten all about it.

Well, so they were married. And for eleven months the girl had all she liked to eat, and all the gowns she liked to get, and all the company she liked to keep. But when the time was getting over, she began to think about the skeins and to wonder if he had 'em in mind. But not one word did he say about 'em, and she thought he'd wholly forgotten 'em. However, the last day of the last month he takes her to a room she'd never set eyes on before. There was nothing in it but a spinning wheel and a stool. And says he: "Now, my dear, here you'll be shut in to-morrow with some victuals and some flax, and if you haven't spun five skeins by the night, your head 'll go off."

And away he went about his business.

Well, she was that frightened, she'd always been such a gatless girl, that she didn't so much as know how to spin, and what was she to do to-morrow with no one to come nigh here to help her? She sat down on a stool in the kitchen, and law! how she did cry!

However, all of a sudden she heard a sort of a knocking low down on the door. She upped and oped it, and what should she see but a small little black thing with a long tail. That looked up at her right curious, and that said:

"What are you a-crying for?"

"What's that to you?" says she.

"Never you mind," that said, "but tell me what you're a-crying for."

"That won't do me no good if I do," says she.

"You don't know that," that said, and twirled that's tail round.

"Well," says she, "that won't do no harm, if that don't do no good," and she upped and told about the pies, and the skeins, and everything.

"This is what I'll do," says the little black thing, "I'll come to your window every morning and take the flax and bring it spun at night."

"What's your pay?" says she.

That looked out of the corner of that's eyes, and that said: "I'll give you three guesses every night to guess my name, and if you haven't guessed it before the month's up, you shall be mine."

Well, she thought she'd be sure to guess that's name before the month was up. "All right," says she, "I agree."

"All right," that says, and law! how that twirled that's tail.

Well, the next day, her husband took her into the room, and there was the flax and the day's food.

"Now there's the flax," says he, "and if that ain't spun up this night, off goes your head." And then he went out and locked the door.

He'd hardly gone, when there was a knocking against the window. She upped and she oped it, and there sure enough was the little old thing sitting on the ledge.

"Where's the flax?" says he.

"Here it be," says she. And she gave it to him.

Well, come the evening a knocking came again to the window. She upped and she oped it, and there was the little old thing with five skeins of flax on his arm.

"Here it be," says he, and he gave it to her.

"Now, what's my name?" says he.

"What, is that Bill?" says she.

"Noo, that ain't," says he, and he twirled his tail.

"Is that Ned?" says she.

"Noo, that ain't," says he, and he twirled his tail.

"Well, is that Mark?" says she.

"Noo, that ain't," says he, and he twirled his tail harder, and away he flew.

Well, when her husband came in, there were the five skeins ready for him. "I see I shan't have to kill you to-night, my dear," says he; "you'll have your food and your flax in the morning," says he, and away he goes.

Well, every day the flax and the food were brought, and every day that there little black impet used to come mornings and evenings. And all the day the girl sate trying to think of names to say to it when it came at night. But she never hit on the right one. And as it got towards the end of the month, the impet began to look so maliceful, and that twirled that's tail faster and faster each time she gave a guess.

At last it came to the last day but one. The impet came at night along with the five skeins, and that said:

"What, ain't you got my name yet?"

"Is that Nicodemus?" says she.

"Noo, t'ain't," that says.

"Is that Sammie?" says she.

"Noo, t'ain't," that says.

"A-well, is that Methusalem?" says she.

"Noo, t'ain't that neither," that says. Then that looks at her with that's eyes like a coal o' fire, and that says: "Woman, there's only to-morrow night, and then you'll be mine!" And away it flew.

Well, she felt that horrid. However, she heard the king coming along the passage. In he came, and when he sees the five skeins, he says, says he:

"Well, my dear," says he. "I don't see but what you'll have your skeins ready to-morrow night as well, and as I reckon I shan't have to kill you, I'll have supper in here to-night."

So they brought supper, and another stool for him, and down the two sate. Well, he hadn't eaten but a mouthful or so, when he stops and begins to laugh.

"What is it?" says she.

"A-why," says he, "I was out a-hunting to-day, and I got away to a place in the wood I'd never seen before. And there was an old chalk-pit. And I heard a kind of a sort of a humming. So I got off my hobby, and I went right quiet to the pit, and I looked down. Well, what should there be but the funniest little black thing you ever set eyes on. And what was that doing, but that had a little spinning wheel, and that was spinning wonderful fast, and twirling that's tail. And as that span that sang:

> "Nimmy nimmy not
> My name's Tom Tit Tot."

Well, when the girl heard this, she felt as if she could have jumped out of her skin for joy, but she didn't say a word.

Next day that there little thing looked so maliceful when he came for the flax. And when night came, she heard that knocking against the windowpanes. She oped the window, and that come right in on the ledge. That was grinning from ear to ear, and Oo! that's tail was twirling round so fast.

"What's my name?" that says, as that gave her the skeins.

"Is that Solomon?" she says, pretending to be afeard.

"Noo, t'ain't," that says, and that come further into the room. "Well, is that Zebedee?" says she again.

"Noo, 'tain't," says the impet. And then that laughed and twirled that's tail till you couldn't hardly see it.

"Take time, woman," that says; "next guess, and you're mine." And that stretched out that's black hands at her.

Well, she backed a step or two, and she looked at it, and then she laughed out, and says she, pointing her finger at it:

"Nimmy Nimmy Noy
Your name's Tom Tit Tot."

Well, when that heard her, that gave an awful shriek and away that flew into the dark, and she never saw it any more.

Kinkach Martinko (1896)[113]

Alexander Chodźko

Once upon a time there was a poor woman who had an only daughter, named Helen, a very lazy girl. One day when she had refused to do a single thing, her mother took her down to the banks of a stream and began to strike her fingers with a flat stone, just as you do in beating linen to wash it.

The girl cried a good deal. A prince, Lord of the Red Castle, happened at that moment to pass by, and inquired as to the cause of such treatment, for it horrified him that a mother should so ill-use her child.

"Why should I not punish her?" answered the woman. "The idle girl can do nothing but spin hemp into gold thread."

"Really?" cried he. "Does she really know how to spin gold thread out of hemp? If that be so, sell her to me."

"Willingly. How much will you give me for her?"

"Half a measure of gold."

"Take her," said the mother, and she gave him her daughter as soon as the money was paid.

The prince placed the girl behind him on the saddle, put spurs to his horse, and took her home.

On reaching the Red Castle, the prince led Helen into a room filled from floor to ceiling with hemp, and having supplied her with distaff and spinning wheel, said, "When you have spun all this hemp into gold thread I will make you my wife."

Then he went out, locking the door after him.

On finding herself a prisoner, the poor girl wept as if her heart would break. Suddenly she saw a very odd-looking little man seated on the windowsill. He wore a red cap, and his boots were made of some strange sort of material.

"Why do you weep so?" he asked.

"I cannot help it," she replied, "I am but a miserable slave. I have been ordered to spin all this hemp into gold thread, but it is impossible, I can never do it, and I know not what will become of me."

"I will do it for you in three days, on condition that at the end of that time you guess my right name, and tell me what the boots I am wearing now are made of."

---

113. *Slav Peasants and Herdsmen*, trans. Emily Harding (London: George Allen, 1896).

Without for one moment reflecting as to whether she would be able to guess aright she consented. The uncanny little man burst out laughing, and taking her distaff set to work at once.

All day as the distaff moved the hemp grew visibly less, while the skein of gold thread became larger and larger.

The little man spun all the time, and, without stopping an instant, explained to Helen how to make thread of pure gold. As night drew on he tied up the skein, saying to the girl, "Well, do you know my name yet? Can you tell me what my boots are made of?"

Helen replied that she could not, upon which he grinned and disappeared through the window. She then sat and looked at the sky, and thought, and thought, and thought, and lost herself in conjecturing as to what the little man's name might be, and in trying to guess what was the stuff his boots were made of. Were they of leather? or perhaps plaited rushes? or straw? or cast iron? No, they did not look like anything of that sort. And as to his name—that was a still more difficult problem to solve.

'What shall I call him?' said she to herself—'John? Or Henry? Who knows? perhaps it is Paul or Joseph.'

These thoughts so filled her mind that she forgot to eat her dinner. Her meditations were interrupted by cries and groans from outside, where she saw an old man with white hair sitting under the castle wall.

"Miserable old man that I am!" cried he. "I die of hunger and thirst, but no one pities my sufferings."

Helen hastened to give him her dinner, and told him to come next day, which he promised to do.

After again thinking for some time what answers she should give the little old man, she fell asleep on the hemp. The little old man did not fail to make his appearance the first thing next morning, and remained all day spinning the gold thread. The work progressed before their eyes, and it was only when evening came that he repeated his questions. Not receiving a satisfactory answer, he vanished in a fit of mocking laughter. Helen sat down by the window to think; but think as she might, no answer to these puzzling questions occurred to her.

While thus wondering, the hungry old man again came by, and she gave him her dinner. She was heart-sick, and her eyes were full of tears, for she thought she would never guess the spinner's name, nor of what stuff his boots were made, unless perhaps God would help her.

"Why are you so sad?" asked the old man when he had eaten and drunk. "Tell me the cause of your grief, dear lady."

For a long time she would not tell him, thinking it would be useless, but at last, yielding to his entreaties, she gave a full account of the conditions under which the gold thread was made, explaining that unless she could answer the little old man's questions satisfactorily she feared some great misfortune would befall her. The old man listened attentively, then, nodding his head, he said: "In coming through the forest to-day I passed close to a large pile of burning wood, round which were placed nine iron pots. A little man in a red cap was running round and jumping over them, singing these words:

> "My sweet friend, fair Helen, at the Red Castle near,
>> Two days and two nights seeks my name to divine.
> She'll never find out, so the third night 'tis clear
>> My sweet friend, fair Helen, can't fail to be mine.
> Hurrah! for my name is KINKACH MARTINKO,
> Hurrah! for my boots are of doggies' skin O!"

"Now that is exactly what you want to know, my dear girl; so do not forget, and you are saved."

And with these words the old man vanished.

Helen was greatly astonished, but she took care to fix in her memory all that the good fellow had told her, and then went to sleep, feeling that she could face to-morrow without fear.

On the third day, very early in the morning, the little old man appeared and set busily to work, for he knew that all the hemp must be spun before sunset, and that then he should be able to claim his rights. When evening came all the hemp was gone, and the room shone with the brightness of the golden thread.

As soon as his work was done, the queer little old man with the red cap drew himself up with a great deal of assurance, and with his hands in his pockets strutted up and down before Helen, ordering her to tell him his right name and to say of what stuff the boots were made, but he felt certain that she would not be able to answer aright.

"Your name is KINKACH MARTINKO, and your boots are made of dog-skin," she replied without the slightest hesitation.

At these words he spun round on the floor like a bobbin, tore out his hair, and beat his breast with rage, roaring so that the very walls trembled.

"It is lucky for you that you have guessed. If you had not, I should have torn you to pieces on this very spot!" So saying he rushed out of the window like a whirlwind.

Helen felt deeply grateful towards the old man who had told her the answers, and hoped to be able to thank him in person. But he never appeared again.

The Prince of the Red Castle was very pleased with her for having accomplished her task so punctually and perfectly, and he married her as he had promised.

Helen was truly thankful to have escaped the dangers that had threatened her, and her happiness as a princess was greater than she had dared hope. She had, too, such a good stock of gold thread that she never had occasion to spin any more all her life long.

Translated by Emily Harding.

10. THE REVENGE AND REWARD OF NEGLECTED DAUGHTERS

ATU 510A—CINDERELLA

This tale type is clearly related to a cycle of stories that concern the reincarnation of a dead mother as a bird/cow/tree who protects her daughter from a stepmother and stepsisters. The plot varies according to the belief systems of the culture in which the tale is told, but it generally contains the following elements: (1) a mother dies and promises to look after her daughter; (2) the father remarries a wicked stepmother who has two or three daughters; (3) the stepmother and stepdaughters maltreat the girl—and sometimes threaten to kill her—and give her a nickname such as Cinderella associated with ashes/dirt/slut; (4) the stepsisters go to a ball where a prince will choose his future bride, or they go to a church, where the prince is in attendance; (5) Cinderella manages to go to the ball/church three times with the help of her dead mother/animals/fairies and attracts the prince; (6) the prince tries to discover the identity of Cinderella, who is not recognized by anyone; (7) Cinderella loses her golden/glass slipper/shoe which is found by the prince; (8) the prince orders all the women in the realm to try on the slipper/shoe, but it only fits Cinderella; (9) the prince weds Cinderella; and (10) the stepmother and stepsisters are punished.

There are thousands of oral and literary versions of "Cinderella," one of the most popular fairy tales in the world. Early versions may have originated in ancient China or Egypt. The shoe or slipper test may have been connected to a marriage custom in which the bridegroom takes off the bride's old shoes and replaces them with new ones. But this thesis has never been completely verified, and depending on the society and customs, shoes are used in many different ways in marriage celebrations. In the various literary and oral versions the shoes are leather, gold, silver, and glass. Charles Perrault invented the glass slippers most likely as an ironic joke, since a glass slipper was likely to break if it were to fall off a foot.

What most of the tales, oral and literary, have in common is the conflict between a young girl and her stepmother and siblings about her legacy. Cinderella must prove that she is the rightful successor in a house in which she has been deprived of her rights. She receives help from her dead mother in the guise of doves, fairies, and godmothers. Belief in the regeneration of the dead who can help the living in the form of plants or animals underlies one of the key motifs of the fairy tale.

In the European literary tradition, which first began with Bonaventure des Périers' *Les Nouvelles Recréations et Joyeux Devis* (*New Recreations and Joyous Games*, 1558), it is clear that Giambattista Basile's version, "The Cat Cenerentola," *Lo Cunto de li Cunti* (1634), played a role in influencing Charles Perrault's

"Cinderella, or The Glass Slipper," *Histoires ou contes du temps passé* (1697) and Mme d'Aulnoy's "Finette Cendron," *Les Contes de fées* (1698). They, in turn, had some effect on the Grimms' tale. Significant in Basile's tale is the active role that Cinderella plays in determining her future: she kills her stepmother and stops her father's ship from returning from Sardinia. Some of this activism, in contrast to Perrault's narrative, can be seen in the Grimms' version. Since there were so many different versions by the time that the Grimms composed their "Cinderella"—for instance, they may have also been influenced by the Bohemian version "Laskopal und Miliwaka" in *Sagen der böhmischen Vorzeit aus einigen Gegenden alter Schlösser und Dörfer* (1808)—it is difficult to establish one particular source for their work. Aside from an anonymous variant that the Grimms received in 1812 from the wife of the director of the Elisabeth Hospital in Marburg, the Grimms may have been influenced by various versions that appeared in popular magazines and also tales that were in oral circulation. By 1819, they began changing the story from their first edition of 1812 through tales they heard from Dorothea Viehmann.

Clearly, many different literary and oral tales fostered a huge Cinderella cycle in the East and the West. As early as 1893, Marian Cox published her significant study, *Cinderella: Three Hundred and Forty-Five Variants of Cinderella, Catskin, and Cap o' Rushes*, which included medieval sources. Alan Dundes' *Cinderella: A Folklore Casebook* (1982) provides valuable background information and discussions about the cycle and different interpretations. The early literary work of Basile, d'Aulnoy, and the Grimms certainly played a role in the creation of nineteenth-century plays and musical adaptations such as Nicolas Isouard's popular fairy opera *Cendrillon* (1810), as well as in the equally successful operas *La Cenerentola* (1817) by Gioacchino Antonio Rossini and *Cendrillon* (1896) by Jules Massenet. The stories below indicate how widely the tale was adapted and in circulation throughout nineteenth-century Europe, and they are only the tip of the iceberg.

******

Cinderella (1812)[114]
Jacob and Wilhelm Grimm

Once upon a time there was a rich man who lived happily with his wife for a long time, and they had one little girl together. Then the wife became ill, and as she became deathly ill, she called her daughter and said, "Dear child, I must leave you, but when I am up in heaven, I shall look after you. Plant a little tree on my grave, and whenever you wish for something, shake it, and you'll have what you wish. And whenever you are otherwise in a predicament, then I'll send you help. Just stay good and pious."

---

114. "Aschenputtel," *Kinder- und Haus-Märchen. Gesammelt durch die Brüder Grimm*, 2 vols. (Berlin: Realschulbuchandlung, 1812/1815).

After she said this, she closed her eyes and died. Her child wept and planted a little tree on her grave and didn't need to water it, for her tears were good enough.

The snow covered the mother's grave like a little white blanket, and by the time the sun had taken it off again, and the little tree had become green for the second time, the man took a second wife. However, the stepmother already had two daughters from her first husband. They had beautiful features but proud, nasty, and wicked hearts. When the wedding had now been celebrated, and all three entered the house, a difficult time began for the poor child.

"What's this terrible and useless thing doing in our rooms?" the stepmother said. "Off with you into the kitchen. Whoever wants to eat bread must first earn it. She can be our maid."

The stepsisters took away her clothes and dressed her in an old gray smock.

"You look good in that!" they said while mocking her and leading her to the kitchen, where the poor child had to do heavy work: she had to get up before dawn, carry the water into the house, make the fire, cook, and wash. Meanwhile her sisters did everything imaginable to cause her grief and make her look ridiculous. They poured peas and lentils into the ashes of the hearth so she had to sit there the entire day and separate them. In the evening, when she was tired, there was no bed for her, and she had to lie next to the hearth in the ashes. Since she always rummaged in dust and looked dirty, they named her Cinderella.

At a certain time the king decided to organize a magnificent ball that was to last three days, and his son was supposed to choose a bride at this event. The two proud stepsisters were also invited to it.

"Cinderella," they called to her, "come up here! Comb out our hair, brush our shoes, and fasten our buckles! We're going to see the prince at the ball."

Cinderella worked hard and cleaned and brushed as good as she could. However, the stepsisters continually scolded her, and when they were finished dressing, they asked her in a mocking tone: "Cinderella, wouldn't you like to go to the ball?"

"Oh, yes," Cinderella replied. "But how can I go? I don't have any clothes."

"No," said the eldest daughter. "That's all we'd need for you to show up there! If the people heard that you were our sister, we'd be ashamed. You belong in the kitchen where there's a bowl full of lentils. When we return, they must be sorted, and take care that we don't find a bad one among them. Otherwise, you'll get nothing good."

After that the stepsisters left, and Cinderella stood there and looked after them, and when she could no longer see them, she went sadly into the kitchen and shook the lentils on to the hearth, and they formed a very large pile.

"Oh," she sighed and said, "I'll have to sort them until midnight, and I won't be able to shut my eyes no matter how much they may hurt. If my mother knew about this!"

Then she knelt down in the ashes in front of the hearth and wanted to begin sorting. Just then two white pigeons flew through the window and landed next to the lentils on the hearth. They nodded with their little heads and said, "Cinderella, would you like us to help you sort the lentils?"

"Yes," answered Cinderella:

"The good ones for the little pot,
the bad ones for your little crop."

And peck, peck! Peck, peck! They began and ate the bad ones and let the good ones remain. And in a quarter of an hour the lentils were so clean that there was not a bad one among them, and Cinderella could smooth them out in the little pot. Now the pigeons said to her, "Cinderella, if you want to see your sisters dance with the prince, then climb up to the pigeon coop."

Cinderella followed them and climbed to the top of the ladder of the pigeon coop and could see the ballroom from there. Indeed, she could see her sisters dance with the prince, and a thousand chandeliers glittered and glistened before her eyes. And after she had seen enough, she climbed down the ladder. Her heart was heavy, and she laid herself down in the ashes and fell asleep.

The next morning the two sisters went into the kitchen, and when they saw that Cinderella had cleanly sorted the lentils, they were angry because they would have liked to have scolded her. Since they couldn't do that, they began to tell her about the ball and said, "Cinderella, that was so much fun, especially the dance. The prince, who's the most handsome in the world, led us out onto the dance floor, and one of us will become his bride."

"Yes," Cinderella said. "I saw the chandeliers glimmer. That must have been splendid."

"What! How did you manage that?" the eldest sister asked.

"I climbed up to the pigeon coop."

When the sister heard this, she was filled with jealousy, and she immediately ordered the pigeon coop to be torn down.

However, Cinderella had to comb and clean again, and the youngest sister, who had a little sympathy in her heart, said, "Cinderella, when it turns dark, you can go to the ball and look in through the windows."

"No," said the eldest. "That will only make her lazy. Here's a sack of sweet peas, Cinderella. Sort the good from the bad and work hard. If you don't have them sorted cleanly by tomorrow, then I'll spill them all into the ashes, and you'll have to starve until you've fished them out of the ashes."

Cinderella sat down in distress on the hearth and poured the peas out of the sack. Then the pigeons flew in to the kitchen once again and asked in a friendly way: "Cinderella, do you want us to sort the peas?"

"Yes."

> "The good ones for the little pot,
> the bad ones for your little crop."

Peck, peck! Peck, peck! It all went so quickly as if twelve hands were there. And when they were finished, the pigeons said: "Cinderella, do you want to go and dance at the ball?"

"Oh, my God!" she cried out. "But how can I go there in my dirty clothes?"

"Go to the little tree on your mother's grave. Shake it and wish for clothes. However, you must return before midnight."

So, Cinderella went to the grave, shook the little tree, and spoke:

> "Shake and wobble, little tree!
> Let beautiful clothes fall down for me."

No sooner had she said all this than a splendid dress lay right before her along with pearls, silk stockings, silver slippers, and everything else that belonged to her outfit. Cinderella carried everything into the house, and after she had washed herself and dressed herself, she was as beautiful as a rose washed by the dew. And when she stepped outside, a carriage stood there drawn by six black horses adorned with feathers and servants dressed in blue and silver, who helped her inside. Then off they galloped to the king's castle.

Meanwhile, the prince saw the carriage come to a halt before the gate and thought that a strange princess had come traveling to the ball. So, he himself went down the stairs, helped Cinderella out of the carriage, and led her into the ballroom. And when the glitter of the four thousand chandeliers fell upon her, she was so beautiful that everyone there was amazed, and the sisters also stood there and were annoyed that someone was more beautiful than they. However, they didn't think in the least that it might be Cinderella who was presumably at home in the ashes. Now the prince danced with Cinderella and showed her royal honor. As he danced, he thought to himself, 'I'm supposed to choose a bride, and I know she's the only one for me.' On the other hand, Cinderella had lived for such a long time in ashes and sadness, and now she was in splendor and joy. But when midnight came, before the clock struck twelve, she stood up and bowed good-bye. Even though the prince begged and begged, she refused to remain any longer. So the prince led her down the stairs. The carriage was below and waiting for her, and it drove off in splendor as it had come.

When Cinderella arrived home, she went once again to the little tree on her mother's grave.

"Shake and wobble, little tree!
Take these clothes back from me."

Then the tree took the clothes, and Cinderella had her gray smock on again. And she returned to the kitchen with it, put some dust on her face, and laid herself down to sleep.

In the morning the sisters came. They looked morose and kept quiet. Then Cinderella said, "You must have had an enjoyable time last night."

"No, a princess was there, and the prince almost always danced with her. Nobody had ever seen her or knew where she came from."

"Was it perhaps that lady who arrived in the splendid carriage pulled by six black horses?" Cinderella asked.

"How do you know this?"

"As I was standing in the entrance to the house, I saw her drive by."

"In the future stay inside working," said the eldest sister, who looked angrily at Cinderella. "What business do you have to stand in the entrance to the house?"

For a third time Cinderella had to dress up the two sisters, and as a reward they gave her a bowl with peas that she was to sort. "And don't you dare to leave your work!" the eldest daughter cried out to her.

Cinderella thought, 'if only my pigeons would return!' And her heart beat somewhat. However, the pigeons came as they had the previous night and said, "Cinderella, do you want us to sort the peas?"

"Yes."

"The good ones for the little pot,
the bad ones for your little crop."

Once more the pigeons pecked the bad ones out, and once they were finished, they said, "Cinderella, shake the little tree. It will throw down even more beautiful clothes. Go to the ball, but take care that you return before midnight."

Cinderella went to her mother's grave:

"Shake and wobble, little tree!
Let beautiful clothes fall down for me."

Then a dress fell down, and it was even more glorious and splendid than the previous one. It was made out of gold and precious gems. In addition there were golden gusseted stockings and gold slippers. And after Cinderella was completely dressed, she glistened really like the sun at midday. A carriage drawn by six white horses that had plumes on their heads stopped in front of the house, and the servants were dressed in red and gold. When Cinderella arrived, the prince was already on the stairs and led her into the ballroom. And if everyone had been astonished by her beauty yesterday, they were even more astounded this evening, and the sisters stood in a corner and were pale out of envy. If they had known that it was Cinderella, who was supposed to be at home in the ashes, they would have died out of envy.

Now the prince wanted to know who the strange princess was, where she came from, and where she drove off to. So he had people stationed on the road, and they were to pay attention to her whereabouts. Moreover, he had the stairs painted with black pitch so that she wouldn't be able to run so fast. Cinderella danced and danced with the prince and was filled with joy so much so that she didn't think about midnight. All of a sudden, as she was in the middle of a dance, she heard the clock begin to strike. She was reminded of the pigeons' warning and was terrified. So, she rushed to the door and flew down the stairs. However, since they were covered with pitch, one of her golden slippers got caught, and Cinderella didn't stop to take it with her out of fear. Indeed, just as she reached the last step of the stairs, the clock struck twelve. Consequently, the carriage and horses disappeared, and Cinderella stood in her gray smock on the dark road. In the meantime, the prince had rushed after her, and he found the golden slipper on the steps. He ripped it from the pitch and carried it with him, but by the time he made it down the stairs, everything had disappeared. Even the people who had stood guard came and said that they had seen nothing.

Cinderella was glad that nothing worse had happened, and she went home. Once there she turned on her dim oil lamp, hung it in the chimney, and laid herself down in the ashes. It didn't take long before the two sisters also returned and called out: "Cinderella, get up and light the way."

Cinderella yawned and pretended that she had been wakened from her sleep. As she showed them the way, she heard one of the sisters say, "God knows who the presumable princess is. If she were only in her grave! The prince only danced with her, and after she had gone, he didn't want to remain, and the entire ball came to an end."

"It was really as if all the lights had suddenly been blown out," the other said.

Meanwhile, the prince was thinking, 'if everything else has gone wrong for you, now the slipper will help you find your bride.' So he had a proclamation announced that whichever maiden's foot fit the golden slipper was to become his wife. But the slipper was much too small for anyone who tried it on. Indeed, many could not even slip their foot into the slipper, and could not have done so even if the single slipper were two. Finally, it was the turn of the two sisters to take the test. They were glad because they had small beautiful feet and believed that it couldn't go wrong for them and that the prince should have gone to them right away.

"Listen," said the mother secretly, "here's a knife, and if the slipper is still too tight for you, then cut off a piece of your foot. It will hurt a bit. But what does that matter? It will soon pass, and one of you will become queen."

So the eldest sister went into the chamber and tried on the slipper. Her toe slipped inside, but the heel was too large. So, she took the knife and cut off a part of her heel until she could force her foot into the slipper. Then she went out of the chamber to the prince, and when he saw that she had the slipper on her foot, he said that she was her bride. Then he led her to his carriage and wanted to drive off. However, when he came to the gate, the pigeons were above and called out:

> "Looky, look, look
> at the shoe that she took.
> There's blood all over, the shoe's too small.
> She's not the bride that you met at the ball."

The prince leaned over and saw that blood was spilling out of the slipper, and he realized that he had been deceived. So he brought the false bride back to the house. However, the mother said to her second daughter, "Take the slipper, and if it's too short for you, then cut off one of your toes."

So the sister took the slipper into her chamber, and since her foot was too large, she bit her lips and cut off a large part of her toes. Then she quickly slipped her foot into the slipper. When she came out of her chamber, the prince thought she was the right bride and wanted to drive off with her. However, when he came to the gate, the pigeons called out again:

> "Looky, look, look
> at the shoe that she took.
> There's blood all over, and the shoe's too small.
> She's not the bride you met at the ball."

The prince looked down and saw that the stockings of the bride were colored red and that her blood was streaming out of the slipper. So the prince brought her to her mother and said, "She, too, is not the right bride. But is there another daughter in your house?"

"No," said the mother, "there's just a nasty Cinderella. She sits below in the ashes. I'm sure the slipper can't fit her."

The mother didn't want to have her called, but the prince demanded that she do so. Therefore, Cinderella was summoned, and when she heard that the prince was there, she washed her face and hands quickly so that they were fresh and clean. When she entered the room, she curtsied. Then the prince handed her the golden slipper and said, "Try it on! If it fits, you'll become my wife."

So Cinderella took off the heavy shoe from her left foot and put this foot into the golden slipper, and after she pressed a bit, her foot fit as though it had been made for her. And when she stood up, the prince looked at her face and recognized the beautiful princess once again and cried: "This is the right bride!"

The stepmother and the two haughty sisters were horrified and became pale, but the prince led Cinderella away. He helped her into the carriage, and as they drove off through the gate, the pigeons called out:

> "Looky, look, look,
> there's no blood at all.
> The golden shoe's not too small.
> She's truly the bride you met at the ball."

Cinderella (1857)[115]
Jacob and Wilhelm Grimm

The wife of a rich man fell ill, and when she felt her end approaching, she called her only daughter to her bedside and said, "Dear child, be good and pious. Then the dear Lord will always assist you, and I shall look down from heaven and take care of you." She then closed her eyes and departed.

After her mother's death the maiden went every day to visit her grave and weep, and she remained good and pious. When winter came, snow covered the grave like a little white blanket, and by the time the sun had taken it off again in the spring, the rich man had a second wife, who brought two daughters with her. They had beautiful and fair features but nasty and wicked hearts. As a result a difficult time lay ahead for the poor stepsister.

"Why should the stupid goose be allowed to sit in the parlor with us?" they said. "Whoever wants to eat bread must earn it. Out with this kitchen maid!"

They took away her beautiful clothes, dressed her in an old gray smock, and gave her wooden shoes.

"Just look at the proud princess and how decked out she is!" they exclaimed with laughter, and led her into the kitchen.

They expected her to work hard there from morning till night. As a result, she had to get up before dawn, carry the water into the house, make the fire, cook, and wash. Besides this, her sisters did everything imaginable to cause her grief and make her look ridiculous. For instance, they poured peas and lentils into the ashes of the hearth so she had to sit there and pick them out. In the evening, when she was exhausted from working, they took away her bed, and she had to lie next to the hearth in the ashes. This is why she always looked so dusty and dirty and why they all called her Cinderella.

One day it happened that her father was going to the fair and asked his two stepdaughters what he could bring them.

"Beautiful dresses," said one.

"Pearls and jewels," said the other.

115. "Aschenputtel," *Kinder- und Hausmärchen gesammelt durch die Brüder Grimm*, 7th ed., 3 vols. (Göttingen: Verlag der Dieterich'schen Buchhandlung, 1857).

"And you, Cinderella?" he asked. "What do you want?'

"Father," she said, "just break off the first twig that brushes against your hat on your way home and bring it to me."

So he bought beautiful dresses, pearls, and jewels for the two stepsisters, and as he was riding through some green bushes on his return journey, a hazel twig brushed against him and knocked off his hat. So he broke off that twig and took it with him. When he arrived home, he gave his stepdaughters what they had requested, and Cinderella received the twig from the hazel bush. She thanked him, went to her mother's grave, planted the twig on it, and wept so hard that the tears fell on the twig and watered it. Soon the twig grew and quickly became a beautiful tree. Three times every day Cinderella would go and sit beneath it and weep and pray, and each time, a little white bird would also come to the tree. Whenever Cinderella expressed a wish, the bird threw her whatever she had requested.

In the meantime, the king had decided to sponsor a three-day ball, and all the beautiful young girls in the country were invited so that his son could choose a bride. When the two stepsisters learned that they, too, had been summoned to make an appearance, they were in good spirits and called Cinderella.

"Comb out our hair, brush our shoes, and fasten our buckles!" they said. "We're going to the festival at the king's castle."

Cinderella obeyed but wept because she, too, wanted to go to the ball with them, and so she asked her stepmother for permission to go.

"You, Cinderella!" she said. "You're all dusty and dirty, and yet you want to go to the ball? How can you go dancing when you've got no clothes or shoes?"

When Cinderella kept pleading, her stepmother finally said, "I've emptied a bowlful of lentils into the ashes. If you can pick out all the lentils in two hours, you may have my permission to go."

The maiden went through the back door into the garden and cried out, "Oh, you tame pigeons, you turtledoves, and all you birds under heaven, come and help me pick

> the good ones for the little pot
> the bad ones for your little crop."

Two white pigeons came flying to the kitchen window, followed by the turtledoves. Eventually, all the birds under heaven swooped down, swarmed into the kitchen, and settled around the ashes. The pigeons bobbed their heads and began to peck, peck, peck, peck, and all the other birds also began to peck, peck, peck, peck, and they put all the good lentils into the bowl. It didn't take longer than an hour for the birds to finish the work, whereupon they flew away. Happy, because she thought she would now be allowed to go to the ball, the maiden brought the bowl to her stepmother. But her stepmother said, "No, Cinderella. You don't have any clothes, nor do you know how to dance. Everyone would only laugh at you."

When Cinderella started crying, the stepmother said, "If you can pick two bowlfuls of lentils out of the ashes in one hour, I'll let you come along." But she thought, 'She'll never be able to do it.'

Then the stepmother dumped two bowlfuls of lentils into the ashes, and the maiden went through the back door into the garden and cried out, "Oh, you tame pigeons, your turtledoves, and all you birds under heaven come and help me pick

> the good ones for the little pot,
> the bad ones for your little crop."

Two white pigeons came flying into the kitchen window, followed by the turtledoves. Eventually, all the birds under heaven swooped down, swarmed into the kitchen, and settled around the ashes. The pigeons bobbed their heads and began to peck, peck, peck, peck, and all the other birds also began to peck, peck, peck, peck, and they put all the good lentils into the bowl. Before half an hour had passed, they finished their work and flew away. Happy, because she thought she would now be allowed to go to the ball, the maiden carried the bowls to her stepmother. But the stepmother said, "Nothing can help you. I can't let you come with us because you don't have any clothes to wear and you don't know how to dance. We'd only be ashamed of you!"

Then she turned her back on Cinderella and hurried off with her two haughty daughters. When they had all departed, Cinderella went to her mother's grave beneath the hazel tree and cried out:

> "Shake and wobble, little tree!
> Let gold and silver fall all over me."

The bird responded by throwing her a gold and silver dress and silk slippers embroidered with silver. She hastily slipped into the dress and went to the ball. She looked so beautiful in her golden dress that her sisters and stepmother did not recognize her and thought she must be a foreign princess. They never imagined it could be Cinderella; they thought she was sitting at home in the dirt picking lentils out of the ashes.

Now, the prince approached Cinderella, took her by the hand, and danced with her. Indeed, he would not dance with anyone else and would not let go of her hand. Whenever someone came and asked her to dance, he said, "She's my partner."

She danced well into the night, and when she wanted to go home, the prince said, "I'll go along and escort you," for he wanted to see whose daughter the beautiful maiden was. But she managed to slip away from him and got into her father's dovecote. Now the prince waited until her father came, and he told him that the unknown maiden had escaped into his dovecote. The old man thought, 'Could that be Cinderella?' And he ordered a servant to bring him an ax and pick so he could chop it down. However, no one was inside, and when they went into the house, Cinderella was lying in the ashes in her dirty clothes, and a dim little oil lamp was burning on the mantel of the chimney. Cinderella had swiftly jumped out of the back of the dovecote and had run to the hazel tree. There she had taken off the beautiful clothes and laid them on the grave. After the bird had taken them away, she had made her way into the kitchen, where she had seated herself in the gray ashes wearing her gray smock.

The next day when the ball had begun again and her parents and sisters had departed, Cinderella went to the hazel tree and cried out:

> "Shake and wobble, little tree!
> Let gold and silver fall all over me."

The bird responded by throwing her a dress that was even more splendid than the one before. And when she appeared at the ball in this dress, everyone was amazed by her beauty. The prince had been waiting for her, and when she came, he took her hand right away and danced with no one but her. When others went up to her and asked her to dance, he said, "She's my partner."

When evening came and she wished to leave, the prince followed her, wanting to see which house she went into, but she ran away from him and disappeared into the garden behind the house. There she went to a beautiful tall tree covered with the most wonderful pears, and she climbed up into the branches as nimbly as a squirrel. The prince didn't know where she had gone, so he waited until the father came and said, "The unknown maiden has slipped away from me, and I think she climbed the pear tree."

The father thought, 'Can that be Cinderella?' And he ordered a servant to bring him an ax and chopped the tree down, but there was no one in it. When they went into the kitchen, Cinderella was lying in the ashes as usual, for she had jumped down on the other side of the tree, brought the beautiful clothes back to the bird, and put on her gray smock.

On the third day, when her parents and sisters had departed, Cinderella went to her mother's grave again and cried out to the tree:

> "Shake and wobble, little tree!
> Let gold and silver fall all over me."

The bird responded by throwing her a dress that was more magnificent and radiant than all the others she had received, and the slippers were pure gold. When she appeared at the ball in this dress, the people were so astounded they didn't know what to say. The prince danced with no one but her, and whenever someone asked her to dance, he said, "She's my partner."

When it was evening and Cinderella wished to leave, the prince wanted to escort her, but she slipped away from him so swiftly that he couldn't follow her. However, the prince had prepared for this with a trick: he had all the stairs coated with pitch, and when Cinderella went running down the stairs, her left slipper got stuck there. After the prince picked it up, he saw it was small and dainty and made of pure gold.

Next morning he carried it to Cinderella's father and said, "No one else shall be my wife but the maiden whose foot fits this golden shoe."

The two sisters were glad to hear this because they had beautiful feet. The oldest took the shoe into a room to try it on, and her mother stood by her side. However, the shoe was too small for her, and she couldn't get her big toe into it. So her mother handed her a knife and said, "Cut your toe off. Once you become queen, you won't have to walk anymore."

The maiden cut her toe off, forced her foot into the shoe, swallowed the pain, and went out to the prince, who took her on his horse as his bride and rode off. But they had to pass the grave where the two pigeons were sitting on the hazel tree, and they cried out:

> "Looky, look, look
> at the shoe that she took.
> There's blood all over, and the shoe's too small.
> She's not the bride you met at the ball."

He looked down at her foot and saw the blood oozing out. So he turned his horse around, brought back the false bride, and said that she was definitely not the right one and the other sister should try on the shoe. Then the second sister went into a room and was fortunate enough to get all her toes in, but the heel was too large. So her mother handed her a knife and said, "Cut off a piece of your heel. Once you become queen, you won't have to walk anymore."

The maiden cut off a piece of her heel, forced her foot into the shoe, swallowed the pain, and went out to the prince. He took her on his horse as his bride, and rode off with her. As they passed the hazel tree, the two pigeons were sitting there, and they cried out:

> "Looky, look, look
> at the shoe that she took.
> There's blood all over, and the shoe's too small.
> She's not the bride you met at the ball."

He looked down at her foot and saw the blood oozing out of the shoe and staining her white stockings all red. Then he turned his horse around and brought the false bride back home.

"She isn't the right one either," he said. "Don't you have any other daughters?"

"No," said the man. "There's only Cinderella, my dead wife's daughter, who's deformed, but she can't possibly be the bride."

The prince told him to send the girl to him, but the mother responded, "Oh, she's much too dirty and really shouldn't be seen."

However, the prince demanded to see her, and Cinderella had to be called. First she washed her hands and face until they were clean, and then she went and curtsied before the prince, who handed her the golden shoe. She sat down on a stool, took her foot out of the heavy wooden shoe, and put it into the slipper that fit her perfectly. After she stood up and the prince looked her straight in the face, he recognized the beautiful maiden who had danced with him.

"This is my true bride!" he exclaimed.

The stepmother and the two sisters were horrified and turned pale with rage. However, the prince took Cinderella on his horse and rode away with her. As they passed the hazel tree, the two white pigeons cried out:

> "Looky, look, look
> at the shoe that she took.
> The shoe's just right, and there's no blood at all.
> She's truly the bride you met at the ball."

After the pigeons had made this known, they both came flying down and landed on Cinderella's shoulders, one on the right, the other on the left, and there they stayed.

On the day that the wedding with the prince was to take place, the two false sisters came to ingratiate themselves and to share in Cinderella's good fortune. When the bridal couple set out for the church, the oldest sister was on the right, the younger on the left. Suddenly the pigeons appeared and pecked out one eye from each of them. And as they came back from the church later on, the oldest was on the left and the youngest on the right, and the pigeons appeared and pecked out the other eye from each sister. Thus they were punished with blindness for the rest of their lives due to their wickedness and malice.

Vasilisa the Fair (1855–1864)[116]

Alexander Afanas'ev

Once upon a time there was a merchant who had been married for twelve years and had only one daughter, Vasilisa the Fair. When her mother died, the girl was eight years old. On her deathbed the mother called the maiden to her, took a doll out of her counterpane, said: "Vasilisushka, hear my last words. I am dying, and I will leave you my mother's blessing and this doll. Keep this doll always by you, but show it to nobody, and no misfortune can befall you. Give it food and ask it for advice. After it has eaten, it will tell you how to avoid your evil."

Then the wife kissed her daughter and died. After the wife's death the merchant mourned as it behooved, and then he thought of a second wife. He was a handsome man and found many brides, but he liked one widow more than anyone. She was no longer young and had two daughters of about the same age

---

116.   Leonard Magnus, *Russian Folk-Tales* (New York: E. P. Dutton, 1916).

as Vasilisa. So she was an experienced housewife and mother. The merchant married her, but he had made a mistake, for she was not a good mother to his own daughter.

Vasilisa was the fairest damsel in the entire village, and therefore the stepmother and the sisters envied her. They used to torture her by piling all the work they could on her so that she might grow thin and ugly and might be tanned by the wind and the sun. And the child lived a hard life. Vasilisa, however, did all her work without complaining and always grew more beautiful and plumper, while the stepmother and her daughters, out of sheer spite, grew thinner and uglier. Yet there they sat all day long with their hands folded, just like fine ladies. How could this be?

It was the doll that had helped Vasilisa. Without her the maiden could never have done her tasks. Vasilisa often ate nothing herself and kept the tastiest morsels for the doll; and when at night they had all gone to bed, she used to lock herself up in her cellaret below, give the doll food to eat, and say, "Dollet, eat and listen to my misery. I am living in my father's house, and my lot is hard. My evil stepmother is torturing me out of the white world. Teach me what I must do in order to bear this life."

Then the doll gave her good advice, consoled her, and did all her morning's work for her. Vasilisa was told to go walking and to pluck flowers; and all her flower-beds were done in time, all the coal was brought in, and the water-jugs carried in, and the hearthstone was hot. Further, the doll taught her herb-lore. So, thanks to her doll, she had a merry life; and the years went by.

Vasilisa grew up, and all the lads in the village sought her. But nobody would look at the stepmother's daughters, and the stepmother grew more evil than ever and answered all her suitors: "I will not give my youngest daughter before I give the elders."

So she sent all the suitors away, and to show how pleased she was, rained blows on Vasilisa.

One day the merchant had to go away on business for a long time. So, in the meantime, the stepmother went over to a new house near a dense, slumberous forest. In the forest there was a meadow, and on the meadow there was a hut, and in the hut Baba Yaga lived, who would not let anybody in, and ate up men as though they were poultry. Whilst she was moving, the stepmother sent her hated stepdaughter into the wood, but she always came back perfectly safe, for the doll showed her the way by which she could avoid Baba Yaga's hut.

So one day the harvest season came, and the stepmother gave all three maidens their task for the evening: one was to make lace and the other to sew a stocking, and Vasilisa was to spin. Each was to do a certain amount. The mother put all the fires out in the entire house, and left only one candle burning where the maidens were at work, and herself went to sleep. The maidens worked on. The candle burned down, and one of the stepmother's daughters took the snuffers in order to cut down the wick. But the stepmother had told her to put the light out as though by accident.

"What is to be done now?" they said. "There is no fire in the house, and our work is not finished. We must get a light from the Baba Yaga."

"I can see by the needles," said the one who was making lace.

"I also am not going," said the second, "for my knitting needles give me light enough. You must go and get some fire. Go to the Baba Yaga!"

And they turned Vasilisa out of the room. Therefore, Vasilisa went to her room, put meat and drink before her doll, and said : "Dolly dear, eat it and listen to my complaint. They are sending me to Baba Yaga for fire, and the Baba Yaga will eat me up."

Then the Dollet ate, and her eyes glittered like two lamps, and she said: "Fear nothing, Vasilisushka. Do what they say, only take me with you. As long as I am with you, Baba Yaga can do you no harm."

Vasilisa put the doll into her pocket, crossed herself, and went tremblingly into the darksome forest. Suddenly a knight on horseback galloped past her all in white. His cloak was white, and his horse and the reins, and it became light. She went further, and suddenly another horseman passed by, who was all in red, and his horse was red as well as his clothes. And the sun rose.

Vasilisa went on through the night and the next day. Next evening she came to the meadow where Baba Yaga's hut stood. The fence round the hut consisted of human bones, and on the stakes skeletons glared out of their empty eyes. And, instead of the doorways and the gate, there were feet, and instead of bolts there were hands, and instead of the lock there was a mouth with sharp teeth. And Vasilisa was stone-cold with fright.

Suddenly another horseman pranced by on his way. He was all in black, on a jet-black horse, with a jet-black cloak. He sprang to the door and vanished as though the earth had swallowed him up. And it was night. But the darkness did not last long, for the eyes in all the skeletons on the fence glistened, and it became as light as day all over the green.

Vasilisa trembled with fear, but remained standing, for she did not know how she could escape. Suddenly a terrible noise was heard in the forest, and the tree-boughs creaked and the dry leaves crackled. And out of the wood Baba Yaga drove in inside the mortar with the pestle, and with the broom swept away every trace of her steps. At the door she stopped, sniffed all the way round, and cried out:

"Fee, Fo, Fi, Fum, I smell the blood of a Russian mum!
Who is there?"

Vasilisa, shuddering with dread, stepped up to her, bowed low to the ground, and said. "Mother, I am here. My stepmother's daughters sent me to you to ask for fire."

"Very well," said Baba Yaga. "I know them. Stay with me, work for me, and I will give you fire. Otherwise I shall eat you up."

Then she went to the door, and she cried out: "Ho! My strong bolts, draw back, my strong door, spring open!"

And the door sprang open, and Baba Yaga went in whistling and whirring, and Vasilisa followed her.

Then the door closed, and Baba Yaga stretched herself in the room and said to Vasilisa : "Give me whatever there is in the oven. I am hungry."

So Vasilisa lit a splinter from the skulls on the hedge and fetched Baba Yaga food out of the oven, and there was food enough there for ten men. Out of a cellar she fetched *kvas,* mead, and wine. Baba Yaga ate and drank it all up. But all there was left for Vasilisa was a little of some kind of soup, and a crust of bread, and a snippet of pork.

Baba Yaga lay down to sleep and said: "In the morning, to-morrow, when I go away you must clean the courtyard, brush out the room, get dinner ready, do the washing, go to the field, get a quarter of oats, sift it all out, and see that it is all done before I come home. Otherwise I will eat you up."

And, as soon as she had given all the orders, she began snoring.

Vasilisa put the rest of the dinner in front of the doll and said: "Dollet, eat it up and listen to my woe. Heavy are the tasks which the Baba Yaga has given me, and she threatens to eat me up if I don't carry them all out. Help me!"

"Have no fear, Vasilisa, thou fair maiden. Eat, pray, and lie down to sleep, for the morning is wiser than the evening."

Very early next day Vasilisa woke up. Baba Yaga was already up and was looking out of the window. The glimmer in the eyes of the skulls had dimmed; the white horseman raced by, and it dawned. Baba Yaga went into the courtyard, and whistled, and the mortar, the pestle, and the besom appeared at once, and the red horseman came by. And the sun rose.

Baba Yaga sat in the mortar and went by, thrusting the mortar with the pestle, and with the besom she removed every trace of her steps. Vasilisa, left all by herself, looked over the house of the Baba Yaga, wondered at all the wealth gathered in, and began to consider what she should start with. But all the work was already done, and the doll had sifted out the very last of the ears of oats.

"Oh, my savior!" said Vasilisa. "You have helped me in my great need."

"You now have only to get dinner ready," the doll answered and clambered back into Vasilisa's pocket. "With God's help get it ready, and stay here quietly waiting."

In the evening Vasilisa laid the cloth and waited for Baba Yaga. The gloaming came, and the black horseman reached by, and it at once became dark, but the eyes in the skulls glowed. The trees shuddered, the leaves crackled. Baba Yaga drove in, and Vasilisa met her.

"Is it all done?" Baba Yaga asked.

"Yes, grandmother. Look!" said Vasilisa.

Baba Yaga looked round everywhere and was rather angry that she had nothing to find fault with and said: "Very well." Then she cried out: "Ye my faithful servants, friends of my heart! Store up my oats."

Then three pairs of hands appeared, seized the oats and carried them off. Baba Yaga had her supper, and, before she went to sleep, once more commanded Vasilisa: "To-morrow do the same as you did to-day, but also take the hay which is lying on my field, clean it from every trace of soil, every single ear. Somebody has, out of spite, mixed earth with it."

And, as soon as she had said it, she turned round to the wall and was snoring. Vasilisa at once fetched her doll, who ate, and said as she had the day before: "Pray and lie down to sleep, for the morning is wiser than the evening. Everything shall be done, Vasilisushka."

Next morning Baba Yaga got up and stood at the window, and then went into the courtyard and whistled. And the mortar, the besom, and the pestle appeared at once, and the red horseman came by. And the sun rose.

Baba Yaga sat in the mortar and went off, sweeping away her traces as before. Vasilisa got everything ready with the help of her doll. Then the old woman came back, looked over everything, and said: "Ho, my faithful servants, friends of my heart! Make me some poppy-oil."

Then three pairs of hands came, laid hold of the poppies, and carried them off. Baba Yaga sat down to supper, and Vasilisa sat silently in front of her.

"Why do you not speak? Why do you stay there as if you were dumb?" Baba Yaga asked.

"I did not venture to say anything, but if I might, I should like to ask some questions."

"Ask, but not every question turns out well: too knowing is too old."

"Still, I should like to ask you of some things I saw. On my way to you I met a white horseman, in a white cloak, on a white horse: who was he?"

"The bright day."

"Then a red horseman, on a red horse, in a red cloak, overtook me. Who was he?"

"The red sun."

"What is the meaning of the black horseman who overtook me as I reached your door, grandmother?"

"That was the dark night. Those are my faithful servants."

Vasilisa then thought of the three pairs of hands and said nothing.

"Why don't you ask any further?" Baba Yaga asked.

"I know enough, for you say yourself 'too knowing is, too old.'"

"It is well you asked only about things you saw in the courtyard, and not about things without it, for I do not like people to tell tales out of school, and I eat up everybody who is too curious. But now I shall ask you, how did you manage to do all the work I gave you?"

"By my mother's blessing!"

"Ah, then, get off with you as fast as you can, blessed daughter. No one blessed may stay with me!"

So she turned Vasilisa out of the room and kicked her to the door, took a skull with the burning eyes from the fence, put it on a staff, gave it her and said, "Now you have fire for your stepmother's daughters, for that was why they sent you here."

Then Vasilisa ran home as fast as she could by the light of the skull, and the flash in it went out with the dawn. By the evening of the next day she reached the house, and was going to throw the skull away, when she heard a hollow voice coming out of the skull and saying: "Do not throw me away. Bring me up to your stepmother's house."

And she looked at her stepmother's house and saw that there was no light in any window and decided to enter with the skull. She was friendlily received, and the sisters told her that ever since she had gone away, they had had no fire. They were able to make none, and all they borrowed of their neighbours went out as soon as it came into the room.

"Possibly *your* fire may burn!" said the stepmother.

So they took the skull into the room, and the burning eyes looked into the stepmother's and the daughters' and singed their eyes out. Wherever they went, they could not escape it, for the eyes followed them everywhere, and in the morning they were all burned to cinders. Vasilisa alone was left alive.

Then Vasilisa buried the skull in the earth, locked the house up, and went into the town. And she asked a poor old woman to take her home and to give her food until her father came back.

"Mother," she said to the old woman, "sitting here idle makes me feel dull. Go and buy me some of the very best flax. I should like to spin."

So the old woman went and bought good flax. Vasilisa set herself to work, and the work went merrily along, and the skein was as smooth and as fine as hair, and when she had a great deal of yarn, no one would undertake the weaving, so she turned to her doll, who said: "Bring me some old comb from somewhere, some old spindle, some old shuttle, and some horse mane, and I will do it for you."

Vasilisa went to bed, and the doll in that night made a splendid spinning stool, and by the end of the winter all the linen had been woven, and it was so fine that it could be drawn like a thread through the eye of a needle. And in the spring they bleached the linen, and Vasilisa said to the old mistress: "Go and sell the cloth, and keep the money for yourself."

The old woman saw the cloth and admired it, and said : "Oh, my child! nobody except the Tsar could ever wear such fine linen. I will take it to Court."

The old woman went to the Tsar's palace and kept walking up and down in front of it. When the Tsar saw her, he said: "Oh, woman, what do you want?"

"Almighty Tsar, I am bringing you some wonderful goods, which I will show to nobody except you."

The Tsar ordered the old woman to be given audience, and as soon as he saw the linen, he admired it very much.

"What do you want for it?" he asked her.

"It is priceless, Bityushka," she said. "I will give it you as a present."

And the Tsar thought it over and sent her away with rich rewards. Now the Tsar wanted to have shirts made out of this same linen, but he could not find any seamstress to undertake the work. And he thought for long, and at last he sent for the old woman again, and said: "If you can spin this linen and weave it, perhaps you can make a shirt out of it?"

"I cannot weave and spin the linen," said the old woman. "Only a maiden can who is staying with me."

"Well, she may do the work."

So the woman went home and told Vasilisa everything.

"I knew that I should have to do the work!" said Vasilisa. And she locked herself up in her little room, set to work, and never put her hands again on her lap until she had sewn a dozen shirts.

The old woman brought the Tsar the shirts, and Vasilisa washed and combed herself, dressed herself, and sat down at the window, and waited. Then there came a henchman of the Tsar's, who entered the room and said: "The Tsar would fain see the artist who has sewn him the shirts, and he wants to reward her with his own hands."

Vasilisa the Fair went to the Tsar. When he saw her, he fell deeply in love with her.

"No, fairest damsel, I will never part from you. You must be my wife."

So the Tsar took Vasilisa, with her white hands, put her next to him, and bade the bells ring for the wedding. Vasilisa's father came back home, rejoiced at her good luck, and stayed with his daughter. Vasilisa also took the old woman to live with her, and the doll remained in her pocket forever.

Cinderella (1864)[117]

Johann Georg von Hahn

Once upon a time there was an old woman who had three daughters. Since she loved the youngest more than the other two, those sisters were jealous and sought to kill their mother in some way or another. Therefore, they decided to go on top of the roof of their house and to bring their spindles with them. Whichever one of them ripped their thread in two was to be eaten by the others. Well now, the mother was old and weak, and it was easy to predict that her thread would

---

117. "Aschenbrödel," *Griechische und albanesische Märchen* (Leipzig: W. Engelmann, 1864).

be ripped. So they took their spindles, climbed to the top of the roof, and so, indeed, the poor old woman did rip the thread in two with her weak hands.

"Oh, little mother," the two sisters said to her. "We're now going to eat you up!"

"Oh, dear daughters," she said to them, "show some mercy this first time, and if I tear the thread the next time, you can eat me up."

So they continued spinning and let down the thread from the roof, and the old woman's thread was ripped in two again.

"Oh, little mother," the two sisters said to her, "now we're going to eat you up."

"Oh, dear daughters," the old woman answered, "have mercy on me this time as well, and if I tear the thread a third time, you can eat me up!"

So once again they began letting down the thread, and once again the thread broke.

"Now we're no longer going to show you any mercy!" the daughters exclaimed. "We're going to eat you!" And they grabbed hold of the mother and began making preparations to slaughter her. When their mother realized that they were serious, she called the youngest maiden to her and said: "Come here, dear daughter, I want to say something to you!" Then she continued: "Right after your sisters have slaughtered and devoured me, collect all the bones that they throw away, if my blessing means anything to you. Put them carefully into a container and smoke them for forty nights and days. And don't ever let them out of your sight. After the time is over, open the vessel and see what's become of the bones."

"I'll do what you command," the daughter said and began to weep for her mother.

"Don't weep, my dear daughter," the mother said. "What do you want to do? Your sisters have decided to kill me."

So the sisters slaughtered their mother, cooked her, and began to devour her.

"Come, sister," they said. "Eat with us! You'll see just how good it tastes."

"No," she answered. "May God be my witness that I haven't eaten my mother."

Instead, she collected the bones with utmost care and placed them in a container without her sisters noticing what she was doing. When they had finished eating, they stood up and left. But what did the youngest sister do? She started a big fire, smoked the bones day and night, and sat there continually without leaving the container for a moment. Of course, her sisters said to her: "Get up, Cinderella. Get dressed. We want to go out."

But she answered: "May Heaven protect me! You've devoured my mother, and I feel no urge to go out with you. So go!"

Well, the sisters got dressed up and went out while the youngest sister remained by the fire and minded the bones. When the forty days and nights were over and the smoking of the bones was done, she let her sisters go out one day, and then she opened the container and looked inside. What did she see? Well, all the bones had become nothing but gold and diamonds.

About this time, however, it so happened that a wedding was to take place, and the sisters were invited to it. The two eldest said to the youngest: "Get up, Cinderella, and come with us to the wedding!"

"No," she answered. "I'm not going with you! If you want to go, then go. I'm staying home."

Consequently, the sisters went off to the wedding. But no sooner were they away than Cinderella opened the container and chose the most beautiful gown made of silk and gold and diamonds. Then she adorned herself with the jewels and also went to the wedding. When the people saw her arrive there, they didn't know who she was and where she came from. Meanwhile the time to return home had arrived. So she stood up, said her farewells, and departed. However, a prince who had seen her in such a magnificent gown, rushed after her, and since she didn't want to be recognized, she ran as quickly as possible. When she lost a shoe, she didn't bother to turn around and look for it. But the prince bent over and picked it up. Soon thereafter he summoned a peddler and gave the shoe to this woman and ordered her to look for its owner and to tell him who it was.

The peddler went from house to house but didn't find what she was looking for until she finally came to the right place where the two older sisters first tried on the shoe, and since it didn't fit them, she at last turned to the youngest sister. Well, the shoe fit her as if it had been made for her, so that once the peddler left the house, she ran directly to the prince and reported this. In turn he began making preparations for a wedding without delay.

After the wedding was celebrated, the newly married couple took two or three servants from the palace with them and went to the house of Cinderella's sisters where she opened the container she knew and took out its contents. When her sisters saw this, they were extremely astonished and had no idea whatsoever where their sister had found such a great treasure which had been inside the container. So she said to them: "All this comes from our mother's bones and her blessing!"

After saying this, she gave them some of the treasure that she thought was good, and then took the rest with her and went back to the royal castle where she then led a happy life, and where we left her before we came here.

La Cenorientola (1874)[118]

Rachel Busk

They say there was a merchant who had three daughters. When he went out into foreign countries to buy wares, he told them he would bring them rare presents whatever they might ask for. The eldest asked for precious jewels, the second for rich shawls, but the youngest, who was always kept out of sight in

---

118.   *The Folk-Lore of Rome. Collected by Word of Mouth from the People* (London: Longmans, Green, 1874).

the kitchen by the others and made to do the dirty work of the house, asked only for a little bird.

"So you want a little bird, do you! What is the use of a little bird to you!" said the sisters mocking her, "and Papa will have something else to think of than minding little birds on a long journey."

"But you *will* bring me a little bird, won't you, papa?" pleaded the little girl, "and I can tell you that if you don't, the boat you are on will stand still and will neither move backwards nor forwards."

The merchant went away into a far country and bought precious wares, but he forgot all about the little bird. It was only when he had got on board a boat to go down a mighty river on his homeward way, and the captain found the boat would not move by any means, that he remembered what his daughter had said to him. Then while the captain was wondering how it was the boat would not move, he went to him and told him what he had done. But the captain said, "That is easily set right. Here close by is a garden full of thousands of birds. You can easily creep in and carry off one that will never be missed among so many thousands."

The merchant followed his directions and went into the garden where there were so many thousand birds that he easily caught one. The captain gave him a cage, and he brought it safely home and gave it to his daughter.

That night the elder sisters said as usual, "We are going to the ball while you will stay at home and sweep up the place and mind the fire."

Now all the birds in the garden which the captain had pointed out to the merchant were fairies. So when the others were gone to the ball and the youngest daughter went into her room to her bird, she said to it:

> "Give me splendid raiment,
> And I will give you my rags."

Immediately, the bird gave her the most beautiful suit of clothes, with jewels and golden slippers, and a splendid carriage and prancing horses. With these the maiden went to the ball which was at the king's palace. The moment the king saw her, he fell in love with her, and would dance with no one else. The sisters were furious with the stranger because the king danced all night with her and not with them, but they had no idea it was their sister.

The second night she did the same, only the bird gave her a yet more beautiful dress, and the king did all he could to find out who she was, but she would not tell him. Then he asked her name, and she said, "They call me Cenorientola."

"Cenorientola," said the king. "What a pretty name! Never heard it before."

He had also told the servants that they must run after her carriage and see where it went; but though they ran fast as the wind, they could not come near the pace of her horses.

The third night the sisters went to the ball and left her at home, and she staid at home with her little bird and said to it:

"Give me splendid raiment,
And I will give you my rags."

Then the bird gave her a more splendid suit still, and the king paid her as much attention as ever. But to the servants he had said, "If you don't follow fast enough tonight to see where she lives, I will have all your heads cut off."

So they used such extra diligence that she in her hurry to get away dropped one of her golden slippers, which the servants picked up and brought to the king.

The next day the king sent a servant into every house in the city till he should find her whom the golden slipper fitted, but there was not one. Last of all he came to the merchant's house, and he tried it on the two elder daughters and it would fit neither. Then he said "There must be some other maiden in this house." But they only shrugged their shoulders.

"It is impossible! Another maiden there must be, for every maiden in the city we have seen and the slipper fits none. Therefore one there must be here."

Then they said: "In truth we have a little sister who sits in the kitchen and does the work. She is called Cenorientola, because she is always smutty. We are sure she never went to a ball, and it would only soil the beautiful gold slipper to let her put her smutty feet into it."

"It may be so," replied the king's servant, "but we must try, nevertheless."

So they fetched her, and the king's servant found that the shoe fitted her. So, they went and told the king all.

The moment the king heard them say *Cenorientola*, he said, "That is she! It is the name she gave me."

So he sent a carriage to fetch her in all haste. The bird meantime had given her a more beautiful dress than any she had had before, and priceless jewels, so that when they came to fetch her she looked quite fit to be a queen.

Date, Oh Beautiful Date (1875)[119]

Giuseppe Pitrè

Once upon a time there was a merchant who had three grown-up daughters: the eldest was called Rosa, the middle daughter, Giovanna, and the youngest, Ninetta, who was also the most beautiful of them all.

One day this merchant went and purchased a great deal of goods, but when he returned home, he appeared to be very disturbed.

"What's wrong, father?" his daughters asked.

"Nothing, my daughters, I purchased some excellent merchandise, but I can't do anything with the goods because I can't leave you by yourselves."

119. "Gràttula-Beddàtula," *Fiabe, novelle e racconti popolari siciliani*, 4 vols. (Palermo: Lauriel, 1875).

"Why are you getting so upset, my lord?" the eldest daughter asked. "Just leave enough provisions here for the time you are gone. Then have the doors sealed, and if it's God's will, we shall see you again."

So this is what the father did. He stored a great quantity of provisions of food and ordered one of his servants to appear on the street below their window every morning and to call the eldest daughter and run errands for whatever his daughters wanted. Before he took his leave, he said, "Rosa, what do want me to bring you?"

"Three dresses with different colors," she said.

"And you Giovannina?"

"Whatever your lordship wants to bring me."

"And you Ninetta?"

"I want a beautiful branch of dates in a silver vase. And if you forget them, may your ship be prevented from moving forward or backward."

"Oh, you shameful creature!" her sisters said. "What kind of bad spell are you casting on our father?"

"It's nothing," the father responded. "Don't take her seriously. She's still young, and we need to indulge her."

The father took his leave and journeyed to the country of his destination where he carried out his business and then bought three beautiful dresses for Rosa and three for Giovannina. But what did he forget? Indeed, the branch of dates for Ninetta. Later, after he boarded a ship, a terrible storm broke out in the middle of the sea—lightning, flashes, thunderbolts, rain, and huge waves—and the ship was unable to move forward or backward.

The captain became desperate and said, "Where did this bad weather come from?"

Then the merchant remembered his daughter's spell and replied, "Captain, I forgot to buy something. My advice is that we turn around and see what happens."

And, it was a miracle! As soon as they turned around, the weather changed, and they sailed with a fair wind. The merchant went ashore, bought a branch with dates, put it into a silver vase, and went back on board the ship. The sailors unfurled the sails, and after three days they reached their country in favorable weather.

After he arrived, the merchant had the doors unsealed, opened the windows, and gave the gifts to all his daughters, the dresses to Rosa and Giovannina and the branch with dates in a silver vase to Ninetta.

Ah, excuse me. I almost forgot the best part of my tale. While the merchant was on his journey, the eldest sister was sewing by the well. Indeed, their father had made this well for them so they would not lack any water. Well, one time she dropped her thimble into this well, and Ninetta said to her sisters, "Don't worry. Lower me into the well, and I'll get the thimble."

"Are you joking?" the eldest sister said.

"No, I want to go down and fetch it."

They said, no. She said, yes. Back and forth they went. Finally, they had to lower her down into the well. As soon as she touched the water, she grabbed the thimble. But when she pulled out her hand from the water, she noticed some light that was coming from a hole. She removed some stones and saw a marvelous garden, really a delightful garden, for there were all kinds of flowers, trees, and fruit. At once, she slipped inside and began gathering the most beautiful flowers, fruit, and other fine things. After she had an apron full, she returned to the well without making a sound, replaced the stones, and cried out, "Pull me up!" And she reappeared fresh as a rose.

When her sisters saw the apron full of fine things, they said, "Where did you get these beautiful things?"

"What does it matter to you? Tomorrow, you'll lower me back down, and I'll get the rest."

Now, the garden belonged to the son of the king of Portugal, and when he discovered that someone had damaged his garden, he began scolding the poor gardener, who told him that he didn't know anything about what had happened. So the prince ordered him to pay more attention in the future, otherwise he would be in trouble.

The next day Ninetta prepared to descend into the well again in order to explore the garden.

"Sisters, lower me down!"

"Are you crazy or drunk?"

"I'm neither crazy nor drunk. Lower me down!"

They told her, no, and she told them yes. Back and forth they went. Finally, they had to lower her down. Again she removed some stones and entered the garden. After she gathered an apron full of flowers and fruit, she had her sisters pull her up.

The prince, who had been watching from a window, saw her in the middle of the garden as she was slinking off. He ran down from the palace, but he couldn't find anyone. So he called the gardener.

"Where did that young woman come from?"

"What young woman, your majesty?"

"The one who was gathering flowers and fruit in my garden."

"I didn't see a thing, your majesty!" and he began to swear on his life that he hadn't seen a single thing. The prince realized he was innocent and retired to his rooms. However, the next day he personally kept watch and muttered to himself, "If you return, you won't escape."

On the third day Ninetta insisted again and told her sisters to lower her into the well. She had liked the adventure of the previous day. They kept saying, no, and she kept saying, yes, until they had to lower her down. She removed some stones, slipped into the garden, and gathered some wonderful things, better than the other day, until she had an apron full without realizing that the prince was laying in wait for her. When she heard a sound, she turned and saw that the prince was heading her way and about to grab her. But in one leap she made it back through the hole, closed it with a stone, and got away.

After this encounter the poor prince couldn't find any peace of mind, and he became grief-stricken because the maiden seemed to him to be a real fairy. None of the doctors in the kingdom were able to cure him, and once the king realized that his son was losing his senses, he called all the wise men and philosophers of his kingdom together to discuss the prince's illness. First this one spoke, then another, until an old sage with a long white beard said, "Your majesty, try to find out whether your son likes some young maiden, and then we might approach this differently."

The king called his son to him and questioned him. In response his son told him the entire story and concluded by saying that he'd never be cured if he couldn't find this maiden. Consequently, the sage said, "Your majesty, I advise you to hold a festive ball for three consecutive days at your palace and issue a proclamation that all the mothers and fathers from all social classes must bring their daughters under pain of death."

The king agreed and issued the proclamation.

Now let us return to the merchant's daughters. When they had the dresses that their father had brought to them, they began to sew things on them for the first night of the ball. On the other hand, Ninetta retired to her room with her vase and dismissed the festive ball as something trivial. Her father and sisters could barely put up with her. Finally, they were convinced that she was sort of crazy and let her do what she wanted.

At the time that the proclamation had been issued by the king, the father had told his daughters. "Girls, the king is going to hold three days of festivities at his palace, and he wants every father and mother to bring their daughters. Whoever keeps a daughter away will be condemned to death."

"How wonderful!" cried Rosa and Giovannina, but Ninetta shrugged her shoulders and said, "You three go. As for me, I don't want to go."

"No, my daughter," her father said. "I'll be punished by death if you don't go, and you don't joke with death!"

"It doesn't matter to me. Besides, who knows that you have three daughters? Pretend that you only have two."

"You must go."

"No, I'm not going."

They argued back and forth until Ninetta won and remained at home with her vase of dates that were her delight.

However, as soon as her father and sisters had departed, she turned to the vase and said:

> "Date, oh beautiful date,
> Come out and dress your Nina.
> Make her more glamorous than ever before."[120]

Well, what do you think came out of the vase? Suddenly, many fairies appeared carrying dresses and jewels without equal. They washed her, combed her hair, and dressed her—and within moments she was completely covered with a necklace, diamonds, and precious stones. After she looked like gold, she got into a carriage and arrived at the royal palace. When she entered everyone looked at her in astonishment. The prince recognized her and told this to the king. Then he approached her, took her by the arm, and asked, "My lady, how are you?"

"Like the winter."

"What do you call yourself?"

"With a name."

"Where do you live?"

"In a house with a door."

"In what street?"

"In the street with a cloud of dust."

"How strange you are! You will be the death of me."

"May you croak!"

They danced together the entire night. The prince got tired, but she remained lively because she was enchanted. Finally she sat down near her sisters. When the party was over, the king secretly ordered his servants to follow her to find out where she lived. She left the palace and got into the carriage. But as soon as she became aware that the servants were following her, she shook her golden braids and let pearls and precious stones fall onto the road. When the servants saw this, they threw themselves upon them like chickens pecking grain. And good-bye lady! She ordered the horses to be spurred on, and she was back at her home in a flash. As soon as she arrived she said:

> "Oh date, beautiful date,
> Come and undress Nina.
> Make her as she was before this evening."[121]

Within that same moment she found herself in the clothes that she wore around the house.

Now let us turn to her sisters who soon arrived home.

---

120.   *Gràttula-beddàttula,*
Acchiana susu e vesti a Nina,
E falla cchiù galanti ch'un era assira.

121.   *Gràttula-beddàttula,*
Spogghia a Nina,
E falla com'era assira.

"Ninetta, Ninetta, what a beautiful ball! There was a lady there who looked just like you! If we hadn't known that you were here, we would have said that it was you!"

"What are you saying?" Ninetta said. "I stayed here with my vase."

"But tomorrow evening, you should come, you know!"

Let us now turn to the king who was waiting for his servants. When they came back to the palace, they threw themselves at his feet and told him what had happened. Then the king said, "Worthless people! Won over by money! If you do the same thing tomorrow, you'll be in trouble!"

The next evening the sisters insisted that Ninetta go with them, but she didn't want to hear anything about this. Finally, her father ended the discussion by saying, "Don't you see that she's lost her mind over this vase? Who knows but I'll get into some trouble because of it.... No matter, let's go!" And they left.

As soon as they departed, Ninetta approached the vase:

"Date, oh beautiful date,
Come out and dress your Nina.
Make her more glamorous than ever before."

Immediately many fairies emerged from the vase. They combed her hair and dressed her in garments more splendid than before and covered her with jewels. After she was completely dressed, she got into a carriage and went to the royal palace. When she appeared, everyone was astounded, especially her sisters and her father. The prince approached her and was very content.

"My lady, how are you?"

"Like the winter."

"What are you called?"

"With a name."

"Where do you live?"

"In a house with a door."

"In what street?"

"In the street with a cloud of dust."

"How strange you are! You will be the death of me."

"May you croak!"

But he paid no attention to what she said and invited her to dance. And they danced the entire evening. Afterward, she went and sat down next to her sisters.

"Madonna!" one of them said. "She looks exactly like Ninetta."

When the ball was over, Ninetta was among the first to leave. As the king accompanied her to the door, he made a signal to the servants. But Ninetta noticed this, and after she got into the carriage, she saw them approaching. So she took out a number of sacks with gold coins that she had in the carriage and threw them in the face of the servants, who broke each other's noses and hit one another in the eyes to get at the gold. So, the servants could not follow the carriage and had to crawl back to the palace like whipped dogs.

When the king saw them, he took pity on them and said, "It doesn't matter! Tomorrow is the last evening, and in one way or another I'll get to the bottom of this."

Let us turn now to Ninetta who just arrived at her home and said to the vase:

"Oh date, beautiful date,
Come and undress Nina
And make her as she was before this evening."

Within seconds her clothes were changed, and she was wearing the dress she usually wore around the house. When her sisters arrived, they said, "Ninetta, Ninetta, what a beautiful ball! The lady who looked exactly like you returned. She was your spitting image—the eyes, the hair, the mouth, everything, even the way she talked. She was wearing a dress that we've never seen before. And she had jewels and precious stones that sparkled like a mirror!"

"Why are you telling me?" responded Ninetta. "I've had fun with my vase, and I don't care about attending either balls or parties."

"All right, but tomorrow you should go!"

"Really! As if it's the only thing I can think about!"

After she ate, she went to bed.

The next evening Rosa and Giovannina wore the best dresses that their father had brought them, and they went to the party.

Ninetta refused to attend. But as soon as they left, she ran to the vase.

"Date, oh beautiful date,
Come out and dress your Nina.
Make her more glamorous than ever before."

Immediately numerous fairies appeared. They combed her hair, washed her, and dressed her. Afterward they put her into the carriage. At the palace she was so radiant, the people were dazzled, and she was wearing a dress and jewels that nobody had ever seen in their lives.

The prince was waiting for her, and as soon as she saw her, he asked, "My lady, how are you?"

"Like the winter."

"How are you called?"

And they had the same conversation as they had before.

They danced and danced, for it was the last night. Finally, she sat down near her father and her sisters, who continued to speak among themselves.

"She is the exact image of Ninetta," they kept saying.

The king and his son also kept looking at her, and at a certain point the king took her by the arm with the excuse that he wanted to bring her into another room to give her something. When they were alone, Ninetta wanted to take her leave so she could return home, but the king was resolved to finish everything there and said, "For two nights you've led me in circles, but you won't succeed on the third night!"

"What's the meaning of this, your majesty?"

"The meaning is that I know who you are. You are the beautiful young lady who has driven my son crazy. You must become his wife!"

"For a favor, your majesty."

"What favor do you want?"

"I'm not free. I'm obliged to my father and two sisters."[122]

"You have nothing to fear," the king said, and he immediately summoned her father.

The summons of a king is not always a good sign, so they say. The father broke out into a cold sweat because he had committed a few illegal acts and didn't have a clear conscience. But the king told him how things stood and that he would pardon anything he had done if he allowed Ninetta to become the prince's wife.

Indeed, the next day the royal chapel was opened, and the prince and Ninetta were wed.

> Well, they remained content and in peace,
> While we still sit here and pick our teeth.

Told by Agatuzza Messia in Palermo.

The Hearth-Cat (1882)[123]

Consiglieri Pedroso

There was once a schoolmistress who was a widow and had daughter who was very plain. This mistress had a pupil who was very pretty and the daughter of a traveler. The mistress was very attached to her father and every day would beg the girl to ask him to marry her, promising to give her porridge made with honey. The girl went home to ask her father to marry her schoolmistress since she would then give her porridge made with honey. To this request the father replied that he would not marry her, for he well knew that, though she said now that she would give her porridge made with honey, later on she would give her porridge with gall. Yet, since the child began to cry, begging her father to consent, the father, who loved his child very much, in order to comfort her, replied that he would order a pair of boots to be made of iron and hang them up until the boots would rust to pieces with age. Only then would he marry the mistress.

---

122.   The youngest sister in a family was generally not allowed to marry before her elder sisters had found husbands.

123.   *Portuguese Folk-Tales*, trans. Henriqueta Monteiro (London: Folklore Society, 1882).

The little girl, very pleased to hear this, went immediately to tell the mistress, who then instructed her pupil to wet the boots every day. The little girl did so, and after a while the boots fell to pieces, and she went and told her father of it. He then said that he would marry the mistress, and on the following day he married her. So long as the father was at home, the child was treated with kindness and affection, but the moment he went out, the mistress was very unkind to her and treated her badly.

One day she sent her to graze a cow and gave her a loaf, which she desired her to bring back whole, and an earthen pot with water, out of which she expected her to drink, and yet was to bring back full. One day the mistress told the girl that she wished her to employ herself in winding some skeins of thread until the evening. The little girl went away crying and bewailing her lot, but the cow comforted her and told her not to be distressed and to fix the skein on her horns and unravel the thread. After that the good cow took out all the crumbs from the loaf by making a small hole with one of her horns and then stopped the aperture and gave the girl the loaf back again entire.

In the evening the girl returned home. When her stepmother saw that she had finished her task and brought all the thread ready wound, she was very vexed and wanted to beat her, saying that she was sure the cow had had something to do with it. So the next day she ordered the animal to be killed. Upon hearing this the girl began to cry very bitterly, but the stepmother told her that she would have to clean and wash the cow's entrails in a tank they had, however grieved she might feel for the loss of the animal.

Once again the cow told the girl not to be troubled, but to go and wash her entrails and to be careful to save whatever she saw come out of them. The girl did so, and when she was cleaning them, she saw a ball of gold come out and fall into the water. The girl went into the tank to search for it, and there she saw a house with everything in it in disorder. So, she began to arrange and make the house look tidy. She suddenly heard footsteps, and in her hurry she hid herself behind the door. The fairies entered and began to look about, and a dog came in also with them and went up to where she was and began to bark, saying: "Bow-wow, bow-wow, behind the door hides somebody who did us good and will yet render us more services. Bow-wow, bow-wow, behind the door hides somebody who has done us good and will yet render us more services."

Upon hearing the dog bark, the fairies searched about and discovered where the girl was hiding. Then one fairy said to her, "I endow you by the power I possess, with the gift of beauty, making you the most lovely maiden ever seen."

Then another fairy said, "I cast a sweet spell over you, so that when you open your mouth to speak, pearls and gold shall drop from your lips."

The third fairy came forward and said, "I endow you with every blessing, making making you the happiest maiden in the world. Take this wand. It will grant you whatever you may ask."

The girl then left the enchanted region and returned home. As soon as the mistress's daughter saw her approach, she commenced to cry out to her mother to come quickly and see the hearth-cat, who had come back at last. The mistress ran to greet her and asked her where and what she had been doing all that time. The girl related the contrary of what she had seen, as the fairies had instructed her to do, that she had found a tidy house, and that she had disarranged everything in it, to make it look untidy.

Now the mistress sent her own daughter there, and she had hardly arrived at the house when she began at once to do as her half-sister had told her. She disarranged everything, to make the house look untidy and uncared for. And when she heard the fairies coming in, she hid behind the door. The little dog saw her and barked at her, "Behind the door stands one who has done us much harm," he said, "and will still continue to molest us. Bow-wow, bow-wow, behind the door stands one who has done us much harm and will continue to molest us on the first opportunity."

Upon hearing this the fairies approached her, and one began to say, "I throw a spell over you which will render you the ugliest maid that can be found."

The next one took up the word and said, "I bewitch you, so that when you attempt to speak all manner of filth shall fall out of your mouth."

And the third fairy said, "I also bewitch you, and you shall become the poorest and most wretched maid in existence."

The mistress's daughter returned home, thinking she was looking quite a beauty, but when she came up close to her mother and began to speak, the mother burst out crying on seeing her own daughter so disfigured and wretched. Full of rage, she sent her stepdaughter to the kitchen and called her the hearth-cat, and told her that she should take care that she kept there, as the only place which was fit for her.

On a certain day the mistress and her daughter repaired to some races which were then taking place, but when the girl saw that they had left the house, she asked her divining rod to give her a very handsome dress, boots, a hat, and everything complete. She dressed and adorned herself with all she had, went to the races, and stood in front of the royal stand. The mistress's daughter instantly saw her and began to exclaim and cry out at the top of her voice in the midst of all the people present, "Oh, mother, mother! That beautiful maiden over there is our very hearth-cat."

The mother, to quiet her, told her to be calm and that the maiden was not her stepsister because she had remained at home under lock and key. The races were hardly over when the girl departed home, but the king, who had seen her, was in love with her.

The moment the mother reached home, she asked the hearth-cat whether she had been out. She replied that she had not and showed her face besmeared with smut. Next day the girl asked the wand to strike and give her another dress which would be more splendid than the previous one. She put on her things and repaired to the races. The moment the king perceived her, he felt very pleased, indeed, but the races were hardly concluded than she retired in haste and went into her carriage and drove home, leaving the king more in love than ever with her.

The third day the girl asked the divining rod to give her a garment which should surpass the other two in richness and beauty and other shoes. Then she went and attended the races. When the king saw her, he was delighted but was again disappointed to see her depart before the races were concluded. In her hurry to enter her carriage quickly, she let fall one of her slippers. The king picked it up and returned to the palace and fell lovesick. The slipper had some letters upon it which said, "This shoe will only fit its owner."

The whole kingdom was searched to find the lady whose foot would be found to fit the slipper exactly, yet no one was found. The schoolmistress went to the palace to try the slipper on, but all her efforts were in vain. After her, her daughter followed and endeavored her best to fit the slipper on, but with no better success. Only the hearth-cat remained.

The king inquired who was the next to try on the slipper and asked the mistress if there was any other lady left in her house who could fit on the slipper. The schoolmistress then said that there only remained a hearth-cat in her house, but that she had never worn such a slipper. The king ordered the girl to be brought to the palace, and the mistress had no alternative but to do so. The king himself insisted on trying the slipper on the girl's foot, and the moment she put her little foot into the slipper and drew it on, it fitted exactly. The king then arranged that she should remain in the palace and married her. And he ordered the mistress and her daughter to be put to death.

Little Saddleslut (1884)[124]

Edmund Martin Geldart

There were once three sisters spinning flax, and they said, "Whoever spindle falls, let us kill her and eat her."

The mother's spindle fell, and they left her alone.

Again they sat down to spin, and again the mother's spindle fell, and again and yet again.

"Ah, well!" said they, "let us eat her now!"

"No!" said the youngest, "do not eat her; eat me, if flesh you will have."

But they would not; and two of them killed their mother and cooked her for eating. When they had sat down to make a meal of her, they said to the youngest, "Come and eat too!"

---

124. *Folk-Lore of Modern Greece* (London: W. Swan Sonnenschein, 1884).

But she refused, and sat down on a saddle which the fowls were covering with filth, and wept, and upbraided them. Many a time they said to her, "Come and eat!" but she would not; and when they had done eating, they all went away.

Then the youngest, whom they called Little Saddleslut, gathered all the bones together and buried them underneath the grate, and smoked them every day with incense for forty days; and after the forty days were out, she went to take them away and put them in another place. And when she lifted up the stone, she was astonished at the rays of light which it sent forth, and raiment was found there, like unto the heavens and the stars, the spring with its flowers, the sea with its waves; and many coins of every kind; and she left them where she found them.

Afterwards her sisters came and found her sitting on the saddle, and jeered at her. On Sunday her sisters went to church; then she, too, arose; she washed and attired herself, putting on the garment that was as the heavens with the stars, and went to church, taking with her a few gold pieces in her purse. When she went into the church all the people were amazed, and could not gaze upon her by reason of the brightness of her garments. When she left the church, the people followed her to see whither she went. Then she filled her hand with money from her bag and cast it in the way, and so she kept throwing it down all the way she went, so that they might not get near her. Then the crowd scrambled for the coins, and left her alone. And straightway she went into her house, and changed her clothes, and put on her old things, and sat down upon the saddle.

Her sisters came home from church and said to her, "Where are you, wretch? Come and let us tell you how there came into the church a maiden more glorious than the sun, who had such garments on as you could not look on, so brightly did they gleam and shine, and she strewed money on the way! Look, see what a lot we have picked up! Why didn't you come too? Worse luck to you!"

"You are welcome to what you picked up; I don't want it," said she.

Next Sunday they went to church again, and she did the same. Then they went another Sunday, and just as she was flinging the money, she lost her shoe among the crowd, and left it behind her.

Now the king's son was following her, but could not catch her, and only found her shoe. Then said he to himself, "Whosoever foot this shoe exactly fits, without being either too large or too small, I will take her for my wife."

And he went to all the women he knew and tried it on, but could not manage to fit it. Then her sisters came to her and spoke as follows to her, "You go and try; perhaps it will fit you!"

"Get away with you!" said she. "Do you think he will put the shoe on me, and get it covered with filth? Do not make fun of me."

The prince had taken all the houses in turn, and so he came at length to the house of Little Saddleslut, and his servants told her to come and try on the shoe.

"Do not make fun of me," she says.

However she went down, and when the prince saw her, he knew the shoe was hers, and said to her, "Do you try on the shoe."

And with the greatest ease she put it on, and it fitted her.

Then said the prince to her, "I will take you to wife."

"Do not make fun of me," she answered, "so may your youth be happy!"

"Nay, but I will marry you," said he, and he took her and made her his wife.

Then she put on her fairest robes. When a little child was born to the princess, the sisters came to see it. And when the princess was helpless and alone they took her and put her into a chest, and carried her off and threw her into a river, and the river cast her forth upon a desert.

There was a half-witted old woman there, and when she saw the chest, she thought to cut it up for firewood and took it away for that purpose. And when she had broken it open, and saw someone alive in it, she got up and made off.

So the princess was left alone, and heard the wolves howling, and the swine and the lions, and she sat and wept and prayed to God, "Oh God, give me a little hole in the ground that I may hide my head in it, and not hear the wild beasts," and he gave her one.

Again she said, "Oh God, give me one a little larger, that I may get in up to my waist."

And he gave her one. And she besought him again a third time, and he gave her a cabin with all that she wanted in it; and there she dwelt, and whatever she said, her bidding was done forthwith. For instance, when she wanted to eat, she would say, "Come, table with all that is wanted! Come food! Come spoons and forks, and all things needful," and straightway they all got ready, and when she finished she would ask, "Are you all there?" and they would answer, "We are."

One day the prince came into the wilderness to hunt, and seeing the cabin he went to find out who was inside; and when he got there he knocked at the door. And she saw him and knew him from afar, and said, "Who is knocking at the door?"

"It is I, let me in," said he.

"Open, doors!" said she, and in a twinkling the doors opened and he entered. He went upstairs and found her seated on a chair.

"Good day to you," said he.

"Welcome!" said she, and straightway all that was in the room cried out, "Welcome!"

"Come chair!" she cried, and one came at once.

"Sit down," she said to him and down he sat. And when she had asked him the reason of his coming, she bade him stay and dine, and afterwards depart.

He agreed, and straightway she gave her orders: "Come table with all the covers," and forthwith they presented themselves, and he was sore amazed.

"Come basin," she cried. "Come jug, pour water for us to wash! Come food in ten courses!" and immediately all that she ordered made its appearance.

Afterwards when the meal was ended, the prince tried to hide a spoon, and put it into his shoe; and when they rose from table, she said "Table, have you all your covers?"

"Yes I have." "Spoons, are you all there?"

"All," they said, except one which said, "I am in the prince's shoe."

Then she cried again, as though she had not heard, "Are you all there, spoons and forks?"

And as soon as the prince heard her, he got rid of it on the sly and blushed.

And she said to him "Why did you blush? Don't be afraid. I am your wife."

Then she told him how she got there and how she fared. And they hugged and kissed each other, and she ordered the house to move and it did move. And when they came near the town all the world came out to see them. Then the prince gave orders for his wife's sisters to be brought before him, and they brought them, and he hewed them in pieces. And so henceforward they lived happily, and may we live more happily still.

Cinderella (1889–1890)[125]
Achille Millien

Once upon a time there was a widower and widow who were neighbors. Each of them had a daughter, and one day they got married. But the wife detested her husband's daughter whom they called Cinderella. This poor girl had to tend the sheep the entire week, and Sundays she remained at home to work while her mother and sister dressed up and went to mass.

Every morning, when she was sent to the fields, her stepmother said to her, "Here's your work for the day: seven reels of thread and a bundle of sticks."

Now, Cinderella was a good worker, and in the evening she brought back seven reels of thread in her apron and the bundle of sticks on her back. One day, when she arrived in a field, her spindle slipped from her hands. She stooped down to pick it up, but it began to roll and roll and roll even more.

"All right, keep going. May God keep you safe!" she cried out. "Wherever you go, I'll follow you!"

It fell into a hole, a kind of vault. Cinderella descended, and what did she see? Well, there were fairies seated around a fire, and when the fairies caught sight of the little shepherdess, they said to her: "Do you want to warm yourself with us, little friend?"

"I don't have time, my ladies. I have to look after my sheep."

"Sit down just for a moment, little friend."

"I can't. I also have to spin seven reels of thread and gather a bundle of sticks."

"Come. That will all be done, little friend. That will all be done."

---

125. "La Cendrillon," *Cahiers de Pougues* (1889–1890).

Cinderella sat down among the fairies next to the fire, and one of them asked her: "Would you delouse me, my friend? Would you delouse me?"

"I shall be glad to, godmother."

During those times everyone was more polite than they are now, and the young people always said to their elders: "Good day, godfather, good day, godmother."

The fairy placed her head on Cinderella's knees. There were nothing but fleas, nits, and scabies.

"What have you found, my little friend?"

"Gold and silver, godmother, gold and silver."

"Gold and silver you will have, my friend, gold and silver you will have."

"What do we wish for her?" the fairy asked the other fairies.

One of them wished her a beautiful coach drawn by six horses with two coachmen, all contained in a nutshell. Another wished for two golden slippers; another, a glittering dress like the moon; another, a glittering dress like the stars; another a glittering dress like the sun; another a comb to gild her hair; another, a chest to keep all her possessions and all the things that were given to her.

In the evening, Cinderella left the hole, and she found her sheep all gathered together, her seven reels filled with thread, and her sticks in a bundle. Then she returned home with her work done.

From then on she returned to the same field and spent all her time with her friends, the fairies. And every day her work was done.

Her stepmother was very astonished, and she chided her own daughter: "You couldn't do any of this better than her."

"I could do it if I wanted to," she responded.

"Very well! It's your turn to go to the field, and we'll see just how you do."

Her mother gave her the same chore: seven reels to spin and a bundle of sticks to gather while looking after the sheep. Her daughter departed reluctantly. Upon arriving at the field, her spindle slipped from her hands, and when she went to pick it up, the spindle began to roll and roll and roll even more. So, she kicked it.

"Keep going, and may the devil get you! I'll follow you wherever you go!"

The spindle fell into the hole, and the maiden descended.

"Come and sit by the fire, good girl," the fairies said to her.

"I don't have time. I have to look after my sheep, my seven reels of thread, and my bundle of sticks."

"That will be done, good girl. That will be done. Stay with us and warm yourself."

She sat down near the fire, and one of the fairies said to her: "Will you delouse me, my good girl?"

And the fairy put her head on the maiden's knees. There were nothing but fleas, nits, and scabies.

"What have you found, my good girl?"

"Fleas, nits, and scabies, my lady. Fleas, nits, and scabies."

"Fleas, nits, and scabies you will have, my good girl. Fleas, nits, and scabies you will have."

And this came to pass right away. That evening, when she climbed out of the hole, her work had not been done. Her sheep were scattered all over the field, and she could not recover them. When she returned home, her mother scolded her.

"What did you do to become as dirty as you are?"

"My spindle fell into a hole where there were these nasty women, and they kept me there and prevented me from working. And they were the ones who gave me these vermin and this filth."

Her mother had to console her.

On Sunday the mother and her daughter wanted to go to mass. They put on their most beautiful outfits and their most beautiful jewels.

"Cinderella," said the mother, "you take care of the kitchen. Here is a liter of lentils to cook. They are to be ready by the end of the mass."

And she poured the lentils into a pile of ashes. Then she departed with her daughter, and Cinderella began to sort out the lentils. But she didn't make much progress and was upset. All at once she saw one of her fairy friends arrive.

"What are you doing, my friend?"

"Godmother, I want to sort out the lentils, but I can't manage to do it. And they must be cooked by the end of the mass."

"Let it be, my friend. Let it be. Get dressed and go to the mass. It will all be done without you, my friend. It will all be done without you."

Cinderella opened her chest, and she combed herself so that her hair glittered with gold, and she put on her beautiful lunar dress and the golden slippers. Then she opened her nutshell, and the beautiful coach drawn by six horses with two coachmen emerged. Then she hugged the fairy, got into the coach, and departed.

It was on that very day that the prince attended mass. When Cinderella entered the church, everyone gazed at her and admired her. As she passed her sister, she put a silver coin in her hand. The prince was enchanted and couldn't take his eyes off her.

Cinderella was the first to leave the church, a little before the end of mass. She got into the coach and drove off very quickly. The prince left the church after her and wanted to talk with her, but she was gone. He searched everywhere and asked people about her, but nobody knew her and had no idea where she had gone. So now the prince decided to order two of his men to keep an eye out for her the following Sunday and to pull off one of her slippers if they couldn't stop her from leaving.

In the meantime, Cinderella had returned home very quickly, and she had enough time to take off her clothes and to put on her kitchen clothes. The lentils were ready.

"My old Cinderella," her sister said to her, "if you had seen the beautiful lady who had been at mass! . . . she gave me a silver coin!"

The following Sunday, mother and daughter went to mass again They left a liter of lentils in a pile of ashes for Cinderella that she was to sort out and prepare for the end of the mass.

Cinderella began sorting them out, but the fairy arrived.

"What are you doing, my friend?"

"Oh, godmother! I have a good deal of work to do."

"Just let it be, my friend. Let it be. Get dressed and go to the mass. It will be done without you, my friend. It will be done without you."

Cinderella opened her chest, combed her hair so that it glittered like gold and put on her dress of stars and her golden slippers. Then she departed in her coach.

The prince kept admiring her again all during mass. And again she left the church before the end of the mass, and the prince's two men couldn't stop her.

"On the following Sunday, I'll have eight men instead of two watching for her!" declared the prince.

The following Sunday Cinderella had to sort out a liter of lentils from a pile of ashes and cook them during mass. Once again, the fairy arrived.

"Let it be, my friend. Let it be. Get dressed and go to mass. It will all be done without you, my friend. It will all be done without you."

This time Cinderella went to mass in her dress of the sun. Everyone admired her, and the prince was hopelessly attracted to her. Once again, Cinderella left before the end of the mass, but the prince's eight men managed to pull off one of her golden slippers just as she was getting into the coach. Nevertheless, she departed to take her place in the kitchen corner next to the fire.

The prince brought the slipper to his father and told him everything but everything and declared that he loved the young maiden who attended mass and that he would marry no one but her. Consequently, the king issued a proclamation that announced all the maidens in the country were to present themselves at the castle to try on the slipper: whoever's foot the slipper fit was to become the prince's wife. So, the maidens came from all over—the cities, the villages, and the farms, but none of them had a foot that was thin enough. Soon only Cinderella and her sister were left, and the neighbors said to the mother: "You should take your daughter."

So, she got ready and took her daughter, but the slipper was still too small. Then the king's men asked her: "Don't you have another daughter?"

"Oh, yes! But she is so ugly and so dirty that I don't dare to present her."

"Have her come as well!"

The mother and daughter returned to the house.

"Cinderella," said the mother, "now it's your turn to go to the castle."

"What's the use?" replied Cinderella, who didn't want to go.

"Who knows what the use is? But it's the king who's ordered you to go."

Finally, Cinderella decided to go and departed. She tried on the slipper, and her foot was the exact fit.

"Here is the maiden whose foot fits the slipper," said the king. "Here is the maiden who will marry my son."

"First, before you take me to the prince," Cinderella replied, "I'd like to go and fetch my dresses."

She returned to the house and went to her chest. Then she combed her hair with the comb that made it glitter with gold and put on her dress of the sun and the other golden slipper. After that she opened her nutshell and got into her beautiful coach drawn by six horses with two coachmen. Her sister and step-mother were stupefied as they watched her depart.

When she was brought to the king's son, the prince was delighted to see her get out of the coach, and he rushed toward her, took her hand, and never wanted to let it go. They were married immediately thereafter.

Narrated by Monsieur Doux, the father.

Rushen Coatie (1890)[126]
Joseph Jacobs

There was once a king and a queen, as many a one has been; few have we seen, and as few may we see. But the queen died, leaving only one bonny girl, and she told her on her deathbed: "My dear, after I am gone, there will come to you a little red calf, and whenever you want anything, speak to it, and it will give it you."

Now, after a while, the king married again an ill-natured wife, with three ugly daughters of her own. And they hated the king's daughter because she was so bonny. So they took all her fine clothes away from her, and gave her only a coat made of rushes. So they called her Rushen Coatie, and made her sit in the kitchen nook, amid the ashes. And when dinner-time came, the nasty step-mother sent her out a thimbleful of broth, a grain of barley, a thread of meat, and a crumb of bread. But when she had eaten all this, she was just as hungry as before, so she said to herself: "Oh! how I wish I had something to eat." Just then, who should come in but a little red calf, and said to her: "Put your finger into my left ear."

She did so, and found some nice bread. Then the calf told her to put her finger into its right ear, and she found there some cheese, and made a right good meal off the bread and cheese. And so it went on from day to day.

Now the king's wife thought Rushen Coatie would soon die from the scanty food she got, and she was surprised to see her as lively and healthy as ever. So she set one of her ugly daughters on the watch at meal times to find out how Rushen Coatie got enough to live on. The daughter soon found out that the red calf gave food to Rushen Coatie, and told her mother. So her mother went to the king and told him she was longing to have a sweetbread from a red calf. Then the king

126. *English Fairy Tales* (London: David Nutt, 1890).

sent for his butcher, and had the little red calf killed. And when Rushen Coatie heard of it, she sat down and wept by its side, but the dead calf said:

> "Take me up, bone by bone,
> And put me beneath yon grey stone;
> When there is aught you want,
> Tell it me, and that I'll grant."

So she did so, but could not find the shank-bone of the calf.

Now the very next Sunday was Yuletide, and all the folk were going to church in their best clothes, so Rushen Coatie said: "Oh! I should like to go to church too."

But the three ugly sisters said: "What would you do at the church, you nasty thing? You must bide at home and make the dinner."

And the king's wife said: "And this is what you must make the soup of, a thimbleful of water, a grain of barley, and a crumb of bread."

When they all went to church, Rushen Coatie sat down and wept, but looking up, who should she see coming in limping, lamping, with a shank wanting, but the dear red calf? And the red calf said to her: "Do not sit there weeping, but go, put on these clothes, and above all, put on this pair of glass slippers, and go your way to church."

"But what will become of the dinner?" said Rushen Coatie.

"Oh, do not worry about that," said the red calf, "all you have to do is to say to the fire:

> 'Every peat make t'other burn,
> Every spit make t'other turn,
> Every pot make t'other play,
> Till I come from church this good Yuleday,'

and be off to church with you. But mind you come home first."

So Rushen Coatie said this, and went off to church, and she was the grandest and finest lady there. There happened to be a young prince there, and he fell at once in love with her. But she came away before service was over, and was home before the rest, and had off her fine clothes and on with her rushen coatie, and she found the calf had covered the table, and the dinner was ready, and everything was in good order when the rest came home. The three sisters said to Rushen Coatie: "Eh, lassie, if you had seen the bonny fine lady in church today, that the young prince fell in love with!"

Then she said: "Oh! I wish you would let me go with you to the church tomorrow," for they used to go three days together to church at Yuletide.

But they said: "What should the like of you do at church, nasty thing? The kitchen nook is good enough for you."

So the next day they all went to church, and Rushen Coatie was left behind, to make dinner out of a thimbleful of water, a grain of barley, a crumb of bread, and a thread of meat. But the red calf came to her help again, gave her finer clothes than before, and she went to church, where all the world was looking at her, and wondering where such a grand lady came from, and the prince fell more in love with her than ever, and tried to find out where she went to. But she was too quick for him, and got home long before the rest, and the red calf had the dinner all ready.

The next day the calf dressed her in even grander clothes than before, and she went to the church. And the young prince was there again, and this time he put a guard at the door to keep her, but she took a hop and a run and jumped over their heads, and as she did so, down fell one of her glass slippers. She didn't wait to pick it up, you may be sure, but off she ran home, as fast as she could go, on with the rushen coatie, and the calf had all things ready.

Then the young prince put out a proclamation that whoever could put on the glass slipper should be his bride. All the ladies of his court went and tried to put on the slipper. And they tried and tried and tried, but it was too small for them all. Then he ordered one of his ambassadors to mount a fleet horse and ride through the kingdom and find an owner for the glass shoe. He rode and he rode to town and castle, and made all the ladies try to put on the shoe. Many a one tried to get it on that she might be the prince's bride. But no, it wouldn't do, and many a one wept, I warrant, because she couldn't get on the bonny glass shoe. The ambassador rode on and on till he came at the very last to the house where there were the three ugly sisters. The first two tried it and it wouldn't do, and the queen, mad with spite, hacked off the toes and heels of the third sister, and she could then put the slipper on, and the prince was brought to marry her, for he had to keep his promise. The ugly sister was dressed all in her best and was put up behind the prince on horseback, and off they rode in great gallantry. But ye all know, pride must have a fall, for as they rode along a raven sang out of a bush:

> "Hacked Heels and Pinched Toes Behind the young prince rides,
> But Pretty Feet and Little Feet Behind the cauldron bides."

"What's that the birdie sings?" said the young prince.

"Nasty lying thing," said the stepsister, "never mind what it says."

But the prince looked down and saw the slipper dripping with blood, so he rode back and put her down. Then he said: "There must be someone that the slipper has not been tried on."

"Oh, no," said they, "there's none but a dirty thing that sits in the kitchen nook and wears a rushen coatie."

Now the prince was determined to try it on Rushen Coatie, but she ran away to the grey stone, where the red calf dressed her in her bravest dress, and she went to the prince, and the slipper jumped out of his pocket on to her foot, fitting her without any chipping or paring. So the prince married her that very day, and they lived happy ever after.

Fair, Brown, and Trembling (1894)[127]

Joseph Jacobs

King Hugh Curucha lived in Tir Conal, and he had three daughters, whose names were Fair, Brown, and Trembling. Fair and Brown had new dresses, and went to church every Sunday. Trembling was kept at home to do the cooking and work. They would not let her go out of the house at all; for she was more beautiful than the other two, and they were in dread she might marry before themselves. They carried on in this way for seven years. At the end of seven years the son of the king of Emania fell in love with the eldest sister.

One Sunday morning, after the other two had gone to church, the old hen-wife came into the kitchen to Trembling, and said: "It's at church you ought to be this day, instead of working here at home."

"How could I go?" said Trembling. "I have no clothes good enough to wear at church; and if my sisters were to see me there, they'd kill me for going out of the house."

"I'll give you," said the henwife, "a finer dress than either of them has ever seen. And now tell me what dress will you have?"

"I'll have," said Trembling, "a dress as white as snow, and green shoes for my feet."

Then the henwife put on the cloak of darkness, clipped a piece from the old clothes the young woman had on, and asked for the whitest robes in the world and the most beautiful that could be found, and a pair of green shoes.

That moment she had the robe and the shoes, and she brought them to Trembling, who put them on. When Trembling was dressed and ready, the henwife said: "I have a honey-bird here to sit on your right shoulder, and a honey-finger to put on your left. At the door stands a milk-white mare, with a golden saddle for you to sit on, and a golden bridle to hold in your hand."

Trembling sat on the golden saddle; and when she was ready to start, the henwife said: "You must not go inside the door of the church, and the minute the people rise up at the end of Mass, do you make off, and ride home as fast as the mare will carry you."

When Trembling came to the door of the church there was no one inside who could get a glimpse of her but was striving to know who she was; and when they saw her hurrying away at the end of Mass, they ran out to overtake her. But no use in their running; she was away before any man could come near her. From the minute she left the church till she got home, she overtook the wind before her, and outstripped the wind behind.

She came down at the door, went in, and found the henwife had dinner ready. She put off the white robes, and had on her old dress in a twinkling.

---

127. *More English Fairy Tales* (London: David Nutt, 1894).

When the two sisters came home, the henwife asked: "Have you any news to-day from the church?"

"We have great news," said they. "We saw a wonderful grand lady at the church-door. The like of the robes she had we have never seen on woman before. It's little that was thought of our dresses beside what she had on; and there wasn't a man at the church, from the king to the beggar, but was trying to look at her and know who she was."

The sisters would give no peace till they had two dresses like the robes of the strange lady; but honey-birds and honey-fingers were not to be found.

Next Sunday the two sisters went to church again, and left the youngest at home to cook the dinner.

After they had gone, the henwife came in and asked: "Will you go to church to-day?"

"I would go," said Trembling, "if I could get the going."

"What robe will you wear?" asked the henwife.

"The finest black satin that can be found, and red shoes for my feet."

"What colour do you want the mare to be?"

"I want her to be so black and so glossy that I can see myself in her body."

The henwife put on the cloak of darkness, and asked for the robes and the mare. That moment she had them. When Trembling was dressed, the henwife put the honey-bird on her right shoulder and the honey-finger on her left. The saddle on the mare was silver, and so was the bridle.

When Trembling sat in the saddle and was going away, the henwife ordered her strictly not to go inside the door of the church, but to rush away as soon as the people rose at the end of Mass, and hurry home on the mare before any man could stop her. That Sunday, the people were more astonished than ever, and gazed at her more than the first time; and all they were thinking of was to know who she was. But they had no chance; for the moment the people rose at the end of Mass she slipped from the church, was in the silver saddle, and home before a man could stop her or talk to her.

The henwife had the dinner ready. Trembling took off her satin robe, and had on her old clothes before her sisters got home.

"What news have you to-day?" asked the henwife of the sisters when they came from the church.

"Oh, we saw the grand strange lady again! And it's little that any man could think of our dresses after looking at the robes of satin that she had on! And all at church, from high to low, had their mouths open, gazing at her, and no man was looking at us."

The two sisters gave neither rest nor peace till they got dresses as nearly like the strange lady's robes as they could find. Of course they were not so good; for the like of those robes could not be found in Erin.

When the third Sunday came, Fair and Brown went to church dressed in black satin. They left Trembling at home to work in the kitchen, and told her to be sure and have dinner ready when they came back.

After they had gone and were out of sight, the henwife came to the kitchen and said: "Well, my dear, are you for church to-day?"

"I would go if I had a new dress to wear."

"I'll get you any dress you ask for. What dress would you like?" asked the henwife.

"A dress red as a rose from the waist down, and white as snow from the waist up; a cape of green on my shoulders; and a hat on my head with a red, a white, and a green feather in it; and shoes for my feet with the toes red, the middle white, and the backs and heels green."

The henwife put on the cloak of darkness, wished for all these things, and had them. When Trembling was dressed, the henwife put the honey-bird on her right shoulder and the honey-finger on her left, and, placing the hat on her head, clipped a few hairs from one lock and a few from another with her scissors, and that moment the most beautiful golden hair was flowing down over the girl's shoulders. Then the henwife asked what kind of a mare she would ride. She said white, with blue and gold-coloured diamond-shaped spots all over her body, on her back a saddle of gold, and on her head a golden bridle.

The mare stood there before the door, and a bird sitting between her ears, which began to sing as soon as Trembling was in the saddle, and never stopped till she came home from the church.

The fame of the beautiful strange lady had gone out through the world, and all the princes and great men that were in it came to church that Sunday, each one hoping that it was himself would have her home with him after Mass.

The son of the king of Emania forgot all about the eldest sister, and remained outside the church, so as to catch the strange lady before she could hurry away. The church was more crowded than ever before, and there were three times as many outside. There was such a throng before the church that Trembling could only come inside the gate.

As soon as the people were rising at the end of Mass, the lady slipped out through the gate, was in the golden saddle in an instant, and sweeping away ahead of the wind. But if she was, the prince of Emania was at her side, and, seizing her by the foot, he ran with the mare for thirty perches, and never let go of the beautiful lady till the shoe was pulled from her foot, and he was left behind with it in his hand. She came home as fast as the mare could carry her, and was thinking all the time that the henwife would kill her for losing the shoe.

Seeing her so vexed and so changed in the face, the old woman asked: "What's the trouble that's on you now?" "Oh! I've lost one of the shoes off my feet," said Trembling.

"Don't mind that; don't be vexed," said the henwife; "maybe it's the best thing that ever happened to you."

Then Trembling gave up all the things she had to the henwife, put on her old clothes, and went to work in the kitchen. When the sisters came home, the henwife asked:

"Have you any news from the church?"

"We have indeed," said they, "for we saw the grandest sight to-day. The strange lady came again, in grander array than before. On herself and the horse she rode were the finest colours of the world, and between the ears of the horse was a bird which never stopped singing from the time she came till she went away. The lady herself is the most beautiful woman ever seen by man in Erin."

After Trembling had disappeared from the church, the son of the king of Emania said to the other kings' sons: "I will have that lady for my own."

They all said: "You didn't win her just by taking the shoe off her foot; you'll have to win her by the point of the sword; you'll have to fight for her with us before you can call her your own."

"Well," said the son of the king of Emania, "when I find the lady that shoe will fit, I'll fight for her, never fear, before I leave her to any of you."

Then all the kings' sons were uneasy, and anxious to know who was she that lost the shoe; and they began to travel all over Erin to know could they find her. The prince of Emania and all the others went in a great company together, and made the round of Erin; they went everywhere—north, south, east, and west. They visited every place where a woman was to be found, and left not a house in the kingdom they did not search, to know could they find the woman the shoe would fit, not caring whether she was rich or poor, of high or low degree.

The prince of Emania always kept the shoe; and when the young women saw it, they had great hopes, for it was of proper size, neither large nor small, and it would beat any man to know of what material it was made. One thought it would fit her if she cut a little from her great toe; and another, with too short a foot, put something in the tip of her stocking. But no use; they only spoiled their feet and were curing them for months afterwards.

The two sisters, Fair and Brown, heard that the princes of the world were looking all over Erin for the woman that could wear the shoe, and every day they were talking of trying it on; and one day Trembling spoke up and said: "Maybe it's my foot that the shoe will fit."

"Oh, the breaking of the dog's foot on you! Why say so when you were at home every Sunday?"

They were that way waiting and scolding the younger sister, till the princes were near the place. The day they were to come, the sisters put Trembling in a closet and locked the door on her. When the company came to the house, the prince of Emania gave the shoe to the sisters. But though they tried and tried, it would fit neither of them.

"Is there any other young woman in the house?" asked the prince.

"There is," said Trembling, speaking up in the closet; "I'm here."

"Oh! we have her for nothing but to put out the ashes," said the sisters.

But the prince and the others wouldn't leave the house till they had seen her; so the two sisters had to open the door. When Trembling came out, the shoe was given to her, and it fitted exactly.

The prince of Emania looked at her and said: "You are the woman the shoe fits, and you are the woman I took the shoe from."

Then Trembling spoke up, and said: "Do stay here till I return."

Then she went to the henwife's house. The old woman put on the cloak of darkness, got everything for her she had the first Sunday at church, and put her on the white mare in the same fashion. Then Trembling rode along the highway to the front of the house. All who saw her the first time said: "This is the lady we saw at church."

Then she went away a second time, and a second time came back on the black mare in the second dress which the henwife gave her. All who saw her the second Sunday said: "That is the lady we saw at church."

A third time she asked for a short absence, and soon came back on the third mare and in the third dress. All who saw her the third time said: "That is the lady we saw at church." Every man was satisfied and knew that she was the woman.

Then all the princes and great men spoke up, and said to the son of the king of Emania: "You'll have to fight now for her before we let her go with you."

"I'm here before you, ready for combat," answered the prince.

Then the son of the king of Lochlin stepped forth. The struggle began, and a terrible struggle it was. They fought for nine hours; and then the son of the king of Lochlin stopped, gave up his claim, and left the field. Next day the son of the king of Spain fought six hours, and yielded his claim. On the third day the son of the king of Nyerfói fought eight hours, and stopped. The fourth day the son of the king of Greece fought six hours, and stopped. On the fifth day no more strange princes wanted to fight; and all the sons of kings in Erin said they would not fight with a man of their own land, that the strangers had had their chance, and, as no others came to claim the woman, she belonged of right to the son of the king of Emania.

The marriage-day was fixed, and the invitations were sent out. The wedding lasted for a year and a day. When the wedding was over, the king's son brought home the bride, and when the time came a son was born. The young woman sent for her eldest sister, Fair, to be with her and care for her. One day, when Trembling was well, and when her husband was away hunting, the two sisters went out to walk; and when they came to the seaside, the eldest pushed the youngest sister in. A great whale came and swallowed her.

The eldest sister came home alone, and the husband asked, "Where is your sister?"

"She has gone home to her father in Ballyshannon; now that I am well, I don't need her."

"Well," said the husband, looking at her, "I'm in dread it's my wife that has gone."

"Oh! no," said she; "it's my sister Fair that's gone."

Since the sisters were very much alike, the prince was in doubt. That night he put his sword between them, and said: "If you are my wife, this sword will get warm; if not, it will stay cold."

In the morning when he rose up, the sword was as cold as when he put it there.

It happened, when the two sisters were walking by the seashore, that a little cowboy was down by the water minding cattle, and saw Fair push Trembling into the sea; and next day, when the tide came in, he saw the whale swim up and throw her out on the sand. When she was on the sand, she said to the cowboy: "When you go home in the evening with the cows, tell the master that my sister Fair pushed me into the sea yesterday; that a whale swallowed me, and then threw me out, but will come again and swallow me with the coming of the next tide; then he'll go out with the tide, and come again with to-morrow's tide, and throw me again on the srand. The whale will cast me out three times. I'm under the enchantment of this whale, and cannot leave the beach or escape myself. Unless my husband saves me before I'm swallowed the fourth time, I shall be lost. He must come and shoot the whale with a silver bullet when he turns on the broad of his back. Under the breast-fin of the whale is a reddish-brown spot. My husband must hit him in that spot, for it is the only place in which he can be killed."

When the cowboy got home, the eldest sister gave him a draught of oblivion, and he did not tell.

Next day he went again to the sea. The whale came and cast Trembling on shore again. She asked the boy, "Did you tell the master what I told you to tell him?"

"I did not," said he; "I forgot."

"How did you forget?" asked she.

"The woman of the house gave me a drink that made me forget."

"Well, don't forget telling him this night; and if she gives you a drink, don't take it from her."

As soon as the cowboy came home, the eldest sister offered him a drink. He refused to take it till he had delivered his message and told all to the master. The third day the prince went down with his gun and a silver bullet in it. He was not long down when the whale came and threw Trembling upon the beach as the two days before. She had no power to speak to her husband till he had killed the whale. Then the whale went out, turned over once on the broad of his back, and showed the spot for a moment only. That moment the prince fired. He had but the one chance, and a short one at that; but he took it, and hit the spot, and the whale, mad with pain, made the sea all around red with blood, and died.

That minute Trembling was able to speak and went home with her husband, who sent word to her father what the eldest sister had done. The father came and told him any death he chose to give her to give it. The prince told the father he would leave her life and death with himself. The father had her put out then on the sea in a barrel with provisions in it for seven years.

In time Trembling had a second child, a daughter. The prince and she sent the cowboy to school and trained him up as one of their own children, and said: "If the little girl that is born to us now lives, no other man in the world will get her but him."

The cowboy and the prince's daughter lived on till they were married. The mother said to her husband, "You could not have saved me from the whale but for the little cowboy; on that account I don't grudge him my daughter."

The son of the king of Emania and Trembling had fourteen children, and they lived happily till the two died of old age.

Cinderella (1907)[128]

Karel Erben

Several girls were once gathered together by a moat to spin, and as they conversed together, an old greybeard came and said to them: "Girls, when you spin and converse be careful about the moat, for if anyone of you lets her spindle fall into it, her mother will become a cow."

Thus he said and passed on his way. After this the girls, surprised at his words, collected together round the moat and looked down into it, and without intending it, one of them, who was the prettiest, dropped her spindle into the moat. In the evening, when she went away, she observed a cow, her mother, before the gate and drove it to pasture with the rest of the cattle.

After some time the father of this girl married a widow, who brought him a daughter. This second wife hated her husband's daughter particularly, because she was prettier and more diligent than her own. So, she continually sought pretexts to bully and scold her, and gave her nothing to wash or comb herself with, nor any change of clothes. Once she sent her with the cattle, gave her a wallet full of flax and said: "If, to-day, you do not spin this flax and wind it on to the spindle, you needn't come to supper or I'll kill you!"

The poor girl, as she followed the cattle, racked her brain to think how she could finish the task. In the afternoon, when the cattle lie down to chew the cud, she looks into the wallet and sees what there is to be done. But when she sees that it is impossible for her to accomplish it, she begins to cry. When the cow, that was her mother, sees her crying, it asks her what she is crying for. She tells the cow all about it. Then the cow says to her: "Fear not, I will help you. I will take the flax in my mouth and chew it, and the thread will come out at my ear; you will seize it and wind it on the spindle, and will thus finish in time."

---

128. *Russian and Bulgarian Folk-lore Stories*, ed. and trans. Walter Strickland (London: Standring, 1907).

As she said, so it was. She began to chew the flax bit by bit. The thread came out at her ear, and the girl drew it, wound it, and so finished her task. In the evening she went away and brought it to her stepmother, who was astonished to see that she had finished it all. The next time she gave her a similar quantity of flax to spin. The girl spun in the forenoon, and in the afternoon, when the cattle lay down to chew the cud, the cow approached and began to chew. The thread came out at her ear, and the girl drew it off, wound it, and so finished in time. In the evening she went away and gave her stepmother all the flax spun and wound. The stepmother was astonished to see the whole task completed. The third day she gave her still more and sent her own daughter to see who helped her. The daughter sallied forth, crept aside, and saw how it was that the girl completed her task in the day. She saw how the cow took the flax in its mouth and chewed it, and how the thread came out at its ear, and the girl drew and wound it.

Then the girl went and told her mother. When she had learnt this from her daughter, she urged her husband to kill the cow. He tried in every way to persuade her not to have it killed but could not dissuade her. At last, when he perceived that there was nothing else to be done, he promised her that he would kill the cow someday. The girl, when she heard that they were going to kill the cow, began to cry. Then she went off and told the cow that they were going to kill it.

"Hold your tongue and do not cry," it said to the girl. "If they kill me, don't eat of my flesh, but collect my bones and bury them behind the house. Then, if trouble overtakes you, go to my grave, and from there help will come to you."

One day they killed the cow, prepared its flesh, brought it into the dining hall and began to eat. Only the girl did not eat, because it had been forbidden her. Instead, she collected the bones, and, without letting anyone see her, carries them away and buries them behind the house, in the place where the cow (her mother) had ordered her to bury them. This girl was called Maria. Afterwards, when all the drudgery of the house was imposed upon her—namely, to sweep, fetch water, cook, and wash up the earthenware—she became scorched and smudgy from excessive labour by the fire, and so her stepmother rechristened her Cinderella, and this name stuck to her. One day her stepmother and daughter sallied forth to go to church, and before setting off, the stepmother took a pan full of millet, strewed it on the floor in the house, and said to Cinderella: "Hey you, Cinderella! If you do not collect this millet and prepare our dinner for us when we have returned from church, don't venture into my presence, or I will kill you."

So saying she departed. Poor Cinderella, when she looked at all the millet, howled and wept and lamented: "I will sweep, and I will cook, and do all their drudgery for them, but how can a poor girl pick up all that millet?"

When she had wept herself to silence, all at once it occurred to her what the cow had said to her—to go to her grave, that there she would find relief in her trouble. Cinderella hurries off to the grave. Arrived, just fancy what she sees! On the grave stands an open trunk, full of all sorts of rich dresses; and two doves, as white as snow, are standing on the lid. These said to her: "Maria! Take dresses from here, array yourself and go to church, and we will pick up the millet and cook the dinner."

She stretched out her hands and took the top dress, which was of pure silks and satins, dressed herself, and went to church. In church great and small wondered at her beauty and her dress, and, above all, because no one had the least idea who she was nor where she came from. And, most of all, the czar's son admired her and could not take his eyes off her. When the service was over, she crept away and ran quickly home again, hastily undressed, stuffed the dress into the trunk, and the trunk in an instant vanished. She then went to the kitchen, and what do you think she saw there? The millet all picked up, the dinner cooked, and all the household work completed.

After a short time, lo! Her stepmother comes with her daughter from church, sees everything tidied up as it should be, and is much surprised. Next Sunday, when she would go to church with her daughter, she takes a larger pan of millet, scatters it on the floor, and threatens Cinderella that, if she does not collect it all and cook the dinner, she will kill her. The stepmother then goes off to church with her daughter, and Cinderella to the cow's grave. By the grave she finds the two doves and the trunk open, with the dresses in it. The doves bid her dress herself and go to church, and they will pick up the millet and cook the dinner.

She takes a dress of pure silver, puts it on and goes to church. And now great and small wonder more than before, and the czar's son cannot take his eyes off her. The service concludes, and she slips through the choir and so home. There she undresses, stuffs the dress into the trunk, and the trunk vanishes. Soon after, lo! Her stepmother, who looks and looks. All the millet was picked up, dinner cooked, and Cinderella by the kitchen stove! She is much surprised at seeing so great a task completed. And now, for the third time, the stepmother goes to church, but before setting off she takes a pan full of millet, three times larger than before, scatters the millet on the ground, and says to Cinderella: "Cinderella, if this millet be not all collected and the dinner cooked, and everything tidied up when I come home from church, don't venture into my presence, or I will kill you!"

Then she set off to church. After this, Cinderella also went off to the cow's grave, and there sees the trunk open and the two doves upon it. They bid her dress and go to church, and that they will pick up the millet and cook the dinner. She takes a dress of pure gold, and goes to church. There, when they look upon her, they are astonished, for nobody knows who she is and where she comes from. The czar's son cannot take his eyes off her, and determines, when service is over, to follow her, in order to see whither she disappears. Service over, she steals off among the choir boys, and hurries away to get home before her stepmother; but as she struggled through the choir one of her shoes came off, and the czar's son picked it up.

She returned home with one shoe, hastily undressed, stuffed the dress into the trunk, and the trunk vanished. Then she went and looked into the house. The millet was all collected, the dinner cooked, and the whole place tidied up. She seats herself by the kitchen fire, and, lo! Her stepmother comes in, looks all round. The millet is all picked up, the dinner cooked, everything in order; she cannot find a single thing awry to scold Cinderella for.

The czar's son goes home, unrobes, takes the shoe and goes from house to house and tries it on to see who it may belong to. And so, when he had gone and made enquiries, he tried the shoe on the feet of pretty nearly all the girls, but it fitted none of them. For some it was too big, for others too small, for some too narrow, for some too broad. And so, at last, he comes to the house of Cinderella. Her stepmother, on seeing him, clapped Cinderella under a trough. He enquired if they had any girls there. She replied that they had and introduced her daughter. He tried on the shoe, but it would not even go over her toes. Then he asks again if they have no other girl, and she says that they have not. Just as she said to the czar's son that they had no other girl, the cock which had hopped on to the trough pipes out: "Cock-a-doodle-do! There's a pretty girl under the trough, though, too!"

The stepmother screamed: "Ish! May the eagles take you."

And the czar's son, as soon as he heard what the cock had said, approached, and turned over the tub. And, lo! There was the very girl he had seen at church, in those beautiful dresses, only that on one of her feet she had no shoe. He tried the shoe on, which, when he had fitted it, was exactly like the one on the other foot. Then the czar's son took her by the hand, led her away to the court and married her, but the stepmother was punished for her evil heart.

Translated by Walter Strickland.

11. INCESTUOUS FATHERS AND BROTHERS

ATU 510B—PEAU D'ASNE, ALSO CALLED THE DRESS OF GOLD, OF SILVER, AND OF STARS (CAP O' RUSHES)

This tale type belongs to a huge general cycle of stories about persecuted heroines in which modes of survival are depicted. In this case a young maiden, not only from the upper class but also from lower classes, is threatened with incest by her father and sometimes by her brother. She receives the help and advice from a nanny/fairy/priest/friend and disguises herself in some kind of animal skin—donkey/cat/mouse/bear. Sometime she hides in a wooden chest or carved figure. She makes her way to a foreign country where she is hired to do menial work at the castle of a prince/king, who maltreats her until he learns through some object that she is the gifted and beautiful maiden, who has overwhelmed him at a ball. She manages to attract his attention through cooking and/or through curing his sickness. In the end she marries him, and sometimes there is a reconciliation with her father/brother.

In the Western world the theme of incest took on significance in literature during the eleventh century. There were undoubtedly oral tales about incest circulating before this period, and such tales continued to be told up through the twenty-first century. Stories dealing with this topic appeared in the works of Giovan Francesco Straparola (*Le piacevoli notti*, 1550/1553), Francesco Maria Molza (a novella of 1547), Francesco Sansovino (*Cento novelle scelti da i più nobilit scrittori, 1561*), Giambattista Basile (*Cunto de li cunti*, 1634), Charles Perrault (*Contes du temps* passé, 1697), and the Grimms. Most important are the works of Ser Giovanni Fiorentino, "Dionigia and the King of England" in *Il Pecorone* (1385), and the fifteenth-century verse romance of *Belle Hélène de Constantinople*, of which there are also prose manuscripts. It became a very popular story and was published in chapbooks and folk collections up to the nineteenth century.

There is generally one plot outline followed in most of the publications: Emperor Antoine of Constantinople falls in love with his daughter Hélène and manages to obtain a papal dispensation so that he may be allowed to marry her. However, Hélène flees to England before the wedding and meets King Henry but does not reveal that she is from a royal family and why she has fled Constantinople. Henry falls in love with her and marries her against his mother's wishes. When the pope is besieged by the Saracens, Henry goes off to war to help him. While he is absent, Hélène gives birth to twins, but the queen mother sends a message to her son that Hélène has brought two monsters into the world. Henry writes back that Hélène is to be kept under guard, but his mother changes his message into an execution order. When the Duke of Gloucester, who is the acting regent, reads the order, he has Hélène's right hand chopped off as proof that he has slain her. In reality he sends her off in a boat with her two sons and hangs the hand around the youngest son's neck. In the meantime, he has the hand of his own niece chopped off as replacement, and she is also burned at the stake.

After a shipwreck, Hélène's sons are abducted by a wolf and lion who bring them to a hermit who names the boy with the hand around his neck Brac and the other Lion. Meanwhile, Hélène makes her way to Nantes. When Henry learns about Hélène's fate from the Duke of Gloucester, he has his mother executed. By chance he meets Emperor Antoine, who is looking for his daughter. Together Henry and Antoine search for Hélène for a year. At the same time, Brac and Lion commence their quest for their mother. When they come to Tours, they enter the service of the Archbishop Martin de Tours, who names them Brice and Martin. Unknown to all, Hélène has also moved to Tours. When Henry and Antoine encounter Brice and Martin in Tours, they notice the hand around one of the boy's necks, and Henry is united with his sons. Soon Hélène comes upon them, and she is reunited with her sons, father, and husband, and her hand his restored to her through a miracle.

Many of the motifs in this legend stem from Byzantine and Greek tales and medieval legends. There is some connection to the marriage customs in the ruling houses in the pre-Hellenistic period. Other important sources are the legend of the famous eighth-century King Offa, John Gower's *Confesso Amantis*, written in the fourteenth century, and Geoffrey Chaucer's *Canterbury Tales* (1387–1389). The father's incestuous desire has always been depicted as sinful, and the second half of the story, the transformation of the princess into a mutilated person or squalid, animal-like servant, has parallels with the Cinderella tales. However, for the most part the heroine is a princess, and the plot revolves around her fall from and return to royalty. Her purity and integrity are tested, and she proves through a ring or shoe test that she is worthy of her rank. Depending on the attitude of the writer, the incestuous father is punished or forgiven.

Most of the tales dealing with incest are also clearly related to another cycle of tales concerned with "The Maiden without Hands" (ATU 706). One of the key literary sources here is Philippe de Rémi's verse romance *La Manekine* (c. 1270), which may have been based on oral tales in Brittany connected to the motif of the persecuted woman. In her essay "The Donkey-Skin Folktale Cycle" (ATU 510B), Christine Goldberg demonstrates that the tales about incest, which she calls the Donkey-Skin cycle, are also connected to the Cinderella cycle, and she also pays a great deal of attention to other motifs such as the King Lear motif of "Love Like Salt," the old woman's skin and disguised flayer, the hiding box, and the spying. However, she does not deal with the legend of *Belle Hélène*, which clearly is crucial for understanding the historical background of incest tales.

The Brothers Grimm based their version on a story that was embedded in Carl Nehrlich's novel *Schilly* (1798) and an oral tale provided in 1812 by Henriette Dorothea Wild. They included "Princess Mouseskin," which combines the story of "King Lear" with the tale type of "Donkey-Skin," and as can be seen in the other versions that follow, this kind of combination was not unusual. What is significant, however, is that the young maiden depends on her own resources to fend for herself. Her identity, which is taken away from her when she is compelled to disguise herself as an animal, is recovered and she displays more grace and civility than other members at the king's court.

******

All Fur (1812)[129]

Jacob and Wilhelm Grimm

Once upon a time there was a king who had the most beautiful wife in the world, and her hair was pure gold. They had a daughter together, and she was just as beautiful as her mother, and her hair was just as golden. One time the queen became sick, and when she felt she was about to die, she called the king to her and requested that if he wanted to marry again after her death, he should only take someone who was as beautiful as she was and who had golden hair like hers. Once the king promised her that, she died.

For a long time the king was so distressed that he didn't think about a second wife. Finally, his councilors urged him to remarry. So, messengers were sent to all the princesses, but none of them were as beautiful as the dead queen. Nor could they find such golden hair anywhere in the world.

Now one time the king cast his eyes on his daughter, and when he saw that her features were very similar to those of her mother and that she also had such golden hair, he thought, 'Since you won't find anyone as beautiful in the world, you must marry your daughter.' And right then he felt such a great love for her that he immediately informed his councilors and the princess of his decision.

The councilors wanted to talk him out of it, but it was in vain. The princess was totally horrified about his godless intention. However, since she was smart, she told the king that he first had to provide her with three dresses, one as golden as the sun, one as white as the moon, and one as bright as the stars, and then a cloak made up of a thousand kinds of pelts and furs, and each animal in the kingdom had to contribute a piece of its skin to it.

The king had such a passionate desire for her that everyone in his realm was set to work. His huntsmen had to catch all the animals and take a piece of their skin. Thus a cloak was made from their fur, and it didn't take long before the king brought the princess what she had demanded.

Now the princess said that she would marry him the next day. However, during the night, she collected the gifts that she had received from her fiancé from another kingdom: a golden ring, a little golden spinning wheel, and a little golden reel, and the three dresses, all of which she put into a nutshell. Then she blackened her face and hands with soot, put on the coat made of all kinds of fur, and departed. She walked the whole night until she reached a great forest, where she was safe. Since she was tired, she climbed into a hollow tree and fell asleep.

---

129. "Allerlei-Rauh," *Kinder- und Haus-Märchen. Gesammelt durch die Brüder Grimm*, 2 vols. (Berlin: Realschulbuchandlung, 1812/1815).

She continued to sleep until it became broad daylight. As it so happened, the king, her bridegroom,[130] was out hunting in the forest. When his dogs came to the tree, they started to sniff and run around it. The king sent his huntsmen to see what kind of animal was hiding in the tree. When they returned to him, they said that there was a strange animal lying in it, and they had never seen anything like it in their lives. Its skin was made up of a thousand different kinds of fur, and it was lying there asleep. Then the king ordered them to catch it and tie it on the back of the wagon. The huntsmen did this, and as they pulled it from the tree, they saw it was a maiden. Then they tied her on the back of the wagon and drove home with her.

"All Fur," they said, "you're good for the kitchen. You can carry wood and water and sweep up the ashes."

Then they gave her a little stall beneath the steps.

"You can live and sleep there."

So she had to work in the kitchen, where she helped the cook, plucked the chickens, tended the fire, sorted the vegetables, and did all the dirty work. Since she did everything so diligently, the cook was good to her and sometimes called All Fur to him in the evening and gave her some of the leftovers to eat. Before the king went to bed, she had to go upstairs and pull off his boots, and as soon as she would pull one off, he would always throw it at her head. And so All Fur led a miserable life for a long time. Ah, you beautiful maiden, what shall become of you?

At one time a ball was held in the castle, and All Fur thought, 'Perhaps now I could see my dear bridegroom once again.' So she went to the cook and asked him to allow her to go upstairs for a while to see the splendor from the doorway.

"Go ahead," said the cook, "but you can't stay longer than half an hour. You've got to sweep up the ashes tonight."

So All Fur took her little oil lamp, went into her little stall, and washed the soot off her so that her beauty came to light again like flowers in springtime. Then she took off the fur coat, opened the nut, and took out the dress that shone like the sun. When she was fully dressed, she went upstairs, and everyone made way for her, for they believed that she was nothing less than a distinguished princess who had just come into the ballroom. The king immediately offered her his hand and led her forth to dance. And as he was dancing with her, he thought, 'This unknown princess resembles my dear bride,' and the longer he gazed at her, the more she resembled her so that he was almost certain it was her. When the dance ended, he wanted to ask her. However, as she finished the dance, she curtsied and disappeared before the king could begin to ask. Then he asked the guards, but nobody had seen the princess leave the castle. She had quickly run to her little stall, had taken off her dress, blackened her face and hands and put on the fur coat once again. Then she went into the kitchen and wanted to sweep up the ashes.

---

130.   Evidently the princess is not aware that she has reached the realm of her fiancé (bridegroom).

"Let it be until morning," the cook said. "I want to go upstairs and take a look at the dance. Make a soup for the king, but don't let any hairs fall in, otherwise you'll get nothing more to eat."

All Fur cooked a bread soup for the king, and then at the end, she slipped the golden ring into the soup that the king had given to her as a present. When the ball came to an end, the king had his bread soup brought to him, and it tasted so good that he was convinced that he had never eaten one so good. However, when he had finished, he found the ring at the bottom of the bowl. As he looked at it carefully, he saw that it was his wedding ring and was puzzled.[131] He couldn't grasp how the ring came to be there, and so he had the cook summoned, and the cook became angry with All Fur.

"You must have certainly let a hair fall into the soup. If that's true, you'll get a beating!"

However, when the cook went upstairs, the king asked him who had cooked the soup because it had been better than usual. So the cook had to confess that All Fur had made it, and the king ordered him to send All Fur up to him. When she came, the king said: "Who are you and what are you doing in my castle? Where did you get the ring that was in the soup?"

Then she replied: "I'm nothing but a poor child whose mother and father are dead. I am nothing and am good for nothing except for having boots thrown at my head. I also know nothing about the ring."

Upon saying that she ran away.

Some time later there was another ball, and once again All Fur asked the cook's permission to go upstairs. The cook allowed her but only for half an hour, and then she was to return and cook the bread soup for the king. So, All Fur went to her little stall, washed herself clean, took out the dress as silvery as the moon and cleaner and more sparkling than fallen snow. When she appeared upstairs, the dance had already begun. The king offered his hand to her again and danced with her. He no longer doubted that she was his bride, for nobody in the world except her had such golden hair. However, when the dance was over, the princess was also gone once again, and despite all his efforts, the king could not find her, and he had not even spoken a single word with her.

Indeed, she was All Fur again with blackened hands and face. She stood in the kitchen and cooked the bread soup for the king while the cook went upstairs to watch the dance. When the soup was done, she put the golden spinning wheel into the bowl. The king ate the soup, and it seemed even better this time. When he found the golden spinning wheel at the bottom, he was even more astounded because he had one time given it to his bride as a present. The cook was summoned, and then All Fur, but once again she replied that she knew nothing about it, and that she was only there to have boots thrown at her head.

---

131. This was the ring that he had sent to her as a gift.

When the king held a ball for the third time, he hoped his bride would come again, and he wanted to make sure to hold on to her. All Fur asked the cook again to let her go upstairs, but he scolded her and said: "You're a witch. You always put something in the soup and can cook it better than I do."

However, since she pleaded so passionately and promised to behave herself, he let her go upstairs again for half an hour. Thereupon she put on the dress that sparkled as bright as the stars in the night and went upstairs and danced with the king. He thought he had never seen her more beautiful. As they were dancing, however, he slipped a ring onto her finger and had ordered that the dance was to last for a very long time. Nevertheless, he couldn't hold onto her, nor could he speak a single word to her, for when the dance was over, she mingled with the people so quickly that she vanished before he turned around.

All Fur ran to her little stall, and since she had been away longer than half an hour, she undressed quickly. In her hurry she could not blacken herself completely so that a finger remained white. When she went into the kitchen, the cook was already upstairs, and she quickly cooked the bread soup and put the golden reel into it.

Just as he had found the ring and the golden spinning wheel, the king also found the reel. Now he knew for sure that his bride was nearby, for nobody else could have had the presents. All Fur was summoned and wanted once again to get out of the jam and run away. However, as she tried to run off, the king caught sight of the white finger on her hand and held her tight. He found the ring that he had slipped onto her finger and tore off her fur coat. Then her golden hair toppled down, and she was his dearly beloved bride. Now the cook was richly rewarded, and the king held the wedding and they live happily until their death.

Princess Mouseskin (1812)[132]

Jacob and Wilhelm Gimm

A king had three daughters, and he wanted to know which one loved him most. So he summoned them to him and began asking. The oldest daughter said she loved him more than the whole kingdom. The second said she loved him more than all the jewels and pearls in the world. But the third said she loved him more than salt. The king was furious that she compared her love for him to such a meager thing. Consequently, he handed her over to a servant and ordered him to take her into the forest and kill her.

When they reached the forest the princess begged the servant to spare her life. Since he was devoted to her, he wouldn't have killed her anyway. Indeed, he said he would go with her and do her bidding. But the princess demanded nothing except a garment made out of mouseskin. When he fetched it for her, she

---

132. "Prinzessin Mäusehaut," *Kinder- und Haus-Märchen. Gesammelt durch die Brüder Grimm*, 2 vols. (Berlin: Realschulbuchandlung, 1812/1815).

wrapped herself in the skin and went straight to a neighboring kingdom. Once there she pretended to be a man and asked the king to employ her. The king consented, and she was to be his personal servant. In the evening, whenever she pulled off his boots, he always tossed them at her head. One time he asked her where she came from.

"From the country where one doesn't toss boots at people's heads."

Her remark made the king suspicious. Finally, the other servants brought him a ring that Mouseskin had lost. It was so precious that they thought she had stolen it. The king called Mouseskin to him and asked how she had obtained the ring. Mouseskin could no longer conceal her true identity. She unwrapped the mouseskin, and her golden hair streamed down. As she stepped out of the skin, he could see that she was beautiful, indeed so beautiful that he immediately took off his crown, put it on her head, and declared her to be his wife.

When the wedding was celebrated, Mouseskin's father was also invited to attend. he believed that his daughter had died a long time ago and didn't recognize her. However, at the dinner table all the dishes put before him were unsalted, and he became irritated and said, "I'd rather die than eat such food!"

No sooner had he uttered those words than the queen said to him, "Well, now you say you can't live without salt, but when I said I loved you more than salt, you wanted to have me killed."

All at once, he recognized his daughter, kissed her, and begged her forgiveness. Now that he had found her again, she was more dear to him than his kingdom and all the jewels in the world.

All Fur (1857)[133]

Jacob and Wilhelm Grimm

Once upon a time there was a king whose wife had golden hair and was so beautiful that her equal could not be found anywhere on earth. Now, it happened that she became sick, and when she felt she was about to die, she called the king to her and said, "If you desire to marry again after my death, I'd like you to take someone who is as beautiful as I am and who has golden hair like mine. Promise me that you will do this."

After the king had promised her, she closed her eyes and died. For a long time the king could not be consoled and didn't think about remarrying. Finally, his councilors said, "This cannot continue. The king must marry again so that we may have a queen."

Messengers were sent far and wide to search for a bride who might equal the beauty of the dead queen. Yet, they couldn't find anyone like her in the world, and even had they found such a woman, she certainly would not have had such golden hair. So the messengers returned with their mission unaccomplished.

---

133.   "Allerleirauh," *Kinder- und Hausmärchen gesammelt durch die Brüder Grimm*, 7th ed., 3 vols. (Göttingen: Verlag der Dieterich'schen Buchhandlung, 1857).

Now the king had a daughter who was just as beautiful as her dead mother, and she also had the same golden hair. When she had grown up, the king looked at her one day and realized that her features were exactly the same as those of his dead wife. Suddenly he fell passionately in love with her and said to his councilors, "I'm going to marry my daughter, for she is the living image of my dead wife."

When the councilors heard that, they were horrified and said, "God has forbidden a father to marry his daughter. Nothing good can come from such a sin, and the kingdom will be brought to ruin."

When she heard of her father's decision, the daughter was even more horrified, but she still hoped to dissuade him from carrying out his plan. Therefore, she said to him, "Before I fulfill your wish, I must have three dresses, one as golden as the sun, one as silvery as the moon, and one as bright as the stars. Furthermore, I want a cloak made up of a thousand kinds of pelts and furs, and each animal in your kingdom must contribute a piece of its skin to it." She thought, 'He'll never be able to obtain all those furs, and by demanding this, I shall divert my father from his wicked intentions.'

The king, however, persisted, and the most skillful women in his realm were assembled to weave the three dresses, one as golden as the sun, one as silvery as the moon, and one as bright as the stars. His huntsmen had to catch all the animals in his entire kingdom and take a piece of their skin. Thus a cloak was made from a thousand kinds of fur. At last, when everything was finished, the king ordered the cloak to be brought and spread out before her. Then he announced, "The wedding will be tomorrow."

When the king's daughter saw that there was no hope whatsoever of changing her father's inclinations, she decided to run away. That night, while everyone was asleep, she got up and took three of her precious possessions: a golden ring, a tiny golden spinning wheel, and a little golden reel. She packed the dresses of the sun, the moon, and the stars into a nutshell, put on the cloak of all kinds of fur, and blackened her face and hands with soot. Then she commended herself to God and departed. She walked the whole night until she reached a great forest, and since she was tired, she climbed into a hollow tree and fell asleep.

When the sun rose, she continued to sleep and sleep until it became broad daylight. Meanwhile, it happened that the king who reigned over this forest was out hunting in it, and when his dogs came to the tree, they started to sniff and run around it and bark.

"Go see what kind of beast has hidden itself there," the king said to his huntsmen.

The huntsmen obeyed the king's command, and when they returned to him, they said, "There's a strange animal lying in the hollow tree. We've never seen anything like it. Its skin is made up of a thousand different kinds of fur, and it's lying there asleep."

"See if you can catch it alive," said the king. "Then tie it to the wagon, and we'll take it with us."

When the huntsmen seized the maiden, she woke up in a fright and cried to them, "I'm just a poor girl, forsaken by my father and mother! Please have pity on me and take me with you."

"You'll be perfect for the kitchen, All Fur," they said. "Come with us, and you can sweep up the ashes there."

So they put her into the wagon and drove back to the royal castle. There they showed her to a little closet beneath the stairs that was never exposed to daylight.

"Well, you furry creature," they said, "you can live and sleep here."

Then she was sent to the kitchen, where she carried wood and water, kept the fires going, plucked the fowls, sorted the vegetables, swept up the ashes, and did all the dirty work. All Fur lived there for a long time in dire poverty. Ah, my beautiful princess, what shall become of you?

At one time a ball was being held in the castle, and All Fur asked the cook, "May I go upstairs and watch for a while? I'll just stand outside the door."

"Yes," said the cook. "Go ahead, but be back in half an hour. You've go to sweep up the ashes."

All Fur took her little oil lamp, went to her closet, took off her cloak, and washed the soot from her face and hands so that her full beauty came to light again. Then she opened the nut and took out the dress that shone like the sun. When that was done, she went upstairs to the ball, and everyone made way for her, for they had no idea who she was and believed that she was nothing less than a royal princess. The king approached her, offered her his hand, and led her forth to dance. In his heart he thought, 'Never in my life have my eyes beheld anyone so beautiful!' When the dance was over, she curtsied, and as the king was looking around, she disappeared, and nobody knew where she had gone. The guards who were standing in front of the castle were summoned and questioned, but no one had seen her.

In the meantime, the princess had run back to her closet and had undressed quickly. Then she blackened her face and hands, put on the fur coat, and became All Fur once more. When she went back to the kitchen, she resumed her work and began sweeping up the ashes.

"Let that be until tomorrow," said the cook. "I want you to make a soup for the king. While you're doing that, I'm going upstairs to watch a little. You'd better not let a single hair drop into the soup or else you'll get nothing more to eat in the future!"

The cook went away, and All Fur made the soup for the king by brewing a bread soup as best she could. When she was finished, she fetched the golden ring from the closet and put it into the bowl in which she had prepared the soup. When the ball was over, the king ordered the soup to be brought to him, and as he ate it, he was convinced that he had never eaten a soup that tasted as good. However, he found a ring lying at the bottom of the bowl when he had finished eating, and he couldn't imagine how it got there. He ordered the cook to appear before him, and the cook became terrified on learning that the king wanted to see him.

"You must have let a hair drop into the soup," he said to All Fur. "If that's true, you can expect a good beating!"

When he went before the king, he was asked who had made the soup.

"I did," answered the cook.

However, the king said, "That's not true, for it was much different from your usual soup and much better cooked."

"I must confess," responded the cook. "I didn't cook it. The furry creature did."

"Go and fetch her here," said the king.

When All Fur appeared, the king asked, "Who are you?"

"I'm just a poor girl that no longer has a mother or father."

"Why are you in my castle?" the king continued.

"I'm good for nothing but to have boots thrown at my head," she replied.

"Where did you get the ring that was in the soup?" he asked again.

"I don't know anything about the ring," she answered. So the king couldn't learn a thing about her and sent her away.

Some months later there was another ball, and like the previous time, All Fur asked the cook's permission to go and watch.

"Yes," he answered. "But come back in half an hour and make the bread soup that the king likes so much."

She ran to the little closet, washed herself quickly, took the dress as silvery as the moon out of the nut, and put it on. When she appeared upstairs, she looked like a royal princess. The king approached her again and was delighted to see her. Since the dance had just begun, they danced together, and when the dance was over, she again disappeared so quickly that the king was unable to see where she went. In the meantime, she returned to the little closet, made herself into the furry creature again, and returned to the kitchen to make the bread soup. While the cook was still upstairs, she fetched the tiny golden spinning wheel, put it into the bowl, and covered it with the soup. Then the soup was brought to the king, and he ate it and enjoyed it as much as he had the previous time. Afterward he summoned the cook, who again had to admit that All Fur had made the soup. Now All Fur had to appear before the king once more, and she merely repeated that she was good for nothing but to have boots thrown at her and that she knew nothing about the tiny golden spinning wheel.

When the king held a ball for the third time, everything happened just as it had before. To be sure, the cook now asserted, "Furry creature, I know you're a witch. You always put something in the soup to make it taste good and to make the king like it better than anything I can cook."

However, since she pleaded so passionately, he let her go upstairs at a given time. Thereupon she put on the dress as bright as the stars and entered the ballroom wearing it. Once again the king danced with the beautiful maiden and thought that she had never been more beautiful. While he danced with her, he put a golden ring on her finger without her noticing it. He had also ordered the dance to last a very long time, and when it was over, he tried to hold on to her hands, but she tore herself away and quickly ran into the crowd, vanishing from his sight. However, she had stayed upstairs too long, more than half an hour, and she couldn't take off her beautiful dress but had to throw her fur cloak over it. Moreover, she was in such a hurry, she couldn't make herself completely black, and one of her fingers was left white. Then All Fur ran into the kitchen and cooked the soup for the king. While the cook was away, she put the golden reel into the bowl. So, when the king found the reel at the bottom of the bowl, he summoned All Fur and saw the ring that he had put on her finger during the dance. Then he seized her hand and held it tight, and when she tried to free herself and run away, the fur cloak opened a bit, and the dress of bright stars was unveiled. The king grabbed the cloak and tore it off her. Suddenly her golden hair toppled down, and she stood there in all her splendor unable to conceal herself any longer. After she had wiped the soot and ashes from her face, she was more beautiful than anyone who had ever been glimpsed on earth.

"You shall be my dear bride," the king said, "and we shall never part from each other!"

Thereupon the wedding was celebrated, and they lived happily until their death.

By Command of the Prince Daniel (1855–1864)[134]

Alexander Afanas'ev

Once upon a time there was an aged queen who had a son and a daughter, who were fine, sturdy children. But there was also an evil witch who could not bear them, and she began to lay plots how she might contrive their overthrow.

So she went to the old Queen and said, "Dear cousin, I'm giving you a ring. Put it on your son's hand, and he will then be rich and generous. Only he must marry the maiden whom this ring fits."

The mother believed her and was extremely glad, and at her death she bade her son marry only the woman whom the ring fitted.

Time went by, and the boy grew up. He became a man and looked at all the maidens. Indeed, he liked very many of them, but as soon as he put the ring on their fingers, the finger was either too broad or too narrow. So he travelled from village to village and from town to town to search out all the fair damsels, but he couldn't find his chosen one and returned home in a reflective mood.

"What's the matter, brother?" his sister asked him.

So he told her of his trouble and explained his sorrow.

---

134. Leonard Magnus, *Russian Folk-Tales* (New York: E. P. Dutton, 1916).

"What a wonderful ring you have!" said the sister. "Let me try it on."

Immediately after she tried it on her finger, the ring was firmly fixed as if it had been soldered on, as though it had been made for her.

"Oh, sister! You are my chosen bride, and you must be my wife."

"What a horrible idea, brother! That would be a sin."

But the brother wouldn't listen to a word she said. He danced for joy and told her to make ready for the wedding. In contrast, she wept bitter tears, went in front of the house, and sat on the threshold, and let her tears flow. Meanwhile, two old beggars came up, and she gave them something to eat and to drink. They asked what her trouble was, and she needs must tell the two.

"Now, weep no more," they said after hearing her. "Do what we say. Make up four dolls and put them in the four corners of the room. After your brother calls you in for the betrothal, go. If he calls you into the bridal chamber, ask for time, trust in God, and follow our advice." And the beggars departed.

The brother and sister were betrothed, and he went into the room and cried out, "Sister mine, come in!"

"I'll come in a moment, brother. I'm only taking off my earrings."

And the dolls in the four corners began to sing:

> Coo-Coo—Prince Danílo
> Coo-Co—Govorílo
> Coo-Coo—'Tis a brother
> Coo-Coo—Weds his sister,
> Coo-Coo—Earth must split asunder
> Cooo—And the sister lie hid under.

Then the earth rose up and slowly swallowed the sister.

And the brother cried out again, "Sister mine, come in to the feather-bed!"

"In a minute, brother. I am undoing my girdle."

Then the dolls began to sing:

> Coo-Coo—Prince Danílo
> Coo-Coo—Govorílo
> Coo-Coo—'Tis a brother
> Coo-Coo—Weds his sister:
> Coo-Coo—Earth must split asunder
> Cooo—And the sister lie hid under.

Only she had vanished now, all but her head. And the brother cried out again: "Come into the feather-bed."

"In a minute, brother. I'm taking off my shoes."

And the dolls went on cooing, and she vanished under the earth. The brother kept crying out and crying out, and crying out. And when she didn't return, he became angry and ran out to fetch her. However, he could see nothing but the dolls, which kept singing. So he knocked off their heads and threw them into the stove.

The sister went farther under the earth, and she saw a little hut standing on cocks' feet and turning round.

"Hut!" she cried out. "Stand as you should with your back to the wood."

So the hut stopped, and the doors opened, and a fair maiden looked out. She was knitting a cloth with gold and silver thread. She greeted the guest friendlily and kindly, but sighed and said, "Oh, my darling, my sister! Oh, I'm so glad to see you. I'll be so glad to look after you and to care for you as long as my mother isn't here. But as soon as she flies in, woe to you and me, for she is a witch."

When she heard this, the maiden was frightened but couldn't fly anywhere. So she sat down and began helping the other maiden at her work. They chatted for some time, and soon, at the right time before the mother came, the fair maiden turned her guest into a needle, stuck her into the broom, and put it on one side. But scarcely had this been done, when Baba Yaga came in.

"Now, my fair daughter, my little child, tell me at once, why does the room smell so of Russian bones?"

"Mother, there have been strange men journeying past who wanted a drink of water."

"Why didn't you keep them?"

"They were too old, mother, much too tough a snack for your teeth."

"Henceforth, entice them all into the house and never let them go. I must now get about again and search for other booty."

As soon as she had gone, the maidens set to work again knitting, talking, and laughing. Then the witch came into the room once more. She sniffed about the house, and said, "Daughter, my sweet daughter, my darling, tell me at once, why does it smell so much of Russian bones?"

"Old men who were just passing by wanted to warm their hands. I did my best to keep them, but they wouldn't stay."

So the witch was angry, scolded her daughter, and flew away. In the meantime her unknown guest was sitting in the broom.

Once more the maidens set to work, sewed, laughed, and thought how they might escape the evil witch. This time they forgot how the hours were flying by, and suddenly the witch stood in front of them.

"Darling, tell me, where have the Russian bones crept away?"

"Here, my mother, a fair maiden is waiting for you."

"Daughter mine, darling, heat the oven quickly. Make it very hot."

So the maiden looked up and was frightened to death because Baba Yaga with the wooden legs and a nose that rose to the ceiling stood in front of her. Now mother and daughter carried firewood made of logs of oak and maple inside the hut. They made the oven ready till the flames shot up merrily. Then the witch took her broad shovel and said in a friendly voice, "Go and sit on my shovel, fair child."

So the maiden obeyed, and as the Baba Yaga was about to shove her into the oven, the girl stuck her feet against the wall of the hearth.

"Will you sit still, girl?"

But it was in vain, for Baba Yaga couldn't put the maiden into the oven. So she became angry, thrust her back, and said, "You are simply wasting time! Just look at me and see how it's done."

Down she sat on the shovel with her legs nicely trussed together. So the maidens instantly put her into the oven, shut the oven door, and slammed her inside. Then they ran away taking their knitting, comb, and brush with them.

They ran as fast as they could, but when they turned round there was Baba Yaga running after them. She had set herself free. "Hoo, Hoo, Hoo! There run the two!"

So the maidens, in their need, threw the brush away, and a thick, dense coppice arose which Baba Yaga could not break through. So she stretched out her claws, scratched herself a way through, and again ran after them. Where could the two poor girls flee?

They flung their comb behind them, and a dark, murky oak forest grew up, so thick, no fly could ever have flown its way through. Then the witch whetted her teeth and set to work. And she went on tearing up one tree after another by the roots, and she made a way through and again set out after them and was almost catching up with them.

Now the girls had no strength left to run, so they threw the cloth behind them, and a broad sea stretched out, deep, wide, and fiery. The old woman rose up, wanted to fly over it, but fell into the fire and was burned to death.

The poor maidens, poor homeless doves! They didn't know where to go. So they sat down to rest, and a man came and asked them who they were. Then he went and told his master, who turned out to be the maiden's brother, that two little birds had fluttered on to his estate, two fairest damsels similar in form and shape, eye for eye and line for line. One was his sister, but which was it? He couldn't guess. So the master went to view them both. One was the sister—which?

The servant had not lied; he didn't know them, and the maiden was angry with him and wouldn't say who she was.

"What shall I do?" the master asked his servant.

"Master, I will pour blood into an ewe-skin, put that under my armpit, and talk to the maiden. In the meantime I'll go by and stab you in the side with my knife causing blood to flow. Then your sister will reveal who she is."

"Very well!"

As soon as it was said, it was done. The servant stabbed his master in the side, and the blood poured forth, and he fell down. Then his sister flung herself over him and cried out, "Oh, my brother, my darling!"

Then the brother jumped up again healthy and well. He embraced his sister, gave her a proper husband, and he married her friend, for the ring fitted her just as well. So they all lived splendidly and happily.

Translated by Leonard Magnus.

The King Who Wished to Marry His Daughter (1860)[135]

John Francis Campbell

There was a king before now, and he married, and he had but one daughter. When his wife departed, he would marry none but one whom her clothes would fit. His daughter one day tried her mother's dress on, and she came and she let her father see how it fitted her. It was fitting her well. When her father saw her, he would marry no woman but her. She went crying where her muime was; and her foster mother said to her: "What's the matter with you?"

"My father's insisting on marrying me," she said.

Her muime told her to say, "She wouldn't marry him until he gets get her a gown of the swan's down."

He went, and at the end of a day and a year he came, and the gown with him. She went again to take the counsel of her muime.

"Say to him," said her muime, "that thou wilt not marry him till he gets thee a gown of the moorland canach."

She said this to him. He went, and at the end of a day and year he returned, and a gown of the moorland canach with him.

"Say to him now," said her muime, "that thou wilt not marry him till he brings thee a gown of silk that will stand on the ground with gold and silver."

At the end of a day and year he returned with the gown.

"Say to him now," said her muime, "that thou wilt not marry him till he brings thee a golden shoe, and a silver shoe."

He got her a golden shoe and a silver shoe.

"Say to him now," said her muime, "that thou wilt not marry him unless he brings thee a kist that will lock without and within, and for which it is all the same to be on sea or on land."

When she got the kist, she folded the best of her mother's clothes and of her own clothes in it. Then she went herself into the kist, and she asked her father to put it out on the sea to try how it would swim. Her father put it out, and when it was put out, it was going, and going, till it went out of sight. It went on shore on the other side; and a shepherd came where it was, intending to break it, in hopes that there were findings in the chest.

When he was going to break it, she called out, "Do not so, but say to thy father to come here, and he will get that which will better him for life."

---

135. *Popular Tales of the West Highlands: Orally Collected*, 4 vols. (Edinburgh: Edmonston and Douglas, 1860–1862).

His father came, and he took her with him to his own house. It was with a king that he was shepherd, and the king's house was near him.

"If I could get," said she, "leave to go to service to this great house yonder."

"They want none," said the shepherd, "unless they want one under the hand of the cook."

The shepherd went to speak for her, and she went as a servant maid under the hand of the cook. When the rest were going to the sermon; and when they asked her if she was going to it, she said "that she was not; that she had a little bread to bake, and that she could not go to it."

When they went away, she took herself to the shepherd's house, and she put on a gown of the down of the swan. She went to the sermon, and she sat opposite the king's son. The king's son took love for her. She went a while, and before the sermon ended, she returned to the shepherd's house and changed her clothes. So, she was in before them. When the rest of the people came home, they talked about the gentlewoman that was at the sermon.

The next Sunday they asked her whether "she was going to the sermon," and she said "that she was not, that she had a little bread to bake."

When they went away, she went to the shepherd's house, and she put on a gown of the moorland canach; and she went to the sermon. The king's son was seated where he was the Sunday before, and she sat opposite to him. She came out before them, and she changed, and she was at the house before them; and when the rest of the people came home, they talked about the great gentlewoman that was at the sermon.

The third Sunday, they "asked her whether she was going to the sermon," and she said "that she was not, that she had a little bread to bake."

When they went away, she went to the shepherd's house. She put on the gown that would stand on the ground with gold and silver, and the golden shoe and the silver shoe, and she went to the sermon. The king's son was seated where he was the Sunday before, and she sat where he was. A watch was set on the doors this Sunday. She arose, she saw a cranny, and she jumped out at the cranny; but they kept hold of one of the shoes.

The king's son said, "Whomsoever that shoe would fit, she it was that he would marry."

Many were trying the shoe on and taking off their toes and heels to try if it would fit them; but there were none whom the shoe would fit. There was a little bird on the top of a tree, always saying as everyone was trying on the shoe, "*Beeg beeg ha nan doot a heeg ach don tjay veeg a ha fo laiv a hawchkare.*"—Wee wee, it comes not on thee; but on the wee one under the hand of the cook.

When he could get none whom the shoe would fit, the king's son lay down, and his mother went to the kitchen to talk over the matter.

"Won't you let me see the shoe?" said she. "I will not do it any harm at all events."

"Thou! thou ugly dirty thing, that it should fit thee." She went down, and she told this to her son.

"Is it not known," said he, "that it won't fit her at all events? And can't you give it her to please her?"

As soon as the shoe went on the floor, the shoe jumped on her foot.

"What will you give me," said she, "to let you see the other one?"

She went to the shepherd's house, and she put on the shoes, and the dress that would stand on the floor with gold and silver. When she returned, there was nothing to do but to send word for a minister, and she herself and the king's son married.

Translated by John Francis Campbell.

Besom-Cast, Brush-Cast, Comb-Cast (1863)[136]

Theodor Vernaleken

In a castle there once lived a count, named Rudolf, whose lady had a golden cross upon her brow. Her daughter Adelaide had the like sign also upon her brow. When she was twenty years of age her mother suddenly died, and the grief of the count and his daughter was boundless. When the mother had been buried, the father and child shut themselves up in their rooms, and seldom saw anyone. At the end of a month the count sent for his daughter and said, "Dear child, thou knowest how I loved thy mother. I cannot live without a consort, and therefore I am about to go forth into the wide world and seek a wife, who shall, like thy mother, have a golden cross upon her brow. And if within a year and a day I find none such, then I shall marry thee."

When Adelaide heard these words, she was greatly dismayed and departed in silence. Count Rudolf journeyed forth next morning with the promise to return within a year and a day. When Adelaide was alone, she considered whether it were possible that her father should find a lady with the mark of the cross. Then she remembered that her mother had once told her that beside herself and Adelaide, no living person had such a cross. So she determined to go forth, and rather earn her bread with the labor of her hands than eat the smallest morsel at her father's table as his spouse. She intrusted a devoted servant with her plan and made all preparations for the journey. She secretly placed her jewels and ornaments, her gold and dresses, in several large carriages, caused them to be driven forward in the nighttime, and departed, accompanied by her servant Gotthold, and several others who were devoted to her. They came into a great city, where she took a house, and went into it with her servants.

Adelaide had often said that she would earn her bread with her own hands. So Gotthold looked out for a situation for his mistress in the city. He found that in the castle of Prince Adolf the place of a cook-maid was vacant. So he

---

136. "Besenwurf, Bürstenwurf, Kammwurf," *Kinder-und Hausmärchen in den Alpenländern* (Vienna: Braumüller, 1863). Translation in *In the Land of Marvels: Folktales from Austria and Bohemia*, trans. Edwin Johnson (London: Swan Sonnenschein, 1884).

went to the head-cook and asked him whether he was inclined to take his niece (so he called the countess) into service. Looking at the head-cook more closely, he recognized in him a friend whom he had not seen for many years. He now told him that his brother was dead and had left him his daughter to look after. The head-cook agreed, and with joy the faithful servant of the countess departed and stayed in the house she had rented. Adelaide now painted her face, her neck, and her hands brown, hid her golden cross and her hair in a large cap, put on old, dirty, and torn clothes instead of her own fine ones, and went to the head-cook. A small room was allotted her, in which she slept and kept her things. Gradually she became used to service, although she was very tired by the hard labor.

Hitherto she had not seen the prince. One day he invited all his friends and acquaintances to a grand ball. On the morning of the day Adelaide was sweeping the stairs, when the prince, without being observed by her came up the stairs and overturned the vessel which held the sweepings, so that his boots were covered with dust. Adelaide fled, and he, in his anger, took the besom and threw it after her.

When in the evening the saloons were gradually filling with guests, the young countess went to the head-cook, and begged for permission to assist at the ball. But he answered, "No, no; that I cannot allow. Suppose the prince should know of it!"

But Adelaide persevered with her request, till at last he said, "Go, then; but do not be late back, and if you get anything, bring me a part of it."

She now went to Gotthold's dwelling, put on her grand clothes, washed away the paint, and hired a fine coach, in which she betook herself to the prince's. When the guests saw the splendid carriage approaching, they all ran down and cried, "A strange lady, a beautiful lady!"

The prince ran to meet her, handed her out of the carriage, and escorted her up the staircase. She had to dance with him the whole evening, and sit by him at table. After supper he asked her name and abode. "Adelaide is my name, and I come from Besom-cast," replied the countess.

About twelve o'clock she departed, and with her the majority of the guests. On getting back home she quickly colored herself brown again, took three gold pieces and gave them to the head-cook, with the remark that she had stood behind a door, and had received the gold from an old woman.

Next morning the prince looked on his map for Besom-cast, but could not find it. He now wished to ask the lady again the name of her birthplace, but as he did not know where she lived, he sent out invitations for a second ball. On the morning of this second ball Adelaide was brushing her clothes when the prince came unobserved up the staircase. She turned round, and the brush fell from her hand on the prince's foot. In anger Adolf took the brush and threw it at the head of the confused countess.

In the evening the head-cook allowed her again to go to the ball, and she availed herself of the permission. The prince told her that he had not found Besom-cast on the map, and she replied, "How could you look for Besom-cast? I certainly said Brush-cast." Again they danced together, and towards midnight she went home and brought the head-cook a golden ring, saying it had been given her as a present.

Next morning the prince looked for Brush-cast, but could not find it. He then invited his friends to a third ball, which was to be much more splendid than the two first. In the evening of the day, shortly before the beginning of the festival, Adelaide, contrary to her custom, was combing her hair; and the prince, vexed that the strange lady was so long in coming, went downstairs, just as the countess let her comb drop. Adolf picked it up and threw it at the head of the cook-maid. Swiftly she went, dressed herself, and hastened to the ball. At table the prince said that he had nowhere found Brush-cast.

"I believe it," said she. "I certainly called the place Comb-cast."

He would not believe it, but she contended so long with him that at last he gave way. Before she departed he placed a ring on her finger, without her noticing it. Next morning the prince was unwell, and he bade the head-cook make him some broth. The latter mentioned this in the kitchen, and Adelaide begged for permission to make it. But the cook said, "If you put in anything that does not belong to the broth, I shall have to suffer for it."

She replied, "I will not put in anything wrong," and prepared the broth, but, unobserved, cast in the ring of the prince. The prince poured out the broth into a plate and heard something rattle. He stirred about, and fished out the ring. Then he asked, in wonder, who had prepared the broth.

"The cook-maid," was the answer.

"Bring her hither," said the count. In haste she put on the dress she had worn the evening before, and as the prince gazed at her, he recognized his partner in the dance. She had now to tell him the story of her life in all its particulars, and soon after he took her for his consort.

Her father meanwhile had returned home, and learning that his daughter was already married, he had to submit to his fate.

Translated by Edwin Johnson.

All Fur (1864)[137]

Johann Georg von Hahn

Once upon a time there was a king whose wife died and left him only with a little daughter. This girl grew gradually into a beautiful young woman. When her father saw that she was so beautiful, he said to her: "I want to marry you, and you must become my wife."

---

137. "Allerleirauh," *Griechische und albanesische Märchen* (Leipzig: W. Engelmann, 1864).

"How can you take me to become your wife," the maiden responded, "when I'm already your daughter?"

"It's all the same to me. I want to marry you."

"But this is impossible," the maiden said. "Go to the bishop and listen to what he says. If he says that you have the right to do this, then you may have me in God's name."

So the king went to the bishop and asked: "If someone has a lamb and looks after it himself and raises it until it is grown, is it better that he is the one to consume it, or someone else?"

"It's better that the person who's raised the lamb is the one to consume it," replied the bishop.

So the king went back to his daughter and said: "He told me that I have the right to take you as my wife."

"If he really said that you have the right to take me, then you may take me in God's name. But before you do, I want two dresses made of gold with pockets filled with gold coins. I also want a bed and a shaft made for me. The shaft is to be ten fathoms deep in the ground."

When the king had everything prepared for her, the maiden took the clothes, got into the bed, and moved on top of it into the shaft.

"Earth, open up wider!" she cried.

And the earth opened itself so that she could move further and come out at another place, and there she remained.

One day, when the prince was hunting in this place, he found the maiden wrapped in an animal skin. So he went over to her and asked: "Are you human?"

"Yes, I am," she answered. "May I come with you?"

"If you like, come with me," he responded and took her with him to look after the geese.

Then, one day when the king held a feast and the women began to dance, the maiden slipped out of her animal skin, put on a golden dress, and joined in the dance. The prince saw her dancing there and said to himself: 'Who might that be? When she leaves the dance, I'm going to follow her.'

So, when the dance was over, the maiden left, and the prince sneaked after her. However, the maiden noticed him and began to run. He pursued her, but the maiden took a handful of coins and threw them on the ground. When the prince stopped to pick up the gold coins, she escaped and slipped back into the animal skin.

So the prince declared: "Tomorrow I'm going to hold another feast to I can learn who that maiden is."

And that's what happened. The maiden came again and joined in the dance, and when she left the dance, the prince followed her. However, she threw gold coins on the ground again, and while the prince stopped to pick them up, she got away and slipped into the animal skin once more.

"I'm going to hold another feast to find out who that maiden is," the prince stated.

When it came time for the feast again, the maiden came and danced, and as she left the dance, the prince followed her. This time she lost a shoe as she was running, and when the prince stopped to pick it up, she got away half barefoot and slipped on the animal skin once more.

The prince took the shoe and tried it on all the young women to see if it fit any of them. But he couldn't find one whose foot fit.

Now, when the servants and maids went to carry the washing water to the king before dinner, the animal skin split open a bit around the maiden's knee so that her golden dress could be seen. She went to the maids and asked them to let her carry the water. However, they said: "What you, the goose girl, want to bring the water to the king?"

"What's the matter?" the king asked.

"The goose girl wants to bring the water to you."

"Well, let her do it. Let her come."

When she knelt down before the king, the golden dress glimmered through the split. As the prince saw this, he cried out: "You certainly have tortured me long enough!"

Soon after he took her to become his wife.

Betta Pilusa (1870)[138]

Laura Gonzenbach

Once upon a time there was a rich man, who had a good and pious wife and an only daughter, who was very beautiful. After some time passed, his poor wife happened to become sick and was about to die. So she called her husband and said, "Dear husband, soon I shall die, and I am placing our child in your hands. Promise me that you will not marry again until a woman comes who can wear this ring."

Upon saying this, she showed him a ring that she placed with her other jewels and died. His daughter became more beautiful with each passing day, and at one time it occurred to her to take a look at the jewels that had belonged to her mother. When she opened up the little jewelry box, she saw the ring, which her mother had shown to her father upon her deathbed, and tried it on. And imagine this: the ring slid very easily onto her finger, but when she wanted to take it off, she couldn't manage to do it. Now she became scared and thought, 'What will my father say?'

And to make sure he wouldn't see it, she wrapped a piece of cloth around her finger. Yet, when her father saw the cloth, he asked why she had wrapped her finger with it, and she answered, "It's nothing, dear father. I just cut my finger."

---

138. "Von der Betta Pilusa," *Sicilianische Märchen*, 2 vols. (Leipzig: W. Engelmann, 1870).

"Let me take a look," the father said.

She didn't want to let him, but her father became angry and ripped the cloth off the finger. All at once he saw the ring and cried out, "You're wearing the ring. Now you must become my wife."

The maiden was terrified and said, "Oh, dear father, how could you possibly propose such a sinful thing?"

However, he didn't listen to her and only kept repeating, "You must become my wife."

"At least allow me first to go to my father confessor," she said.

So she went to the priest and began to weep and tell him about her father's desires. The father confessor was extremely shocked and said, "We've got to put him off until he comes to his senses again. So, I advise you to demand from him a dress the color of the sky with the sun, moon, and stars on it. If he can provide this, tell him you'll become his wife."

The poor girl went to her father and said, "Father, if you bring me a dress with the color of the sky and you can see the sun, moon, and stars on it, I'll become your wife."

The father went and searched for the dress, but no matter what shop he visited, he couldn't find this particular dress anywhere. He became very sullen and walked into the fields and kept thinking of some way to obtain the dress. All of a sudden a gentleman joined him and asked him why he was hanging his head so low. So the father told him about his troubles.

"Oh," responded the gentleman, "if that's all there's to it, I can get it for you. Just wait here for me."

The man went away, and after a short while, he reappeared with the dress. To be sure, the strange gentleman was the devil, who wanted to lure the father into committing a sin. So, now the father brought his daughter the dress, and the girl was horrified, but she only said, "Dear father, I must go to my father confessor again."

So she went and said, "What am I to do now? My father brought me the dress and still wants to marry me."

"Demand another dress from him," the priest replied. "This time ask him for one that has the color of the sea and all the fish and plants of the sea on it."

So she went to her father and asked him for this particular dress. The father looked for the dress in all the shops, and since he couldn't find it, he went to the place where he had met the sinister man. Once again he found him there, and when he told him about his wish, the devil brought him the dress which had the color of the sea, and all the fish and plants of the sea could be seen on it.

When he brought the dress to his daughter, she said once more: "Dear father, let me first go to confession."

Then she asked her father confessor for advice, and he said she should demand a dress from her father with the color of the earth and with all the animals and flowers of the earth on it. She did this, but her father went straight to the devil and had another dress made for her. Now the poor maiden no longer knew what she should do. Once again she went to her father confessor and revealed to him that everything had been in vain. In response the priest said, "Demand a dress made from the fur of a gray cat."

She did this, and her father went once more to the devil, who also provided him a dress made from the fur of a gray cat. Meanwhile, the daughter went to the father confessor and complained that her father still persisted in marrying her.

"Demand that he bring you two barrels full of pearls and jewels," the father confessor advised her.

When she requested the two barrels full of pearls and jewels from her father, he had the devil provide them for him and brought them to her as well. Now she really did not know how she could help herself, and so she decided to flee. She made a bundle out of the three dresses and pearls and jewels and waited until morning arrived. As soon as dawn came, she stood up, filled a bowl with water, and placed two pigeons inside. Suddenly, her father knocked on the door and asked her whether she was ready.

"I'm still washing myself, dear father," she answered while slipping into the dress made of gray cat fur. Then she took the bundle with her and ran through a back door into the open, and since it was still somewhat dark, nobody saw her. In the meantime, her father waited for her in his house. Whenever he came near her door, he heard the pigeons splashing and thought that his daughter was still washing herself. Finally, he lost his patience and had the door broken down, but there was nobody inside, and her father exploded with rage, but his rage did not help him.

Well, let's leave the father and see what became of his poor daughter.

With tears in her eyes she made her way until she came to a dense forest. It so happened that on this day the young king was hunting in this forest, and when he saw the strange-looking creature in the gray fur coat, he thought it was an animal and wanted to shoot it. All at once, however, the maiden cried out, "Don't shoot!"

Now he was even more astonished by an animal who could speak and called out to her, "I swear in the name of God that you had better tell me who you are."

"Don't you swear to God!" she replied. "I am a baptized soul."

"What's your name?" the king asked.

"My name is Betta Pilusa."[139]

"Do you want to come with me to my castle?" the king asked.

"Yes," she answered. "You can let me be your maid."

So the king took her to his castle and asked her, "Where do you want to live?"

---

139. German: *Die haarige Bertha*; English: Hairy Bertha.

"In the chicken coop," she answered.

From then on she lived in the chicken coop and looked after the chickens. The king went to her every day, brought her delicious bits of food, and conversed with her. One day he came to her and said, "You know, Betta Pilusa, my wedding will take place soon, and there will be three days of festivities. Today there will be a ball. Do you want to come?"

"How could I possibly appear at your dance?" Betta Pilusa grumbled. "Leave me in peace."

When it had become evening, however, she threw off the cat fur and wished for a chambermaid, for whoever possessed the three dresses could wish for whatever she wanted, and the wish would be granted. All at once a chambermaid appeared, and she washed and combed Betta Pilusa. Then she helped Betta Pilusa put on the dress with the sun, moon, and stars and adorned her with her mother's jewels. Now Betta Pilusa wished for a coach and beautiful horses and coachmen in uniforms, and they drove her to the ball. As soon as she appeared in the dance hall, she was so stunningly beautiful that everybody stared at her, and the king left his bride standing and danced the entire evening only with her and gave a golden needle as gift. When the ball was finished, however, she broke away from him and drove off in her coach.

"Follow that lady!" the king cried out to his servants, "and find out where she's going."

But Betta Pilusa threw so many pearls and jewels from her coach that the servants were dazzled and couldn't see where she went. When they were out of sight, the maiden sprang into the chicken coop and hurriedly put on her gray fur coat. Now that the ball had been finished, the king came to her again and said, "Oh, Betta Pilusa, if you could only have seen what a beautiful lady appeared at the ball! And nobody knows where she comes from."

"What do I care about your beautiful women," grumbled Betta Pilusa. "You've woken me from my sleep!"

The next day the king came again and said, "Betta Pilusa, today is the second ball. Do you want to come?"

"Do you want to make a laughingstock out of me?" she said. "Leave me in peace."

However, in the evening she dressed herself up even more beautifully than she was the first time and wore the dress on which all the animals and plants of the sea were to be seen. Moreover, she put on beautiful jewelry, and when she entered the ballroom, everyone was astounded by her stunning beauty, and the king danced with her and gave her a gold watch as a present. Of course, his bride was filled with envy and rage. The king had told his servants in advance to pay careful attention to where the beautiful lady was heading when she bounded away, but once again she threw such precious stones in their eyes that they were dazzled. Consequently, the king became very angry, but it didn't help. The maiden made her way back to the chicken coop and dressed herself in the gray fur coat. Now the king came to

Betta Pilusa once again to tell her about the beautiful lady. In response she just growled at him.

The next morning he came to her again and said, "Betta Pilusa, today there's another ball, and today I must learn who this unknown lady is."

So he called all his servants together and said, "If you don't find out tonight who this lady is, you'll all lose your heads!"

That evening Betta Pilusa put on the dress with all the animals and flowers of the earth on it and adorned herself with her jewelry, and when she appeared at the ball, she was even more beautiful than on the previous evenings. The bride was in complete despair, for the king danced only with the strange woman and gave her a precious ring as gift. When she broke away from him, his servants couldn't follow her because she dazzled them just like she had done before and fled to the chicken coop. This time, however, she did not take off the beautiful dress. Instead, she pulled the gray fur coat over it. When the king heard that she had disappeared again without a trace, he was furious. The servants fell to their knees and told him that they hadn't been able to do anything. The beautiful lady had dazzled them and blinded them. So the king went sadly to Betta Pilusa and said, "Oh, Betta Pilusa, I'm very sick. The beautiful lady disappeared again without a trace."

But she just grumbled, "What do I care about your beautiful lady? Leave me in peace!"

The king became very melancholy and could only think about the beautiful maiden. The next morning, when the cook was kneading the bread that was to be brought to the king's table, Betta Pilusa came into the kitchen and asked him: "Give me a little bit of the dough. I'd like to make a bun for myself."

"Go away," the cook answered. "What do you want to bake with your dirty hands? That would really be beautiful!"

However, she persisted and kept asking so that he finally gave her a piece of dough just to get rid of her. Then she began to knead the bread with her dirty hands while she hid the gold needle that the king had given to her at the ball in the middle of it.

"All right," she said, "now you also have to shove this bread into the oven."

The cook did what she said, and imagine what happened! When the cook returned and opened the oven, all the bread had been burned, but the small dirty little bread that belonged to Betta Pilusa had become a wonderful loaf of white bread. So the cook called Betta Pilusa and said, "Oh, Betta Pilusa, give me your bread so that I can bring it to the king."

"No, no," she answered. "I want to eat my bread myself. What do care if all your bread has been burned."

Then the cook pleaded, "Oh, Betta Pilusa, I'll lose my job if you don't give me your bread. Please give it to me."

So she let herself be persuaded and gave him the bread. The cook sent it right away to the king's table. When the king saw the bread, he said, "Today the bread is really beautiful," and he took a slice of it, and the gold needle fell out. The king recognized it immediately, and he called for the cook.

"Who baked this wonderful bread," he asked.

The cook didn't want to tell the truth and answered, "Your majesty, it was I who baked it."

The king thought for sure that this was probably not true, but he kept silent and kept the gold needle. The next morning Betta Pilusa went into the kitchen, while the cook was kneading the bread and said, "Yesterday, you took away my little bread. So now you have to give me some dough again. But let me tell you something. Today I'm going to eat my own bread."

The cook gave her a piece of dough, and she made bread out of it and stuck the gold watch in the middle. When the time came to take the bread out of the oven, everything had been burned again, and only the dirty dough that Betta Pilusa had kneaded had become a beautiful loaf of white bread. Once again the cook implored Betta Pilusa to give him the bread. She made him beg for a long time, and finally she gave it to him. When the king found the gold watch in the middle of the bread, he summoned the cook and asked him who had baked the bread. The cook replied that it was he who had done it.

The third day Betta Pilusa baked another bread and stuck the ring inside. Just like the other days, the cook's bread was burned, and only the bread with the ring became white and soft. The cook begged Betta Pilusa for her bread, and she refused for a long time. Finally she grumbled but gave it to him. The king was very impatient for he thought, "Today the ring must be in the bread," and he was right. When he cut open the bread, he found the ring. So he summoned the cook and said, "If you don't tell me the truth about who baked the bread, then I'll fire you from your job on the spot."

The cook became frightened and told the king about everything that had happened.

"Send Betta Pilusa up to me right away," the king commanded.

When she appeared before the king, he closed all the doors and said, "For three days I've found a gold needle, a watch, and a ring in the middle of the bread that you baked, all which I had given to the beautiful lady at the ball. You're not the simple maid that you want us to believe you are. So now, tell me who you are."

"I'm just plain Betta Pilusa," she answered, "and I don't know a thing about what you're saying."

Then the king threatened her, "If you don't tell me right away who you are, I'll have your head cut off!"

So, all at once, she threw off the gray cat's fur[140] and appeared as she really was, young and beautiful, in her glistening dress. When the king saw her, he

---

140.   In another version Betta Pilusa had a wooden chest made for her with moveable legs instead of a dress or coat made of cat's fur. She would hide herself in the chest whenever she

recognized her immediately, locked her in his arms, and said, "You are to become my bride."

Then he called his mother to him, and she was delighted to see her son healthy and cheerful again. Soon thereafter they celebrated a beautiful wedding. The other bride had to return to her home. The king and the young queen lived happily and content, but we were left without a cent.

The Golden Bull (1877)[141]
Emmanuel Cosquin

Once upon a time there was a king whose wife was the most beautiful woman in the world. She gave birth only to one very pretty little girl, whose beauty increased from day to day. When the princess became of age to be married, the queen fell ill. Sensing that she was going to die, she called the king to her bed and made him swear to marry again only if he found a woman as beautiful as she herself. He promised, and soon after, she died.

The king didn't wait much time to abandon widowhood and ordered his people to search everywhere for a woman more beautiful than his deceased wife. But all the searches were in vain. Only the king's daughter was more beautiful. So, the king, who was determined to remarry, but also to keep his word, declared that he would marry his daughter.

When the princess heard this news, she was very distressed and ran to her godmother to ask for some means to prevent this marriage. Her godmother advised her to say to the king that, before the wedding, she desired to have a dress the color of the sun. The king had his people search all over, and they finally found a dress the color of the sun. When the king brought her this dress, the princess was in despair: she wanted to flee the chateau, but her godmother advised her to wait and to request a dress the color of the moon. The king succeeded again to obtain a dress that the princess had desired. So, the princess now demanded that she be given a golden bull.

The king had all of the jewels of his kingdom that had been made of gold brought to him—bracelets, necklaces, rings, earrings—and he ordered a goldsmith to make a golden bull. While the goldsmith was occupied by this work, the princess went to him in secret and persuaded him to make the bull hollow. On the day of her wedding, she opened a little door that had been concealed on the side of the bull, and she shut herself inside. When the servants came to look for her, they couldn't find her anywhere. The king sent all his men into the countryside, but they couldn't find her no matter where they looked. So, he fell into a deep depression.

---

fled. Due to her long stay in the forest, the chest became completely covered with moss. She was regarded as a strange-speaking wild beast at the king's court.

141.   "Le Traureau d'Or," *Romania, recueil trimestrielconsacré à l'étude des langues et des littératures romanes* (Paris: 1877).

About this time there was a prince in a neighboring realm who had become sick. One day he whimsically asked his parents for a golden bull. The king, the father of the princess, heard talk of the prince's desire, and he gave up his golden bull because he didn't intend to keep it. The princess was still in her hiding place.

The prince had the golden bull installed in his room so that he could always look at it. Ever since his sickness he refused to have anyone with him, and he ate alone. The servants brought his meals to his room. From the first day the princess took advantage of the times that the prince dozed off to leave the golden bull, take a plate of food, and bring it back with her into her hiding place. She kept doing this day after day. The prince was so astonished to see his plates disappear every day that he changed rooms. However, since he had the golden bull brought into his new room, the plates kept disappearing. Finally, he decided to pretend to sleep so that he could discover the thief.

When the servants brought him his meal, he closed his eyes and feigned that he was asleep. As soon as that happened, the princess quietly got out of the golden bull to grab one of the plates that was on the table. However, when she saw that the prince was awake, she became very frightened. She threw herself at his feet and told him about her adventures.

"Don't be afraid," the prince said to her. "Nobody knows that you're here. From now on I'll order two plates for each thing, one for you and the other for me."

The prince soon became cured and got ready to depart for the war.

"When I return," he told the princess, "I'll knock three times on the golden bull to alert you."

During his absence, the prince's father wanted to show the golden bull to some foreign lords who had come to visit him. One of them wanted to see if the bull was hollow, and he knocked on it three times with his cane. The princess thought that it was the prince who had returned, and as soon as she heard the knocks, she left her hiding place. Indeed, she was totally terrified when she realized that she had been mistaken. The king was very surprised and had her tell her story and said that she could stay at the chateau as long as she desired.

Now, for some time there was a young maiden at the court that the king and queen had raised to marry the prince. When this maiden saw the attention that the princess was receiving from the king and queen, she became mortally jealous. So, one day when she went walking together with the princess in the woods, she led the princess to the edge of a large hole and told her to look down at the bottom. When the princess leaned over to look, the maiden pushed her over and fled.

The princess fell down into the hole without hurting herself, and she cried for help. A coalman who was passing nearby heard her cries, and he pulled her out of the hole and returned her to the chateau. It was just at that time that the war had ended, and the prince had returned home. Everyone was preparing for his wedding with his fiancée. A large fire of celebration had been set aflame in front of the chateau. When the prince learned what the maiden had done to the princess, he ordered the wicked girl to be thrown into the fire. Then he married the beautiful princess. His father let the father of the princess know that she was married. He took it well, and that was for the best.

Maria Wood (1877)[142]
Rachel Busk

They say, there was a king, whose wife, when she came to him, said to him,

"When I am dead, you will want to marry again; but take my advice: marry no woman but her whose foot my shoe fits."

However, she said this because the shoe was under a spell, and would fit no one whom he could marry.

Meanwhile, the king caused the shoe to be tried on all manner of women; and when the answer always was that it would fit none of them, he grew quite bewildered and strange in his mind.

After some years had passed, his young daughter, having grown up to girl's estate, came to him one day, saying,

"Oh, papa; only think! Mamma's shoe just fits me!"

"Does it!" replied the simple king; "then I must marry you."

"Oh, that cannot be, papa," said the girl, and ran away.

But the simple king was so possessed with the idea that he must marry the woman whom his wife's shoe fitted, that he sent for her every day and said the same thing.

But the queen had not said that he should marry the woman whom her shoe fitted, but that he should not marry any whom it did not fit.

When the princess found that he persevered in his silly caprice, she said at last,

"Papa, if I am to do what you say, you must do something for me first."

"Agreed, my child," replied the king; "you have only to speak."

"Then, before I marry," said the girl, "I want a lot of things, but I will begin with one at a time. First, I want a dress of the colour of a beautiful noontide sky, but all covered with stars, like the sky at midnight, and furnished with a parure (jewels or jewelry that match) to suit it."

Such a dress the king had made and brought to her.

"Next," said the princess, "I want a dress of the colour of the sea all covered with golden fishes, with a fitting parure."

Such a dress the king had made, and brought to her.

"Next," said the princess, "I want a dress of a dark blue, all covered with gold embroidery and spangled with silver bells, and with a parure to match."

Such a dress the king had made and brought to her.

---

142. *The Folk-Lore of Rome. Collected by Word of Mouth from the People* (London: Longmans, Green, 1874).

"These are all very good," said the princess, "but now you must send for the most cunning artificer in your whole kingdom, and let him make me a figure of an old woman just like life, fitted with all sorts of springs to make it move and walk when one gets inside, just like a real woman."

Such a figure the king had made, and brought it to the princess.

"That is just the sort of figure I wanted," said she; "and now I don't want anything more."

And the simple king went away quite happy.

As soon as she was alone, however, the princess packed all three dresses and many of her other dresses, and all her jewelry and a large sum of money, inside the figure of the wood woman, and then she got into it and walked away. No one seeing an old woman walking out of the palace thought she had anything to do with the princess, and thus she got far away without anyone thinking of stopping her.

On, on, on she wandered till she came to the palace of a great king, and just at the time that the king's son was coming in from hunting.

"Have you a place in all this fine palace to take in a poor old body?" whined the princess inside the figure of the old woman.

"No, no! Get out of the way! How dare you come in the way of the prince!" said the servants, and drove her away.

But the prince took compassion on her, and called her to him.

"What's your name, good woman?" said the prince.

"Maria Wood is my name, your Highness," replied the princess.

"And what can you do, since you ask for a place?"

"Oh, I can do many things. First, I understand all about poultry, and then—"

"That'll do," replied the prince; "take her, and let her be the henwife, and let her have food and lodging, and all she wants."

So they gave her a little hut on the borders of the forest, and set her to tend the poultry.

But the prince as he went out hunting often passed by her hut, and when she saw him pass, she never failed to come out and salute him, and now and then he would stop his horse and spend a few moments to gossip with her.

Before long it was Carneval time, and as the prince came by, Maria Wood came out and wished him a "good Carneval."

The prince's mind was on the pleasure that he expected and stopped his horse and said: "To-morrow, you know, we have the first day of the feast."

"To be sure I know it; and how I should like to be there: won't you take me?" answered Maria Wood.

"You shameless old woman," replied the prince, "to think of your wanting to go to a *festino* at your time of life!" and he gave her a cut with his whip.

The next day Maria put on her dress of the colour of the noontide sky, covered with stars like the sky at midnight, with the parure made to wear with it, and came to the feast. Every lady made way for her because of her dazzling appearance, and the prince alone dared to ask her to dance. With her he danced all the evening, and fairly fell in love with her, nor could he leave her side; and as they sat together, he took the ring off his own finger and put it on to her hand. She appeared equally satisfied with his attentions, and seemed to desire no other partner. Only when he tried to gather from her whence she was, she would only say she came from the country of Whipblow, which set the prince wondering very much, as he had never heard of such a country. At the end of the ball, the prince sent his attendants to watch her so that he might learn where she lived, but she disappeared so swiftly that it was impossible for them to tell what had become of her.

When the prince came by Maria Wood's hut next day, she did not fail to wish him again a "good Carneval."

"To-morrow we have the second *festino*, you know," said the prince.

"Well I know it," replied Maria Wood; "shouldn't I like to go! Won't you take me?"

"You contemptible old woman to talk in that way!" exclaimed the prince. "You ought to know better!" and he struck her with his boot.

Next night Maria put on her dress of the colour of the sea, covered all over with gold fishes, and the parure made to wear with it, and went to the feast. The prince recognised her at once, and claimed her for his partner all the evening, nor did she seem to wish for any other, only when he tried to learn from her whence she was, she would only say she came from the country of Bootkick. The prince could not remember ever to have heard of the Bootkick country, and thought she meant to laugh at him; however, he ordered his attendants to make more haste this night in following her; but what diligence soever they used she was too swift for them.

The next time the prince came by Maria Wood's hut, she did not fail to wish him again a "good Carneval."

"To-morrow we have the last *festino*!" exclaimed he, with a touch of sadness, for he remembered it was the last of the happy evenings that he could feel sure of seeing his unknown fair lady.

"Ah! you must take me. But, what'll you say if I come to it in spite of you?" answered Maria Wood.

"You incorrigible old woman!" exclaimed the prince; "you provoke me so with your nonsense, I really cannot keep my hand off you," and he gave her a slap.

The next night Maria Wood put on her dress of a dark blue, all covered with gold embroidery and spangled with silver bells, and the parure made to wear with it. The prince claimed her as his partner for the evening as before, nor did she seem to wish for any other, only when he wanted to learn from her whence she was, all she would say was that she came from Slapland. This night the prince told his servants to make more haste following her, or he would discharge them all. But they answered, "It is useless to attempt the thing, as no mortal can equal her in swiftness."

After this, the prince fell ill of his disappointment, because he saw no hope of hearing any more of the fair lady with whom he had spent three happy evenings, nor could any doctor find any remedy for his sickness.

Then Maria Wood sent him word, saying, "Though the prince's physicians cannot help him, let him but take a cup of broth of my making, and he will immediately be healed."

"Nonsense! how can a cup of broth, or how can any medicament help me!" exclaimed the prince. "There is no cure for my ailment."

Again Maria Wood sent the same message; but the prince said angrily, "Tell the silly old thing to hold her tongue; she doesn't know what she's talking about."

But again, the third time, Maria Wood sent to him, saying, "Let the prince but take a cup of broth of my making, and he will immediately be healed."

By this time the prince was so weary that he did not take the trouble to refuse. The servants, finding him so depressed began to fear that he was sinking, and they called to Maria Wood to make her broth. Though they had little faith in her promise, they knew not what else to try. So Maria Wood made the cup of broth she had promised, and they put it down beside the prince.

Presently the whole palace was roused; the prince had started up in bed, and was shouting,

"Bring hither Maria Wood! Quick! Bring hither Maria Wood!"

So they ran and fetched Maria Wood, wondering what could have happened to bring about so great a change in the prince. But the truth was that Maria had put into the cup of broth the ring the prince had put on her finger the first night of the feast, and when he began to take the broth, he found the ring with the spoon. When he saw the ring, he knew at once that Maria Wood could tell him where to find his fair partner.

"Wait a bit! There's plenty of time!" said Maria, when the servant came to fetch her in all haste; and she took her time to put on her dress of the colour of the noontide sky.

The prince was beside himself with joy when he saw her, and would have the betrothal celebrated that very day.

Translated by Rachel Busk.

The Princess Who Would Not Marry Her Father (1882)[143]
Consiglieri Pedroso

There was once a king and a queen. But a few years after their marriage the queen died. At her death she placed a ring on a table and bade the king marry whomsoever that ring should fit. It happened that their daughter, the princess, approached the table by chance, saw the ring, and tried it on. She then ran to the

143. *Portuguese Folk-Tales*, trans. Henriqueta Monteiro (London: Folklore Society, 1882).

king, her father, and said: "Sire, do you know that a ring which I found on the table fits me as though it had been made expressly for me! . . ."

On hearing this, the king replied: "Oh my daughter, you will have to marry me, because your mother, before she died, expressed a wish that I should marry whoever this ring would fit."

Greatly depressed, the princess shut herself up in a room which had the window looking into the garden, and gave vent to her grief. Soon, however, a little old woman appeared to her, and asked her: "Why do you weep, royal lady?"

To which the princess replied: "Well, what else can I do? My father says that I must marry him."

The little old woman then said to her: "Listen to me, royal lady, go and tell your father that you will only marry him on condition that he buys you a dress of the color of the stars in the heavens."

And after saying this she departed. The princess then went up to the king, who asked her: "Well, my daughter, are we to be married?"

To which she replied: "Well, father, I shall marry you when you bring me a dress of the color of the stars in the heavens."

On hearing this, the king went out, bought her the dress, and gave it to her ready made. The princess again went to her room to cry. The little old woman again appeared to her, and asked her, "What ails you, royal lady?"

She replied: "What can ail me! My father has bought me the dress I asked him for, and he wishes to marry me."

The old lady rejoined: "Never mind, you must now ask him to bring you a dress of the color of the flowers that grow in the fields."

The princess again went to her father and told him that she could only marry him on condition of his bringing her a robe of the color of wild flowers. The king bought the dress and gave it to her made up and quite ready to be put on. The princess, again in trouble, retired to her chamber to weep. The old lady again appeared and demanded: "What ails you, royal lady?"

To which the princess replied: "What can ail me, indeed! My father has bought me the second robe and is determined to marry me."

The good old lady rejoined: "Ask your father now for a robe of various colors."

The princess did so, and asked for a robe of various colors, and the king bought her the dress and brought it to her ready to be put on. The princess returned to her chamber to weep over her new trouble, but the little old woman came to her and asked her what troubled her. The princess replied that the king had bought her the third robe she required of him and was now determined that the marriage should take place.

"And what should I do to prevent it?" inquired the princess.

"Royal lady," the little old woman replied, "you must now send for a carpenter and order him to make you a dress of wood. Get inside it, and go to the palace of the king who lives yonder and requires a servant to tend the ducks."

The princess did as she was told and had a dress made of wood. She put all her jewels and everything else she would require inside, and got inside it herself. Then, one fine day she ran away.

She walked on and on until she arrived at the said palace. She knocked at the door and told the servants to ask his majesty the king if he required a maid to mind the ducks. He replied that he did and asked her what her name was. She rejoined that her name was Maria do Pau, and after this the king sent her to tend the ducks which were in a field next to the palace gardens. The moment the princess reached it, she took off everything she had on, and the wooden dress also. She washed herself, for she was travel-stained, and then put on the richest robe she had, which was the one the color of the stars. The king was taking a walk in the garden, and noticed a lovely maiden who was in the field driving the ducks, and heard her repeat:

"Ducks here, ducks there,
The daughter of a king tends the ducks,
A thing never seen before!"

When she had finished saying this, she killed one of the ducks, then took off her robes, and again got into her wooden dress. At night she went indoors, saying: "Oh king! I have killed one of the ducks."

The king asked her: "Maria do Pau, who was that beautiful maiden so splendidly robed that minded the ducks?"

To this she said: "Indeed there was no one else there but myself in disguise."

Next day the king again sent Maria do Pau to tend the ducks. And when she was in the field, she did the same thing as the day before. She took off her wooden dress, washed and combed herself carefully, put on the robe the color of wild flowers, and went about driving the ducks, saying as before:

"Ducks here, ducks there,
The daughter of a king tends the ducks,
A thing never seen before."

Afterward she killed another duck. Next day she did as the day before, put on the robe of many colors, and killed another duck. In the evening when she went indoors, the king said to her: "I do not wish you to take care of the ducks any longer, for every day we find a duck has been killed! Now you shall remain locked up in the house. We are to have a feast which will last three days, but I promise you that you shall not enjoy it, for I shall not allow you to go to it."

To this she said to the king: "Oh, my liege! Do let me go."

But the king replied, "No, indeed, you shall not go."

On the first day of the feast she again begged of the king to allow her to repair to it, and his majesty replied: "God, preserve me! What would be the consequences of taking Maria do Pau to the feast!"

The king put on his gala robes and then sent for her to his chamber He asked her what dress she would like to put on, and the princess replied by asking him to give her a pair of boots, which the king threw at her and took his departure for the feast. She then repaired to her chamber and removed from inside the dress made of wool a wand she had, which the little old woman, who was a fairy, had given her, and holding it up she said: "Oh! divining rod, by the virtue that God gave you, send me here the best royal carriage, which is the very one that took the king to the feast."

The carriage was instantly in sight, and entering it she made her appearance at the feast, in the robe of the color of the stars. The king, who had his eyes continually fixed upon her, went out to the guards and told them not to allow the maiden to pass. But when she wished to get out, she threw them a bag of money, and the guards allowed her to pass, but they asked her to what country she belonged, to which she replied that she came from the land of the boot.

The king went home, and on arriving found the princess was already in the palace. The king, who wished to find out whether the lovely maiden, whom he had seen at the feast, could possibly be Maria do Pau, went to see if she was safe in her chamber, and afterwards sent for her and said to her: "Oh, Maria do Pau! Do you happen to know where the land of the boot is situated?"

"Oh, my liege! Do not come troubling me with your questions. Is it possible that your majesty does not know where the land of the boot is situated?"

The king replied: "I do not. A maiden was at the feast. I asked her where she came from, and she said that she came from the land of the boot, but I do not know where that is."

Next day the king again attended the feast, but before leaving he said to Maria do Pau: "You shall not be allowed to go there."

"Do allow me for once," replied she.

The king then asked her to give him the towel, and as she presented him with it, he threw it at her and departed for the feast. The princess repaired to her room, struck the divining rod, and put on the robe, which was the color of the wild flowers. The king, who had been charmed with her on the first day of the feast, now admired her all the more, because she appeared more beautiful than ever. He went out to the guards and told them to ask the beautiful maiden when she passed to what country she belonged. And when she went out, she informed them that she was from the land of the towel. As soon as the king was told of this, he returned to the palace to think over and try to guess, if possible, where the land of the towel could be situated. And when he arrived at the palace, the first thing he did was to ask his maid if she knew where the land of the towel could be found. To his inquiries she replied: "Well, well! Here comes a king who does not know and cannot tell, where the land of the towel is situated! Neither do I know."

The king now said: "Oh Maria do Pau, every time that I have been at the feast I have seen such a pretty maiden. If the one I saw yesterday was beautiful, the one of to-day is perfectly lovely, and much more charming than the first."

Next day as the king was on the point of going out, the princess said to his majesty: "Oh, my liege! Let me go to the feast so that I may see the maiden that is so beautiful!"

The king replied: "God, preserve me! What would be the result if I were to present you before that maiden?"

After which he asked her to give him his walking-stick, and as he was going out, he struck her with it. He went to the feast, and when he was there, the princess presented herself before him in the robe of many colors. If on the previous days she appeared most beautiful, on this day of the feast she looked perfectly ravishing and more interesting than ever. The king fixed his eyes upon her so as not to lose sight of her, as he wished to see her go out, and follow her to where she lived, as it was the last day of the feast. But the king missed seeing her depart after all, and he could find her nowhere. He went to the guards and asked them what she had said, but the guards replied that she had come from the land of the walking-stick. The king returned to the palace and inquired of his maid where the land of the walking-stick could be found, but she replied: "Oh, my liege! How could I know where the land of the walking-stick is situated? Does not my liege know? Well, neither do I."

The king again asked her: "Do you really not know? To-day I again saw the same girl who is so beautiful, but I begin to think it cannot be the same one every time, because at one time she says that she comes from the land of the boot, next time that she is from the land of the towel, and lastly she says she is from the land of the walking-stick.

The princess repaired to her room, washed and combed herself, and dressed herself in the robe she had on the first day of the feast. The king went to look through the key-hole to find out why she was so long away and remained in her chamber so quiet, and also to see what she was at. He saw a lovely maiden, the same one who had appeared at the feast dressed in the robe the color of the stars in the heavens, sitting down busy with some embroidery. When the princess left her chamber to repair to the dinner-table again disguised, the king said to her: "Oh, Maria do Pau, you must embroider a pair of shoes for me!"

She replied: "Do I know how to embroider shoes?"

And she left the parlor to go back to her chamber. Every day she put on one of the dresses she had worn at the feast, and on the last day she robed herself with the one of many colors. The king begged her every day to embroider him a pair of shoes, and she always returned the same answer. He had a key made to open the princess's room, and one day when he saw through the key-hole that she was robed in her best, he suddenly opened the door without her perceiving it and entered the chamber. The princess startled, and very much frightened, tried to run away, but the king said to her:

"Do not be troubled, for you shall marry me! But I wish you first to tell me your history, and why it is that you wear a wooden dress."

The princess recounted all the events of her life, and the king married her. The king next sent for the little old woman, who had given her the wand, to come and live in the palace, but she refused to live there because she was a fairy.

Translated by Henriqueta Monteiro.

Catskin (1890)[144]

Joseph Jacobs

Well, there was once a gentleman who had fine lands and houses, and he very much wanted to have a son to be heir to them. So when his wife brought him a daughter, bonny as bonny could be, he cared naught for her, and said, "Let me never see her face."

So she grew up a bonny girl, though her father never set eyes on her till she was fifteen years old and was ready to be married. But her father said, "Let her marry the first that comes for her."

And when this was known, who should be first but a nasty rough old man. So she didn't know what to do, and went to the henwife and asked her advice. The henwife said, "Say you will not take him unless they give you a coat of silver cloth."

Well, they gave her a coat of silver cloth, but she wouldn't take him for all that, but went again to the henwife, who said, "Say you will not take him unless they give you a coat of beaten gold."

Well, they gave her a coat of beaten gold, but still she would not take him, but went to the henwife, who said, "Say you will not take him unless they give you a coat made of the feathers of all the birds of the air."

So they sent a man with a great heap of peas; and the man cried to all the birds of the air, "Each bird take a pea, and put down a feather."

So each bird took a pea and put down one of its feathers; and they took all the feathers and made a coat of them and gave it to her; but still she would not, but asked the henwife once again, who said, "Say they must first make you a coat of catskin."

So they made her a coat of catskin; and she put it on, and tied up her other coats, and ran away into the woods.

So she went along and went along and went along, till she came to the end of the wood, and saw a fine castle. So there she hid her fine dresses, and went up to the castle gates, and asked for work. The lady of the castle saw her, and told her, "I'm sorry I have no better place, but if you like, you may be our scullion." So down she went into the kitchen, and they called her Catskin, because of her dress. But the cook was very cruel to her, and she led her a sad life.

Well, it happened soon after that the young lord of the castle was coming home, and there was to be a grand ball in honour of the occasion. And when

---

144. *English Fairy Tales* (London: David Nutt, 1890).

they were speaking about it among the servants, "Dear me, Mrs. Cook," said Catskin, "how much I should like to go."

"What! you dirty impudent slut," said the cook, "you go among all the fine lords and ladies with your filthy catskin? A fine figure you'd cut!" And with that she took a basin of water and dashed it into Catskin's face. But she only briskly shook her ears, and said nothing.

When the day of the ball arrived, Catskin slipped out of the house and went to the edge of the forest where she had hidden her dresses. So she bathed herself in a crystal waterfall, and then put on her coat of silver cloth, and hastened away to the ball. As soon as she entered, all were overcome by her beauty and grace, while the young lord at once lost his heart to her. He asked her to be his partner for the first dance, and he would dance with none other the livelong night.

When it came to parting time, the young lord said, "Pray tell me, fair maid, where you live." But Catskin curtsied and said:

"Kind sir, if the truth I must tell,
At the sign of the 'Basin of Water' I dwell."

Then she flew from the castle and donned her catskin robe again, and slipped into the scullery again, unbeknown to the cook.

The young lord went the very next day to his mother, the lady of the castle, and declared he would wed none other but the lady of the silver dress, and would never rest till he had found her. So another ball was soon arranged for in hope that the beautiful maid would appear again.

So Catskin said to the cook, "Oh, how I should like to go!"

Whereupon the cook screamed out in a rage, "What, you, you dirty impudent slut! You would cut a fine figure among all the fine lords and ladies." And with that she up with a ladle and broke it across Catskin's back. But she only shook her ears, and ran off to the forest, where she first of all bathed, and then put on her coat of beaten gold, and off she went to the ballroom.

As soon as she entered all eyes were upon her; and the young lord soon recognised her as the lady of the "Basin of Water," and claimed her hand for the first dance, and did not leave her till the last. When that came, he again asked her where she lived. But all that she would say was:

"Kind sir, if the truth I must tell,
At the sign of the 'Broken Ladle' I dwell,"

and with that she curtsied, and flew from the ball, off with her golden robe, on with her catskin, and into the scullery without the cook's knowing.

Next day when the young lord could not find where was the sign of the "Basin of Water," or of the "Broken Ladle," he begged his mother to have another grand ball, so that he might meet the beautiful maid once more.

All happened as before. Catskin told the cook how much she would like to go to the ball, the cook called her "a dirty slut," and broke the skimmer across her head.

But she only shook her ears and went off to the forest, where she first bathed in the crystal spring, and then donned her coat of feathers, and so off to the ballroom.

When she entered every one was surprised at so beautiful a face and form dressed in so rich and rare a dress; but the young lord soon recognised his beautiful sweetheart, and would dance with none but her the whole evening. When the ball came to an end, he pressed her to tell him where she lived, but all she would answer was:

"Kind sir, if the truth I must tell,
At the sign of the 'Broken Skimmer' I dwell,"

and with that she curtsied, and was off to the forest. But this time the young lord followed her, and watched her change her fine dress of feathers for her catskin dress, and then he knew her for his own scullery-maid.

Next day he went to his mother, the lady of the castle, and told her that he wished to marry the scullery-maid, Catskin.

"Never," said the lady, and rushed from the room.

Well, the young lord was so grieved at that, that he took to his bed and was very ill. The doctor tried to cure him, but he would not take any medicine unless from the hands of Catskin. So the doctor went to the lady of the castle and told her that her son would die if she did not consent to his marriage with Catskin. So she had to give way and summoned Catskin to her. Now she put on her coat of beaten gold and went to the lady, who soon was glad to wed her son to so beautiful a maid.

Well, so they were married, and after a time a dear little son came to them and grew up a bonny lad. One day, when he was four years old, a beggar woman came to the door, so Lady Catskin gave some money to the little lord and told him to go and give it to the beggar woman. So he went and gave it, but put it into the hand of the woman's child, who leant forward and kissed the little lord. Now the wicked old cook—why hadn't she been sent away?—was looking on, so she said, "Only see how beggars' brats take to one another."

This insult went to Catskin's heart, so she went to her husband, the young lord, and told him all about her father and begged he would go and find out what had become of her parents. So they set out in the lord's grand coach and travelled through the forest till they came to Catskin's father's house, and put up at an inn near, where Catskin stopped, while her husband went to see if her father would own her.

Now her father had never had any other child, and his wife had died. So, he was all alone in the world and sate moping and miserable. When the young lord came in he hardly looked up, till he saw a chair close to him, and asked him, "Pray, sir, had you not once a young daughter whom you would never see or own?"

The old gentleman said, "It is true; I am a hardened sinner. But I would give all my worldly goods if I could but see her once before I die."

Then the young lord told him what had happened to Catskin, and took him to the inn, and brought his father-in-law to his own castle, where they lived happily ever afterwards.

12. WILD AND GOLDEN MEN

ATU 502 AND ATU 314—THE WILD MAN AND GOLDENER

These two tale types generally blend together to form hybrid tales that either focus on a mysterious wild man, a savage, whom people seek to capture and tame, or on a young boy, who is banished from his family/kingdom because he helps an imprisoned savage, who reciprocates by mentoring him through magic so that he rises to become a champion knight. Many other folk motifs have been added by storytellers and writers since the medieval period, and most of the stories in the two cycles of the wild man and the goldener (the golden youth) are woven together by themes of compassion, freedom, initiation, reciprocity, and humility. A young boy, out of pity or naiveté, frees a wild man, who returns to nature or an unknown domain. He is joined by the young boy because his father, often a king or aristocrat, seeks to punish him by death for having freed the wild man. In reciprocity the wild man promises to help the boy, who sometimes makes a mistake causing his hair to turn to gold. The boy often takes a humble job as gardener or shepherd in disguise and works for a king. The king's daughter falls in love with him and perceives that he is more than what he appears to be. Frequently, the king goes off to a war that he may lose. So, the boy calls upon the wild man for help so that he may come to the rescue of the king. The wild man responds by giving him three different horses and the armor of a knight. The disguised boy is victorious and eventually claims the princess for his bride. Sometimes the boy must rescue the princess from a dragon or monster. The wild man disappears, and we never learn who he is. The prince marries the princess and is often reunited with his father.

Literary sources can be found in medieval romances and stories, especially about the wild man. The first fully developed fairy tale was Giovan Francesco Straparola's "Guerrino and the Savage Man" in *Le Piacevoli Notti* (1550). Other tales that preceded the Grimms' "The Wild Man" are Jean de Mailly's "Prince Guerini" in *Les Illustres fées, contes galans* (1698) and Christian August Vulpius' "The Iron Man, or the Reward of Obedience" in *Ammenmärchen* (1791).

In 1815, the Brothers Grimm published "The Wild Man" in dialect, a tale that they had obtained from Jenny von Dröste-Hülshoff, a member of a prominent aristocratic family in Münster. The Grimms kept publishing this tale in the following editions of the *Children and Household Tales* until 1843. Then they eliminated it in favor of "Iron Hans," a tale which Wilhelm virtually wrote by himself using the dialect version of "The Wild Man," another oral story that the Grimms had collected from a member of the Hassenpflug family of Kassel, and Friedmund von Arnim's "Iron Hans" in *Hundert neue Mährchen im Gebirge gesammelt* (1844). Wilhelm synthesized literary and oral versions that folklorists have traced to the two basic tale types 314 and 502. Given the evidence we have from the Brothers Grimm, Wilhelm's "Iron Hans" is mainly based on tales that focus on the golden-haired youth. As usual, there is a debate among folklorists about the origins of this tale type. Some place the tale's creation in India, while others argue that it originated during the latter part of the Roman Empire. However, almost all folklorists agree that, as far as Wilhelm Grimm's version is concerned, the major plot line and motifs of the tale were formed during the Middle Ages in Europe. Furthermore, they may have been influenced by a literary tradition, in particular a twelfth-century romance entitled *Robert der Teufel* (*Robert the Devil*), which gave rise to many different literary and oral versions in medieval Europe.

In *Robert der Teufel*, Count Hubertus of Normandy and his wife become skeptical about God's powers because they cannot conceive a child. They lose their faith in the Almighty, and the wife says that she would accept a child even if it were provided by the devil. Indeed, she gives birth to a son named Robert, who is possessed by the devil and has extraordinary powers. No one can control him, and he cannot master himself. Soon he is known by the name of Robert the Devil. When he turns seventeen and is made a knight, he terrorizes the region and commits many crimes. However, all this changes when his mother tells him to kill her because she is so ashamed of him and herself. She reveals the story of his birth, and he decides to make a pilgrimage to Rome. As repentance for his crimes, a holy hermit tells him that he must live the life of a fool or madman. So Robert travels to the emperor's court, where he acts the fool and lives with dogs. Only the emperor's daughter, who cannot speak, knows that Robert is someone other than he pretends to be. After seven years, a treacherous seneschal attempts to overthrow the emperor with the help of the Saracens. God commands Robert to help the emperor and gives him white armor and a white horse. As a result, Robert saves the Holy Roman Empire, and the emperor's daughter reveals that he is the true savior when his identity is doubted. Eventually, Robert marries the emperor's daughter and returns to Normandy, where he and his wife give birth to a son named Richard.

As can be seen from this brief summary, this popular romance contains most of the important motifs and features that one can find not only in the Grimms' "Iron Hans" but also in Straparola's "Guerrino" and Mailly's imitation "Prince Guerini." All these tales are a blend of Christian legendary material and medieval folk tales dealing with the initiation of a golden-haired youth, who becomes a stalwart knight, and the mysterious wild man, who may either be a friend, mentor, or demonic figure. In some cases, as in Ignaz and Josef Zingerele's "Goldener," it is a wise woman of the forest and her magic book that assist a poor and needy young man. There are hundreds of oral versions of this tale in France, Germany, and the Scandinavian countries, and they have also spread to North America.

******

The Wild Man (1815)[145]

Jacob and Wilhelm Grimm

Once upon a time there was a wild man who was under a spell, and he went into the gardens and wheat fields of the peasants and destroyed everything. The peasants complained to their lord and told him that they could no longer pay their rent. So the lord summoned all the huntsmen and announced that whoever caught the wild beast would receive a great reward. Then an old huntsman arrived and said he would catch the beast. He took a bottle of brandy, a bottle of wine, and a bottle of beer and set the bottles on the bank of a river, where the beast went every day. After doing that the huntsman hid behind a tree. Soon the beast came and drank up all the bottles. He licked his mouth and looked around to make sure everything was all right. Since he was drunk, he lay down and fell asleep. The huntsman went over to him and tied his hands and feet. Then he woke the wild man and said, "You, wild man, come with me, and you'll get such things to drink every day."

The huntsman took the wild man to the royal castle, and they put him into a cage. The lord then visited the other noblemen and invited them to see what kind of beast he had caught. Meanwhile, one of his sons was playing with a ball, and he let it fall into the cage.

"Wild man," said the child, "throw the ball back out to me."

"You've got to fetch the ball yourself," said the wild man.

"All right," said the child. "But I don't have the key."

"Then see to it that you fetch it from your mother's pocket."

The boy stole the key, opened the cage, and the wild man ran out.

"Oh, wild man!" the boy began to scream. "You've got to stay here, or else I'll get a beating!"

The wild man picked up the boy and carried him on his back into the wilderness. So the wild man disappeared, and the child was lost.

The wild man dressed the boy in a coarse jacket and sent him to the gardener at the emperor's court, where he was to ask whether they could use a gardener's helper. The gardener said yes, but the boy was so grimy and crusty that the others would not sleep near him. The boy replied that he would sleep in the straw. Then early each morning he went into the garden, and the wild man came to him and said, "Now wash yourself, now comb yourself."

And the wild man made the garden so beautiful that even the gardener himself could not do any better. The princess saw the handsome boy every morning, and she told the gardener to have his little assistant bring her a bunch of flowers. When the boy came, she asked him about his origins, and he replied that he didn't know them. Then she gave him a roast chicken full of ducats. When he

145. "De wilde Mann," *Kinder- und Haus-Märchen. Gesammelt durch die Brüder Grimm*, 2 vols. (Berlin: Realschulbuchhandlung, 1812/1815).

got back to the gardener, he gave him the money and said, "What should I do with it? You can use it."

Later he was ordered to bring the princess another bunch of flowers, and she gave him a duck full of ducats, which he also gave to the gardener. On a third occasion she gave him a goose full of ducats, which the young man again passed on to the gardener. The princess thought that he had money, and yet he had nothing. They got married in secret, and her parents became angry and made her work in the brewery, and she also had to support herself by spinning. The young man would go into the kitchen and help the cook prepare the roast, and sometimes he stole a piece of meat and brought it to his wife.

Soon there was a mighty war in England, and the emperor and all the great armies had to travel there. The young man said he wanted to go there too and asked whether they had a horse in the stables for him. They told him that they had one that ran on three legs that would be good enough for him. So he mounted the horse, and the horse went off, *clippety-clop*. Then the wild man approached him, and he opened a large mountain in which there was a regiment of a thousand soldiers and officers. The young man put on some fine clothes and was given a magnificent horse. Then he set out for the war in England with all his men. The emperor welcomed him in a friendly way and asked him to lend his support. The young man defeated everyone and won the battle, whereupon the emperor extended his thanks to him and asked him where his army came from.

"Don't ask me that," he replied. "I can't tell you."

Then he rode off with his army and left England. The wild man approached him again and took all the men back into the mountain. The young man mounted his three-legged horse and went back home.

"Here comes our hobbley-hop again with his three-legged horse!" the people cried out, and they asked, "Were you lying behind the hedge and sleeping?"

"Well," he said, "if I hadn't been in England, things would not have gone well for the emperor!"

"Boy," they said, "be quiet, or else the gardener will really let you have it!"

The second time, everything happened as it had before, and the third time, the young man won the whole battle, but he was wounded in the arm. The emperor took his kerchief, wrapped the wound, and tried to make the boy stay with him.

"No, I'm not going to stay with you. It's of no concern to you who I am."

Once again the wild man approached the young man and took all his men back into the mountain. The young man mounted his three-legged horse once more and went back home. The people began laughing and said, "Here comes our hobbley-hop again. Where were you lying asleep this time?"

"Truthfully, I wasn't sleeping," he said. "England is totally defeated, and there's finally peace."

Now, the emperor talked about the handsome knight who provided support, and the young man said to the emperor, "If I hadn't been with you, it wouldn't have turned out so well."

The emperor wanted to give him a beating, but the young man said, "Stop! If you don't believe me, let me show you my arm."

When he revealed his arm and the emperor saw the wound, he was amazed and said, "Perhaps you are the Lord Himself or an angel whom God has sent to me," and he asked his pardon for treating him so cruelly and gave him a whole kingdom.

Now the wild man was released from the magic spell and stood there as a great king and told his entire story. The mountain turned into a royal castle, and the young man went there with his wife, and they lived in the castle happily until the end of their days.

Iron Hans (1857)[146]
Jacob and Wilhelm Grimm

Once upon a time there was a king who had a large forest near his castle, and in the forest all sorts of game could be found. One day he sent a huntsman there to shoot a deer, but he did not return. "Perhaps he met with an accident," said the king, and on the following day he sent two other huntsmen into the forest to look for the missing one, but they, too, did not return. So, on the third day the king assembled all his huntsmen and said to them, "Comb the entire forest and don't stop until you've found all three of them." But these huntsmen were never seen again, nor were the dogs from the pack of hounds that went with them. From that time on nobody dared venture into the forest, and it stood there solemnly and desolately, and only every now and then could an eagle or a hawk be seen flying over it.

This situation lasted for many years, and then a huntsman, a stranger, called on the king seeking employment and offered to go into the dangerous forest. However, the king wouldn't give his consent and said, "The forest is enchanted, and I'm afraid the same thing would happen to you that happened to the others, and you wouldn't return."

"Sire," replied the huntsman, "I'll go at my own risk. I don't know the meaning of fear."

So the huntsman went into the forest with his dog. It was not long before the dog picked up the scent of an animal and wanted to chase it, but after the dog had run just a few steps, it came upon a deep pool and could go no further. Then a long, bare arm reached out of the water, grabbed the dog, and dragged it down. When the huntsman saw that, he went back to the castle and got three men to come with buckets and to bale the water out of

146. "Der Eisenhans," *Kinder- und Hausmärchen gesammelt durch die Brüder Grimm*, 7th ed., 3 vols. (Göttingen: Verlag der Dieterich'schen Buchhandlung, 1857).

the pool. When they could see to the bottom, they discovered a wild man lying there. His body was as brown as rusty iron, and his hair hung over his face down to his knees. They bound the wild man with rope and led him away to the castle, where everyone was amazed by him. The king had him put into an iron cage in the castle courtyard and forbade anyone to open the cage under the penalty of death. The queen herself was given the key for safekeeping. From then on the forest was safe, and everyone could go into it again.

One day the king's son, who was eight years old, was playing in the courtyard, and as he was playing, his golden ball fell into the cage. The boy ran over to it and said, "Give me back my ball."

"Only if you open the door," answered the man.

"No," said the boy. "I won't do that. The king has forbidden it." And he ran away.

The next day he came again and demanded his ball. The wild man said, "Open my door," but the boy refused.

On the third day, when the king was out hunting, the boy returned and said, "Even if I wanted to, I couldn't because I don't have the key."

"It's under your mother's pillow," said the wild man. "You can get it."

"The boy, who wanted to have the ball again, threw all caution to the winds and brought him the key. It was difficult to open the door, and the boy's finger got stuck. When the door was open, the wild man stepped out, gave him the golden ball, and hurried away. But the boy became afraid, screamed, and called after him, "Oh, wild man, don't go away; otherwise, I'll get a beating!"

The wild man turned back, lifted him onto his shoulders, and sped into the forest with swift strides. When the king came home, he noticed the empty cage and asked the queen what had happened. She knew nothing about it and looked for the key, but it was gone. Then she called the boy, but nobody answered. The king sent people out into the fields to search for him, but they did not find him. By then it was not all that difficult for the king to guess what had happened, and the royal court fell into a period of deep mourning.

When the wild man reached the dark forest again, he set the boy down from his shoulders and said to him, "You won't see your father and mother again, but I'll keep you with me because you set me free, and I feel sorry for you. If you do everything that I tell you, you'll be all right. I have plenty of treasures and gold, more than anyone in the world."

He made a bed out of moss for the boy, and the child fell asleep on it. The next morning, the man led him to a spring and said, "Do you see this golden spring? It's bright and crystal clear. I want you to sit there and make sure that nothing falls in; otherwise, it will become polluted. I'll come every evening to see if you've obeyed my command."

The boy sat down on the edge of the spring, and once in a while he saw a golden fish or a golden snake, but he made sure that nothing fell in. While he was sitting there, his finger began to hurt him so much that he dipped it into the water without meaning to. He pulled it out quickly but saw that it had turned to gold, and no matter how hard he tried, he could not wipe off the gold. It was in vain.

In the evening Iron Hans returned, looked at the boy, and said, "What happened to the spring?"

"Nothing, nothing," the boy answered as he held his finger behind his back so that the man would not see it.

But Iron Hans said, "You dipped your finger in the water. I'll let it go this time, but make sure that you don't let anything else fall in."

At the crack of dawn the next day the boy was already sitting by the spring and guarding it. His finger began hurting him again, and he brushed his head with it. Unfortunately, a strand of his fair fell into the spring. He quickly pulled it out, but it had already turned completely into gold. When Iron Hans came, he already knew what had happened. "You've let a hair fall into the spring," he said. "I'll overlook it once more, but if this happens a third time, the spring will become polluted, and you'll no longer be able to stay with me."

On the third day the boy sat at the spring and didn't move his finger even when it hurt him a great deal. However, he became bored and began looking at his face's reflection in the water. As he leaned farther and farther over the edge of the pool to look himself straight in the eye, his long hair fell down from his shoulders into the water. He straightened up instantly, but his entire head of hair had already turned golden and shone like the sun. You can imagine how terrified the boy was. He took his handkerchief and tied it around his head so that Iron Hans would not be able to see it. When the man arrived, however, he already knew everything and said, "Untie the handkerchief."

The golden hair came streaming out, and no matter how much the boy apologized, it didn't help. "You've failed the test and can no longer stay here. Go out into the world, and you'll learn what it means to be poor. However, since you're not bad at heart, and since I wish you well, I'll grant you one thing: whenever you're in trouble, go to the forest and call, 'Iron Hans,' then I'll come and help you. My power is great, greater than you think, and I have more than enough gold and silver."

Then the king's son left the forest and traveled over trodden and untrodden paths until he came to a large city. He looked for work there but could not find any. Nor had he been trained in anything that might enable him to earn a living. Finally, he went to the palace and asked for work and a place to stay. The people at the court didn't know how they might put him to good use, but they took a liking to him and told him to stay. At length the cook found work for him and had him carry wood and water and sweep away the ashes. Once, when nobody else was available, the cook told him to carry the food to the royal table. Since the boy did not want anyone to see his golden hair, he kept his cap on. The king had never seen anything like this and said, "When you come to the royal table, you must take off your cap."

"Oh, sire," the boy answered, "I can't, for I have an ugly scab on my head."

The king summoned the cook, scolded him, and asked him how he could have taken such a boy into his service. He told the cook to dismiss him at once. The cook, however, felt sorry for him and had him exchange places with the gardener's helper.

Now the boy had to plant and water the garden, hoe and dig, and put up with the wind and bad weather. One summer day, while he was working in the garden all alone, it was so hot that he took off his cap to let the breeze cool his head. When the sun shone upon his hair, it glistened and sparkled so much that the rays shot into the room of the king's daughter, and she jumped up to see what it was. Then she spotted the boy and called to him, "Boy, bring me a bunch of flowers."

Hastily he put on his cap, picked a bunch of wild flowers, and tied them together. As he was climbing the stairs, he came across the gardener, who said, "How can you bring the king's daughter a bunch of common flowers? Quick, get some others and choose only the most beautiful and rarest that you can find."

"Oh, no," answered the boy. "Wild flowers have a stronger scent, and she'll like them better."

When he entered her room, the king's daughter said, "Take off your cap. It's not proper for you to keep it on in my presence."

He replied, as he had before, "I've got a scabby head."

However, she grabbed his cap and pulled it off. Then his hair rolled forth and dropped down to his shoulders. It was a splendid sight to behold. He wanted to run away, but the king's daughter grabbed his arm and gave him a handful of ducats. He went off with them, but since he didn't care for gold, he gave them to the gardener and said, "Here's a gift for your children. They can have fun playing with the coins."

The next day the king's daughter called to him once again and told him to bring her a bunch of wild flowers, and as he entered her room with them, she immediately lunged for his cap and wanted to take it away from him, but he held it tight with both hands. Again she gave him a handful of ducats, but he didn't keep them. Instead, he gave them to the gardener once more as play-things for his children. The third day passed just like the previous two: she could not take his cap from him, and he did not want her gold.

Not long after this the country became engaged in a war. The king assembled his soldiers but was uncertain whether he would be able to withstand the enemy that was more powerful and had a large army. Then the gardener's helper said, "I'm grown up now and want to go to war. Just give me a horse."

The others laughed and said, "When we've gone, you can have your horse. We'll leave one for you in the stable."

When they had departed, he went into the stable and led the horse out. One foot was lame, and it limped *hippety-hop, hippety-hop*. Nevertheless, he mounted it and rode toward the dark forest. When he reached the edge of the forest, he yelled, "Iron Hans!" three times so loudly that the trees resounded with his call. Immediately the wild man appeared and asked, "What do you want?"

"I want to go to war, and I need a strong steed."

"You shall have what you want and even more."

Then the wild man went back into the forest, and it was not long before a stable boy came out leading a horse that snorted through its nostrils and was so lively that it could barely be controlled. They were followed by a host of knights wearing iron armor and carrying swords that flashed in the sun. The young man gave the stable boy his three-legged horse, mounted the other, and rode at the head of the troop of knights. As he approached the battlefield, he saw that a good part of the king's men had already fallen, and it would not have taken much to have forced the others to yield as well. So the youth charged forward with his troop of iron knights. They broke like a storm over the enemy soldiers, and the young man struck down everything in his way. The enemy took flight, but the young man remained in hot pursuit and didn't stop until there was no one left to fight. However, instead of returning to the king, he led the troop back to the forest by roundabout ways and called Iron Hans.

"What do you want?" asked the wild man.

"Take back your horse and your troop, and give me my three-legged horse again."

He received all that he had desired and rode home on his three-legged horse. Meanwhile, when the king returned to his castle, his daughter came toward him and congratulated him on his victory.

"I'm not the one who brought about the victory," he said. "It was some unknown knight who came to my aid with his troop."

The daughter wanted to know who the unknown knight was, but the king had no idea and said, "He went in pursuit of the enemy, and I never saw him after that."

She asked the gardener about his helper, and he laughed and said, "He's just returned home on his three-legged horse, and the others all made fun of him crying out, 'Here comes *hippety-hop, hippety-hop* again.' Then they asked, 'What hedge were you sleeping behind?'

"And he replied, 'I did my best, and without me, things would have gone badly.'"

"Then they laughed at him even more."

The king said to his daughter, "I'm going to celebrate our victory with a great festival that will last three days, and I want you to throw out a golden apple. Perhaps the unknown knight will come."

When the festival was announced, the young man went to the forest and called Iron Hans.

"What do you want?" he asked.

"I want to catch the princess's golden apple."

"It's as good as done," said Iron Hans. "You shall also have a suit of red armor and ride on a lively chestnut horse."

When the day of the festival arrived, the young man galloped forward, took his place among the knights, and went unrecognized. The king's daughter stepped up and threw a golden apple to the knights, but only he could catch it. However, as soon as he had it, he galloped away. On the second day Iron Hans provided him with a suit of white armor and gave him a white horse. Once again only he could catch the apple, and again he did not linger long but galloped away with it. The king became angry and said, "I won't allow this. He must appear before me and tell me his name." So, the king gave orders that his men were to pursue the knight if he caught the apple again, and if he didn't come back voluntarily, they were to use their swords and spears on him.

On the third day the young man received a suit of black armor and a black horse from Iron Hans. Again he caught the apple, but this time the king's men pursued him when he galloped away with it. One of them got near enough to wound him with the point of his sword. Nevertheless, he escaped them, and his horse reared so tremendously high in the air that his helmet fell off his head, and they saw his golden hair. Then they rode back and reported everything to the king.

The next day the king's daughter asked the gardener about his helper.

"He's working in the garden. The strange fellow was at the festival too, and he didn't get back until last night. Incidentally, he showed my children three golden apples that he won there."

The king had the young man summoned, and when he appeared, he had his cap on. But the king's daughter went up to him and took it off. Then his golden hair swooped down to his shoulders, and he was so handsome that everyone was astonished.

"Are you the knight who came to the festival every day in a different-colored armor and caught the three golden apples?" asked the king.

"Yes," he replied. "And here are the apples."

He took them out of his pocket and handed them to the king. "If you want more proof than this, you can have a look at the wound that your men gave me as they pursued me. And I'm also the knight who helped you defeat your enemy."

"If you can perform such deeds, you're certainly no gardener's helper. Tell me, who is your father?"

"My father is a mighty king, and I have all the gold I want."

"I can see that," said the king. "I owe you a debt of gratitude now. Is there any favor that I can do for you?"

"Yes," he replied. "You can indeed. You can give me your daughter for my wife."

Then the maiden laughed and said, "He doesn't stand on ceremony, does he? But I already knew from his golden hair that he wasn't a gardener's helper." Then she went over and kissed him.

The young man's mother and father came to the wedding and were filled with joy, for they had given up all hope of ever seeing their dead son again. And, while they were sitting at the wedding table, the music suddenly stopped, and the doors swung open as a proud king entered with a great retinue. He went to the young man, embraced him, and said, "I am Iron Hans and was turned into a wild man by a magic spell. But you released me from the spell, and now all the treasures that I possess shall be yours."

Iron Hans (1844)[147]

Friedmund von Arnim

There was once a king who had a great forest that would not put up with any hunters entering it. Whoever went into it would disappear along with the hounds. Therefore, the king decided not to send any more hunters into the forest and to let the forest alone. But one day a man showed up who wanted to serve the king as hunter.

"It will cost your life," said the king. "I can't really take you in."

"Now, that's my worry," replied the hunter.

So he went hunting with his hound, and when the hound came upon a scent, he sprang over a pool, but a bare arm stretched itself out and dragged the hound down into it. Immediately thereafter some men were sent for from the city, and they had to drain the pool where they found a wild man. Then they brought him into the city to the king, who had a big cage built and locked the wild man inside.

Then he commanded that the wild man was not to be let out of the cage, or if anyone did this, it would cost him his life. Now the king had a prince, who was six years old, and when the prince came to the cage one time, the wild man was playing with a golden ball. Then the prince said, "Give me the ball."

"If you let me out," the wild man said.

"I can't do that. If I do, it will cost me my life."

Meanwhile the king returned from a hunt, and nothing had happened in the forest. The next day they went hunting again, and they found plenty of game. Now the prince went to the cage once more.

"Give me the ball."

"Only when you let me out."

"I'm not allowed to do it," the prince said again, and soon he was irritated that he did not get the golden ball.

---

147. "Der eiserne Hans," *Hundert neue Mährchen im Gebirge gesammelt* (Charlottenburg: Egbert Bauer, 1844).

On the third day the king and his company went hunting again, and as soon as they were gone, the prince went to the cage once more.

"I really want the ball!" the prince declared.

This time the wild man gave him the ball, and the prince let him out. Then the wild man said, "If you are ever in great trouble, you're to go to the edge of the forest and cry out 'Iron Hans,' and then I'll help you."

When the king returned, he headed straight to the cage, but the wild man was gone. So he went to the queen and immediately asked whether she knew what had happened to the wild man. She was very terrified and stood there petrified because this could cost her her life since the wild man had escaped. Nobody else had been there except the prince, and he must have let him out. Indeed, the golden ball revealed that he had done it.

So the king sent the hunter into the forest with the prince and ordered him to kill his son. The hunter went into the woods with him, but he only cut off a finger, shot a young hog, and took out its tongue and heart that he brought and showed to the king along with the finger. Meanwhile the boy went deeper into the forest and kept crying out, "Iron Hans, do you hear me?"

Finally, Iron Hans came and said, "Come, I'll give you some work to do."

Now he led him to a small spring and said, "You're not to let anything fall into the water. If you do and I come again, you'll regret it."

But his finger hurt him so much that he put it into the water. Immediately it turned to gold. Then Iron Hans returned.

"What have you done to the spring?" asked Iron Hans.

"Nothing, nothing," said the prince.

"You dipped your finger into it," Iron Hans replied. "I'm going away again. If you let anything fall into the water again, it will be too bad for you."

Then the boy took a little piece of hair and dipped it into the water, and it turned into gold right away.

"You've dipped some hair into the spring," said Iron Has when he returned. "Now you'd better believe me. This is the last time I'm going away. Don't dishonor the spring."

As soon as Iron Hans was gone, the boy dipped his entire head of hair into the spring and now had a splendid golden head as if the sun were really shining upon it. He didn't know, however, how to conceal it so that Iron Hans wouldn't notice it right away.

"What have you done to the spring?" Iron Hans asked when he came back. "Take off the kerchief!" The boy had put a kerchief on his head. "Go away. You're a disobedient son. But if things go bad for you, you may go to the edge of the forest again and call for me."

Now the boy went away and walked deeper into the forest through thick and thin until he came to another country and finally reached a royal city. Once there he asked where he could find some work, and he found a job in the royal kitchen and became a kitchen helper. But he was supposed to carry the food to the table many times and he always kept a cap on his head.

"When you come to the table," said the king, "you must take off the cap."

"Yes, I know," said the boy, "but I have a horrible-looking head. I have the scabs and can't take off my cap."

This was quite bad for the cook who had hired a helper who couldn't serve at the table. Therefore, he sent the boy to the garden in exchange for the garden helper. There the boy had to dig and work hard. One time the sun shone so strongly that he became hot. So he took off his cap, and when the sun shone upon his head, it glistened so much that it cast a great reflection on the windows. When the princess saw this, she rushed outside to see what was glistening and radiating. It was the gardener's helper with his golden hair.

"My boy," she cried, "bring a bouquet of flowers up to my room."

So he made a bundle out of the most ordinary flowers. When the gardener came, he showed them to him and told him that he was supposed to bring the princess a bouquet. The gardener said, "But those are just plain wild flowers."

"Well," responded the boy, "they have a strong scent."

Then he went to the princess, and when he entered her room, she said, "My boy, take off your cap."

He didn't take it off and said that he had something wrong with his head. But she had seen his head and knew that this wasn't true. So she tried to tear it off his head. He jumped away from her. She called him back and gave him a handful of ducats as a tip for bringing the flowers. When he returned to the gardener, he said, "I was given some money as a tip, and I'd like to give them to your children so that they can play with them."

The gardener said that was fine with him, for he thought, 'Let him first give them to my children!' Then he took the money away from them.

The next day the princess called the gardener's helper again, and he had to make another bouquet. As soon as he entered, she tried to take off his cap and wanted to snatch him and pluck off the cap. However, she didn't get it and gave him another handful of ducats. Then he went away and gave the money to the children once more. On the third day he had to bring her a bouquet again, and again she wanted to take the cap. But he held on to it tightly.

So now the princess decided to have a ball game and invited many people. All sorts of noble and royal people appeared. Meanwhile the gardener's helper asked the gardener to let him go along. When he was told he could, he went to the forest, called Iron Hans, and asked him for help him get the balls from the princess.

"They're yours already," said Iron Hans as soon as he appeared. Then he gave the gardener's helper a brown horse, a brown coat, and changed him into a knight. Later, when the princess threw out the ball, our dear prince got it. None of the other knights got a ball, for the prince rode back to Iron Hans on his brown steed. On the next day there was another game. So the boy went to the edge of the forest and called Iron Hans. Then he received a white horse and a pure white coat. And again he got the ball, and nobody got one. The king didn't know what was happening, nor did the princess. So the third day came, and the king issued an order: if the knight rides off and doesn't stop, his men were to chop him down, shoot him, or stab him. Meanwhile the boy went to the edge of the forest again and called out to Iron Hans. This time he received a black stallion and a pitch dark black coat and had to ride bareheaded. He looked quite charming. Then our dear princess threw the ball again. Fortunately, he got it, and there was a great uproar. Not one nobleman, not one prince, nobody got the ball. But when our prince rode away with it, he was wounded on his leg.

Since everyone was upset again that nobody among them had gotten the ball, the gardener said, "My helper was there at the game."

So the king summoned the helper, and he had the three balls.

"Tell me," said the king, "were you the knight who won the ball three times?"

Now he had a wound on his leg, and it was clear that he was indeed the knight.

"Where do you come from?" asked the king.

"I am the prince whose realm has no end," he said, for Iron Hans had told him everything that he was to say. Since he had the balls, however, he got the princess.

Soon he was made vice-king, and he was assured that he would become the ruling king when his father-in-law died. Then the king asked him where he was born.

"The king of Sicily is my father," he said, "and I was banished because I had freed the wild man, who is always ready to help me."

Soon the time arrived for the marriage to be celebrated, and the young man's father was invited. Then the son sat next to his father, and his father-in-law asked what such a father was worth who had a son and had him killed because he had freed a wild man. The young man's father replied that he should have his tongue cut out, for he thought that his son had long since disappeared from the face of the earth.

"You are my father, and I'm the prince," his son revealed himself. "And you will be punished the way that you have chosen."

Now the matter was settled, and the prince became king of both realms.

The Golden Youth (1852)[148]

Ignaz and Joseph Zingerle

Once there was a very poor boy who went walking through the green forest. He was extremely sad, and his eyes were filled with tears. While he was wandering with a heavy heart, a little old woman suddenly appeared before him. Her

148.   "Goldener," *Tirols Volksdichungen und Volksgebräuche: Kinder- und Hausmärchen*, vol. 1 (Innsbruck: Verlag der Wagner'schen Buchhandlung, 1852).

hair was as hoary as old moss on a tree, and there were no longer any teeth wobbling in her mouth.

"Why are you so sad, my child?" the little grandma asked in a cozy tone and looked at the boy in a compassionate way.

The young boy summoned his courage and responded, "Well, it's easy to guess. My father is dead, and my mother can't earn enough to support the both of us. That's why I must go begging, and I don't like to do that at all because people look at me as though I were some sort of a scoundrel."

The little grandma seemed to have even more compassion for him now and said, "If that's the only thing that's bothering you, you'll soon be helped. Just come with me."

And she took the boy with her and led him further into the forest. They must have gone for half an hour when they came to a large beautiful house that was completely built from marble and was as white as snow. The little grandma went inside ahead of the boy who followed her. He was extremely delighted, for he had never seen such a beautiful house. After they entered a large room, the little grandma said to the curious boy: "If you want, you can stay here. You won't have much to do except to fan the flames of the fire beneath the cauldron in the kitchen. There are also two other things that you must promise me no matter what. You must never look into the cauldron, and you must never open the little chest standing along the wall near the hearth. If you faithfully follow my instructions, you'll receive a large reward at the end of the year because you'll see me again at that time."

The boy was very satisfied with the proposal and promised to follow her instructions diligently. The little grandma led him into the kitchen, showed him the cauldron and the chest, and then went away.

The boy was now all alone in the castle and lived like a count. He had an abundance of food and drink and a soft little bed in the night. Of course, he faithfully carried out his duties and fanned the flames with pleasure. The fire continued to burn and crackle cheerfully, and inside the cauldron you could hear the boiling and bubbling as if it were a church day.

This was how the days passed one after the other, and before the boy realized it, a year had gone by, and the old little grandma stood before him.

"You've done your duty well," she said and gave the boy a hundred and fifty gold ducats. "If you continue to work this way and are diligent, I'll give you exactly the same amount when I come again."

No sooner did she say this than she went off again, and the boy had no idea where she had gone. However, he was very delighted with his reward and worked even harder the second year. He fanned and fanned the flames and otherwise lived quite cheerfully and happily. So the days passed one after the other, and before he was aware of it, a year had gone by, and the little grandma stood before him. It seemed as if she were very pleased and said: "You've done very well, my child! If you continue to be so diligent, I shall give you double what I've already given you."

Then she gave him three hundred gold ducats and disappeared once again.

The boy continued to work in the castle and fanned the fire so that it really blazed, and it would have been impossible to think it would ever go out. This was how another year passed, and on the last day the little grandma came once more. She saw how everything was in order and gave her approval with a smile.

"You're a good boy," she said. "Take these six hundred gold ducats, and if you remain faithful to me for another year and serve me honestly, I'll give you twice as much money."

After saying this, the little grandma disappeared. The boy was extremely pleased that he had received six hundred gold ducats and intended to be as diligent as possible. But no matter how much he tried to be obedient and loyal, he kept thinking about what was in the cauldron and in the little chest. 'I wonder what I'd see if I peeked inside,' he often thought, and yet, he couldn't bring himself to do it.

One time, however, he kept thinking about the cauldron, and he finally peeked into it. But he couldn't see anything. So he stuck his finger inside and saw that it was completely golden when he withdrew it. What was to be done? He washed and scraped the finger—but it was all in vain. He didn't know any other way except to bind his golden finger with a small piece of cloth so that the old woman wouldn't notice it.

Then he opened the little chest that was along the wall next to the hearth, and he found a book in which he read: "Whoever has this book can demand whatever he likes and wants." So he took this book of magic from the chest and stuck it into his pants pocket, for he thought: 'I'll certainly be able to make use of this.' However, no sooner had he hidden the book than the little grandma stood before him and was furious. Her eyes had turned crimson out of anger. She chased him out of the kitchen and threw the cauldron at his head. All at once his hair turned so beautifully yellow that one would have thought his hair was pure gold. The boy now ran through the forest and wanted to find somewhere else to stay. He covered his head with a tree bark so that his hair wouldn't become dirty, and after this he never took off the bark.

He had already been walking for a long time when darkness fell in the valley, and he came to an open space where he saw the most beautiful gardens, and in the middle there was a proud castle. Now this castle belong to the king who lived there with his daughter and many, many servants and maids.

So now the young man went up to the castle and asked if he could enter into the king's service. Since the steward liked him, the young man was hired at the beginning as a shepherd. The young man was satisfied and tended the sheep and lambs outside on a hill. And lo and behold, the animals became more and more beautiful, and none of them were ever lost. When the steward saw this, he praised the golden youth and promoted him to gardener.

The golden youth now worked in the garden and tended the plants and flowers and took pleasure in doing this. The beautiful princess often came down into the garden and was delighted that everything was so clean and tidy and that the flowers were so carefully looked after. From day to day she became more inclined to like the gardener because he worked so diligently in the garden. One day when she was in the garden again, she noticed his beautiful golden hair, and ever since then she liked the gardener even better, and she couldn't see him often enough.

About the same time the king wanted to search for a successor and a husband for his daughter, for he was already old and had become tired of ruling the land. He thought about this time and again but couldn't find anyone that he or his daughter liked. In particular, the beautiful princess didn't want to approve of anyone, for she constantly thought about the golden-haired gardener. Finally, the old king became weary of making a choice and said to his daughter: "If you like none of the men that I've proposed, name one of your own choice."

The princess didn't have to reflect about this very long and named the gardener with the golden hair. Then the king became so angry and furious that he ordered his daughter to keep away from him and no longer recognized her as his very own child. He wanted to banish her from the castle. But she begged and pleaded so long until he allowed her to remain in the castle. In return, she had to work like a maid in the kitchen and perform the most burdensome chores. However, the king aged noticeably, for grief tore his heart apart.

Not long after this incident, war erupted, and the king had to arm himself for the battle. Soon he gathered together a large army and inspected it in front of the castle. When the golden youth saw the sparkling helmets and suits of armor and the flags flap in the wind, he felt a great desire to depart with them. So he went to the king and asked for his permission to join the departing army. The king was quite angry when he saw the gardener. However, he granted the youth's request. 'I'll certainly manage to find some trifle for you,' he thought to himself and gave the golden youth a horse that had only three feet and a sword that was entirely rusty. The warriors mocked him, but the golden youth's face turned serious as if everything had to be this way.

Now the army departed. The king rode at the head while the golden youth limped onward riding his three-legged nag at the end. They marched this way for a long time until they came to a marshy region. The army continued to ride, but the golden youth's three-legged horse got stuck in the bog and could not move forward and get out. The army was not far away, and all at once the hostile king made his move, and soon the decisive battle began. When the golden youth saw this and heard the noise, he remembered his book and wished for a fast, strong horse, a beautiful, sharp sword, and a crimson garment interwoven with silver. No sooner did he make this wish than he saw himself on a valiant steed; he had a splendid, sharp sword in his hand and was wearing a magnificent outfit that was incomparably beautiful. Now he spurred his horse on, and he was instantly carried into the battle, and his golden hair flew high in the air. He sprung all over like lightning and was here, there, and everywhere, and he spilled blood all about him and wounded many enemy soldiers. The battle did not last long now, and the enemy troops retreated howling in flight, and the glorious victory was attained.

The king didn't know whether he was awake or dreaming and whether the unknown rescuer was a human or an angel. As he was thinking about all this, the golden youth rode by him, and since he didn't stop when the king called to him, the king hurled his sword at him to mark him. The weapon wounded the rider's heel. The blade sprung and its point remained stuck in the golden youth's foot. However, the golden youth didn't care about this and jumped from his horse to his three-footed nag. Then he took off his garment and sat down on the old horse—and sword, crimson garment, and the beautiful steed had vanished. The golden youth now sat there just as he had at the beginning of the battle, and the army and king rode by him and laughed at him. When they had all passed by him, he also wanted to return home, and two days later he finally found his way back to the king's castle. His wound, however, had become much worse, and the gardener called for a doctor. When the king heard this, he had to laugh out loud. It seemed so odd to him that the gardener, who had watched the battle from afar, was supposed to be wounded. He could hardly believe it, and out of curiosity he went down to the gardener's room to get to the bottom of the matter.

Just imagine the king's expression when he saw the wound and the point of the sword on which his royal name had been written drawn from the wound!

Now the king interrogated the wounded young man and asked whether he had been in the battle, and the gardener told him everything to the last detail. Then the old king kissed the sick young man, had his daughter summoned to the room, and cherished her more than ever before. Meanwhile the golden youth was treated as if he were the king's son. And when the wound had healed, the wedding was held, and the king was extremely pleased with the wedding couple. And so all three lived happily together for many years. When the old king died, the golden youth became king and was so powerful, wise, and pious that no one before him or after him ever had the good fortune to be like him.

The Princess on the Glass Mountain (1853)[149]
Benjamin Thorpe

From South Småland

There was once a king, who was so devoted to the chase that he knew of no greater pleasure than hunting the beasts of the forest. Early and late he would stay out in the field with hawk and hound and always had good success. It nevertheless one day happened that he could start no game, though he sought on all sides from early morn. When evening was drawing on, and he was about to

149.   *Yule-Tide Stories: A Collection of Scandinavian and North German Popular Tales and Traditions from the Swedish, German, and Danish* (London: Henry G. Bohn, 1853).

return home with his attendants, he suddenly perceived a dwarf, or "wild man," running before him in the forest. Putting spurs to his horse, the king instantly went in pursuit of him, and caught him. His extraordinary appearance caused no little surprise, for he was little and ugly as a troll, and his hair resembled shaggy moss. To whatever the king said to him he would return no answer, good or bad. At this the king was angry, and the more so as he was already out of humour, in consequence of his bad luck at the chase. He therefore commanded his followers to keep a strict watch over the wild man, so that he might not escape, and then returned to his palace.

In those times it was an old-established custom for the king and his men to hold drinking meetings till a late hour in the night, at which much was said, and still more drunk. As they were sitting at one of these meetings and making themselves merry, the king, taking up a large horn, said: "What think ye of our sport today? When could it before have been said of us, that we returned home without some game?"

The men answered: "It is certainly true as you say, and yet, perhaps, there is not so good a sportsman as you to be found in the whole world. You must not, however, complain of our day's luck, for you have caught an animal, whose like was never before seen or heard of."

This discourse pleased the king exceedingly, and he asked what they thought he had best do with the dwarf. One of the courtiers answered: "You should keep him confined here in the palace so that it may be known far and near what a great hunter you are, provided that you can guard him so that he does not escape, for he is crafty and perverse withal."

On hearing this, the king for some time sat silent and then, raising the horn, said: "I will do as thou sayest, and it shall be through no fault of mine, if the wild man escapes. But this I vow, that if anyone lets him loose, he shall die, even if it be my own son."

Having said this, he emptied the horn, so that it was an inviolable oath. But the courtiers cast looks of doubt on each other, for they had never before heard the king so speak and could plainly see that the mead had mounted to his head.

On the following morning, when the king awoke, he recollected the vow he had made at the drinking party and accordingly sent for timber and other materials, and caused a small house or cage to be constructed close by the royal palace. The cage was formed of large beams and secured by strong locks and bars so that no one could break through. In the middle of the wall there was a little opening or window for the purpose of conveying food to the prisoner. When all was ready, the king had the wild man brought forth, placed him in the cage, and took the keys himself. There must the dwarf now sit day and night, both goers and comers stopping to gaze on him, but no one ever heard him complain, or even utter a single word.

Thus did a considerable time pass, when war broke out, and the king was obliged to take the field. When on the eve of departure, he said to his queen:

"Thou shalt rule over my realm, and I will leave both land and people in thy care. But thou shalt promise me one thing, that thou wilt keep the wild man, so that he escape not while I am absent."

The queen promised to do her best both in that and all things besides, and the king gave her the keys of the cage. He then pushed his barks from the shore, hoisted sail on the gilded yards, and went far, far away to distant countries; and to whatever place he came, he was there victorious. But the queen stood on the shore, looking after him as long as she could see his pendants waving over the ocean, and then, with her attendants, returned to the palace, there to sit sewing silk on her knee, awaiting her consort's return.

The king and queen had an only child, a prince, still of tender age, but who gave good promise of himself. After the king's departure, it one day happened that the boy, in his wanderings about the palace, came to the wild man's cage and sat down close by it playing with his gold apple. While he was thus amusing himself, his apple chanced to pass through the window of the cage. The wild man instantly came forwards and threw it out. This the boy thought a pleasant pastime and threw his apple in again, and the wild man cast it back, and thus they continued for some time. But at length pleasure was turned to sorrow, for the wild man kept the apple and would not throw it back. When neither threats nor prayers were of any avail, the little one burst into tears. Seeing this, the wild man said: "Thy father has acted wickedly towards me, in making me a prisoner, and thou shalt never get thy apple again, unless thou procurest my liberty."

The boy answered: "How shall I procure thy liberty? Only give me my gold apple! My gold apple!"

"Thou shalt do as I now tell thee," replied the wild man. "Go to the queen, thy mother, and desire her to comb thee. Be on the watch, and steal the keys from her girdle. Then come and open the door. Thou canst afterwards restore the keys in the same manner, and no one will be the wiser."

In short, the wild man succeeded in persuading the boy, who stole the keys from his mother, ran down to the cage, and let the wild man come out. At parting, the dwarf said: "Here is thy gold apple, as I promised, and thou hast my thanks for allowing me to escape. Another time, when thou art in trouble, I will help thee in return."

And then he ran off.

When it was known in the royal palace that the wild man had fled, there was a great commotion. The queen sent people on the roads and ways to trace him, but he was away and continued away. Thus some time passed, and the queen was more and more troubled, for she was in daily expectation of her consort's return. At last she descried his ships come dancing on the waves, and a multitude of people were assembled on the shore to bid him welcome. On landing, his first inquiry was, whether they had taken good care of the wild man, and the queen was obliged to confess what had taken place. At this intelligence the king was highly incensed, and declared he would punish the perpetrator, be he whoever he might. He then caused an investigation to be made throughout the palace and every man's child was called forth to bear witness, but no one knew anything. At last the little prince came forward. On appearing before his father he said: "I know that I have incurred my father's anger. Nevertheless, I cannot conceal the truth; for it was I who let the wild man escape."

On hearing this the queen grew deadly pale, and every other with her, for the little prince was the favourite of all. At length the king spoke: "Never shall it be said of me that I broke my vow, even for my own flesh and blood, and thou shalt surely die as thou deservest."

Thereupon he gave orders to his men to convey the young prince to the forest, and there slay him, but to bring his heart back as a proof that his order had been fulfilled.

Now there was sorrow among the people such as the like had never before been experienced; everyone interceded for the young prince, but the king's word was irrevocable. The young men had, therefore, no alternative. So, taking the prince with them, they set out on their way. When they had penetrated very far into the forest, they met a man driving swine, whereupon one of the men said to his companion: "It seems to me not good to lay violent hands on a king's son. Let us rather purchase a hog, and take its heart; for no one will know it not to be the prince's heart."

This to the other seemed wisely said. So they bought a hog of the man, slaughtered and took out its heart. They then bade the prince go his way and never return. The king's son did as they had directed him; he wandered on as far as he was able, and had no other sustenance than the nuts and wild berries, which grew in the forest. When he had thus travelled a long distance, he came to a mountain, on the summit of which stood a lofty fir. He then thought to himself: 'I may as well climb up into this fir, and see whether there is any path.' No sooner said than done. When he reached the top of the tree and looked on all sides, he discerned a spacious palace lying at a great distance, and glittering in the sun. At this sight he was overjoyed and instantly bent his steps thither. On his way he met with a boy following a plough, with whom he exchanged clothes. Thus equipped he at length reached the palace, entered it, and asked for employment, and so was taken as a herd-boy, to watch the king's cattle. Now he ranged about the forest both late and early, and as time went on he forgot his sorrow, and grew, and became tall and vigorous, so that nowhere was to be found his like.

Our story now turns to the king, to whom the palace belonged. He had been married, and by his queen had an only daughter. She was much fairer than other damsels and was both kind and courteous so that he might be regarded as fortunate, who should one day possess her. When she had completed her fifteenth winter, she had an innumerable host of suitors, whose number, although she gave each a denial, was constantly increasing so that the king at length knew not what answer to give them. He one day, therefore, went up to his daughter in her bower and desired her to make a choice, but she would not. In his anger at her refusal he said: "As thou wilt not thyself make a choice, I will make one for thee, although it may happen not to be altogether to thy liking."

He was then going away, but his daughter held him back and said, "I am well convinced that it must be as you have resolved; nevertheless, you must not imagine that I will accept the first that is offered, as he alone shall possess me, who is able to ride to the top of the high glass mountain fully armed."

This the king thought a good idea, and, yielding to his daughter's resolution, he sent a proclamation over the whole kingdom, that whosoever should ride fully armed to the top of the glass mountain, should have the princess to wife.

When the day appointed by the king had arrived, the princess was conducted to the glass mountain with great pomp and splendour. There she sat, the highest of all, on the summit of the mountain with a golden crown on her head and a golden apple in her hand and appeared so exquisitely beautiful that there was no one present who would not joyfully have risked his life for her sake. Close at the mountain's foot were assembled all the suitors on noble horses and with splendid arms, which shone like fire in the sunshine; and from every quarter the people flocked in countless multitudes to witness the spectacle. When all was ready, a signal was given with horns and trumpets, and in the same instant the suitors galloped up the hill one after another. But the mountain was high and slippery as ice and was, moreover, exceedingly steep so that there was no one, who, when he had ascended only a small portion, did not fall headlong to the bottom. It may, therefore, well be imagined there was no lack of broken legs and arms. Hence arose a noise of the neighing of horses, the outcry of people and the crash of armour that was to be heard at a considerable distance.

While all this was passing, the young prince was occupied in tending his cattle. On hearing the tumult and the rattling of arms, he sat on a stone, rested his head on his hand, and wept, for he thought of the beautiful princess, and it passed in his mind how gladly he would have been one of the riders. In the same moment he heard the sound of a footstep, and, on looking up, saw the wild man standing before him.

"Thanks for the past," said he. "Why sittest thou here lonely and sad?"

"I may well be sad," answered the prince. "For thy sake I am a fugitive from my native land and have now not even a horse and arms so that I might ride to the glass mountain, and contend for the princess."

"Oh," said the wild man, "that's a remedy may easily be found. Thou hast helped me, I will now help thee in return."

Thereupon, taking the prince by the hand, he led him to his cave deep down in the earth and showed a suit of armour hanging on the wall, forged of the hardest steel, and so bright that it shed a bluish light all around. Close by it stood a splendid steed, ready saddled and bridled, scraping the ground with his steel-shod hoofs, and champing his bit.

The wild man then said to him: "Arm thyself quickly, and ride away, and try thy fortune. I will, in the meantime, tend thy cattle."

The prince did not require a second bidding, but instantly armed himself with helm and harness, buckled spurs on his heels, and a sword by his side, and felt as light in his steel panoply as a bird in the air. Then vaulting into the saddle, he gave his horse the rein, and rode at full speed to the mountain.

The princess's suitors had just ceased from their arduous enterprise, in which none had won the prize, though each had well played his part, and were now standing and thinking that another time fortune might be more favourable, when on a sudden they see a young knight come riding forth from the verge of the forest directly towards the mountain. He was clad in steel from head to foot, with shield on arm and sword in belt, and bore himself so nobly in the saddle that it was a pleasure to behold him. All eyes were instantly directed towards the stranger knight, each asking another who he might be, for no one had seen him before. But they had no long time for asking, for scarcely had he emerged from the forest, when, raising himself in the stirrups, and setting spurs to his horse, he darted like an arrow straight up the glass mountain. Nevertheless, he did not reach the summit, but when about half way on the declivity, he suddenly turned his charger and rode down the hill, so that the sparks flew from his horse's hoofs. He then disappeared in the forest as a bird flies.

Now, it is easy to imagine, there was a commotion among the assembled multitude, of whom there was not one that was not stricken with wonder at the stranger, who, I hardly need say it, was no other than the prince. At the same time all were unanimous that they had never seen a nobler steed or a more gallant rider. It was, moreover, whispered abroad that such was also the opinion of the princess herself, and that every night she dreamed of nothing but the venturous stranger.

The time had now arrived when the suitors of the princess should make a second trial. As on the first occasion, she was conducted to the glass mountain, the attempt to ascend which by the several competitors was attended with a result similar in every respect to what has been already related.

The prince in the meanwhile was watching his cattle and silently bewailing his inability to join in the enterprise, when the wild man again appeared before him, who, after listening to his complaints, again conducted him to his subterranean abode, where there hung a suit of armour formed of the brightest silver, close by which stood a snow-white steed ready saddled and fully equipped, pawing the ground with his silver-shod hoofs and champing his bit. The prince, following the directions of the wild man, having put on the armour and mounted the horse, galloped away to the glass mountain.

As on the former occasion, the youth drew on him the gaze of every one present, and he was instantly recognised as the knight who had already so distinguished himself, but he allowed them little time for observation, for setting spurs to his horse, he rode with an arrow's speed up the glassy mountain, when, having nearly reached the summit, he made an obeisance to the princess, turned his horse, rapidly rode down again, and again disappeared in the forest.

The same series of events took place a third time, excepting that on this occasion the prince received from the wild man a suit of golden armour, in which he, on the third day of trial, rode to the mountain's summit, bowed his knee before the princess, and from her hand received the golden apple. Then casting himself on his horse, he rode at full speed down the mountain, and again disappeared in the forest.

Now arose an outcry on the mountain! The whole assemblage raised a shout of joy; horns and trumpets were sounded, weapons clashed, and the king caused it to be proclaimed aloud that the stranger knight in the golden armour had won the prize. What the princess herself thought on the occasion, we will leave unsaid, though we are told that she turned both pale and red, when she presented the young prince with the golden apple.

All that now remained was to discover the gold-clad knight, for no one knew him. For some time hopes were cherished that he would appear at court, but he came not. His absence excited the astonishment of all. The princess looked pale and was evidently pining away; the king became impatient; and the suitors murmured every day. When no alternative appeared, the king commanded a great assemblage to be held at his palace, at which every man's son, high or low, should be present, that the princess might choose among them. At this meeting there was not one who did not readily attend, both for the sake of the princess, and in obedience to the king's command so that there was assembled an innumerable body of people. When all were gathered together, the princess issued from the royal palace in great state and with her maidens passed among the whole throng; but although she sought in all directions, she found not what she sought. She was already surveying the outermost circle, when suddenly she caught sight of a man who was standing concealed amid the crowd. He wore a broad-brimmed hat and was wrapped in a large grey cloak like those worn by herdsmen, the hood of which was drawn up over his head so that no one could discern his countenance.

But the princess instantly ran towards him, pulled down his hood, clasped him in her arms and cried: "Here he is! Here he is!"

At this all the people laughed, for they saw that it was the king's herd-boy, and the king himself exclaimed: "Gracious heaven support me! What a son-in-law am I like to have!"

But the young man said with a perfectly unembarrassed air: "Let not that trouble you! You will get a good king's son as you yourself are a king."

At the same moment he threw aside his cloak, and where were now the laughers when, in place of the grey herdsman, they saw before them a comely young prince clad in gold from head to foot and holding in his hand the princess's apple! All now recognised in him the youth who had ridden up the glass mountain.

Now, it is easy to imagine there was joy, the like of which was never known. The prince clasped his beloved in his arms with the most ardent affection and told her of his family and all that he had undergone.

The king allowed himself no rest, but instantly made preparations for the marriage, to which he invited all the suitors and all the people. A banquet was then given such as has never been heard of before or after.

Thus did the prince gain the king's daughter and half the kingdom, and when the feastings had lasted about seven days, the prince took his fair young bride in great state to his father's kingdom, where he was received as may easily be conceived, both the king and queen weeping for joy at seeing him again. They afterwards lived happily, each in his kingdom. But nothing more was heard of the wild man.

Translated by Benjamin Thorpe.

The Wild Man of the Marsh (1876)[150]
Svend Grundtvig

Once upon a time there lived a King of England who had in his domain a dismal, wild, and pathless swamp. No one would go near the place, for it was said that every living thing, whether man or beast, that ventured to set foot there would surely perish, and that instantly, and folks called it the Wild Marsh.

Well, one day the king made up his mind to have this marsh, or swamp, thoroughly explored; so he gave orders for his soldiers to pour down into the marsh from all sides.

When they had got half-way through, they came upon a gigantic Wild Man, lying asleep, and before he could awake, they had bound him fast, hand and foot, and then they brought him to the king's castle. He was a strange fellow to look at—in form like a man, only much, much bigger, and covered with hair from top to toe; and he had but one eye, and that was in the middle of his forehead.

The king was very pleased with the capture he had made. He felt certain that the Wild Man possessed vast hidden treasures, and he longed to have some of them himself. But to all they said, the Wild Man spoke never a word in answer. So the king had him put in a big iron cage, which he placed in a tower built of huge blocks of granite. Every day food and drink were thrust through the iron cage, but the keys of the tower were in the king's own keeping.

Now it so fell out that the king had to go away to the wars, to help another king in defending his land, for in those days there were many kings in England. The keys of the tower he gave into the queen's keeping, bidding her take good care of them, for he vowed a solemn vow that if anyone, whosoever it might be, let the Wild Man escape, he should thereby forfeit his own life. So the queen promised she would never let the keys out of her keeping, day or night.

---

150. *Fairy Tales from Afar*, trans. Jane Mulley (London: Hutchison, 1900).

Now this king and queen had an only child, a pretty, clever little fellow of seven years. He was in the garden one day playing ball with a golden apple, and quite by accident he threw the apple so that it fell between the bars of the iron cage in the tower. The boy ran to the cage and begged the Wild Man to throw the apple back to him. But the Wild Man said no, he should not have his apple again unless he came in and fetched it; and then he told him how to steal the keys of the tower from his royal mother.

So the prince ran and laid his head in the queen's lap, and said: "Oh, mother, something is tickling my ear! Do see what it is!"

Then the queen looked and said: "No, there is nothing there."

Meanwhile the boy had stolen the keys out of her pocket; and he ran away to the tower, and opened the outer door.

"Now give me my golden apple," said he.

"No, you must open the next door, too!" replied the Wild Man.

The prince did so, and then asked again for his apple. But the Wild Man answered: "You must first open the innermost door."

And when the prince had done this he got back his golden apple. But at the same moment the Wild Man stepped out of his cage, and he gave the prince a little whistle, saying:

"If ever you find yourself in trouble, just sound this whistle, and call me. I will come to your assistance."

And with that the Wild Man ran off to the marsh.

The prince grew hot with fright when he saw the Wild Man make off, for he knew what his father had vowed concerning anyone who should set the captive free. Then he locked all the doors again, and, running back to the queen, he laid his head in her lap, and said: "Oh, there is something tickling my ear! Do see what it is!"

So the queen looked. "Nonsense! there is nothing there," she said.

But meanwhile the prince had managed to slip the keys back into his mother's pocket. Next day, when they went to feed the Wild Man, they found he had gone, and no one could conceive how he had got through the locked doors. The queen was dreadfully frightened, but she had her suspicions as to how it had happened. However, she said nothing, neither to her son nor to anyone else, but waited quietly till the king should come home from the wars.

The king was furious when he learned that the Wild Man was gone, and he said what he had sworn, that he would hold to, and that the queen, who had had possession of the keys, must answer for what had happened; she must know who had let him out. But the queen said she had not done it, that she had never let anyone have the keys, and that she knew nothing whatever about it.

Then the king condemned her to pay the forfeit with her life, and she was led away to the place of execution. But now the prince stepped forward and said that his mother was innocent; that he had stolen the keys out of her pocket, and slipped them in again; and that he had unlocked the doors of the Wild Man's cage to get back his golden apple. So the queen was set free.

But now, according to the king's vow, her son must pay the forfeit with his life. His father, however, would not shed his blood, but commanded that he should be immediately conveyed to the wild marsh and driven down into it, where he would certainly perish, and thus the king's oath would be kept.

So the Prince was led away to the wild marsh; and he was told that, supposing he made his escape, if he, on any pretext whatever, showed himself outside the marsh, his life would forthwith pay the forfeit.

It was already getting toward evening when the prince was set down in the wild marsh, and by the time he had gone as far as he could find his way, it was quite dark. So, he set about climbing a tree, where he might remain till daylight came again.

Then he found that something he had about him had caught in a little twig of this tree, and when he looked to see what it might be, he saw it was the whistle the Wild Man had given him. He had never given it a thought before, but now he set to and blew the best he could, and then he shouted at the top of his voice, "Wild Man! Wild Man!"

At the same instant the Wild Man stood before him, looking at him in the most friendly manner. "Get up on my back," said he.

And the boy was not slow to obey, clasping him round the neck with both legs, and holding on to his shaggy locks with both hands. So the Wild Man ran with him farther into the marsh; and then all at once down they sank, deep down below the earth, for it was there the Wild Man lived in a grand castle of his own.

There the prince was served with a good meal, and a comfortable bed was given him, where he slept soundly all the night through. In the morning the Wild Man came to the prince, and said:

> "Here shalt thou live, and here shalt thou stay
> Till seven long years have passed away."

Then he took the boy to the stables and showed him all his horses. After that he led him round the outside of the castle. There were meadows and gardens; there were also a fencing-court and a racecourse. Every day the prince took lessons in riding and racing, in fighting and fencing; he also learned to swim and to shoot, and how to handle lance and spear.

Seven years had passed away thus, and the prince was now fourteen years old; but he might well have passed for eighteen, so tall and so strong, so straight and so slim, so handsome and graceful was he. Then the Wild Man said to him: "Now you must dip your head in this stream."

And he did so, and his hair became the color of the purest gold. After that the Wild Man presented him with a suit of clothes, very plain and simple in make and material, and told him he must put them on and then set out to seek his fortune through the wide world. That same evening the Wild Man took the prince upon his back, and he ran with him all through that night, till the gray dawn broke. Then the Wild Man set him down, and bade him farewell.

"There is a king's castle close by," said he. "You must go and take service there; take whatever you can get, whatever they offer you. Never speak of your home, nor where you came from; and so long as you remain in a lowly station, so long must you keep your hat upon your head, that none may get a glimpse of your golden hair. All that I possess, horses or armor or weapons, you can always obtain by wishing for them, and you can be rid of them again whenever you will."

With that the Wild Man vanished, and the youth went his way to the king's castle, and asked if he might take service there. Yes, he might be the gardener's boy. He was very pleased at this and went and presented himself to the head-gardener.

"Off with your hat when you speak to me," said the head-gardener.

"I may not take off my hat, for I am bald-headed," said the prince.

"Ugh! What a misfortune!" cried the head-gardener. "Well, I can't have you in my house, but you may sleep in the outhouse!"

The gardener's apprentice paid great attention to his duties, and every one marveled to see the amount of work he could get through, and how everything prospered that he undertook. And this is how it happened. When he stuck his spade into the earth, he just wished that the piece of ground was all dug up, and that very instant it was all dug! When he stuck a stick into the ground, he just wished it might grow, and so it always came to pass that what he planted in the evening was full-grown by the following morning. The gardener soon saw this, and was much pleased to have such an apprentice. Early one morning, after passing the night as usual in the outhouse, the prince came out and washed himself in the stream, and then he took off his hat, and combed his long golden locks.

Now it so happened that the king's youngest daughter (he had three daughters, all young and fair to look upon) had risen very early that morning and stood at her window, which looked out upon the garden. She saw something shining through the trees, and thought at first it was the sunrise. But on looking again, she saw it was the under-gardener's long hair, that shone like the purest, gold. She was greatly struck by this, for she had always noticed that on meeting her sisters or herself in the garden, the youth had never once lifted his hat— indeed, he declined to bare his head to royalty as resolutely as he had refused to take off his hat to the head-gardener. From that hour she watched him closely, and she could not help thinking him the very handsomest serving-man she had ever seen, and she felt sure that he was not what he gave himself out to be. Both her sisters teased her for casting an eye of favor upon a poor bald-headed serving-man, for she could not help looking at him when they met him. And once, when she was taking a noon-day stroll in the garden with her father and her two sisters, and they came upon the gardener's boy lying asleep on a grassy bank, she even could not refrain from going up to him and lifting his cap. Her sisters laughed at her, and her father scolded her soundly for having anything to do with a mere peasant; but she cared not a jot, for she had caught a glimpse of his golden hair.

At last the king determined to marry his three daughters to the three most gallant knights who should win the three best prizes in a tournament. The tournament was to last three days, and whoever remained victor, should receive a golden apple from the hand of that princess whose day it was, and he should be her betrothed husband.

On the first day the hand of the eldest princess was to be contended for. A great many princes and knights were gathered together from the king's own land and from other lands. Then the gardener's boy went out into the wood and wished for his brown horse out of the Wild Man's stables, with accoutrements and coat-of-mail of glittering steel. Springing into the saddle, he galloped off to the spot where the tournament was being held. It was a lance tournament, and they rode and they strove and the knight on the brown charger was victorious over all, and to him was given the princess's golden apple. Then he galloped off and vanished, none knew whither. But as he went, he threw the golden apple to a knight in brave attire who had not entered the lists at all.

The following day they were to strive for the hand of the second princess, and there were as many combatants as the day before. Then gardener's boy went out into the wood again, and he wished for his coal-black steed out of the Wild Man's stables, with coat-of-mail and accoutrements of shining silver. And he rode and he strove with the other knights till he had conquered them all, and so he won the second golden apple. He gave that to an earl's son.

The third day the youngest princess was to be fought for. She was the most beautiful of the three, and there was no less rivalry among the combatants than on the previous days. That day the gardener's boy wished for his milk-white steed out of the Wild Man's stables and for a coat-of-mail and accoutrements of purest gold. Then he loosed his golden hair, so that it fell down over his shoulders and galloped to the courtyard where the tournament was being held. And he rode, and he strove so well that none could withstand him. And so he received the golden apple from the hand of the youngest princess. But he did not give that away; he held it fast in his closed hand and galloped away, none knew whither.

And now those knights who had won the prizes on the three days were summoned to appear. And the duke's son, who had been so bravely appareled, and the earl's son, who had been unhorsed, stepped forward with haughty mien, each carrying his golden apple. So they were betrothed each to his princess. But no knight in golden armor made his appearance; no one knew what had become of him.

The two eldest princesses were delighted with their betrothed husbands, and they made great fun of their sister, whom "no one would have," they said. "But, after all, you have a lover too!" cried they. "There is your bald-headed gardener's boy. Send for him."

And they did send for him, and he came in his old clothes and wearing his fur cap, but in his hand was the princess's golden apple. Then the king came to him in haste and said:

"You found that in the courtyard. It does not belong to you."

And the gardener's boy answered: "Nay, but I won it in the courtyard, and the princess belongs to me."

Then the youngest princess went up to him, gave him her hand, and said that he who had her golden apple was her true love. The king, felt convinced that the Golden Knight had lost the apple and was even now searching for it, and that this was the reason why he had not come, but that he would come, sooner or later.

The days went on, but no Golden Knight made his appearance. The king was terribly put out, and the sisters taunted the youngest princess, saying: "He would neither win thee nor woo thee, so he threw the apple away, but thou hast still thy bald-headed gardener's boy."

"Aye, surely I have, and he is good enough for me," said she.

One morning, soon after this, the youngest princess went down into the garden and sought out the gardener's boy, and as she came, he saw her, and he lifted his cap, and his golden hair rolled down on to his shoulders. He kissed her hand, and he kissed her mouth, and he told her who he was—that, like herself, he was of royal birth, and that he would bring no shame upon her. He told her also that it was he who had won all three golden apples, but that he had given a way the first two, as he did not wish to have either of the two elder princesses; he only wanted her whom he had now won, and who had been to him so loving and so true. Not many days hence, he said, they should give him the place of honor at the king's table.

The following morning the two high-born lovers rode forth to the hunt, and the two eldest princesses, anxious to carry on their merry jests of yesterday, declared that the third lover must go too. So the gardener's boy was sent for, and they equipped him for the hunt in a style that these laughter-loving princesses deemed appropriate. They gave him a gray donkey to ride, and, instead of a gun, they fetched a pitchfork from the cow house, and thus equipped he rode out of the courtyard with the two young noblemen.

When they had got a little distance from the king's castle, they came to two crossroads—to the right was a beautiful wood, to the left a wild marsh overgrown with brushwood. The two young nobles struck off to the right, but the gardener's boy turned his donkey to the left—the road leading to the marsh. And when he had gone a little way, he wished for his good crossbow from the Wild Man's castle, and then he wished he might see some hares and stags and foxes and wild boars, and he very soon had bagged as much game as his donkey could carry.

Towards evening the two noblemen came riding homewards with a crest-fallen air; they had not killed even a hare. When they saw the donkey so laden with game, they begged the boy, to sell it to them. He was quite willing to do this, but they must give him their golden apples in exchange, or they should not have so much as a single hare. And they were obliged to agree to that. Then they shared the game between them and rode proudly into the castle yard.

Next day the two noblemen went hunting again, and again the gardener's boy had to go with them, riding his little gray donkey and carrying his pitchfork on his shoulder. And exactly the same thing happened again. In the evening, when the noblemen tried to bargain with him again to buy the game, he would not sell it unless they each gave him a strip of their skins.

"I will cut it off where it won't be seen," said he.

And so, since they could make no easier bargain and wished to be considered as skillful sportsmen as they were gallant knights, they consented to that arrangement. The next day there was to be a great banquet given in the king's castle in honor of the betrothal of the two princesses. But that same night came news of an invasion of the king's domains by a horde of sea-robbers, who were ravaging the land with fire and sword. So all the king's soldiers set out to meet the enemy, and the two highborn lovers were forced to go too. Then the gardener's boy mounted his little gray donkey, took his pitchfork, and rode forth with them.

The way led along by a great peat-marsh, and when they came to a steep bank, the two noblemen set upon the gardener's boy and rode him down, so that the donkey stuck fast in the bog; and the more the poor beast struggled to free himself, the deeper he sank into the mire. Then the gardener's boy begged the two noblemen to help him out, but they saw that he would be sure to sink to the bottom so that no one would ever hear about their golden apples, or about their skin that had been stripped off; so they rode away and left him.

As soon as they were out of sight, the gardener's boy wished himself back on dry ground; then he wished for his milk-white steed and for his harness and coat-of-mail, all of purest gold. And he rode on till he came to the battlefield.

There things were going badly for the king's men. The enemy were pressing them hard, and a part of the royal army had retreated. But the knight in golden armor dashed to the front, cutting his way through the enemy right and left, and roused the sinking courage of the king's soldiers. The fortune of the day turned once more, and the enemy turned and fled back to their ships.

All agreed that to the Golden Knight was due the honor of the victory, and he was invited to return to the king's castle. And the king himself came out to receive him when he arrived at the castle. The news of the battle had already reached him, and he had also been told that the Golden Knight who had won it was the same who, some days before, had won the youngest princess.

And the king now led forth his youngest daughter by the hand and betrothed her to the unknown prince. Then there was a splendid banquet given, where the Golden Prince was seated at the head of the table, opposite the king, and all showed him the deepest respect. During the feast he drew forth the golden apple he had received from his betrothed when he won her in the tournament, and at the same time also the golden apple he had played ball with in his father's castle yard, and upon which his name and crown were engraved; and he presented them both as a betrothal gift to his youthful bride.

The king sat there expecting to see the two knights do the same, but they sat on, pretending not to take any notice. So, after a while, the Golden Prince drew forth another golden apple, and then again another, and gave them to his young bride, saying: "Like seeks like; these two shall also be thine."

The king thought he recognized these apples, and when they were given to him to look at, he discovered the names of his two eldest daughters engraved on them, and so he knew they were the same golden apples he had given to the victors on the first and second days of the tournament. He asked how the prince had come by them.

Then the prince told the whole story, and when the king heard it he was furious and declared that the two good-for-nothings should leave his castle directly, and that they might take their betrothed brides with them. But the King of England's son was married to the youngest princess, and they live there still, in great joy and splendor, he and his true-hearted queen.

Translated by Jane Mulley.

The Grateful Tartaro and the Heren-Suge (1879)[151]
Wentworth Webster

Like many of us who are, have been, and shall be in the world, there was a king, and his wife, and three sons. The king went out hunting one day, and caught a Tartaro. He brings him home, and shuts him up in prison in a stable, and proclaims, by sound of trumpet, that all his court should meet the next day at his house, that he would give them a grand dinner, and afterwards would show them an animal such as they had never seen before.

The next day the two sons of the king were playing at ball against the wall of the stable where the Tartaro was confined, and the ball went into the stable. One of the boys goes and asks the Tartaro: "Throw me back my ball, I beg you."

He says to him, "Yes, if you will deliver me."

He replies, "Yes, yes," and he threw him the ball.

A moment after, the ball goes again to the Tartaro. He asks for it again; and the Tartaro says: "If you will deliver me, I will give it you."

The boy says, "Yes, yes," takes his ball, and goes off.

---

151. *Basque Legends: Collected Chiefly in the Labourd* (London: Griffith and Farran, 1877).

The ball goes there for the third time, but the Tartaro will not give it before he is let out. The boy says that he has not the key. The Tartaro says to him: "Go to your mother, and tell her to look in your right ear, because something hurts you there. Your mother will have the key in her left pocket, and take it out."

The boy goes, and does as the Tartaro had told him. He takes the key from his mother, and delivers the Tartaro. When he was letting him go, he said to him:

"What shall I do with the key now? I am undone."

The Tartaro says to him: "Go again to your mother, and tell her that your left ear hurts you, and ask her to look, and you will slip the key into her pocket."

The Tartaro tells him, too, that he will soon have need of him, and that he will only have to call him, and he will be his servant forever.

The boy puts the key back; and everyone came to the dinner. When they had eaten well, the king said to them that they must go and see this curious thing. He takes them all with him. When they are come to the stable, he finds it empty. Judge of the anger of this king, and of his shame. He said: "I should like to eat the heart, half cooked, and without salt, of him who has let my beast go."

Some time afterwards the two brothers quarreled in presence of their mother, and one said to the other: "I will tell our father about the affair of the Tartaro."

When the mother heard that, she was afraid for her son, and said to him:

"Take as much money as you wish."

And she gave him the Fleur-de-lys.[152]

"By this you will be known everywhere as the son of a king."

Petit Yorge[153] goes off, then, far, far, far away. He spends and squanders all his money, and does not know what to do more. He remembers the Tartaro, and calls him directly. He comes, and Petit Yorge tells him all his misfortunes; that he has not a penny left, and that he does not know what will become of him. The Tartaro says to him: "When you have gone a short way from here you will come to a city. A king lives there. You will go to his house, and they will take you as gardener. You will pull up everything that there is in the garden, and the next day everything will come up more beautiful than before. Also, three beautiful flowers will spring up, and you will carry them to the three daughters of the king, and you will give the most beautiful to the youngest daughter."

He goes off, then, as he had told him, and he asks them if they want a gardener.

They say, "Yes, indeed, very much."

He goes to the garden, and pulls up the fine cabbages, and the beautiful leeks as well. The youngest of the king's daughters sees him, and she tells it to her father, and her father says to her:

---

152. This Fleur-de-lys was supposed by our narrator to be some mark tattooed or impressed upon the breast of all kings' sons.

153. This, of course, is "Little Goerge," and makes one suspect that the whole tale is borrowed from the French; though it is just possible that only the names and some of the incidents may be.

"Let him alone, we will see what he will do afterwards." And, indeed, the next day he sees cabbages and leeks such as he had never seen before. Petit Yorge takes a flower to each of the young ladies. The eldest said: "I have a flower that the gardener has brought me, which has not its equal in the world."

And the second says that she has one, too, and that no one has ever seen one so beautiful. And the youngest said that hers was still more beautiful than theirs, and the others confess it, too. The youngest of the young ladies found the gardener very much to her taste. Every day she used to bring him his dinner. After a certain time she said to him,

"You must marry me."

The lad says to her, "That is impossible. The king would not like such a marriage."

The young girl says, too, "Well, indeed, it is hardly worthwhile. In eight days I shall be eaten by the serpent."

For eight days she brought him his dinner again. In the evening she tells him that it is for the last time that she brought it. The young man tells her, "No," that she will bring it again; that somebody will help her.

The next day Petit Yorge goes off at eight o'clock to call the Tartaro. He tells him what has happened. The Tartaro gives him a fine horse, a handsome dress, and a sword, and tells him to go to such a spot, and to open the carriage door with his sword, and that he will cut off two of the serpent's heads.

Petit Yorge goes off to the said spot. He finds the young lady in the carriage. He bids her open the door. The young lady says that she cannot open it—that there are seven doors, and that he had better go away; that it is enough for one person to be eaten.

Petit Yorge opens the doors with his sword, and sits down by the young lady's side. He tells her that he has hurt his ear and asks her to look at it; and at the same time he cuts off seven pieces of the seven robes which she wore without the young lady seeing him. At the same instant comes the serpent and says to him,

"Instead of one, I shall have three to eat."

Petit Yorge leaps on his horse, and says to him, "You will not touch one; you shall not have one of us."

And they begin to fight. With his sword he cuts off one head, and the horse with his feet another; and the serpent asks quarter till the next day. Petit Yorge leaves the young lady there. The young lady is full of joy; she wishes to take the young man home with her. He will not go by any means (he says); that he cannot; that he has made a vow to go to Rome; but he tells her that "to-morrow my brother will come, and he will be able to do something, too."

The young lady goes home, and Petit Yorge to his garden. At noon she comes to him with the dinner, and Petit Yorge says to her,

"You see that it has really happened as I told you—he has not eaten you."

"No, but to-morrow he will eat me. How can it be otherwise?"

"No, no! To-morrow you will bring me my dinner again. Some help will come to you."

The next day Petit Yorge goes off at eight o'clock to the Tartaro, who gives him a new horse, a different dress, and a fine sword. At ten o'clock he arrives where the young lady is. He bids her open the door. But she says to him that she cannot in any way open fourteen doors; she is there, and that she cannot open them, and he should go away; that it is enough for one to be eaten; that she is grieved to see him there. As soon as he has touched them with his sword, the fourteen doors fly open. He sits down by the side of the young lady and tells her to look behind his ear, for it hurts him. At the same time he cuts off fourteen bits of the fourteen dresses she was wearing. As soon as he had done that, the serpent comes, saying joyfully,

"I shall eat not one, but three."

Petit Yorge says to him, "Not even one of us."

He leaps on his horse and begins to fight with the serpent. The serpent makes some terrible bounds. After having fought a long time, at last Petit Yorge is the conqueror. He cuts off one head, and the horse another with his foot. The serpent begs quarter till the next day. Petit Yorge grants it, and the serpent goes away.

The young lady wishes to take the young man home to show him to her father; but he will not go by any means. He tells her that he must go to Rome and set off that very day; that he has made a vow, but that to-morrow he will send his cousin, who is very bold and is afraid of nothing.

The young lady goes to her father's, Petit Yorge to his garden. Her father is delighted and cannot comprehend it at all. The young lady goes again with the dinner.

The gardener says to her, "You see you have come again to-day, as I told you. To-morrow you will come again, just the same."

"I should be very glad of it."

On the morrow Petit Yorge went off at eight o'clock to the Tartaro. He said to him that the serpent had still three heads to be cut off, and that he had still need of all his help.

The Tartaro said to him, "Keep quiet, keep quiet; you will conquer him."

He gives him a new dress, finer than the others, a more spirited horse, a terrible dog, a sword, and a bottle of good-scented water. Then he says to him,

"The serpent will say to you, 'Ah! if I had a spark between my head and my tail, how I would burn you and your lady, and your horse and your dog.' And you, you will say to him then, 'I, if I had the good-scented water to smell, I would cut off a head from thee, the horse another, and the dog another.' You will give this bottle to the young lady, who will place it in her bosom, and, at the very moment you shall say that she must throw some in your face, and on the horse, and on the dog as well."

He goes off then without fear because the Tartaro had given him this assurance. He comes then to the carriage. The young lady says to him, "Where are you going? The serpent will be here directly. It is enough if he eats me."

He says to her, "Open the door."

She tells him that it is impossible; that there are twenty-one doors. This young man touches them with his sword, and they open of themselves. This young man says to her, giving her the bottle, "When the serpent shall say, 'If I had a spark between my head and my tail, I would burn you,' I shall say to him, 'If I had a drop of the good-scented water under my nose'; you will take the bottle, and throw some over me in a moment."

He then makes her look into his ear, and, while she is looking, he cuts off twenty-one pieces from her twenty-one dresses that she was wearing. At the same moment comes the serpent, saying, with joy, "Instead of one, I shall have four to eat."

The young man says to him, "And you shall not touch one of us, at any rate."

He leaps on his spirited horse, and they fight more fiercely than ever. The horse leaps as high as a house, and the serpent, in a rage, says to him, "If I had a spark of fire between my tail and my head, I would burn you and your lady, and this horse and this terrible dog."

The young man says, "I, if I had the good-scented water under my nose, I would cut off one of your heads, and the horse another, and the dog another."

As he said that, the young lady jumps up, opens the bottle, and very cleverly throws the water just where it was wanted. The young man cuts off a head with his sword, his horse another, and the dog another; and thus they make an end of the serpent. This young man takes the seven tongues with him and throws away the heads.

Judge of the joy of this young lady. She wants to go straight to her father with her preserver (she says), that her father must thank him too; that he owes his daughter to him. But the young man says to her that it is altogether impossible for him; that he must go and meet his cousin at Rome; that they have made a vow, and that, on their return, all three will come to her father's house. The young lady is vexed, but she goes off without losing time to tell her father what has happened. The father is very glad that the serpent was utterly destroyed; and he proclaims in all the country that he who has killed the serpent should come forward with the proofs of it.

The young lady goes again with the dinner to the gardener. He says to her, "I told you true, then, that you would not be eaten? Something has, then, killed the serpent?"

She relates to him what had taken place. But, lo! some days afterwards there appeared a black charcoal-burner, who said that he had killed the serpent and had come to claim the reward. When the young lady sees the charcoal-burner, she says immediately, that most certainly it was not he; that it was a fine gentleman, on horseback, and not a pest of a man like him. The charcoal-burner shows the heads of the serpent; and the king says that, in truth, this must be the man. The king has only one word to say, she must marry him. The young lady says she will not at all, and the father begins to compel her, saying that no other man came forward. But, as the daughter would not consent, to make a delay, the king proclaims in all the country that he who killed the serpent would be capable of doing something else, too, and that, on such a day, all the young men should assemble, that he would hang a diamond ring from a bell, and that whosoever riding under it should pierce the ring with his sword, should certainly have his daughter.

From all sides arrive the young men. Our Petit Yorge goes off to the Tartaro and tells him what has happened, and that he has again need of him. The Tartaro gives him a handsome horse, a superb dress, and a splendid sword. Equipped thus, Petit Yorge goes with the others. He gets ready. The young lady recognizes him immediately and says so to her father. He has the good luck to carry off the ring on his sword; but he does not stop at all, but goes off galloping as hard as his horse can go. The king and his daughter are in a balcony, looking on at all these gentlemen. They see that he still went on. The young lady says to her father: "Papa, call him!"

The father says to her, in an angry tone, "He is going off, because apparently he has no desire to have you." And he hurls his lance at him. It strikes him on the leg. He still rides on. You can well imagine the chagrin of the young lady. The next day she goes with the gardener's dinner. She sees him with his leg bandaged. She asks him what it is. The young lady begins to suspect something and goes to tell to her father how the gardener had his leg tied up, and that he must go and ask the gardener what is the matter. That he had told her that it was nothing.

The king does not want to go and says that she must get it out of the gardener; but to please his daughter, he says he will go there. He goes then, and asks him, "What is the matter?"

He tells him that a blackthorn has run into him. The king gets angry and says "that there is not a blackthorn in all his garden, and that he is telling him a lie."

The daughter says to him, "Tell him to show it us."

He shows it to them, and they are astonished to see that the lance is still there. The king did not know what to think of it all. This gardener has deceived him, and he must give him his daughter. But Petit Yorge, uncovering his bosom, shows the "Fleur-de-lys" there. The king does not know what to say; but the daughter says to him, "This is my preserver, and I will marry no one else than him."

Petit Yorge asks the king to send for five dressmakers, the best in the town, and five butchers. The king sends for them. Petit Yorge asks the dressmakers if they have ever made any new dresses which had a piece out; and on the dressmakers saying "No," he counts out the pieces and gives them to the dressmakers, asking if it was like that that they had given the dresses to the princess. They say, "Certainly not."

He goes, then, to the butchers, and asks them, if they have ever killed animals without tongues? They say, "No!"

He tells them, then, to look in the heads of the serpent. They see that the tongues are not there, and then he takes out the tongues he has. The king, having seen all that, has nothing more to say. He gives him his daughter.

Petit Yorge says to him that he must invite his father to the wedding, but on the part of the young lady's father; and that they must serve him up at dinner a sheep's heart, half cooked, and without salt. They make a great feast and place this heart before this father. They make him carve it himself, and he is very indignant at that. The son then says to him: "I expected that," and he adds, "Ah! my poor father, have you forgotten how you said that you wished to eat the heart, half cooked, and without salt, of him who let the Tartaro go? That is not my heart, but a sheep's heart. I have done this to recall to your memory what you said, and to make you recognize me."

They embrace each other and tell each other all their news, and what services the Tartaro had done him. The father returned happy to his house, and Petit Yorge lived very happily with his young lady at the king's house; and they wanted nothing, because they always had the Tartaro at their service.

Translated by Wentworth Webster.

Georgik and Merlin (1915)[154]

François Cadic

In a forest full of mystery near the chateau of a rich lord, a bird was singing cheerfully. Its voice went straight to the heart as did its caressing music. It would have made the most melodious of nightingales jealous.

"Now there's a nice neighbor that I'd be glad to have even closer to me," the lord used to say. "I'd give a great deal to whoever would help me catch it."

Indeed, a soldier who had recently returned from serving the king fulfilled his desire by capturing the bird. So, they built a beautiful cage with golden latticework, and they put various kinds of food in it along with fresh water in cups that glistened like crystal. Vain precautions! No sooner did the bird take a beak full than it stopped singing. Its musical chords were lost with its freedom. Its body was imprisoned, but its soul still dwelled deep in the mysterious forest.

The lord was still very much attached to his prisoner. He would not separate himself from the bird for all the gold in the world.

He would often say, "Woe to anyone who lets it escape! Death will be the punishment!"

This lord was a hard man, and nothing in the world would have prevented him from carrying out this sentence even if it were against the most beloved in his family, even if it were against his own son. In fact, he did have a son named

---

154.   "Georgik et Merlin," *La Paroisse Bretonne* (February 1915).

George, a ten-year-old child, who did not have his equal on earth with regard to the qualities of his heart and mind.

One day when the lord was on a journey, the little boy and the bird found themselves alone together, and the bird began to talk: "Georgik, Georgik, open the door of the cage, and I'll sing a beautiful song for you."

"I'll gladly do this," the child responded without thinking about it, and he released the prisoner.

Full of joy, the bird flew away crying out: "Thank you, my friend. "You've done me the greatest of services. Rest assured that you've not helped an ingrate!"

Then the bird pulled out a feather from its wing and said something more: "Take this. When you have need of my services, you only have to shake this feather and say these words: *Merlin, Merlin, come quickly to my aid!* And I'll be with you in an instant."

Before the boy knew it, the little bird had flown toward the forest singing the most melodious refrains. Then the child understood the seriousness of his error. He understood it even better when he saw his mother burst into tears.

"My son, my son," the poor woman sobbed, "what have you done? Have you forgotten your father's threats? You will now have to die!"

A salt merchant who happened to be in this region selling his salt heard all this moaning.

"To condemn a child to death for a mere thoughtless act," he cried, "would be an abominable crime. If you would like, I'll help you out of this trouble. Give me your son for some days. Then I'll be far from here, and your husband will never hear anyone talk about it."

The proposal was accepted as if it were a favor granted by heaven. Georgik was entrusted to the merchant with a sack of a hundred coins to cover the boy's expenses, and the two of them set out searching for adventure in new lands. However, along the way, the salt merchant thought to himself: 'I doubt that it was a good idea to take this kid under my wing. I'll abandon him at the first opportunity and take his coins with me.'

The opportunity presented itself very soon. They arrived before an old chateau whose large towers were reflected in the water of a pond at the edge of a forest. After leaving his little companion at the door, the merchant entered the chateau.

"Do you need a shepherd?" he asked.

"Yes, indeed," he was told, "providing that he's strong."

"Why strong?"

"Because our fields are infested by wolves, and he will undoubtedly have to protect himself against them."

"He is smart and good. Take him anyway."

This is how the boy, without his knowing it, was hired as a shepherd at this desolate chateau. Immediately, the salt merchant took off without caring about him anymore.

"And my money!" Georgik yelled after him. "Aren't you going to leave it here, too?"

A threatening gesture was his only answer.

"Merlin, Merlin, come help me!" the little boy cried out and shook the feather.

There was a rustling of wings, and all at once the bird of the forest appeared, and an invisible hand holding a hard club began vigorously beating the back of the thief. The salt merchant had to yield and return the hundred coins to the boy.

The next day the little shepherd led his sheep to the pasture.

"Beware of the wolves!" he was told. "Otherwise they will eat you."

"We shall certainly see," he replied, and once again he cried out: "Merlin, Merlin! come help me!"

And the bird came running.

"I'd like to have a whistle," the boy said, "then I'll call the wolves and put muzzles on them to prevent them from biting."

You can imagine the surprise of the servant who came to bring him his lunch at noon. He saw the boy playing on the side of the sheep which were grazing peacefully in the middle of the field, and around them was a pack of wolves, seated on their behinds, each with a muzzle on its mouth, and they seemed to be guarding them.

"Why aren't these ferocious beasts devouring the flock?"

"Because I haven't given them the permission," the boy responded.

Now, in those days, a serpent lived deep in the forest, and it was the terror of the countryside. It was a hideous monster that had seven heads. Each year, to avoid the consequences of its rage, the inhabitants were compelled to give him a young maiden to devour. This had been going on for a long time, and for a long time Georgik had been carrying out his duties to the great satisfaction of his master, when his daughter's turn came. She was precisely the one who brought the shepherd his lunch in the field every day. The poor creature wept more and more as the fatal day approached, and the shepherd did not cease comforting her.

"Pray, pray," he advised. "You'll see that God will protect you."

Finally, the designated day arrived, and the victim had to submit and set out on her way. She walked sadly toward the dragon's lair and had abandoned hope when suddenly she heard the gallop of a horse running at full speed. It was Georgik. The brave boy had asked his bird to give him everything he needed: a horse, a black cloak, and a steel sword. And now, he was prepared to confront the most formidable dangers.

"Mount behind me!" he said to the young maiden. "We shall find out whether the serpent will attack an armed man so willingly as he attacks weak women."

The hideous beast was waiting at the entrance to his lair.

"Come on!" Georgik cried out. "Come on, you cruel dragon, come for your prey!"

But the dragon certainly didn't think he'd see his victim appear in such company, and it recoiled.

"No," it responded, "I don't want her until tomorrow. Today I don't have much of an appetite."

Georgik dug his spurs into his horse's flanks and briskly departed. Shortly thereafter, he put the girl down at the edge of the forest and disappeared. The poor maiden had been so troubled that she had not recognized him in his disguise. However, she had had enough presence of mind to cut a piece of his black cloak and to bring it to her father.

At noon as on the previous days, she returned to the field to bring Georgik his lunch and told the shepherd about her unusual adventure.

"What did I tell you?" he declared. "Prayer brings good things. So, pray."

Early the next day the maiden began her sad pilgrimage once again. She heard the dragon's terrible roars of rage, and her entire body trembled, but no sooner was she in the middle of the forest than the knight, who wore a gray cloak over his shoulders, joined her and invited her to mount behind him.

The third day came, and the victim had to take the path through the forest. For the third time she encountered her savior dressed in a superb red cloak. Since they had to pass near a house where a man was busy heating his oven and holding a long iron fork, the knight stopped.

"Will you lend me your fork an instant?" he asked the man. "I've got to get rid of a criminal."

"Yes, yes, I'd be glad to," the man consented. "As long as it concerns a good deed, I'm your servant. . . . Take it."

The dragon had taken refuge in the depths of his lair as soon as it heard the horse's gallop. It was frightened.

"Here I am again, cruel beast," Georgik cried out at the entrance. "I've brought you your prey. If you want her, come and take her."

"I'm not in a hurry," the monster responded. "Another day, perhaps, when I feel myself better disposed."

Georgik felt his soul being filled with a violent anger.

"Do you think, you damned creature, that I'll permit you to mock us any longer?"

And, he seized the fork, forced it down one of the dragon's throats, and dragged the monster outside. His steel sword did the rest. After seven blows, seven heads fell. In disdain, the victor pushed the dead beast back with his foot, cut off the seven tongues, which he put in a kerchief, and suddenly took leave of the young maiden. As before, she had cut off a piece of his red cloak without his noticing it.

It had been announced everywhere by order of the lord of the chateau that whoever got rid of the cruel dragon from the country would wed his daughter. For proof it would be sufficient for the victor to bring back the dragon's seven heads.

Now, a coalman whose hut of branches stood in the forest and who had watched the fight from his hiding spot thought that he had found a good deal. He gathered the seven heads and went to the chateau claiming that he was the victor.

"The victor," exclaimed the young maiden. "That can't be! The man who killed the beast carried off the dragon's tongues not the heads."

"I have eaten the tongues," the imposter responded. "Only the heads are left."

To clear up everything, the lord ordered a great banquet to which he invited gentlemen and peasants of the country. There was a chance that the black knight might also attend. Indeed, Georgik went, but he was so well disguised that it was impossible to recognize his features. However, the young maiden didn't have any difficulty recognizing the black cloak.

"There he is!" she cried. "I'm not mistaken!"

The piece of cloth was an exact fit for the cloak. Who was this man? They didn't have time to find out because Georgik had disappeared.

Some time later, the lord held a second banquet. The people came to it in large numbers as before. Among the crowd there was a splendid knight dressed in a gray cloak that the young maiden recognized immediately.

"That must be he," she murmured in her father's ears.

Indeed, a cut she made in his cloak produced an exact fit with the piece she had detached.

"Are you the one who saved my daughter?" the father asked.

"Perhaps," the knight responded and he briskly vanished.

As she watched him go away, the young maiden remained pensive.

"I don't know whether I'm mistaken," she said, "but it seems to me that it was Georgik."

A third festival took place, and as many people as before attended this event. The coalman was also there, but one could sense that that he wasn't going to fatten himself in his corner because the outcome was approaching. A distinguished gentleman with his shoulders covered by a rich red cloak drew the particular attention of the people.

"I'm sure it's him!" the young maiden exclaimed with joy.

Indeed, the red cloak had a cut in it that corresponded exactly with the piece of cloth that she was holding in her hand.

Upon being discovered, the mysterious stranger wanted to flee again, but there were guards everywhere. As he was trying to go through the door, one of them threw a lance across his legs, and they had no difficulty in stopping him. It was indeed Georgik, and he was clearly her savior, and the best proof was the seven tongues that he had in his kerchief. As for the impostor, he cleared off without making a sound.

Now the young maiden rightfully belonged to the valiant young man.

Some days after the marriage had been celebrated, the couple was living happily when suddenly the lord of the chateau fell gravely ill. The doctors could do nothing despite their expertise. So, they called upon an old sorcerer.

"Three things are needed to cure him," he declared. "A piece of orange from the orange tree of the Armenian Sea, water from the Fountain of Life, and a slice of bread from the Yellow Queen with a bit of her wine. Just so you know, the Fountain of Life is not very far from the palace of the Yellow Queen."

The lord had two other sons-in-law who were very jealous of Georgik and who claimed the honor of seeking these remedies. They departed, but they didn't return for months. The first got lost in a country that was dry and cold, and he lived there half-dead at the foot of a mountain. The second embarked by ship on the ocean and was cast on a deserted shore by a storm.

When Georgik took his turn, he went on the prayers of his wife. He had a horse called Giletik that ran as fast as the wind. When Georgik was crossing through a forest, he came upon a hermit.

"I know the goal of your quest," the saint said to Georgik, "and I want to support your generous mission. So, first take the seaside oath. Here is a wand that will always go ahead of you. Follow it, and it will lead you to the orange tree. There you are to pick an orange and cut it into four pieces and bring one back. As you continue straight ahead, you will arrive at the Fountain of Life. It will not be easy to approach it because it is guarded by a gigantic lion whose body covers seven leagues of the countryside and only leaves a small path to reach the water. But before you try to get the water, you are to first go to the Yellow Queen's palace, where you'll find her lance near the hearth that you must bring back. Then, you are to cut a slice of her bread and fill a bottle of her wine, repeating: 'Yellow Queen, Yellow Queen, it's for my father-in-law's health.' When you are outside, you will see a stag tied to a post near the house. You are to get on its back and to take care that you leave your horse on the road so as not to frighten the stag. Then you are to return to the fountain. The lion will be sleeping. If it wakes up, you are to hide behind a bush and attack it without warning. With your lance it should be easy for you to do away with it. Once the lion's dead, make sure that you divide his body into four parts and to make three cuts in its tail. Then nothing will hinder you from getting water from the Fountain of Life."

Everything happened just as the hermit had predicted. Georgik arrived without much difficulty at the orange tree of Armenian Sea and at the palace of the Yellow Queen. He took the lance, the bread, the wine, the princess's stag and went to the fountain where the lion was sleeping.

'Everything's going well,' he said to himself, and he approached the water on tiptoe. Unfortunately, as he was pouring the water, there was some gurgling. The ferocious beast woke up with a roar, and Georgik hardly had time to slip behind a hawthorn bush. Five minutes later, the lion was asleep again.

This was the moment. Georgik stuck the lance straight into the lion's heart, and it was dead. Now he divided its body just as he had been instructed to do and left to search for his horse. He had left it grazing in the grass, but during his absence a hungry wolf had devoured the poor Giletik. So, now he only had one way to leave the place: he had to take the wolf in place of his horse. When he blew his whistle, the wolf came running. Then he climbed on the wolf's back, and there you have it: he galloped along the road on his way home.

The first man that they encountered was one of the brothers-in-law. The unfortunate soul was reduced to nothing and at the end of his strength. The water from the Fountain of Life and the Yellow Queen's wine restored his health. He couldn't restrain himself from expressing his contentment and admiration even if it was mixed with envy.

"Give me your remedies, Georgik, and I'll pay you whatever price they are worth."

Georgik had a grudge against this brother-in-law who up to this day had never stopped humiliating him.

"I shall gladly give you a little of my water, but I am going to set heavy conditions. I demand your wedding ring and the tip of your ear."

The brother-in-law uttered a deep sigh and accepted.

A little further on the travelers encountered the second brother-in-law who was also in bad condition. Thanks to the precious remedy, he was soon on his feet, and in turn, he asked: "What do you want in exchange for your water, your bread, and your wine?"

This brother-in-law hadn't treated Georgik any better than the first.

"The price that I demand for a little bread and some drops of wine," Georgik replied, "will be one of your toes."

After a moment of hesitation, the brother-in-law accepted the bargain.

Content at having humiliated these two arrogant men, Georgik let them cure their father-in-law and take pleasure in bragging about how they went themselves to search for the marvelous remedy. But he was only waiting to give them an unpleasant surprise again.

"I am warning you," the hermit had told Georgik, "the power of this water, this bread, and this wine will last only a month. Moreover, if you haven't returned them, the Yellow Queen will arrive at the end of this time to get them and beware of her anger."

Of course, the brothers-in-law were not aware of anything, and they hadn't returned the water, bread, and wine at the end of the month. So, the Yellow Queen arrived at their homes, enraged and with a whip in her hand. Georgik was not there. Suspecting what might happen, he had gone to work in the field with his wolf.

"My water, my bread, my wine!" screamed the queen.

The first brother-in-law brought her some drops of the water, the second, a little of wine and crumbs of the bread.

"Is that all that I gave you?" the queen asked. "I don't like to be mocked!"

And she violently whipped the shoulders of these two unfortunate men, who howled in vain.

"Georgik has the rest! Georgik has the rest!"

But the whip continued to hit them with such violence that they had to run to the field where their brother-in-law was working.

"Georgik, I beg you," they cried out. "Give back the Yellow Queen's water, bread, and wine!"

"Gladly," Georgik responded, "and above and beyond our agreement I'm going to return the ear, the wedding ring, and the toe. The first lesson that you deserved for your disdain and your pride was not sufficient to mend your ways. May the second be more beneficial for you! It is never beneficial for anyone to magnify himself at the expense of others."

Told by Méliau Le Cam, a tailor, at Plunéliau (Morbihan).

13. EXTRAORDINARY HEROES

ATU 513—THE EXTRAORDINARY COMPANIONS,
ATU 513A—HOW SIX GO THROUGH THE WORLD,
ATU 513B—THE LAND AND WATER SHIP

The key motifs in all the related tale types of this sort, which assumed many different forms in Europe, are a flawed hero, men with extraordinary talents, and an unusual boat. No matter the specific type, in these tales the hero (prince, commoner, bumpkin) cannot accomplish his goal without the help of godlike superhumans, who are generally altruistic. It is because the hero is basically good-natured and inadequate that a wild man, wise woman, dwarf, or saint will guide him to resourceful and potent individuals and enable him to develop his integrity. The young protagonist learns through experience as a cook/gardener to mobilize forces so that he can cleanse his reputation, gain revenge, and attract a young woman/princess who becomes his wife. Some folklorists have labeled these tale types as comic tales or tales of courting. Yet, the primary goal of the young man is to prove himself worthy as a son/knight, even if he may want to marry a king's daughter by building a boat that sails on land. It is the challenge or the desire to be worthy and recognized as having more talent than one suspects that draws the young man to engage in competition.

Some of the more important literary versions of these tale types are Giovanni Sercambi's "De Bono Facto," *Novelle* (1384); Giambattista Basile's "Lo 'gnorante" and "Lo Polece," *Lo cunto de li cunti* (1634), and Marie-Catherine d'Aulnoy, "Belle-Belle ou le Chevalier fortuné," *Les Contes de fées* (1697). There is also an incident in the *Mabingion* (c. 1100), in which extraordinary Arthurian knights assist the hero in his pursuit of a bride.

In the Grimms' final notes to the 1857 edition of *Children's and Household Tales*, they indicate that "How Six Made Their Way through the World" was provided by the talented storyteller Dorothea Viehmann and "The Six Servants" by the Family von Haxthausen. Wilhelm makes clear that he and Jacob knew several German variants as well as literary tales written by Basile and d'Aulnoy. It does not appear that they were familiar with the epic poem *Argonautica* by Apollonius of Rhodes. However, it is clear that this poem, along with oral tales and legends, played a major role in the formation of folk and fairy tales that gave rise to "How Six Made Their Way in the World," "The Six Servants," and myriad tales about the cooperation of superheroes. Apollonius' epic poem written some time during the third century BCE bears the markings of legends, oral tales, and literary works such as Homer's *Iliad* and *Odyssey*, and it is strange that the Grimms did not cite the Greco-pagan origins in the notes to "How Six Made Their Way in the World." This may be due to the fact that they were always looking for Nordic origins of the tales that they collected. Whatever the case may be, it is clear that the *Argonautica* became a foundational story for fairy tales about superheroes and collective action that flourish throughout the world as well as for chapbooks, dime novels, comics, cartoons, and films. A short summary of the poem reveals just how pregnant it is with fairy-tale motifs:

Once upon a time there was a nasty king named Pelias who had usurped the throne of Iolkos in Thessaly from his half-brother Aeson. Warned by an oracle that Aeson's baby son, Diomedes, would kill him one day, Pelias seeks to murder the baby. However, his mother smuggles him to Mount Pelion, where he is raised under the name of Jason by the centaur Chiron. When Jason turns twenty, an oracle sends him back to Iolkos in disguise. Along the way he loses a sandal because he kindly helps an old woman, the goddess Hera in disguise. In gratitude, Hera, who bears a grudge against Pelias, will assist Jason in the future. When Jason arrives in Iolkos, he attends a celebration and games to honor Poseidon, god of the sea, and is recognized by Pelias because an oracle had informed him that a young man with one sandal would kill him one day. Therefore, Pelias devises a plan to make sure Jason will die by sending him on a perilous mission to obtain the Golden Fleece in Colchis, guarded by a vicious dragon that never sleeps. To reach Colchis, Jason needs the help of the great shipmaker Argus, who builds the ship *Argo*. Then Jason recruits fifty of the most extraordinary superhuman and divine heroes to accompany him. Among this valiant group are Actor, Amphion, Heracles, Pollux, Nestor, Telamon, Atalanta, Lynceus, Phineas, Castor, Philias, Iphitos, Peleus, Orpheus, and so on. They are all committed to this quest because they understand that they will be righting a wrong. They are champions of justice. They have numerous adventures in which Jason plays but a minor role, and they encounter all sorts of obstacles, including the clashing rocks through which the *Argo* must sail. It is only thanks to his shipmates that Jason arrives in Colchis, where he faces another obstacle: King Aeetes of Colchis demands that Jason perform three impossible tasks if he is to receive the Golden Fleece. Fortunately, Hera intercedes in his behalf and has Medea, the witch-daughter of Aeetes, fall in love with Jason. Consequently, she assists him in completing the tasks, and after he puts the ferocious dragon to sleep with a magic potion, Jason sails away in the *Argo* with Medea on board. However, King Aeetes pursues them, until Medea chops up her brother Apsyrtus and scatters his pieces in the sea, compelling Aeetes to stop and pick them up. So, Jason and Medea escape and eventually return to Iolkos, where Medea uses her sorcery again to trick Pelias' daughters to chop up their father and cook him in a cauldron. However, there is no happy end to this tale, for Medea and Jason must flee to Corinth, where Jason betrays her by becoming engaged to Creusa, the daughter of the king of Corinth. Medea, unlike the forgotten brides in later folk and fairy tales, takes her revenge by using her sorcery to burn Creusa and her father to death. Then she kills the two sons that she bore to Jason and flees to Athens. Jason later dies, a miserable and lonely flawed hero, when a piece of the rotting ship *Argo* falls upon him while he is sleeping.

There are hundreds if not thousands of versions of this tale, which may have been a variant itself, and these tales have come down to us in the present; some even predate Apollonius' version. The theme has also been interpreted in manifold ways as an initiation voyage or a shamanistic exploration of the other world. But there is one consistent element of shared intentionality and collaboration that is at the basis of all the stories and accounts for its appeal. During the twentieth century, figures such as Superman, Captain Marvel, Batman, and other superheroes such as the X-Men and the Avengers clearly owe a debt to the Greco-Roman gods and titans who entered into the popular storytelling traditions throughout Europe in the medieval period.

******

How Six Made Their Way through the World (1819)[155]
Jacob and Wilhelm Grimm

Once upon a time there was a man who had mastered all kinds of skills. He had fought in the war and had conducted himself correctly and courageously, but when the war was over, he was discharged and received three pennies for traveling expenses.

"Just you wait!" he said. "I won't put up with that. If I find the right people, I'll force the king to turn over all the treasures of his kingdom to me."

Full of rage, he went into the forest, and there he saw a man tearing up six trees as if they were blades of wheat.

"Will you be my servant and travel with me?" he asked.

"Yes," the man answered. "But first I want to bring this little bundle of firewood home to my mother."

He took one of the trees and wrapped it around the others, lifted the bundle onto his shoulders, and carried it away. Then he returned and went off with his master, who said, "We two shall certainly make our way anywhere in the world."

After they had walked for a while, they found a huntsman who was kneeling down and taking aim at something with his gun.

"Huntsman, what are you going to shoot?" the master asked him.

"There's a fly sitting on the branch of an oak tree two miles from here. I want to shoot out its left eye," he answered.

"Oh, come with me," said the man. "If we three stick together, we'll certainly make our way anywhere in the world."

The huntsman was willing and went with him. As they approached seven windmills, they saw the sails rotating swiftly, even though there was no wind coming from any direction, nor was there a leaf stirring.

"What in the world can be driving those windmills? There's not a breeze around," the man said. He continued on with his servants for about two miles,

---

155. "Sechse kommen durch die Welt," *Kinder- und Haus-Märchen. Gesammelt durch die Brüder Grimm*, 2 vols. (Berlin: G. Reimer, 1819).

and then they saw a man sitting on a tree. He was holding one nostril closed while blowing through the other.

"My goodness! What are you doing up there?" the man asked.

"Two miles from here are seven windmills," he said. "I'm blowing them so that they'll turn."

"Oh, come with me," said the man. "If we four stick together, we'll certainly make our way anywhere in the world."

So the blower got down from the tree and went along with them. After some time they saw a man standing on one leg, while the other was lying unbuckled on the ground next to him.

"You've made things comfortable for yourself," said the man. "Time for a rest, I suppose?"

"I'm a runner," he answered, "and I've unbuckled my leg so that I don't run too fast. When I run with two legs, I go faster than any bird can fly."

"Oh, come with me. If we five stick together, we certainly shall make our way anywhere in the world."

So he went along with them, and shortly thereafter they met a man who was wearing a cap that completely covered one of his ears.

"Where are your manners?" the master asked him. "You shouldn't drape your cap over one ear like that. You look like a dunce."

"It's got to be this way," said the man. "If I put on my cap straight, then a tremendous frost will come, and all the birds in the air will freeze and drop down dead to the ground."

"Oh, come with me," said the master. "If we six stick together, we'll certainly make our way anywhere in the world."

Now the six came to a city where the king had proclaimed that whoever ran a race against his daughter and won would become her husband. But whoever lost would have to pay for it with his head. Then the man appeared before the king and said, "I want to race but under the condition that one of my servants runs for me."

The king answered, "Then his life must also be placed at stake, and you and he will forfeit your lives if you lose."

When they agreed on the terms and everything was set, the master buckled on the runner's other leg and said to him, "Now show us how quick you are and help us win."

It had been determined that whoever was the first to bring back water from a distant well would be the victor. The runner and the king's daughter were both given jugs and set off running at the same time. Yet, within seconds after the king's daughter had run but a short stretch, the spectators could no longer see the runner, for he had soared by them just like the wind. In a short time he arrived at the spring, filled the jug with water, and turned around. Halfway back, however, he was overcome by fatigue, put the jug on the ground, lay down, and fell asleep. For his pillow he had taken a dead horse's skull that had been lying on the ground so that he wouldn't be too comfortable and would wake up in time to continue the race. In the meantime, the king's daughter, who was much better at running than ordinary people, had reached the spring and was hurrying back with her jug full of water. When she saw the runner lying asleep on the ground, she was delighted and said, "Now the enemy's been delivered into my hands." She emptied his jug and continued running. Everything would have been lost for the runner if the huntsman had not by chance been standing on the top of the castle and if he had not seen everything with his sharp eyes.

"I'll make sure that the king's daughter doesn't defeat us!" he said, and he loaded his gun and aimed so carefully that he shot the horse's skull out from under the runner's head without hurting him. The runner awoke, jumped up, and saw that his jug was empty and that the king's daughter was way ahead of him. However, he didn't lose heart, but ran back to the spring with the jug, filled it anew with water, and managed to beat the king's daughter home with ten minutes to spare.

"You see," he said, "it was about time that I really started using my legs. I wouldn't exactly call that running, what I was doing before."

However, the king was vexed and—his daughter, even more so—that a common discharged soldier should win the race. Therefore, they consulted with each other, seeking a way to get rid of him and all his companions as well. Finally, the king said to her, "I've got an idea. Don't fret. They'll never see their homes again."

Then he went to the six and said, "I want you to eat, drink, and be merry," and he led them to a room that had an iron floor. The doors were also made of iron, and the windows were lined with iron bars. In the room there was a table covered with delicious food, and the king said to them, "Go inside and enjoy yourselves."

When they were inside, the king had the door locked and bolted. Then he summoned the cook and commanded him to make a fire and keep it going under the room until the iron became burning hot. The cook did that, and it began to get hot in the room. The six, who were sitting at the table, felt very warm, but they thought this was due to the food. However, when the heat became greater and greater and they wanted to leave the room, they found the doors and windows locked. Now they realized that the king had devised something evil and meant to suffocate them.

"He won't succeed!" said the man with the cap. "I'm going to let a frost come that will put the fire to shame and send it crawling away."

So he put his cap on straight, and immediately there was a frost, causing all the heat to disappear and the food on the table to freeze. After two hours had passed and the king thought they had all perished in the heat, he commanded that the door be opened and looked in himself to see how they were. Yet, when the door was opened, all six of them were well and vigorous. Indeed, they declared that it would be nice to get outside and warm themselves, for the food had frozen to the dishes because of the cold conditions in the room. The king stormed furiously down the stairs, scolded the cook, and asked him why he had not done what he had ordered. But the cook answered, "There's more than enough heat. Just look for yourself."

The king saw a tremendous fire blazing under the iron room and realized that he couldn't get the better of the six by doing something like that. So he tried to think of something new to get rid of the unwelcome guests. He summoned the master and said, "If you will accept gold and give up your claim to my daughter, you can take away as much gold as you like."

"That's fine with me, Your Majesty," he answered. "If you give me as much as my servant can carry, I won't claim your daughter."

The king was satisfied with that, and the master added, "In two weeks I shall return here to fetch the gold."

Then he summoned all the tailors in the entire kingdom, and for two weeks they had to sit and sew a sack. When it was finished, the strong man, who could tear up trees, swung the sack over his shoulder and went to the king, who said, "Who's that powerful fellow carrying such a bundle of canvas on his shoulder?" Suddenly he became horrified and thought, 'What a lot of gold he'll carry away!' So the king ordered a ton of gold be brought, and all of that took sixteen of his strongest men to carry, but the strong man grabbed it with one hand, put it into the sack and said, "Why don't you bring more right away? This will barely cover the bottom."

Gradually, the king had his whole treasure brought, and the strong man tossed it all into the sack, but it only became half full.

"Bring some more!" the strong man cried. "These few crumbs aren't enough to fill the sack."

So seventeen thousand wagons of gold from all over the kingdom had to be driven to the spot, and the strong man stuffed them all into the sack along with the oxen that were harnessed to the wagons.

"Since I don't have the time to inspect everything," he said, "I'll just take what comes until the sack's completely full."

When everything was in the sack, there was still room for a lot more, but the strong man said, "I think it's time to put an end to this. Sometimes one has to tie up a sack even if it's not quite full."

Then he hoisted it onto his back and went away with his companions. When the king saw one single man carrying away all the treasures of his kingdom, he was furious and ordered his cavalry to pursue the six and take the sack away from the strong man. Two of the king's regiments soon caught up with the six and called to them:

"You're our prisoners! Put down the sack with the gold, or else you'll be cut to pieces!"

"What did you say?" asked the blower. "We're your prisoners? Before that ever happens, all of you will soon be dancing around in the air."

With that he held one nostril and blew through the other at the two regiments, sending them flying in every which direction, up into the blue and over hill and dale. Some were scattered this way, others that way, while a sergeant begged for mercy. Since he was a brave fellow, who had nine wounds and didn't deserve to be humiliated, the blower let up a bit, and the sergeant came out of it without being harmed. Then the blower said to him, "Now go home to the king and tell him, all he has to do is send a few more regiments, and I'll blow them all sky high!"

When the king received the message, he said, "Let those fellows go. There's something extraordinary about them."

So the six brought their wealth back home, divided it among themselves, and lived happily until their death.

How Six Made Their Way through the World (1857)[156]
Jacob and Wilhelm Grimm

Once upon a time there was a man who had mastered all kinds of skills. He had fought in the war and had conducted himself correctly and courageously, but when the war was over, he was discharged and received three pennies for traveling expenses.

"Just you wait!" he said. "I won't put up with that. If I find the right people, I'll force the king to turn over all the treasures of his kingdom to me."

Full of rage, he went into the forest, and there he saw a man tearing up six trees as if they were blades of wheat. "Will you be my servant and travel with me?" he asked.

"Yes," the man answered. "But first I want to bring this little bundle of firewood home to my mother."

He took one of the trees and wrapped it around the others, lifted the bundle onto his shoulders, and carried it away. Then he returned and went off with his master, who said, "We two shall certainly make our way anywhere in the world."

After they had walked for a while, they found a huntsman who was kneeling down and taking aim at something with his gun.

"Huntsman, what are you going to shoot?" the master asked him.

"There's a fly sitting on the branch of an oak tree two miles from here. I want to shoot out its left eye," he answered.

"Oh, come with me," said the man. "If we three stick together, we'll certainly make our way anywhere in the world."

The huntsman was willing and went with him. As they approached seven windmills, they saw the sails rotating swiftly, even though there was no wind coming from any direction, nor was there a leaf stirring.

---

156.   "Sechse kommen durch die Welt," *Kinder- und Hausmärchen gesammelt durch die Brüder Grimm*, 7th ed., 3 vols. (Göttingen: Verlag der Dieterischen Buchhandlung, 1857).

"What in the world can be driving those windmills? There's not a breeze around," the man said. He continued on with his servants for about two miles, and then they saw a man sitting on a tree. He was holding one nostril closed while blowing through the other.

"My goodness! What are you doing up there?" the man asked.

"Two miles from here are seven windmills," he said. "I'm blowing them so that they'll turn."

"Oh, come with me," said the man. "If we four stick together, we'll certainly make our way anywhere in the world."

So the blower got down from the tree and went along with them. After some time they saw a man standing on one leg, while the other was lying unbuckled on the ground next to him.

"You've made things comfortable for yourself," said the man. "Time for a rest, I suppose?"

"I'm a runner," he answered, "and I've unbuckled my leg so that I don't run too fast. When I run with two legs, I go faster than any bird can fly."

"Oh, come with me. If we five stick together, we certainly shall make our way anywhere in the world."

So he went along with them, and shortly thereafter they met a man who was wearing a cap that completely covered one of his ears.

"Where are your manners?" the master asked him. "You shouldn't drape your cap over one ear like that. You look like a dunce."

"It's got to be this way," said the man. "If I put on my cap straight, then a tremendous frost will come, and all the birds in the air will freeze and drop down dead to the ground."

"Oh, come with me," said the master. "If we six stick together, we'll certainly make our way anywhere in the world."

Now the six came to a city where the king had proclaimed that whoever ran a race against his daughter and won would become her husband. But whoever lost would have to pay for it with his head. Then the man appeared before the king and said, "I want to race but under the condition that one of my servants runs for me."

The king answered, "Then his life must also be placed at stake, and you and he will forfeit your lives if you lose."

When they agreed on the terms and everything was set, the master buckled on the runner's other leg and said to him, "Now show us how quick you are and help us win."

The runner and the king's daughter were both given jugs and set off running at the same time. Yet, within seconds after the king's daughter had run but a short stretch, the spectators could no longer see the runner, for he had soared by them just like the wind. In a short time he arrived at the spring, filled the jug with water, and turned around. Halfway back, however, he was overcome by fatigue, put the jug on the ground, lay down, and fell asleep.

For his pillow he had taken a dead horse's skull that had been lying on the ground so that he wouldn't be too comfortable and would wake up in time to continue the race. In the meantime, the king's daughter, who was much better at running than ordinary people, had reached the spring and was hurrying back with her jug full of water. When she saw the runner lying asleep on the ground, she was delighted and said, "Now the enemy's been delivered into my hands." She emptied his jug and continued running. Everything would have been lost for the runner if the huntsman had not by chance been standing on the top of the castle and if he had not seen everything with his sharp eyes.

"I'll make sure that the king's daughter doesn't defeat us!" he said, and he loaded his gun and aimed so carefully that he shot the horse's skull out from under the runner's head without hurting him. The runner awoke, jumped up, and saw that his jug was empty and that the king's daughter was way ahead of him. However, he didn't lose heart, but ran back to the spring with the jug, filled it anew with water, and managed to beat the king's daughter home with ten minutes to spare.

"You see," he said, "it was about time that I really started using my legs. I wouldn't exactly call that *running*, what I was doing before."

However, the king was vexed and—his daughter, even more so—that a common discharged soldier should win the race. Therefore, they consulted with each other, seeking a way to get rid of him and all his companions as well. Finally, the king said to her, "I've got an idea. Don't fret. They'll never show their faces around here again."

Then he went to the six and said, "I want you to eat, drink, and be merry," and he led them to a room that had an iron floor. The doors were also made of iron, and the windows were lined with iron bars. In the room there was a table covered with delicious food, and the king said to them, "Go inside and enjoy yourselves."

When they were inside, the king had the door locked and bolted. Then he summoned the cook and commanded him to make a fire and keep it going under the room until the iron became burning hot. The cook did that, and it began to get hot in the room. The six, who were sitting at the table, felt very warm, but they thought this was due to the food. However, when the heat became greater and greater and they wanted to leave the room, they found the doors and windows locked. Now they realized that the king had devised something evil and meant to suffocate them.

"He won't succeed!" said the man with the cap. "I'm going to let a frost come that will put the fire to shame and send it crawling away."

So he put his cap on straight, and immediately there was a frost, causing all the heat to disappear and the food on the table to freeze. After two hours had passed and the king thought they had all perished in the heat, he commanded that the door be opened and looked in himself to see how they were. Yet, when the door was opened, all six of them were well and vigorous. Indeed, they declared that it would be nice to get outside and warm themselves, for the food had frozen to the dishes because of the cold conditions in the room. The king stormed furiously down the stairs, scolded the cook, and asked him why he had not done what he had ordered. But the cook answered, "There's more than enough heat. Just look for yourself."

The king saw a tremendous fire blazing under the iron room and realized that he couldn't get the better of the six by doing something like that. So he tried to think of something new to get rid of the unwelcome guests. He summoned the master and said,

"If you will accept gold and give up your claim to my daughter, you can take away as much gold as you like."

"That's fine with me, Your Majesty," he answered. "If you give me as much as my servant can carry, I won't claim your daughter."

The king was satisfied with that, and the master added, "In two weeks I shall return here to fetch the gold." Then he summoned all the tailors in the entire kingdom, and for two weeks they had to sit and sew a sack. When it was finished, the strong man, who could tear up trees, swung the sack over his shoulder and went to the king, who said, "Who's that powerful fellow carrying such a bundle of canvas on his shoulder? Why, it's as big as a house!" Suddenly he became horrified and thought, 'What a lot of gold he'll carry away!'

So the king ordered a ton of gold be brought, and all of that took sixteen of his strongest men to carry, but the strong man grabbed it with one hand, put it into the sack and said, "Why don't you bring more right away? This will barely cover the bottom."

Gradually, the king had his whole treasure brought, and the strong man tossed it all into the sack, but it only became half full.

"Bring some more!" the strong man cried. "These few crumbs aren't enough to fill the sack."

So seventeen thousand wagons of gold from all over the kingdom had to be driven to the spot, and the strong man stuffed them all into the sack along with the oxen that were harnessed to the wagons.

"Since I don't have the time to inspect everything," he said, "I'll just take what comes until the sack's completely full."

When everything was in the sack, there was still room for a lot more, but the strong man said, "I think it's time to put an end to this. Sometimes one has to tie up a sack even if it's not quite full." Then he hoisted it onto his back and went away with his companions.

As soon as the king saw one single man carrying away all the treasures of his kingdom, he was furious and ordered his cavalry to pursue the six and take the sack away from the strong man. Two of the king's regiments soon caught up with the six and called to them:

"You're our prisoners! Put down the sack with the gold, or else you'll be cut to pieces!"

"What did you say?" asked the blower. "We're your prisoners? Before that ever happens, all of you will soon be dancing around in the air." With that he held one nostril and blew through the other at the two regiments, sending them flying in every which direction, up into the blue and over hill and dale. Some were scattered this way, others that way, while a sergeant begged for mercy. Since he was a brave fellow, who had nine wounds and didn't deserve to be humiliated, the blower let up a bit, and the sergeant came out of it without being harmed. Then the blower said to him, "Now go home to the king and tell him, all he has to do is send a few more regiments, and I'll blow them all sky high!"

When the king received the message, he said, "Let those fellows go. There's something extraordinary about them."

So the six brought their wealth back home, divided it among themselves, and lived happily until their death.

The Six Servants (1812)[157]
Jacob and Wilhelm Grimm

An old queen, who was a sorceress, had a daughter, who was the most beautiful maiden under the sun. However, whenever a suitor came to court her daughter, she gave him a task to perform, and if he failed, she showed him no mercy. He had to kneel down, and his head was cut off.

Now it so happened that there was a prince who wanted to court her. But his father did not permit him to leave.

"No," said the king. "If you go, you'll never return."

Then the son withdrew to his bed and became deathly ill for seven years. When his father saw that he might die, he said, "Go there. Perhaps you'll have luck."

The prince immediately became healthy, got up from his bed, and went on his way. Now he had to go through some woods where he saw a man lying on the ground. He was immensely fat and really a small mountain. The man called out to him and asked him whether he wanted to have a servant.

"What can I do with such a fat man like you?" the prince said. "How did you become so fat?"

"Oh," said the Fat Man, "this is nothing. When I really want to expand, I'm three thousand times as fat."

"Well, then come with me," the prince said.

So the two men continued on their way and found another man who was lying on the ground with his ear glued to the grass.

"What are you doing there?" asked the prince.

---

157. "Die sechs Diener," *Kinder- und Haus-Märchen. Gesammelt durch die Brüder Grimm*, 2 vols. (Berlin: Realschulbuchhandlung, 1812/1815).

"Hey! I'm listening," answered the man. "I can hear the grass grow and every-thing that is just happening in the world, and that's why people call me the Listener."

"Tell me what's happening at the old queen's court," said the prince.

"A suitor is having his head cut off. I hear the swishing of a sword," he answered.

"Come with me," said the prince, and they continued on their way until they found a man lying on the ground who was so very long that they had to go quite far until they could reach his head from his feet.

"Why are you so tall?" asked the prince.

"Oh," he said. "When I really want to stretch out my limbs, I'm three thou-sand times as tall, taller than the highest mountain on earth."

"Come with me," said the prince, and so they continued on their way and came across a blindfolded man sitting beside the road.

"Why do you have that piece of cloth around your eyes?" the prince asked.

"Oh," he responded. "My glance is so powerful that it shatters whatever I gaze upon with my eyes. That's why I can't keep them open."

"Come with me," said the prince.

So the five of them continued on their way and encountered a man basking under the hot sun, but he was freezing and shivering so much that his entire body was shaking.

"How can you be freezing when the sun is shining?" asked the prince.

"Ah," answered the man, "the hotter it is, the more I freeze, and the colder it is, the hotter I am. In the midst of ice, I can't stand the heat, and in the midst of hot flames, I can't stand the cold."

"Come with me," said the prince, and the six of them continued on their way until they saw a man standing there and looking in different directions and over all the mountains.

"What are you looking at?" asked the prince.

"I have such sharp eyes," said the man, "that I can see over all the forests and fields, valleys and mountains, and throughout the whole world."

"Come with me," said the prince, "I've been needing someone just like you."

Now the prince and his six servants entered the city where the beautiful and dangerous maiden lived. But the prince went before the old queen and said that he wanted to court her daughter.

"Yes, you may," she answered. "I shall give you three tasks, and if you perform each one of them, the princess is yours. The first task is to bring back a ring that I dropped into the Red Sea."

"I'll carry out this task," and as he said this, he called his servant with the sharp eyes, and after looking into the sea all the way to the bottom, Sharp Eyes saw the ring lying next to a stone. After that the Fat Man put his mouth to the sea and let the waves rush inside until he had drunk everything so that the sea was as dry as a meadow. Then the Tall Man bent over a little and picked up the ring with his hand. After that the prince brought it to the old woman, who was astonished and said, "Yes, that's the right ring. You've performed the first task all right, but now comes the second. Do you see the three hundred fat oxen grazing on the meadow in front of my castle? You must devour them, skin and bones, hair and horns. And you can invite only one guest to eat with you. Then, down in my cellar there are three hundred barrels of wine that you must drink up as well. If one hair is left from the oxen or one little drop from the wine, your life will be forfeited to me."

"I'll accomplish this as well," said the prince, and he invited the Fat Man to be his guest.

Fat Man ate the three hundred oxen without leaving a single hair anywhere and drank the wine right out of the barrels without a glass. When the old sorceress saw that, she was astonished and said to the prince, "No one has ever gotten this far, but there's still one task left." And she thought to herself, 'I'll turn you to stone yet.' Then she said aloud, "Tonight I'm going to bring the maiden into your room, and you're to put your arms around her. While you sit there with her, be sure not to fall asleep. I shall come at the stroke of midnight, and if she's no longer in your arms, you'll lose your life."

'This task is not too difficult,' the prince thought. 'I'll certainly be able to keep my eyes open. Nevertheless, it's wise to be cautious.'

When the maiden was led into his room that evening, the prince called all his servants to enter, and the Tall Man had to form a circle around the two, and Fat Man had to place himself in front of the door so that no living soul could enter. The couple sat there, and the beautiful maiden didn't say a word, but the moon shone through the window on her face so that the prince could gaze at her wonderful beauty. They all stayed awake until eleven o'clock. Then the old woman cast a sleeping spell over their eyes that they couldn't fend off. They all slept soundly until a quarter of twelve, and when they all awoke, the princess was gone, for she had been taken away by the old woman.

The prince and the servants began to moan, but Listener said, "Be quiet!" And he listened and said: "She's sitting inside a rock three hundred miles from here and is lamenting her fate."

"I'll help," said Tall Man, and he lifted his blindfolded companion onto his back, and in no time they were in front of the enchanted rock. Then Tall Man took off the blindfold, and no sooner did Sharp Eyes gaze at the rock than it shattered into a thousand pieces. Tall Man fetched the princess from the depths of the rock and carried her back to the prince within three minutes. When the clock struck twelve, the old woman entered into the room and thought she'd find the prince fast asleep, but there he was, cheerfully holding her daughter tightly in his arms. To be sure, she had to keep quiet now, but she felt sorry for her daughter, and the princess was also upset that a commoner had won her.

The next morning the princess had three hundred cords of wood gathered together and said to the prince that, even though he had performed the three tasks, she would not become his wife until someone was ready to sit in the middle of the woodpile and, once it was lit, withstand the fire. She was convinced that none of his servants would let himself be burned for the prince's sake and that the prince would have to sacrifice himself on the woodpile out of love for her. Then she'd be free.

But when the servants heard that, they said, "We've all done something with the exception of Frosty. Now he's got to do his share."

Then they took him and placed him in the middle of the heap of wood and set fire to it. The flames began to burn, and they burned for three days until all the wood had been consumed, and when the flames died down, Frosty stood in the middle of the ashes trembling like an aspen leaf and said, "Never in my life have I endured such a frost, and if it had lasted much longer, I'd have been frozen stiff."

Now the beautiful maiden had to marry the prince. Still, as they drove off to the church, the old woman said, "I can't let this happen," and she sent her soldiers after them to bring back her daughter and to strike down anyone that opposed them. However, Listener had pricked up his ears and had heard everything that the old woman had said. Then he told it to Fat Man, who spat on the ground once or twice and a huge amount of water came flowing out and caused the soldiers to drown. When they didn't return, the old woman sent her knights in armor, but Listener heard them coming and undid the blindfold of Sharp Eyes, who took a piercing look at the enemy, and they shattered like glass. Thus the prince and his bride could continue on their way undisturbed, and when the couple had been blessed in church, the six servants took their leave to seek their fortune in the world.

Half an hour from the prince's castle was a village, and outside the village a swineherd was tending his pigs. When the prince and his wife arrived there, he said to her, "Do you know who I really am? I'm not the son of a king but a swineherd, and the man with the pigs over there is my father. You and I must now get to work and help my father look after the pigs."

Then the prince took lodgings at the inn and secretly told the innkeeper and his wife to take away his wife's royal garments during the night. When she awoke the next morning, she had nothing to put on, and the innkeeper's wife gave her an old skirt and a pair of woolen stockings. At the same time the woman acted as if she were giving the princess a great gift. After that the princess believed that her husband really was a swineherd, and so she tended the pigs with him and said, "I've deserved this because of my arrogance."

All of this lasted a week, by which time she could no longer stand it, for her feet had become all sore. Then some people came and asked whether she knew who her husband was.

"Yes," she answered. "He's a swineherd, and he's gone out to do a little trading."

However, they asked her to come with them, and they took her to the castle. When they entered the hall, the prince was standing there in his royal attire, but she didn't recognize him until he took her into his arms, kissed her, and said, "I suffered a great deal for you, and it was only right that you should also suffer for me."

Now the wedding was truly celebrated, and you can imagine that the person who told this tale would have liked to have been there, too.

Ashiepattle and His Goodly Crew (1848)[158]

Peter Christen Asbjørnsen

Once upon a time there was a king, and this king had heard about a ship which went just as fast by land as by water, and he wished to have one like it. He promised his daughter and half the kingdom to anyone who could build one for him. And this was given out at every church all over the country. There were many who tried, as you can imagine, for they thought it would be a nice thing to have half the kingdom, and the princess wouldn't be a bad thing in the bargain. But they all fared badly.

Now there were three brothers, who lived far away on the borders of a forest; the eldest was called Peter, the second Paul, and the youngest Espen Ashiepattle, because he always sat in the hearth, raking and digging in the ashes.

It so happened that Ashiepattle was at church on the Sunday when the proclamation about the ship, which the king wanted, was read. When he came home and told his family, Peter the eldest asked his mother to get some food ready for him, for now he was going away to try if he could build the ship and win the princess and half the kingdom. When the bag was ready, he set out. On the way he met an old man who was very crooked and decrepit.

"Where are you going?" the man asked.

"I'm going into the forest to make a trough for my father. He doesn't like to eat at table in our company," said Peter.

"Trough it shall be!" said the man. "What have you got in that bag of yours?" he added.

"Dung," said Peter.

"Dung it shall be," said the man. Peter then went into the forest and began to cut and chop away at the trees and work away as hard as he could, but in spite of all his cutting and chopping, he could only turn out troughs. Toward dinnertime he wanted something to eat and opened his bag. But there was not a crumb of food in it. As he had nothing to live upon and as he did not turn out anything but troughs, he became tired of the work, took his ax and bag on his shoulder and went home to his mother.

Paul then wanted to set out to try his luck at building the ship and winning the princess and half the kingdom. He asked his mother for provisions, and

---

158.   Originally published in Peter Christen Asbjørnsen, *Norske huldreeventyr of folkesagn* (Christiania: C. A. Oybwad, 1848). The English translation is to be found in *Fairy Tales from the Far North*, trans. H. L. Bræstad (London: D. Nutt, 1897).

when the bag was ready, he threw it over his shoulder and went on his way to the forest. On the road he met the old man, who was very crooked and decrepit.

"Where are you going?" the man asked.

"Oh, I'm going into the forest to make a trough for our sucking pig," said Paul.

"Pig-trough it shall be," said the man. "What's in that bag of yours?" added the man.

"Dung," said Paul.

"Dung it shall be," said the man.

Paul then began felling trees and working away as hard as he could, but no matter how he cut and how he worked, he could only turn out pig-troughs. He didn't give in, however, but worked away till far into the afternoon before he thought of taking any food. Then, all at once, he became hungry and opened his bag, but not a crumb could he find. Paul became so angry he turned the bag inside out and struck it against the stump of a tree. Then he took his ax, went out of the forest, and set off homeward.

As soon as Paul returned, Ashiepattle wanted to set out and asked his mother for a bag of food.

"Perhaps I can manage to build the ship and win the princess and half the kingdom," said he.

"Well, I never heard the like," said his mother. "Are you likely to win the princess, you, who never does anything but root and dig in the ashes! No, you shan't have any bag with food!"

Ashiepattle didn't give in, however, and prayed and begged till he got leave to go. He didn't get any food, not he, but he stole a couple of oatmeal cakes and some flat beer and set out.

When he had walked awhile he met the same old man, who was so crooked and tattered and decrepit.

"Where are you going?" the man asked.

"Oh, I was going into the forest to try if it were possible to build a ship which can go as fast by land as by water," said Ashiepattle. "The king has proclaimed that anyone who can build such a ship shall have the princess and half the kingdom."

"What have you got in that bag of yours?" asked the man.

"Not much worth talking about. There ought to be a little food in it," answered Ashiepattle.

"If you'll give me a little of it, I'll help you," said the man.

"With all my heart," said Ashiepattle, "but there's nothing but some oatmeal cakes and a drop of flat beer."

It didn't matter what it was, the man told him. If he only got some of it, he would be sure to help Ashiepattle. Afterward they came up to an old oak in the wood, and the man said to the lad, "Now you must cut off a chip and then put it back again in exactly the same place, and when you have done that, you can lie down and go to sleep." Ashiepattle did as he was told and then lay down to sleep, and in his sleep he thought he heard somebody cutting and hammering and sawing and carpentering, but he couldn't wake up till the man called him; then the ship stood quite finished by the side of the oak.

"Now you must go on board, and you must take everyone you meet with you," said the man.

Espen Ashiepattle thanked him for the ship, said he would do so, and then sailed away. When he had sailed some distance he came to a long, thin tramp, who was lying near some rocks, eating stones.

"What sort of a fellow are you, that you lie there eating stones?" asked Ashiepattle.

The tramp said he was so fond of meat he could never get enough. Therefore, he was obliged to eat stones. And then he asked if be might go with him in the ship.

"If you want to go with us, you must make haste and get on board," said Ashiepattle.

Yes, that he would, but he must take with him some large stones for food.

When they had sailed some distance, they met one who was lying on the side of a sunny hill, sucking at a bung.[159]

"Who are you," asked Ashiepattle, "and what's the good of lying there sucking that bung?"

"Oh, when one hasn't got the barrel, one must be satisfied with the bung," said the man. "I'm always so thirsty, I can never get enough beer and wine." And then he asked for leave to go with him in the ship.

"If you want to go with me, you must make haste and get on board," said Ashiepattle.

Yes, that he would. And so he went on board and took the bung with him to allay his thirst.

When they had sailed awhile again, they met one who was lying with his ear to the ground, listening.

"Who are you, and what's the good of lying there on the ground listening?" Ashiepattle asked.

"I'm listening to the grass, for I have such good ears that I can hear the grass growing," said the man. And then he asked for leave to go with him in the ship. Ashiepattle couldn't say nay to that, and so he responded:

"If you want to go with me, you must make haste and get on board."

Yes, that he would. And he also went on board.

When they had sailed some distance, they came to one who was standing taking aim with a gun.

"Who are you, and what's the good of standing there aiming like that?" asked Ashiepattle.

---

159. A stopper or plug.

So the man said: "I have such good eyes that I can hit anything, right to the end of the world." And then he asked for leave to go with him in the ship.

"If you want to go with me, you must make haste and get on board," said Ashiepattle.

Yes, that he would. And he went on board.

When they had sailed some distance again, they came to one who was hopping and limping about on one leg, and on the other he had seven-ton weights.

"Who are you," said Ashiepattle, "and what's the good of hopping and limping about on one leg with seven-ton weights on the other?"

"I am so light," said the man, "that if I walked on both my legs, I should get to the end of the world in less than five minutes." And then he asked for leave to go with him in the ship.

"If you want to go with us, you must make haste and get on board," said Ashiepattle.

Yes, that he would. And so he joined Ashiepattle and his crew on the ship.

When they had sailed on some distance, they met one who was standing holding his hand to his mouth.

"Who are you?" said Ashiepattle, "and what's the good of standing there, holding your mouth like that?"

"Oh, I have seven summers and fifteen winters in my body," said the man. "So I think I ought to keep my mouth shut, for if they get out all at the same time, they would finish off the world altogether." And then he asked for leave to go with him in the ship.

"If you want to go with us, you must make haste and get on board," said Ashiepattle.

Yes, that he would, and then he joined the others on the ship.

When they had sailed a long time, they came to the king's palace, and Ashiepattle went straight in to the king and said the ship stood ready in the courtyard outside, and now he wanted the princess, as the king had promised.

The king didn't like this very much, for Ashiepattle did not cut a very fine figure. He was black and sooty, and the king didn't care to give his daughter to such a tramp. So, he told Ashiepattle that he would have to wait a little and added, "You can have her all the same, if by this time to-morrow you can empty my storehouse of three hundred barrels of meat."

"I suppose I must try," said Ashiepattle; "but perhaps you don't mind my taking one of my crew with me?"

"Yes, you can do that, and take all six if you like," said the king, for he was quite sure that, even if Ashiepattle took six hundred with him, it would be impossible. So Ashiepattle took with him the one who ate stones and always hungered after meat.

When they came next morning and opened the storehouse, they found he had eaten all the meat, except six small legs of mutton, one for each of his companions. Ashiepattle then went to the king and said the storehouse was empty, and he supposed he could now have the princess.

The king went into the storehouse and, sure enough, it was quite empty. But Ashiepattle was still black and sooty, and the king thought it was really too bad that such a tramp should have his daughter. So, he said he had a cellar full of beer and old wine, three hundred barrels of each kind, which he would have him drink first.

"I don't mind your having my daughter if you can drink them up by this time tomorrow," said the king.

"I suppose I must try," responded Ashiepattle, "but perhaps you don't mind my taking one of my crew with me?"

"Yes, you may do that," said the king, for he was quite sure there was too much beer and wine even for all seven of them. Ashiepattle took with him the one who was always sucking the bung and was always thirsty, and the king then shut them down in the cellar, where the thirsty one drank barrel after barrel, as long as there was any left. But he left a couple of pints to each of his companions in the last barrel.

In the morning the cellar was opened, and Ashiepattle went at once to the king and said he had finished the beer and wine, and now he supposed he could have the princess as the king had promised.

"Well, I must first go down to the cellar and see," said the king, for he couldn't believe it. But, when he got there, he found nothing but empty barrels. Nevertheless, Ashiepattle was both black and sooty, and the king thought it wouldn't do for him to have such a son-in-law. So he said that if Ashiepattle could get water from the end of the world in ten minutes for the princess's tea, he could have both her and half the kingdom, for he thought that task would be quite impossible.

"I suppose I must try," responded Ashiepattle, and sent for the one of his crew who limped about on one leg and had seven ton weights on the other, and told him that he must take off the weights and use his legs as quickly as he could, for he must have water from the end of the world for the princess's tea in ten minutes.

So he took off the weights, got a bucket, and set off, and the next moment he was out of sight. Then they waited and waited for him to return, but he didn't appear. At last there were only three minutes left for him to return, and the king became as pleased as if he had won a big wager. Then Ashiepattle called the one who could hear the grass grow and told him to listen and find out what had become of their companion.

"He has fallen asleep at the well," said he who could hear the grass grow; "I can hear him snoring, and a troll is scratching his head."

Ashiepattle then called the one who could shoot to the end of the world and told him to send a bullet into the troll. He did so and hit the troll right in the eye. The troll gave such a yell that he woke the man who had come to fetch the water for the tea, and when he returned to the palace, there was still one minute left out of the ten.

Ashiepattle went straight to the king and said: "Here's the water," and now he supposed he could have the princess, for surely the king would not make any more

fuss about it now. But the king thought that Ashiepattle was just as black and sooty
as ever, and didn't like to have him for a son-in-law. So, he said he had three hundred fathoms of wood with which he was going to dry in the bakehouse, and he
wouldn't mind Ashiepattle having his daughter if he would first sit in the bakehouse
and dry all the wood. Then he should have the princess, and that without fail.

"I suppose I must try," responded Ashiepattle, "but perhaps you don't mind
my taking one of my crew with me?"

"Oh, no, you can take all six," said the king, for he thought it would be warm
enough for all of them.

Ashiepattle took with him the one who had fifteen winters and seven summers in his body, and in the evening he went across to the bakehouse. However,
the king had piled up so much wood on the fire that you might almost have
melted iron in the room. They couldn't get out of it, for no sooner were they
inside than the king fastened the bolt and put a couple of padlocks on the door
besides. Ashiepattle then said to his companion: "You had better let out six or
seven winters, so that we may get something like summer weather here."

They were then just able to exist, but during the night it got cold again, and
Ashiepattle then told the man to let out a couple of summers, and so they slept
far into the next day. But when they heard the king outside Ashiepattle said: "Let
out a couple more winters, but you must manage it so that the last winter you
let out strikes the king right in the face."

He did so, and when the king opened the door, expecting to find Ashiepattle
and his companion burned to cinders, he saw them huddling together and shivering with cold till their teeth chattered. The same instant Ashiepattle's companion with the fifteen winters in his body let loose the last one right in the king's
face, which swelled into a big chilblain.[160]

"Can I have the princess now?" asked Ashiepattle.

"Yes, take her and keep her and the kingdom into the bargain," said the
king, who dared not refuse any longer. And so the wedding took place, and they
feasted and made merry and fired off guns.

While the people were running about searching for waddling for their guns,
they took me instead, gave me some porridge in a bottle and some milk in a
basket, and fired me right across here so that I could tell you how it all happened.

Translated by H. L. Brœstad.

The Four Brothers (1852)[161]

Ernst Meier

There were once four brothers who were called Hans, Jorg, Jokel, and Michel.
The first was a sharpshooter, the second, a wind-blower, the third, a runner, the

160.   A swelling produced by exposure to cold.
161.   "Die vier Brüder," *Deutsche Volksmärchen aus Schwaben* (Stuttgart: E. B. Scheitlin's
Verlagshandlung, 1852).

fourth, Michel, was so strong that he could pluck the largest oak trees from the ground as if they were blades of grass. All four brothers went out together into the world.

At one time a game-keeper came across Hans, who had just got his rifle ready as if to shoot into the air, and therefore, the game-keeper asked him what he was aiming at.

"Well, a hundred hours from here there's a sparrow sitting on the top of a church steeple in Berlin, and I want to shoot it."

And in that very moment he squeezed the trigger, and after a short time he said, "It's lying on the ground."

However, the game-keeper refused to believe that he had hit anything. So the sharpshooter called his brother, the runner, over to him and sent him off to Berlin to fetch the sparrow that he had shot. He immediately ran off, and after two hours he was back again and brought the sparrow with him. The shot had been so perfect that the sparrow's head had fallen from the church steeple to the right, and the body to the left.

Afterward the game-keeper accompanied the two brothers part of their way, and they came upon Jorg, who was standing next to seven windmills and seemed to be looking idly into the sky and holding a reed steadily in front of his mouth.

"Hey, friend, what are you doing there?" the game-keeper asked.

"Well, I'm blowing the windmills so that they won't stand still because there's no wind blowing today."

Not far from there the game-keeper also encountered Michel, who had wrapped a huge rope around seventy acres of the forest. The game-keeper had no idea what the meaning of all this was, and so he asked him what he intended to do.

"Oh," Michel said, "I wanted to fetch a little bundle of wood to make a little fire when it gets cold in the winter." Then he tore down the entire forest so that it crashed, and he carried it away.

The game-keeper was completely astounded and rushed home as fast as he could. Meanwhile the four brothers wandered further and soon came to Berlin.

It so happened that the king of Prussia had become very sick, and his personal doctor declared: "The king will have to die unless the grass of life that grows on top of Mount Saint Gotthardt in Switzerland is brought to him within eight hours."

So the king immediately issued a proclamation: "Whoever fetches the grass of life within eight hours from Mount Saint Gotthardt in Switzerland will receive as much money as he wants."

Upon hearing this the runner Jokel reported to the king and declared that he was ready to fetch the grass of life if he could have a written guarantee that he would receive the reward that had been announced. This was soon done.

Immediately thereafter Jokel raced off, and within two hours he reached the top of Mount Saint Gotthardt and soon found the grass of life. Then he hurried back, but when he was about a hundred hours far from Berlin, he sat down to rest awhile beneath an oak tree and fell asleep. Meanwhile, his brothers began worrying that he was taking too much time. Consequently, the sharpshooter looked for him and saw that he was fast asleep. So he quickly took his rifle and shot a bullet at his brother's coattails. The runner felt as though someone was yanking at his coattails, and so he woke up and looked at his watch. It was high time, and he ran off and arrived in Berlin in two hours with plenty of time to spare and delivered the grass. Then the doctor prepared a medicine from it, and thanks to the medicine the king became completely healthy again.

Now the king was very happy and let the runner know that he should come and fetch his reward. However, Jokel had a sack made before he went to the king. In order to do this he needed two hundred cubit yards of twilled cotton fabric. Then he took his brother Michel, who had torn out the oak trees, with him to carry the money in the sack that the king had promised to give him, namely as much money as one could carry. Once they appeared in the castle, the king led them into his treasure chamber and said: "Here, take as much as you can carry!"

Then Michel opened up his huge sack and took tons of gold one after the other with his hands as if they were marbles and threw the gold into the sack. But the sack was hardly full at all, and Michel could carry much more. Therefore, they went into a second treasure chamber and stuck all the money that they found there into the sack as they had previously done. When they went into the third chamber, however, and still could not get enough money, the king became angry and ordered two regiments of infantrymen and two regiments of the cavalry to assemble before the castle. It took them two hours until they were all organized. In the meantime Michel had thrown the sack over his shoulder and had departed. But since the sack was so thick and wide, he could not get out of the castle without hindrance and had to pull the sack a little. To be sure, the sack made its way through, but the entire castle door along with eight pillars came along with it.

Michel continued on his way with the sack until he came to the castle gate, and the gateway was once again too small. So he pushed firmly and lifted the entire castle gate from its sockets and carried it on his shoulder along with the eight pillars, the castle door, and the tons of gold. He carried this burden to the sea and said: "I want to rest here a little while until Jokel and Jorg come. Also this dumb little sack is bothering my shoulder a bit."

And as he put down the sack, he saw for the first time all the other things that had become attached to the sack, and when his brothers now arrived, they had to have a good laugh about strong Michel.

It didn't take long, however, until the four regiments of soldiers reached the sea and sought to retrieve the money. Then Jorg merely took the wind reed and blew all the soldiers into the sea so that they died a miserable death. Afterward the four brothers moved on, divided the money among themselves, and lived happily as rich people until the end of their lives.

The King of Lochlin's Three Daughters (1860–1862)[162]

John Francis Campbell

There was a king of Lochlin, who had three daughters. One day, when they were out for a walk, they were carried off by three giants, and no one knew where they had gone. The king consulted a storyteller, and this wise man told him that the giants had taken them under the earth.

"The only way to reach them," said he, "is to build a ship that will sail on land and sea."

So the king sent out a proclamation that any man who could make such a ship could marry his eldest daughter. Now there was a widow who had three sons. The eldest went to his mother and said: "Bake me an oatcake and roast me a cock. I am going to cut wood and build a ship to sail on land and sea."

"A large oatcake with a curse, or a small oatcake with a blessing?" asked his mother.

"A large oatcake will be small enough before I've built the ship!"

Away he went with his oatcake and roasted cock to a wood by the river. He sat down to eat, when a great water goblin came up out of the water.

"Give me a share of your oatcake," said the goblin.

"I'll not do that," said he. "There's little enough for myself."

After he had eaten, he began to chop down a tree, but as soon as he felled a tree it was standing again. At night he gave up and went home. The next day the second son asked his mother to bake him an oatcake and roast him a cock.

"A large oatcake with a curse, or a small oatcake with a blessing?" she asked.

"A large one will be little enough," said he.

And away he went with the bannock and roasted cock, to the wood by the river. He sat down to eat, when a great goblin came up out of the water.

"Give me a share of your oatcake," said she.

"There's less than enough for myself," he replied.

The same thing happened to him as to his eldest brother. As fast as he cut down a tree, it was standing again. So he gave up and went home. Next day the youngest son asked his mother to bake him an oatcake and roast him a cock. But he chose the wee oatcake with a blessing.

Away he went to the wood by the river. There he sat down to eat, when a great goblin came up out of the water, and said: "Give me a share of your oatcake."

"You shall have that," said the lad, "and some of the cock too, if you like."

After the goblin had eaten, she said: "Meet me here at the end of a year and a day, and I shall have a ship ready to sail on land and sea."

---

162. *Popular Tales of the West Highlands: Orally Collected*, 4 vols. (Edinburgh: Edmonston and Douglas, 1860–1862).

At the end of a year and a day, the youngest son found that the goblin had the ship ready. He went aboard, and sailed away. He had not sailed far when he saw a man drinking up a river.

"Come with me," said the lad. "I'll give you meat and wages, and better work than that."

"Agreed!" said the man.

They had not sailed far when they saw a man eating all the oxen in a field.

"Come with me," said the lad. "I'll give you meat and wages, and better work than that."

"Agreed!" said the man.

They had not sailed much farther when they saw a man with his ear to the ground. "What are you doing?" asked the lad.

"I'm listening to the grass coming up through the earth," said the man.

"Come with me," said the lad. "I'll give you meat and wages, and better work than that."

So he went with the lad and the other two men, and they sailed on till the Listener said: "I hear the giants and the king's three daughters under the earth."

So they let a basket down the hole, with four of them in it, to the dwelling of the first giant and the king's eldest daughter.

"You've come for the king's daughter," said the giant, "but you'll not get her unless you have a man that can drink as much water as I."

The lad set the Drinker to compete with the giant. Before the Drinker was half full, the giant burst. They freed the eldest daughter and went to the house of the second giant.

"You've come for the king's daughter," said he, "but you'll not get her till you find a man who can eat as much as I."

So the lad set the Eater to compete with the giant. Before he was half full, the giant burst. They freed the second daughter and went to the house of the third giant.

"You've come for the king's daughter," said the giant, "but you'll not get her unless you are my slave for a year and a day."

"Agreed!" said the lad.

Then he sent the Listener, the Drinker and the Eater up in the basket, and after them the three princesses. The three men left the lad at the bottom of the hole and led the princesses back to their father, the king of Lochlin. They told the king of all the brave deeds they had done to rescue his daughters.

Now, at the end of a year and a day, the lad told the giant he was leaving, and the giant said: "I've an eagle that will carry you to the top of the hole."

The lad mounted the eagle's back, taking fifteen oxen to feed the eagle, but the eagle had eaten them before she had flown half way. So the lad had to return.

"You'll be my slave for another year and a day," said the giant.

At the end of that time the lad mounted the eagle's back, taking thirty oxen to feed the eagle, but the eagle ate them all before she had flown three quarters of the way. So they returned.

"You must be my slave for another year and a day," said the giant.

At the end of that time, the lad mounted the eagle's back, taking sixty oxen to feed the eagle on the way, and they had almost reached the top when the meat was finished. Quickly the lad cut a piece from his own thigh and gave it to the eagle. With one breath they were in the open air. Before leaving him, the eagle gave the lad a whistle.

"If you are in difficulty," said she, "whistle, and I'll help you."

When the lad reached the king of Lochlin's castle, he went to the smith and asked him if he needed a lad to blow the bellows. The smith agreed to take him. Shortly after, the king's eldest daughter ordered the smith to make her a golden crown, like the one she had worn under the earth.

"Bring me the gold, and I'll make the crown," said the new lad to the smith.

The smith brought the gold. Then the lad whistled, and the eagle came at once. "Fetch the gold crown that hangs behind the first giant's door."

The eagle returned with the crown, which the smith took to the king's eldest daughter.

"This looks like the crown I had before," said she.

Then the second daughter ordered the smith to make her a silver crown like the one she had worn under the earth.

"Bring me the silver, and I'll make the crown," said the lad.

The smith brought the silver. Then the lad whistled, and the eagle came.

"Fetch the silver crown that hangs behind the second giant's door," said the lad.

The eagle returned with the crown, which the smith took to the king's second daughter.

"This looks like the crown I had before," said she.

Then the king's youngest daughter ordered the smith to make her a copper crown like the one she had worn under the earth.

"Bring me the copper, and I'll make the crown," said the lad.

The smith brought the copper. Then the lad whistled, and the eagle came at once.

"Fetch the copper crown that hangs behind the third giant's door," said the lad.

The eagle returned with the crown, which the smith took to the king's youngest daughter.

"This looks like the crown I had before," said she.

"Where did you learn to make such fine crowns?" the king asked the smith.

"It was my lad who made them," said he.

"I must see him," said the king. "I must ask him to make me a crown."

The king sent a coach and four to fetch the lad from the smithy, but when the coachmen saw how dirty he looked, they threw him into the coach like a dog. So he whistled for the eagle, who came at once.

"Get me out of this," said the lad, "and fill the coach with stones."

The king came to meet the coach, but when the door was opened for the lad, a great heap of stones tumbled out instead. Other servants were sent to fetch the lad, but they treated him just as badly, so he whistled for the eagle.

"Get me out of this," said he, "and fill the coach with rubbish from the midden."

Again the king came to meet the coach, but when the door was opened for the lad, a great mound of rubbish fell out on to the king. The king then sent his trusted old servant to fetch the lad. He went straight to the smithy and found the lad blowing the bellows, his face black with soot.

"The king wishes to see you," said the king's servant, "but first, clean a little of the soot off your face."

The lad washed himself and went with the servant to the king. On the way he whistled for the eagle.

"Fetch me the gold and silver clothes belonging to the giants," said he.

The eagle returned with the clothes, and when the lad put them on, he looked like a prince. The king came to meet him and took him to the castle, where he told the king the whole story from beginning to end. The Drinker, the Eater and the Listener were punished. The king gave his eldest daughter to the lad, so they were married, and the wedding lasted twenty days and twenty nights.

How St. Joseph Helped a Young Man Win the Daughter of a King (1870)[163]

Laura Gonzenbach

Once upon a time there was a man who was very rich and had three sons. When he was about to die, he divided his wealth and property among the three brothers and gave each one an equal share.

Now it so happened that the king issued a proclamation in the entire country that whoever built a ship that could sail on the sea and on land could have his daughter for his wife. Thereupon, the eldest brother thought, 'I have such a large amount of money that I might as well try to build this ship.'

So he called together all the master shipbuilders in the entire land and had them begin to construct the ship. Old people also came and asked him, "Your lordship, can we also work on the ship so that we can earn a living?"

But he turned them away with hard words and said, "I can't use you because you don't have enough strength."

Then very young boys and apprentices came and asked him for work, but he responded, "I can't use you because you're much too weak."

163. *Sicilianische Märchen*, 2 vols. (Leipzig: W. Engelmann, 1870).

And when workers came who were not very skillful, he chased them away with hard words. Finally, a very little old man with a white beard arrived and said to him, "Are you also going to turn me away like the others so that I can't earn a living?"

Indeed, the young man did turn him away like the others.

When the ship was finally finished and was ready to sail, there was a sudden explosion, and the entire ship collapsed. Now the young man had nothing anymore and had become a poor man. So he returned to his brothers who gave him a place to live and kept him with them. Meanwhile, the second brother thought, 'My brother certainly managed things in a clumsy way, and that's why the ship collapsed. Now I'm going to try my luck, and if I succeed, then the beautiful princess will be mine.' Shortly thereafter he called together all the master shipbuilders again and ordered them to build a new ship. However, he was just as cold-blooded as his brother, and when old men, young apprentices, or clumsy workers came, he chased them away with hard words. Finally even the old little man with the long white beard came and asked for work. But he, too, was turned away.

When the ship was finished, there was another explosion, and the entire ship collapsed. The second brother was now just as poor as the older one, and both had to be supported by the youngest. Now, he began to think: 'How shall I be able to support my brothers by myself? I want to try my luck, too. If I succeed in getting the king's beautiful daughter for my bride, I'll have enough money for me and my brothers. If I don't succeed, we shall at least, all three of us, be equally poor.'

Soon thereafter he called together all the master shipbuilders to construct a new ship for him. Since very old people came and asked for work, he said to them, "Certainly, there's enough work for everyone here." And when young boys came and asked, "Master, let us work to earn our bread," he gave them work as well. And he didn't even turn back the clumsy workers. Rather, he let them work to earn their bread. Finally the old little man arrived and asked, "Let me work to earn my living."

"No, old father,"[164] he responded. "You're not to work. I want you to manage all the other workers and to oversee the entire construction."

Now the old man was actually St. Joseph, who had come to help the young man because he was so kind and pious and devoted to St. Joseph,[165] and kept a lamp lit at his bedside day and night to honor St. Joseph.

When the ship was finished, St. Joseph said to the young man, "Now you can sail away and fetch the beautiful princess."

"Oh, old father," the young man requested, "don't leave me. I'd prefer it if you accompanied me to the king."

---

164. *Patri granni.*
165. *Era divotu di S. Giuseppe.*

"Good," St. Joseph said. "I'll do that, but only under the condition that you give me half of what you get, whatever it may be."

The young man promised to do this, and shortly thereafter, they began their journey, and the ship sailed on the sea as well as on land. Meanwhile, the young man continued to keep a lamp burning in front of the image of St. Joseph day and night.

After they had gone some distance, they saw a man, who stood in a thick fog and had a large sack that he was filling with fog.

"Oh, old father," the young man cried out, "what is he doing there?"

"Ask him," answered St. Joseph.

"What are you doing there, handsome lad?" the young man called out.

"I'm gathering fog in a sack. That's my talent."

"Ask him if he wants to come along with us," St. Joseph said.

Then the young man asked, and the man answered, "Yes, if you'll give me food and drink, I'll come along."

So they took him on board the ship, and the young man said, "Old man, there were two of us, and now there's three."

After a while they saw a man coming toward them. He had ripped out half a forest and was carrying all the tree trunks on his shoulders.

"Old father," cried the young man, "just look at that man who's carrying all those trees!"

"Ask him why he's ripped out all the trees."

So the young man asked the man, who answered, "I just wanted to gather together a small handful of twigs."

"Ask him if he will come along with us," St. Joseph said.

The young man did this, and the strong man answered, "Yes, if you'll give me food and drink, I'll come along."

So they took him on board the ship, and the young man said, "Old father, there were three of us, and now we're four."

After they had traveled another distance, they saw a man drinking out of a river, and he had drunken almost half the river.

"Old father," the young man exclaimed, "just look at how the man can drink!"

"Ask him what he's doing."

So the young man asked, and the other fellow answered, "I've just had a drop of water to drink."

"Ask him whether he'll come along with us."

The young man did that, and the man answered, "Yes. If you'll give me food and drink, I'll come along."

So they took him on board the ship, and the young man said, "Old father, there were four of us, and now we're five."

Once more they traveled for a while until they saw a man who stood on the side of a stream and was aiming his gun into the water.

"Old father," the young man said, "what is the man aiming at?"

"Ask him yourself," St. Joseph said.

So the young man called out to this fellow, "Handsome lad, what are you aiming at?"

"Shhh! Shhh!" the man said and made a sign for him to keep quiet.

However, the young man asked him again, "What are you aiming at?"

"Now you've scared it away!" the man said reluctantly. "There was a quail sitting on a tree in the underworld. I wanted to shoot it. That's my talent. I can hit anything I aim at."

"Ask him whether he'll come along with us."

The young man did this, and the man said, "Yes. If you'll give me food and drink, I'll come along."

So they took him on board the ship, and the young man said, "Old father, there were five of us, and now we're six."

After they had gone somewhat further again, they saw a man coming their way who took such long strides that he stood with one foot in Catania and the other near Messina.

"Old father, just look at those long strides that man is taking!"

"Ask him what he's doing."

So the young man asked the fellow who answered, "I'm just taking a little walk."

"Ask him whether he'll come along with us."

The young man did this, and the man said, "If you'll give me food and drink, I'll come along."

So they took him also on board, and the young man said, "Old father, there were six of us, and now we're seven."

St. Joseph knew quite well why he took them along, and the ship continued to sail over land and sea due to his power. Blessed is he whom it carried!

Finally they came to the city where the king was living with his beautiful daughter. The young man sailed in front of the palace, went to the king, and said, "Your majesty, I've fulfilled your wish and built a ship that can sail on land and on water. Now give me the reward that I deserve, namely your daughter."

But the king thought, 'Should I give my daughter to this stranger? I don't know whether he's rich or poor, whether he's a cavalier or a beggar.' Therefore, he contemplated how he might keep his daughter from this young man and said, "It's not enough that you've built this ship. You must fulfill one more condition. You must provide me with a runner who's capable of delivering this letter to the Count of the Underworld and can bring back the answer in an hour."

"But this condition was not part of your proclamation," responded the poor young man.

"If you don't want to fulfill this condition," the king declared, "I won't give you my daughter."

So the young man became despondent and went straight to St. Joseph and said, "Old father, the king won't give me his daughter unless I provide him with a runner who's capable of bringing a letter to the Count of the Underworld and who can bring the answer within an hour."

"You fool," said St. Joseph. "Accept the condition. You can send the man who stands with one foot near Catania and the other foot near Messina."

All at once the young man was happy and called the man and took him with him to the king and said, "I want to fulfill the condition, and here's the runner."

The king gave him a letter for the Count of the Underworld, and the man went off with great strides. When he arrived in the underworld, the count spoke to him, "Wait a while until I've finished writing the answer."

However, the man was so tired from so much fast running that he fell asleep while he was waiting and completely forgot about going home. At the same time the young man waited for the runner full of anxiety and worries. Indeed, the hour was nearly up, and the runner still did not appear. Then St. Joseph spoke to the shooter who hit everything he aimed at: "Look and see why the runner is staying away for so long."

The shooter looked and said, "He's still in the underworld, in the count's palace, and he's sleeping. I'll wake him right away."

So he shot and hit the runner with a bullet right in his knee. The runner woke up immediately, and once he realized that the hour was nearly up, he jumped up, asked for the answer, and ran back to the palace so fast that he arrived before the hour was up.

Now the young man was very happy, but the king was bent on keeping his daughter from him and said, "You have fulfilled this condition, but it is not enough. Now you must provide a man who is capable of drinking up half my cellar."

"This condition was not in your proclamation," the young man complained.

"If you don't want to fulfill this condition," the king replied, "I won't give my daughter to you."

So the young man went sadly to St. Joseph and told him his dilemma.

"You fool," St. Joseph said. "You can take the man who drank up half the river."

So the young man called the fellow and said to him, "Do you think you can drink up half the cellar?"

"Certainly," the man answered. "I'm so thirsty I could even drink more if there is any more."

Now they went to the king, who led them into the cellar, and the man drank up all the barrels until they were empty—wine, vinegar, and oil, everything that could be found in the cellar. The king became frightened and said, "I can no longer refuse to give you my daughter. But you must know that I can only give as much dowry as a man can carry."

"But, your royal highness," the young man spoke, "even if a man is very strong, he can't carry much more than a hundred or so pounds. What kind of a king's daughter is she?"

But the king insisted: "I'm only going to give her as much as a man can carry. If you won't agree to this condition, I won't give you my daughter."

Once again the young man was distressed and went back to St. Joseph and said, "The king will give his daughter only so much dowry as a man can carry. Now I've spent my entire fortune to build the ship. How can I return to my brothers this way?"

"You fool!" said St. Joseph. "Call the man who carried half the woods on his shoulders."

The young man became very happy and took the man with him.

"Load as much as you can on your shoulders," he said. "You must clean out the entire palace."

The strong man promised to do this, and he packed everything on his shoulders that he could: closets, tables, chairs, gold, and silver, even the king's gold crown, and when he had cleaned out the entire palace, he ripped the gate from its hinges and threw it on top. Then he carried everything to the ship, and the young man brought the princess there as well, and they sailed away in good spirits. However, the king became furious when he saw his palace empty, and he summoned all his warships and ordered his soldiers to follow him on a ship to pursue the young man and regain all his treasures.

When the warships had almost overtaken the young man's ship, St. Joseph said to him, "Turn around, and tell me what you see."

As soon as the young man saw all the ships, he became scared and cried out, "Oh, old father, I see a lot of warships following us, and they've almost caught up with us."

All at once, St. Joseph ordered the man who had gathered together the fog to open his sack. As soon as he did this, a thick fog arose around the ship so that the soldiers could no longer see it and had to return to the king without accomplishing their mission. Meanwhile, St. Joseph used his power to enable the ship to sail on until it finally reached home safely.

"So," said St. Joseph, "now you're home again, and I want you to fulfill your promise and give me half of all your treasures."

"I'm glad to do this, old father," the young man responded and divided all the treasures into two equal parts. The last thing was the gold crown, and the young man took his sword and split the crown in two. He took one half and gave the other to St. Joseph.

"Old father," he said, "I've now divided everything, and there's nothing left."

"What do you mean there's nothing left?" St. Joseph asked. "You've forgotten the best!"

"The best!" the young man exclaimed. "Old father, I don't see anything more that we haven't divided."

"What about the king's daughter?" St. Joseph asked. "Wasn't the condition that you would share everything that you got?"

All at once, the young man became very despondent because he had fallen in love with the princess with all his heart. Nevertheless, he thought, 'I made a promise, and I've got to keep my promise.' So, he pulled out his sword and wanted to slice the princess in half, but when St. Joseph saw his pious and simple heart, he cried out: "Stop! The beautiful princess is yours, and all the treasures as well. You see, I'm St. Joseph, and I don't need any of this. I've helped you because I recognized that you have a kind, humble heart. Whenever you're in trouble, you just have to turn to me, and I'll help you."

Upon saying all this, he blessed the couple and disappeared. Now the young man married the beautiful princess. Then he took his brothers to his home to care for them and always remained devoted to St. Joseph, and he honored him by keeping a lamp burning day and night.

The Flying Ship (1874)[166]
Peter Polevoi

There was once upon a time an old man and an old woman, and they had three sons. Two were clever, but the third was a fool. The old woman loved the first two and quite spoiled them, but the latter was always hardly treated.

One day, they heard that a writing had come from the Tsar which said, "Whoever builds a ship that can fly, to him will I give my daughter the Tsarevna to wife."

The elder brothers resolved to go and seek their fortune, and they begged a blessing of their parents. The mother got ready their things for the journey and gave them something to eat on the way and a flask of wine. And the fool began to beg them to send him off, too. His mother told him he couldn't go.

"Whither would you go, fool?" said she. "Why, the wolves would devour you!"

But the fool was always singing the same refrain: "I want to go, I want to go!"

His mother saw that she could do nothing with him, so she gave him a piece of dry bread and a flask of water and quickly thrust him out of the house.

The fool went and went, and at last he met an old man. They greeted each other. The old man asked the fool, "Whither are you going?"

"Look now!" said the fool. "The Tsar has promised to give his daughter to him who shall make a flying ship!"

"And can you then make such a ship?"

"No, I can't, but they'll make it for me somewhere."

"And where is that somewhere?"

"God only knows."

---

166.   R. Nisbet Bain, ed., *Russian Fairy Tales: From the Skazki of Polevoi* (London: Lawrence and Bullen, 1893).

"Well, in that case, sit down here. Rest and eat a bit. Take out what you have in your knapsack."

"Nay, it is such stuff that I am ashamed to show it to people."

"Nonsense! Take it out! What God has given is quite good enough to be eaten."

The fool undid his knapsack and could scarcely believe his eyes! There, instead of the dry crust of bread, lay white rolls and divers savory meats, and he gave of it to the old man. So they ate together, and the old man said to the fool, "Go into the wood, right up to the first tree, cross yourself thrice, and strike the tree with your axe, then fall with your face to the ground and wait till you are aroused. Then you will see before you a ship quite ready. Sit in it and fly wherever you like, and gather up everything you meet on your road."

So our fool blessed the old man, took leave of him, and went into the wood. He went up to the first tree and did exactly as he had been commanded. He crossed himself three times, struck the tree with his axe, fell with his face to the ground, and went to sleep. In a little while someone or other woke him. The fool rose up and saw the ship quite ready, and without thinking long about it, he sat in it, and the ship flew up into the air. It flew and flew, and look!—There on the road below, a man was lying with his ear to the damp earth.

"Good-day, uncle!"

"Good-day."

"What are you doing?"

"I'm listening to what is going on in the world."

"Take a seat in the ship beside me."

The man didn't like to refuse, so he sat in the ship, and they flew on farther. They flew and flew, and look!—A man was coming along hopping on one leg, with the other leg tied tightly to his ear.

"Good-day, uncle. Why are you hopping on one leg?"

"Well, if I were to untie the other, I should stride half round the world at a single stride."

"Come and sit with us."

The man sat down, and they flew on. They flew and flew, and look!—A man was standing with a gun and taking aim, but at what they could not see.

"Good-day, uncle. What are you aiming at? Not even a bird is to be seen."

"What! I am shooting at short range. I could hit bird or beast at a distance of one hundred leagues. That's what I call shooting!"

"Sit down with us."

This man also sat with them, and they flew on farther. They flew and flew, and look!—A man was carrying on his back a whole sack-load of bread.

"Good-day, uncle. Whither are you going?"

"I am going," he said, "to get some bread for dinner."

"But you've got a whole sack-load on your back already!"

"That! Why I should think nothing of eating all that at a single mouthful."

"Come and sit with us."

The Gobbler sat in the ship, and they went flying on farther. They flew and they flew, and look!—A man was walking round a lake.

"Good-day, uncle. What are you looking for?"

"I want to drink, but I can't find any water."

"But there's a whole lake before you. Why don't you drink of it?"

"That! Why that water would not be more than a mouthful to me!"

"Then come and sit with us."

He sat down, and again they flew on. They flew and flew, and look!—A man was walking in the forest, and on his shoulders was a bundle of wood.

"Good-day, uncle. Why are you dragging about wood in the forest?"

"But this is not common wood."

"What sort is it then?"

"It is of such a sort that if you scatter it, a whole army will spring up."

"Sit down with us then."

He sat down with them, and they flew on farther. They flew and flew, and look!—A man was carrying a sack of straw.

"Good-day, uncle. Whither are you carrying that straw?"

"To the village."

"Is there little straw in the village then?"

"Nay, but this straw is of such a kind that, if you scatter it on the hottest summer day, cold will immediately set in, with snow and frost."

"Won't you sit with us then?"

"Thank you, I will."

Soon they flew into the Tsar's courtyard. The Tsar was sitting at table just then. He saw the flying ship, was much surprised, and sent out his servant to ask who was flying on that ship. The servant went to the ship and looked, and brought back word to the Tsar that 'twas but a single, miserable little muzhik[167] who was flying the ship. The Tsar fell a-thinking. He didn't relish the idea of giving his daughter to a simple muzhik and began to consider how he could get rid of this wretched son-in-law for a whole year. And so he thought, 'I'll give him many grievous tasks to do.' So he immediately sent out to the fool with the command to get him, by the time the imperial meal was over, living and singing water.

Now, at the very time when the Tsar was giving this command to his servant, the first comrade whom the fool had met (that is to say, the one who was listening to what was going on in the world) heard what the Tsar said and told it to the fool.

"What shall I do now?" said the fool. "Why, if I search for a year, and for my whole life as well, I'll never find such water."

"Don't be afraid," said Swift-of-foot to him. "I'll manage it for you."

The servant came and made known the Tsar's command.

---

167. A peasant.

"Say I'll fetch it," replied the fool, and his comrade untied his other leg from his ear, ran off, and in a twinkling he drew from the end of the world some of the living and singing water.

"I must make haste and return presently," said he, and he sat down under a water-mill and went to sleep.

The Tsar's dinner was drawing to a close, and still Swift-of-foot did not turn up though they were all waiting. Those on board the ship grew uneasy. The first comrade bent down to the earth and listened. "Oh ho! So you are asleep beneath the mill, are you?"

Then the Marksman seized his gun, shot into the mill, and woke Swift-of-foot with his shooting. Swift-of-foot set off running, and in a moment he had brought the water. The Tsar had not yet risen from the table, and his command could not therefore have been more exactly fulfilled. But it was all to no purpose. Another task had to be imposed. The Tsar bade them say to the fool, "Come now, as you are so smart, show what you're made of! You and your comrades must eat at one meal twenty roast oxen and twenty large measures of baked bread."

The first comrade heard and told this to the fool. The fool was terrified and said, "Why, I can't eat even one whole loaf at one meal!"

"Don't be afraid," said Gobbler, "that will be very little for me."

The servant came and delivered the Tsar's command.

"Good!" said the fool. "Let us have it, and we'll eat it."

And they brought twenty roasted bullocks, and twenty measures of baked bread. Gobbler alone ate it all up.

"Ugh," he said, "precious little! They might have given us a little more."

The Tsar bade them say to the fool that he must now drink forty barrels of wine, each barrel holding forty buckets. The first comrade of the fool heard these words and told them to him beforehand. The fool was horrified.

"Why, I couldn't drink a single bucketful," said he.

"Don't be frightened," said the Drinker, "I'll drink for all. It will be little enough for me."

So, they poured out the forty barrels of wine. The Drinker came and drank the whole lot at one draught. He drank it right to the dregs and said, "Ugh! Little enough, too! I should have liked as much again."

After that the Tsar commanded the fool to get ready for his wedding and go to the bathroom to have a good wash. Now this bathroom was of cast iron, and the Tsar commanded that it should be heated hotter than hot so that the fool might be suffocated therein in a single instant. So they heated the bath red-hot. The fool went to wash himself, and behind him came the muzhik with the straw.

"I must straw the floor," said he, and they locked them both in the bathroom. The muzhik scattered the straw, and it became so cold that the fool was scarcely able to wash himself properly, because the water in the bath froze so hard. He crept up on the stove, and there he passed the whole night. In the morning they opened the bath, and they found the fool alive and well, lying on the stove and singing songs. They brought word thereof to the Tsar.

Now the Tsar was sore troubled, for he didn't know how to rid himself of the fool. He thought and thought and then commanded him to produce a whole army of his own devising.

'How will a simple muzhik be able to form an army?' thought he. 'He'll certainly not be able to do that.'

As soon as the fool heard of this, he was very alarmed. "Now I'm quite lost," said he. "You have delivered me from my straits more than once, my friends, but it is plain that nothing can be done now."

"You're a pretty fellow," said the man with the bundle of wood. "Why, you've clean forgotten me, haven't you?"

The servant came and told the fool the Tsar's command: "If you will have the Tsarevna to wife, you must put on foot a whole army by morning."

"Agreed. But if the Tsar even after this should refuse, I will conquer his whole Tsardom and take the Tsarevna by force."

At night the fool's companion went out into the fields, took his bundle of wood, and began scattering the faggots in different directions—and immediately a countless army appeared, both horse and foot. In the morning the Tsar saw it and was terrified in his turn, and in all haste he sent to the fool precious ornaments and raiment and bade them lead him to court and marry him to the Tsarevna.

The fool attired himself in these costly ornaments, and they made him look handsomer than words can tell. He appeared before the Tsar, wedded the Tsarevna, received a large wedding-gift, and became clever and witty. The Tsar and the Tsarista[168] grew very fond of him, and the Tsarevna lived with him all her life and loved him as the apple of her eye.

Translated by R. Nisbet Bain.

Long, Broad, and Sharpsight (1890)[169]
Karel Erben

There was a king, who was already old, and had but one son. Once upon a time he called this son to him and said to him, "My dear son! You know that old fruit falls to make room for other fruit. My head is already ripening, and maybe the sun will soon no longer shine upon it, but before you bury me, I should like to see your wife, my future daughter. My son, marry!"

The prince said, "I would gladly, father, do as you wish, but I have no bride and don't know any."

---

168. The consort of the tsar.

169. Albert Henry Wratislaw, *Sixty Folk-Tales from Exclusively Slavonic Sources* (Boston: Houghton, Mifflin, 1890)

The old king put his hand into his pocket, took out a golden key, and showed it to his son with the words: "Go up into the tower, to the top story, look round there, and then tell me which you fancy."

The prince went without delay. Nobody within the memory of man had been up there, or had ever heard what was up there. When he got up to the last story, he saw in the ceiling a little iron door like a trapdoor. It was closed. He opened it with the golden key, lifted it, and went up above it. There was a large circular room. The ceiling was blue like the sky on a clear night, and silver stars glittered on it; the floor was a carpet of green silk, and around in the wall were twelve high windows in golden frames, and in each window on crystal glass was a damsel painted with the colors of the rainbow, with a royal crown on her head, in each window a different one in a different dress, each handsomer than the other, and it was a wonder that the prince did not let his eyes dwell upon them. When he had gazed at them with astonishment, the damsels began to move as if they were alive, looked down upon him, smiled, and did everything but speak.

Now the prince observed that one of the twelve windows was covered with a white curtain. So, he drew the curtain to see what was behind it. There was a damsel in a white dress, girt with a silver girdle, with a crown of pearls on her head. She was the most beautiful of all, but was sad and pale, as if she had risen from the grave. The prince stood long before the picture, as if he had made a discovery, and as he thus gazed, his heart pained him, and he cried, "This one will I have, and no other."

As he said the words the damsel bowed her head, blushed like a rose, and instantly all the pictures disappeared. When he went down and related to his father what he had seen and which damsel he had selected, the old king became sad, bethought himself, and said, "You have done ill, my son, in uncovering what was curtained over, and have placed yourself in great danger on account of those words. That damsel is in the power of a wicked wizard and kept captive in an iron castle. From all who have attempted to set her free, not one has hitherto returned. But what's done cannot be undone; the plighted word is a law. Go! Try your luck, and return home safe and sound!"

The prince took leave of his father, mounted his horse, and rode away in search of his bride. It came to pass that he rode through a vast forest, and through the forest he rode on and on till he lost the road. And as he was wandering with his horse in thickets and amongst rocks and morasses, not knowing which way to turn, he heard somebody shout behind him, "Hi! Stop!"

The prince looked round and saw a tall man hastening after him.

"Stop and take me with you, and take me into your service, and you won't regret it!"

"Who are you," said the prince, "and what can you do?"

"My name is Long, and I can extend myself. Do you see a bird's nest in that pine yonder? I will bring you the nest down without having to climb up."

Long then began to extend himself; his body grew rapidly till it was as tall as the pine. He then reached the nest and in a moment contracted himself again and gave it to the prince.

"You know your business well, but what's the use of birds' nests to me, if you can't conduct me out of this forest?"

"Ahem! That's an easy matter," said Long, and he began to extend himself till he was thrice as high as the highest fir in the forest, looked round, and said, "Here on this side we have the nearest way out of the forest."

He then contracted himself, took the horse by the bridle, and before the prince had any idea of it, they were beyond the forest. Before them was a long and wide plain, and beyond the plain tall gray rocks, like the walls of a large town, and mountains overgrown with forest trees.

"Yonder, sir, goes my comrade!" said Long and pointed suddenly to the plain. "You should take him also into your service. I believe he would serve you well."

"Shout to him, and call him hither so that I may see what he is good for."

"It is a little too far, sir," said Long. "He would hardly hear me, and it would take a long time before he came because he has a great deal to carry. I'll jump after him instead."

Then Long again extended himself to such a height that his head plunged into the clouds, made two or three steps, took his comrade by the arm, and placed him before the prince. He was a short, thick-set fellow, with a paunch like a sixty-four-gallon cask.

"Who are you?" demanded the prince, "and what can you do?"

"My name, sir, is Broad. I can widen myself."

"Give me a specimen."

"Ride quick, sir, quick, back into the forest!" cried Broad, as he began to blow himself out.

The prince didn't understand why he was to ride away, but seeing that Long made all haste to get into the forest, he spurred his horse and rode full gallop after him. It was high time that he did ride away, or else Broad would have squashed him, horse and all, as his paunch rapidly grew in all directions. It filled everything everywhere, just as if a mountain had rolled up. Broad then ceased to blow himself out and took himself in again, raising such a wind that the trees in the forest bowed and bent, and became what he was at first.

"You've played me a nice trick," said the prince. "But I shan't find such a fellow every day. Come with me."

They proceeded further. When they approached the rocks, they met a man who had his eyes bandaged with a handkerchief.

"Sir, this is our third comrade," said Long. "You ought to take him also into your service. I'm sure he won't eat his victuals for naught."

"Who are you?" the prince asked him. "And why are your eyes bandaged?"

"You don't see your way!"

"No, sir, quite the contrary! It is just because I see too well that I am obliged to bandage my eyes. I see with bandaged eyes just as well as others with unbandaged eyes, and if I unbandage them, I look everything through and through, and when I gaze sharply at anything, it catches fire and bursts into flame, and what can't burn splits into pieces. For this reason my name is Sharpsight."

He then turned to a rock opposite, removed the bandage, and fixed his flaming eyes upon it. The rock began to crackle; pieces flew on every side; and in a very short time nothing of it remained but a heap of sand, on which something glittered like fire. Sharpsight went to fetch it and brought it to the prince. It was pure gold.

"Heigh! You're a fellow that money can't purchase!" said the prince. "He is a fool who wouldn't make use of your services, and if you have such good sight, look and tell me whether it is far to the iron castle, and what is now going on there?"

"If you rode by yourself, sir," answered Sharpsight, "maybe you wouldn't get there within a year, but with us you'll arrive to-day—they're just getting supper ready for us."

"And what is my bride doing?"

> "An iron lattice is before her,
> In a tower that's high
> She doth sit and sigh,
> A wizard watch and ward keeps o'er her."

The prince cried, "Whoever is well disposed, help me to set her free!"

They all promised to help him. They guided him among the gray rocks through the breach that Sharpsight had made in them with his eyes, and further and further on through rocks, through high mountains and deep forests, and wherever there was any obstacle in the road, forthwith it was removed by the three comrades. And when the sun was declining towards the west, the mountains began to become lower, the forests less dense, and rocks concealed themselves amongst the heath. When it was almost on the point of setting, the prince saw not far before him an iron castle, and when it was actually setting, he rode by an iron bridge to the gate, and as soon as it had set, up rose the iron bridge of itself, the gate closed with a single movement, and the prince and his companions were captives in the iron castle.

When they had looked round in the court, the prince put his horse up in the stable, where everything was ready for it, and then they went into the castle. In the court, in the stable, in the castle hall, and in the rooms, they saw in the twilight many richly-dressed people, gentlemen and servants, but not one of them stirred—they were all turned to stone. They went through several rooms, and came into the supper-room. This was brilliantly lighted up, and in the midst was a table, and on it plenty of good meats and drinks, and covers were laid for four persons. They waited and waited, thinking that someone would come, but when nobody came for a long time, they sat down and ate and drank what the palate fancied.

When they had done eating, they looked about to find where to sleep. Thereupon the door flew open unexpectedly all at once, and into the room came the wizard, a bent old man in a long black garb, with a bald head, a gray beard down to his knees, and three iron hoops instead of a girdle. By the hand he led a beautiful, very beautiful damsel, dressed in white. She had a silver girdle round her waist, and a crown of pearls on her head, but was pale and sad, as if she had risen from the grave. The prince recognized her at once, sprang forward, and went to meet her, but before he could utter a word the wizard addressed him: "I know for why you have come. You want to take the princess away. Well, be it so. Take her, if you can keep her in sight for three nights, so that she doesn't vanish from you. If she vanishes, you will be turned into stone as well as your three servants like all who have come before you."

He then motioned the princess to a seat and departed. The prince could not take his eyes off the princess, so beautiful was she. He began to talk to her and asked her all manner of questions, but she neither answered nor smiled, nor looked at anyone any more than if she had been of marble. He sat down by her and determined not to sleep all night long lest she should vanish from him, and, to make surer, Long extended himself like a strap and wound himself round the whole room along the wall. Broad posted himself in the doorway, swelled himself up, and stopped it up so tight that not even a mouse could have slipped through while Sharpsight placed himself against a pillar in the midst of the room on the lookout. But after a time they all began to nod, fell asleep, and slept the whole night, just as if the wizard had thrown them into the water.

In the morning, when it began to dawn, the prince was the first to wake, but—as if a knife had been thrust into his heart—the princess was gone! He forthwith awoke his servants and asked what was to be done.

"Never mind, sir," said Sharpsight, and he looked sharply out through the window, "I see her already. A hundred miles hence is a forest, in the midst of the forest an old oak, and on the top of the oak an acorn, and she is that acorn."

Long immediately took him on his shoulders, extended himself, and went ten miles at a step, while Sharpsight showed him the way. No more time elapsed than would have been wanted to move once round a cottage before they were back again, and Long delivered the acorn to the prince.

"Sir, let it fall on the ground."

The prince let it fall, and that moment the princess stood beside him. And when the sun began to show itself beyond the mountains, the folding doors flew open with a crash, and the wizard entered the room and smiled spitefully, but when he saw the princess, he frowned, growled, and bang! One of the iron hoops which he wore splintered and sprang off him. He then took the damsel by the hand and led her away.

The whole day after the prince had nothing to do but walk up and down the castle, and round about the castle, and look at the wonderful things that were there. It was everywhere as if life had been lost in a single moment. In one hall he saw a prince, who held in both hands a brandished sword, as if he intended to cleave somebody in twain, but the blow never fell. He had been turned into stone. In one chamber was a knight turned into stone, just as if he had been fleeing from someone in terror, and, stumbling on the threshold, had taken a downward direction, but not fallen. Under the chimney sat a servant, who held in one hand a piece of roast meat, and with the other lifted a mouthful towards his mouth, which never reached it when it was just in front of his mouth; he had also been turned to stone. Many others he saw there turned to stone, each in the position in which he was when the wizard said, "Be turned into stone." He likewise saw many fine horses turned to stone, and in the castle and round the castle all was desolate and dead. There were trees, but without leaves; there were meadows, but without grass; there was a river, but it did not flow. Nowhere was there even a singing bird, or a flower, the offspring of the ground, or a white fish in the water.

Morning, noon, and evening the prince and his companions found good and abundant entertainment in the castle. The viands came of themselves, the wine poured itself out. After supper the folding doors opened again, and the wizard brought in the princess for the prince to guard. And although they all determined to exert themselves with all their might, not to fall asleep, yet it was of no use, fall asleep again they did. And when the prince awoke at dawn and saw the princess had vanished, he jumped up and pulled Sharpsight by the arm, "Hey! Get up, Sharpsight, do you know where the princess is?"

He rubbed his eyes, looked, and said, "I see her. There's a mountain two miles off, and in the mountain a rock, and in the rock a precious stone, and she's that precious stone. If Long carries me thither, we shall obtain her."

Long took him at once on his shoulders, extended himself, and went twenty miles at a step. Sharpsight fixed his flaming eyes on the mountain, and the mountain crumbled, and the rock in it split into a thousand pieces, and amongst them glittered the precious stone. They took it up and brought it to the prince, and when he let it fall on the ground, the princess again stood there. When afterwards the wizard came and saw her there, his eyes flashed with spite, and bang! again an iron hoop cracked upon him and flew off. He growled and led the princess out of the room.

That day all was again as it had been the day before. After supper the wizard brought the princess in again, looked the prince keenly in the face, and scornfully uttered the words, "It will be seen who's a match for whom and whether you are victorious or I," and with that he departed.

This day they all exerted themselves still more to avoid going to sleep. They wouldn't even sit down. They wanted to walk about all night long, but all in vain. They were bewitched: one fell asleep after the other as he walked, and the princess vanished away from them. In the morning the prince again awoke earliest, and when he didn't see the princess, woke Sharpsight.

"Hey! Get up, Sharpsight! Look where the princess is!"

Sharpsight looked out for a long time.

"Oh sir," says he, "she is a long way off, a long way off! Three hundred miles off is a black sea, and in the midst of the sea a shell on the bottom, and in the shell is a gold ring, and she's the ring. But never mind! We shall obtain her, but today Long must take Broad with him as well; we shall want him."

Long took Sharpsight on one shoulder, and Broad on the other and went thirty miles at a step. When they came to the black sea, Sharpsight showed him where he must reach into the water for the shell. Long extended his hand as far as he could, but could not reach the bottom.

"Wait, comrades! Wait only a little, and I'll help you," said Broad, and he swelled himself out as far as his paunch would stretch. He then lay down on the shore and drank. In a very short time the water fell so low that Long easily reached the bottom and took the shell out of the sea. Out of it he extracted the ring, took his comrades on his shoulders, and hastened hack. But on the way he found it a little difficult to run with Broad, who had half a sea of water inside him, so he cast him from his shoulder onto the ground in a wide valley. Thump! he went like a sack let fall from a tower, and in a moment the whole valley was under water like a vast lake. Broad himself barely crawled out of it.

Meanwhile the prince was in great trouble in the castle. The dawn began to display itself over the mountains, and his servants had not returned. The more brilliantly the rays ascended, the greater was his anxiety. A deadly perspiration came out upon his forehead. Soon the sun showed itself in the east like a thin strip of flame—and then with a loud crash the door flew open, and on the threshold stood the wizard. He looked round the room, and seeing the princess was not there, laughed a hateful laugh and entered the room. But just at that moment, pop! the window flew in pieces, the gold ring fell on the floor, and in an instant there stood the princess again.

Sharpsight, seeing what was going on in the castle, and in what danger his master was, told Long. Long made a step and threw the ring through the window into the room. The wizard roared with rage, till the castle quaked, and then bang! went the third iron hoop that was round his waist, and sprang off him. The wizard turned into a raven and flew out and away through the shattered window.

Then, and not till then, did the beautiful damsel speak and thank the prince for setting her free, and blushed like a rose. In the castle and round the castle everything became alive again at once. He who was holding in the hall the outstretched sword, swung it into the air, which whistled again, and then returned it to its sheath; he who was stumbling on the threshold, fell on the ground, but immediately got up again and felt his nose to see whether it was still entire; he who was sitting under the chimney put the piece of meat into his mouth and went on eating; and thus everybody completed what he had begun doing, and at the point where he had left off. In the stables the horses merrily stamped and snorted; the trees round the castle became green like periwinkles; the meadows were full of variegated flowers, high in the air warbled the skylark, and abundance of small fishes appeared in the clear river. Everywhere was life, everywhere enjoyment.

Meanwhile a number of gentlemen assembled in the room where the prince was, and all thanked him for their liberation. But he said, "You have nothing to thank me for. If it had not been for my trusty servants, Long, Broad, and Sharpsight, I too should have been what you were."

He then immediately started on his way home to the old king, his father, with his bride and servants. On the way they met Broad and took him with them. The old king wept for joy at the success of his son, for he had thought he would return no more. Soon afterwards there was a grand wedding, the festivities of which lasted three weeks. All the gentlemen that the prince had liberated were invited. After the wedding Long, Broad, and Sharpsight announced to the young king that they were going again into the world to look for work. The young king tried to persuade them to stay with him. "I will give you everything you want, as long as you live," said he. "You needn't work at all."

But they didn't like such an idle life, took leave of him, went away and have been ever since knocking about somewhere or other in the world.

Translated by Albert Henry Wratislaw.

14. SHREWD CATS AND FOXES

ATU 545B—PUSS IN BOOTS

As types of fairy-tale telling evolved and crystallized, the genre of the fairy tale borrowed and used motifs, themes, characters, expressions, and styles from other narrative forms and genres—and it still does. A good example is "Puss in Boots," which has a close connection to the fable and legend. As is well known, the basic plot of this tale involves an anthropomorphized cat or fox, who helps the destitute third son in a family of peasants impress a pompous king through flattery and tricks so that the king will believe that the young peasant is a rich lord. The peasant is often portrayed as an awkward dunce while the supernatural cat, sometimes a fairy or fox in different European, Middle Eastern, and Asian variants, is clever and instructs the peasant how to speak and dress, for underlying the fairy tale is the proverb, "clothes make the person." Once the king believes that the peasant is a nobleman, the cat leads the king, his daughter, and the peasant to the large estate of an ogre/dragon/witch. The cat rushes ahead of the party, outwits the ogre, and kills him. Once the king, princess, and peasant arrive, the cat tells them that the castle and grand estate belong to the peasant, and the king, of course, gives his daughter to the peasant as his bride. They live happily ever after, and the cat is generally rewarded, for the animal is the actual hero/protagonist of the story.

Some critics interpret this tale as a "rise tale," in which the peasant is elevated and becomes a nobleman. But he is not the driving force of the tale. It is the cat/fox which moves the action, for he/she is often threatened with death by the peasant at the beginning of the tale and must use his/her cunning to avoid death and find a rightful position for himself or herself. Quite often the cat/fox becomes a matchmaker, indicating a ritual role in marriage. Indeed, whether a cat or fox, this is a tale about the use of brains by cunning "people" in adapting to difficult situations, and the active cat/fox exposes the contradictions and pretensions of the upper-class figures.

There are three major literary versions, crystallizations of oral folk tales that have made this tale memetically traditional in the Western world: Giovan Francesco Straparola's "Constantino Fortunato" in *Le piacevoli notti* (1550–1553), Giambattista Basile's "Cagliuso" in *Lo Cunto de li cunti* (1634), and Charles Perrault's "The Master Cat, or Puss in Boots" in *Histoires ou Contes du temps passé* (1697). They are all unique and have specific cultural differences. For instance, in Straparola's tale, the cat is a fairy; in Basile's story, the cat is almost killed by the ungrateful peasant, while Perrault's cat becomes a royal messenger in the service of a French king. But they all have some very common features that reveal how they are closely bound to European, Middle Eastern, and Asian oral storytelling traditions about animal protagonists, and they all circulated hundreds of years before the tale was shaped by three educated writers in print. Nobody is certain when the first oral tale was created, and nobody will ever be able to determine its exact origins. Nevertheless, there are clues, fragments, and indications that this hybrid tale type which involves motifs and themes such as an animal as helper, grateful recognition, the civilization of an uncouth lad, ruthless behavior for gain, and other popular themes was disseminated widely throughout the world. There are hundreds of versions that can be found in Europe, the Middle East, North and South Asia, North Africa, and North America. The Grimms obtained their version from Johanna Hassenpflug in 1812 and deleted it from the second edition because it was too similar to Charles Perrault's 1697 tale. Despite this deletion, the tale remained popular in Germany in chapbooks, broadsheets, and illustrated books. In 1845 Ludwig Bechstein, the bestselling author of fairy tales in Germany, re-appropriated it as a "German" tale in *Deutsches Märchenbuch*.

******

Puss in Boots (1812)[170]

Jacob and Wilhelm Grimm

A miller had three sons, a mill, a donkey, and a cat. The sons had to grind grain, the donkey had to haul the grain and carry away the flour, and the cat had to catch the mice. When the miller died, the three sons divided the inheritance: the oldest received the mill, the second the donkey, and nothing was left for the third but the cat. This made the youngest sad, and he said to himself, 'I certainly got the worst part of the bargain. My oldest brother can grind wheat, and my second brother can ride on his donkey. But what can I do with the cat? Once I make a pair of gloves out of his fur, it's all over.'

The cat, who had understood all he had said, began to speak. "Listen, there's no need to kill me when all you'll get will be a pair of poor gloves from my fur. Have some boots made for me instead. Then I'll be able to go out, mix with people, and help you before you know it."

The miller's son was surprised the cat could speak like that, but since the shoemaker happened to be walking by, he called him inside and had him fit the cat for a pair of boots. When the boots were finished, the cat put them on. After that he took a sack, filled the bottom with grains of wheat, and attached a piece of cord to the top, which he could pull to close it. Then he slung the sack over his back and walked out the door on two legs like a human being.

At that time there was a king ruling the country, and he liked to eat partridges. However, there was a grave situation because no one had been able to catch a single partridge. The whole forest was full of them, but they frightened so easily that none of the huntsmen had been able to get near them. The cat knew this and thought he could do much better than the huntsmen. When he entered the forest, he opened the sack, spread the grains of wheat on the ground,

---

170. "Der gestiefelte Kater," *Kinder- und Haus-Märchen. Gesammelt durch die Brüder Grimm*, 2 vols. (Berlin: Realschulbuchandlung, 1812/1815).

placed the cord in the grass, and strung it out behind a hedge. Then he crawled in back of the hedge, hid himself, and lay in wait. Soon the partridges came running, found the wheat, and hopped into the sack, one after the other. When a good number were inside, the cat pulled the cord. Once the sack was closed tight, he ran over to it and wrung their necks. Then he slung the sack over his back and went straight to the king's castle. The sentry called out, "Stop! Where are you going?"

"To the king," the cat answered curtly.

"Are you crazy? A cat to the king?"

"Oh, let him go," another sentry said. "The king's often very bored. Perhaps the cat will give him some pleasure with his meowing and purring."

When the cat appeared before the king, he bowed and said, "My lord, the Count"—and he uttered a long, distinguished name—"sends you his regards and would like to offer you these partridges, which he recently caught in his traps."

The king was amazed by the beautiful, fat partridges. Indeed, he was so over-come with joy that he commanded the cat to take as much gold from his trea-sury as he could carry and put it into the sack. "Bring it to your lord and give him my very best thanks for his gift."

Meanwhile, the poor miller's son sat at home by the window, propped his head up with his hand, and wondered why he had given away all he had for the cat's boots when the cat would probably not be able to bring him anything great in return. Suddenly, the cat entered, threw down the sack from his back, opened it, and dumped the gold at the miller's feet.

"Now you've got something for the boots. The king also sends his regards and best of thanks."

The miller was happy to have such wealth, even though he didn't understand how everything had happened. However, as the cat was taking off his boots, he told him everything and said, "Surely you have enough money now, but we won't be content with that. Tomorrow I'm going to put on my boots again, and you shall become even richer. Incidentally, I told the king you're a count."

The following day the cat put on his boots, as he said he would, went hunting again, and brought the king a huge catch. So it went every day, and every day the cat brought back gold to the miller. At the king's court he became a favorite, so that he was permitted to go and come and wander about the castle wherever he pleased. One day, as the cat was lying by the hearth in the king's kitchen and warming himself, the coachman came and started cursing, "May the devil take the king and princess! I wanted to go to the tavern, have a drink, and play some cards. But now they want me to drive them to the lake so they can go for a walk."

When the cat heard that, he ran home and said to his master, "If you want to be a rich count, come with me to the lake and go for a swim."

The miller didn't know what to say. Nevertheless, he listened to the cat and went with him to the lake, where he undressed and jumped into the water completely naked. Meanwhile, the cat took his clothes, carried them away, and hid them. No sooner had he done it than the king came driving by. Now the cat began to wail in a miserable voice, "Ahh, most gracious king! My lord went for a swim in the lake, and a thief came and stole his clothes that were lying on the bank. Now the count is in the water and can't get out. If he stays in much longer, he'll freeze and die."

When the king heard that, he ordered the coach to stop, and one of his servants had to race back to the castle and fetch some of the king's garments. The miller put on the splendid clothes, and since the king had already taken a liking to him because of the partridges that, he believed, had been sent by the count, he asked the young man to sit down next to him in the coach. The princess was not in the least angry about this, for the count was young and handsome and pleased her a great deal.

In the meantime, the cat went on ahead of them and came to a large meadow, where there were over a hundred people making hay.

"Who owns this meadow, my good people?" asked the cat.

"The great sorcerer."

"Listen to me. The king will be driving by, and when he asks who the owner of this meadow is, I want you to answer, 'The count.' If you don't, you'll all be killed."

Then the cat continued on his way and came to a wheat field so enormous that nobody could see over it. There were more than two hundred people standing there and cutting wheat.

"Who owns this wheat, my good people?"

"The sorcerer."

"Listen to me. The king will be driving by, and when he asks who the owner of this wheat is, I want you to answer, 'The count.' If you don't do this, you'll all be killed."

Finally, the cat came to a splendid forest where more than three hundred people were chopping down large oak trees and cutting them into wood.

"Who owns this forest, my good people?"

"The sorcerer."

"Listen to me. The king will be driving by, and when he asks who the owner of this forest is, I want you to answer, 'The count.' If you don't do this, you'll all be killed."

The cat continued on his way, and the people watched him go. Since he looked so unusual and walked in boots like a human being, they were afraid of him. Soon the cat came to the sorcerer's castle, walked boldly inside, and appeared before the sorcerer, who looked at him scornfully and asked him what he wanted. The cat bowed and said, "I've heard that you can turn yourself into a dog, fox, or even a wolf, but I don't believe that you can turn yourself into an elephant. That seems impossible to me, and this is why I've come: I want to be convinced by my own eyes."

"That's just a trifle for me," the sorcerer said arrogantly, and within seconds he turned himself into an elephant.

"That's great, but can you also turn yourself into a lion?"

"Nothing to it," said the sorcerer, and he suddenly stood before the cat as a lion. The cat pretended to be terrified and cried out, "That's incredible and unheard of! Never in my dreams would I have thought this possible! But you'd top all of this if you could turn yourself into a tiny animal, such as a mouse. I'm convinced that you can do more than any other sorcerer in the word, but that would be too much for you."

The flattery had made the sorcerer quite friendly, and he said, "Oh, no, dear cat, that's not too much at all," and soon he was running around the room as a mouse.

All at once the cat ran after him, caught the mouse in one leap, and ate him up.

While all this was happening, the king had continued driving with the count and princess and had come to the large meadow.

"Who owns the hay?" the king asked.

"The count," the people all cried out, just as the cat had ordered them to do.

"You've got a nice piece of land, Count," the king said.

Afterward they came to the large wheat field.

"Who owns that wheat, my good people?"

"The count."

"My! You've got quite a large and beautiful estate!"

Next they came to the forest.

"Who owns these woods, my good people?"

"The count."

The king was even more astounded and said, "You must be a rich man, Count. I don't think I have such a splendid forest as yours."

At last they came to the castle. The cat stood on top of the stairs, and when the coach stopped below, he ran down, opened the door, and said, "Your majesty, you've arrived at the castle of my lord, the count. This honor will make him happy for the rest of his life."

The king climbed out of the coach and was amazed by the magnificent building, which was almost larger and more beautiful than his own castle. The count led the princess up the stairs and into the hall, which was flickering with lots of gold and jewels.

The princess became the count's bride, and when the king died, the count become king, and the Puss in Boots was his prime minster.

Count Martin von der Katze (1867)[171]

Christian Schneller

When a poor father died, he left his two sons nothing but a bench and a cat.

"Share this small inheritance between you," the father had said as his eyes were already closing. "Let no quarreling over it flare up between you."

---

171. "Graf Martin von der Katze," *Märchen und Sagen aus Wälschtirol* (Innsbruck: Verlag der Wagner'schen Universitäts-Buchhandlung, 1867).

Then the eldest said, "I'll take the bench. At least I can sit down on it and take a rest as often as I want."

"And I'll take the cat," spoke the younger son, whose name was Martin. "Anyway I'm attached to her, and she follows me all over the place."

Both went off in different directions into the world. The elder son carried the bench with him, and whenever he became tired, he sat down on it and rested. Martin went his own way with the cat and had every reason to be glad about his choice. Whenever he became hungry, the cat went into the houses where the table was set and carried food right away to his master in front of the eyes of the astonished people. Therefore, Martin never lacked for food or drink. But the cat also provided clothes for him by grabbing a beautiful garment here and there and brought it to her master so that he could dress like a real gentleman. This is why the cat said to him: "When people ask you your name, then tell them that you are called Count Martin von der Katze."

He was all right with this and fond of the name.

'I would have never let myself dream of this!' he said to himself with a laugh. 'Who would have believed that I'd become a count thanks to my cat.'

One day they came upon a wide plain with beautiful green meadows and fields, and they asked the people who owned this land.

"Such and such count," they answered.

And Martin and his cat continued on their way until they reached some beautiful woods. After that they came across some more beautiful pastures with herds of animals and shepherds, and whenever they asked who the owner of the land was, they learned that it all belonged to the same count. Finally, they came to a castle, where the rich old count lived with his wife, and they received the hospitality they requested. When the old lord went down into the cellar to fetch some wine, the cat took the opportunity to sneak after him and strangle him. Then the count's wife went down into the cellar to see why her husband was spending so much time there, and the cat jumped on her and strangled her, too. Afterward the cat went upstairs and said to her master: "The two of them in the cellar are dead. Now you're the lord of the castle and should conduct yourself as a lord. Leave the rest to me."

Then she sprang out of the castle and ran through fields and meadows and woods and everywhere, meeting reapers, woodcutters, and shepherds, and she called out to them: "The old count and his wife are dead, and they have left everything to my lord, the Count Martin von der Katze. He is now the legal lord of the castle and has ordered me to announce this so that you know his name and obey only him!"

Everywhere the cat went, the people answered: "At your service, Madame Cat! If our old lord has died, then he's clearly dead. Long live our new lord!"

Count Martin von der Katze now had the most glorious life in the world. One day his brother arrived at the castle, and he was still carrying the bench with him and was still very poor. He no longer recognized Martin, who welcomed him in the very best way and placed him in charge of a beautiful court, where he could also have the best kind of life and sit on his bench as often as he wanted.

After some time had passed, the cat said to her master: "I feel that I have gotten old and that my life is coming to an end. Since I've helped you attain such great happiness, I'd be grateful if you would bury me properly and erect a beautiful monument on my grave because I've certainly earned it."

Meanwhile, the cat had decided to test her master, and so one day she laid down on the balcony and stretched herself out as if she were dead. When Martin came across her and saw her, he said: "Well, that atrocious animal is finally dead!" And he wanted to throw the cat down into the courtyard.

But the cat sprang to her feet and yelled: "How ungrateful can you be! Is this the way you treat me even though you owe everything to me!"

And she poured forth a flood of reproach which he swallowed without saying a word, for he felt that he had earned this scolding. Finally, he told her that he was sorry and asked for forgiveness.

"Certainly," he promised her in the most solemn way, "I shall bury you properly after your death, and I'll have a beautiful monument erected in your honor."

Once again, some time passed, and the cat really died. And, indeed, Count Martin kept his promise and had the cat buried with great ceremony.

I almost don't want to say, but I was told that he even had her buried in a church with a beautiful gravestone. And all the cat's accomplishments were carved into the stone in resplendent letters. Today the gravestone can no longer be found, and nobody can remember to have seen it or at least to have heard about what happened to it.

Count Piro (1870)[172]

Laura Gonzenbach

Once upon a time there was a poor man who had only one son. However, this son was dumb and ignorant. When the father was about to die, he said to the youth, "My son, I must die and have nothing to leave you except this little house and the pear tree that's standing next to it."

The father died, and his son remained in the cottage. Since he couldn't earn a living by himself, the dear Lord in his mercy let the pear tree bear fruit throughout the entire year, and this is how the young man nourished himself.

Now one day, as he was sitting in front of the door to the house, a fox came by. To be sure it was in the middle of winter, and yet, the pear tree was still covered with the most beautiful and largest fruit.

"Oh!" cried the fox. "Fresh pears in this time of the season! Give me a basket of the pears, and your fortune will be made."

"Oh, little fox, if I give you a basket full of pears, what shall I have to eat?" the young man said.

---

172. "Graf Birnbaum," *Sicilianische Märchen*, 2 vols. (Leipzig: W. Engelmann, 1870).

"Be quiet, and do what I tell you to do," the fox answered. "You'll see, your fortune will be made."

So the young man gave the little fox a basket of beautiful pears, and the fox carried it to the king.

"Your majesty, my master sends you this little basket of pears, and asks you to have the good grace to accept this fruit," the fox said to the king.

"Pears! In this time of the season!" cried the king. "I've never seen anything like this before! Who is your master?"

"Count Piro,"[173] the fox answered.

"How did he manage to get pears at this time of the year?" the king asked.

"Oh, he always gets what he wants," replied the fox. "He's much richer than you yourself are, your majesty."

"What could I give him as a gift as thanks for his pears?" the king asked.

"Nothing, your royal highness," the sly fox responded. "You should know that he would be insulted if you sent him a gift for his gift."

"Well then, tell your count that I thank him for his gorgeous pears."

When the fox returned to the house, the young man cried out, "Oh, little fox, what am I supposed to eat if you carry away my pears?"

"Be quiet, and let me take care of everything," said the fox, and he took another large basket full of the most beautiful pears. Then he went to the king and said, "Your majesty, since you accepted the first basket so kindly, my master, Count Piro, has taken the liberty to send you another basket full of pears."

"Oh my, how's that possible?!" the king exclaimed. "Fresh pears at this time of the year!"

"Oh, that's nothing," said the fox. "This is just a drop in the bucket compared to the other treasures that he has. However, he would like to ask your permission to make your daughter his wife."

"If the count is so rich," the king replied, "even richer than I am, I cannot in any way accept this honor."

"Forget that, your royal highness," the fox said. "My lord wishes to have your daughter for his wife, and he doesn't care whether your dowry is more or less because he is so wealthy."

"Is he really so rich?" the king asked.

"Oh, your royal majesty, if you only knew! He's much richer than you!"

"Well then, I'd like to invite him to come and dine with me."

So the fox went to the young man and said, "I told the king that you are the Count Piro and that you would like to marry his daughter."

"Oh, little fox, what have you done?" screamed the poor boy. "If the king sees me, he'll rip my head off my shoulders!"

---

173.   Count Pear.

"Let me take care of things, and be quiet," the fox said, and he went into the city to a tailor and said, "My master, the Count Piro, wants you to make him the most elegant suit ready to wear. I'll bring you the money for it another time."

Well, the tailor gave him a splendid suit, and the fox continued on his way to a horse trader and was able to obtain the most magnificent horse there was to find in the same way as before. Then the young man had to put on the fine garments, mount the horse, and ride to the castle, while the fox ran in front of him.

"Oh, little fox, what should I say to the king?" the young man cried out. "I can't speak the way noble people are supposed to speak."

"Let me speak, and you keep quiet," said the fox. "You just say 'good day' and 'your majesty,' and leave the rest to me."

When they came to the castle, the king rushed toward Count Piro and greeted him with honor. Then he led him to the dinner table where the beautiful princess was seated. However, he remained silent and didn't say a thing.

"Little Fox," the king said quietly to the fox, "Count Piro doesn't seem to speak."

"Of course not," the fox responded. "He's got too much to think about, especially his treasures and all his wealth."

After they had eaten, Count Piro took his leave and rode back to his house. The next morning, the fox said to him, "Give me another basket full of pears to bring to the king."

"Do what you want, little fox," the young man answered, "but you'll see, it's going to cost me my life."

"Oh, just be quiet!" the fox cried. "When I say, your fortune will be made, I mean it."

So the young man picked the pears, and the fox brought them to the king and said, "My master, Count Piro, has sent you this little basket of pears and would like to have an answer to his marriage proposal."

"Tell the count that the wedding can take place whenever he wants," the king replied, and the fox was very pleased to bring the news to Count Piro.

"But, little fox, where am I supposed to bring my bride?" the young man asked. "I can't take her to this poor old house."

"Let me take care of it. What's your concern anyway? Haven't I done very well for you thus far?" the fox said.

So a splendid wedding was celebrated, and Count Piro married the beautiful princess. After a few days passed, the fox said, "My master wants to take his young bride to his castle."

"Good," said the king. "I shall accompany them."

Soon after they all mounted their horses, and the king brought a large retinue of his knights with him, and so they rode off into the plains.[174] Meanwhile, the

---

174. The plains of Catania.

sly fox ran way ahead of them. When he came to a large herd with thousands of sheep, he asked the shepherds, "Who is the owner of this herd of sheep?"

"The ogre," they answered.

"Be quiet!" whispered the fox. "Do you see all those knights who are following me? If you say to them that the herd belongs to the ogre, they'll murder you. You'd better say they belong to Count Piro."

Shortly after, when the king came riding up to the shepherds, he asked, "Who is the owner of this wonderful herd of sheep?"

"Count Piro," the shepherds cried out.

"Well, I say, he must be rich!" the king declared and was happy.

A little further on the fox came across a herd of pigs that was just as large, and he asked the swineherds, "Who is the owner of this herd?"

"The ogre."

"Be quiet! Do you see all those knights who are following me? If you say to them that the herd belongs to the ogre, they'll murder you. You'd better say they belong to Count Piro."

When the king soon reached the swineherds, he asked who owned the herd, and they answered, "Count Piro," and the king was very happy about his rich son-in-law.

A little further on the fox came to a large herd of horses and asked the men tending them who was the owner of the herd.

"The ogre."

"Be quiet! Do you see all those knights who are following me? If you say to them that the herd belongs to the ogre, they'll murder you. You'd better say they belong to Count Piro."

When the king arrived and asked who owned the horses, the men responded, "Count Piro," and the king was glad that his daughter had married such a rich man.

Meanwhile, the fox kept running ahead and came to a large herd of cattle.

"Who's the owner of this large herd of cattle?"

"The ogre."

"Be quiet! Do you see all those knights who are following me? If you say to them that the herd belongs to the ogre, they'll murder you. You'd better say they belong to Count Piro."

Soon after the king came riding by and asked who owned the herd of cattle.

"Count Piro," they said, and the king was happy about his rich son-in-law.

Finally, the fox came to the palace of the ogre, who lived there with his wife. Immediately he rushed in to see them and cried out, "Oh, you poor people! You have a terrible fate!"

"What's happened?" the ogre cried out with fright.

"Do you see all those knights who are following me?" the fox asked. "The king has sent them to murder you."

"Oh, little fox, dear fox, help us," the two ogres began to moan and groan.

"I have an idea!" said the fox. "Crawl into that large baking oven and hide. After they've left, I'll call you."

They agreed and crawled into the oven and asked the fox to stuff the opening of the oven with wood so that they wouldn't be seen. This was exactly what the fox had wanted, and he filled the entire opening with wood. Then he stood in front of the door to the palace, and when the king came riding up to the door, the fox said, "Your majesty, please get down and rest here. This is the palace of Count Piro."

So they dismounted and went up the stairs and found such great splendor and wealth that the king was completely astounded and thought, "My own palace cannot compare to the beauty of this one." Then he asked the fox, "How come there are no servants here?"

"My master didn't want to set up the household without knowing what the wishes of his beautiful wife were," he answered. "She can now do just as she pleases."

After they had examined everything, the king returned to his castle, and Count Piro remained in the beautiful palace. During the night, however, the fox crept to the oven, lit the wood, and started a large fire so that the ogre and his wife were burned to death. The next morning the fox said to Count Piro and his wife, "You're now happy and rich. But you must promise me one thing. When I die, you must put me into a beautiful coffin and bury me with all the honor I deserve."

"Oh, little fox, don't talk about dying," the princess said, for she had become very fond of the fox.

After some time had passed, the fox wanted to put Count Piro to the test and pretended to be dead. When the princess saw the fox, she cried out, "Oh, the little fox is dead. The poor little thing! Now we must quickly have a beautiful coffin made for him."

"A coffin for that beast?" Count Piro cried out. "Take him by his legs and throw him out the window!"

All at once the fox jumped up and screamed, "Oh, you ungrateful dirty beggar, you miserable starving hound! Have you forgotten that it was me who made your fortune? It was me who helped you get everything that you have? You ungrateful wretch!"

"Oh, little fox, just calm down," Count Piro pleaded. "I didn't mean it that way. I just spoke without thinking about what I was saying."

The fox let himself be calmed down and continued to live for a long time in Count Piro's palace, and when he really died, his master had a beautiful coffin made for him and buried him with all the honors he deserved. As for Count Piro, he and his beautiful wife lived happy and content, but we were left without a cent.

Count Joseph Pear (1875)[175]
Giuseppe Pitrè

There were once three brothers who owned a pear tree and lived off their pears. One day one of the brothers went to pick some pears and saw that some had been taken.

"My brothers! What shall we do? Somebody's picked our pears!"

Indeed, they had been stolen, and that night the eldest went to the garden to guard the pear tree. However, he fell asleep, and the next morning the middle brother came and said, "What were you doing, brother? Now look at what's happened! More pears have been picked. Well, tonight I'm going to stand guard."

So, that night the second brother was on the lookout. The next morning the youngest brother went to the garden and saw that more of the pears had been picked.

"And you said you were going to keep close watch over everything!" he said to his brother. "Get out of here! Now I'm going to spend the night guarding the tree, and we'll see whether the thief can pull the wool over my eyes!"

That night, to keep himself awake, the youngest brother began to play and dance under the pear tree. After he stopped for a moment, a female fox, who thought the young man had gone to sleep, came out of a hiding place, climbed the tree, and picked the rest of the pears. As she was descending the tree, the young man quickly aimed his gun at her and was about to shoot.

"Don't shoot!" cried the fox. "Please don't shoot me, Count Joseph. Yes, I shall call you Count Joseph Pear from now on, and I'll see to it that you'll marry the king's daughter."

"But if I let you go, I'll probably never see you again. Besides, as soon as the king sees you, he'll kick you out and make you disappear."

Despite saying all these things, Count Joseph Pear took pity on the fox and let her go. As soon as she went to the forest, the fox caught all sorts of game—squirrels, rabbits, and pheasants—and carried them to the king, who was quite pleased by the sight.

"Your majesty," said the fox, "Count Joseph Pear asked me to bring you this game that he caught."

"Listen, little fox," the king replied, "I'll take this game you brought, even though I've never heard of your Count Joseph Pear before."

The fox left the game there and returned to Count Joseph.

"Listen, Count Joseph, I've taken the first step," the fox reported. "I went to the king and with a gift, and he took it."

---

175.   "Don Giuseppi Piru," *Fiabe, novelle e racconti popolari siciliani*, 4 vols. (Palermo: Lauriel, 1875).

A week later the fox went to the forest, caught some more animals—squirrels, rabbits, birds—and told Count Joseph he wanted to take them to the king, which he did.

"Your majesty, Count Joseph Pear sent me to offer you another present," the fox said.

"Oh, my little fox," the king replied, "I don't know who this Count Joseph Pear is. I'm afraid your count's been sending you to the wrong king. However, I'll tell you what we'll do: you bring Count Joseph Pear here so I can at least make his acquaintance."

The fox left the game and said, "I'm not mistaken, your majesty. My master sent me here, and in exchange for his generosity, he would like to wed your daughter, the princess."

The little fox returned to Count Joseph and said to him, "Listen, things are going well. After I see the king one more time, the matter will be settled."

"I won't believe you until I have my wife," Count Joseph responded.

Now the fox went back into the forest to an ogress[176] and said, "My friend, my friend, isn't it time for us to divide our money and put the gold coins with the gold and the silver with the silver?"

"Certainly," the ogress said to the fox. "Go fetch a scale so we can weigh and put the gold with the gold and the silver with the silver."

The little fox went to the king, but she didn't say, "The ogress wants to borrow your scale." Instead, she said, "Count Joseph Pear wants to borrow your scale to weigh and divide the gold and silver."

"How did Count Joseph Pear become so wealthy? Is he richer than I am?"

The king gave the fox the scale. When he was alone with his daughter, they talked and talked, and he said to her, "I see that this Count Joseph Pear is very rich because he's weighing and dividing the gold and silver."

In the meantime the fox carried the scale to the ogress, who began to weigh and divide the gold and silver. When she was finished, the fox went to Count Joseph Pear and dressed him in new clothes and gave him a watch with diamonds, some rings, an engagement ring for the princess, and everything that was needed for the marriage."

"Listen to me, Count Joseph Pear," the fox said. "I'm going out before you to prepare the way. You're to go to the king, get your bride, and go to the church."

So Count Joseph went to the king, got his bride, and they went to the church. After they were married, the princess got into the carriage, and the bridegroom mounted his horse. The fox made a sign to Joseph and cried out, "I'll ride ahead, and you follow me. Let the carriages and horses come after."

They started on their way and came to a sheep farm which belonged to the ogress. When the shepherd, who was tending the sheep, saw the fox approach, he threw a rock at her. The fox began to weep.

---

176. *Mammadràa*, which is a special ogress in Sicily.

"Now I'll have you killed!" she said to the shepherd. "Do you see those horsemen behind me? They are mine, and I'll have you killed!"

The shepherd was frightened and said, "If you don't harm me, I won't throw stones at you anymore."

The fox turned and responded, "This is what you must do if you don't want to be killed," the fox replied. "When the king passes by and asks you who the owner of the sheep farm is, you must tell him that the farm belongs to Count Joseph Pear. He's the king's son-in-law, and the king will reward you."

Soon the cavalcade passed by, and the king asked the boy, "Who is the owner of this sheep farm?"

"Count Joseph Pear," the shepherd replied, whereupon the king gave him some money.

The fox kept about ten feet in front of Count Joseph, who turned to her and whispered, "Where are you taking me, fox? How can you make them believe that I'm rich? Where are we going?"

"Listen to me," replied the fox. "Leave everything to me."

They went on and on, and the fox saw another farm of cattle with a herdsman. The same thing happened there as with the other shepherd. The herdsman threw a stone, and the fox threatened him. The king passed by and asked, "Herdsman, who owns all these fields?"

"Count Joseph Pear," the herdsman responded, and the king, astonished by his son-in-law's wealth, gave the herdsman a piece of gold.

On the one hand, Joseph was pleased, but on the other, he was confused and wasn't sure how things would end. When the fox turned around, Joseph said, "Where are you taking me, fox? You're going to be the ruin of me."

The fox kept on as if she hadn't heard a thing. Then she came to a horse farm, and the boy who was tending the stallions and mares threw a stone at the fox, who, in turn, frightened him with a threat just as she had done with the others. When the boy saw the king, he said that the farm belonged to Count Joseph Pear.

They kept on traveling, and soon the fox came to a well. The ogress was sitting next to it. The fox began to run and pretended to be tremendously afraid of some rogues.

"Friend! Friend!" she cried out to the ogress. "Do you see them coming after me? Those horsemen will kill us! Quick, let's hide down inside the well."

"Yes, let's do it, friend!" the ogress responded in fear. "We've got to save ourselves."

"Shall I throw you down first?" the fox asked.

"Certainly, friend," the ogress said.

So the fox threw the ogress down the well and then entered her palace. Count Joseph Pear followed the fox with his wife, father-in-law, and all the horsemen. The fox showed them through the apartments, displaying all the riches. Of course, Count Joseph was happy because he had found his fortune, and the king was even happier because his daughter had married a very rich man. There was a celebration for a few days, and then the king, who was most satisfied, returned to his own castle, and his daughter remained with her husband.

One day soon after the king's departure, the fox was looking out the window, and Joseph and his wife were going up to the terrace. Joseph took some dirt and threw it at the fox's head. The fox raised her eyes.

"What's the meaning of this?" she said to Count Joseph. "You're disgusting! Why are you doing this after all the good things that I've done for you? Watch out, or I'll talk!

"What does the fox have to talk about?" the wife said to Count Joseph.

"Nothing," he said to his wife. "I threw a little dirt at her, and she got angry."

Then Joseph picked up some more dirt and threw it at the fox's head.

The fox became angry and cried out, "Well, little Joey, now I'm going to talk and tell everyone that you're just the common owner of a pear tree."

Joseph became very frightened because the little fox began to tell his wife everything. As she was talking, he picked up a vase and threw it at the little fox's head, and the vase crushed her skull. Thus Joseph repaid her kindness by killing her, and he continued to enjoy all his wealth with his wife.

And those who tell this tale and whoever caused it to be told
Will not die a terrible death whenever they get old.[177]

Told by Angela Smiraglia, eighteen-years-old, a villager, in Capa.

The Gilded Fox (1880–1882)[178]

Paul Sébillot

There was once a man who had three sons. At his death he left an inheritance that consisted of a cock, a cat, and a cherry tree. It wasn't necessary to hire a lawyer to determine how the inheritance was to be shared, for his sons divided everything amiably. And each time one of them took possession of his share, he tried to make the best out of it.

The eldest son whose share had been the cock set out on his way to seek his fortune. He travelled far, very far, and then even further than I can say, and he finished his travels by arriving at a house where he asked for a night's lodging. However, no sooner had he fallen asleep than he heard the people say that they had to get up in the dark before sunrise of the next day.

"Why do you need to get up so early in the morning?" he asked.

"It's because we're obliged to go to the seaside to earn our living in our carts," they responded.

---

177. *E cu' l'ha dittu e cu' l'ha fattu diri/Di mala morti nun pozza muriri.*
178. "Le Renard doré," *Contes populaires de la Haute-Bretagne* (Paris: Charpentier, 1880).

"You don't need to get up until the sun rises," he told them. "I have a small animal with feathers that's called a cock in my country. The day doesn't begin until he begins to crow."

The people of this country were very anxious to know whether this was the truth, and since they were afraid they might miss the crowing of the cock, they couldn't fall asleep that night. In the morning the cock began to crow. As soon as the people of the house looked at the sun rising and saw that the day had arrived, they rushed to tell the lord of the country all about of this. Then the lord summoned the young man and asked to buy the animal who made the day arrive.

"I'll be glad to give you the cock," he said, "but on condition that you give me a horse loaded with gold."

"A horse loaded with gold is yours!" responded the lord.

And the young man was delighted to have become rich thanks to his cock.

The son who had inherited the cat also set out on the road with his cat. He travelled far, very far, and further than I can say. He finished by arriving on an island and knocking on the door of a house where he asked for a place to sleep.

"Gladly," said the owner of the house, "but I must warn you that as soon as night falls, some small animals come and gnaw at everything and don't let anyone sleep."

"I have with me a small animal that's called a cat in my country," said the young man. "He knows just how to fight rats and mice."

When night arrived, the rats and mice came out of all the corners of the house. Immediately the young man let his cat loose, and it strangled so many rats and mice in the house that one couldn't move a foot without stepping on their dead bodies.

When the lord of this country had learned of a stranger who possessed such a marvelous animal, he summoned him to his castle. There had been so many mice and rats there that when the lord was dining at his table, the mice ran on the plates, and the rats put their paws into the soup.

The young man went to the castle. His cat strangled more than a hundred mice and just as many rats, nothing less. So the lord asked to buy the cat.

"I'll gladly sell it," said the young man, "but on condition that you give me two good mules loaded with gold."

"Gladly," answered the king. "But you must first search for the animal's family so that the entire country will have one of its species."

The young man left his cat at the castle and returned to his home country where he bought a female cat belonging to his neighbors. Then he travelled back to the country of the lord who had his cat.

"She's very nice," said the lord, "but you must live with me until this cat gives birth to kittens."

The young man remained in the castle, and at the end of two months there were pretty little kittens. There was great rejoicing on the entire island to celebrate this occasion, and the lord gave the young man two good mules packed with gold.

The cherry tree bore fruit in every season, and the son who had inherited the tree ate as much of the cherries that he desired, and he easily sold the rest because the quality of the cherries was very good. His neighbors called him the Marquis of Carabas.

One day when he was climbing up his cherry tree, Renard the fox passed by and said to him: "What are you doing on this tree, Marquis de Carabas?"

"I'm picking the cherries. Would you like some, Renard?"

"Gladly, thank you."

The young man gave him some of the most beautiful cherries, and Renard the fox ate them, and then he took the cherries that remained to the king.

"Sire," he said, "here are some gifts that the Marquis de Carabas has sent to you."

"He must be very rich, this marquis, if he has such beautiful cherries. What would you like for your efforts, Renard the fox?"

"I desire," he said, "to have the end of my tail gilded."

The goldsmith came to gild the fox's tail, and everything went very well. His tail shone like the sun. As he was returning to his home, he encountered some partridges along the way.

"Renard," they said, "how handsome you are! Your tail is like gold."

"If you want to come with me, you can also become beautiful and gilded like me," he responded.

The partridges followed him, and the fox led them to the king.

"Sire," Renard said, "here are the partridges of the Marquis de Carabas that you desired."

"He must be very rich, this Marquis de Carabas!" the king replied. "What would you like for your efforts, Renard the fox?"

"I would like to have my four paws gilded."

The goldsmith came and gilded Renard the fox's four paws, and he was even more handsome than before. On his return home he passed by a field where there was a group of rabbits.

"Ah, Renard the fox!" they cried out. "How handsome you are! Your tail and your paws appear to be made of gold."

"If you want to come with me, you can also become as beautiful and gilded as I am."

The rabbits followed him, and along the way they told other rabbits about the gold, and they joined in order to become gilded. So, Renard the fox arrived at the royal court with a regiment of rabbits and said to the king: "Sire, here are the rabbits that the Marquis of Carabas has sent you."

"He must be very rich, this Marquis de Carabas," said the king. "What would you like for your efforts, Renard the fox? I shall not refuse you anything."

"Sire," the fox responded, "I'd like to have the rest of my body gilded."

The goldsmith came and gilded the fox who was now completely yellow and shone like the sun. Soon after he went to find the Marquis de Carabas and told him that the king wanted to speak to him. The young man followed him, and as they were approaching the court, Renard the fox told him to get undressed. When the young man was completely nude, the fox began to cry out: "Help! Help!"

The king's men arrived, and the fox said to them: "When the Marquis de Carabas arrived in his coach, some bandits attacked and robbed him and left him just as naked as a newborn baby!"

The king's men went and fetched some clothes from the castle and carried them to Renard the fox, who said: "The clothes that were stolen were much more beautiful. No matter. These clothes will keep the marquis from catching a cold."

The Marquis de Carabas and the Renard the fox went to the court, where the king received the marquis in the best manner and told him that he would like very much to view his castle The young man responded that he would like nothing better, for he was confident that Renard the fox would always do his best for him.

They set out on their way, and Renard the fox, completely gilded, walked ahead of them. He reached a pasture where the washerwomen were hanging out the laundry to dry.

"Have you seen the king pass by?" he asked them.

"No, we haven't seen him."

"He's going to pass by in his coach. If you don't tell him that the laundry belongs to the Marquis de Carabas, he'll kill you."

When the king arrived at the field, he said to the washerwomen: "Who's the owner of this beautiful pasture and the beautiful laundry?"

"The Marquis de Carabas."

"Ah!" said the king. "You have a beautiful piece of property here."

"That's just a little part," replied the Marquis.

Renard the Fox continued on his way until he reached a field where many people were cutting the wheat.

"Have you seen the king pass by?"

"No," they responded. "We haven't seen him."

"He's going to pass by soon in his coach. If you don't say that all this wheat belongs to the Marquis de Carabas, he will kill you."

When the king arrived at the field, he asked the peasants: "Who's the owner of this wheat?"

"The Marquis de Carbas."

"Ah!" said the king. "You have a beautiful harvest."

"Ah, sire!" replied the Marquis de Carabas. "That's just a little of what I have."

Renard the fox now went to a pasture where the cattle were grazing, and he said to the herdsmen: "Have you seen the king pass by?"

"No," they responded. "We haven't seen him."

"He's going to pass by soon in his coach. If you don't say that all the cattle belongs to the Marquis de Carabas, he will kill you."

When the king arrived at the place where the cattle were grazing, he asked the herdsmen: "Who's the owner of these cattle?"

"The Marquis de Carabas."

"Ah!" said the king. "You have quite beautiful cattle."

"Ah, sire, that's just a little of what I have."

Meanwhile, Renard the fox reached a convent of monks, just as beautiful as a king's palace, where he said to them:

"Have you seen the king pass by?"

"No," they responded. "We haven't seen him."

"He's going to pass by soon in his coach, and he's going to kill you because he detests monks. If you want to avoid being found, you must hide yourselves in the middle of this pile of straw, and you're not to budge. He won't think of searching for you there."

The monks got under the straw while Renard the fox entered the convent and said to the servants: "The king will soon be here, and if you don't say that this convent belongs to the Marquis de Carabas, he'll kill you."

The king arrived at the convent where he was treated as if he were at home. After the meal, he went for a walk, and as he was passing by the pile of straw, Renard the fox said to him: "There are a bunch of rats in this pile that are devouring everything around."

"What do we have to do to get rid of them?" the king asked.

"We must set the pile on fire."

So, the straw was set on fire, and the monks were grilled except for two or three who escaped, and the Marquis de Carabas remained master of the convent with his companion Renard the Fox who was completely gilded and shone like the sun.

Prince Csihan (Nettles) (1889)[179]

W. Henry Jones

There was once—I don't know where, at the other side of seven times seven countries, or even beyond them, on the tumble-down side of a tumble-down stove—a poplar-tree, and this poplar-tree had sixty-five branches, and on every branch at sixty-six crows; and may those who don't listen to my story have their eyes picked out by those crows!

There was a miller who was so proud that had he stept on an egg he would not have broken it. There was a time when the mill was in full work, but once as he was tired of his mill-work he said, "May God take me out of this mill!"

179. *The Folk-Tales of the Magyars: Collected by Kriza, Erdélyi, and Others* (London: Elliot Stock, 1889).

Now, this miller had an auger, a saw, and an adze, and he set off over seven times seven countries and never found a mill. So his wish was fulfilled. On he went, roaming about, till at last he found on the bank of the Gagy, below Martonos, a tumbledown mill, which was covered with nettles. Here he began to build, and he worked, and by the time the mill was finished all his stockings were worn into holes, and his garments all tattered and torn. He then stood expecting people to come and have their flour ground, but no one ever came.

One day the twelve huntsmen of the king were chasing a fox, and it came to where the miller was and said to him:

"Hide me, miller, and you shall be rewarded for your kindness."

"Where shall I hide you?" said the miller, "seeing that I possess nothing but the clothes I stand in?"

"There is an old torn sack lying beside that trough," replied the fox. "Throw it over me, and, when the dogs come, drive them away with your broom."

When the huntsmen came, they asked the miller if he had seen a fox pass that way.

"How could I have seen it? Behold, I have nothing but the clothes I stand in."

With that the huntsmen left, and in a little while the fox came out and said, "Miller, I thank you for your kindness, for you have preserved me and saved my life. I am anxious to do you a good turn if I can. Tell me, do you want to get married?"

"My dear little fox," said the miller, "if I could get a wife, who would come here of her own free will, I don't say that I would not—indeed, there is no other way of my getting one because I can't go among the spinning-girls in these clothes."

The fox took leave of the miller, and, in less than a quarter of an hour, he returned with a piece of copper in his mouth. "Here you are, miller," said he. "Put this away. You will want it ere long."

The miller put it away, and the fox departed, but before long, he came back with a lump of gold in his mouth.

"Put this away, also," said he to the miller, "as you will need it before long. . . . And now, wouldn't you like to get married?"

"Well, my dear little fox," said the miller, "I am quite willing to do so at any moment, as that is my special desire."

The fox vanished again, but soon returned with a lump of diamond in his mouth.

"Well, miller," said the fox, "I will not ask you any more to get married. I will get you a wife myself. And now give me that piece of copper I gave you."

Then, taking it in his mouth, the fox started off over seven times seven countries, and travelled till he came to King Yellow Hammer's castle.

"Good day, most gracious King Yellow Hammer," said the fox. "My life and death are in your majesty's hands. I have heard that you have an unmarried daughter. I am a messenger from Prince Csihan, who has sent me to ask for your daughter as his wife."

"I will give her with pleasure, my dear little fox," replied King Yellow Hammer. "I will not refuse her. On the contrary, I give her with great pleasure, but I would do so more willingly if I saw to whom she is to be married—even as it is, I will not refuse to let her get married."

The fox accepted the king's proposal, and they fixed a day upon which the prince and the fox would fetch the lady.

"Very well," said the fox, and, taking leave of the king, set off with the ring to the miller.

"Now then, miller," said the fox, "you are no longer a miller, but Prince Csihan, and on a day and hour you must be ready to start, but, first of all, give me that lump of gold I gave you that I may take it to His Majesty King Yellow Hammer so that he may not think you are a nobody."

The fox then started off to the king.

"Good day, most gracious king, my father. Prince Csihan has sent this lump of gold to my father the king that he may spend it in preparing for the wedding, and that he might change it, as Prince Csihan has no smaller change, his gold all being in lumps like this."

"Well," reasoned King Yellow Hammer, "I am not sending my daughter to a bad sort of place, for although I am a king, I have no such lumps of gold lying about in my palace."

The fox then returned home to Prince Csihan.

"Now then, Prince Csihan," said he, "I have arrived safely, you see. Prepare yourself to start to-morrow."

Next morning he appeared before Prince Csihan.

"Are you ready?" asked he.

"Oh yes, I am ready. I can start at any moment, as I got ready long ago."

With this they started over seven times seven lands. As they passed a hedge the fox said, "Prince Csihan, do you see that splendid castle?"

"How could I help seeing it, my dear little fox."

"Well," replied the fox, "in that castle dwells your wife."

On they went, when suddenly the fox said, "Take off the clothes you have on. Let us put them into this hollow tree, and then burn them, so that we may get rid of them."

"You are right, we won't have them, nor any like them."

Then said the fox, "Prince Csihan, go into the river and take a bath."

Having done so the prince said, "Now I'm done."

"All right," said the fox. "Go and sit in the forest until I go into the king's presence."

The fox set off and arrived at King Yellow Hammer's castle.

"Alas! My gracious king, my life and my death are in thy hands. I started with Prince Csihan with three loaded wagons and a carriage and six horses, and I've just managed to get the prince naked out of the water."

The king raised his hands in despair, exclaiming, "Where hast thou left my dear son-in-law, little fox?"

"Most gracious king, I left him in such-and-such a place in the forest."

The king at once ordered four horses to be put to a carriage and then looked up the robes he wore in his younger days and ordered them to be put in the carriage; the coachman and footman to take their places, the fox sitting on the box. When they arrived at the forest, the fox got down, and the footman, carrying the clothes upon his arm, took them to Prince Csihan. Then said the fox to the servant, "Don't you dress the prince, he will do it more becomingly himself."

He then made Prince Csihan arise and said, "Come here, Prince Csihan, don't stare at yourself too much when you get dressed in these clothes, else the king might think you were not used to such robes."

Prince Csihan got dressed and drove off to the king. When they arrived, King Yellow Hammer took his son-in-law in his arms and said, "Thanks be to God, my dear future son-in-law, for that He has preserved thee from the great waters. Now let us send for the clergyman and let the marriage take place."

The grand ceremony over, they remained at the court of the king. One day, a month or so after they were married, the princess said to Prince Csihan, "My dear treasure, don't you think it would be as well to go and see your realm?"

Prince Csihan left the room in great sorrow and went towards the stables in great trouble to get ready for the journey he could no longer postpone. Here he met the fox lolling about. As the prince came, his tears rolled down upon the straw.

"Hollo! Prince Csihan, what's the matter?" cried the fox.

"Quite enough," was the reply. "My dear wife insists upon going to see my home."

"All right," said the fox. "Prepare yourself, Prince Csihan, and we will go."

The prince went off to his castle and said, "Dear wife, get ready. We will start at once."

The king ordered out a carriage and six, and three wagons loaded with treasure and money, so that they might have all they needed. Then they started off, and the fox said: "Now, Prince Csihan, wherever I go you must follow."

So they went over seven times seven countries. As they travelled, they met a herd of oxen.

"Now, herdsmen," said the fox, "if you won't say that this herd belongs to the Vasfogu Baba, but to Prince Csihan, you shall have a handsome present."

With this the fox left them and ran straight to the Vasfogu Baba.

"Good day, my mother," said he.

"Welcome, my son," replied she. "It's a good thing for you that you called me your mother, else I would have crushed your bones smaller than poppy-seed."

"Alas!" said the fox. "My mother, don't let us waste our time talking such nonsense, the French are coming!"

"Oh! My dear son, hide me away somewhere!" cried the old woman.

'I know of a bottomless lake,' thought the fox, and he took her and left her on the bank, saying, "Now, my dear old mother, wash your feet here until I return."

The fox then left the Vasfogu Baba and went to Prince Csihan, whom he found standing in the same place where he left him. He began to swear and rave at him fearfully.

"Why didn't you drive on after me? Come along at once."

They arrived at the Vasfogu's great castle and took possession of a suite of apartments. Here they found everything the heart could wish for, and at night all went to bed in peace. Suddenly the fox remembered that the Vasfogu Baba had no proper abode yet and set off to her.

"I hear, my dear son," said she, "that the horses with their bells have arrived. Take me away to another place."

The fox crept up behind her, gave her a push, and she fell into the bottomless lake and was drowned, leaving all her vast property to Prince Csihan.

"You were born under a lucky star, my prince," said the fox, when he returned, "for you see, I have placed you in possession of all this great wealth."

In his joy the prince gave a great feast to celebrate his coming into his property so that the people from Banczida to Zsukhajna were feasted royally, but he gave them no drink.

'Now,' said the fox to himself, 'after all this feasting I will sham illness, and see what treatment I shall receive at his hands in return for all my kindness to him.'

So Mr. Fox became dreadfully ill. He moaned and groaned so fearfully that the neighbors made complaint to the prince.

"Seize him," said the prince, "and pitch him out on the dunghill."

So the poor fox was thrown out on the dunghill.

One day Prince Csihan was passing that way.

"You a prince!" muttered the fox. "You are nothing else but a miller. Would you like to be a householder such as you were at the nettle-mill?"

The prince was terrified by this speech of the fox, so terrified that he nearly fainted.

"Oh! dear little fox, do not do that," cried the prince, "and I promise you on my royal word that I will give you the same food as I have, and that so long as I live you shall be my dearest friend, and you shall be honored as my greatest benefactor."

He then ordered the fox to be taken to the castle and to sit at the royal table, nor did he ever forget him again. So they lived happily ever after, and do yet, if they are not dead. May they be your guests to-morrow!

Translated by W. Henry Jones.

Bukutschichan (1919)[180]

Adolf Dirr

There was once a miller called Lause-Hadschi[181] And it happened on one occasion that the rags he had gathered together in heaps disappeared.

"That must not be allowed to pass," he said, "I must find the thief," and he hid himself behind the door. He had not long to wait till he saw a fox slink in, and the fox had no hair underneath, and his coat was all disheveled on his back.

"Aha! You mangy wretch! It is you, is it?" said Lause-Hadschi, and he flung himself with a cudgel on the fox.

"Slowly, miller, slowly!" cried the fox. "The rapid river does not find the sea, as the proverb says. Will you kill me because of these few rags I have carried away from you? I will make you rich because of them. I will marry you to the chan's daughter. I will make you great and famous. Under one condition, however— you must feed me with kurdjuk[182] as long as I live, and when I die you must bury me in one."

The miller gladly agreed to all this. Then the fox ran away and scraped about in a dust-heap till he found an abbas.[183] He ran with it to the chan's castle, which lay on the other side of the river. He said to the chan: "Forgive me for making so free, but I came to ask you for a measure with which to measure Bukutschichan's silver. I have tried everywhere to get one, but could not hear of one anywhere."

"Who is this Bukutschichan, then?" asked the chan. "I have never heard anything about him."

"He exists, nevertheless," answered the fox. "I am his vizier."

Then he took the measure and ran away. In the evening he brought back the measure after he had stuck the abbas into a crack in it.

"I should like to know if it is true what that good-for-nothing fox told me," said the chan and shook his measure. The coin at once fell out. 'It must seemingly be true, then,' he said thoughtfully to himself, 'but I wonder who this Bukutschichan is?'

Next day the fox came again. This time he wanted a measure to measure his master's gold. When he had got what he asked for, he searched and searched till he found a gold coin, stuck it too into a crack in the measure, and brought the measure back to its owner.

"We have only just got finished before dark by working very hard," he lied.

The fox had hardly gone, when the chan shook the measure again, and the gold coin fell out. How astonished the chan was! After a time the fox came back

---

180.   "Bukutschichan," *Caucasian Folk-Tales*, trans. Lucy Menzies (London: Dent, 1925).

181.   The pilgrims to Mecca are called *Hadschi,* because they have made the pilgrimage.

182.   The fat tail of a special breed of sheep.

183.   The present name of the twenty-kopek piece in the Caucasus.

again. But this time he came to ask the hand of the chan's daughter in marriage for his master. The chan nearly died with joy.

"I will come to-morrow with Bukutschichan," said the fox and ran away home. The following day he made a robe of state for Lause-Hadschi out of brightly colored Alpine flowers. Then he made him a set of weapons from the wood of a lime tree with cords of bast and many other similarly artificial things. Bukutschichan—for that was what he was called now—looked like a rainbow when seen from a distance. When everything was ready the fox said to him: "The chan will ride with his retinue to meet you as far as the river. But as you ride through the river cry, 'Help! Help! The river is carrying me away!' and dive underneath. Then the chan's retinue will pull you out of the water, and everything will be all right."

And so it all happened. When Bukutschichan got to the middle of the river, he pretended that the stream was carrying him off and cried for help. The river naturally washed off everything he had on, and when the chan's people pulled him out of the water, he was as naked as when he was born. But they at once offered him clothing and weapons. Bukutschichan dressed himself and now looked a fine fellow. But as he had never had anything to wear except a mangy skin, the new clothes seemed strange to him, and he could not hide his awkwardness. He tugged here and pulled there, smoothed out here and pushed to the side somewhere else.

"What is he doing?" the chan's followers asked the fox. "It looks as if he had never had proper clothes to put on before."

"What were his clothes made of?" asked the followers another time. "He looked like a rainbow."

"They were priceless," lied the fox, "covered all over with diamonds and precious stones. But he has plenty of clothes like that. It does not matter having lost those. What I am sorry about is his sword. That was an ancient Stamboul sword, which he inherited from his ancestors. There will never be another like it!"

"Yes, yes! It must have been made of pure silver," said the followers. "We noticed how it glittered in the sun."

When they arrived at the chan's palace, Bukutschichan was still more astonished. He looked up at the roof and down at the floor. His glance swept along the walls, and he examined everything most particularly.

"Whatever is he doing?" the chan's followers asked.

"He is behaving as if he had never seen a house before," the chan said to the fox.

"No, no, it is not that at all!" answered the fox. "It is only that . . . yours does not please him."

And Bukutschichan married the chan's daughter. The wedding festivities lasted a whole week. The bride got a magnificent trousseau, and when the newly married pair went away, they had every kind of escort imaginable—riders and pedestrians, drummers, flute-players, singers, youths, maidens, and a great crowd of people.

"I will hurry on in front and get the house in order," said the fox. "You can follow after."

He had no sooner spoken than he tore away as fast as his legs could carry him. Whether he ran for a long time or a short time, who knows? At any rate, he came at last to a plain on which a great herd was grazing.

"To whom do these cattle belong?" he asked.

"To the dragon," the shepherd answered.

"Take care, take care!" said the fox. "Don't mention the name of the dragon again. He is as good as dead. The army of the seven kings is coming to kill him with cannons and mortars, with powder and lead. If you say you are the dragon's shepherd, they will certainly put you to death and carry off your herd. But there is a chan—he is called Bukutschichan—whom even the kings are afraid of. If anyone asks you who the cattle belong to, say only they belong to Bukutschichan. Then no one will do you any harm."

The fox then rushed on and came to a drove of the dragon's horses, then to his flocks of sheep, then to his harvesters, and everywhere he told the same story. He ran on further and further till at last he came to the dragon's palace.

"Dragon!" he cried, "Dragon! I have not forgotten your hospitality, and I have come to warn you. The army of the seven kings is coming on behind me with cannons, mortars, guns, and so on. What will you do?"

"Alas! What can I do?" answered the dragon. "Against such an army I can do nothing! Do you not know some place, Mr. Fox, where I could hide myself?"

"Hide yourself here," said the fox, and pointed to a mountainous stack of hay which stood in the middle of the court. "Only be quick about it, for the army is following close on my heels."

The dragon hid himself as quickly as he could, and the fox . . . set a light to the haystack at all four corners. The dragon was roasted like a sausage in the gigantic fire.

And now the newly married pair were advancing, with music and drums, with outriders and singers. There was a great commotion round about them, shouting, and volleys of firing. When they came to the great plain where the cattle were grazing they asked who the herd belonged to. "To Bukutschichan," was the answer. When they came to the drove of horses and asked the same question, they got the same answer. And when they came to the flocks of sheep and asked whom they belonged to, the answer was still the same: "To Bukutschichan." When they came to the harvesters and asked to whom these fields and meadows belonged, they were told again: "To Bukutschichan." And the retinue was not a little astonished at the unheard-of riches of its master. He himself had no idea how it had all come about: he came near to losing his reason with it all. Finally they came to the dragon's castle. There the fox awaited them. Then he sent back the retinue of the young couple and established Bukutschichan and his wife upstairs while he made himself at home below. Bukutschichan had a splendid time there; he had nothing to do, for the fox took all burdens on his own shoulders.

But the fox was anxious to know what Bukutschichan really thought of him. For that reason he lay down once in the middle of the court and pretended to be dead.

"Look, there lies our fox. He looks as if he were dead," said Mrs. Bukutschichan to her husband.

"And if he were seven times dead it would be all the same to me," answered Bukutschichan. "I have been tired of that useless creature for a long time."

Hardly had he spoken, when the fox sprang to his feet and began a little song:

> Shall I or shall I not
> Tell the story of Lause-Hadschi
> And of the wooden gun?
> Of the miller who was in a scrape?
> Who fell on his knees?
> Who begged, who implored the fox not to give him away?
> Lause-Hadschi.
> And who generously forgave?
> The fox.

But everything comes to an end. . . . One day the fox really died. But Bukutschichan, who thought it was another trick, rolled him up in a kurdjuk. And the fox is supposed to be in it still to this day.

Translated by Lucy Menzies.

15. THE WISHES OF FOOLS
ATU 675—THE LAZY BOY

This tale type is loaded with social-class conflict that is played out in different ways. The basic plot involves a young man considered to be dumb and lazy by his brothers, relatives, and neighbors. However, he is much more clever than he seems and more thoughtful than those around him. Though treated badly, he treats others with kindness. Often he helps fairies from becoming sunburned or catches a fish and returns it to the sea. Because of his thoughtfulness, he is granted magic powers to obtain whatever he desires or wishes for. When a king's daughter mocks him because of his odd behavior and looks, he wishes her pregnant. The result is a baby boy. Consequently, the furious king orders a paternity test to discover the father because the princess does not know who impregnated her. Once the eccentric seemingly dumb lad is revealed to be the father, the king orders him, the princess, and their son to be put into a barrel/vat and set out to sea to die. However, due to the odd young man's powers, they reach land, and he erects a castle and often transforms himself into an elegant man. The remorseful king often stumbles by chance onto the new castle without recognizing either his daughter or the young man. His daughter purposely has the eccentric young man use his magic powers to plant a golden object (cup, spoon, apple) in the king's pocket/boot and accuses her father of stealing. The king complains that he has been unjustly accused, and his daughter explains that she, too, had been unjustly accused. They are then reunited. Sometimes the eccentric man marries the princess, but often she marries a suitor from the upper classes.

This tale has a significant literary tradition that probably emanated from oral storytelling in southern Europe and the Mediterranean. The class conflict and positive portrayal of the "dumb" hero are indications that the perspective of the storytellers stemmed from the lower classes. The most important early literary versions are Straparola's "Pietro the Fool," *Le Piacevoli Notti* (1550); Basile's "Pervonto," *Lo Cunto de li Cunti* (1634); Marie-Catherine d'Aulnoy's "Le Dauphin," *Suite des Contes Nouveaux ou des Fées à la mode* (1698); and Christoph Martin Wieland's *Pervonte oder die Wünsche* (1778). The Brothers Grimm received their version from one of the Hassenpflug sisters in 1812 and omitted it in the second edition because they may have found the pregnancy distasteful and the moral about justice somewhat ambivalent. Moreover, the debt to Wieland's poem was obvious. Another interesting German tale about a mysterious pregnancy written during the romantic period was Heinrich von Kleist's "Die Marquise von O" (1810–1811). Though not a fairy tale, it raises all the same pertinent questions about the responsibility for an unexpected pregnancy that the tales in this cycle pose.

The mysterious pregnancy of a daughter was a real concern for many noble families and commoners as well. A woman's body was regarded as a possession of the male, and any violation of a female body was a violation of patriarchal authority. At stake was the legacy and honor of a family. In the cycle of tales that involve a fool, often called Emil, Peter, or Hans, who seeks his luck by wishing that a princess becomes pregnant, there are other motifs that recall King Lear's harsh treatment of his innocent daughter as well as the cycle of tales that deal with a proud princess or noblewoman who needs to learn humility. However, the revenge motif is dominant: the eccentric young peasant is humiliated by the princess and seeks revenge or social justice. Once the princess learns her lesson, she, too, wants social justice. Interestingly, many of the storytellers are hesitant to allow the peasant to wed the princess in the end because it would breach the principles of the upper class. Only if the peasant transforms himself into a nobleman is he allowed to marry the woman whom he made pregnant. Very few tales concern the unwanted pregnancies of peasant women, who were commonly violated by so-called noblemen.

******

Simple Hans (1812)[184]
Jacob and Wilhelm Grimm

Once a king lived happily with his daughter, who was his only child. Then, all of a sudden she gave birth to a baby, and no one knew who the father was. For a long time the king didn't know what to do. At last he ordered the princess to take the child and go to the church. There a lemon was to be given to the child, who was to offer it to anyone around him, and the man who took it was to be considered the child's father and the princess's husband. Everything was arranged accordingly, and the king also gave orders to allow only highborn people into the church.

However, there was a little, crooked hunchback living in the city who was not particularly smart and was therefore called Simple Hans. Well, he managed to push his way into the church among the others without being noticed, and when the child offered the lemon, he handed it to Simple Hans. The princess was mortified, and the king was so upset that he had his daughter, the child, and Simple Hans stuck into a barrel, which was cast into the sea. The barrel soon floated off, and when they were alone at sea, the princess groaned and said, "You nasty, impudent hunchback! You're to blame for my misfortune! Why did you force your way into the church? My child's of no concern to you."

"That's not true," said Simple Hans. "He does concern me because I once made a wish that you would have a child, and whatever I wish comes true."

"Well, if that's the case, wish us something to eat."

---

184. "Hans Dumm," *Kinder- und Haus-Märchen. Gesammelt durch die Brüder Grimm*, 2 vols. (Berlin: Realschulbuchhandlung, 1812/1815).

"That's easily done," replied Simple Hans, and he wished for a dish full of potatoes. The princess would have liked to have something better. Nevertheless, she was so hungry that she joined him in eating the potatoes. After they had stilled their hunger, Simple Hans said, "Now I'll wish us a beautiful ship!"

No sooner had he said this than they were sitting in a splendid ship that contained more than enough to fulfill their desires. The helmsman guided the ship straight toward land, and when they went ashore, Simple Hans said, "Now I want a castle over there!"

Suddenly there was a magnificent castle standing there, along with servants dressed in golden uniforms. They led the princess and her child inside, and when they were in the middle of the main hall, Simple Hans said, "Now I wish to be a young and clever prince!"

All at once his hunchback disappeared, and he was handsome, upright, and kind. Indeed, the princess took such a great liking to him that she became his wife.

For a long time they lived happily together, and then one day the old king went out riding, lost his way, and arrived at their castle. He was puzzled because he had never seen it before and decided to enter. The princess recognized her father immediately, but he did not recognize her, for he thought she had drowned in the sea a long time ago. She treated him with a great deal of hospitality, and when he was about to return home, she secretly slipped a golden cup into his pocket. After he had ridden off, she sent a pair of knights after him. They were ordered to stop him and search him to see if he had stolen the golden cup. When they found it in his pocket, they brought him back. He swore to the princess that he hadn't stolen it and didn't know how it had gotten into his pocket.

"That's why," she said, "one must beware of rushing to judgment." And she revealed to him that she was his daughter. The king rejoiced, and they all lived happily together, and after his death, Simple Hans became king.

Emilian the Fool (1855–1864)[185]

Alexander Afanas'ev

There were once three brothers, of whom two were sharp-witted, but the third was a fool. The elder brothers set off to sell their goods in the towns down the river and said to the fool: "Now Mind, fool! Obey our wives and pay them respect as if they were your own mothers. We'll buy you red boots and a red caftan and a red shirt."

The fool said to them, "Very good, I'll pay them respect."

They gave the fool their orders and went away to the downstream towns, while the fool stretched himself on top of the stove and remained lying there. His brothers' wives said to him: "What are you about, fool! Your brothers ordered

---

185. William R. S. Ralston, *Russian Folk-Tales* (London: Smith, Elder, 1873).

you to pay us respect, and in return for that each of them was going to bring you a present, but there you lie on the stove and don't do a bit of work. Go and fetch some water, at all events."

The fool took a couple of pails and went to fetch the water. As he scooped it up, a pike happened to get into his pail.

"Glory to God!" said the fool. "Now I'll cook this pike and will eat it all myself. I won't give a bit of it to my sisters-in-law. I'm savage with them!"

"Don't eat me, fool!" the pike said to him with a human voice. "If you'll put me back again into the water, you shall have good luck!"

"What sort of good luck shall I get from you?" asked the fool.

"Why, this sort of good luck—whatever you say, that shall be done. Say, for instance, 'By the Pike's command, at my request, go home, ye pails, and be set in your places.'"

As soon as the fool had said this, the pails immediately went home of their own accord and became set in their places. The sisters-in-law looked and wondered: "What sort of a fool is this? Why, he's so knowing! Look how his pails have come home and gone to their places of their own accord!"

The fool came back and lay down on the stove, and again his brothers' wives began saying to him: "What are you lying on the stove for, fool? There's no wood for the fire. Go and fetch some."

The fool took two axes and got into a sledge, but without harnessing a horse to it.

"By the Pike's command," he said, "at my request, drive into the forest, oh sledge!"

Away went the sledge at a rattling pace, as if urged on by someone. The fool had to pass by a town, and the people he met were jammed into corners by his horseless sledge in a way that was perfectly awful. They began crying out: "Stop him! Catch him!"

But they couldn't lay hands on him. The fool drove into the forest, got out of the sledge, sat down on a log, and said: "One of you axes fell the trees, while the other cuts them up into billets!"

Well, the firewood was cut up and piled on the sledge. Then the fool said, "Now then, one of you axes, go and cut me a cudgel just as heavy as I can lift."

The axe went and cut him a cudgel, and the cudgel came and lay on top of the load. The fool took his seat and drove off. He drove by the town, but the townspeople had met together and had been looking out for him for a long time. So they stopped the fool, laid hands upon him, and began pulling him about.

"By the Pike's command," the fool said, "at my request, go, oh cudgel, and bestir thyself."

Out jumped the cudgel and began thumping and smashing and knocked over a great many people. There they lay on the ground, strewed about like so many sheaves of corn. The fool got clear of them and drove home, heaped up the wood, and then lay down on the stove.

Meanwhile, the townspeople got up a petition against him and denounced him to the king by declaring: "Folks say there's no getting hold of him the way we tried. We must entice him by cunning, and the best way of all will be to promise him a red shirt and a red caftan, and red boots."

So the king's messengers went to the fool and said: "Go to the king. He will give you red boots, a red caftan, and a red shirt."

Well, the fool, who was seated on the stove at that time, said, "By the Pike's command, at my request, oh stove, go to the king!"

So, the stove went, and the fool arrived on the stove at the king's court. The king was going to put him to death, but he had a daughter, and she took a tremendous liking to the fool. So she began begging her father to give the fool to her in marriage. Her father flew into a passion. He had them married and then ordered them both to be placed in a tub, and the tub to be tarred over and thrown into the water; all which was done.

Long did the tub float about on the sea, and wife began to beseech the fool: "Do something to get us cast on shore!"

"By the Pike's command, at my request," said the fool, "cast this tub ashore and tear it open!"

He and his wife stepped out of the tub. Then she again began imploring him to build some sort of a house. So the fool said: "By the Pike's command, at my request, let a marble palace be built, and let it stand immediately opposite the king's palace!"

This was all done in an instant. In the morning the king saw the new palace and sent a messenger to enquire who it was that lived in it. As soon as he learnt that his daughter lived there, he summoned her and her husband that very minute. Soon after they arrived, the king pardoned them, and they all began living together and flourishing.

Translated by William R. S. Ralston.

The Half Man (1864)[186]

Johann Georg von Hahn

Once upon a time there was a woman who had not given birth to any children and was so distressed by her condition that she prayed to God one day: "Dear God, please give me a child even if the infant would be just half a baby."

Well, God gave her a boy with half a head, half a nose, half a mouth, half a body, one hand, and one foot, and since he was so deformed, his mother always kept him at home and didn't send him out to work. One day, however, he became so bored that he said to his mother: "Mother, I don't want to stay at home. Give me an axe and a mule. I want to go out into the forest and fetch wood."

---

186. "Der halbe Mensch," *Griechische und albanische Märchen* (Leipzig: W. Engelmann, 1864).

But the mother responded: "How can you chop wood, my dear child? You're only half a man."

Nevertheless, he pleaded so long until his mother finally gave him an axe and a mule. Then he took them, went into the forest, chopped wood, and brought it back home. And since he did this work very well, his mother let him keep doing it.

One day, when he went to fetch some wood, he passed by the castle of the king's daughter, and when the princess saw him with one foot and one arm sitting on the mule, she laughed a great deal and called her maids: "Come and look at that half man!"

When they saw him, they almost burst from laughter. All this baffled the half man so much that his axe fell to the ground. He thought about this for some time and asked himself: 'Should I get off the mule and pick up the axe, or should I just keep sitting here?' Finally, he decided not to dismount. Instead, he left the axe lying on the ground and rode on. Then the princess said to the maids: "Just look at the half man. He let the axe drop and doesn't even get off the mule to pick it up!"

The half man became even more baffled by these remarks and let his rope fall as well. Then he thought about this awhile and said to himself: 'Should I get off the mule and pick up the rope, or should I just keep sitting here?' Finally, he continued to ride on and left the rope lying on the ground.

Then the princess called out to her maids: "Just look at the half man. He's let his axe and his rope fall to the ground and doesn't dismount to pick them up."

Half man rode to the place where he usually chopped wood, and when he arrived there, he said to himself: 'What are you going to use now to chop wood? What are you going to use to bind the wood?'

There happened to be a sea nearby, and as half man was thinking and staring into the water, he noticed a fish swimming toward the bank. Quickly he threw his raggedy coat on top of the fish and caught it. The fish began immediately to plead for its life and said: "Let me loose, half man! If you do, I'll teach you a skill, and if you learn to use it, everything will happen just as you desire."

In response half man said: "All right, then load my mule with wood so that I can see whether you're telling the truth."

And the fish said: "Upon the first word of God and the second of the fish, the mule is to be loaded with wood!"

And lo and behold he had barely finished saying this than the mule was loaded with wood. When half man saw this, he said to the fish: "If you teach me this skill, I'll set you free."

And the fish responded: "Whenever you want something to happen, you're to say: 'Upon the first word of God and the second of the fish, so and so is to happen!' And whatever you wish for will happen."

After the fish told him this, half man let the fish go, took his loaded mule by his hand, and walked past the castle of the king's daughter once again. When the princess caught sight of him, she called her maids: "Come quickly and look at the half man and how he's walking along now with his mule without his axe and rope."

Then they broke into laughter and continued laughing until they couldn't anymore. All this annoyed half man so much that he cried out: "Upon the first word of God and the second of the fish, the princess is to become pregnant!"

And after nine months, she gave birth to a child without anyone knowing who was responsible for getting her pregnant. Then her father summoned her and wanted to question her about this, but she continually answered: "I've never even spoken to a man. So I have no idea where the baby has come from."

When the baby grew, the king had all the people of his kingdom come to the major city, and after they were all gathered together, he gave the child an apple and said: "Now go and give this apple to your father."

As the child now ran around and played with the apple, it fell to the ground and rolled away. When the child ran after it, the apple came to a corner where half man was standing, and the apple stopped right before him. The child leaned over to pick up the apple, and as he lifted his head, he looked at half man and said: "Here papa! Take the apple!"

When the people heard this, they grabbed half man and brought him to the king, who immediately said: "Since it was half man who did this, we must kill all of them, him, the princess, and the child!"

However, his councilors said to him: "What you've said is not right! The princess is your daughter, and you shouldn't spill your own blood! So, have an iron barrel made and have the princess, half man, and the child stuck into it. Then have them thrown into the sea and give them nothing but a wreath of figs for the child so that he doesn't die all too quickly."

The king was pleased by this advice. So he had the barrel made, and then the three were put into it and thrown into the sea. Now, when they were sitting together in the barrel, the princess said to half man: "I've never seen you before. So how is it that we're now sitting here together?"

"Give me a fig," responded half man. "Then I'll tell you."

And so the princess gave him a fig that she had taken with her for the child. After half man had eaten it, he said: "Don't you remember that you laughed at me when I rode by your castle and my axe and rope fell to the ground?"

"Yes, I remember," the princess responded.

"Well, I now know a magic saying and when I use it, everything I want happens the way I want it. So, back then I wished that you would become pregnant, and that's why you became pregnant."

In response the princess said: "If you know such a saying that brings about everything that you want, then say it now so that we can get out of this barrel and reach land."

Half man answered: "Give me a fig, and then I'll say it."

So the princess gave him a fig, and after he had eaten it, he said to himself in secret: "Upon the first word of God and the second of the fish, the barrel is to swim to land and open up so that we can step outside."

Immediately thereafter the barrel headed for the shore and opened up, and they climbed out of it. As they stood outside, it began to rain. So the princess asked half man: "Say something so that we can find shelter somewhere and don't get wet."

Half man replied: "Give me a fig, and then I'll say something."

So the princess gave him a fig, and he said to himself: "Upon the first word of God and the second of the fish, let there be shelter."

And immediately they had some shelter and sat down beneath it. Once again the princess said to half man: "Up to now you've done very well! But now say something so that we can get a large castle with stones and beams and all house utensils that can speak!"

And half man responded: "Give me a fig, and then I'll say it."

So she gave him another fig, and after he ate it, he said to himself: "Upon the first word of God and the second of the fish, let there be a castle with stones, beans, and house utensils that can speak!"

A castle arose immediately, and everything in it spoke. So they went inside and began living there. Half man produced everything they needed and whatever the princess wished for.

One day the king went hunting and caught sight of a distant castle that he had never seen before. He became curious about who the owner might be. So he said to two of his servants: "Take these two partridges. Go to that castle over there, and roast them. Take a good look to see what kind of a castle it is because I've often been hunting around here and have never noticed it before."

Then the servants whom the king had called to him took the partridges and went to the castle. And when they came to the castle gate, it asked them: "What do you want here?"

"The king sent us here to roast a pair of partridges," they declared.

However, the castle gate responded: "Stay here. First I must ask my wife."

Right after this the castle gate said something to the first inside door, which turned to the second inside door, which turned to the third, and so it went from door to door, until the question reached the housewife, who commanded the gate and all the doors to let the strangers come inside, and immediately all the doors opened by themselves and let the strangers in. They were very astonished when they heard that even the beams and stones welcomed them. Then they went into the kitchen, and when they were there, one of the king's servants said to the other: "Where will we find some wood?"

Then some logs cried out: "Here we are!"

And when the king's servants said to one another, "We don't have any salt or butter," the salt and butter cried out, "Here we are!"

After the servants prepared the partridges, put them on spits, and stuck them into the fire, they wanted to look around the rooms near the kitchen more closely to see if there were other things in the castle that spoke. But they found so many and stayed away from the kitchen for such a long time that the partridges were burned to ashes before they remembered to return to the kitchen. They became very embarrassed and didn't know how they were to excuse themselves before the king and tell him that they had burned the partridges. Finally they decided to go straight to the king and to tell him about everything that they had seen.

However, the king refused to believe them and sent some other servants to the castle. But they experienced the exact same things that the first servants had, and when the king heard them say the same things that the first had said, he decided to go there himself and to convince himself with his own eyes and ears.

When he came to the castle, the gate said to him: "Welcome, your majesty!"

And when the king went inside, all the stones and beams cried out "welcome," and the king was very astounded that wood and stones could speak.

As soon as the princess heard that the king himself had come, she approached him to greet him. Then she led him into her stately apartments but didn't reveal herself to him. For his part, the king was very much astonished by her respectable behavior and her refined way of speaking.

Meanwhile the servants in the kitchen wanted to roast the partridges that the king had brought with him. However, they experienced the same thing that the other servants had and let the partridges burn to ashes because they had been caught up in the astonishment of what they saw.

When the king learned that the partridges had been burned to ashes, he became furious because he was hungry, and now there was nothing to eat. However, the princess said: "Please, your majesty, do us the favor of dining with us in our meager house."

And when the king accepted, she went looking for half man who had crawled into hiding, and said: "I've invited the king to eat with us. Now say something so that there will be a splendid meal with all the necessary servants, musicians, dancers, and everything else that is appropriate."

"Give me a fig, and then I'll do what you ask," half man replied.

So the princess gave him a fig. After he ate it, he wished for all that the princess wanted, and immediately a splendid meal and everything that went along with it appeared. When the princess sat down with the king and when the servants were in attendance, the musicians began to play, and they played so beautifully that the king was astonished and said: "I am a king, but I've never heard such music in my castle."

Soon afterward the dancers began to dance, and they danced so beautifully that the king said to the princess: "I am a king, but I don't have such dancers like these in my castle. Tell me how you've managed to come upon them."

"My father left them to me as part of my inheritance," said the princess.

Then she went to half man and said to him: "I want you to say something so that a spoon gets stuck in the king's boot."

And half man responded: "Give me a fig, and then I'll make it happen."

So the princess gave him a fig, and he fulfilled her wish so that a spoon stuck itself inside the king's boot.

When the king was now ready to take his leave, the princess said to him: "Wait a second. I think that I'm missing something."

The king became rather surly when he heard these words, and he said: "No, that's not possible. We are not people of that kind!"

But the princess didn't let herself be led astray and cried out: "Bowls, are you all here?"

"Yes!"

"Plates, are you all here?"

"Yes!"

"Spoons, are you all here?"

Then the spoon called out from the king's boot: "I'm stuck in the king's boot!"

Now the princess began to scold the king and said: "I've welcomed you into my house, prepared a meal for you, and bestowed you with all sorts of honors, and you steal a spoon from me! Aren't you ashamed of yourself?"

"That's not possible!" the king cried. "Someone stuck the spoon into my boot. You're treating me unjustly!"

In response the princess said: "And you also treated me unjustly when you stuck me with half man in the barrel even though I had done nothing wrong."

The king was so astonished that he remained speechless for a long time. However, the princess led half man before him, and half man told him how everything had happened.

The king was very astounded by this story and took his daughter back to his court and wed her to one of his great noblemen. As for half man, he appointed him to his number one bodyguard and gave him his most beautiful slave for a wife.

Sioccolone (1874)[187]

Rachel Busk

Once upon a time there were three brothers, who were woodmen; their employment was not one which required great skill, and they were none of them very clever, but the youngest was the least brilliant of all. So simple was he that all the neighbours, and his very brothers—albeit they were not so very superior in intelligence themselves—gave him the nickname of 'Sioccolone,' the great simpleton, and accordingly Sioccolone he was called wherever he went.

---

187. *The Folk-Lore of Rome. Collected by Word of Mouth from the People* (London: Longmans, Green, 1874).

Every day these three brothers went out into the woods to their work, and every evening they all came home, each staggering under his load of wood, which he carried to the dealer who paid them for their toil. Thus one day of labour passed away just like another in all respects. So it went on for years.

Nevertheless, one day came at last which was not at all like the others, and if all days were like it, the world would be quite upside down, or be at least a very different world from what it is. Oime! that such days never occur now at all! Basta, this is what happened.

It was in the noontide heat of a very hot day, the three simple brothers committed the imprudence of going out of the shelter of the woods into the world beyond, and there, lying on the grass in the severest blaze of the burning sun, they saw three beautiful peasant girls lying fast asleep.

"Only look at those silly girls sleeping in the full blaze of the sun!" cried the eldest brother.

"They'll get bad in their heads in this heat," said the second.

But Scioccolone said: "Shall we not get some sticks and boughs, and make a little shed to shelter them?"

"Just like one of Scioccolone's fine ideas!" laughed the eldest brother scornfully.

"Well done, Scioccolone! That's the best thing you've thought of this long while. And who will build a shed over us while we're building a shed for the girls, I should like to know?" said the second.

But Scioccolone said: "We can't leave them there like that. They will be burnt to death. If you won't help me, I must build the shed alone."

"A wise resolve, and worthy of Scioccolone!" scoffed the eldest brother.

"Good-bye, Scioccolone!" cried the second, as the two elder brothers walked away together. "Good-bye for ever! I don't expect ever to see you alive again, of course."

And they never did see him again, but what it was that happened to him you shall hear.

Without waiting to find a retort to his brothers' gibes, Scioccolone set to work to fell four stout young saplings, and to set them up as supports of his shed in four holes he had previously scooped with the aid of his bill-hook. Then he rammed them in with wedges, which he also had to cut and shape. After this he cut four large bushy branches, which he tied to the uprights with the cord he used for tying up his faggots of logs; and as the shade of these was scarcely close enough to keep out all the fierce rays of the sun, he went back to the wood and collected all the large broad leaves he could find, and came back and spread them out over his leafy roof. All this was very hard labour indeed when performed under the dreaded sun, and just in the hours when men do no work; yet so beautiful were the three maidens that, when at last he had completed his task, he could not tear himself away from them to go and seek repose in the shade of the wood, but he must needs continue standing in the full sun gazing at them open-mouthed.

At last the three beautiful maidens awoke, and when they saw what a fragrant shade had refreshed their slumbers, they began pouring out their gratitude to their devoted benefactor.

Do not run at hasty conclusions, however, and imagine that of course the three beautiful maidens fell in love on the spot with Scioccolone, and he had only to pick and choose which of them he would have to make him happy as his wife. A very proper ending, you say, for a fairy tale. It was not so, however. Scioccolone looked anything but attractive just then. His meaningless features and uncouth, clownish gait were never at any time likely to inspire the fair maidens with sudden affection; but just then, after his running hither and thither, his felling, digging, and hammering in the heat of the day, his face had acquired a tint which made it look rougher and redder and more repulsive than anyone ever wore before.

Besides this, the three maidens were fairies, who had taken the forms of beautiful peasant girls for some reason of their own. But neither did they leave his good deed unrewarded. By no means. Each of the three declared she would give him such a precious gift that he should own to his last hour that they were not ungrateful. So they sat and thought what great gift they could think of which should be calculated to make him very happy indeed.

At last the first of the three got up and exclaimed that she had thought of her gift, and she did not think anyone could give him a greater one, for she would promise him he should one day be a king.

Wasn't that a fine gift!

Scioccolone, however, did not think so. The idea of his being a king! Simple as he was, he could see the incongruity of the idea, and the embarrassment of the situation. How should he the poor clown, everybody's laughingstock, become a king? And if he did, kingship had no attractions for him. He was too kind-hearted, however, to say anything in disparagement of the well-meant promise, and too straightforward to assume a show of gratitude he did not feel. So after the first little burst of hilarity which he was not sufficiently master of himself to suppress, he remained standing open-mouthed after his awkward manner.

Then the second fairy addressed him and said: "I see you don't quite like my sister's gift, but you may be sure she would not have promised it if it had not been a good gift, after you have been so kind to us, and when it comes true, it will somehow all turn out very nice and right. But now, meantime, that I may not similarly disappoint you with my gift by choosing it for you, I shall let you choose it for yourself. So say what shall it be."

Scioccolone was almost as much embarrassed with the second fairy's permission of choosing for himself as he had been with the first fairy's choice for him. First he grinned, and then he twisted his great awkward mouth about, and then he grinned again, till, at last, ashamed of keeping the fairies waiting so long for his answer, he said, with another grin: "Well, to tell you what I should really like, it would be that when I have finished making up my faggot of logs this evening, instead of having to stagger home carrying it, it should roll along by itself, and then I get astride of it, and that it should carry me."

"That would be fine!" he added, and he grinned again as he thought of the fun it would be to be carried home by the load of logs instead of carrying the load as he had been wont.

"Certainly! That wish is granted," replied the second fairy readily. "You will find it all happen just as you have described."

Then the third fairy came forward and said: "And now choose what shall my gift be? You have only to ask for whatever you like and you shall have it."

Such a heap of wishes rose up in Scioccolone's imagination at this announcement, that he could not make up his mind which to select. As fast as he fixed on one thing, he remembered it would be incomplete without some other gift, and as he went on trying to find some one wish that should be as comprehensive as possible, he suddenly blurted out: "Promise me that whatever I wish may come true. That'll be the best gift, and so if I forget a thing one moment, I can wish for it the next. That'll be the best gift to be sure!"

"Granted!" said the third fairy. "You have only to wish for anything, and you will find you get it immediately, whatever it is."

The fairies then took leave and went their way, and Scioccolone was reminded by the lengthening shades that it was time he betook himself to complete his day's work. Scarcely succeeding in collecting his thoughts, so dazzled and bewildered was he by the late supernatural conversation, he yet found his way back to the spot where he had been felling wood.

'Oh, dear! how tired I am!' he said within himself as he walked along. 'How I wish the wood was all felled and the faggots tied up!' and though he said this mechanically as he might have said it any other day of his life, without thinking of the fairy's promise, which was, indeed, too vast for him to put it consciously to such a practical test then, full of astonishment as he was, yet when he got back to his working place, the wood was felled and laid in order and tied into a faggot in the best manner.

"Well to be sure!" soliloquised Scioccolone. "The girls have kept their promise indeed! This is just exactly what I wished. And now, let's see what else did I wish? Oh, yes, that if I got astride on the faggot, it should roll along by itself and carry me with it. Let's see if that'll come true too!"

With that he got astride on the faggot, and sure enough the faggot moved on all by itself, and carried Scioccolone along with it pleasantly enough. Only there was one thing Scioccolone had forgotten to ask for, and that was power to guide the faggot. And now, though it took a direction quite contrary to that of his homeward way, he had no means of inducing it to change its tack. After some time spent in fruitless efforts in schooling his unruly mount, Scioccolone began to reason with himself. 'After all, it does not much matter about going home.

I only get laughed at and called "Scioccolone." Maybe in some other place they may be better, and as the faggot is acting under the orders of my benefactress, it will doubtless all be for the best.'

So he committed himself to the faggot to take him wherever it would. On went the faggot surely and steadily, as if quite conscious where it had to go, and thus, before nightfall, it came to a great city where were many people, who all came out to see the wonder of the faggot of logs moving along by itself, and a man riding on it.

In this city was a king, who lived in a palace with an only daughter. Now this daughter had never been known to laugh. What pains soever the king her father took to divert her were all unavailing. Nothing brought a smile to her lips.

Now, however, when all the people ran to the windows to see a man riding on a faggot, the king's daughter ran to look out too, and when she saw the faggot moving by itself and the uncouth figure of Scioccolone sitting on it, and heard all the people laughing at the sight, then the king's daughter laughed too, laughed for the first time in her life.

But Scioccolone passing under the palace, heard her clear and merry laugh resounding above the laughter of all the people, he looked up and saw her, and when he saw her looking so bright and fair he said within himself: 'Now, if ever the fairy's power of wishing is to be of use to me, I wish that I might have a little son, and that the beautiful princess should be the mother.'

But he did not think of wishing to stop there that he might look at her, so the faggot carried him past the palace and past all the houses into the outskirts of the city, till he got tired and weary, and just then passing a wood merchant's yard, the thought rose to his lips, 'I wish that wood merchant would buy this faggot of me!'

Immediately the wood merchant came out and offered to buy the faggot, and as it was such a wonderful faggot that he thought Scioccolone would never consent to sell it, he offered him such a high price that Scioccolone had enough to live on like a prince for a year.

After a time there was again a great stir in the city. Everyone was abroad in the streets whispering and consulting. To the king's daughter was born a little son, and no one knew who the father was, not even the princess herself. Then the king sent for all the men in the city and brought them to the infant, and said, "Is this your father?" but the babe said "No" to them all.

Last of all, Scioccolone was brought, and when, the king took him up to the babe and said, "Is this your father?" the babe rose joyfully from its cradle and said, "Yes, that is my father!"

When the king heard this and saw what a rough ugly clown Scioccolone was, he was very angry with his daughter and said she must marry him and go away for ever from the palace. It was all in vain that the princess protested she had never seen him but for one moment from the top of the palace. The babe protested quite positively that he was his father. So the king had them married and sent them away from the palace forever, and the babe was right, for though Scioccolone and the princess had never met, Scioccolone had wished that he might have a son, of whom she should be the mother, and by the power of the spell, the child was born.

Scioccolone was only too delighted with the king's angry decree. He felt quite out of place in the palace and was glad enough to be sent away from it. All he wanted was to have such a beautiful wife, and he willingly obeyed the king's command to take her away, a long, long way off.

The princess, however, was quite of a different mind. She could not cease from crying, because she was given to such an uncouth, clownish husband that no tidy peasant wench would have married.

When, therefore, Scioccolone saw his beautiful bride so unhappy and distressed, he grew distressed himself, and in his distress he remembered once more the promise of the fairy, that whatever he wished he might have, and he began wishing away at once. First he wished for a pleasant villa, prettily laid-out, and planted, and walled; then, a little house in the midst of it, prettily furnished, and having plenty of pastimes and diversions; then, for a farm, well-stocked with beasts for all kinds of use; for carriages and servants, for fruits and flowers, and all that can make life pleasant.

Yet, when he found with all these things the princess did not seem much happier than before, he bethought himself of wishing that he might be furnished with a handsome person, polished manners, and an educated mind, altogether such as the princess wished. All his wishes were fulfilled, and the princess now loved him very much, and they lived very happily together.

After they had been living thus some time, it happened one day that the king, going out hunting, observed this pleasant villa on the edge of the wood where heretofore all had been bare, unplanted, and unbuilt.

"How is this!" cried the king, and he drew rein and went into the villa intending to inquire how the change had come about.

Scioccolone came out to meet him, not only so transformed that the king never recognised him, but so distinguished by courtesy and urbanity, that the king himself felt ashamed to question him as to how the villa had grown up so suddenly. However, he accepted his invitation to come and rest in the house, and there they fell to conversing on a variety of subjects, till the king was so struck with the sagacity and prudence of Scioccolone's talk that when he rose to take leave, he said: "Such a man as you I have long sought to succeed me in the government of the kingdom. I am growing old and have no children, and you are worthy in all ways to wear the crown. Come up, therefore, if you will, to the palace, and live with me, and when I die, you shall be king."

Scioccolone, now no longer feeling himself so ill-adapted to live in a palace, willingly consented, and a few days after, with his wife and his little son, he went up to the palace to live with the king.

But the king's delight can scarcely be imagined when he found that the wife of the polished stranger was indeed his very own daughter.

After a few years the old king died, and Scioccolone reigned in his stead. And thus the promises of all the three fairies were fulfilled.

Translated by Rachel Busk.

The Fig-and-Raisin Fool (1875)[188]
Giuseppe Pitrè

Once upon a time there was a foolish son who would eat nothing but figs and raisins. His friends said to him, "Do you want to come with us to collect wood?" and he answered, "Will there be figs and raisins there?"

"If you want them," they replied, "we'll certainly get you some."

"All right, then, I'm coming," was his answer.

So he went with them to collect wood, and with much effort he amassed a huge bunch of branches.

"You dolt!" his friends exclaimed. "How do you expect to carry all of that back? Why don't you go find even more to pile on?" And then they went off to another spot.

Now the young fool, in his search for more wood, came upon a fountain, and there he saw three nymphs sleeping nearby in the shade with their faces exposed to the sun. So the young man took some leaves and covered their faces. When the nymphs woke up, they realized that someone had passed by and had kindly shaded their faces to keep the sun from burning them. And so they said, "May the person who was so kind to us be granted whatever wish his heart desires."

Now at this moment the foolish boy had tied up his entire bundle of wood, and when he looked at its size, he exclaimed, "Now that you're all tied up, who's going to carry you? You should be carrying me!"

All at once the bundle of wood got underneath him and carried him all the way back to Palermo and right to his own front door. On the way, however, they passed through the street where the king's daughter happened to be looking out the window, and she burst out laughing at him.

"I wish I could make that maiden pregnant!" was the lad's response when he saw her.

And that's exactly what happened. As soon as the king became aware of his daughter's condition, he scolded her a great deal, while she insisted on her innocence. When she finally gave birth, the king proclaimed that once they found the man who was responsible, both he and the princess would be placed in a bronze barrel and thrown into the sea.

Then the king devised a scheme for discovering who the man was. He organized a three-day banquet. The first day was to be for the nobility, the second

---

188. "Lu loccu di li pàssuli e ficu," *Fiabe, novelle e racconti popolari siciliani*, 4 vols. (Palermo: Lauriel, 1875).

day for the merchant class, and the third day for the common people. At each banquet he told his daughter's child to walk around and find his father.

At the banquet for the nobility, the child made the rounds without identifying anyone. At the banquet for the merchants, the same thing happened. At the banquet for the common folk, the fool's friends all said, "Look, today all the commoners are invited to dine at the royal palace. Aren't you going to come?"

"Will there be figs and raisins there?" asked the young man.

"Oh, good grief! Always figs and raisins, raisins and figs! Of course they'll have that to eat as well, so why don't you come along with us?"

Once they were inside the palace, the young fool began to feel uncomfortable. He twisted this way and that, he stretched and he yawned, until finally it was time for the banquet, and the king said to the child, "Go and find your father."

The innocent young boy walked this way and that way and ended up directly in front of the fool. "This is my father," he declared.

"Oh, you stupid creature!" said the king to his daughter. "Were your eyes screwed in backwards? You've managed to fall in love with a total fool! Oh, what a disaster! But just wait—I have a remedy for this."

And he ordered a bronze barrel to be built. Once it was finished, he had the fool and his daughter packed inside it and tossed into the sea. Now the fool was able to recount his whole story to the princess, beginning with his going to collect wood and his encounter with the nymphs.

"Do you recall," he asked, "when you saw me go by riding on the bundle of wood and you laughed at me? Well, that's when I said, 'I wish I could make that maiden pregnant.'"

"Oh," replied the princess, "so those were the words I saw you muttering under your breath! Well, if you have such powers, why don't you bring this barrel back to dry land?"

And all at once they were back on land.

"Now make the barrel open and release us."

"If I do, will you give me figs and raisins?"

"Yes, my husband. Of course I will."

And in an instant they were outside the barrel.

Now that they were free, they purchased a large palace and surrounded it with a magnificent garden filled with every kind of delectable plant. Then they hired a guard to stand at the entrance and direct every passerby to read what was written above the portal:

You may look, but you must not touch! Take a pear or a bunch of grapes, and you lose your life!

Well, various people visited the garden, and among them was the father of the fool's wife, the king himself. The fool recognized him and said, "Could the king's pocket be hiding a bunch of grapes?" And in fact this was true.

"Seize that thief!" he shouted to his guard. "Hold him right there!"

The king was at a loss for what to do, and when they searched his pockets, they found the grapes. The fool now declared that the king must be put to death. The king begged for mercy, asking the fool to take pity on him and spare his life. The fool consented, revealing his true identity to the king.

> And so they all lived on, happy and content,
> While we cannot even pay our rent.

Collected by Giuseppe-Vincenzo Marotta in Cerda.

The Baker's Idle Son (1882)[189]
Consiglieri Pedroso

There was a woman baker who had a very indolent son. When the other boys went to gather firewood and he was told to go also, he would never go. The mother was very unhappy to have such a lazy son and really did not know what she should do with him. As she one day insisted upon his joining the other boys, he went along with them, but the moment they reached the wood, whilst the other boys were collecting the sticks and small branches of trees for firewood, he went to lie down by the side of a brook and began to eat what he had brought with him. While he was doing so, a fish came close to him and began to eat up all the crumbs he let fall, until at last he caught it.

The fish entreated him not to kill him and that he would do for him all he could wish for. The lazy boy, who did not trust the fish, said to it, "In the name of my God, and of my fish, I wish that this very moment a faggot of wood, larger than any of the ones held by the other boys, shall appear before me, and that the bundle shall proceed without my being seen under it."

All at once a faggot made its appearance ready tied, and he then allowed the fish to go back into the sea. Then he turned to go home, and as he passed the palace, the king, who was at the window with the princess, was very much astonished to see the faggot move along by itself, and the princess was so very much amused at it that she laughed. The lazy boy then said: "In the name of God, and of my fish, let the princess have a son without its being known whose son he is."

The princess then began to feel that she was with child, and the king became very displeased with her and ordered her to be imprisoned in a tower with her maids of honor. After a time she gave birth to a male child. The lazy boy returned to the wood, and the fish again appeared and told him that the princess had given birth to a son. The lazy boy, being instructed by the fish, ordered a palace to be erected which should be more splendid than the one belonging to the king. There was a garden in this palace replete with flowers of every color and shade, and, wonderful to relate, there was an orchard full of fruit trees in which

---

189. *Portuguese Folk-Tales*, trans. Henriqueta Monteiro (London: Folklore Society, 1882).

grew an orange tree with twelve golden oranges. All this was brought about by the fish and the fairies.

The lazy boy went to this palace transformed into a prince, and no one knew him to be anything else. The king sent a message asking to see the palace, and he replied that he would be most happy to show him over it and sent his majesty an invitation to breakfast and to all his court. The king and his chamberlains were much surprised on their arrival to see so much luxury and splendor. After they had inspected the whole palace, they went into the garden. They were charmed with the variety of flowers in it, but were much more astonished to see an orange tree bearing golden oranges. The lazy boy informed the king and his courtiers that they could take of everything in the garden which they might desire, except gathering any of the oranges. They all returned to the palace and sat down to the breakfast. When the breakfast was over, and the king was taking his departure to return to his own palace, the lazy boy told the king that he was much surprised to find that after he had treated them so luxuriously they should have gathered one of the golden oranges. The courtiers all commenced to deny that any of them had taken the orange and took off their coats that he might see for himself that they had not been guilty of the accusation. The king, who felt very much abashed, was now the only one who had not been examined. He took off his coat and nothing was found on examination in its pockets, but the lazy boy asked him to look carefully again when he had put his coat on, because since his courtiers had not taken the orange, it must be himself who had. The king then put his hands again into his pocket and drew out the orange, very much confused and ashamed, for he could not imagine how it could have come there as he had not touched the oranges. The lazy boy then said to him that the very same thing had happened to the princess, who had borne a son without knowing by whom. The spell under which the fish was bound was then broken, and the fish was transformed into a prince and married the princess. The lazy boy returned home a rich man.

Translated by Henriqueta Monteiro.

The Fairy Tale about Falchetto (1885)[190]
Giuseppe Pitrè

One day Falchetto saw some nude ladies bathing in a river and only saw their backs. (They were fairies.) Falchetto wanted to cover them, but he didn't have the courage to spring into the water. Finally, he saw a fig tree, and once he climbed it and was above the fairies, he picked many figs and said: "Ladies, is the sun burning your backs?"

"Yes."

"Well then, take these fig leaves."

The fairies were grateful for Falchetto's kind thought.

---

190.   "La Favola del Falchetto," *Novelle Popolari Toscane* (Florence: G. Babèra, 1885).

"What should we give to this young man who's been so considerate?"

After they had thought about this, they decided to grant him whatever he wished and left him there. Then Falchetto went into the forest where he chopped a good deal of wood until he had a large bundle. But he didn't have any means to transport it home. So Falchetto got on top of the bundle and said to the wood: "Oh, if you would only carry me off that would be a beautiful thing!"

Well, the wood began to walk, and he began laughing like the fool he was and said: "Oh, how good this is! How good!"

As he passed through a city, curious people came out to see him and burst into laughter. When he passed beneath the window of the king's daughter, she laughed just like the others. But when Falchetto saw this maiden laugh, he said to her:

"Oh, you who are laughing, also you, I wish you'd have a baby as handsome as me."

When Falchetto finally returned home, his mother laughed like a mad-woman.

After some time had passed, the king's daughter did not feel very well. The doctor realized that she was pregnant but didn't know how to tell her. Finally, he spilled the beans to her father, who became very upset. Indeed, after nine months, the princess gave birth to a baby boy. She gave birth, and in a short time she began trying to discover who the father might have been. Nothing! So, they charmed the boy and had him pass by all the noblemen of the realm. However, the boy didn't recognize any of them as his father. Then they tried something else, but it was in vain. So the king summoned all the rich and poor men to the court and presented them to the boy. Falchetto was the last one to remain, and as was to be expected, he was dirty and dressed in rags.

"How is it possible," the king asked, "that he could have been my daughter's lover?!"

But it was indeed Falchetto as the boy indicated.

Just imagine the scandal at the court! Everyone said that Falchetto deserved to be put to death, but there was a large vat nearby totally covered with tar, and Falchetto, the princess, and the boy were put inside and then thrown into the river. The poor princess cried her eyes out while Falchetto laughed and jumped about like a madman, content to have three flasks of wine and bread that had been put into the vat. After the princess wept and wept, she resigned herself to her situation and started a conversation with Falchetto and attempted at the very least to discover why she had been condemned to this terrible death. In the process Falchetto told her about his adventure with the fairies.

"You know what you should do?" the princess said to him. "You should order the vat to stop."

And upon Falchetto's command, the vat stopped.

"Now order the vat to transport us to a beautiful meadow."

And the vat transported them to a beautiful meadow. Afterward the princess told Falchetto to have a beautiful palace usher from beneath the ground so that they could live in it, and she asked him to change himself into a handsome nobleman. And suddenly the most beautiful palace in the world appeared before them, and Falchetto became not only a handsome young man, but also the most handsome young man anyone had ever seen. And he and the princess began to love each other very much like a married couple, and soon they had three sons.

In the meantime the princess's mother died from grief, and the poor king lived a melancholy life tormented by remorse. One day he thought he'd go hunting to distract himself. The king's daughter knew about everything that happened in her home because Falchetto was now a sorcerer. So, she ordered her husband to bring about a huge rainstorm.

The king and his retinue were forced to take shelter in Falchetto's palace. The princess received the king with his retinue, and as they were chatting there, she asked her father if he had ever had a daughter. And the old man told her that he had once had a daughter whom he had condemned to death. As soon as he said this, the princess revealed herself to her father. The boys ran and embraced the king's knees and called him grandpa. And his daughter told him everything he needed to know. From then on, Falchetto, his wife, his father-in-law, and his sons lived a life of complete happiness.

The Sluggard (1896)[191]

Alexander Chodźko

On the banks of a certain river, where there was always good fishing, lived an old man and his three sons. The two eldest were sharp-witted, active young men, already married; the youngest was stupid and idle, and a bachelor. When the father was dying, he called his children to him and told them how he had left his property. The house was for his two married sons with a sum of three hundred florins each. After his death he was buried with great pomp, and after the funeral there was a splendid feast. All these honors were supposed to be for the benefit of the man's soul.

When the elder brothers took possession of their inheritance, they said to the youngest: "Listen, brother, let us take charge of your share of the money, for we intend going out into the world as merchants, and when we have made a great deal of money, we will buy you a hat, a sash, and a pair of red boots. You will be better at home, and mind you, do as your sisters-in-law tell you."

For a long time this silly fellow had been wanting a cap, a sash, and a pair of red boots, so he was easily persuaded to give up all his money. The brothers set out on their travels and crossed the sea in search of fortune. The "fool"

191. *Slav Peasants and Herdsmen*, trans. Emily Harding (London: George Allen, 1896).

of the family remained at home, and since he was an out-and-out sluggard, he would lie whole days at a time on the warm stove without doing a stroke of work, and only obeying his sisters-in-law with the greatest reluctance. He liked fried onions, potato soup, and cider, better than anything else in the world.

One day his sisters-in-law asked him to fetch them some water. It was winter and a hard frost; moreover, the sluggard did not feel at all inclined to go out. So he said, "Go yourselves, I prefer to stay here by the fire."

"Stupid boy, go at once. We will have some onions, potato soup, and cider ready for you when you come back. If you refuse to do what we ask you, we shall tell our husbands, and then there will be neither cap, sash, nor red boots for you."

At these words the sluggard thought he had better go. So he rolled off the stove, took a hatchet and a couple of pails, and went down to the river. On the surface of the water, where the ice had been broken, was a large pike. The sluggard seized him by the fins and pulled him out.

"If you will let me go," said the pike, "I promise to give you everything you wish for."

"Well then, I should like all my desires to be fulfilled the moment I utter them."

"You shall have everything you want the moment you pronounce these words:

'At my behest, and by the orders of the pike,
May such and such things happen, as I like.'"

"Just wait one moment while I try the effect," said the sluggard, and began at once to say:

"At my behest, and by the orders of the pike,
Bring onions, cider, soup, just as I like."

That very moment his favorite dishes were before him. Having eaten a large quantity, he said, "Very good, very good indeed, but will it always be the same?"

"Always," replied the pike.

The sluggard put the pike back into the river, and turning towards his buckets, said:

"At my behest, and by the orders of the pike,
Walk home yourselves, my pails—that I should like."

The pails and the strong rod to which they were fastened, immediately set off and walked solemnly along, the sluggard following them with his hands in his pockets. When they reached the house, he put them in their places and again stretched himself out to enjoy the warmth of the stove. Presently the sisters-in-law said, "Come and chop some wood for us."

"Bother! Do it yourselves."

"It is not fit work for women. Besides, if you don't do it, the stove will be cold, and then you will be the chief sufferer. Moreover, pay attention to what we say, for if you do not obey us, there will be no red boots, nor any other pretty things."

The sluggard then just sat up and said:

> "At my behest, and by the orders of the pike,
> Let what my sisters want be done—that's what I like."

Instantly the hatchet came out from behind a stool and chopped up a large heap of wood, put a part of it on the stove, and retired to its corner. All this time the sluggard was eating and drinking at his ease.

Another day some wood had to be brought from the forest. Our sluggard now thought he would like to show off before the villagers, so he pulled a sledge out of the shed, loaded it with onions and soup, after which he pronounced the magic words. The sledge started off, and passing through the village at a rattling pace, ran over several people, and frightened the women and children.

When the forest was reached, our friend looked on while the blocks of wood and faggots cut, tied, and laid themselves on the sledge, after which they set off home again. But when they got to the middle of the village the men, who had been hurt and frightened in the morning, seized hold of the sluggard and pulled him off the sledge, dragging him along by the hair to give him a sound thrashing.

At first he thought it was only a joke, but when the blows hurt his shoulders, he said:

> "At my behest, and by the orders of the pike,
> Come, faggots, haste, and my assailants strike."

In a moment all the blocks of wood and faggots jumped off the sledge and began to hit right and left, and they hit so well that the men were glad to get out of the way as best they could. The sluggard laughed at them till his sides ached. Then he remounted his sledge and was soon lying on the stove again.

From that day he became famous, and his doings were talked about all through the country. At last even the king heard of him, and, his curiosity being aroused, he sent some of his soldiers to fetch him.

"Now then, booby," said the soldier, "come down off that stove and follow me to the king's palace."

"Why should I? There is as much cider, onions, and soup as I want at home."

The man, indignant at his want of respect, struck him. Upon which the sluggard said:

> "At my behest, and by the orders of the pike,
> May this man get a taste of what a broom is like."

A large broom, and not particularly clean, immediately hopped up, and first dipping itself in a pail of water, beat the soldier so mercilessly that he was obliged to escape through the window, whence he returned to the king. His majesty, amazed at the sluggard's refusal, sent another messenger. This man was "cuter" than his comrade, and first made inquiries as to the sluggard's tastes. Then he went up to him and said, "Good-day, my friend, will you come with me to see the king? He wishes to present you with a cap, a waistband, and a pair of red boots."

"With the greatest pleasure. You go on, and I will soon overtake you."

Then he ate as much as he could of his favorite dishes and went to sleep on the stove. He slept so long that at last his sisters-in-law woke him up and told him he would be late if he did not at once go to see the king. The lazy fellow said nothing but these words:

"At my behest, and by the orders of the pike,
This stove to carry me before the king I'd like."

At the very same instant the stove moved from its place and carried him right up to the palace door. The king was filled with amazement, and running out, followed by the whole court, asked the sluggard what he would like to have.

"I have merely come to fetch the hat, waistband, and red boots you promised me."

Just then the charming princess Gapiomila came to find out what was going on. Directly the sluggard saw her, he thought her so enchanting that he whispered to himself:

"At my behest, and by the orders of the pike,
That this princess so fair may love me, I should like."

Then he ordered his stove to take him back home, and when there he continued to eat onions and soup and to drink cider. Meanwhile the princess had fallen in love with him and begged her father to send for him again. As the sluggard would not consent, the king had him bound when asleep and thus brought to the palace. Then he summoned a celebrated magician, who at his orders shut the princess and sluggard up in a crystal cask, to which was fastened a balloon well filled with gas, and sent it up in the air among the clouds.

The princess wept bitterly, but the fool sat still and said he felt very comfortable. At last she persuaded him to exert his powers, so he said:

"At my behest, and by the orders of the pike,
This cask of crystal earth at once must strike
Upon the friendly island I should like."

The crystal cask immediately descended and opened upon a hospitable island where travelers could have all they wanted by simply wishing for it. The princess and her companion walked about, eating when hungry, and drinking when athirst. The sluggard was very happy and contented, but the lady begged him to wish for a palace. Instantly the palace made its appearance. It was built of white marble, with crystal windows, roof of yellow amber, and golden furniture. She was delighted with it. Next day she wanted a good road made, along which she could go to see her father. Immediately there stretched before them a fairy-like bridge made of crystal, having golden balustrades set with diamonds, and leading right up to the king's palace. The sluggard was just about to accompany the princess when he began to think of his own appearance, and to feel ashamed that such an awkward, stupid fellow as he should walk by the side of such a lovely and graceful creature. So he said:

"At my behest, and by the orders of the pike,
To be both handsome, wise, and clever I should like."

Suddenly he became as handsome, wise, and clever as it was possible to be. Then he got into a gorgeous carriage with Gapiomila, and they drove across the bridge that led to the king's palace. There they were received with every mark of joy and affection. The king gave them his blessing, and they were married the same evening. An immense number of guests were invited to the wedding feast. I, too, was there, and drank freely of wine and hydromel. And this is the story I have done my best to tell you as faithfully as possible.

Translated by Emily Harding.

16. EVIL STEPMOTHERS AND MAGIC MIRRORS

ATU 709—SNOW WHITE

This tale type often combines motifs from "Hansel and Gretel," "The Maiden without Hands," and "The Golden Children," all which touch on themes related to child abuse or the persecuted heroine. In "Snow White" the focus is more on the conflict between mother and daughter and mother-in-law and daughter with regard to envy and beauty. The plot develops in eight phases: (1) A queen wishes for a daughter with skin as white as snow, lips as red as blood, and hair as black as ebony. (2) After she gives birth, she becomes jealous of her daughter because a magic mirror reveals that her daughter is more beautiful than she is, or she dies and is replaced by a stepmother, who is also envious. Whether mother or stepmother, the woman wants her daughter killed. (3) The mother/stepmother orders a huntsman, servant, maid to take the daughter into a forest and abandon or kill her. But the "hired" killer takes pity on the girl because she is kind and beautiful. The persecuted heroine is abandoned in a forest while the servant returns with animal parts to deceive the queen. (4) The maiden finds her way to a cottage in the woods that belongs to seven dwarfs, robbers, or a wise old man/woman or angel, who try to protect her. (5) The wicked mother/stepmother discovers that she has survived, and so she disguises herself and endeavors to kill her daughter/stepdaughter three times. (6) The persecuted heroine succumbs to the devious designs of her mother/stepmother and appears to have died after taking a bite of an apple. (7) The maiden is revived though a lucky accident or by a prince, or the prince's mother. (8) The maiden marries the prince, and her persecutor is severely punished.

Throughout the different variants, the wicked queen is motivated not only by her envy but also by the magic mirror, which arbitrarily decides who is more beautiful. In other words, the conflict is generally played out as a reflection of women seeking male approval within the frame of a patriarchal society. In the Grimms' depiction of Snow White, she embodies the ideal qualities of the domestic housewife in the nineteenth century, for she is innocent, hardworking, obedient, honest, clean, and cheerful. In effect, she proves her worth through her passivity and submission.

Though there are not too many literary versions that document a strong oral tradition of "Snow White," there are ample traces of the tale type that hark back to the Greco-Roman period, as Graham Anderson has clearly documented in *The Fairytale in the Ancient World*, and there are numerous oral variants that were collected in Western Asia, Northern Africa, and Europe during the nineteenth century that reveal the popularity of this tale type. One of the earliest literary versions was Giambattista Basile's "The Young Slave" in *Cunto de li Cunti* (1634). However, the Grimms were more influenced by Johann Karl August Musäus'

"Richilde" in *Volksmärchen der Deutschen* (1782) and Albert Ludwig Grimm's fairy-tale play *Snow White*, published in *Kindermährchen* (1809).

Jacob Grimm became aware of the tale as early as 1806 through a version given to him by his brother Ferdinand. He copied it and sent it to his mentor Carl von Savigny. Later, in 1812, this tale was revised by Wilhelm, who had gathered some other versions. Throughout the following six editions of *Kinder- und Hausmärchen*, Wilhelm kept revising "Snow White," basing his revisions on other variants that he received. In the notes to the second edition of 1822, Wilhelm records a version that is worth quoting in full:

> A count and a countess drove by three cottages covered by white snow, and the count said: "I wish for a little girl as white as this snow." Soon thereafter they went by three graves with red blood, and the count spoke again: "I wish for a little girl with cheeks as red as this blood." Finally three black ravens flew above them, and he wished for a girl "with hair as black as these ravens." As they continued traveling for some time, they came upon a girl as white as snow, with cheeks as red as blood, and with hair as black as the ravens, and that was Snow White. The count had her take a seat in the coach right away and was very fond of her, while the countess did not take to her kindly at all. She only thought of how she might get rid of the girl. Finally, she let her glove fall out of the coach and ordered Snow White to go and look for it. As the girl did this, the coachman was ordered to drive on quickly. Now Snow White was alone and came to the dwarfs, etc.

This fragment is significant not only because it indicates the variety of beginnings for this tale type in the nineteenth century but also because it is the source of Angela Carter's superb rendition, "The Snow Child," which she published in her fascinating collection *The Bloody Chamber and Other Stories* (1979).

******

Snow White, Snow White, or The Unfortunate Child (1808)[192]
Jacob Grimm

Once upon a time it was winter, and snow fell from heaven. A queen was sitting at a window made of ebony and sewing. She very much wanted to have a child. While she thought about this, she stuck her finger accidentally with the needle, and some drops of blood fell upon the snow. So she made a wish and said, "Oh, if only I could have a child as white as this snow, as red-caked as this red blood, and as black-eyed as this ebony window frame!"

---

192.   Included in an 1806 letter from Jacob Grimm to Carl von Savigny, his mentor at the University of Marburg. This handwritten version was given to Jacob Grimm by his brother Ferdinand, and Jacob sent it to Savigny with some small corrections. See Wilhelm Schoof, ed., *Briefe der Brüder Grimm an Savigny* (Berlin, 1953).

Soon thereafter she gave birth to a wonderful and beautiful little daughter as white as snow, as red as blood, and as black as ebony, and the daughter was called Snow White. The queen was the most beautiful woman in the entire land, but Snow White was a hundred thousand times more beautiful, and when the queen asked her mirror,

> "Mirror, mirror on the wall,
> who is the most beautiful woman in England?"

The little mirror answered,

> "The queen is the most beautiful,
> but Snow White is a hundred thousand times more beautiful."

The queen could no longer stand this because she wanted to be the most beautiful in the realm. So, when the king went off to war one time, she had the horses harnessed to her carriage and ordered her driver to take her and Snow White deep into a dark forest, which was filled with many beautiful red roses. When the queen arrived with her daughter at a spot where the roses were growing, she said to her, "Oh, Snow White, climb out and pick me one of the beautiful roses."

As soon as she obeyed her mother's command and climbed out of the carriage, she heard the wheels of the carriage roll off in great speed, for the queen had ordered the driver to do so and hoped that the wild animals would eat her.

Since Snow White was now all alone in the large forest, she began to weep and kept weeping as she walked and walked until she became very tired and reached a small cottage. There were seven dwarfs who lived in this cottage, but they were not at home right then, for they had gone to work in a mine. As Snow White entered the cottage, she saw a table, and on the table were seven plates with seven spoons, forks, knives, and glasses, and in another room there were seven little beds. Snow White ate some vegetables and bread from each plate and drank a drop from each one of the glasses. Finally, she wanted to lay down to sleep because she was so tired. But when she tried all the little beds, she did not find any one of them right except for the last one where she fell asleep.

When the seven dwarfs now returned home from their day's work, they said to each other:

"Who ate something from my plate?
Who took some of my bread?
Who ate with my fork?
Who cut something with my fork?
Who drank something from my little cup?"

and then the first dwarf said,

> "Who was on my bed?"

And the second said,

"Hey, somebody also slept in my bed."

And the third, fourth, fifth and sixth dwarfs repeated this until they came to the seventh bed and found Snow White lying there. However, they took such a great liking to her that they let her lie there out of pity, and the seventh dwarf had to sleep with the sixth as best he could.

After a good night's sleep Snow White awoke the next morning, and the dwarfs asked how she had come to the cottage. Thereupon, she told them everything and how the queen her mother had left her alone in the forest and had driven away. The dwarfs took pity on her and asked her to stay with them and to cook for them when they went to work in the mine. However, she would have to beware of the queen and not let anyone into the house.

When the queen learned that Snow White was living with the seven dwarfs and had not perished in the forest, she put on some clothes from an old peddler and went to the cottage and asked to enter with her wares. Snow White didn't recognize her and spoke to her from the window.

"I'm not allowed to let anyone inside."

"Oh, my dear child," said the peddler, "Look at the pretty ribbons and laces that I have. I'll let you have them cheaply!"

Snow White thought, 'I could use some laces, and there's no harm if I let the woman enter. I can make a good bargain.' So she opened the door and bought some laces. And just as she bought them, the peddler began to speak, "Oh, look at how sloppily you are laced. That doesn't make you look so good. Come, I'll lace you up better."

Thereupon, the old woman, who was actually the queen, took the laces of the corset and tied them so tight that Snow White fell to the ground as if she were dead, and the woman left.

When the dwarfs came home and saw Snow White lying on the ground, they all knew who had been there right away and untied the laces quickly so that Snow White came to herself again. Then they warned her to take better precaution in the future.

After the queen learned that her daughter was alive again, she couldn't rest and returned to the cottage in disguise and wanted to sell Snow White a splendid comb. Since Snow White liked the comb so much, she let the woman trick her and opened the door. When the old woman entered and began to comb the girl's golden hair, she stuck the comb into it until Snow White sunk dead to the ground.

When the seven dwarfs came home, they found the door open and Snow White lying on the ground. Of course, they knew right away who had caused this disaster. So they pulled the comb out of Snow White's hair right away, and the girl returned to life. But they told her that if she let herself be fooled one more time, they wouldn't be able to help her.

Now the queen was very angry when she learned that Snow White was alive again and she disguised herself a third time as a peasant woman. Then she took an apple with her that was half poisoned on the red side. This time Snow White took care and wouldn't open the door for the old woman. But the queen had been able to disguise herself so well that she couldn't be recognized and handed Snow White the apple through the window. Snow White bit the apple where it was red and sank to the ground dead.

When the seven dwarfs returned home, they could no longer help Snow White and were very sad and suffered a great deal. They placed Snow White in a glass coffin in which she was able to keep her form. Then they wrote her name and place of birth on it and guarded the coffin carefully day and night.

One day Snow White's father returned to his realm and had to go into the same forest in which the seven dwarfs lived. When he caught sight of the coffin and its inscription, he became greatly saddened by the death of his beloved daughter. However, he had some very experienced doctors in his entourage. They asked permission to take the corpse from the dwarfs. When they took the body, they tied a rope to the four corners of the room, and Snow White came to life again. Thereupon, they all continued on their way to the castle. Soon Snow White was married to a handsome prince, and at the wedding a pair of shoes were made glowing hot by a fire. The queen had to put them on and dance in them until she died.

Snow White (1812)[193]
Jacob and Wilhelm Grimm

Once upon a time, in the middle of winter, when snowflakes were falling like feathers from the sky, a beautiful queen was sitting and sewing at a window with a black ebony frame. And as she was sewing and looking out the window at the snow, she pricked her finger with the needle, and three drops of blood fell on the snow. The red looked so beautiful on the white snow that she thought to herself, 'If only I had a child as white as snow, as red as blood, and as black as the wood of the window frame!' Soon thereafter she gave birth to a little daughter who was as white as snow, as red as blood, and her hair as black as ebony. That's why the child was called Snow White.

The queen was the most beautiful woman in the entire land and very proud about her beauty. She also had a mirror, and every morning she stepped in front of it and asked:

"Mirror, mirror, on the wall,
who in this land is fairest of all?"

The mirror would answer:

"You, my queen, are the fairest of all."

193. "Sneewittchen," *Kinder- und Haus-Märchen. Gesammelt durch die Brüder Grimm*, 2 vols. (Berlin: Realschulbuchhandlung, 1812/1815).

And then she knew for certain that there was nobody more beautiful in the entire world. However, Snow White grew up, and when she was seven years old, she was so beautiful that her beauty surpassed even that of the queen, and when the queen asked her mirror:

"Mirror, mirror, on the wall,
who in this land is fairest of all?"

The mirror answered:

"You, my queen, may have a beauty quite rare,
but Snow White is a thousand times more fair."

When the queen heard the mirror speak this way, she became pale with envy, and from that hour onward, she hated Snow White, and when she looked at her and thought that Snow White was to blame that she the queen was no longer the most beautiful woman in the world, her heart turned against Snow White. Her jealousy kept upsetting her, and so she summoned the huntsman and said: "Take the child out into the forest to a spot far from here. Then stab her to death and bring me back her lungs and liver as proof of your deed. After that I'll cook them with salt and eat them."

The huntsman took Snow White and led her out into the forest, but when he drew his hunting knife and was about to stab her, she began to weep and pleaded so much to let her live and promised never to return but to run away deeper into the forest, the huntsman was moved to pity, also because she was so beautiful. Anyway, he thought the wild beasts in the forest would soon devour her. 'I'm glad that I won't have to kill her.' Just then a young boar came dashing by, and the huntsman stabbed it to death. He took out the lungs and liver and brought them to the queen as proof that the child was dead. Then she boiled them in salt, ate them, and thought that she had eaten Snow White's lungs and liver.

Meanwhile, Snow White was so all alone in the huge forest that she became afraid and began to run and run over sharp stones and through thorn bushes. She ran the entire day. Finally, as the sun was about to set, she came upon a little cottage that belonged to seven dwarfs. However, they were not at home but had gone to the mines. When Snow White entered, she found everything tiny, but dainty and neat. There was a little table with a white tablecloth, and on it were seven little plates with seven tiny spoons, seven tiny knives and tiny forks and seven tiny cups. In a row against the wall stood seven little beds recently covered with sheets. Since she was so hungry and thirsty, Snow White ate some vegetables and bread from each of the little plates and had a drop of wine to drink out of each of the tiny cups. And since she was so tired, she wanted to lay down and sleep. So she began trying out the beds, but none of them suited her until she found that the seventh one was just right. So she laid down in it and fell asleep.

When it turned night, the seven dwarfs returned home from their work and lit their seven little candles. Then they saw that someone had been in their house.

The first dwarf said: "Who's been sitting in my chair?"

"Who's eaten off my plate?" said the second.

"Who's eaten some of my bread?" said the third.

"Who's eaten some of my vegetables?" said the fourth.

"Who's been using my little fork?" said the fifth.

"Who's been cutting with my little knife?" said the sixth.

"Who's had something to drink from my little cup?" said the seventh.

Then the first dwarf looked around and said, "Who's been sleeping in my bed?"

Then the second cried out, "Someone's been sleeping in my bed!"

And he was followed by all of them until the seventh dwarf. When he looked at his bed, he saw Snow White lying there asleep. The others came running over to him, and they were so astounded that they screamed and fetched their seven little candles to observe Snow White.

"Oh, my Lord! Oh, my Lord!" they exclaimed. "How beautiful she is!"

They took great delight in her but didn't wake her up. Instead, they let her sleep in the bed, while the seventh dwarf spent an hour in each one of his companions' beds until the night had passed. When Snow White awoke, they asked her who she was and how she had managed to come to their cottage. Then she told them how her mother had wanted to have her killed, how the huntsman had spared her life, and how she had run all day until she had eventually arrived at their cottage.

Then the dwarfs took pity on her and said, "If you'll keep house for us, cook, sew, make the beds, wash, and knit, and if you'll keep everything neat and orderly, you can stay with us, and we'll provide you with everything you need. When we come home in the evening, dinner must be ready. During the day we're in the mines and dig for gold, you'll be alone and have to watch out for the queen and not let anyone enter the cottage."

However, the queen believed that she was once again the most beautiful woman in the land and stepped before her mirror and asked:

"Mirror, mirror, on the wall,
who in this land is fairest of all?"

The mirror answered:

"You, my queen, may have a beauty quite rare,
but beyond the seven mountains, this I must tell,
Snow White is living and doing quite well.
And yes, she's still a thousand times more fair."

When the queen heard this, she was horrified, for she saw that she had been deceived and that the huntsman had not killed Snow White. Since nobody but the seven dwarfs lived in the seven mountains region, the queen knew immediately that Snow White was dwelling with them and began once again plotting ways to kill her. As long as the mirror didn't say that she was the most beautiful woman in the land, she would remain disturbed. Since she couldn't be absolutely certain and didn't trust anyone, she disguised herself as an old peddler woman, painted her face so that nobody could recognize her, and went to the cottage of the seven dwarfs, where she knocked at the door and cried out, "Open up! Open up! I'm an old peddler woman. I've got pretty wares for sale!"

Snow White looked out of the window: "What do you have for sale?"

"Staylaces, dear child!" the old woman replied and took out a lace woven from yellow, red, and blue silk. "Do you want it?"

"Well, yes," said Snow White and thought, 'I can certainly let this good old woman inside. She's honest enough.'

So Snow White unbolted the door and bought the lace.

"My goodness, you're so sloppily laced up!" said the old woman. "Come, I'll lace you up properly for once."

Snow White stood in front of the old woman who took the lace and tied it around Snow White so tightly that she lost her breath and fell down as if dead. Then the queen was satisfied and left.

Not long after nightfall the dwarfs came home, and when they saw their dear Snow White lying on the ground, they were horrified, for she seemed to be dead. They lifted her up, and when they saw that she was laced too tightly, they cut the staylace in two. At once she began to breathe a little, and after a while she had fully revived.

"That was nobody else but the queen," they said. "She wanted to take your life. Take care, and don't let anyone else enter the cottage."

Now the queen asked her mirror:

> "Mirror, mirror, on the wall,
> who in this land is fairest of all?"

The mirror answered:

> "You, my queen, may have a beauty quite rare,
> But Snow White's alive, this I must tell,
> She's with the dwarfs and doing quite well.
> And yes, she's still a thousand times more fair."

The queen was so horrified that all her blood rushed to her heart when she realized that Snow White was alive once again. So she began thinking day and night how she could catch Snow White. Finally, she made a poisoned comb, disguised herself in a completely different shape, and went off to the dwarfs' cottage once again. When she knocked on the door, however, Snow White called out: "I'm not allowed to let anyone enter!"

The queen then took out the comb, and when Snow White saw it shine and that the woman was someone entirely different, she opened the door and bought the comb.

"Come," said the peddler woman, "I'll also comb your hair."

But no sooner did the old woman stick the comb in Snow White's hair than the maiden fell down and was dead.

"Now you'll remain lying there," the queen said, and her heart had become lighter as she returned home.

However, the dwarfs came just in the nick of time. When they saw what had happened, they pulled the poison comb out of Snow White's hair, and she opened her eyes and was alive again. She promised the dwarfs that she would certainly not let anyone inside again.

Now the queen stepped in front of her mirror once more and asked:

"Mirror, mirror, on the wall,
who in this land is fairest of all?"

The mirror answered:

"You, my queen, may have a beauty quite rare,
But Snow White's alive, this I must tell,
She's with the dwarfs and doing quite well.
And yes, she's still a thousand times more fair."

When the queen heard this once again, she trembled and shook with rage. "Snow White shall die!" she exclaimed. "Even if it costs me my own life!"

Then she went into a secret chamber where no one was allowed to enter. Once inside she made a deadly poisonous apple. On the outside it looked beautiful with red cheeks. Anyone who saw it would be enticed to take a bite. Thereafter, she disguised herself as a peasant woman, went to the dwarfs' cottage, and knocked on the door. Snow White looked and said, "I'm not allowed to let anyone inside. The seven dwarfs have strictly forbidden me."

"Well, if you don't want to let me in, I can't force you," answered the peasant woman. "I'll surely get rid of my apples in time. But let me give you one to test."

"No," said Snow White. "I'm not allowed to take anything. The dwarfs won't let me."

"You're probably afraid," said the old woman. "Look, I'll cut the apple in two. You eat the beautiful red half."

However, the apple had been made with such cunning that only the red part was poisoned. When Snow White saw the peasant woman eating her half, and when her desire to taste the apple grew stronger, she finally let the peasant woman give her the other half through the window. As soon as she took a bite of the apple, she fell to the ground and was dead.

The queen rejoiced, went home, and asked the mirror:

"Mirror, mirror, on the wall,
who in this land is the fairest of all?"

And the mirror answered:

"You, my queen, are now the fairest of all."

"Now I can rest in peace," she said. "Once again I'm the most beautiful in the land, and Snow White will remain dead this time."

When the dwarfs came home from the mines that evening, they found Snow White lying on the ground, and she was dead. They unlaced her and tried to find something poisonous in her hair, but nothing helped. They couldn't revive her. So they laid her on a bier, and all seven of them sat down beside it and wept and wept for three whole days. Then they intended to bury her, but she looked so alive not like a dead person, and she still had such pretty red cheeks. So, instead they made a glass coffin and placed her inside so that she could easily be seen. Then they wrote her name on the coffin in gold letters and added the family name of her origins. One of the dwarfs remained at home every day to keep watch over her.

So Snow White laid in the coffin for a long, long time but did not rot. She was still so white as snow and so red as blood, and if her eyes could have opened, they would have been so black as ebony, for she laid there as if she were sleeping.

Now it happened that a prince came to the dwarfs' cottage one day and wanted to spend the night there. When he entered the room and saw Snow White lying in the coffin and the seven little candles casting their light right on her, he couldn't get enough of her beauty. Then he read the golden inscription and saw that she was a princess. So he asked the dwarfs to sell him the coffin with the dead Snow White inside. But they wouldn't accept all the gold in the world for it. Consequently, he pleaded with them to give Snow White to him as a gift because he couldn't live without gazing upon her, and he would honor her and hold her in high regard as his most beloved in the world. Well, the dwarfs took pity on him and gave him the coffin, and the prince had it carried to his castle. It was then placed in his room where he himself sat the entire day and couldn't take his eyes off her. And when he had to leave the room and couldn't see Snow White, he became sad. Indeed, he couldn't eat a thing unless he was standing near the coffin. However, the servants, who constantly had to carry the coffin all around the castle, became angry about this, and at one time a servant opened the coffin, lifted Snow White into the air, and said: "Why must we be tormented so much all because of a dead maiden?" On saying this he shoved Snow White's back with his hand, and out popped the nasty piece of apple that had been stuck in Snow White's throat, and she was alive once again. Then she went to the prince, and when he saw his dear Snow White alive, he rejoiced so much that he didn't know what to do. Soon after they sat down at the dinner table and ate with delight.

The wedding was planned for the next day, and Snow White's godless mother was also invited to attend. Before she went, she stepped before the mirror and said:

"Mirror, mirror, on the wall,
who in this land is the fairest of all?"

And the mirror replied:

"You, my queen, may have a beauty quite rare,
but Snow White is a thousand times more fair."

When the queen heard this, she was horrified, and she was so afraid, so very afraid that she didn't know what to do. However, her jealousy drove her so much that she wanted to be seen at the wedding. After she arrived, she saw that Snow White was the bride. Iron slippers were then heated over a fire. The queen had to put them on and dance in them, and her feet were miserably burned, but she had to keep dancing in them until she danced herself to death.

Snow White (1857)[194]
Jacob and Wilhelm Grimm

Once upon a time, in the middle of winter, when snowflakes were falling like feathers from the sky, a queen was sitting and sewing at a window with a black ebony frame. And as she was sewing and looking out the window, she pricked her finger with the needle, and three drops of blood fell on the snow. The red looked so beautiful on the white snow that she thought to herself, 'If only I had a child as white as snow, as red as blood, and as black as the wood of the window frame!'

Soon after she gave birth to a little daughter who was as white as snow, as red as blood, and her hair as black as ebony. Accordingly, the child was called Snow White, and right after she was born, the queen died. When a year had passed, the king married another woman, who was beautiful but proud and haughty, and she couldn't tolerate anyone else who might rival her beauty. She had a magic mirror and often she stood in front of it, looked at herself, and said:

"Mirror, mirror, on the wall,
who in this realm is fairest of all?"

Then the mirror would answer:

"You, my queen, are the fairest of all."

---

194. "Schneewittchen," *Kinder- und Hausmärchen gesammelt durch die Brüder Grimm*, 7th ed. 3 vols. (Göttingen: Verlag der Dieterischen Buchhandlung, 1857).

That reply would make her content, for she knew the mirror always told the truth. In the meantime, Snow White grew up and became more and more beautiful. By the time she was seven years old, she was as beautiful as the day is clear and more beautiful than the queen herself. One day when the queen asked her mirror:

> "Mirror, mirror, on the wall,
> who in this realm is fairest of all?"

The mirror answered:

> "You, my queen, may have a beauty quite rare,
> but Snow White is a thousand times more fair."

The queen shuddered and became yellow and green with envy. From that hour on, her hate for the girl became so great that her heart throbbed and turned in her breast each time she saw Snow White. Like weeds, the envy and arrogance grew so dense in her heart that she no longer had any peace, day or night. Finally, she summoned a huntsman and said, "Take the child out into the forest. I never want to lay eyes on her again. You are to kill her and to bring me back her lungs and liver as proof of your deed."

The huntsman obeyed and led Snow White out into the forest, but when he drew his hunting knife and was about to stab Snow White's innocent heart, she began to weep and said, "Oh, dear huntsman, spare my life, and I'll run into the wild forest and never come home again."

Since she was so beautiful, the huntsman took pity on her and said, "You're free to go, my poor child!" Then he thought, 'The wild beasts will soon eat you up.' Nevertheless, he felt as if a great weight had been lifted off his heart, because he didn't have to kill her. Just then a young boar came dashing by, and the huntsman stabbed it to death. He took out the lungs and liver and brought them to the queen as proof that the child was dead. The cook was ordered to boil them in salt, and the wicked woman ate them and thought that she had eaten Snow White's lungs and liver.

Meanwhile, the poor child was all alone in the huge forest. When she looked at all the leaves on the trees, she was petrified and didn't know what to do. Then she began to run, and she ran over sharp stones and through thorn bushes. Wild beasts darted by her at times, but they didn't harm her. She ran as long as her legs could carry her, and it was almost evening when she saw a little cottage and went inside to rest. Everything was tiny in the cottage and indescribably dainty and neat. There was a little table with a white tablecloth, and on it were seven little plates. Each plate had a tiny spoon next to it, and there were also seven tiny knives and forks and seven tiny cups. In a row against the wall stood seven little beds covered with sheets as white as snow. Since she was so hungry and thirsty, Snow White ate some vegetables and bread from each of the little plates and had a drop of wine to drink out of each of the tiny cups, for she didn't want to take everything from just one place. After that she was tired and began trying out the beds, but none of them suited her at first: one was too long, another too short, but at last, she found that the seventh one was just right. So she stayed in that bed, said her prayers, and fell asleep.

When it was completely dark outside, the owners of the cottage returned. They were seven dwarfs who searched in the mountains for minerals with their picks and shovels. They lit their seven little candles, and when it became light in the house, they saw that someone had been there, for none of their things was in the exact same spot in which it had been left.

"Who's been sitting in my chair?" said the first dwarf.

"Who's been eating off my plate?" said the second.

"Who's been eating my bread?" said the third.

"Who's been eating my vegetables?" said the fourth.

"Who's been using my fork?" said the fifth.

"Who's been cutting with my knife?" said the sixth.

"Who's been drinking from my cup?" said the seventh.

Then the first dwarf looked around and noticed that his bed had been wrinkled and said, "Who's been sleeping in my bed?"

The others ran over to their beds and cried out, "Someone's been sleeping in my bed, too!"

But when the seventh dwarf looked at his bed, he saw Snow White lying there asleep. So he called the others over to him, and when they came, they were so astounded that they fetched their seven little candles to allow more light to shine on Snow White.

"Oh, my Lord! Oh, my Lord!" they exclaimed. "What a beautiful child!"

They were so delirious with joy that they didn't wake her up. Instead, they let her sleep in the bed, while the seventh dwarf spent an hour in each one of his companions' beds until the night had passed. In the morning Snow White awoke, and when she saw the seven dwarfs, she was frightened. But they were friendly and asked, "What's your name?"

"My name's Snow White," she replied.

"What's brought you to our house?" the dwarfs continued.

She told them how her stepmother had ordered her to be killed, how the huntsman had spared her life, and how she had run all day until she had eventually discovered their cottage.

Then the dwarfs said, "If you'll keep house for us, cook, make the beds, wash, sew, and knit, and if you'll keep everything neat and orderly, you can stay with us, and we'll provide you with everything you need."

"Yes," agreed Snow White, "with all my heart."

So she stayed with them and kept their house in order. In the morning they went to the mountains to search for minerals and gold. In the evening they returned, and their dinner had to be ready. During the day Snow White was alone, and the good dwarfs made sure to caution her.

"Beware of your stepmother," they said. "She'll soon know that you're here. Don't let anybody in!"

Since the queen believed she had eaten Snow White's liver and lungs, she was totally convinced that she was again the most beautiful woman in the realm. And when she went to her mirror, she said:

"Mirror, mirror, on the wall,
who in this realm is the fairest of all?"

The mirror answered:

"You, my queen, may have a beauty quite rare,
but beyond the mountains, where the seven dwarfs dwell,
Snow White is thriving, and this I must tell:
Within this realm she's still a thousand times more fair."

The queen was horrified, for she knew that the mirror never lied, which meant that the huntsman had deceived her and Snow White was still alive. Once more she began plotting ways to kill her. As long as Snow White was the fairest in the realm, the queen's envy would leave her no peace. Finally, she thought up a plan. She painted her face and dressed as an old peddler woman so that nobody could recognize her. Then she crossed the seven mountains in this disguise and arrived at the cottage of the seven dwarfs, where she knocked at the door and cried out, "Pretty wares for sale! Pretty wares!"

Snow White looked out of the window and called out, "Good day, dear woman, what do you have for sale?"

"Nice and pretty things! Staylaces in all kinds of colors!" she replied and took out a lace woven from silk of many different colors.

'I can certainly let this honest woman inside,' Snow White thought. She unbolted the door and bought the pretty lace.

"My goodness, child! What a sight you are!" said the old woman. "Come, I'll lace you up properly for once."

Snow White didn't suspect anything, so she stood in front of the old woman and let herself be laced with the new staylace. However, the old woman laced her so quickly and so tightly that Snow White lost her breath and fell down as if dead.

"Well, you used to be the fairest in the realm, but not now!" the old woman said and rushed off.

Not long after, at dinnertime, the dwarfs came home, and when they saw their dear Snow White lying on the ground, they were horrified. She neither stirred nor moved and seemed to be dead. They lifted her up, and when they saw that she was laced too tightly, they cut the staylace in two. At once she began to breathe a little, and after a while she had fully revived. When the dwarfs heard what had happened, they said, "The old peddler woman was none other than the wicked queen! Beware, don't let anyone in when we're not with you!"

When the evil woman returned home, she went to her mirror and asked:

> "Mirror, mirror, on the wall,
> who in this realm is the fairest of all?"

Then the mirror answered as usual:

> "You, my queen, may have a beauty quite rare,
> but beyond the mountains, where the seven dwarfs dwell,
> Snow White is thriving, and this I must tell:
> Within this realm she's still a thousand times more fair."

When the queen heard that, she was so upset that all her blood rushed to her heart, for she realized that Snow White had recovered.

"This time I'm going to think of something that will destroy her," she said, and by using all the witchcraft at her command, she made a poison comb. Then she again disguised herself as an old woman and crossed the seven mountains to the cottage of the seven dwarfs, where she knocked at the door and cried out, "Pretty wares for sale! Pretty wares!"

Snow White looked out the window and said, "Go away! I'm not allowed to let anyone in."

"But surely you're allowed to look," said the old woman, and she took out the poison comb and held it up in the air. The comb pleased the girl so much that she let herself be carried away and opened the door. After they agreed on the price, the old woman said, "Now I'll give your hair a proper combing for once."

Poor Snow White didn't give this a second thought and let the old woman do as she wished. But no sooner did the comb touch her hair than the poison began to take effect, and the maiden fell to the ground and lay there unconscious.

"You paragon of beauty!" said the wicked woman. "Now you're finished!" And she went away.

Fortunately, it was nearly evening, the time when the seven dwarfs began heading home. And, when they arrived and saw Snow White lying on the ground as if she were dead, they immediately suspected the stepmother and began looking around. As soon as they found the poison comb, they took it out, and Snow White instantly regained consciousness. She told them what had happened, and they warned her again to be on her guard and not to open the door for anyone.

In the meantime, the queen returned home, went to the mirror, and said:

> "Mirror, mirror, on the wall,
> who in this realm is the fairest of all?"

Then the mirror answered as before:

> "You, my queen, may have a beauty quite rare,
> but beyond the mountains, where the seven dwarfs dwell,
> Snow White is thriving, and this I must tell:
> Within this realm she's still a thousand times more fair."

When she heard the mirror's words, she trembled and shook with rage. "Snow White shall die!" she exclaimed. "Even if it costs me my own life!"

Then she went into a secret and solitary chamber where no one else ever went. Once inside she made a deadly poisonous apple. On the outside it looked beautiful—white with red cheeks. Anyone who saw it would be enticed, but whoever took a bite was bound to die. When the apple was ready, the queen painted her face and dressed herself up as a peasant woman and crossed the seven mountains to the cottage of the seven dwarfs. When she knocked at the door, Snow White stuck her head out of the window and said, "I'm not allowed to let anyone inside. The seven dwarfs have forbidden me."

"That's all right with me," answered the peasant woman. "I'll surely get rid of my apples in time. But let me give you one as a gift."

"No," said Snow White. "I'm not allowed to take anything."

"Are you afraid that it might be poisoned?" said the old woman. "Look, I'll cut the apple in two. You eat the red part, and I'll eat the white."

However, the apple had been made with such cunning that only the red part was poisoned. Snow White was eager to eat the beautiful apple, and when she saw the peasant woman eating her half, she could no longer resist, stretched out her hand, and took the poisoned half. No sooner did she take a bite than she fell to the ground dead. The queen stared at her with a cruel look, then burst out laughing and said, "White as snow, red as blood, black as ebony! This time the dwarfs won't be able to bring you back to life!"

When she got home, she asked the mirror:

> "Mirror, mirror, on the wall,
> who in this realm is the fairest of all?"

Then the mirror finally answered, "You, my queen, are now the fairest of all." So her jealous heart was satisfied as much as a jealous heart can be satisfied.

When the dwarfs came home that evening, they found Snow White lying on the ground. There was no breath coming from her lips, and she was dead. They lifted her up and looked to see if they could find something poisonous. They unlaced her, combed her hair, washed her with water and wine, but it was to no avail. The dear child was dead and remained dead. They laid her on a bier, and all seven of them sat down beside it and mourned over her. They wept for three whole days, and then they intended to bury her, but she looked so alive and still had such pretty red cheeks that they said, "We can't possibly bury her in the dingy ground."

Instead, they made a transparent glass coffin so that she could be seen from all sides. Then they put her in it, wrote her name on it in gold letters, and added that she was a princess. They carried the coffin to the top of the mountain, and from then on one of them always stayed beside it and guarded it. Some animals came also and wept for Snow White. There was an owl, then a raven, and finally a dove. Snow White lay in the coffin for many, many years and didn't decay. Indeed, she seemed to be sleeping, for she was still as white as snow, as red as blood, and her hair as black as ebony.

Now it happened that a prince came to the forest one day, and when he arrived at the dwarfs' cottage, he decided to spend the night. Then he went to the mountain and saw the coffin with beautiful Snow White inside. After he read what was written on the coffin in gold letters, he said to the dwarfs, "Let me have the coffin, and I'll pay you whatever you want."

But the dwarfs answered, "We won't give it up for all the gold in the world."

"Then give it to me as a gift," he said, "for I can't go on living without being able to see Snow White. I'll honor her and cherish her as my dearly beloved."

Since he spoke with such fervor, the good dwarfs took pity on him and gave him the coffin. The prince ordered his servants to carry the coffin on their shoulders, but they stumbled over some shrubs, and the jolt caused the poisoned piece of apple that Snow White had bitten off to be released from her throat. It was not long before she opened her eyes, lifted up the lid of the coffin, sat up, and was alive again.

"Oh, Lord! Where am I?" she exclaimed.

The prince rejoiced and said, "You're with me," and he told her what had happened. Then he added, "I love you more than anything else in the world. Come with me to my father's castle. I want you to be my wife."

Snow White felt that he was sincere, so she went with him, and their wedding was celebrated with great pomp and splendor.

Now, Snow White's stepmother had also been invited to the wedding celebration, and after she had dressed herself in beautiful clothes, she went to the mirror and said:

> "Mirror, mirror, on the wall,
> who in this realm is the fairest of all?"

The mirror answered:

> "You, my queen, may have a beauty quite rare,
> but Snow White is a thousand times more fair."

The evil woman uttered a loud curse and became so terribly afraid that she didn't know what to do. At first she didn't want to go to the wedding celebration. But she couldn't calm herself until she saw the young queen. When she entered the hall, she recognized Snow White. The evil queen was so petrified with fright that she couldn't budge. Iron slippers had already been heated over a fire, and they were brought over to her with tongs. Finally, she had to put on the red-hot slippers and dance until she fell down dead.

The Death of the Seven Dwarfs (1856)[195]
Ernst Ludwig Rochholz

There were once seven dwarfs who lived together in a small cottage on one of the plateaus between Brugg and Waldshut near the Black Forest. Late one evening a nice young peasant girl happened to lose her way. She was hungry and asked for a night's lodging. The dwarfs only had seven beds, and so they began quarreling among one another because each of them wanted to offer her his bed. Finally, the eldest dwarf took her into his bed, but no sooner had they begun to fall asleep than a peasant woman knocked on the door and asked to enter. The girl stood up immediately and told her that there were no more places for anyone because the seven dwarfs only had seven beds for themselves.

The woman became very angry about this and scolded the girl. She suspected that she was the mistress of the seven men and accused her of being a slut. So she threatened that she would soon make an end to such a nasty business and went away in a rage. Then, that very night, she returned with two men, whom she had fetched from the bank of the Rhine River. These men broke into the house right away and slew the dwarfs. Then they dragged their corpses outside into the little garden and burned down the house. While all this was happening, the girl disappeared, and people never saw her again.

The Three Sisters (1867)[196]
Christian Schneller

A father had three daughters, and they lived in a beautiful house near the king's palace. One time it so happened that the father had to travel because of some important business. The king had a son, who was a handsome young prince, and he informed the maidens that he was going to visit them after their father had departed. In preparation for his visit, the young women began to get dressed in splendid clothes, and the two eldest sisters arranged everything so that the youngest would have to sit in the middle. They did this because they thought that the prince would have to sit next to one of them. However, when the prince came, he sat down in the middle next to the youngest sister because she was the most beautiful and charming among them. The two of them talked about all sorts of things for a long time.

195.   "Tod der sieben Zwerge," *Schweizersagen aus dem Aargau* (Aarau: Druck und Verlag von H. R. Sauerländer, 1856).
196.   "Die drei Schwestern," *Märchen und Sagen aus Wälschtirol* (Innsbruck: Verlag der Wagner'schen Universitäts-Buchhandlung, 1867).

The next day the prince promised to come again, and the two older sisters arranged everything so that Marie—this was the name of the youngest sister—would have to sit on the side. However, once again the prince sat down next to her and continued to do this with each and every visit. Then, one time the two older sisters hid Marie's beautiful clothes, and she had to appear in front of the prince in simple house clothes. Nevertheless, to the annoyance of the two older sisters, he talked much more and was more friendly with Marie this time than he ever had before, and it was quite clear that his visits were meant mainly for Marie's sake.

"How is it that the youngest of us will become queen and not me or you?" the two older sisters said to each other. Indeed, they were furious and thought of doing something nasty to Marie.

Now they had an old maid in their house, and she was a witch. So, one evening they summoned her and asked her: "Whom do you love more, the two of us, or our younger sister?"

"Oh, you two, for sure," the maid replied, and so they immediately ordered her to take Marie into the forest the next morning to pick strawberries.

"Lead her deep into the forest," they said. "Then leave there alone so that she can't find her way back anymore. Meanwhile we're going to make a coffin and bury her in a grave. As soon as our father returns, we'll tell him that Marie died, and if he doesn't believe it, we'll dig up the grave and show him the coffin."

The next morning Marie went into the forest with the maid to pick strawberries. They went deeper into the woods, and while Marie busily picked the red berries, the maid withdrew from her without being noticed and returned home. Marie wept and called out to her, but it was in vain. She wandered about the entire day and couldn't find a way out of the forest. Instead she strayed even deeper into the dark forest that had no paths and was full of tall trees whose branches did not permit the rays of the sun to penetrate the moist, mossy ground. Finally she sat down, exhausted and distressed, on the long roots of a hundred-year-old pine tree. As she wept, she surrendered to her bitter fate. However, all of a sudden she saw a venerable old man with a long white beard standing in front of her, and he asked her in a friendly way how she had got there. She told him everything, and he said: "My child, your sisters thought up this evil plot against you because they are jealous of you. And they would certainly bring about your ruin if you were to find the way back home. Stay with me, and you'll lead a quiet and solitary life, but you will be happy."

Marie gladly agreed, and the old man led her to his little cottage that stood in the middle of the forest. So she stayed with him. The smart old man knew a great deal to tell her and treated her lovingly like a father and respectfully as if she were a queen. Marie was only alone from time to time, for the old man left her only to gather wood or to fetch food. However, he forbade her to open the door to strangers, no matter who they were.

Now Marie's two sisters learned that she was still alive and where she was. Enraged, they ordered the maid to disguise herself and to take a basket with bewitched things to the little cottage in the forest and offer them for sale to Marie.

Now, one day when the old man left the cottage and Marie was all alone at home, a woman came with a basket and cried out: "Rings, needles, and yarn for sale! I have beautiful and cheap things!"

At first Marie didn't want to open the door, but the woman knew how to coax her until she finally opened it to look at the merchandise. There was a ring that she liked the most, but when she put the ring on her finger, she fell to the ground as if she were dead, and the maid—for this was the woman—took off as quickly as she could.

When the old man came home and saw Marie lying on the ground as if she were dead, he soon suspected what must have taken place. Then he noticed that a finger on her hand was swollen and took off the ring. All at once, Marie awoke as if she had been in a deep sleep and told the old man everything that had happened. Once again he warned her and forbade her not to open the door to anyone when he was absent.

The two sisters soon learned that Marie was still alive and sent the maid into the forest once more. It so happened that the old man had just gone off, and Marie was alone in the house. A woman came again, and she looked totally different from the one who had come before, and she had other things to sell such as clothes. Marie let the woman cry out and knock at the door for a long time. But finally Marie looked out a window, and when she saw such beautiful things, she forgot the old man's orders and opened the door. Among the things that she saw, there was a pretty corset that seemed to be made just for her, and she immediately tried it on. No sooner than she had tied it around her body than she fell to the ground as if she were dead. The wicked maid fled as fast as her feet could carry her. When the old man returned home, he looked at her in horror and began to examine her right away. Then he untied the corset and took it off Marie, who once again woke up as if she had been in a deep sleep. And once again the old man repeated his warning and orders with even more urgency than before.

Meanwhile her father had returned home and shed bitter tears when the two daughters told him that Marie had died. Some time went by, and the sisters learned once more that Marie was alive. Enraged they summoned the maid and said: "Go into the forest and disguise yourself as only you can so that she will open the door. Then persuade her to let you comb her hair, and when you start combing, you're to thrust this bewitched needle into her head. The old man will certainly not find it."

One day Marie was alone in the cottage again and looked through the window where she saw an old woman dragging herself with great effort on crutches, and all of a sudden she collapsed. Marie ran outside right away. She lifted the old woman from the ground and led her into the cottage where she refreshed her with food and drink. The old woman soon regained her strength and thanked Marie warmly: "Oh, if only I could repay you with a favor, my good child!" she said. "I see that your beautiful hair has become tousled. I'll comb your hair so that it is properly beautiful and then braid it."

Marie resisted, but finally gave in and let it happen. Then the maid—for it was she who was the old woman—stuck the needle into Marie's head and rushed off. The old man arrived and saw Marie lying on the ground as if she were dead. He examined her entire body but couldn't find anything. He became very sad and decided to keep her in the house, for she didn't resemble a dead person but rather someone asleep. He laid her beautifully dressed on a bed, bought many large candles in the city, and placed them around the bed, where he let them burn day and night.

One day the king's son went hunting and got lost in the forest. At one point he passed by the little cottage and noticed the burning candles. So, out of curiosity he looked through the window and saw the most beautiful maiden asleep on a bed. When the old man opened the door for him, the prince went inside and could not stop gazing at the beautiful sleeping corpse. So he pressed the old man with thousands of pleas and promises to let him have the sleeping beauty. But it was all in vain and the prince sadly went home. However, he returned the next day with his servants who carried precious gifts, and he began pleading again. Finally, the old man gave in with tears in his eyes, not because of the gifts, but because he could no longer refuse the prince this favor.

The beautiful sleeping corpse was brought to the royal castle in the city. The prince had her splendidly dressed and placed in a sumptuous glass case that he himself had made. He often stood for hours before the beautiful image and couldn't get enough of her so that he became more and more sad. He wouldn't allow anyone to enter the room, not even his mother, and always kept the key to the room with him.

One day the prince went off hunting for a long time. So he entrusted the key to his mother with the order that she wasn't to enter the room unless there was some kind of emergency. After he departed, the queen's curiosity got the better of her, and she entered the room and gazed at the beautiful image in the glass case with astonishment.

"Oh, what a beautiful maiden!" she exclaimed time and again. "She's not dead and yet not alive. What is she? And what splendid hair she has!" she added and began touching the hair with her fingers.

As she was doing this, she felt something hard and saw that there was a large needle in it. So she slowly withdrew the needle, and all at once, Marie awoke from her enchanted sleep and looked around her with fright. But the queen spoke to her in a friendly way, and Marie told her everything that had happened.

About this time the prince returned home, and the queen ordered Marie to hide herself quickly. The prince entered the room, and his first angry looks fell upon his mother and the glass case,

"Where is the body?" he yelled with rage when he saw that the case was empty.

The queen told him to calm down, and he suppressed his anger but couldn't stop the burst of tears of pain. So the queen gave a signal to Marie, and the maiden came out of her hiding place and approached the prince. At first he was so overcome by joyful fright that he didn't know what to do. However, he soon recognized Marie and embraced her as his bride.

And now our story has a sad and happy ending. The sad part is that the prince immediately summoned the two older sisters and ordered that their heads to be cut off then and there. The wicked witch was burned at a stake in the public square. Afterward, a merry wedding was held. As for me, they didn't even give me a bit of the banquet meal, just a bone that they threw at me, and my back is still hurting me because of it.

Maria, the Evil Stepmother, and the Seven Robbers (1870)[197]
Laura Gonzenbach

Once upon a time there was a man, whose wife died, and he was left only with a small maiden called Maria.

Maria went to a school where she learned sewing and knitting from a woman. When she went home each evening, this woman told her time and again, "Make sure you give my warm greetings to your father."

Since she seemed to be so kind, Maria's father thought, 'She'd make for a good wife,' and so he married her. But when they were married, the woman became quite nasty to poor Maria, for that's the way stepmothers have always been, and finally she couldn't stand Maria at all. So she said to her husband, "The girl eats too much of our bread. We've got to get rid of her."

But the man said, "I'm not going to kill my own child!"

"Take her with you tomorrow into the fields," the woman said. "Leave her there alone. She won't be able to find her way back home."

The next day the man called his daughter and said to her, "Let's go work in the forest, and we'll take some food with us."

Then he took a large loaf of bread with him, and they set out on their way. However, Maria was shrewd and had filled her pockets with bran. As she walked behind her father, she threw heaps of bran on the path from time to time. After they had walked for several hours, they came to a steep cliff where the man let the loaf of bread fall over and cried out, "Oh, Maria, the bread fell over the cliff!"

"Don't worry, father," Maria said, "I'll climb down and fetch it."

197. "Maria, die böse Stiefmutter und die sieben Räuber," *Sicilianische Märchen*, 2 vols. (Leipzig: W. Engelmann, 1870).

She went down to the bottom of the cliff and found the bread. When she, however, returned to the top, her father had disappeared, and Maria was alone. She began to weep, for she was very far from their house and in a strange spot. But then she thought about the heaps of bran, and she summoned her courage again. Slowly she followed the bran and returned home late at night.

"Oh, father!" she said. "Why did you leave me so alone?"

The man comforted her and talked to her until she calmed down. But the stepmother was angry that Maria had found her way back home. After some time had passed, she said to her husband once again that he should take Maria into the fields and leave her alone in the forest. The next morning the man called his daughter again, and they set out on their way. The father carried a loaf of bread with him once more, but Maria forgot to take bran with her. Once they were deeper in the forest and reached another even steeper cliff, the father let the loaf of bread fall again, and Maria had to climb down to fetch it. When she returned to the top, the man had left, and she was alone. So she began to weep bitter tears and ran around for a long time looking for the way home, but she only managed to go deeper into the dark forest. Gradually as it turned dark, he suddenly saw a light, and when she went toward it, she came upon a cottage, in which she found a table set for dinner and seven beds. But there were no people. Indeed, the house belonged to seven robbers, and therefore, Maria hid herself behind the baking tray. Soon the robbers came home. They ate and drank and then lay down to bed. The next morning they went forth and left their youngest brother there so that he could cook and clean the house. While they were away, the youngest brother also left to buy a few things. Then Maria came out from behind the baking tray and began cleaning the entire house. She finished by sweeping the room and setting the kettle on the fire to cook the beans. Then she hid behind the baking tray again.

When the youngest robber returned, he was astonished to see everything so clean, and when his brothers came home, he told them what had happened. They were all very puzzled and couldn't imagine how all this had come to pass. The next day the second youngest brother remained behind. He pretended that he also had to go away, but he returned right away and saw Maria come out of her hiding place to bring things in order. Maria was terrified when she caught sight of the robber.

"Oh," she pleaded, "please don't kill me. For God's sake!"

Then she told him about her evil stepmother, and how her father had abandoned her in the forest, and how she had hid herself for two days behind the baking tray.

"You don't need to be afraid of us," the robber said. "Stay with us. Be our sister, and cook, sew, and wash for us."

When the other brothers came home, they, too, were satisfied with Maria, and so Maria remained with the seven robbers, kept house for them, and was always quiet and diligent.

One day, as she was sitting at the window and sewing, a poor woman came by and asked for alms.

"Oh!" said Maria. "I don't have much, for I myself am a poor, unfortunate maiden. But I'll be glad to give you whatever I have."

"Why are you so unfortunate?" asked the beggar woman.

Then Maria told her how she had left home and had made her way to the robber's house. The poor woman left and later told the evil stepmother that Maria was still alive. When the stepmother heard that, she was very angry and gave the beggar woman a ring that she was to bring to poor Maria. This ring was a magic ring. After a week passed, the beggar woman went to Maria again to ask for alms, and when Maria gave her something, she said, "Look, my child, I have a beautiful ring. Since you have been so kind to me, I want to give it to you as a gift."

Without suspecting anything, Maria took the ring, but when she put it on her finger, she fell down dead. After the robbers returned home and found Maria on the floor, they were very distressed and shed bitter tears. Then they made a beautiful coffin, and after they had adorned her with the most beautiful jewels and placed a great deal of gold inside, they put Maria into the coffin and placed it on a cart drawn by two oxen. When they approached the king's castle, they saw that the door to the stable was wide open and drove the oxen and the cart inside. All this caused the horses to become unsettled, and they began to kick and make noise. When the king heard the racket, he sent a servant to the stable to ask the stable master what had happened. The stable master replied that a cart had come into the stable and nobody was driving it. But there was a beautiful coffin on the cart. So the king ordered his men to bring the coffin into his room and had them open it.

When he glanced at the beautiful dead maiden in the coffin, he began to weep bitter tears and couldn't bear to leave her. Then he ordered four large wax candles to be set up and lit on the four corners of the coffin. Afterward he sent all the people out of the room, locked the door, fell on his knees next to the coffin, and burst into tears. When it came time for dinner, his mother sent servants to him and told him to come. But he didn't even answer. Instead, he kept weeping all the more uncontrollably. So the old queen herself came and knocked on the door and asked him to open up. Still, he didn't answer. Then she looked through the keyhole, and when she saw that her son was kneeling next to a corpse, she had her servants break open the door. However, as soon as she saw the beautiful maiden, she herself was very touched and leaned over Maria and took her hand. When she noticed the beautiful ring, she thought it would be a shame to have the ring buried with the girl. So she slipped it off. All of a sudden the dead Maria was alive again, and the young king was extremely pleased and said to his mother. "This maiden is to be my bride!"

"Then it will be as you say!" his mother responded and embraced Maria.

So Maria became the wife of the king and a queen as well, and they lived in glory and happiness until the end of their days.

Child Margarita (1875)[198]

Giuseppe Pitrè

Once upon a time there was a merchant with a wife and three daughters. The oldest was extraordinarily beautiful so that people called her "Child Margarita." When the children reached the proper age, they began school. Their teacher was a young woman and began doing them special favors. After some time, the girls' mother died. Then the teacher, who had plans of her own, began doing them even more favors than before. One day she said to Child Margarita, "Margarita, if your father plans to re-marry, he should consider marrying me."

The girl dutifully reported this to her father. And the man decided to do just that, noting that his daughters had not fared badly with this teacher. But the minute they were married, the woman felt a visceral hatred for Margarita because she thought the girl considered herself special.

One day she sent Margarita on a walk with the maid, who was instructed to abandon the child in a deserted part of the countryside. This she did, and the child, alone and afraid, began crying pitifully. Finally an old woman appeared and asked, "Why are you crying?"

"Why shouldn't I cry? My stepmother sent me on a walk with the maid, and I got lost."

"In that case, do as I say: go to that nearby palace, and all will turn out well for you."

The girl went to the palace, entered, and found one beautiful room after another. When she called out, "Greetings!" nobody answered. She looked further and then heard someone groaning. Peering into the back of a room, she saw a poor lady lying in bed all covered with blood. The girl searched the drawers of a chest for clean linen and changed her bed sheets.

"May the good Lord reward you for this, dear girl," said the woman. Then Margarita went into the kitchen, washed the sheets, and proceeded to clean up the whole house.

Now let's return to the stepmother, who was enjoying the fact that her step-daughter had disappeared. One day she went to her mirror and said:

> "Mirror of mine, so nice and round,
> Can anyone prettier than me be found?"

And the mirror responded:

> "There is the sun, and there is the moon,
> And then there is Child Margarita."

---

198. "La infanti Margarita," *Fiabe, novelle e racconti popolari siciliani*, 4 vols. (Palermo: Lauriel, 1875).

"What? Margarita is still alive?" the stepmother exclaimed.

"Certainly she's alive," answered the mirror, "and she's living in a palace as if she owned the place."

Meanwhile, Margarita was working every day as a servant for the poor woman with the wounds. It turns out that this woman was a condemned soul who was serving out her term of punishment. So, when the stepmother learned about this, she went to her mirror and said,

> "Mirror of mine, so nice and round,
> Can anyone prettier than me be found?"

Then the mirror responded:

> "There is the sun, and there is the moon,
> And then there is Child Margarita."

"Oh, what must I do to rid myself of this creature?" the stepmother asked.

"Summon an old witch, give her this enchanted braid of hair, and order her to bring it to Child Margarita."

This is exactly what the stepmother did, and the old witch went off to find the child. Now the time had arrived, and the wounded woman completed her term of suffering. She embraced Child Margarita and said, "My suffering is now over. Because of all the good you have done for me, I am leaving this entire palace to you with all its contents. But you must be very careful because your stepmother has evil designs on you."

With these words, she vanished.

One day Margarita was sitting at her window when the old woman came along. She claimed to be her grandmother, and the girl, who had a trusting nature, invited her inside.

"How lovely you are, my child, and what lovely hair you have! Here, let me brush it for you."

The girl believed her and let her brush her hair. At the right moment the old witch inserted the enchanted braid, and Margarita fell into an enchanted sleep. The old woman, quiet as a cat, went back to her house.

A few days later the liberated soul returned and removed the braid, and Margarita was revived.

"Didn't I tell you? Your stepmother has evil designs on you. Be very careful now, because the next time I won't be able to come back again to revive you."

Now the stepmother went to her mirror and said,

> "Mirror of mine, so nice and round,
> Can anyone prettier than me be found?"

The mirror responded:

> "There is the sun, and there is the moon,
> And then there is Child Margarita."

"What? How can she still be alive?" the stepmother exclaimed.

"She is. But here's what you must do. Call the old woman, give her this long pin, and tell her to stick it into Margarita's head."

So that terrible old woman went there again, pretending this time to be someone in need of lodging for the night. Child Margarita welcomed her and was completely taken in by her pretenses. She let her caress her with "How lovely you are!" and the like, and finally the old woman got to touch her hair. In the twinkling of an eye the deceitful old woman inserted the long pin, and the girl fell into an enchanted sleep. The old witch put seven veils in front of the girl's face and departed. And now the liberated soul was unable to return to free Margarita from the spell.

Now, let's leave her there, enchanted, and take up the story of a prince who liked to go hunting. On one of his outings he encountered a dreadful storm, and where did he find shelter? In the very palace where Margarita lay sleeping. When he entered and saw the girl he said, "Oh, what a rare and lovely face! Could she be embalmed?" and he touched her head. As he stroked her hair, he noticed the pin and pulled it out. All at once she awakened and was startled to find herself alone with a man.

"Don't be afraid," he said, "I'm a prince and will do you no harm. But tell me, how is it you've come to be here alone?"

After she told him the whole story, the prince said, "Oh my poor girl! But take courage now because I am with you."

Things followed their usual course, ending up with "Do you love me?" "Yes, and do you love me, too?" So they hugged and kissed, and the prince left for home, leaving her safely shut within her palace.

When he got home, he told the whole story to his mother, who said, "Well, let's go see her first, and then we can discuss it."

They went together, and when the queen saw the maiden, she said, "My son, no need to discuss it further, this is the wife for you."

So the wedding was arranged, carriages were summoned, and off they went. Meanwhile the stepmother picked up her mirror and said,

> "Mirror of mine, so nice and round,
> Can anyone prettier than me be found?"

And the mirror responded:

> "There is the sun, and there is the moon,
> And then there is Child Margarita."

"But how can this girl still be alive?" the stepmother exclaimed.

"She is, and there's nothing you can do about it. She's marrying a prince, and you can whistle all you want."

When she heard this, the stepmother went into a frenzy and smashed her head against the wall until it split open.

Once the prince and Margarita were married, she said to him, "If you truly love me you'll do me a great favor. My sisters are suffering terribly because they are in the hands of our dreadful stepmother." (Indeed, she was unaware that the stepmother had already split her head open). "Send for them to come and live with us here."

The prince sent for them and provided rooms for them in his palace, and they all lived like princesses.

> So they lived on, in contentment and peace,
> While we just sit here, picking our teeth.

Told by Agatuzza Messia in Palermo.

Maroula and the Mother of Eros (1877)[199]

Bernhard Schmidt

There once was a princess who was by far the most beautiful woman among all the women in the world. When the mother of Eros learned about her, she decided to kill her because she would not tolerate any woman more beautiful than she was. In order to carry out her plans she disguised herself as an old woman and went to the princess's castle with a poisoned golden apple and offered it for sale. The princess was an orphan, but she had many brothers who protected her and locked her in the palace whenever they left it so that nobody could come and do her harm. This is why she was locked inside when the old woman arrived below the castle and showed her the golden apple. Since the princess wanted to buy the apple, Eros' mother told her to drop a rope from the window. Then she would tie it to the rope, and the princess could pull it up to her. And this is what happened. But with the first bite that the princess took, she fell unconscious to the floor. It was in this condition that her brothers found poor Maroula—for that was her name—when they returned home. When they noticed the apple, they thought that it might be poisoned and had somehow harmed their sister. So they took out the piece of the apple from her mouth that she had bitten off, and she immediately came back to life.

Meanwhile the mother of Eros wanted to know for certain whether the beautiful princess had really died when she had taken a bite of the apple. Therefore, she held a mirror in front of the sun and said:

> "Oh, sun of mine that shines so bright,
> Tell me with your eyes of light,
> Who's the most beautiful woman in the world?"

"You are indeed beautiful," the sun answered, "but Maroula has no equal in the world."

---

199.   "Maroula und die Mutter des Érotas," *Griechische Märchen, Sagen und Volkslieder* (Leipzig: Teubner, 1877). Érotas is Love (Eros, Cupid), and his mother is the Greek goddess Venus.

When the mother of Eros heard that Maroula was still alive, she became even more angry at her and went once again to the palace with an enchanted ring. The princess bought the ring, but no sooner than she put the ring on her finger than she sank lifeless to the ground. But this time the brothers didn't notice that the ring on their sister's finger had been enchanted. And since they abandoned hope of ever being able to restore her life, they laid her down in a large gold coffin and placed the coffin in a meadow near their castle.

One day, a prince who had been out hunting became aware of the coffin when a bird flew down from the sky and landed on it. He ordered his servants to pick it up and bring it to his palace. Once there he opened it and saw the beautiful maiden lying inside. Quite by accident he pulled the ring from her finger, and she came back to life right away. Soon after the prince married her, and after they had been living together for a while, the young woman became pregnant and gave birth to twins.

However, the prince's mother was very indignant that her son had shown her very little attention because of his love for his wife, and she decided to ruin her daughter-in-law's life. So, one evening she went into her room, cut off the heads of her two children, and threw the knife with which she had committed the murder onto Maroula's bed in order to throw suspicion for the crime on her. The next morning her son saw what had happened, and since his mother blamed Maroula for the deed, he didn't but doubt that she was the murderer. Therefore, he ordered Maroula's hands to be cut off and the children's heads and bodies to be sewn in a sack along with their mother's hands and the sack tied around Maroula's neck. Then Maroula was to be banished from his land. And his orders were carried out.

As Maroula made her way through a forest, she met a monk and told him everything that had happened. The monk took the heads of the children and placed them back on their bodies. All at once their lives were restored. Then he joined Maroula's hands to her arms. Right after this he hit the ground with his staff, and all at once a large palace emerged. Then he said to Maroula: "Stay here with your boys and live happily! I want you to know that I'm your good angel, and I'll come back to see you."

After saying these words he suddenly disappeared, and Maroula didn't even have the time to say farewell to him.

While she was now living in the castle with her children, her husband, who had chased her out of his house, came walking by with some friends and saw his wife up in the castle but didn't recognize her. However, Maroula recognized him, and upon the advice of the monk, her good angel, who all of a sudden appeared at her side again, she invited her husband to come up and visit her. While her husband climbed the stairs, Maroula instructed her children to grab hold of two balls when he appeared and then to throw them and say: "We hope things are going well for you, father, but we hope our grandmother bursts because she was spurred on by Eros' mother to move you to cut off our mother's hands even though our grandmother was the one who murdered us."

When the prince heard this, he said to his friends: "I want you to know that this is my wife, and these are my children."

And now he told them the entire story of what happened at his castle, and Maroula told him what had happened after he had banished her and how the monk had healed her wound and the wounds of her children. Moreover she told him that the monk revealed to her that it was Eros' mother who had caused her all the troubles because she had been jealous of her beauty.

So now the prince took his wife and children with him and hid them in his castle. Some days later he invited many of his friends to a banquet, told them everything, and demanded that they determine what kind of punishment that her mother deserved. Then they said unanimously that he should stick her in a barrel of tar and set it on fire on the sea. And this is what happened.

From then on the young couple lived happily, for Eros' mother contented herself with the suffering that she had caused Maroula and let her live without contesting her beauty anymore.

The Vain Queen (1882)[200]
Consiglieri Pedroso

There was a very vain queen who, turning towards her maids of honor, asked them, "Is there a face more beautiful than mine?"

To which they replied that there was not; and on asking the same question of her servants they made the same answer. One day she turned towards her chamberlain and asked him, "Is there a more beautiful face than mine?"

The chamberlain replied, "Be it known to your august majesty that there is."

The queen, on hearing this, desired to know who it could be, and the chamberlain informed her that it was her daughter. The queen then immediately ordered a carriage to be prepared, and after placing the princess in it, she ordered her servants to take her far away into the country and there to cut off her head and to bring back her tongue.

The servants departed as the queen had ordered them, but, on arriving at the place agreed upon, they turned towards the princess and said, "Your highness is not aware for what purpose we have brought you here; but we shall do you no harm."

They found a small bitch, killed her, and cut her tongue off. Then they told the princess that they had done this to take it to her majesty, for she had commanded them to behead her, and to take her back the tongue. Now they begged of the princess to flee to some distant part and never to return to the city, so as not to betray them. The maiden departed and went on walking through several lonely wild places until she noticed a small farm-house in the distance, and on approaching it she found nothing whatever inside the hut but the trail of some pigs. She walked on, and, on entering the first room she came to, she found a

---

200. *Portuguese Folk-Tales*, trans. Henriqueta Monteiro (London: Folklore Society, 1882).

very old chest made of pinewood; in the second room she found a bed with a very old straw mattress upon it; and in the third room a fireplace and a table. She went to the table, drew open the drawer, and found some food, which she put on the fire to cook. She laid the cloth, and when she was beginning to eat she heard a man coming in. The maiden, who was very much frightened, hid herself under the table, but the man, who had seen her hiding away, called her to him. He told her not to be ashamed; and they both afterwards dined at the table, and at night they also supped together. At the end of supper the man asked the princess which she would prefer, to remain as his wife or as his daughter. The princess replied that she should like to remain as his daughter. The man then arranged a separate bed for himself, and they each retired to rest. They lived in this way very happily.

One day the man told the maiden to go and take a walk to amuse herself. The maiden replied that the dress she wore was too old to go out in, but the man opening a cupboard showed her a complete suit of a countrywoman's clothes. The maiden dressed herself in them and went out. When she was out walking, she saw a gentleman coming towards her. The maiden immediately turned back very much alarmed and hid herself at home. At night when the man returned home, he asked her if she had enjoyed her walk, to which she replied that she had, but this she said in a timid tone of voice. The next day the man again sent her out to take a walk. The maiden did so and again saw the same gentleman coming towards her, and as before she fled home in great fright to hide herself. When the man saw her in the evening and asked her whether she had enjoyed her walk, the maiden replied that she had not because she had seen a man approach as though he wished to speak to her, and therefore she did not wish ever to go out again. To this the man made no reply.

The gentleman was a prince, who, on returning twice to the same place, and failing to meet the maiden, fell love-sick. The wisest physicians attended him; and they gave an account of the illness the prince was suffering from. The queen immediately commanded a proclamation to be issued to the effect that the country lass who had seen the prince should at once proceed to the palace, for which she would be recompensed and marry the prince.

But since the maiden now never left her home, she knew nothing of the proclamation. The queen, seeing that no one presented herself at the palace, sent a guard to search the place. The guard went and knocked at the door, and told the maiden that her majesty sent for her to the palace, and that she would be well-rewarded if she came. The maiden told the guard to return next day for her answer.

When she saw the man again in the evening, she related to him all that had passed. He told her that when the guard should return for the answer, she was to tell him that the queen must come to her as she would not go to the queen. When the guard returned next day for the answer, the girl told him that she did not dare inform him of her decision. The guard told her to say whatever she liked, that he would repeat it to the queen. The girl then told him what the man had advised her to say. When the guard arrived at the palace, he also feared to give the girl's answer; but the queen obliged him to do so. The guard then recounted all that the girl had said. The queen was very angry, but as at that very moment the prince was attacked with a severe fit of convulsions, and the queen feared he might die of it, she resolved to go.

She ordered a carriage to be brought, and she went to see the maiden; but as she was approaching the house, it was transformed into a palace; the man who had sheltered the girl was turned into a powerful emperor; the pigs, into dukes, the maiden, into a beautiful princess, and all the rest into wealth and riches. When the queen saw all this, she was very astonished and made many apologies for having summoned the girl to the palace. She told the maiden that since her son the prince was so greatly in love with her, she begged of her, if such was pleasing to her, to consent to marry the prince, as otherwise he would most certainly die. The maiden was willing and acceded to the request of the queen, and the marriage was celebrated with great pomp, and they all lived very happily.

Translated by Henriqueta Monteiro.

The Magic Slippers (1885)[201]
Adolpho Francisco Coelho

A long time ago there lived a very beautiful woman, who was the landlady of a roadside inn, principally patronised by muleteers and merchants who passed that way with their merchandise. This woman had a daughter whose great misfortune it was to be still fairer than her mother. The mother was so jealous of this daughter that she kept her shut up in a dark room with all the windows closed so that no one should see her. Poor girl, she often wished she had been born very plain so that she might have her liberty and enjoy life like other young people.

When any muleteers entered her inn, the first question the landlady would put to them was, if they had ever seen any woman more beautiful than herself? And as they generally answered "No," she was satisfied they had not seen her daughter.

One day the girl, however, contrived to open a window, and a muleteer, who came to the inn and was questioned as usual, replied that he had just seen a girl at a window, who far surpassed her in loveliness.

"Ah, I know who that is, then," said the woman. "What business had she to be looking out of the window? She shall pay me for it."

Full of spite and rage, she resolved to kill her daughter. She ordered two of her men to take her to a lonely place on a mountain, a few miles off, and there put her to death.

The men took the girl to the spot indicated, but just as one of them was raising the hatchet to sever her head from her body, the girl sank on her knees and, with tears rolling down her beautiful cheeks, pleaded to have her life spared,

201.   *Tales of Old Lusitania, from the Folklore of Portugal*, trans. Henriqueta Monteiro (London: Sonnenschein Ywan, 1885).

promising never to return to her mother so that they could pretend they had executed her commands. The men were touched by the appeal, and having no ill feeling against her, they raised her from the ground, and said to her, "No, no, we have not the heart to kill you, but you must leave this part of the country, for, if your mother finds you are alive, we shall get into trouble with her."

"I thank you for this good deed," replied the girl, "and I trust some day to have the means of rewarding you."

The girl, being left alone, determined to leave the neighbourhood as quickly as possible. She took a winding path that led to a stream at the foot of the mountain and followed its course till she came in sight of a house situated between two hills. It being now dark, she went up to the house, and finding the door open, she entered as far as the great hall, but seeing no one, she called out, "Will anyone here give a poor girl shelter for the night?"

Since no one answered her call, she walked in further, and roaming from chamber to chamber through dark passages, she found the place was deserted and empty of furniture except here and there a broken chair, or a tumble-down table. She determined to take up her quarters there till the morning and make herself as comfortable as the place admitted. Feeling hungry, she went down to the kitchen, and as she pried into every hole and corner in the store room in hopes of finding some food, she discovered among some rubbish and broken crockery, a brown earthen pot containing meal and a cruse with rancid oil, which to her then was as good as the best and finest. She then went to the garden, and after gathering some sticks and lighting a fire, she made herself a hearth-cake with the meal and oil. But, just as she was laying out her frugal supper on the kitchen table, which, besides the cake, consisted of a few small radishes she had dug up in the garden, and a cupful of water from the well, she heard a noise which so frightened her that she hid herself and listened. She soon found that the noise was made by a band of robbers who were bringing in their booty to hide it in the house.

When they saw supper laid, they cried: "Halloo! Who prepared this supper? If anyone is here, let them show themselves."

The poor girl came out of her hiding place trembling with fear, and stood before the robbers. But the men, struck with admiration at her beautiful face and charming figure, asked her what great stress had brought her there alone and apparently friendless. She then told them her history and how she was without a friend in the world, and the robbers, full of compassion, kindly said to her: "Fear not, and grieve no more. You shall stay with us, and we promise to protect you and treat you as our sister."

What could the poor girl do but consent to their proposal. She stayed with the men and made herself useful by preparing their meals and keeping house for them. The robbers became every day more fond of their newly adopted sister, who was so gentle and good; they treated her with all respect and were careful she should enjoy every comfort they could afford her.

I must now tell you that the girl's mother knew an old woman who often came to her inn, and whose business was to go about doing errands and carrying messages.

"Tell me," said the landlady one day to the old woman, "you, who travel everywhere and see so many different faces, did you ever see a woman more beautiful than myself?"

"Well, if I must tell you the truth, I have seen a handsomer face than yours. Once, at a town in Tras-os-Montes, I saw a girl more charming than any woman I ever saw in my life. She had a lovely figure and the sweetest and smallest feet possible."

"Indeed," replied the landlady, "then I know who she is. I want you to take a present to her the first time you go that way."

She then took out of a drawer a small pair of slippers and gave them to the old woman, saying, "Here, take these to her, and tell her that it is her loving mother who sends them. But you must on no account leave them with her till you have seen her put them on. Be very particular about that point, and I assure you that I shall pay you well if you follow my instructions faithfully."

The woman did as she was told, and going into the house where the girl was living, accosted her thus: "My dear girl, I bring you some slippers which your loving mother sends you, that you may wear them for her sake."

"I am not in want of shoes because my brothers supply me with them whenever I require any, so you may, if you please, take them back to my mother."

But the old woman insisted on her putting them on just to see if they fitted her, and so teased her to do it that at last the girl, to get rid of the old woman, consented and began to try them on. She had hardly put one of the shoes on when one of her eyes was completely closed. She put on the other one, and the other eye was also closed, and that instant she fell on the floor, dead. The old woman, surprised and frightened at what she saw, ran away, and left the neighbourhood as fast as she could.

When the robbers came home and saw their beloved sister lying dead on the floor, they wondered how she had come by her death. They were sorely eyed and wept over her corpse.

"But," said they, "it is a shame for such a face and figure to be hidden underground. We must put her in a coffin with a glass lid, and place it on the hills where the king's son comes to hunt with his nobles. It is right he should see such a rare and lovely flower."

The robbers had a beautiful coffin made, in which they laid the body of their dear sister, and strewed flowers over her, and then, fastening the glass cover down, they carried her to a retired spot on the hills.

Now it so happened that the king's son, as he was hunting one day with a number of courtiers, passed the very spot where the girl's body was laid, and seeing the coffin, they wondered why it was placed in such an unusual way and locality. The prince looked into the coffin and was at once fascinated by the beauty of the dead girl's countenance and the eyelids that were fringed with long silken lashes. He admired her pretty hands and feet and the silver band twined in the luxuriant tresses of her hair. His heart beat fast as he looked into her face and wondered if it were possible to call down a fairy who, with her magic wand, would bring back to life the little beauty whom he sighed to snatch from death and call his own.

When the prince had recovered from his reverie, he determined at least to take with him a keepsake of the beautiful figure, and uncovering the coffin he pulled off one of the pretty little slippers. But he had hardly done so when one of the girl's eyes opened, and the king's son seeing this, immediately pulled off the other slipper, and behold, the other eye opened also, and the girl came to life again. The prince, in the greatest delight, took her by the hand and helped her out of the coffin, and she came forth, if possible, fresher and fairer than ever.

The prince now sent one of his attendants for a carriage to take the maiden to the palace and present her to the king. And a few weeks after this event the prince married the girl amid great rejoicings. Among all the court beauties, there was not one to compare with the sweet little bride in grace and loveliness.

The prince then took his bride to her mother's inn so that the cruel woman might know that she had not succeeded in killing her daughter, who, by her matchless beauty, had captivated and married a prince of royal blood.

The chronicles of those times related that the wicked innlady, steadfast in her stern resolve, tried once more to destroy her daughter, so full was she of jealousy and revenge.

But her daughter was now so far removed from her clutches and her sphere that she could not carry out her cruel purpose, and thus ends this wonderful history of a beauty and her magical slippers.

Translated by Henriqueta Monteiro.

Gold Tree and Silver Tree (1894)[202]

Joseph Jacobs

Once upon a time there was a king who had a wife, whose name was Silver-tree, and a daughter, whose name was Gold-tree. On a certain day of the days, Gold-tree and Silver-tree went to a glen, where there was a well, and in it there was a trout.

Said Silver-tree, "Troutie, bonny little fellow, am not I the most beautiful queen in the world?"

"Oh! indeed you are not."

"Who then?"

"Why, Gold-tree, your daughter."

Silver-tree went home, blind with rage. She lay down on the bed, and vowed she would never be well until she could get the heart and the liver of Gold-tree, her daughter, to eat.

---

202. *More English Fairy Tales* (London: David Nutt, 1894).

At nightfall the king came home, and it was told him that Silver-tree, his wife, was very ill. He went where she was, and asked her what was wrong with her.

"Oh! only a thing—which you may heal if you like."

"Oh! indeed there is nothing at all which I could do for you that I would not do."

"If I get the heart and the liver of Gold-tree, my daughter, to eat, I shall be well."

Now it happened about this time that the son of a great king had come from abroad to ask Gold-tree for marrying. The king now agreed to this, and they went abroad.

The king then went and sent his lads to the hunting-hill for a he-goat, and he gave its heart and its liver to his wife to eat; and she rose well and healthy.

A year after this Silver-tree went to the glen, where there was the well in which there was the trout.

"Troutie, bonny little fellow," said she, "am not I the most beautiful queen in the world?"

"Oh! indeed you are not."

"Who then?"

"Why, Gold-tree, your daughter."

"Oh! well, it is long since she was living. It is a year since I ate her heart and liver."

"Oh! indeed she is not dead. She is married to a great prince abroad."

Silver-tree went home, and begged the king to put the long-ship in order, and said, "I am going to see my dear Gold-tree, for it is so long since I saw her." The long-ship was put in order, and they went away.

It was Silver-tree herself that was at the helm, and she steered the ship so well that they were not long at all before they arrived.

The prince was out hunting on the hills. Gold-tree knew the long-ship of her father was coming.

"Oh!" said she to the servants, "my mother is coming, and she will kill me."

"She shall not kill you at all; we will lock you in a room where she cannot get near you."

This is how it was done; and when Silver-tree came ashore, she began to cry out:

"Come to meet your own mother, when she comes to see you." Gold-tree said that she could not, that she was locked in the room, and that she could not get out of it.

"Will you not put out," said Silver-tree, "your little finger through the key-hole, so that your own mother may give a kiss to it?"

She put out her little finger, and Silver-tree went and put a poisoned stab in it, and Gold-tree fell dead.

When the prince came home, and found Gold-tree dead, he was in great sorrow, and when he saw how beautiful she was, he did not bury her at all, but he locked her in a room where nobody would get near her.

In the course of time he married again, and the whole house was under the hand of this wife but one room, and he himself always kept the key of that room. On a certain day of the days he forgot to take the key with him, and the second wife got into the room. What did she see there but the most beautiful woman that she ever saw. She began to turn and try to wake her, and she noticed the poisoned stab in her finger. She took the stab out, and Gold-tree rose alive, as beautiful as she was ever.

At the fall of night the prince came home from the hunting-hill, looking very downcast.

"What gift," said his wife, "would you give me that I could make you laugh?"

"Oh! indeed, nothing could make me laugh, except Gold-tree were to come alive again."

"Well, you'll find her alive down there in the room."

When the prince saw Gold-tree alive he made great rejoicings, and he began to kiss her, and kiss her, and kiss her.

Said the second wife, "Since she is the first one you had it is better for you to stick to her, and I will go away."

"Oh! indeed you shall not go away, but I shall have both of you."

At the end of the year, Silver-tree went to the glen, where there was the well, in which there was the trout.

"Troutie, bonny little fellow," said she, "am not I the most beautiful queen in the world?"

"Oh! indeed you are not."

"Who then?"

"Why, Gold-tree, your daughter."

"Oh! well, she is not alive. It is a year since I put the poisoned stab into her finger."

"Oh! indeed she is not dead at all, at all."

Silver-tree, went home, and begged the king to put the long-ship in order, for that she was going to see her dear Gold-tree, as it was so long since she saw her. The long-ship was put in order, and they went away. It was Silver-tree herself that was at the helm, and she steered the ship so well that they were not long at all before they arrived.

The prince was out hunting on the hills. Gold-tree knew her father's ship was coming.

"Oh!" said she, "my mother is coming, and she will kill me."

"Not at all," said the second wife; "we will go down to meet her."

Silver-tree came ashore. "Come down, Gold-tree, love," said she, "for your own mother has come to you with a precious drink."

"It is a custom in this country," said the second wife, "that the person who offers a drink takes a draught out of it first."

Silver-tree put her mouth to it, and the second wife went and struck it so that some of it went down her throat, and she fell dead. They had only to carry her home a dead corpse and bury her.

The prince and his two wives were long alive after this, pleased and peaceful. I left them there.

A Tuscan Snow-White and the Dwarfs (1905)[203]

Isabella Anderton

Once upon a time there lived a king who had one little girl called Elisa. She was a dear little girl, and her father and mother loved her very much. But presently her mother died, and the stepmother got quite angry with jealousy of the poor little thing. She thought and she thought what she could do to her, and at last she called a witch and said: "Get rid of Elisa for me."

The witch spirited her away into some meadows a long, long way off, in quite another country, and left her there all alone so that poor little Elisa was very frightened. Presently there came by three fairies who loved her because she was so pretty, and asked her who she was. She said she was a king's daughter, but she did not know where her home was or how she had come to be where she was now, and that she was very unhappy.

"Come with us," said the fairies, "and we will take care of you."

So they led her into another field where was a big hole. They took her down into the hole, and there was the most beautiful palace that Elisa had ever seen in her life.

"This palace is yours," said the fairies. "Live here, and do just as you like."

Well, time went by, and Elisa forgot her home and was very happy, when one night her stepmother had a dream. She dreamt that Elisa was not dead, but alive and happy. She called the witch again, and said "Elisa is not dead, she is alive and well. Take some schiacciata (a kind of cake), put poison in it, and take it to her. She is very fond of schiacciata, and will be sure to eat it."

So the witch went to the hole and called "Elisa."

"What do you want?" said Elisa.

"Here's some schiacciata for you."

"I don't want schiacciata," said Elisa. "I have plenty."

"Well, I'll put it here, and you can take it if you like."

So she put it down and went away. Presently there came by a dog, who ate the schiacciata and immediately fell down dead. In the evening the fairies came home, took up the dog, and showed him to Elisa.

"See you never take anything that anyone brings you," said they, "or this will happen to you, too."

Then they put the dog into their garden.

After a time the queen dreamt again that Elisa was alive and happy, so she called the witch and said: "Elisa is very fond of flowers; pick a bunch and cast a spell upon them so that whoever smells them shall be bewitched."

The witch did as she was told and took the flowers to the hole.

"Elisa," she called down.

"What is it?" said Elisa.

"Here are some flowers for you."

---

203. *Tuscan Folk-lore and Sketches: Together with Some Other Papers* (London: Arnold Fairbairns, 1905).

"Well, you can put them down and go away. I don't want them."

So the witch put them down and went home. Soon some sheep and a shepherd came by. The sheep saw the flowers, smelt them, and became spell-bound. The shepherd went to drive off the sheep and became spell-bound too. When the fairies came home that night, they found the sheep and the shepherd, showed them to Elisa as a warning, and put them too into their garden.

But the queen dreamt a third time, and a third time she called the witch, saying: "Elisa is well and happy. Take a pair of golden slippers this time, pianelle (slippers with a covering for the toe only), bewitch them, and take them to Elisa, for those she will certainly put on."

And the queen was right. When the witch had gone away from the hole, Elisa came up to look at the pretty golden pianelle. First she took them in her hands, and then she put one on, and afterwards the other. As soon as she had done it, she was quite spell-bound and could not move. When the fairies came home, they were very sad. They took her up and put her into the garden with the dog, the sheep, and the shepherd, because they did not know what else to do with her. There she stayed a long time, till one day the king's son rode by as he went out hunting. He looked through the garden gate, and saw Elisa.

"Oh, look," said he to the hunters, "look at that lovely girl who does not move. I never saw anyone so beautiful. I must have her."

So he went into the garden, took Elisa, carried her home, and put her into a glass case in his room. Now he spent all the time in his room and would never come out and would not even let the servants in to make his bed, for he loved Elisa more and more every day and could not bear to leave her, or to let anyone else see her.

"What can be in there?" said the servants. "We can't keep his room clean if we're not allowed to go into it."

So they watched their opportunity, and one day when the prince had gone to take the holy water, they made their way in to dust.

"Oh! Oh!" said they. "The prince was quite wise to keep his room shut up. What a beautiful woman, and what lovely slippers!"

With that one went up, and said, "This slipper's a little dusty. I'll dust it."

While he was doing so, it moved. So, he pushed it a little more, and it came off altogether. Then he took off the other too, and immediately Elisa came back to life. When the prince came home, he wanted to marry her at once, but his father said:

"How do you know who she is? She may be a beggar's daughter."

"Oh, no," said Elisa, "I'm a princess," and she told them her father's name.

Then a grand wedding feast was prepared, to which her father and stepmother were invited, and they came, not knowing who the bride was to be. When they saw Elisa, the father was very glad, but the stepmother was so angry that she went and hanged herself. Nevertheless, the marriage feast went off merrily. Elisa and the prince were very happy and presently united the two kingdoms under their single rule. If they're not alive now, they must be dead, and if they're not dead, they must still be alive.

17. THE TAMING OF SHREWS

ATU 900—KING THRUSHBEARD

This tale type is perhaps one of the most sexist told throughout the Renaissance period and in the following centuries. It generally concerns an arrogant princess who demeans and insults her suitors. Because of her pride, her father banishes her from his kingdom. Sometimes he makes a pact to humiliate his daughter with one of the insulted princes, who disguises himself as a commoner (baker, cook, beggar, performer), and sometimes the insulted prince charms her with extraordinary gifts, sleeps with her, and makes her pregnant. The prince takes her to his own kingdom and compels her to work, often scolding her and beating her. Once she is sufficiently punished, the "commoner" reveals his true identity as prince, and they marry, for she is indeed "fit" to become a queen.

The shaming of a princess by a gardener, fool, lower-class man, or prince disguised as a beggar or peasant became a motif in many oral and literary tales beginning in the medieval period. In the thirteenth-century erotic tale written in middle high German verse "Diu halbe bir" or "Die halbe Birne" ("Half a Pear"), there is a mighty king who decides to offer his daughter in marriage to the knight who shows his valor and wins a tournament. When a knight named Arnold wins the tournament, he is invited to a feast, where pears are served, one for two people. He cuts a pear in half without peeling it. After he eats his half, he offers the princess the other half, and she is so insulted that she berates him before all the guests. Arnold is enraged and departs, swearing revenge. He returns later as a court fool and is allowed to enter the princess's salon to entertain her and her ladies. She becomes so sexually aroused by his antics that she yields to his amorous advances. Then Arnold leaves, discards his disguise, and returns to the court as knight. When the princess sees him again, she begins to mock him as the knight with half a pear. However, he responds with a retort that makes her aware of his amorous conquest of the night before. Consequently, he compels her to become his wife.

A similar version can be found in the fourteenth-century Icelandic legend "Clárus" written by Jón Halldórsson. There is also a fascinating Arabic tale, "Prince Behram and the Princess Al-Datma" (c. twelfth–fourteenth centuries), which was part of a manuscript that formed *The Arabian Nights* and was eventually published in English in Richard Burton's *The Book of the Thousand Nights and a Night* (1885–1886). In this version the extraordinarily beautiful Princess Al-Datma proclaims that she will only marry the prince who can defeat her with his lance and sword in fair battle. For a while nobody can do this, not even the Persian Behram, whom she tricks and humiliates. He then disguises himself as an old man selling trinkets to gain entrance to her garden. Once there he rapes her, and she goes off with him because she does not want to live in dishonor in her own country. Later she is reconciled with her father. Shakespeare used the motif of humiliation in *The Taming of the Shrew* (1605), and Luigi Allemanni's novella "Bianca, figliuola del conte di Tolosa" (1531) had a direct influence on Giambattista's "Pride Punished" in *Lo Cunto de li cunti* (1634).

The popularity of the literary tales had a strong influence on the oral tradition, and the mutual development of different oral and literary versions led to Hans Christian Andersen's "The Swineherd" (1842) and Ludwig Bechstein's "Vom Zornbraten" in *Deutsches Märchenbuch* (1857). Ernst Philippson's *Der Märchentypus von König Drosselbart* is an excellent study of the folklore and literary background of this tale type. For the most part, the tales about so-called "shrews" represented a patriarchal viewpoint of how women, particularly courtly women, were to order their lives according to the dictates and demands of their fathers/husbands. In addition, the women fulfill the dreams of men's imaginations, and the sadism of the tale is often concealed by the humorous manner in which a haughty woman must learn "humility."

The Grimms received their 1812 version from the Family von Haxthausen, and Wilhelm's changes were already evident in the second edition of 1819 where the tale is based on a version he heard from Dorothea Wild. They believed that the name "Drosselbart" may have stemmed from the name "Brösselbart" or "Brotbröseln" (bread crumbs) and may be related to the crumbs that stick to the beard of the prince, indicating shabby manners. However, not all the humiliated princes have a name or are rejected by the princess because of bad manners, as the following European versions indicate. In the end, it is always the princess who is humiliated because she is the one who must learn good manners. This can also be seen in other versions by Gradi, Knust, Nerucci, Coelho, Grundtvig, Kristensen, Zingerele, Kuhn, Pröhle, Sébillot, Dardy, and Luzel.

******

King Thrushbeard (1812)[204]
Jacob and Wilhelm Grimm

A king had a daughter who was marvelously beautiful but so proud and haughty that she rejected one suitor after the other out of stubbornness and ridiculed them as well. Once her father held a great feast and invited all the marriageable young men to the event. They were all lined up according to their rank and class: first came the kings, then the dukes, princes, counts, and barons, and finally the gentry. The king's daughter was led down the line, and she found fault with each one of the suitors there. In particular, she made the most fun of a good king who stood at the head of the line and had a chin that was a bit crooked.

"My goodness!" she exclaimed and laughed. "He's got a chin like a thrush's beak!"

From then on, everyone called him Thrushbeard.

---

204. "König Drosselbart," *Kinder- und Haus-Märchen. Gesammelt durch die Brüder Grimm*, 2 vols. (Berlin: Realschulbuchhandlung, 1812/1815).

When her father saw how she did nothing but ridicule people, he became furious and swore that she would have to marry the very first beggar who came to his door. A few days later a minstrel appeared and began singing beneath the princess's window. When the king heard him, he ordered the man to come up to him immediately. Despite his dirty appearance, his daughter had to accept him as her bridegroom. A minister was summoned right away, and the wedding took place. After the wedding was concluded, the king said to his daughter: "It's not fitting for you to stay in my palace any longer since you're a beggar woman. You must now depart with your husband."

The beggar took her away, and as they walked through a huge forest, she asked the beggar:

> "Tell me, who might the owner of this beautiful forest be?"
> "King Thrushbeard owns the forest and all you can see.
> If you had taken him, it would belong to you."
> "Alas, poor me! What can I do?
> I should have wed King Thrushbeard. If only I knew!"

Soon they crossed a meadow, and she asked again:

> "Tell me, who might the owner of this beautiful green meadow be?"
> "King Thrushbeard owns the meadow and all you can see.
> If you had taken him, it would belong to you."
> "Alas, poor me! What can I do?
> I should have wed King Thrushbeard. If only I knew!"

Then they came to a large city, and she asked once more:

> "Tell me, who might the owner of this beautiful big city be?"
> "King Thrushbeard owns the forest and all you can see.
> If you had taken him, it would belong to you."
> "Alas, poor me! What can I do?
> I should have wed King Thrushbeard. If only I knew!"

The minstrel became very grumpy when he heard that she always desired another man and didn't think that he was good enough for her. Finally they came to a tiny cottage.

> "Oh, Lord! What a wretched tiny house!
> It's not even fit for a mouse."

The beggar answered, "This house is our house, and we shall live here together." Now, make a fire at once and put the water on so you can cook me my meal. I'm very tired."

However, the king's daughter knew nothing about cooking, and the beggar had to lend a hand himself. So things went reasonably well, and after they had eaten, they went to bed. But the next morning she had to get up very early and work. For a few days they lived miserably until the man finally said: "Wife, we can't go on this way any longer. We're eating everything up and not earning anything. You've got to weave baskets."

He went out and cut some willows and brought them home, and she had to begin to weave baskets. However, the rough willows bruised her hands.

"I see that you can't do this work," said the man. "Then you should try spinning. Perhaps you'll be better at that."

She sat down and spun, but her fingers were so soft that the hard thread soon cut her, and blood began to flow.

"You're not fit for any kind of work," the man said with irritation. "I'm going to start a business with earthenware. You're to sit in the marketplace and sell the wares."

The first time everything went well. People gladly bought her pots because she was beautiful, and they paid what she asked. Indeed, many gave her money and didn't even bother to take the pots with them. When everything had been sold, her husband bought a lot of new earthenware. Once again his wife sat down with it at the marketplace and hoped to make a good profit. Suddenly, a drunken hussar came galloping along and rode right over the pots so that they were all smashed to pieces. The woman became terrified, and for the rest of the day she didn't dare to go home. When she finally did, the beggar was nowhere to be seen.

For some time she lived in poverty and in great need. Then a man came and invited her to a wedding. She wanted to take all kinds of leftovers from the wedding and live off them for a while. So she put on her little coat with a pot underneath and stuck a large leather purse with it. The wedding was magnificent and with plenty of good things. She filled the pot with soup and her leather purse with scraps. As she was about to leave with everything, one of the guests demanded that she dance with him. She resisted with all her might, but to no avail. He grabbed hold of her, and she had to go with him. All at once the pot fell so that the soup flowed on the ground, and the many scraps also tumbled out of her purse. When the guests saw all this, they broke out in laughter and ridiculed her.

She was so ashamed that she wished she were a thousand fathoms under the earth. She ran out the door and tried to escape, but a man caught up with her on the stairs and brought her back. When she looked at him, she saw it was King Thrushbeard, and he said: "I and the beggar are the same person, and I was also the hussar who rode over your pots and smashed them to pieces. All this happened to you for your benefit and to punish you because you had ridiculed me some time ago. Now, however, our wedding will be celebrated."

Then her father also appeared with his entire court, and she was cleaned and magnificently dressed appropriate for her position, and the festive event was her marriage with King Thrushbeard.

King Thrushbeard (1857)[205]

Jacob and Wilhelm Grimm

A king had a daughter whose beauty was beyond comparison, but she was so proud and haughty that no suitor was good enough for her. Indeed, she rejected one after the other and ridiculed them as well. Once her father held a great feast and invited all the marriageable young men from far and wide to attend. They were all lined up according to their rank and class: first came the kings, then the dukes, princes, counts, and barons, and finally the gentry. The king's daughter was led down the line, and she found fault with each one of the suitors there. One was too fat for her. "That wine barrel!" she said. Another was too tall. "Tall and thin, he looks like a pin!" The third was too short. "Short and fat, he's built like a vat!" The fourth was too pale. "He resembles death!" The fifth was too red. "What a rooster!" The sixth did not stand straight enough. "Green wood, not good enough to burn!"

There was not a single man whom she didn't criticize, but she made the most fun of a good king who stood at the head of the line and had a chin that was a bit crooked.

"My goodness!" she exclaimed and laughed. "He's got a chin like a thrush's beak!" From then on, everyone called him Thrushbeard.

When her father saw that she did nothing but ridicule people, and that she scorned all the suitors who were gathered there, he was furious and swore that she would have to marry the very first beggar who came to his door. A few days later a minstrel came and began singing beneath the windows to earn some money. As soon as the king heard him, he said, "Have him come up here."

The minstrel, who was dressed in dirty, tattered clothes, entered the hall and sang in front of the king and his daughter. When he was finished, he asked for a modest reward.

"Your singing has pleased me so much," the king said, "that I shall give you my daughter for your wife."

The king's daughter was horrified, but the king said, "I swore I'd give you to the very first beggar who came along, and I intend to keep my word."

All her objections were to no avail. The minister was fetched, and she was compelled to wed the minstrel. When that was done, the king said, "It's not fitting for you to stay in my palace any longer since you're now a beggar woman. I want you to depart with your husband."

205. "König Drosselbart," *Kinder- und Hausmärchen gesammelt durch die Brüder Grimm*, 7th ed., 3 vols. (Göttingen: Verlag der Dieterischen Buchhandlung, 1857).

The beggar took her by the hand, and she had to go with him on foot. When they came to a huge forest, she asked:

> "Tell me, who might the owner of this forest be?"
> "King Thrushbeard owns the forest and all you can see.
> If you had taken him, it would belong to you."
> "Alas, poor me! What can I do?
> I should have wed King Thrushbeard. If only I knew!"

Soon they crossed a meadow, and she asked again:

> "Tell me, who might the owner of this meadow be?"
> "King Thrushbeard owns the meadow and all you can see.
> If you had taken him, it would belong to you."
> "Alas, poor me! What can I do?
> I should have wed King Thrushbeard. If only I knew!"

Then they came to a large city, and she asked once more:

> "Tell me, who might the owner of this city be?"
> "King Thrushbeard owns the city and all you can see.
> If you had taken him, it would belong to you."
> "Alas, poor me! What can I do?
> I should have wed King Thrushbeard. If only I knew!"

"I'm not at all pleased by this," said the minstrel. "Why are you always wishing for another husband? Do you think I'm not good enough for you?"

Finally, they came to a tiny cottage, and she said:

> "Oh, Lord! What a wretched tiny house!
> It's not even fit for a mouse."

The minstrel answered, "This house is mine and yours, and we shall live here together."

She had to stoop to get through the low doorway.

"Where are the servants?" the king's daughter asked.

"What servants?" asked the beggar. "You must do everything yourself if you want something done. Now, make a fire at once and put the water on so you can cook me my meal. I'm very tired."

However, the king's daughter knew nothing about making a fire or cooking, and the beggar had to lend a hand himself if he wanted anything done in a tolerable fashion. After they had eaten their meager meal, they went to bed. But the next morning he got her up very early because she had to take care of the house. For a few days they lived like this and managed as best they could. When they had consumed all their provisions, the man said, "Wife, we can't go on this way any longer. We've used everything up, and we're not earning a thing. You've got to weave baskets."

He went out to cut some willows and brought them home, but the rough willows brushed her tender hands.

"I see that won't work," said the man. "Let's try spinning. Perhaps you'll be better at that."

She sat down at the spinning wheel and tried to spin, but the hard thread soon cut her soft fingers, and blood began to flow.

"See now," said the man. "You're not fit for any kind of work. I made a bad bargain when I got you. But let's see how things go if I start a business with pots and earthenware. You're to sit in the marketplace and sell the wares."

'Oh,' she thought, 'if some people from my father's kingdom come to the marketplace and see me selling wares, they'll surely make fun of me!'

But there was no way to avoid it. She had to obey her husband if she did not want to die of hunger. The first time everything went well. People gladly bought her wares because she was beautiful, and they paid what she asked. Indeed, many gave her money and didn't even bother to take the pots with them. So the couple lived off their earnings as long as they lasted. Then her husband bought a lot of new earthenware. His wife sat down with it at a corner in the marketplace, set her wares around her, and offered them for sale. Suddenly, a drunken hussar came galloping along and rode right over the pots so that they were all smashed to pieces. She began to weep and was paralyzed with fear.

"Oh, what's going to happen to me?" she exclaimed. "What will my husband say?"

She ran home and told him about the accident, and he responded by saying, "In Heaven's name, who would ever sit down at a corner in the marketplace with earthenware? Now stop your weeping. I see full well that you're not fit for proper work. I've already been to the king's castle and have asked whether they could use a kitchen maid, and they've promised me to take you on. In return you'll get free meals."

Now the king's daughter became a kitchen maid and had to assist the cook and do the most menial kind of work. She sewed two little jars inside her pockets and carried home the leftovers so they could have some food to live on. One day it so happened that the king was celebrating his wedding, and the poor woman went upstairs, stood outside the door of the large hall, and wanted to look inside. When the candles were lit, the guests entered, one more exquisitely dressed than the next, and everything was full of splendor. With a sad heart she thought about her fate and cursed her own pride and arrogance for bringing about her humiliation and great poverty. Sometimes the servants threw her pieces of the delicious dishes they were carrying in and out of the hall, and she could also smell the aroma of the food. She put the pieces into her pockets and intended to carry them home.

Suddenly the king entered. He was dressed in velvet and silk and had a golden chain around his neck. And, when he saw the beautiful woman standing in the doorway, he grabbed her by the hand and wanted to dance with her, but she refused. Indeed, she was horrified because she saw it was King Thrushbeard, who had courted her and whom she had rejected with scorn. Although she struggled, it was to no avail, for he pulled her into the hall. Then the string that held her pockets together broke, and the jars fell out, causing the soup to spill and the scraps of food to scatter on the floor. When the people saw that, they laughed a good deal and poked fun at her. She was so ashamed that she wished she were a thousand fathoms under the earth. She ran out the door and tried to escape, but a man caught up with her on the stairs and brought her back. When she looked at him, she saw it was King Thrushbeard again, and he said to her in a friendly way, "Don't be afraid. I and the minstrel who lived with you in the wretched cottage are one and the same person. I disguised myself out of love for you, and I was also the hussar who rode over your pots and smashed them to pieces. I did all that to humble your proud spirit and to punish you for the insolent way you behaved toward me."

Then she shed bitter tears and said, "I've done a great wrong and don't deserve to be your wife."

However, he said, "Console yourself. The bad days are over. Now we shall celebrate our wedding."

The chambermaids came and dressed her in splendid clothes, and her father came along with his entire court, and they wished her happiness in her marriage with King Thrushbeard. Then the real rejoicing began, and I wish that you and I had been there, too.

Hacon Grizzlebeard (1852)[206]

Peter Christen Asbjørnsen and Jørgen Moe

Once upon a time there was a princess who was so proud and pert that no suitor was good enough for her. She made game of them all and sent them about their business, one after the other. But though she was so proud, still new suitors kept on coming to the palace, for she was a beauty, the wicked hussy!

So one day there came a prince to woo her, and his name was Hacon Grizzlebeard. The first night he was there, the princess bade the king's fool cut off the ears of one of the prince's horses and slit the jaws of the other up to the ears. When the prince went out to drive next day, the princess stood in the porch and looked at him.

"Well!" she cried, "I never saw the like of this in all my life. The keen north wind that blows here has taken the ears off one of your horses, and the other has stood by and gaped at what was going on till his jaws have split right up to his ears."

206. *Popular Tales from the Norse*, trans. George Webbe Dasent (Edinburgh: Edmonston & Douglas, 1859).

And with that she burst out into a roar of laughter, ran in, slammed the door, and let him drive off.

So he drove home, but as he went, he thought to himself that he would pay her off one day. After a bit, he put on a great beard of moss, threw a great fur cloak over his clothes, and dressed himself up just like any beggar. He went to a goldsmith and bought a golden spinning wheel. Then he sat down with it under the princess's window and began to file away at his spinning wheel, and to turn it this way and that, for it wasn't quite in order, and besides, it wanted a stand.

So when the princess rose up in the morning, she came to the window, threw it up, and called out to the beggar if he would sell his golden spinning wheel?

"No, it isn't for sale," said Hacon Grizzlebeard, "but if I may have leave to sleep outside your bedroom door tonight, I'll give it you."

Well, the princess thought it a good bargain. There could be no danger in letting him sleep outside her door. So she got the wheel, and at night Hacon Grizzlebeard lay down outside her bedroom. But as the night wore on he began to freeze.

"Hutetutetutetu! It is so cold! Do let me in!" he cried.

"You've lost your wits outright, I think," said the princess.

"Oh, hutetutetutetu! It is so bitter cold, pray do let me in," said Hacon Grizzlebeard again.

"Hush! Hush! Hold your tongue!" said the princess. "If my father were to know that there was a man in the house, I should be in a fine scrape."

"Oh, hutetutetutetu! I'm almost frozen to death! Just let me come inside and lie on the floor," said Hacon Grizzlebeard.

Yes! There was no help for it. She had to let him in, and when he was, he lay on the ground and slept like a top.

Some time after, Hacon came again with the stand to the spinning wheel and sat down under the princess's window, and began to file at it, for it was not quite fit for use. When she heard him filing, she threw up the window and began to talk to him, and to ask what he had there.

"Oh! Only the stand to that spinning wheel which your royal highness bought, for I thought, as you had the wheel, you might like to have the stand too."

"What do you want for it?" asked the princess, but it was not for sale any more than the wheel, but she might have them if she would give him leave to sleep on the floor of her bedroom next night.

Well she gave him leave, only he was to be sure to lie still and not to shiver and call out "hutetu," or any such stuff. Hacon Grizzlebeard promised fair enough, but as the night wore on he began to shiver and shake and to ask whether he might not come nearer and lie on the floor alongside the princess's bed.

There was no help for it. She had to give him leave, lest the king should hear the noise he made. So Hacon Grizzlebeard lay alongside the princess's bed and slept like a top.

It was a long while before Hacon Grizzlebeard came again, but when he came, he had with him a golden wool-winder, and he sat down and began to file away at it under the princess's window. Then came the old story over again. When the princess heard what was going on, she came to the window and asked him how he did, and whether he would sell the golden wool-winder?

"It is not to be had for money, but if you'll give me leave to sleep tonight in your bedroom with my head on your bedstead, you shall have it for nothing," said Hacon Grizzlebeard.

Well! She would give him leave, if he only gave his word to be quiet and make no noise. So he said he would do his best to be still, but as the night wore on he began to shiver and shake, so that his teeth chattered again.

"Hutetutetutetu! It is so bitter cold! Oh, do let me get into bed and warm myself a little," said Hacon Grizzlebeard.

"Get into bed!" said the princess. "Why, you must have lost your wits!"

"Hutetutetutetu!" said Flacon. "Do let me get into bed. Hutetutetutetu!"

"Hush! Hush! Be still for God's sake!" cried the princess. "If father knows there is a man in here, I shall be in a sad plight. I'm sure he'll kill me on the spot."

"Hutetutetutetu! Let me get into bed," said Hacon Grizzlebeard, who kept on shivering so that the whole room shook. Well! There was no help for it. She had to let him get into bed, where he slept both sound and soft. But a little while after, the princess had a child, at which the king grew so wild with rage that he was near making an end of both mother and babe.

Just after this happened, Hacon Grizzlebeard came tramping that way once more, as if by chance, and took his seat down in the kitchen, like any other beggar. So when the princess came out and saw him, she cried, "Ah, God have mercy on me, for the ill-luck you have brought on me! Father is ready to burst with rage. Do let me follow you to your home."

"Oh! I'll be bound! You're too well bred to follow me," said Hacon, "for I have nothing but a log to live in. And how shall I ever get food for you? I can't tell, for it's just as much as I can do to get food for myself."

"Oh yes! It's all the same to me how you get it, or whether you get it at all," she said. "Just let me be with you, for if I stay here any longer, my father will be sure to take my life."

So she got leave to be with the beggar, as she called him, and they walked a long, long way, though she was but a poor hand at tramping. When she passed out of her father's land into another, she asked whose it was?

"Oh! This is Hacon Grizzlebeard's, if you must know," said he.

"Indeed!" said the Princess. "I might have married him if I chose, and then I should not have had to walk about like a beggar's wife."

So, whenever they came to grand castles, woods, and parks, and she asked whose they were, the beggar's answer was still the same: "Oh! They are Hacon Grizzlebeard's." And the princess was in a sad way that she had not chosen the man who had such broad lands. Last of all they came to a palace, where he said he was known, and where he thought he could get her work so that they might have something to live on. Then he built up a cabin by the wood-side for them to dwell in, and every day he went to the king's palace, as he said, to hew wood and draw water for the cook, and when he came back, he brought a few scraps of meat, but they did not go very far.

One day, when he came home from the palace, he said, "Tomorrow I will stay at home and look after the baby, but you must get ready to go to the palace, do you hear? The prince said you were to come and try your hand at baking."

"I bake!" said the Princess. "I can't bake, for I never did such a thing in my life."

"Well, you must go," said Hacon, "because the prince has said it. If you can't bake, you can learn. You have only got to look how the rest bake, and mind, when you leave, you must steal me some bread."

"I can't steal," said the princess.

"You can learn that, too," said Hacon. "You know we live on short commons. But take care that the prince doesn't see you, for he has eyes at the back of his head."

So when she was well on her way, Hacon ran by a shortcut and reached the palace long before her, threw off his rags and beard, and put on his princely robes.

The princess took her turn in the bakehouse and did as Hacon bade her, for she stole bread till her pockets were crammed full. So when she was about to go home, the prince said: "We don't know much of this old wife of Hacon Grizzlebeard's. I think we'd best see if she has taken anything away with her."

So he thrust his hand into all her pockets and felt her all over, and when he found the bread, he was in a great rage, and led them all a sad life. She began to weep and bewail, and said: "The beggar made me do it, and I couldn't help it."

"Well," said the prince at last, "it ought to have gone hard with you, but all the same, for the sake of the beggar, you shall be forgiven this once."

When she was well on her way, he threw off his robes, put on his skin cloak, and his false beard, and reached the cabin before her. When she came home, he was busy nursing the baby.

"Well, you have made me do what it went against my heart to do. This is the first time I ever stole, and this shall be the last." And with that she told him how it had gone with her, and what the prince had said.

A few days later Hacon Grizzlebeard came home and said: "Tomorrow I must stay at home and mind the babe, for they are going to kill a pig at the palace, and you must help to make the sausages."

"I make sausages!" said the princess. "I can't do any such thing. I have eaten sausages often enough, but as to making them, I never made one in my life."

Well, there was no help for it. The prince had said it, and go she must. As for not knowing how, she was only to do what the others did, and at the same time Hacon bade her steal some sausages for him.

"Nay, but I can't steal them," she said. "You know how it went last time."

"Well, you can learn to steal. Who knows but you may have better luck next time," said Hacon Grizzlebeard.

When she was well on her way, Hacon ran by a shortcut, reached the palace long before her, threw off his skin cloak and false beard, and stood in the kitchen with his royal robes before she came in. So the princess stood by when the pig was killed and made sausages with the rest and did as Hacon bade her, and stuffed her pockets full of sausages. But when she was about to go home, the prince said, "This beggar's wife was long-fingered last time. I may as well just see if she hasn't carried anything off."

So he began to thrust his hands into her pockets, and when he found the sausages, he was in a great rage again and made a great to-do, threatening to send for the constable and put her into the cage.

"Oh, God bless your royal highness! Do let me off. The beggar made me do it," she said, and wept bitterly.

"Well," said Hacon, "you ought to smart for it, but for the beggar's sake, you shall be forgiven."

When she was gone, he changed his clothes again, ran by the shortcut, and when she reached the cabin, there he was before her. Then she told him the whole story, and swore, through thick and thin, it should be the last time he got her to do such a thing.

Now, it fell out a little time after, when the man came back from the palace, he said: "Our prince is going to be married, but the bride is sick, so the tailor can't measure her for her wedding gown. And the prince's will is, that you should go up to the palace and be measured instead of the bride, for he says you are just the same height and shape. But after you have been measured, mind you don't go away. You can stand about, you know, and when the tailor cuts out the gown, you can snap up the largest pieces, and bring them home for a waistcoat for me."

"Nay, but I can't steal," she said; "besides, you know how it went last time."

"You can learn then," said Hacon, "and you may have better luck, perhaps."

She thought it bad, but still she went and did as she was told. She stood by while the tailor was cutting out the gown, and she swept down all the biggest scraps, and stuffed them into her pockets. And when she was going away, the prince said:

"We may as well see if this old girl has not been long-fingered this time, too."

So he began to feel and search her pockets, and when he found the pieces, he was in a rage and began to stamp and scold at a great rate, while she wept and said: "Ah, pray forgive me! The beggar bade me do it, and I couldn't help it."

"Well, you ought to smart for it," said Hacon," but for the beggar's sake it shall be forgiven you."

So it went now just as it had gone before, and when she got back to the cabin, the beggar was there before her.

"Oh, heaven help me," she said. "You will be the death of me at last by making me nothing but what is wicked. The prince was in such a towering rage that he threatened me both with the constable and cage."

Some time after, Hacon came home to the cabin at even and said, "Now, the prince's will is that you should go up to the palace and stand for the bride, old lass, for the bride is still sick and keeps her bed, but he won't put off the wedding, and he says, you are so like her that no one could tell one from the other. So tomorrow you must get ready to go to the palace."

"I think you've lost your wits, both the prince and you," said she. "Do you think I look fit to stand in the bride's place? Look at me! Can any beggar's trull look worse than I?"

"Well, the prince said you were to go, and so go you must," said Hacon Grizzlebeard.

There was no help for it. Go she must, and when she reached the palace, they dressed her out so finely that no princess ever looked so smart. The bridal train went to church, where she stood for the bride, and when they came back, there was dancing and merriment in the palace. But just as she was in the midst of dancing with the prince, she saw a gleam of light through the window, and lo! the cabin by the wood-side was all one bright flame.

"Oh! The beggar, and the babe, and the cabin!" she screamed out and was just going to swoon away.

"Here is the beggar, and there is the babe, and so let the cabin burn away," said Hacon Grizzlebeard.

Then she knew him again, and after that the mirth and merriment began in right earnest. But since that time I have never heard tell anything more about them.

Translated by George Webbe Dasent.

The Humiliated Princess (1870)[207]

Laura Gonzenbach

Once upon a time there was a king who had a very beautiful daughter, but she was also very moody and proud. Indeed, she was never satisfied with any of her suitors. No matter how many came to the castle, she would laugh at them,

---

207. "Die gedemüthigte Königstochter," *Sicilianische Märchen*, 2 vols. (Leipzig: W. Engelmann, 1870).

and they would depart feeling ashamed and cursed. The king reproached her, but she didn't listen to him and continued to play the same game with all the suitors who arrived at the castle. Finally, nobody ventured to the castle to court her.

So, the king decided to send pictures of her to foreign countries, where nobody knew anything about her, and he had pictures of handsome princes sent back to him. But they didn't please his daughter. However, finally, since the king reproached her so much, she pointed to the picture of a handsome king and said, "Let him come. I'll take him for my husband."

Consequently, the old king was highly pleased and had the young king brought to his castle with great fanfare and gave him a splendid reception. There were many festivities in his honor, and everything seemed to go well. But one day, when they were sitting at the table, the princess noticed that the young king had taken a chair on which a little feather was lying, and that a drop of sauce fell on his chest while he was eating.

"Oh," she cried out, "feather on the chair, sauce on the breast!" And she didn't want him anymore. As a result, the young king became very annoyed and had to return to his country in great shame. The old king, however, became so enraged that he banished his daughter from his castle and sent her with a chambermaid out into the wide world.

So the princess wandered with the chambermaid until they came to a small city, where she rented a small house. Since they had to earn money to live, the chambermaid went about the city and bought some cloth that she took to the princess who began sewing clothes. And this is the way they lived for some time.

Meanwhile, the young prince had fallen very much in love with the princess and couldn't find peace or quiet without her. When he heard that she had been banished by her father, he disguised himself as a peddler and wandered with his boxes throughout the entire kingdom in order to possibly find her. One day he came to the city in which she was living, and since he cried out that he had various things for sale, it occurred to her that she no longer had any needles, and she called him to her house to buy some. When he saw her, he was very happy and sold her all kinds of things. While they were doing this, he conversed with her, and when he heard that she sewed clothes, he ordered a dozen shirts from her and often came by to see how far she had gotten with the work. However, he wanted to gain revenge on her for causing him to be humiliated, and so he did not reveal himself. Rather, he came by always dressed as a peddler.

After some time had passed, he took the chambermaid aside and said to her, "If it is all right with her, I'd like to marry this young maiden. To be sure, I can't marry her yet, but I'd like to take her back to my country because I can't stay here any longer."

The chambermaid went to her young mistress and persuaded her to marry the peddler.

"If I should die some day," she said to the princess, "you would be alone in the world."

The princess didn't really want to get married, but her pride had been broken, and she said "yes" and went with the peddler out into the wide world. They wandered many, many days until they came to the realm of the young king. The poor princess was so exhausted that she could barely move forward. Then her husband led her into a miserable little cottage and said, "Here you have my dwelling. We've got to make the best of it."

Now the tender princess had to do all the work—cook, wash, and sew, and each morning the peddler wandered about, and when he returned in the evening, he would bring some small thing to eat and say, "You see, that's all that I earned today."

However, he remained in the castle with his mother the entire day and revealed to her that he had brought the young princess who had disturbed him so much.

After some time had passed, he went to the princess one day and said, "We have to leave this place because I can't pay the rent any more. I'm going to the queen to ask her if we can have permission to live in one of the stalls in her stable. She is my patron and won't refuse me."

So he went away, and when he returned, he said, "The queen gave her permission, and from now on we'll live in a stall."

Now the tender princess had to live in a stall and sleep on straw. But she bore all this with patience and thought, 'I've deserved all of this because of my pride.' Meanwhile, her husband went away each day with his boxes to sell things. Yet, he really went just a few steps, and as soon as he was out of her sight, he went through a side door into the castle, dressed himself as king, and always went by her dwelling without her recognizing him as her husband. Instead, she recognized him as one of the suitors whom she had scorned, and she felt she might sink into the ground out of shame.

One day he went to his mother and said, "The princess hasn't been punished enough for her pride. Let her come up into the castle and work as a seamstress."

"Oh, my son," his mother said, "leave the poor girl in peace, and pardon her."

"No," he answered. "I want her to experience the same humiliation that I experienced in her hands."

Then he went to his wife and said, "There are a lot of children's clothes that have to be sewn in the castle because the king has married, and his young queen is expecting a child. The old queen has called for you so that you can help with the work."

"Oh, no," she answered. "Please let me stay here. I'm ashamed to let the young king see me."

"Come now!" he exclaimed. "How are we going to make our living? I want you to go right now. The young king won't care about you in the least. And listen to me, don't be stupid. If you can take a little shirt or a bonnet with you, then do it. You'll be needing it soon."

"Oh no," she said. "How could I do such a thing?"

"Don't make me mad!" the husband yelled. "Do what I say. You can hide it beneath your blouse."

The poor princess went into the castle, and since she was afraid of her husband, she stole a little shirt when nobody was looking and hid it beneath her blouse. When she was sitting there and sewing, however, the young king suddenly entered the room and cried, "Who is this sewing here? I recognize her as a thief."

The poor princess turned red right away, then pale, and the old queen said, "Leave the seamstress in peace, my son. She is a poor maiden who lives in one of our stalls."

"No," he said. "She is a thief, and I'll prove it."

Then he grabbed beneath her blouse and pulled out the little shirt. The poor princess was so terrified that she fainted.

"My son," the queen said. "Don't you see how the poor girl is suffering? Now stop torturing her."

"No," he said. "She hasn't been punished enough." And he had her carried down to the stall.

When it was evening again, she wept and told her husband about her misfortune and said she wouldn't return to the castle. But he was very hard with her and ordered her to go back to the castle the next morning to take something else.

"You can hide it under your apron," he insisted.

She wept bitter tears but had to obey him, and the next morning she went back into the castle, and when nobody was looking, she took two bonnets and hid them beneath her apron. Meanwhile, as she was sewing, the king entered the room and cried out, "Why have you let this thief come back here? Now I'll show you that nothing can be kept safe from her."

He reached beneath her apron and pulled out the bonnets. The princess fainted, and in spite of the pleas of the old queen, the king had her brought back to the stall.

During that night, her time had come, and she gave birth to a marvelous baby boy. Then her husband brought her some meat broth and said, "The queen has sent you this broth, and these old diapers for our son."

There was a sleeping potion in the broth, and after the princess had drunken it, she fell sound asleep. Then the king had her carried back into the castle where a beautiful bed was standing ready for her. Then he had her dressed in a garment made of the finest cloth and placed in the bed. Next to the bed stood a precious cradle for the baby prince who was also clad in garments fit for the son of a king. Finally, the young king took off the peddler's clothes and put on his royal garments. When the princess finally awoke, she looked around her in astonishment and thought she was dreaming. The king entered and asked her in a friendly way how she was feeling, but she couldn't look him in the eyes.

"Don't you recognize me?" the king asked. "I'm your husband, the peddler. I wanted to punish you for your pride. Now all your sufferings are at an end, and you are my dear wife."

When the young queen regained her health, they celebrated a splendid wedding feast, and the parents of the young queen were invited to come and were very happy to see their daughter once again.

> They lived happy and content
> and we're still worrying about the rent.

The Haughty Princess (1870)[208]
Patrick Kennedy

There was once a very worthy king, whose daughter was the greatest beauty that could be seen far or near, but she was as proud as Lucifer, and no king or prince would she agree to marry. Her father was tired out at last and invited every king, and prince, and duke, and earl that he knew or didn't know to come to his court to give her one trial more. They all came, and next day after breakfast they stood in a row in the lawn, and the princess walked along in the front of them to make her choice. One was fat, and says she, "I won't have you, Beer-barrel!" One was tall and thin, and to him she said, "I won't have you, Ramrod!" To a white-faced man she said, "I won't have you, Pale Death!" And to a red-cheeked man she said, "I won't have you, Cockscomb!" She stopped a little before the last of all, for he was a fine man in face and form. She wanted to find some defect in him, but he had nothing remarkable but a ring of brown curling hair under his chin. She admired him a little, and then carried it off with, "I won't have you, Whiskers!"

So all went away, and the king was so vexed, he said to her, "Now, to punish your impudence, I'll give you to the first beggar man or singing *sthronshuch*, that calls," and, as sure as the hearth-money, a fellow all over rags, and hair that came to his shoulders, and a bushy red beard all over his face, came next morning and began to sing before the parlour window.

When the song was over, the hall-door was opened, the singer asked in, the priest brought, and the princess married to Beardy. She roared and she bawled, but her father didn't mind her.

"There," says he to the bridegroom, "is five guineas for you. Take your wife out of my sight, and never let me lay eyes on you or her again."

Off he led her, and dismal enough she was. The only thing that gave her relief were the tones of her husband s voice and his genteel manners.

"Whose wood is this?" said she, as they were going through one. "It belongs to the king you called Whiskers yesterday."

208. *The Fireside Stories of Ireland* (Dublin: M'Glashan and Gill, 1870).

He gave her the same answer about meadows and cornfields, and at last a fine city.

"Ah, what a fool I was!" said she to herself. "He was a fine man, and I might have had him for a husband."

At last they were coming up to a poor cabin, "Why are you bringing me here?" says the poor lady.

"This was my house," said he, "and now it's yours!"

She began to cry, but she was tired and hungry, and she went in with him. Ovoch! There was neither a table laid out, nor a fire burning, and she was obliged to help her husband to light it, and boil their dinner, and clean up the place after. And next day he made her put on a stiff gown and a cotton handkerchief. When she had her house readied up, and no business to keep her employed, he brought home *sallies* [willows], peeled them, and showed her how to make baskets. But the hard twigs bruised her delicate fingers, and she began to cry. Well, then he asked her to mend their clothes, but the needle drew blood from her fingers, and she cried again. He couldn't bear to see her tears, so he bought a creel of earthenware, and sent her to the market to sell them. This was the hardest trial of all, but she looked so handsome and sorrowful, and had such a nice air about her that all her pans, and jugs, and plates, and dishes were gone before noon, and the only mark of her old pride she showed was a slap she gave a buckeen across the face when he asked her to go in an' take share of a quart.

Well, her husband was so glad, he sent her with another creel the next day, but faith, her luck was after deserting her. A drunken huntsman came up riding, and his beast got in among her ware, and made *brishe* of every mother's son of 'em. She went home cryin', and her husband wasn't at all pleased.

"I see," said he, "you're not fit for business. Come along, I'll get you a kitchen-maid's place in the palace. I know the cook."

So the poor thing was obliged to stifle her pride once more. She was kept very busy, and the footman and the butler would be very impudent about looking for a kiss, but she let a screech out of her the first attempt was made, and the cook gave the fellow such a lambasting with the besom that he made no second offer. She went home to her husband every night, and she carried broken victuals wrapped in papers in her side pockets.

A week after she got service there was great bustle in the kitchen. The king was going to be married, but no one knew who the bride was to be. Well, in the evening the cook filled the princess's pockets with cold meat and puddings, and says she, "Before you go, let us have a look at the great doings in the big parlour."

So they came near the door to get a peep, and who should come out but the king himself, as handsome as you please, and no other but King Whiskers himself.

"Your handsome helper must pay for her peeping," says he to the cook, "and dance a jig with me."

Whether she would or no, he held her hand and brought her into the parlour. The fiddlers struck up, and away went him and her. But they hadn't danced two steps when the meat and the *puddens* flew out of her pockets. Every one roared out, and she flew to the door, crying piteously. But she was soon caught by the king, and taken into the back parlour.

"Don't you know me, my darling?" said he. "I'm both King Whiskers, your husband the ballad singer, and the drunken huntsman. Your father knew me well enough when he gave you to me, and all was to drive your pride out of you."

Well, she didn't know how she was with fright, and shame, and joy. Love was uppermost anyhow, for she laid her head on her husband's breast and cried like a child. The maids of honour soon had her away and dressed her as fine as hands and pills could do it; and there were her mother and father, too. And while the company were wondering what end of the handsome girl and the king, he and his queen, who they didn't know in her fine clothes, and the other king and queen came in, and such rejoicings and fine doings as there was, none of us will ever see, anyway.

Blanca the Haughty (1870)[209]
Rachel Busk

The Count of Tolosa had a beautiful daughter called Blanca, and he had promised her in marriage to the son of the Count of Barcelona. Both were young, and rich, and noble, and all the people from both provinces gathered together to celebrate the wedding with every testimony of interest in their happiness. But Blanca was very self-willed; she had always had every thing her own way—a noble palace in the midst of an enchanting country, plenty of servitors to do her bidding, many knights to contend for her favour; and she seemed to fancy that the whole earth and all who lived in it were made for her, and that all must conform themselves to her desires. Nothing was ever good enough to please her.

Her father had thought she would grow out of these foolish ways as she became older and wiser, and had never duly corrected her. Meanwhile, she became more practised in them and chose the occasion of her marriage-fete for the wildest of all her pranks.

While all were seated in the great hall of the castle at the high banquet, and all lips were overflowing with praises, perhaps also with envy at her happiness, the young count, offering her a basket of rich fruits, proposed to divide with her a fine pomegranate. Blanca condescended to give him permission to do so, but the count with all his dexterity could not avoid letting one of the luscious ruby pips fall upon the table. Then, as if afraid of leaving a spot before her eyes as a testimony of his awkwardness, he hastily took up the pip and put it to his mouth.

---

209. *Patranas; or Spanish Stories, Legendary and Traditional* (London: Griffith and Farran, 1870).

Blanca, who had all the morning been on the lookout in vain for some captious pretext on which to found a quarrel and show off her haughty, petulant airs, immediately caught at this one, and exclaimed, she would never be bound to such a parsimonious husband; it was an act unworthy of a noble; a man who was afraid of losing the value of a pomegranate pip must be a sorry mate indeed; he would not do for *her*!

It was vain, the young count tried to pacify her by explaining how utterly false was the view she had taken. Equally vain, that her father reasoned with her on the childishness of her conduct, or that her companions pleaded in favour of the disconcerted bridegroom. Blanca would not listen to reason, and the poor young count found himself at last left alone, an object of derision, or at least of pity, to the whole assembly.

He really loved Blanca and had before this day put up with many caprices out of his affection for her, but this was not only a tax on his patience and good temper, it was an affront on his name and lineage which must not be borne. And yet he loved Blanca too much to resort to any act of hostility which might put a further barrier between them. Uncertain how to act, he went out and rode away, spurring his horse, not caring whither he went, so that he could go far away from the face of his fellow-men and muse over his grief. But all the time there ran ringing in his head,—

"No more a noble count, I trow,
A humble shepherd seem I now!"

though he could not think what the lines meant, yet he went on till he had got far away into a distant forest, where all was savage and wild, and where there was nothing to remind him of the scenes he had passed through. There he alighted from his good steed, and threw himself on the hard ground. The sword which he had been wont to raise so bravely against the enemies of his country clanked listlessly by his side, the sharp rocks cut his cheeks, and his noble blood flowed from the rents, while he felt them not, for his heart bled with other and deeper wounds; but all the time there ran in his head the lines,

"No more a noble count, I trow,
A humble shepherd seem I now!"

After he had lain there some time, and the passion of his sorrow had so far cooled down that he began to take notice of the objects around him, he observed two milk-white doves perched lovingly side by side on the branches over his head, yet fluttering full of fear and trouble. Full of his own recent suffering, he felt singular compassion for the two frightened birds; and searching for the cause of their distress, he perceived a great hawk hovering in the air above, in ever-nearing circles, and with glaring eyes preparing to pounce on his luckless prey. The count at once understood their danger, and picking up a stone, threw it with such force and dexterous aim that it brought down the greedy hawk dead upon the ground.

The doves no sooner found themselves delivered from their pursuer than they gave every token of gladness and delight, hopping from branch to branch, fluttering away and pursuing each other, and then again loving each other in the gentlest way.

The count could not bear to see their happiness, it reminded him of his loss. So he got up and wandered on into a dark cave where he could see nothing, and there laid him down, and the lines running in his head lulled him to sleep.

> "No more a noble count, I trow,
> A humble shepherd seem I now!"

Then in his dream he saw one of the fair doves appear to him in the form of a beautiful woman; her face was of the softest pink and white, like the face of the sky at sunrise, and her eyes were so bright and lustrous that they illumined the whole cave.

"*Caballero, caballero!*" said the bright vision. "You do not recognize me, I fear. Nevertheless, I am indeed one of those poor doves whose lives you saved from the wicked hawk but now, and if I and my mate live in love of each other, it is to you we owe the boon. I am come to pay the debt I owe you, and I know there is only one way in which I can do it, and that is by telling you how to get for *your* mate Blanca, for whose sake you are now so sad. I promise you that in a very little time you shall have it all your own way with her, and she shall become as humble as she now is haughty. Meanwhile, take this ring, which I have enchanted on purpose for you, and whatever you ask of it, you will find that it will do it for you."

Then the beautiful vision disappeared, and the cave immediately became dark and gloomy as before. The moment the count woke, the memory of his vision rose up before him, and he lost no time in feeling whether he had the ring safe. There it was all right on his finger; and when he felt it, he put his confidence in the promise of the vision, and hastened to go back out of the cave and set to work.

He had no sooner found his way again into daylight than he took off his ring, and thus addressed it:

"*Anielliko, anielliko!* Now is the time come to show your devotion to me. You know how Blanca has scorned me, and how I fear to go near her again, lest she should put some fresh affront in her willfulness upon me, and yet I cannot bear to stay away from her. Tell me, ring, what I shall do?"

"Attend, attend," answered the ring. "Watch now what you see passing before your eyes."

As the ring spoke, the count saw a moor-hen scudding away across the plain, and a cock as fast as he could following after her. The hen seemed determined to have nothing to say to the cock; but the cock was so persevering that he came up to her and made her stand still and listen to him, and then he first knocked her about a good deal, and then soothed her down, and at last they both went off together quite amicably. And the ring sang:

> "The cock o'ercomes, though somewhat rough,
> So man, no less, the coy rebuff
>   Of woman!"

"I see," said the count, "what you mean, but I do *not* at all see how you mean me to carry out your plan."

"Leave that to me," said the ring. "Only do as I advise you, and according to the instructions of my lady the dove, I will give you all you wish. And now, in the first instance, you must take off all this fine armour, and all your noble dress, and put on this disguise of a shepherd. Then take this loom, as if you were going, like the poor shepherd, to weave the wool of your flock; and now come along."

As they went along together, the ring told him all that he was to do, and what to say, and it had hardly completed its instructions when they arrived at the gate of the gardens of the Count of Tolosa, every now and then interrupting its discourse to sing:

> "The cock o'ercomes, though somewhat rough,
> So man, no less, the coy rebuff
>   Of woman!"

A gruff old gardener came out to see who called; and when he saw it was only a country bumpkin of a shepherd, he was gruffer than ever, and bid him be gone.

"Gardener, gardener!" said the disguised count in his most insinuating accents, "don't you think, now, if you were to let me come in and help you, you would get through your work much more easily? You have a hard time of it, and get little rest. I am young and strong, and should soon accomplish what you have to do, and then you need not turn out so early in the morning, nor sit up so late at night watching this gate."

"*Pastorcillo, pastorcillo!*" rejoined the old gardener, quite tamed by this appeal, "I cannot say nay to such an offer. So come in."

The count lost no time in obeying and at once began fulfilling his promise by taking the sheep out of the fold and leading them out to pasture. In doing this, he took care to direct them straight towards the windows of the palace. Arrived there, he sat down and placed his loom, and began weaving away diligently after the manner of poor shepherds, and singing the while:

> "The cock o'ercomes, though somewhat rough,
> So man, no less, the coy rebuff
>   Of woman!"

He had not been sitting there long before he observed a postern in the wall which separated the castle-keep from the private gardens, open. How his heart beat! Might it not be Blanca coming out for a walk? No, it was only one of her attendants, who had come to see what the shepherd was weaving.

"Tell me, *Don Villano*,"[210] she cried, as she came near him, "what wondrous kind of stuff, is that you are weaving? Is it a heavenly or an earthly texture?"

"It is a stuff much too fine for such as *you*. It is such a stuff as has not its like in all the world and cannot be bartered for cloth of gold, for whoever wears this stuff, however old they may be, immediately appears young, and if already young, it makes them beautiful too."

And then he went on weaving, without paying any attention to her any more than if he had not seen her, nor seeming to hear any of her questions or entreaties, and singing the while,—

> "The cock o'ercomes, though somewhat rough,
> So man, no less, the coy rebuff
>   Of woman!"

When the *dueña* found she could make no impression on him, she ran off at last to call Blanca, who was not yet out of bed, crying long before she got within hearing, *"Infantina, infantina*! get up and come down quickly, for here in your gardens is a shepherd who is weaving a stuff which cannot be matched in all the world, and cannot be bartered for cloth of gold! Whoever puts on a garment made of it will instantly appear young, how old soever they may have been before. And if they are already young and beautiful, it will make them much more so."

Now the waiting-maid, it must be observed, was neither young nor pretty, and she was most desirous to get possession of the stuff; and as the shepherd would not give it to her, she was dying to make her young mistress get it from him.

Blanca's curiosity was sufficiently whetted by the description to get up in all haste and come down, and see the strange shepherd herself.

The count's heart beat indeed, as she came near, and she looked so handsome and so haughty that the sight brought back the memory of all her cruelty so that he was divided between the inclination to throw himself at her feet and beg her to come and be reasonable, and the resolve to follow the advice of the ring and give her a lesson that should make her a good wife. But the ring adjured him to keep quite quiet, and not even look up at her.

"God be with you, this morning, *villano*!"[211] she exclaimed, rather loud, with a little sharp cough, to attract his attention.

"May He have you in His good keeping, *niña*!"[212] rejoined the disguised shepherd, without looking up from his loom.

Blanca was not accustomed to be treated in this way, and she felt very much inclined to call some of the servants to chastise the supposed shepherd for his rudeness. Nevertheless, there was something about his manner that both awed

---

210. Sir Country Bumpkin.
211. Bumpkin.
212. Child.

as well as interested her to an unaccountable degree, and far too much to let her give up diving farther into the mystery that surrounded him without another attempt.

"*Villano, villano!*" she said, at last, "tell me, I pray, the tissue you are weaving, who taught you to weave it?"

"Seven fairies, lady," replied the feigned shepherd, "who live in seven towers, and who never sleep or dine, but are constantly weaving and singing this refrain, which I sing continually too, lest I should forget it:

> "The cock o'ercomes, though somewhat rough,
> So man, no less, the coy rebuff
>   Of woman!"

And with that he went on working away as before.

"I suppose you want to sell it, don't you, *villano*?" continued Blanca, trying not to look vexed. "Now if you like, I'll buy it of you, and you may ask what you like—money, or jewels, or whatever you will, and I will pay the price." And when she had said that, she thought such a bait would be sufficient to make him obsequious.

But far from this, he drew himself up proudly and told her that all her money and jewels were useless to him, that whoever makes up his mind to contemn riches is richer than all the world; and he who is content with the food and raiment earned by his daily toil cannot be bribed by gold. "But," he continued, speaking a little lower and more softly, "there is one condition on which I part with my fine weft, and only one. The woman I give it to must be *my wife!*" and then he resumed his indifferent manner again and went on weaving and singing the while:

> "The cock o'ercomes, though somewhat rough,
> So man, no less, the coy rebuff
>   Of woman!"

Blanca seemed riveted to the spot. She had long mourned—quite in secret and in silence, the loss of her fond admirer, the Count of Barcelona, and often her heart was—quite in secret and in silence—cut to the quick with the thought, 'Suppose he should never come back to me!' Though she appeared outwardly gay and haughty as before, this care was continually preying on her mind. She treasured up, quite in secret and in silence, every little thing that could remind her of him, and whenever a stranger came to her father's castle, though she pretended scarcely to look at him, she scrutinized him through and through to see if he could be bearer of any tidings from the absent count. Now there was something about the shepherd that re-awakened all her sorrows and all her hopes. She did not know what it was. She was too agitated to suspect that it was he himself, and yet she felt so drawn towards him, she could not tear herself away. The audacity of such words was great, however, coming from one in his humble garb, and she felt she must administer some strong reproof. So, assuming a show of all the indignation she could call to her aid, she half turned away exclaiming, "Begone, *villano*! Nor dare to approach me. If you come but one step nearer, I will call my father's men to kill you!"

"*Soperbica, soperbica!*"[213] replied the shepherd with most provoking coolness. "You are very proud now, but I swear to you that you will not always take that tone. You will talk to me very differently some day. For so the seven fairies promised me when they taught me the song:

> "The cock o'ercomes, though somewhat rough,
> So man, no less, the coy rebuff
>   Of woman!"

The *dueña*, who had been standing by and watching this scene with the greatest anxiety, intent only on getting a chance of possessing some of the weft which was to make her young and beautiful, was driven beyond endurance by the turn matters were now taking. So she called her young mistress aside and descanted so earnestly on the incomparable powers of the cloth and the little probability of ever meeting with such a chance again if she neglected this one, and threw in, too, such clever hints about easy ways of getting over the difficulty—that the simple shepherd could easily be deceived, that she could pretend she was going to listen to his attentions, though it need only be pretence, and in the meantime she would get his priceless treasure out of him—that poor little Blanca was quite bewildered. She was, indeed, so anxious to see more of the mysterious shepherd, and so possessed with the vague fancy that there was some connexion between him and the count of Barcelona, that it was not a very difficult matter to overcome her scruples, particularly as the *dueña* promised to smooth the way a little for her.

The count, who had also been a little frightened, lest he had spoken too abruptly, was also willing to receive the *dueña's* mediation, and in a very little time Blanca had obtained possession of the texture, but the count had also played his game so successfully that Blanca was quite under his influence and could think and dream of nothing else, nor rest till she had an opportunity of meeting him again. Of course this was not difficult, and the *dueña* was ready enough to assist her, as she thought the shepherd might have some other precious gifts to impart.

Nor was she mistaken. The count consulted his ring as to what he should do next, and the ring gave him a fowl which laid pearls for eggs, and the chickens that came out of them had feathers like gold.

When Blanca saw this, she could not forbear coming down into the garden to ask for the beautiful fowl. The shepherd was feeding her with gold corn, and he went on throwing down the grains without taking any notice of her approach, but singing:

---

213. Proud little thing.

> "My fair begins to yield;
> I'm safe to win the field!"

"*Pastorcillo, pastorcillo!* Give me the beautiful fowl!" said Blanca imploringly. "I should *so* like to have her. I shall cry if you won't give her, *pastorcillo*." She continued, as the count turned on his heels, and continued singing:

> "My fair begins to yield;
> I'm safe to win the field!"

"*Pastorcillo,* listen!" repeated the poor child sadly, for though she did not recognize the count, he had so enthralled her that she felt towards the supposed shepherd as she had never felt towards any but him.

"Oh, cease that horrid song, and speak to me," she said at last, and so humbly that the count thought it was time to put in a word.

"Will you come away with me? Because otherwise it is no use talking," he said, somewhat abruptly.

"Never!" retorted Blanca, indignantly. "And you had better take care and not talk so loud, for if my father overheard you, he would send and have you strung up."

But the shepherd did not care a bit, for he had in the meantime spoken to her father and told him what his plan was, and he received from him the hearty approval of his scheme for bringing his incorrigible daughter to reason. So he sang out louder than before:

> "My fair begins to yield;
> I'm safe to win the field!"

Blanca had never been treated in this way and did not know what to make of it. She turned to go away, but then the dread stole over her, suppose the shepherd should go away as mysteriously as he had come, and then there would be no one left to remind her of the count. She could not bear to think of it. So, she turned and said faintly: "*Pastorcillo!* Give me the beautiful fowl! You must give it me!"

"I am going away, Blanca," he replied, but less sternly than before. It was the first time he had called her by her name, and it seemed as if she heard the count speaking.

"Going away!" she exclaimed, in blank despair. "Oh, you must take me with you!"

"Take you with me!" repeated the shepherd. "No, you said you wouldn't come."

"Oh, but I did not know what I was saying!"

"It's too late now," replied the count.

"Oh, but I shall come, whether you will or no," she said pertly, for every time he spoke, his words seemed to rivet more firmly the chain which bound her to her affianced husband. It seemed as if he was his spectre come to avenge him.

"I cannot help it, if you choose to do *that*," was all his answer, and he turned to go.

"Take me, *Pastorcillo!*" she said once more.

"You would not like to come where I have to go," answered the supposed shepherd. "My dwelling is a dark cave, where no light ever enters. My bed is the sharp rock, which cuts through to the bones. My drink is water, muddy and cold; and my meat is grief and mourning. No companions are there where I live, for all men and women hold my way of living in dread."

When Blanca heard this, she turned pale. Nevertheless, she could not see him go without her, and still asked to go.

The shepherd walked on without saying a word. Blanca followed him as if drawn by magic.

Away they went, sad and silent, far, far away; over rocks and declivities, through streams and torrents, past briars and brakes. For months they went on thus. the count going on before, Blanca, sad and silent, after him. They never entered any town, and their only food was the berries they found in the wood, and the water of the brooks they crossed. Blanca's fair soft skin was burnt brown by the sun and parched up by the wind; her hands were torn by the thorns, and her feet bleeding from the unevenness of the way. At last a day came when she could go no farther. She sank down fainting on the earth, but she was so humble now, she did not so much as proffer a word of complaint.

"What is the matter, Blanca?" inquired the count. "Do you give up following me any farther?"

"*Pastorcillo!* Mock me not. You see I would follow you gladly, but you see too my strength is at an end; I can go no farther." And with that her senses failed.

When the count saw her in this condition, he took pity on her, and, lifting her up in his arms, carried her to a shepherd's but at no great distance along the moor, and there the good wife attended to her, putting her in her poor bed, and gently trying to bring her to again. But it was all of no use. Blanca continued in the swoon, and the poor peasant's restoratives were of no avail.

When the count saw this, he was in despair and sitting down under shadow of a rock, he took out his ring to ask it what was to be done, now being almost ready to reproach it for having led him to be so cruel.

But the ring told him to be of good heart, and all the promises of the milk-white dove would be fulfilled.

"Blanca has now learnt a lesson, and acquired a habit of submission which she will not forget all through her life. And besides, after she has given such strong proofs of love and devotion towards you, she will have no inclination to resume the provoking ways with which she tormented you before, so you may safely discover yourself to her now."

Then the good ring suddenly pronounced some words near the peasant's hut, and it became a fine palace, and the bed on which Blanca was lying became covered with beautiful embroidered coverlets, and all around were clothes fit for a countess to wear. The count, too, was provided with a shining suit of armour and a prancing charger, and by its side a palfrey for his bride, and a train of noble knights and dames to attend them. Over Blanca, too, the ring said some words, and her consciousness came back to her, and when she saw the count standing by her side, looking just as he did the day he dropped the pomegranate pip, it seemed as if she had never seen him in any other garb, only that he kept singing a verse the ring had taught him:

> "She spurned me, bridegroom, in her pride!
> Then with a shepherd would abide.
> Yet loved me still, for I have tried
> Her love, as gold is purified!"

till she begged him not to sing it, but so gently and submissively, that he could not resist. So he lifted her on to her palfrey, and the whole noble train moved on towards his father's palace, where she lived by his side all her life, a model of a devoted wife.

Translated by Rachel Busk.

The Crumb in the Beard (1873)[214]

Carolina Coronedi-Berti

There once was a king who had a daughter whose name was Stella. She was indescribably beautiful, but was so whimsical and hard to please that she drove her father to despair. There had been princes and kings who had sought her in marriage, but she had found defects in them all and would have none of them. She kept advancing in years, and her father began to despair of knowing to whom he should leave his crown. So he summoned his council, and discussed the matter, and was advised to give a great banquet, to which he should invite all the princes and kings of the surrounding countries, for, as they said, there cannot fail to be among so many, someone who should please the princess, who was to hide behind a door, so that she could examine them all as she pleased.

When the king heard this advice, he gave the orders necessary for the banquet, and then called his daughter, and said: "Listen, my little Stella, I have thought to do so and so, to see if I can find anyone to please you. Behold, my daughter, my hair is white, and I must have someone to leave my crown to."

Stella bowed her head, saying that she would take care to please him. Princes and kings then began to arrive at the court, and when it was time for the banquet, they all seated themselves at the table. You can imagine what sort of a banquet that was, and how the hall was adorned: gold and silver shone from all their necks; in the four corners of the room were four fountains, which continually

---

214.   "La Fola d'Brisla in Barba," *Novelle popolari Bolognesi* (Bologna: Tipi Fava e Garagnani, 1873).

sent forth wine and the most exquisite perfumes. While the gentlemen were eating, Stella was behind a door, as has been said, and one of her maids, who was near by, pointed out to her now this one, now that one: "See, your Majesty, what a handsome youth that is there."

"Yes, but he has too large a nose."

"And the one near your father?"

"He has eyes that look like saucers."

"And that other at the head of the table?"

"He has too large a mouth; he looks as if he liked to eat."

In short, she found fault with all but one, who, she said, pleased her, but that he must be a very dirty fellow, for he had a crumb on his beard after eating. The youth heard her say this, and swore vengeance. You must know that he was the son of the king of Green Hill, and the handsomest youth that could be seen.

When the banquet was finished and the guests had departed, the king called Stella and asked: "What news have you, my child?"

She replied that the only one who pleased her was the one with the crumb in his beard, but that she believed him to be a dirty fellow and did not want him.

"Take care, my daughter, you will repent it," answered her father, and turned away.

You must know that Stella's chamber looked into a courtyard into which opened the shop of a baker. One night, while she was preparing to retire, she heard, in the room where they sifted the meal, someone singing so well and with so much grace that it went to her heart. She ran to the window and listened until he finished. Then she began to ask her maid who the person with the beautiful voice could be, saying she would like to know.

"Leave it to me, your Majesty," said the maid; "I will inform you to-morrow."

Stella could not wait for the next day; and, indeed, early the next day she learned that the one who sang was the sifter. That evening she heard him sing again and stood by the window until everything became quiet. But that voice had so touched her heart that she told her maid that the next day she would try and see who had that fine voice. In the morning she placed herself by the window and soon saw the youth come forth. She was enchanted by his beauty as soon as she saw him and fell desperately in love with him.

Now you must know that this was none other than the prince who was at the banquet, and whom Stella had called "dirty." So he had disguised himself in such a way that she could not recognize him and was meanwhile preparing his revenge. After he had seen her once or twice he began to take off his hat and salute her. She smiled at him, and appeared at the window every moment she could. Then they began to exchange words, and in the evening he sang under her window. In short, they began to make love in good earnest, and when he learned that she was free, he began to talk about marrying her. She consented at once, but asked him what he had to live on.

"I haven't a penny," said he. "The little I earn is hardly enough to feed me."

Stella encouraged him, saying that she would give him all the money and things he wanted. To punish Stella for her pride, her father and the prince's father had an understanding, and pretended not to know about this love affair, and let her carry away from the palace all she owned. During the day Stella did nothing but make a great bundle of clothes, of silver, and of money, and at night the disguised prince came under the balcony, and she threw it down to him. Things went on in this manner some time, and finally one evening he said to her: "Listen. The time has come to elope."

Stella could not wait for the hour, and the next night she quietly tied a cord about her and let herself down from the window. The prince aided her to the ground, and then took her arm and hastened away. He led her a long ways to another city, where he turned down a street and opened the first door he met. They went down a long passage until they reached a little door, which he opened, and they found themselves in a hole of a place which had only one window, high up. The furniture consisted of a straw bed, a bench, and a dirty table. You can imagine that, when Stella saw herself in this place, she thought she should die. When the prince saw her so amazed, he said: "What is the matter? Does the house not please you? Do you not know that I am a poor man? Have you been deceived?"

"What have you done with all the things I gave you?"

"Oh, I had many debts, and I have paid them, and then I have done with the rest what seemed good to me. You must make up your mind to work and gain your bread as I have done. You must know that I am a porter of the king of this city, and I often go and work at the palace. To-morrow, they have told me, the washing is to be done, so you must rise early and go with me there. I will set you to work with the other women, and when it is time for them to go home to dinner, you will say that you are not hungry, and while you are alone, steal two shirts, conceal them under your skirt, and carry them home to me."

Poor Stella wept bitterly, saying it was impossible for her to do that, but her husband replied: "Do what I say, or I shall beat you."

The next morning her husband rose with the dawn and made her get up, too. He had bought her a striped skirt and a pair of coarse shoes, which he made her put on, and then took her to the palace with him, conducted her to the laundry, and left her. After he had introduced her as his wife, he said that she should remember what awaited her at home. Then the prince ran and dressed himself like a king, and waited at the gate of the palace until it was time for his wife to come. Meanwhile poor Stella did as her husband had commanded, and stole the shirts. As she was leaving the palace, she met the king, who said: "Pretty girl, you are our porter's wife, are you not?"

Then he asked her what she had under her skirt under her skirt and shook her until the shirts dropped out, and the king cried: "See there! The porter's wife is a thief, she has stolen some shirts."

Poor Stella ran home in tears, and her husband followed her when he had put on his disguise again. When he reached home Stella told him all that had happened and begged him not to send her to the palace again; but he told her that the next day they were to bake, and she must go into the kitchen and help, and steal a piece of dough. Everything happened as on the previous day. Stella's theft was discovered, and when her husband returned, he found her crying like a condemned soul and swearing that she had rather be killed than go to the palace again. He told her, however, that the king's son was to be married the next day, and that there was to be a great banquet, and she must go into the kitchen and wash the dishes. He added that, when she had the chance, she must steal a pot of broth and hide it about her so that no one should see it. She had to do as she was told, and had scarcely concealed the pot when the king's son came into the kitchen and told his wife she must come to the ball that had followed the banquet. She did not wish to go, but he took her by the arm and led her into the midst of the festival. Imagine how the poor woman felt at that ball, dressed as she was, and with the pot of broth! The king began to poke his sword at her in jest until he hit the pot, and all the broth ran on the floor. Then all began to jeer her and laugh, until poor Stella fainted away from shame, and they had to go and get some vinegar to revive her.

At last the king's mother came forward and said: "Enough; you have revenged yourself sufficiently." Then turning to Stella: "Know that this is your mother, and that he has done this to correct your pride and to be avenged on you for calling him dirty."

Then she took her by the arm and led her to another room, where her maids dressed her as a queen. Her father and mother then appeared and kissed and embraced her. Her husband begged her pardon for what he had done, and they made peace and always lived in harmony. From that day on she was never haughty and had learned to her cost that pride is the greatest fault.

Translated by Thomas Frederick Crane in Italian Popular Tales *(Boston: Houghton, Mifflin and Co., 1885).*

The Finicky Princess (1875)[215]
Giuseppe Pitrè

This tale's been told time and again about a king, who once upon a time ago had a daughter who was as beautiful as could be. When she had reached an age when it was time to get married, the king summoned her one day and said, "My daughter, you've now reached the age when you need to marry. So, I'm going

---

215. "La rigginotta sghinfignusa," *Fiabe, novelle e racconti popolari siciliani*, 4 vols. (Palermo: Lauriel, 1875).

to inform all the kings, who are friends of mine, that I shall be holding a great celebration and shall invite them with all their families. This way, my daughter, you'll be able to see which prince pleases you the most."

The day arrived, and all the kings came with their families. The king invited them to dine with him later at noon. Meanwhile, his daughter looked them over and fell in love with the son of the King Garnet. So she told her father and well, you know how things spread among friends . . .

In short, the son of King Garnet learned about her choice and was very happy. Just imagine the grand feast that was prepared! At noon everyone sat down to eat at the table. At the end of the meal, pomegranates were served. The prince had never eaten a pomegranate before, and he embarrassed himself when he dropped a seed on the floor. So what did he do? He kneeled down on the floor and picked it up. What a sight! When the princess, who couldn't keep her eyes off him, saw this, she got up from the table, ran to her room, and shut the door. Then her father got up from the table and went to see what was wrong with his daughter. When he saw her, she said, "Papa, I really liked this young man, but now that I've seen his shabby manners, I don't want him anymore."

So, the king thanked all the other monarchs for coming and said farewell to them. But the son of the King Garnet knew what had happened, and therefore, he had no intention of leaving. And what do you think he did? He disguised himself and remained in the kingdom. Moreover, he looked for a way to enter the royal palace. One day, he found out that the royal gardener had left, and the palace was looking for a good gardener to replace him. Well, since the prince knew a good deal about gardening, what do you think he did? He dressed himself as a peasant and applied for the job. They came to an understanding about the salary, and after he asked what he had to do, he became the gardener of the royal palace and was given a cottage where he hid the gifts that he had intended to give his betrothed. He made it seem that the trunk was filled with his own clothing and left it in the cottage in the middle of the garden.

The next morning he spread out a beautiful silk shawl embroidered in gold that glistened brightly. The princess's window faced the garden, and every morning the princess stood by her window. One morning, she got up, went to the window, and noticed the shawl which appealed to her very much. So, she called to the gardener.

"Tell me," she said, "whose shawl is that?"

"That shawl's mine," he replied.

"Do you want to sell it to me?"

"Never."

After she heard this, she commanded her servants to see if they could persuade him to sell it to her. But no matter how much they tried to buy the shawl, it was all in vain. Then they endeavored to get him to exchange it for something else. However, this too was in vain. The only thing he said to them was, "I'll give the shawl to the princess if she lets me sleep in the first room of her apartments."

The servants burst out laughing and ran to their mistress, and after giving her the message and discussing it, the princess agreed. She went to get the shawl and told him that the servants would call him when the time came. That night, after everyone had gone to bed, they called him and let him enter. Early the next morning they woke him and showed him out.

After a week had passed, the gardener spread out another shawl as beautiful as the first but more lavish. The princess wanted it. However, the gardener asked to be allowed to sleep in the second room of her apartments. And she consented.

Another week passed, and he spread out a dress embroidered in gold and ornamented with a large quantity of pearls and diamonds. The princess went crazy about the dress, but there was nothing she could do but to let him sleep in the antechamber of the room where she herself slept. She was not afraid because everyone considered him somewhat insane. Poor boy! This time, however, she paid the price.

After the gardener was convinced that everyone was sleeping, he went to bed and pretended to fall asleep. After some time passed, he began to tremble all over, and since his bed was propped next to the door, everything began to tremble, and the noise woke the princess. She told him to be quiet, but he responded that he felt cold and made even more of a racket. After a while she saw that it was impossible to try to reason with him and make herself heard, and since everyone might hear the noise and would be displeased, especially since the gardener was insane, she got out of her bed and let him into her room. Well, what do you think he did after the princess went back to sleep? In the morning, he got up early and left the room.

Some time later the princess discovered that she was pregnant, and what was she to do? Indeed, she became so angry she stopped eating, but she watched her belly grow and grow and was worried that everyone would notice it. In desperation she went to the gardener and spoke with him, and he told her that there was no other remedy but to flee with him. Even though he was really ugly, the poor princess was afraid of being dishonored. So she agreed to flee with him and took some clothes and a purse filled with money. That night they ran away on foot.

Along the way they met cowherds and shepherds and passed by many estates and fields.

"Who owns all those cattle?"

"They belong to King Garnet."

"Ah!"

"Why? What's wrong?" the gardener asked.

"This was the man I didn't want to marry," she replied.

"Too bad for you!" And this is what the gardener said to her each time she asked him who owned the estates, the fields, the horses, and the sheep they saw.

With the help of God, they managed to make their way. By night they were freezing, sweating, and dead tired. The gardener had told her that he was the son of King Garnet's steward. Finally they reached a tiny hut where there was a little bed, a stove, and a fireplace. Outside there was the hen-house and another dwelling that was the barn. He told her to slaughter a chicken and cook it for him, and she filled the stove with the feathers. After they ate, they went to bed. The next morning, before he left, he told her he would return in the evening. After he departed, some time passed, and soon King Garnet's son, dressed in his royal clothes, appeared and began to ask her who she was.

"I'm the wife of the steward's son."

"As far as I'm concerned you don't seem to be a good woman. You seem like a thief."

Well, what do you think he did? He gathered together all the chickens and counted them. Then he told her that they had all been there the day before, and now one was missing. Then he began to look through the hut, and when he found the feathers in the stove, he gave her hell. Then he beat her and slapped her. Finally, he said to her, "If it wasn't for me, you'd be turned over to the police. You might be able to do something like this in your country, but you had better get to know our laws."

The poor maiden began to cry. Meanwhile, the prince's mother heard all this noise and summoned her. When the princess entered the palace, the queen mother gave her a cup of coffee and told her that her son was strange and she need not worry about him. "Right now I have a daughter-in-law, who is pregnant, and I must get the baby clothes ready. Do you want to help me with the sewing?"

The princess said yes, and the queen mother laid out a good number of baby shirts, pullovers, diapers, and bits of cloth for sewing. When the gardener returned in the evening, she wept and told him about everything that had happened and said that he was to blame.

"I don't want to stay here any longer," she said. "Let's go to another cottage."

After he comforted her, they went to bed.

The next day, before he left, he told her as usual that he would return in the evening. Then he added that she was to steal some baby clothes from the queen and some other things and stuff them beneath her blouse because these things were scarce, very scarce, and since she was pregnant, she would need some clothes for the baby when the time came for it to be born. So after he departed, the queen summoned her, and they began to sew. When the queen wasn't looking, she took some baby clothes and stuffed them beneath her blouse. Just then the prince entered and said to the queen, "Mama, who's this maiden working with you? Why have you hired this thief? She's capable of stealing everything!"

Well, what do you think he did? He grabbed her and stuck his hand beneath her blouse, and he pulled out the baby clothes. Just imagine how mortified the poor maiden felt! Then he gave her a terrible scolding, but the queen his mother did not approve of what he did.

"Enough!" she said. "These are women's affairs, and they don't concern you!"

Then she comforted the maiden who wept her heart out, and after she stopped, the queen told her to come the next day, "We can string some pearls."

That night, when the gardener returned home, his wife told him everything that had happened. Then he responded and said that the king was greedy and that she shouldn't let him trample on her. "Instead," he said, "you should try to steal a string of peals and put them in your pocket."

And this is what she did. The next day, the queen summoned her, and they began to string some pearls. When the queen left her for a moment, she stuck a string of pearls into her pocket. After some time passed and the queen returned, who should come by but the prince. When he saw the maiden, he said to his mother, "You're giving this thief pearls? Let's see how many she's stolen!"

Without much ado, he stuck his hand into her pocket, and he pulled out the string of pearls. I can't tell you or recount what the prince did, and what he said to her, but as far as the maiden is concerned, I can tell you that she fainted. The queen brought her smelling salts and gave her some water to drink. Thank God, she revived!

That night the gardener returned home, and the maiden told him what had happened. Since she didn't feel well, she went to bed without eating. The next day her labor pains began because the time had arrived, and she began to suffer. Meanwhile, her husband, who hadn't noticed her pains, told her that he would return in the evening and left. The pains became more intense so that her cries were heard by the queen who came to her and said, "Good woman, the midwife is here because my daughter-in-law has labor pains. Get up, and we'll have the midwife visit you."

In short, she got up and was embarrassed. When the midwife visited her, she said that the maiden was about to give birth, and in fact, she did give birth to a handsome baby boy, and the queen brought her to the palace where there was a magnificent bed. Soon thereafter the prince arrived and entered the room. When he saw her, he called his mother and said, "How could you give this thief such a bed?"

But the poor maiden started complaining about the prince, and when the queen heard this, she said, "My daughter, this man is your husband whom you wouldn't marry because of the pomegranate seed."

Then the prince told her all that he had done. So he wrote to her father. Indeed, after her family came, they were married in a grand ceremony. All the neighboring monarchs were invited, and there were three days of festivities.

They remained happy and content
While we were left without a cent.

Collected by Professor Ugo Antonio Amico in Erice.

The Princess of England (1886)[216]
Emmanuel Cosquin

Once upon a time there was a princess, who was the daughter of the king of England. When the prince of France sent his ambassadors to ask for her hand in marriage, she replied that he was not even worthy of untying the laces of her shoes.

Well then, the prince traveled to England without revealing himself and had himself announced at the palace as a talented wigmaker from Paris. The princess wanted to see him, and the so-called wigmaker knew the ways of the world so well that he soon wed her in secret. However, when the king learned about what had happened, he became enraged and banished the two of them from the palace.

The wigmaker took his wife to Paris where they lived in a gloomy inn. 'Alas!' the princess thought. 'Was it necessary to have refused the king of France only to become the wife of a wigmaker?'

One day her husband said to her, "My wife, tomorrow I want you to sell the water of life at the square."

She obeyed and set up a place at the square with pitchers of water. Soon after some soldiers arrived and asked for water to drink. They gave her five pennies and drank all the water. Then they smashed the pitchers and the glasses. The poor princess didn't dare to return to the house. She was positive that it was the prince of France, who had sent the soldiers. When she stood standing near the door, her husband asked her: "My wife, why don't you enter?"

"I don't dare," the princess responded.

"How much did you earn today?"

"I earned five pennies."

"That's already quite good for you, my wife. As for me, I earned three gold coins by making wigs for the king."

"Well then," the princess said, "things are going quite well for us! We can pay the innkeeper and go somewhere else."

The next day the wigmaker said to his wife, "I want you to go to the large bridge and clean the mud off the soles of the passers-by."

The princess went there, and no sooner had she arrived than the king, her father-in-law, passed by and had her clean the mud from his shoes. Then he

---

216.   "La Princesse D'Angleterre," *Contes populaires de Lorraine* (Paris: Vieweg, 1886).

gave her a gold coin. The queen came next and gave her three gold coins. Then all the noblemen from the king's court came one after the other, and at the end of the day she had earned sixty gold coins. When night approached, she returned to the inn, but stopped just before the door.

"Well, wife, why don't you enter," her husband asked her.

"I don't dare to."

"How much have you earned today, my wife?"

"I earned sixty gold coins."

"As for me, my wife, I earned thirty gold coins by shaving the men at the king's court."

"Well then," the princess said, "things are going well for us. We can pay the innkeeper and go somewhere else."

Another time the wigmaker sent his wife to sell pottery at the square. No sooner had she laid out the pots than soldiers came and rode over the pottery breaking all her merchandise. It was the prince of France who had given them the orders to do this. The poor maiden went and told her husband about her misfortune and asked him whether the soldiers could be punished.

"I'll talk to the king about this," he said, "but what do you want done to them?"

'Alas!' the princess thought. 'Was it necessary to have refused the king of France only to become the wife of a wigmaker?' Then she said, "Ah, all the better. Things are going better. We'll pay the innkeeper and go somewhere else."

One day the wigmaker said to his wife, "The king is going to hold a grand festival. Since I am well thought of at the palace, I'll ask if they will let you serve at the table. I'll also have leather pockets made for you so that you can put the leftovers into them when they give you some."

Indeed, he had leather pockets made for her, but the pockets were attached by laces so weak that the least little thing could cause them to break off.

So the princess went to serve the table. At the beginning of the dinner she didn't find anything to put in her pockets. There was only a little sauce left on the plates. Later, she was able to put some good pieces of food into her pockets. However, as she was carrying a pile of plates, she slipped and let them fall. The laces were torn, and the contents of her pockets were spread out on the floor. The poor princess didn't know what to do.

All at once the king, her father-in-law, approached her and said: "My daughter, don't feel ashamed. It wasn't a wigmaker whom you married. It was my son, the prince of France."

"Ah! Father," the prince said, "you shouldn't have told her this yet. She said that I was not worthy of undoing the knots of her shoes. Well then, mademoiselle, you've undone knots of others very well."

From this moment onward there was nothing more to do than rejoice, and a magnificent wedding was held.

The Prince, Who Was Supposed to Be Too Young to Marry (1891)[217]

Ulrich Jahn

Once upon a time there was a king who had ten rooms in his castle, and they stood open for everyone. It was only the eleventh room that nobody was allowed to enter with the exception of the king, who always carried the key to it with him throughout the day, and in the evenings he laid the key beneath his pillow. Everyone was curious about what was kept in the room that the king concealed from the eyes of his family, and the most curious of all was his young son. Finally, the prince couldn't resist his desire any longer, and he slipped into his father's bedroom during the night and stole the key from beneath the pillow. Then he lit a candle, went to the door, stuck the key into the lock, turned it, and opened the door. Inside he saw that all the walls were covered with beautiful pictures, but the most beautiful of all was that of the princess of England. It was so beautiful that the prince fell deliriously in love with the princess on the spot and could think of nothing else but marrying her.

To realize his goal he summoned all the painters of the realm to come to his father's castle the next day and ordered them to paint himself exactly as he was. And when the painting was finished, he had a ship equipped for a voyage and placed a first mate in charge of the picture. He was to bring it to the princess of England, who lived overseas. Moreover, the first mate was to tell the princess that the prince had fallen in love with her and wanted to marry her.

The first mate carried out the orders and brought the painting to the princess and told her what his master had instructed him to say. However, the princess burst into laughter when she gazed at the painting and said: "Tell your 'prince milksop' that he's not yet old enough to marry. Young boys who are still green and wet behind the years should wait until they learn to dry themselves!"

The first mate had to return to the ship in disgrace and sail back home. When the prince heard how his messenger had been treated in England, he became pale from anger and exclaimed: "Well, that's certainly backfired on me! I'll make sure that she remembers this milksop!"

Then he went upstairs to the kitchen to see his father's cook, and he learned how to make the most delicious meals for kings so that they would be proud to partake of them. And once he had finished learning all that he could, he left the castle and traveled to England, where he enlisted at the king of England's palace as cook. Now the king was a real gourmand, and when he noticed that the new cook understood the art of cooking better than the old one, he dismissed the elder man, and the prince became the king of England's top chef.

---

217. "Vom Königssohn, der noch zu jung zum Heiraten sein sollte," *Volksmärchen aus Pommern und Rügen* (Leipzig: Diederich Soltau's Verlag, 1891).

Every day after he performed his chores, the prince took his harp and sat down beneath the princess's window and played and sang so beautifully, indeed so marvelously, that the servants and maids forgot all about their work and the people on the street stopped to listen to him. It also didn't take long before the princess desired very much to take a look at the wondrous performer and to get to know who he was. So her lady-in-waiting descended to fetch him but returned immediately and said: "It's only the new cook whom your father recently placed in charge of the kitchen."

However her heart had been enchanted so much by the wondrous song that she said: "So what! A cook, a cook is a human being just as good as anyone else!"

And the lady-in-waiting had to rush down again and bring the singer to her. When he now stood before the princess and played the harp so wonderfully and a song so gloriously, the princess became overcome by a great love for him that she said she'd like to marry him.

"That would be fine, but it can't work," said the cook. "If my lord, the king, hears about our marriage, he'll hang me from the gallows."

The princess agreed, and therefore, she planned to flee with the cook overseas where they would be safe from her father. They soon found a ship, and early the next morning they departed and sailed three days and nights on the wild sea until they caught sight of the city where the prince's father was king. They let themselves be set on land there, and the ship continued its journey. It was, however, a long way from the beach to the city, and they had to travel this distance by foot.

"My little one," the cook said, "you're now no longer a princess! We'll have to find some way to make and save money. So take off your shoes and stockings, and walk in your bare feet so that you can save all this for the holidays."

The princess did what she was told to do, but soon she had wounds on her feet due to the hard pebbles and moaned and groaned. She couldn't go any further.

"Then lay down in the grass and wait for me," he said to her in a rude way. "In the meantime I'll go to the city and see if I can find a job as cook for the king."

After a short time had passed, he returned and said: "There's no possibility for me to work as a cook. The position is already taken, and the king in this country doesn't send his servants away just because another person comes. So, I've rented a small house right outside the city so that we have a place to stay. There will be plenty of room for you and me."

The princess's feet were bleeding, but she had to go with him until they finally reached the small house. It was clean and nicely furnished and had a kitchen, living room, and bedroom.

"My darling," she said to him tenderly, "let's live here happy and content."

"What do you mean, happy and content?" he grumbled. "What are we going to live on? You can't do any hoeing and digging with your wounded feet. I'm going into the woods to cut some willows from the meadow so that you make some baskets out of them."

However, after he had brought the willows to her, the hard rods cut her tender hands so they became sore and she couldn't weave.

"You're really good for nothing!" the man scolded her. "Sore feet, cut-up hands, useless for hoeing and digging the ground, and also useless for weaving baskets! You were born to make my life miserable! What am I to do with you?"

The princess covered her face with her hands and wept and wailed. "Oh, try me with something else!" she said. "I'll learn what to do for sure."

"We'll see about that," the prince said and went into the city where he bought a spinning wheel that she was to learn how to use.

But she had always detested spinning and didn't know anything at all about how to use the spinning wheel. The man chided her and then showed her how to spin, but the hard thread cut her fingers that had already been punctured by the willows from the meadow so deeply that the pain prevented her from continuing.

"Didn't I say," he yelled at her, "that you were a waste of money? You don't understand how to hoe or dig, how to weave or spin. So now sit down behind the oven and let me take care of you!"

Then he took the axe and set it on his shoulder as if he were going into the woods to chop some logs. Instead he went directly to his father's castle. In the evening he returned from there and gave her a thaler that he supposedly had earned from a day's work. And he continued to do this the entire week, and the princess was overjoyed that, by the end of the week, she had six hard shining thalers in her pocket. So her pride and arrogance vanished. However, the prince thought to himself, 'She's not been punished enough. I'm not going to forgive her so easily for calling me a milksop and a boy who's green and still wet behind his ears.'

Therefore, on Monday, he said: "Wife, we now have a good pile of money, and you can begin a small business. I'm going to buy some clay dishes, and you can sell them at the market."

"I'll gladly do this, husband," she said with delight, for she wanted to please the prince. So he went into the city and bought clay dishes for six thalers. Then he hung the dishes up in a stall at the market. Afterward he informed the merchants in the city that on the next day they were to buy up all her stuff with good money. If they didn't, he would show them what he was made of as the king's son.

When the princess came to the market early on Tuesday morning, the people rushed to buy her clay dishes so that she sold out everything in a short time and could close down the stall. Delighted, she hurried back to the small house and told her husband what had happened.

"Let's buy some new dishes," he said, "and tomorrow you'll open your stall at the same spot. Perhaps we'll have the same luck tomorrow."

The prince took care of acquiring the dishes. However, when she opened the stall the next day and had spread out her stuff, she waited a long time, but no buyers appeared. Finally, a splendid coach approached, and the driver directed the coach to roll straight at the stall. He ran over all the dishes, large and small, and smashed them so that not a single piece remained intact.

"Oh, my good man," she screamed. "Have mercy! I'm nothing but a poor woman!"

But the fine gentleman who sat in the coach was none other than the prince himself. He paid no attention to her screams. Instead he drove off without compensating her for the damage.

"That's what you get from the milksop!" he said.

When the princess returned to the small house, her husband was already there and scolded her when he heard about the mishap.

"You're useless for digging and chopping, and for spinning and weaving! And each time when I begin believing that things will work out, then the next time all my hope is thwarted. What are we going to do now? It's just fortunate that I still have some money in my pocket. So I'll use the money to buy beer, schnapps, sausage, bacon, bread, and rolls, and you can open a tavern here in the woods."

The princess was satisfied, and her husband brought her everything that he had mentioned. At the same time he commanded his father's soldiers not to visit any other inn in the evening but to go into the woods and to have their dinner there in the small house.

Toward evening soldier after soldier set out for the little house in the woods, and the princess couldn't slice the food and serve the customers fast enough to satisfy them. Before she knew it, she had sold out everything. Her eyes shone brightly as she counted out the hard thalers on the table to her husband. But he thought: 'You've not been punished enough in the eyes of the green young man.' And he commanded her to fetch new supplies for the next evening.

This time the soldiers received the order that they were not to pay anything for what they ate, and if the woman were to become angry, they were to smash everything to pieces, but they were not to touch a hair of her body. And so the soldiers did this, and in the evening the princess was poorer than she had ever been before. And when she told her husband about the mishap, he didn't want to hear a thing about her anymore. However, she pleaded and kept weeping until he promised that he would do his utmost and give her one more chance.

About this time there was a job as kitchen help that had become open in the castle, and the prince told her that the chief chef wanted to give it to her.

However, she had to keep her husband's needs in mind and tie a little pot on her body and to put the good pieces of the leftovers from the plates into the pot. And the princess promised him that she would do this.

After she had now spent the first day at the castle and wanted to bring the pot to her husband in the woods, she had to walk by the large hall. The door stood open a bit, and she looked inside and watched the fine people turn about and dance. At that very same moment the prince approached her and demanded that she dance with him. She didn't want to because she was wearing such poor clothes and had tied the pot around her body. But her resistance didn't help. She had to dance, and as they were dancing, the prince untied the strings of her bow so that the pot fell to the ground and burst and all the pieces of the roast and dumplings rolled on the ground. All this caused the princess to turn red and blush out of shame. She would have preferred most of all to have sunk into the earth. She wrested herself from the prince's arms and rushed out of the hall. The prince threw a poor cloak over himself as disguise, overtook her on the stairs, and pretended as if he had been waiting for her in the castle.

"The top chef is my friend," he said. "Come and hide in his room. When it becomes dark and the guests go away, we'll get miles away from here, for we can't remain here anymore."

Upon saying this, he led her into a magnificent bedroom, but she saw nothing and heard nothing. She was tired and weak, and she fell into a deep sleep and didn't awake again until the light of the morning sun shone upon her bed.

"Now I'm sure she'll believe that I'm finally dry behind my ears!" the prince laughed, and he sent some maids to his wife. They had to wake her and dress her in splendid clothes appropriate for a queen. And she let them do everything they wanted. However, it seemed to her that she was dreaming. When the prince entered the room with a gold star on his chest and embraced her, she began to weep and said: "Oh, what do you want from me? I'm nothing but a poor woman and the wife of a common man!"

However, the prince touched her shoulders and answered: "That's not the case. The cook and I are one and the same. You could have spared me a great deal of trouble if you hadn't been so arrogant and proud with my messenger."

When the princess heard this, she was overjoyed and kissed her husband. Afterward a splendid meal was prepared and a wedding was celebrated again.

Everything turned out splendidly, and I must know this because I myself was there and helped serve everything. I was given slippers made of glass to put on, and I received a dress made of blotting paper, and they placed a hat made of butter on my head. But I drank too much of the delicious wine, and I became dizzy, and I tripped at the threshold. So my slippers went cling-clang and broke in two. Out of fear I ran into the kitchen to look after the roast, and then the hot steam melted my hat so that it began to run. I began to feel cooking hot and ran into the open air to cool myself off. But it was raining outside, and the dress fell from my body so that I was no longer wearing anything on my body, and I was chased from the court with disgrace. Then I had to work for a long time before I earned enough so that I could once again let myself appear among people.

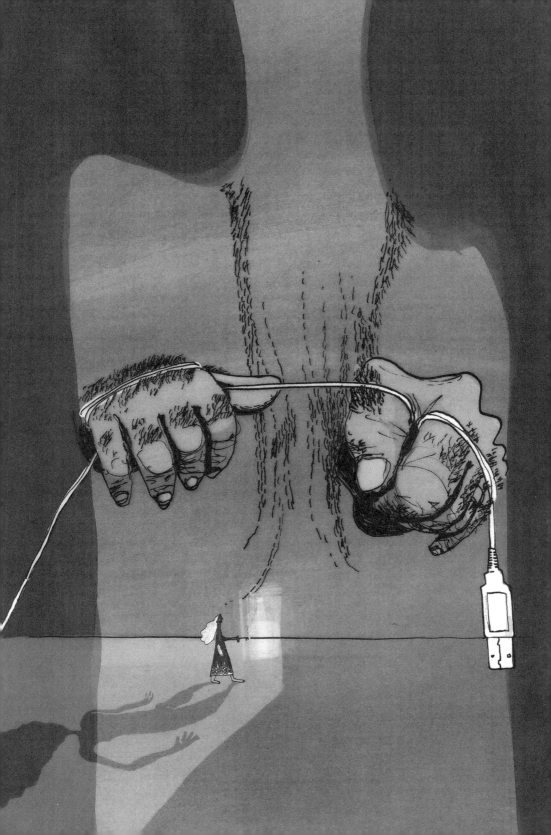

18. BLOODTHIRSTY HUSBANDS AND SERIAL KILLERS

ATU 955—THE ROBBER BRIDEGROOM, ATU 311—RESCUE BY THE SISTER MAIDEN, ATU 312—MAIDEN-KILLER (BLUEBEARD)

All three tales types (ATU 955, ATU 311, and ATU 312) really should be categorized under one title—"Serial Killers"—because they all feature mysterious male killers (kings, dukes, robbers, princes, sextons, monsters) who cannot restrain themselves from murdering helpless women to demonstrate their power. Motifs from all three tale types blend or are woven into one another to form a consistent pattern. A strange man, often marked by a startling characteristic like a blue beard, appears and asks to wed a young woman or kidnaps her. He arouses fear and trembling. The maiden (sometimes three sisters) is taken to a magnificent castle or palace. She is given keys to all the rooms and warned not to enter one chamber or else she will be killed or suffer horrible consequences. The fearsome killer departs on a long journey. The maiden becomes curious and opens the forbidden chamber where she finds numerous corpses of women and blood. Her key becomes accidentally stained with blood. When the killer returns from his journey, he intends to punish his "wife" by cutting off her head. However, her brothers and/or friends arrive in the nick of time to save her. The killer is executed, and the persecuted maiden obtains his treasures. Sometimes she marries one of her rescuers. In various tale types, the youngest kidnapped daughter is clever. She saves her two murdered sisters with a magic salve and outwits the serial killer. In another slightly different variant she goes into the forest and discovers that the fiancé-murderer is a robber, escapes his lair, and returns home to set a trap for him and his companions.

Generally speaking, most folklorists and literary critics tend to trace the tale types of the "exemplary" serial killer to Charles Perrault's "Bluebeard" in *Contes du temps passé* (1697), the first written text, because it encapsulates all of the tales' most significant motifs and because nobody has ever found an oral variant preceding it. However, there were numerous ballads about serial killers in Great Britain and Europe in the medieval and Renaissance periods that prepared the way for Perrault's writing of "Bluebeard." For example, in France there were many stories and rumors about the history of Gilles de Rais, a sadistic mass murderer of children in the fifteenth century. Atrocious and scandalous behavior has always made, and still makes, for sensational news.

Are monsters born monsters, or are they created by circumstances? Are men brutes by nature? Perhaps they become brutal because they are treated brutally when they are young, or they are too easily provoked by women? Perhaps some have insulted a fairy and been turned into a beast? Some scholars have traced motifs in Perrault's tale to the Bible and Greek and Roman myths that deal with the curiosity of women, such as the story of Adam and Eve or Pandora's Box. In fact, the curiosity of scholars has led to multiple studies of the serial killer in the past twenty years. See the following interesting books: Maria Tatar's *Secrets beyond the Door: The Story of Bluebeard and His Wives* (2004); Casie Hermansson's *Bluebeard: A Reader's Guide to the English Tradition* (2009); and Shuli Barzilai's *Tales of Bluebeard and His Wives from Late Antiquity to Postmodern Times* (2009). In addition, Heidi Anne Heiner has produced an important anthology of serial murderer tale types, *Bluebeard Tales from Around the World: Fairy Tales, Myths, Legends and Other Tales about Dangerous Suitors and Husbands* (2011).

The Brothers Grimm published their version of "Bluebeard," which they obtained from the Hassenpflug family, in the first volume of *Children's and Household Tales* in 1812. They deleted it in 1819 because they thought, rightly so, that it too closely resembled Perrault's literary tale of Bluebeard. They also felt that "Fitcher's Bird," which was already part of the first edition, was similar enough to "Bluebeard" and regarded it as a substitute. "Fitcher's Bird" was a combination of two tales provided by Friederike Mannel, a minister's daughter in nearby Allendorf, and by Dorothea Wild of Kassel, who later became Wilhelm's wife. "The Robber Bridegroom," delivered by Marie Hassenpflug, was also published in the first edition and later honed by Wilhelm Grimm. The fact that the Grimms offered two similar tales among others that revealed the horror of male brutality indicates just how popular stories about serial killers became in the nineteenth century. As the selections that follow indicate, there has never been a lack of "Bluebeard-themed tales, then or now."

******

Bluebeard (1812)[218]

Jacob and Wilhelm Grimm

There was once a man who lived in a forest with his three sons and beautiful daughter. One day a golden coach drawn by six horses and attended by several servants came driving up to his house. After the coach stopped, a king stepped out and asked him if he could have his daughter for his wife. The man was happy that his daughter could benefit from such a stroke of good fortune and immediately said yes. There was nothing objectionable about the suitor except for his beard, which was totally blue and made one shudder somewhat whenever one looked at it. At first the maiden also felt frightened by it and resisted marrying

---

218.   "Blaubart," *Kinder- und Haus-Märchen. Gesammelt durch die Brüder Grimm*, 2 vols. (Berlin: Realschulbuchandlung, 1812/1815).

him. But her father kept urging her, and finally she consented. However, her fear was so great that she first went to her brothers, took them aside, and said, "Dear brothers, if you hear me scream, leave everything standing or lying wherever you are, and come to my aid."

The brothers kissed her and promised to do this. "Farewell, dear sister, if we hear your voice, we'll jump on our horses and soon be at your side."

Then she got into the coach, sat down next to Bluebeard, and drove away with him. When she reached his castle, she found everything splendid, and whatever the queen desired was fulfilled. They would have been very happy together if she had only been able to have accustomed herself to the king's blue beard. However, whenever she saw it, she felt frightened.

After some time had passed, he said to her, "I must go on a long journey. Here are the keys to the entire castle. You can open all the rooms and look at everything. But I forbid you to open one particular room, which this little golden key can unlock. If you open it, you will pay for it with your life."

She took the key and promised to obey him. Once he had departed, she opened one door after another and saw so many treasures and magnificent things that she thought they must have been gathered from all over the world. Soon nothing was left but the forbidden room. Since the key was made of gold, she believed that the most precious things were probably kept there. Her curiosity began to gnaw at her, and she certainly would have passed over all the other rooms if she could have only have seen what was in this one. At last her desire became so great that she took the key and went to the room. 'Who can possibly see when I open it?' she said to herself. 'I'll just glance inside.' Then she unlocked the room, and when the door opened, a stream of blood flowed toward her, and she saw dead women hanging along all the walls, some only skeletons. Her horror was so tremendous that she immediately slammed the door, but the key popped out of the lock and fell into the blood. Swiftly she picked it up and tried to wipe away the blood, but to no avail. When she wiped the blood away on one side, it appeared on the other. She sat down, rubbed the key throughout the day, and tried everything possible, but nothing helped: the bloodstains could not be erased. Finally, in the evening she stuck it into some hay, which was supposed to be able to absorb blood.

The following day Bluebeard came back, and the first thing he requested was the bunch of keys. Her heart pounded as she brought the keys, and she hoped that he wouldn't notice that the golden one was missing. However, he counted all of them, and when he was finished, he said, "Where's the key to the secret room?"

As he said this, he looked straight into her eyes, causing her to blush red as blood.

"It's upstairs," she answered. "I misplaced it. Tomorrow I'll go and look for it."

"You'd better go now, dear wife. I need it today."

"Oh, I might as well tell you. I lost it in the hay. I'll have to go and search for it first."

"You haven't lost it," Bluebeard said angrily. "You stuck it there so the hay would absorb the bloodstains. It's clear that you've disobeyed my command and entered the room. Now, you'll enter the room whether you want to or not."

Then he ordered her to fetch the key, which was still stained with blood.

"Now, prepare yourself for your death. You shall die today," Bluebeard declared. He fetched his big knife and took her to the threshold of the house.

"Just let me say my prayers before I die," she said.

"All right. Go ahead, but you'd better hurry. I don't have much time to waste."

She ran upstairs and cried out of the window as loud as she could, "Brothers, my dear brothers! Come help me!"

The brothers were sitting in the forest and drinking some cool wine. The youngest said, "I think I heard our sister's voice. Let's go! We must hurry and help her!"

They jumped on their horses and rode like thunder and lightning. Meanwhile, their sister was on her knees, praying in fear.

"Well, are you almost done?" Bluebeard called from below, and she heard him sharpening his knife on the bottom step. She looked out the window but could only see a cloud of dust as if a herd were coming. So she screamed once again, "Brothers, my dear brothers! Come help me!"

And her fear became greater and greater when Bluebeard called, "If you don't come down soon, I'll be up to get you. My knife's been sharpened!"

She looked out the window again and saw her three brothers riding across the field as though they were birds flying through the air. For the third time she screamed desperately and with all her might, "Brothers, my dear brothers! Come help me!"

The youngest brother was already so near that she could hear his voice. "Calm yourself. Another moment, dear sister, and we'll be at your side!"

But Bluebeard cried out, "That's enough praying! I'm not going to wait any longer. If you don't come, I'm going to fetch you."

"Oh, just let me pray for my three dear brothers!"

However, he wouldn't listen to her. Instead, he went upstairs and dragged her down. Then he grabbed her by the hair and was about to plunge the knife into her heart when the three brothers knocked at the door, charged inside, and tore their sister out of his hands. They then drew out their sabers and cut him down. Afterward he was hung up in the bloody chamber next to the women he had killed. Later, the brothers took their dear sister home with them, and all of Bluebeard's treasures belonged to her.

Fitcher's Bird (1812)[219]

Jacob and Wilhelm Grimm

Once upon a time there was a sorcerer who was a thief, and he used to go begging from house to house in the guise of a beggar. One time a maiden opened the door and gave him a piece of bread. He only had to touch her to force her to jump into his basket. Then he carried her off to his house, where everything was splendid inside, and he gave her whatever she desired.

Some time later he said to her: "I have some business to attend outside the house, and so I must take a trip. Here is an egg. Take good care of it and carry it with you wherever you go. I'm also giving you a key, and if you value your life, don't go into the room that it opens."

Nevertheless, when he was gone, she went and opened up this room, and as she entered it, she saw a large basin in the middle with dead and butchered people lying in it. She was so tremendously horrified that the egg she was carrying plopped into the basin. To be sure she quickly took it out and wiped the blood off, but the blood reappeared instantly. She wiped and scraped, but she couldn't get rid of the stain.

When the man returned from his journey, he demanded the key and the egg. He looked at both of them, and he realized right away that she had been in the bloody chamber.

"Didn't you pay attention to my instructions?" he said angrily. "Now you'll go back into the bloody chamber against your will."

Upon saying this, he grabbed her, led her to the chamber, chopped her into pieces, and tossed her into the basin with the others.

After some time had passed, the man went begging again and captured the second daughter. He took her from the house, and the same thing happened to her. She opened the forbidden door, let the egg fall into the blood, and was chopped to pieces and thrown into the basin.

Now the sorcerer wanted to have the third daughter as well. So he captured her and put her into his basket. After he returned home, he gave her the key and the egg before he set out on his journey. However, the third daughter was smart and cunning. She put the egg into a cupboard and then went into the secret chamber. When she found her sisters in the bloody basin, she looked all over the place for their missing members and put them all together—head, body, arms, and legs. So the two sisters came back to life. Then their sister led them out of the chamber and hid them.

When the man came home and found that there were no bloodstains on the egg, he asked her to become his bride. She said yes, but first he had to fill his basket full of gold and carry it to her parents on his back. In the meantime she

---

219. "Fitchers Vogel," *Kinder- und Haus-Märchen. Gesammelt durch die Brüder Grimm*, 2 vols. (Berlin: Realschulbuchhandlung, 1812/1815).

would make preparations for the wedding. After this she told her sisters that they were to get help from home. Then she stuck them into the basket and covered them with gold.

"Now carry this basket to my parents," she said to the man, "but don't dare to stop and rest along the way. I can see everything from my window."

So the man lifted the basket onto his back and went on his way. It was, however, so heavy that he was almost crushed to death by the weight. At one point he wanted to rest, but one of the sisters immediately cried out from the basket: "I see from my window that you're resting! Get a move on at once!"

He thought that it was his wife who was crying out, and so he immediately continued walking. Whenever he stopped along the way, he heard a voice and had to keep moving.

Back at his place, the bride took a skull, decorated it with jewels and set it on the window. Then she invited the sorcerer's friends to the wedding, and after that was done, she dipped herself into a barrel of honey, cut open a bed, and rolled around in the feathers so that it was impossible to recognize her because she looked so weird. And this is how she set out on her way. Soon she met some of the wedding guests, who asked:

"Where are you coming from, oh, Fitcher's bird?"
"From Fitze Fitcher's house, haven't you heard?"
"And what may the young bride be doing there?"
"She's swept the whole house from top to bottom.
Just now she's looking straight out of the window."

Soon thereafter she met the bridegroom who was on his return home.

"Where are you coming from, oh, Fitcher's bird?"
"From Fitze Fitcher's house, haven't you heard?"
"And what may the young bride be doing there?"
"She's swept the whole house from top to bottom.
Just now she's looking straight out of the window."

The bridegroom looked and saw the decorated skull. He thought it was his bride and waved to her. However, once he and his guests were all gathered inside the house, the help arrived that the sisters had sent. These people locked all the doors of the house and then they set fire to it. And since nobody could get out, they all had to burn to death.

The Robber Bridegroom (1857)[220]

Jacob and Wilhelm Grimm

Once upon a time there was a miller who had a beautiful daughter, and when she was grown up, he wanted to arrange a good marriage for her with a man who

---

220. "Der Räuberbräutigam," *Kinder- und Hausmärchen gesammelt durch die Brüder Grimm*, 7th ed., 3 vols. (Göttingen: Verlag der Dieterischen Buchhandlung, 1857).

would provide for her in an appropriate way. 'If the right suitor comes along and asks to marry her,' he thought, 'I shall give her to him.'

It was not long before a suitor appeared who seemed to be very rich, and since the miller found nothing wrong with him, he promised him that he could wed his daughter. The maiden, however, did not love him the way a bride-to-be should love her bridegroom, nor did she trust him. Whenever she looked at him or thought about him, her heart shuddered with dread.

One day he said to her, "You're my bride-to-be, and yet, you've never visited me."

"I don't know where your house is," the maiden replied.

"My house is out in the dark forest," said the bridegroom.

She tried to make excuses and told him she would not be able to find the way. But the bridegroom said, "Next Sunday I want you to come out and visit me. I've invited the guests, and I shall spread ashes on the ground so you can find the way."

When Sunday arrived and the maiden was supposed to set out on her way, she became very anxious but couldn't explain to herself why she felt so. She filled both her pockets with peas and lentils to mark the path. At the entrance to the forest, she found that the ashes had been spread, and she followed them, while throwing peas right and left on the ground with each step that she took. She walked nearly the whole day until she came to the middle of the forest. There she saw a solitary house, but she didn't like the look of it because it was so dark and dreary. She went inside and found nobody at home. The place was deadly silent. Then suddenly a voice cried out:

> "Turn back, turn back, young bride.
> The den belongs to murderers,
> Who'll soon be at your side!"

The maiden looked up and saw that the voice came from a bird in a cage hanging on the wall. Once again it cried out:

> "Turn back, turn back, young bride.
> The den belongs to murderers,
> Who'll soon be at your side!"

The beautiful bride moved from one room to the next and explored the entire house, but it was completely empty. Not a soul could be found. Finally, she went down into the cellar, where she encountered a very, very old woman, whose head was constantly bobbing.

"Could you tell me whether my bridegroom lives here?" asked the bride.

"Oh, you poor child," the old woman answered. "Do you realize where you are? This is a murderers' den! You may think you're about to celebrate your wedding, but the only marriage you'll celebrate will be with death. Just look! They ordered me to put this big kettle of water on the fire to boil. When they have you in their power, they'll chop you to pieces without mercy. Then they'll cook you and eat you because they're cannibals. If I don't take pity on you and save you, you'll be lost forever."

The old woman then led her behind a large barrel, where nobody could see her.

"Be still as a mouse," she said. "Don't budge or move! Otherwise, it will be all over for you. Tonight when the robbers are asleep, we'll escape. I've been waiting a long time for this chance."

No sooner was the maiden hidden than the godless crew came home, dragging another maiden with them. They were drunk and paid no attention to her screams and pleas. They gave her wine to drink, three full glasses, one white, one red, and one yellow, and soon her heart burst in two. Then they tore off her fine clothes, put her on a table, chopped her beautiful body to pieces, and sprinkled the pieces with salt. Behind the barrel, the poor bride shook and trembled, for she now realized what kind of fate the robbers had been planning for her. One of them noticed a ring on the murdered maiden's little finger, and since he could not slip it off easily, he took a hatchet and chopped the finger off. But the finger sprang into the air and over the barrel and fell right into the bride's lap. The robber took a candle and went looking for it, but he couldn't find it. Then another robber said, "Have you looked behind the barrel as well?"

Immediately the old woman called out, "Come and eat! You can look for it tomorrow. The finger's not going to run away from you."

"The old woman's right," the robbers said, and they stopped looking and sat down to eat. The old woman put a sleeping potion into their wine, and soon they lay down in the cellar, fell asleep, and began snoring. When the bride heard the snoring, she came out from behind the barrel and had to step over the sleeping bodies lying in rows on the ground. She was afraid that she might wake them up, but she got safely through with the help of God. The old woman went upstairs with her and opened the door, and the two of them scampered out of the murderers' den as fast as they could. The wind had blown away the ashes, but the peas and lentils had sprouted and unfurled, pointing the way in the moonlight. They walked the whole night, and by morning they had reached the mill. Then the maiden told her father everything that had happened.

When the day of the wedding celebration came, the bridegroom appeared, as did all the relatives and friends that the miller had invited. As they were all sitting at the table, each person was asked to tell a story. The bride, though, remained still and didn't utter a word. Finally, the bridegroom said, "Well, my dear, can't you think of anything? Tell us a good story."

"All right," she said. "I'll tell you a dream. I was walking alone through the forest and finally came to a house. There wasn't a soul to be found in the place except for a bird in a cage on the wall that cried out:

'Turn back, turn back, young bride.
The den belongs to murderers,
Who'll soon be at your side!'
Then the bird repeated the warning.
(My dear, it was only a dream.)

"After that I went through all the rooms, and they were empty, but there was something about them that gave me an eerie feeling. Finally, I went downstairs into the cellar, where I found a very, very old woman, who was bobbing her heard. I asked her, 'Does my bridegroom live in this house?' 'Oh, you poor child,' she responded, 'you've stumbled on a murderers' den. Your bridegroom lives here, but he wants to chop you up and kill you, and then he wants to cook you and eat you.'

(My dear, it was only a dream.)

"The old woman hid me behind a large barrel, and no sooner was I hidden than the robbers returned home, dragging a maiden with them. They gave her all sorts of wine to drink, white, red, and yellow, and her heart burst in two.

(My dear, it was only a dream.)

"One of the robbers saw that a gold ring was still on her finger, and since he had trouble pulling it off, he took a hatchet and chopped it off. The finger sprang into the air, over the barrel, and right into my lap. And here's the finger with the ring!"

With these words she produced the finger and showed it to all those present.

The robber, who had turned white as a ghost while listening to her story, jumped up and attempted to flee. However, the guests seized him and turned him over to the magistrate. Then he and his whole band were executed for their shameful crimes.

Fitcher's Bird (1857)[221]

Jacob and Wilhelm Grimm

Once upon a time there was a sorcerer who used to assume the guise of a poor man and go begging from house to house to catch beautiful girls. No one knew where he took them since none of the girls ever returned.

One day he appeared at the door of a man who had three beautiful daughters. He looked like a poor, weak beggar and carried a basket on his back as though to collect handouts in it. He begged for some food, and when the oldest daughter came out to hand him a piece of bread, he had only to touch her, and that compelled her to jump into his basket. Then he rushed away with great strides and carried her to his house in the middle of a dark forest. Everything was splendid inside the house, and he gave her whatever she desired.

---

221. "Fitchers Vogel," *Kinder- und Hausmärchen gesammelt durch die Brüder Grimm*, 7th ed., 3 vols. (Göttingen: Verlag der Dieterischen Buchhandlung, 1857).

"My darling," he said, "I'm sure you'll like it here, for there's everything your heart desires."

After a few days had gone by, he said, "I must go on a journey and leave you alone for a short time. Here are the keys to the house. You may go wherever you want and look at everything except one room, which this small key here opens. If you disobey me, you will be punished by death." He also gave her an egg and said, "I'm giving you this egg for safekeeping. You're to carry it wherever you go. If you lose it, then something awful will happen."

She took the keys and the egg and promised to take care of everything. When he was gone, she went all around the house and explored it from top to bottom. The rooms glistened with silver and gold, and she was convinced that she had never seen such great splendor. Finally, she came to the forbidden door. She wanted to walk past it, but curiosity got the better of her. She examined the key, which looked like all the others, stuck it into the lock, turned it a little, and the door sprang open. But, what did she see when she entered? There was a large bloody basin in the middle of the room, and it was filled with dead people who had been chopped to pieces. Next to the basin was a block of wood with a glistening ax on top of it. She was so horrified by this that she dropped the egg she had been holding in her hand, and it plopped into the basin. She took it out and wiped the blood off, but to no avail: the blood reappeared instantly. She wiped and scraped, but she could not get rid of the spot.

Not long after this, the sorcerer came back from his journey, and the first things he demanded from her were the keys and the egg. When she handed them to him, she was trembling, and he perceived right away by the red stains on the egg that she had been in the bloody chamber.

"Since you went into that chamber against my will," he said, "you will go back in, against your will. This is the end of your life."

He threw her down, dragged her along by her hair, cut her head off on the block, and chopped her into pieces so that her blood flowed on the floor. Then he tossed her into the basin with the others.

"Now I shall fetch the second daughter," said the sorcerer.

Once again he went to the house in the guise of a poor man and begged. When the second daughter brought him a piece of bread, he caught her as he had the first, just by touching her. Then he carried her away, and she fared no better than her sister, for she succumbed to her own curiosity. She opened the door to the bloody chamber, looked inside, and had to pay for this with her life when the sorcerer returned from his journey.

Now he went and fetched the third daughter, but she was smart and cunning. After he had given her the keys and the egg and had departed, she put the egg away in a safe place. Then she explored the house and eventually came to the forbidden chamber. But, oh, what did she see? Her two dear sisters lay there in the basin cruelly murdered and chopped to pieces. However, she set to work right away, gathered the pieces together, and arranged them in their proper order: head, body, arms, and legs. When nothing more was missing, the pieces began to move and join together. Both the maidens opened their eyes and were alive again. Then they all rejoiced, kissed, and hugged each other.

When the sorcerer returned, he demanded his keys and egg right away, and when he couldn't discover the least trace of blood, he said, "You've passed the test, and you shall be my bride."

But, he no longer had any power over her and had to do what she requested.

"All right," she answered. "But first I want you to carry a basket full of gold to my father and mother, and you're to carry it on your back by yourself. In the meantime I shall prepare for the wedding."

Then she ran to her sisters, whom she had hidden in a little chamber.

"The time has come when I can save you," she said. "The villain himself will carry you back home. But as soon as you get there, you must send help to me."

She put her two sisters into a basket and covered them completely with gold until nothing could be seen of them at all. Then she called the sorcerer to her and said, "Now take the basket away. But don't you dare stop and rest along the way! I'll be keeping an eye on you from my window."

The sorcerer lifted the basket onto his back and went on his way. The basket, however, was so heavy that sweat ran down his face. At one point he sat down and wanted to rest a while, but one of the sisters called from the basket, "I can see through my window that you're resting. Get a move on at once!"

Whenever he stopped along the way, he heard a voice and had to keep moving. Although he had run out of breath and was groaning, he finally managed to bring the basket with the gold and the two maidens to their parents' house.

Back at his place, the bride was preparing the wedding feast and sent invitations to all the sorcerer's friends. Then she took a skull with grinning teeth, decorated it with jewels and a wreath of flowers, carried it up to the attic window, and set it down so it faced outward. When everything was ready, she dipped herself into a barrel of honey, cut open a bed, and rolled around in the feathers so she looked like a strange bird, and it was impossible to recognize her. Afterward she went out of the house, and on the way she met some of the wedding guests, who asked:

"Where are you coming from, oh, Fitcher's bird?"
"From Fitze Fitcher's house, haven't you heard?"
"And what may the young bride be doing there?"
"She's swept the whole house from top to bottom.
Just now she's looking out the attic window."

Finally, she met the bridegroom who was walking back slowly. He also asked:

"Where are you coming from, oh, Fitcher's bird?"
"From Fitze Fitcher's house, haven't you heard?"
"And what may the young bride be doing there?"
"She's swept the whole house from top to bottom.
Just now she's looking out the attic window."

The bridegroom looked up and saw the decorated skull. He thought it was his bride and nodded and greeted her in a friendly way. However, once he and his guests were all gathered inside the house, the bride's brother and relatives arrived. They had been ready to rescue her, and they locked all the doors of the house to prevent anyone from escaping. Then they set fire to the house, and the sorcerer and all his cronies were burned to death.

King Bluebeard (1852)[222]

Ernst Meier

An old man who had three sons and two daughters lived very close to a large forest. One time they were sitting and were thinking of nothing when suddenly a splendid coach came driving up to their house and stopped. Then a distinguished gentleman stepped out of the coach, entered the house, and held a conversation with the father and his daughters. Since the youngest pleased him so very much, he asked the father whether he would give her to him as his wife.

It seemed to the father that this would be a good marriage, and he had been wishing for a long time that his daughters would be taken care of during his lifetime. But the daughter could not decide whether to say yes, for the strange knight had a beard that was entirely blue, and she was terrified of him, and each time she looked at him she had the creeps.

She went to her brothers who were brave knights and asked for their advice. However, her brothers thought that she should take Bluebeard, and they gave her a little whistle and said: "If any kind of harm should come to you, just blow into this whistle! Then we'll come to your aid!"

So she let herself be persuaded and became the wife of this stranger but arranged it so that her sister was allowed to accompany her when King Bluebeard led her to his castle.

When the young wife arrived there, there was great jubilation throughout the castle, and King Bluebeard was also overjoyed. All this lasted four weeks. Then he wanted to take a journey and turned all the keys of the castle over to his wife.

"You may go anywhere you want to in the castle and open and look at anything you like," he said. "However, if you value your life, you had better not use this little golden key to open this one door to which it belongs."

"Of course not," she responded affirming that she would not open that door.

However, when the king was absent for some time, she became restless and continually thought about what might be in the chamber that was forbidden to her. She was just about to open it when suddenly her sister came and held her back. But the next morning of the fourth day she could no longer stop herself, and so she secretly crept to the room with the key, stuck it into the

222.　"König Blaubart," *Deutsche Volksmärchen aus Schwaben* (Stuttgart: E. B. Scheitlin's Verlagshandlung, 1852).

lock, and opened the door. But you can imagine how horrified she was when she saw that the entire room was full of corpses, and they were all nothing but women.

To be sure she wanted to shut the door right away, but the key fell out of her hand and into some blood. Quickly she picked it up, but it had bloodstains on it, and no matter how much she rubbed and polished it, she could not get rid of the stains. So she went to her sister and moaned and groaned.

When King Bluebeard finally returned from his journey, he immediately inquired about the golden key. But when he saw the bloodstains on it, he said: "Wife, why didn't you listen to my warning? Your time has come! Prepare yourself to die, for you've been in the forbidden chamber."

All at once she broke into tears and went to her sister who lived upstairs in the castle. While she was complaining about her fate, the sister remembered the whistle that her brothers had given Bluebeard's wife, and she said: "Give me the whistle, and I'll send a signal to our brothers. Perhaps they can come and help you."

And she blew the whistle three times so that it emitted a high sound that echoed throughout the forest.

An hour later they heard Bluebeard rushing up the stairs to fetch and slaughter his wife.

"Oh God! Oh God!" she screamed. "Aren't my brothers coming?"

And she rushed to the door and locked it, and then she stood there and fearfully held it closed.

Then Bluebeard pounded on the door and yelled, telling them to open it. And when she didn't do it, he tried to break the door down.

"Oh, sister! Oh, sister! Aren't my brothers coming?" She asked her sister who was standing by the window and looking off into the distance.

"I don't see anyone yet," she responded.

Meanwhile Bluebeard was smashing the door to pieces, and when he was almost through the door and about to enter the room, three knights suddenly appeared in front of the castle, and the sister cried out from the window as loudly as she could: "Help! Help!" And she signaled to them to come up.

Indeed, they stormed up the stairs immediately to the place where they had heard their sister's cries. When they reached the top, they saw King Bluebeard with sword in hand standing before the broken-down door, and they heard their sister scream inside the room. They realized immediately what he was up to and immediately stabbed him in his chest with their daggers.

When the brothers learned afterward what the godless king wanted to do with their sister and that he had already murdered so many women, they destroyed his castle so that there was not one stone left standing on another. Then they took away all his treasures and led their sisters back to their father's house with great delight.

The Widow and Her Daughters (1860–1862)[223]
John Francis Campbell of Islay

There was formerly a poor widow, and she had three daughters, all she had to feed them was a kailyard. There was a great gray horse who was coming every day to the yard to eat the kail.[224] Said the eldest of the daughters to her mother, "I will go to the yard today, and I will take the spinning wheel with me, and I will keep the horse out of the kail."

"Do," said the mother.

She went out. The horse came; she took the distaff from the wheel and she struck him. The distaff stuck to the horse, and her hand stuck to the distaff. Away went the horse till, they reached a green hill, and he called out, "Open, open, oh green hill, and let in the king's son; open, open, oh green hill, and let in the widow's daughter."

The hill opened, and they went in. He warmed water for her feet and made a soft bed for her limbs, and she lay down that night. Early on the morrow when he rose, he was going to hunt. He gave her the keys of the whole house, and he said to her that she might open every chamber inside but the one. "By all she ever saw not to open that one." That she should have his dinner ready when he should come back, and that if she should be a good woman that he would marry her.

When he went away, she began to open the chambers. Every one, as she opened it, was getting finer and finer, till she came to the one that was forbidden. It seemed to her, 'What might be in that she might not open it too.' She opened it, and it was full of dead gentlewomen, and she went down to the knee in blood. Then she came out, and she was cleansing her foot, and though she were cleaning it, still she could not take a bit of the blood off it. A tiny cat came where she was, and she said to her, "If she would give a little drop of milk then she would clean her foot as well as it was before."

"Thou! ugly beast! be off before thee. Doest thou suppose that I won't clean them better than thou?"

"Yes, yes, take thine own away. Thou wilt see what will happen to thee when himself comes home."

He came home, and she set the dinner on the board, and they sat down at it. Before they ate a bit, he said to her, "Wert thou a good woman today?"

"I was," said she.

"Let me see thy foot, and I will tell thee whether thou wert or wert not."

She let him see the one that was clean.

"Let me see the other one," said he.

When he saw the blood, "Oh! Oh!" said he.

---

223. *Popular Tales of the West Highlands: Orally Collected* (Edinburgh: Edmonston and Douglas, 1860–1862).

224. Kale. An edible plant such as cabbage.

He rose and took the axe and took her head off, and he threw her into the chamber with the other dead people. He laid down that night, and early on the morrow he went to the widow's yard again.

Said the second one of the widow's daughters to her mother, "I will go out today, and I will keep the gray horse out of the yard."

She went out sewing. She struck the thing she was sewing on the horse. The cloth stuck to the horse, and her hand stuck to the cloth. They reached the hill. He called as usual to the hill; the hill opened, and they went in. He warmed water for her feet, and made a soft bed for her limbs, and they lay down that night. Early in the morning he was going to hunt, and he said to her that she should open every chamber inside but one, and "by all she ever saw" not to open that one.

She opened every chamber until she came to the little one, and because she thought, 'What might be in that one more than the rest that she might not open it?' she opened it, and it was full of dead gentlewomen, and her own sister amongst them. She went down to the knee in blood. She came round out, and as she was cleaning herself, and the little cat came round about, and she said, "If thou wilt give me a tiny drop of milk I will clean thy foot as well as it ever was."

"Thou! ugly beast! begone. Dost thou think that I will not clean it myself better than thou?"

"Thou wilt see," said the cat, "what will happen to thee when himself comes home."

When he came, she set down the dinner, and they sat at it.

Said he, "Wert thou a good woman today?"

"I was," said she.

"Let me see thy foot, and I will tell thee whether thou wert or wert not."

She let him see the foot that was clean.

"Let me see the other one," said he.

She let him see it.

"Oh! ho!" said he, and he took the axe and sliced her head off. He lay down that night.

Early on the morrow, said the youngest to her mother, as she wove a stocking, "I will go out with my stocking today, and I will watch the gray horse. I will see what happened to my two sisters, and I will return to tell you."

"Do," said the mother, "and see thou doest not stay away."

She went out, and the horse came. She stuck her stocking on the horse. The stocking stuck to the horse, and the hand stuck to the stocking. They went away, and they reached the green hill. He called out as usual, and they got in. He wanted water for her feet, and made a soft bed for her limbs, and they lay down that night. On the morrow he was going to hunt, and he said to her, "If she would behave herself as a good woman till he returned, that they would be married in a few days."

He gave her the keys, and he said to her that she might open every chamber that was within except that little one, "but see that she should not open that one."

She opened every one, and when she came to this one, because she thought, 'What might be in it that she might not open it more than the rest?' she opened it, and she saw her two sisters there dead, and she went down to the two knees in blood. She came out, and she was cleaning her feet, and she could not take a bit of the blood off them. The tiny cat came where she was, and she said to her, "Give me a tiny drop of milk, and I will clean thy feet as well as they were before."

"I will give it thou creature; I will give thee thy desire of milk if thou wilt clean my feet."

The cat licked her feet as well as they were before. Then the king came home, and they set down his dinner, and they sat at it. Before they ate a bit, he said to her, "Wert thou a good woman today?"

"I was middlin," said she; "I have no boasting to make of myself."

"Let me see thy feet," said he.

She let him see her feet.

"Thou wert a good woman," said he; "and if thou holdest on thus till the end of a few days, thyself and I will be married."

On the morrow he went away to hunt. When he went away, the little cat came where she was.

"Now, I will tell thee in what way thou wilt be quickest married to him," said the cat. "There are," said she, "a lot of chests within. Thou shalt take out three of them; thou shalt clean them. Thou shalt say to him next night that he must leave these three chests, one about of them, in thy mother's house, as they are of no use here; that there are plenty here without them; thou shalt say to him that he must not open any of them on the road, or else, if he opens, thou wilt go up into a tree top, and that thou will be looking, and that if he opens any of them that thou wilt see. Then when he goes hunting, thou shalt open the chamber, thou shalt bring out thy two sisters; thou shalt draw on them the magic club, and they will be as lively and whole as they were before; thou shalt clean them then, and thou shalt put one in each chest of them, and thou shalt go thyself into the third one. Thou shalt put of silver and of gold, as much as in the chests as will keep thy mother and thy sisters right for their lives. When he leaves the chests in thy mother's house, and when he returns, he will fly in a wild rage: he will then go to thy mother's house in this fury, and he will break in the door; be thou behind the door, and take off his head with the bar; and then he will be a king's son, as precious as he was before, and he will marry thee. Say to thy sisters, if he attempts the chests to open them by the way, to call out, 'I see thee, I see thee,' and that he wilt think that thou wilt be calling out in the tree."

When he came home he went away with the chests, one after one, till he left them in her mother's house. When he came to a glen, where he thought she in the tree could not see him, he began to let the chest down to see what was in it; she that was in the chest called out, "I see thee, I see thee!"

"Good luck be on thy pretty little head," said he, "if thou canst not see a long way!"

This was the way with him each journey, till he left the chests altogether in her mother's house.

When he returned home on the last journey and saw that she was not before him, he flew in a wild rage; he went back to the widow's house, and when he reached the door, he drove it in before him. She was standing behind the door, and she took his head off with the bar. Then he grew into a king's son, as precious as ever came; there he was within, and they were in great gladness. She and himself married, and they left with her mothers and sisters, of gold and silver, as much as left them well for life.

From Mrs. MacGeachy, famer's wife, Islay.

Bluebeard (1866)[225]

Jean-François Bladé

Once upon a time there was a man six-feet tall with a blue beard that went down to his waist, and that's why he was called Bluebeard. This rich man had an ocean of money. However, he never gave alms to the poor. He never set foot in a church. It was said that he had been married seven times, but nobody knew what had become of his seven wives.

At last the bad rumors about him reached the king of France's ears. As soon as they did, he sent a troupe of soldiers to arrest the wicked man and a royal high judge to interrogate him. For seven years they beat the woods and searched the mountains, but Bluebeard hid himself, and nobody knew where to find him.

When the soldiers and the royal high judge finally returned to Paris, Bluebeard reappeared, more wicked and more terrible than ever before. There came a time when nobody dared to risk coming within seven miles of his chateau.

One morning, Bluebeard rode through the countryside mounted on his large black horse followed by three mastiffs as large and strong as bulls. As he was riding, he passed a young and beautiful lady all alone.

Without saying a word, the rogue seized her by her waist and carried her off to his chateau.

"Listen, I expect you to be my wife. So you'll never leave this place."

Consequently, the young lady married Bluebeard by force and lived as a prisoner suffering like death with tears constantly flowing from her eyes. Every morning at daybreak Bluebeard mounted his horse and departed, and he was followed by his large mastiffs strong as bulls. He always returned at dinnertime. His wife

---

225. "Barbe-bleue," *Contes populaires de la Gascogne*, 3 vols. (Paris: Maisonneuve frères et Ch. Leclerc, 1886).

remained at her window the entire day. She looked out of the window and down into the countryside and had sad thoughts. Sometimes a little shepherdess would come and sit next to her mistress. She was as pretty as a picture and as wise as a saint.

"Madame," she said to her, "I know your thoughts. You don't trust the butlers and the servants of the chateau. And you're not wrong, Madame. But Madame, as far as I am concerned, I wasn't born to betray you. Tell me your troubles, Madame."

The lady kept quiet. But one day she talked.

"My pretty shepherdess, if you betray me, the Good Lord and the Blessed Virgin will punish you. Listen. I'm going to tell you my troubles. Little Shepherdess, I think about my father and my mother day and night. I think about my two brothers who departed seven years ago for foreign countries to serve the king of France. Pretty shepherdess, if you betray me, the Good Lord and the Blessed Virgin will punish you."

"Madame, I won't betray you. Listen, I have great power over a talking crow. If you want, he will fly off and tell everything to your brothers who have gone off to foreign countries to serve the king of France."

"Thank you, my little shepherdess. For the moment let us wait."

From then on the lady and the pretty shepherdess became great friends. But they didn't talk about the lady's problems anymore because they feared that they might be sold out by the butlers and servants of the chateau.

One day Bluebeard said to his wife: "Listen. Tomorrow morning, at daybreak, I'm going to take a long journey. Here are seven keys. The seven big keys open the rooms and the closets in the chateau. You may make use of them as you will. The smallest key is for that little chamber, and I forbid you to enter it. If you disobey me, I'll know about it, and it will be your misfortune."

The next morning at daybreak Bluebeard galloped off on his black horse followed by his three large mastiffs as strong as bulls.

For three months the young lady did as she had been commanded by her master. She used the six keys only to open the rooms and the closets of the chateau. But she thought a hundred times every day: 'I'd like very much to know what's inside that little chamber.' And she couldn't resist for very long.

"Bah!" She said one day. "I've got to satisfy my desire. Bluebeard won't know anything about it."

What was said, was done. The young lady called the pretty shepherdess, took the little key, and opened the door to the small chamber.

"Holy Mary! Eight iron hooks! Seven dead women hung!"

The young lady tried to close the door again. But the little key fell to the ground. The pretty shepherdess picked it up. What bad luck! The little key had a bloodstain on it.

Once they managed to close the door to the small chamber, the lady and the little shepherdess polished the bloodstain until sunset. They polished it with vinegar and salt, with hot ashes, and with horsetail. But nothing worked. The more the two unfortunate women rubbed, the redder the bloodstain became on the iron key.

Finally, the little key spoke: "Rub, ladies. Certainly, you may rub as well as you can. But my bloodstain will never be rubbed out, never. In one week Bluebeard will be here again."

So, the pretty shepherdess said to her mistress: "The right moment has arrived to send for help from the crow.—Caw, caw, caw!"

Right after she uttered this cry, the talking crow flew in through the window.

"Caw, caw, caw. What would you like, pretty shepherdess?"

"Talking crow, I want you to fly off to foreign countries. Fly to the king of France's army. Once you're there, you're to speak to the two brothers of my mistress and tell them to hurry to save their sister who is a prisoner in Bluebeard's chateau."

In the darkness of the night the talking crow sped off. By sunrise he had done his duty.

Seven days later Bluebeard returned to his chateau still mounted on his black horse followed by the three large mastiffs as strong as bulls.

"Wife, return my keys to me!"

The poor wife presented him with the six large keys to the rooms and closets.

"You nasty thing! I've had it with you! The little key! The little key!"

Trembling all over, the unfortunate wife presented him with the little key that had a bloodstain on it.

"You rotten thing! You looked inside the small chamber. Within the next hour you'll be hanging dead on the eighth iron hook!"

Bluebeard descended into the court to sharpen his large knife on a stone, and while he was sharpening it, he said:

> "Sharpen, sharpen, my trusty knife,
> You'll soon cut the throat of my nasty wife."

The young lady and the pretty shepherdess heard all this and trembled.

"Shepherdess, pretty shepherdess, run and climb up to the highest tower."

The pretty shepherdess obeyed. Down in the courtyard Bluebeard continued to sharpen his large knife on the stone.

> "Sharpen, sharpen, my trusty knife,
> You'll soon cut the throat of my nasty wife."

"Shepherdess, pretty shepherdess, what do you see from the tower up high?"

"Madame, in the tower up high I see the sun in the sky. I see the sea. I see mountains and meadows."

So the young lady climbed up seven steps of the stairs.

Down in the courtyard Bluebeard sharpened his knife on the stone.

> "Sharpen, sharpen, my trusty knife,
> You'll soon cut the throat of my nasty wife."

"Shepherdess, my pretty shepherdess, what do you see from the tower up high?"

"Madame, from the tower up high I look below, and below I see your two brothers launched at great speed, galloping on their horses."

So the young lady climbed up seven steps of the stairs.

Down in the courtyard Bluebeard sharpened his knife on the stone.

> "Sharpen, sharpen, my trusty knife,
> You'll soon cut the throat of my nasty wife."

"Shepherdess, my pretty shepherdess, what do you see from the tower up high?"

> "Madame your two brothers are a mile away,
> Save your life if you may."

Down in the courtyard Bluebeard had finished sharpening his knife.

"Come down here, you rotten thing. Come down, or I'll come up!"

But the lady climbed up seven more steps of the stairs."

"My friend, it's time to say my prayers.—Shepherdess, my pretty shepherdess, what do you see from the tower up high?"

> "Madame, your two brothers are not far away.
> Save your life if you may."

So the young lady climbed the stairs to the top. Her two brothers dismounted in front of the door to the chateau.

From the courtyard Bluebeard cried out: "Come down here, you rotten thing. Come down, or I'll come up!"

Now Bluebeard climbed up the stairs and brandished his newly sharpened knife.

"Be brave, my brothers! Come and help me!"

Bluebeard let go of his wife and whistled for his three large mastiffs strong as bulls.

With their swords drawn the two brothers reached the top of the tower.

"Be brave, my brothers! Come and help me!"

For a good hour people and beasts fought against one another. At the end, Bluebeard was killed along with his three large mastiffs as strong as bulls.

"Little sister, we've put an end to this rogue and his beasts. Let us be off."

The eldest brother picked up his sister in his arms. The younger brother took the pretty shepherdess. By sundown they arrived at the chateau of their parents.

"Good day, my father. Good day, my mother. You cried for me because you thought I was dead, and I would have died at Bluebeard's chateau if it hadn't been for the friendship of this pretty shepherdess."

And they all embraced like people who were happy to see each other again.

At dinner the younger son said, "Listen, my father. I'm in love with the pretty shepherdess. If you don't allow me to marry her, I shall go off to war again tomorrow. You'll never see me again. Never!"

"My son, do as you wish. Your pretty shepherdess will receive Bluebeard's chateau as her dowry."

Told by Catherine Sustrac.

The Count's Daughter (c. 1867)[226]
János Erdélyi

There was once, I don't know where, an old tumble-down oven. There was nothing left of its sides; there was also once a town in which a countess lived with an immense fortune. This countess had an exceedingly pretty daughter, who was her sole heiress. The fame of her beauty and her riches being very great the marrying magnates swarmed about her. Among others the three sons of a count used to come to the house, whose castle stood outside the town in a pretty wood. These young men appeared to be richer than one would have supposed from their property, but no one knew where and how the money came to them. The three young men were invited almost every day to the house, but the countess and her daughter never visited them in return, although the young lady was continually asked by them.

For a long time the girl did not accept their invitation, till one day she was preparing for a walk into the wood, in which the young counts' castle was supposed to be. Her mother was surprised to hear that she intended to go into the wood, but as the young lady didn't say exactly where she was going, her mother raised no objection. The girl went, and the prettiness of the wood, and also her curiosity enticed her to go in further and further till at last she discovered the turrets of a splendid castle. Being so near to it her curiosity grew stronger, and at last she walked into the courtyard.

Everything seemed to show that the castle was inhabited, but still she did not see a living soul; the girl went on till she came to the main entrance. The stairs were of white marble, and the girl, quite dazzled at the splendour she beheld, went up, counting the steps.

"One hundred," said the girl, in a half whisper, when she reached the first flight and tarried on the landing. Here she looked round when her attention fell on a bird in a cage.

226. *The Folk-Tales of the Magyars: Collected by Kriza, Erdélyi, and Others*, trans. Henry Jones and Lewis Kropf (London: Elliot Stock, 1889).

"Girl, beware!" said the bird.

But the girl, dazzled by the glitter, and drawn on by her curiosity, again began to mount the stairs, counting them without heeding the bird's words.

"One hundred," again said the girl, as she tarried on the next landing, but still no one was to be seen, but thinking that she might find someone, she opened the first door, which revealed a splendour quite beyond all she had ever imagined, a sight such as she had never seen before, but still no one appeared. She went into another room, and there amongst other furniture she also found three bedsteads, 'This is the three young men's bedroom,' she thought, and went on. The next room into which she stepped was full of weapons of every possible description. The girl stared and went on, and then she came to a large hall which was full of all sorts of garments, clerical, military, civilian, and also women's dresses. She went on still further, and in the next room she found a female figure, made up of razors, which, with extended arms as it seemed, was placed above a deep hole. The girl was horror-struck at the sight, and her fear drove her back. Trembling she went back through the rooms again, but when she came into the bedroom, she heard male voices. Her courage fled, and she could go no further, but hearing some footsteps approach, she crept under one of the beds.

The men entered, whom she recognised as the three sons of the count, bringing with them a beautiful girl, whom the trembling girl recognised by her voice as a dear friend. They stripped her of all, and as they could not take off a diamond ring from her little finger, one of the men chopped it off, and the finger rolled under the bed where the girl lay concealed. One of the men began to look for the ring when another said, "You will find it some other time," and so he left off looking for it.

Having quite undressed the girl they took her to the other room, when after a short lapse of time, she heard some faint screaming, and it appeared to her as if the female figure of razors had snapped together, and the mangled remains of the unfortunate victim were heard to drop down into the deep hole. The three brothers came back, and one of them began to look for the ring while cold sweat broke out on the poor girl hiding under the bed.

"Never mind, it is ours now, and you can find it in the morning," said one of the men, and bade the others go to bed. And so it happened: the search for the ring was put off till next day. They went to bed, and the girl began to breathe more freely in her hiding place. She began to grope about in silence and found the ring and secreted it in her dress, and hearing that the three brothers were fast asleep, she stole out noiselessly leaving the door half ajar.

The next day the three brothers again visited the countess when the daughter told them that she had a dream as if she had been to their castle. She told them how she went up a flight of marble stairs till she counted one hundred, and up the next flight when she again counted one hundred. The brothers were charmed and very much surprised at the dream and assured her that it was exactly like their home.

Then she told them how she went from one room to another and what she saw, but when she came in her dream as far as the razor-maid, they began to feel uneasy and grew suspicious, and when she told them the scene with the girl, and in proof of her tale produced the finger with the ring, the brothers were terrified and exclaimed: "We are betrayed!" Immediately, they took flight. But everything was arranged, and the servants, who were ordered to watch, caught them. After an investigation all their numberless deeds were brought to light, and they were beheaded.

Translated by Henry Jones and Lewis Kropf.

The Story about Oh My (1870)[227]

Laura Gonzenbach

Once upon a time there was a poor old woodcutter, who had three beautiful granddaughters. The youngest was called Maruzza, and she was also the most beautiful and the most clever among them. The grandfather had no way of earning a living, and he also had no money so that he didn't know how to support his granddaughters.

One day, as he was gathering wood in the forest, he became so tired and exhausted that he sat down on a large rock and sighed very loudly, "Oh my!"

All of a sudden a large man appeared and asked him, "Why have you called me?"

"I didn't call you," the woodcutter said, visibly terrified.

"Didn't you cry out 'Ohmy'? That's my name," the huge man said. "You look as though you were a poor lost soul. So I'm going to help you. Bring your oldest granddaughter to me. She will serve my wife. Then I'll reward you with rich gifts. Lead her to this spot. Call out my name. And I'll soon appear."

Upon saying these words, he gave the old man some money. Then the old man rejoiced and ran home to his granddaughters.

"Just think," he said to the oldest granddaughter, "you have been blessed with good luck. A distinguished gentleman wants to hire you to serve his wife. Now you'll be looked after."

When his granddaughter heard this, she kissed the ground and said, "I thank you, my Lord!"

After a few days had passed, she got herself ready, and her grandfather took her into the woods and called out loudly, "Oh my!"

Then Ohmy appeared, and when he saw the beautiful maiden, he said, "You've kept your word, and now your daughter will have it good. You may come here once a week and ask about her." Then he gave the grandfather a beautiful gift, took the girl by the hand, and led her to a large stone wall. Once

---

227. "Die Geschichte von Ohimè," *Sicilianische Märchen*, 2 vols. (Leipzig: W. Engelmann, 1870).

they stood in front of it, the wall opened so that they could enter into splendid rooms that were filled with marvelous treasures and valuable things.

"Where is the mistress of the house?" asked the girl.

"The mistress is you," Ohmy answered. "And if you obey me and do everything I command you to do, you'll also become my wife."

With these words he led her through the entire castle and showed her the beautiful things. Finally, they came to a room in which there were many murdered young women.

"Do you see these women?" Ohmy said. "None of them obeyed me. None of them did their duty. That's why I had to punish them. So let this be a warning to you."

"If they didn't obey you," she said, "then they got what they deserved. I'll certainly do my duty."

So the maiden remained with Ohmy and had a good life. After some days had passed, however, Ohmy came to her and said, "I must go away for three days, and I want you to carry out my orders while I am gone. If you don't do this, you'll pay for it badly."

"What do you want me to do?" she asked.

Ohmy gave her a dead leg and said, "You must eat this leg, and when I return, I don't want to see any trace of it."

Upon saying this, he left her, but she remained full of anxiety.

"How can I eat a dead leg?" she thought. "It's such a dirty, disgusting thing. Well, Ohmy will have to wait an eternity before I eat this!" And since she didn't want to eat it, she threw the leg out the window and believed that Ohmy wouldn't notice it. However, when he returned home, his first question was, "Did you do your duty?"

"Yes, master."

Then Ohmy cried out, "Where are you, leg?"

"I'm here!"

"Come here to me."

Then the leg appeared, and Ohmy said to the maiden, "Since you've lied to me and not done your duty, you shall now receive your punishment!"

Immediately he grabbed hold of her, dragged her into the room, where the numerous dead girls were lying, and murdered her.

After some days had passed, the old woodcutter came back to the woods and cried out for Ohmy, and when the large man appeared, the grandfather asked him, "How are things going with my granddaughter?"

"Oh, she's doing very well," Ohmy answered. "My wife treats her as if she were her very own daughter and would like to hire your middle granddaughter as well. Bring her to me here, and I'll give you another beautiful gift."

The old woodcutter ran home once more full of joy and told the second granddaughter that the distinguished gentleman wanted her as well. She was very content, and the grandfather led her into the woods.

"Oh my!" he cried out, and immediately Ohmy appeared and took charge of the granddaughter. He led her through the stone wall into his palace and showed her the marvelous rooms with many treasures.

"Where is my sister?" she asked.

"I'll show you your sister right away," he answered and led her into the room where she saw her dead sister among all the other corpses.

"You see, your sister didn't obey my commands. That's why I had to punish her this way. And if you don't obey me, you will suffer the exact same fate."

"Oh, I'll certainly do my duty," she replied, but she was trembling in her heart and thought, 'Who knows what terrible command he gave to my poor sister?'

Some days passed, and one morning Ohmy came to her and said, "I must go away for three days. In the meantime I want you to carry out my command. Otherwise, something terrible will happen to you."

With these words, he gave her a foot from a dead person that she was supposed to eat. Then he departed, and the maiden was left full of anxiety and thought, 'How can I eat this disgusting, dirty foot? I'm going to throw it on to the roof and tell that vicious thing Ohmy that I've eaten it.'

So she did this and believed that Ohmy wouldn't notice it. But when he returned home, his first question was: "Did you carry out my command?"

"Yes, master!"

"Foot! Where are you? Come to me right now!"

Then the foot appeared, and Ohmy exclaimed, "Did you think you could really lie to me? Since you didn't do your duty, I'm going to kill you."

Then he dragged her into the room where the other dead young women were and murdered her as well.

After some days had passed the woodcutter returned to the woods to ask about his granddaughters.

"Oh, they're leading a good life," answered Ohmy. "My wife has taken a great liking to them as if they were her own daughters. Now she would like to have your third granddaughter as well."

The poor woodcutter felt he would explode from joy now that all his granddaughters would be well looked after. So he rushed home to his youngest granddaughter and said, "Maruzza, get yourself ready quickly. The distinguished gentleman wants to hire you as well."

Then the grandfather led her into the woods where Ohmy was very friendly to her and led her through the stone wall.

"Where are my sisters?" Maruzza asked.

"I'll show them to you right away," he responded and opened the door to the room in which all the corpses were lying.

"You see your sisters. They're lying there because they didn't do their duty."

Poor Maruzza's heart trembled, but she only said, "You did the right thing by punishing them if they didn't do their duty. You can order me to do anything you want. I'll do whatever you say."

After a several days had passed, Ohmy said to Maruzza, "I've got to go away for three days, and now the time has come when you can show me how obedient you are. You see this dead arm of a person. You must eat it while I'm gone, and I don't want to see the slightest trace of it when I return."

With these words he departed and left poor Maruzza troubled by her worries and thoughts.

"Oh," she thought, "what should I do now? Oh, I'm so unlucky! How can I eat the arm of a dead person! Oh, blessed soul of my mother, come help me and tell me what I should do!"

All of a sudden she heard a voice that called out to her, "Maruzza, don't weep. I shall help you. Heat the oven and make it as hot as possible, and leave the arm inside until it its burned into coals. Then ground the coals into powder and wrap them in a fine cloth around your waist. Ohmy will not notice a thing and won't harm you."

This voice was the blessed soul of her mother, who helped poor Maruzza. Indeed, Maruzza did everything that the voice had told her to do. She heated the oven and placed the arm inside until it was burned into coals. Then she ground the coals, wrapped the powder in a fine cloth, and tied it around her waist.

When Ohmy returned home, he asked right away, "Did you carry out my command?"

"Yes, master!"

"Arm, where are you? Come to me now!"

"I can't come," the arm answered.

"Where are you?"

"I'm in Maruzza's Body."

When Ohmy heard this, he became very happy and cried, "Well, Maruzza, you will become my wife, for now I know that you're honest and obedient."

From then on Maruzza led a good life with him. Ohmy loved her and brought her everything she wished. One day he also showed her all his closets in which he had many bottles with potions and salves.

"Look," he said. "Here is a salve for dead people. When you rub the salve on them, they will return to life. I'm showing it to you because I know that you are loyal to me."

After he had shown her everything, he led her also to a locked door and said, "Look, Maruzza. Everything that's in this castle belongs to you, and you may do whatever you wish with it. However, you may never open this door. If I ever notice that you've opened it, I'll murder you."

No sooner had Ohmy departed on his next trip, however, than Maruzza took her bundle of keys and opened the door. When she entered the room, she saw a marvelously handsome young man, who was lying on the ground as if he were dead, and a dagger was stuck into his heart.

"Oh!" Maruzza thought full of sympathy. "What a poor unfortunate young man! This is why that wicked Ohmy didn't want me to open the door."

So she ran out and fetched some of the salve. Then she returned to the young man, pulled the dagger from his heart, and rubbed the wound with the salve. All of a sudden, the young man opened his eyes and was healed.

"Beautiful maiden," he cried. "You've saved me. I want you to know that I'm a prince, and the evil Ohmy dragged me here and has kept me a prisoner."

"Oh," she responded. "What's the use now that you're cured? Ohmy will soon return, and when he sees that you're healthy and have regained your life, he will kill you and me. So you had better lie down again, and I'll stick the dagger into your heart. Then I'll see what we can do to murder the wicked Ohmy."

And this is what they did. The prince lay down again, and Maruzza stuck the dagger into his heart while shedding many tears, especially because she had fallen passionately in love with him.

When Ohmy returned home, she went with him into the garden and flattered him with many sweet words.

"Tell me, dear master, if you ever had the misfortune of being pursued by someone who wanted to take your life, what would he have to do to kill you?"

"Why are you asking me this?" Ohmy replied. "Do you want perhaps to betray me?"

"Oh, how can you think such a thing like that!? Aren't I your obedient, faithful Maruzza? It was just a thought that went through my head."

"Well, since I know I can trust you, I'll tell you," Ohmy said. "Look, nobody can murder me. But if someone were to take a twig from this herb right here and stuff it into my ear, then I would fall asleep and never wake up again."

"Now, now, don't tell me any more. I don't want to know anything about it," Maruzza responded, but secretly she leaned over, broke off a twig of the herb, and put it into her pocket.

"Now, sit down over here," she said to Ohmy, "and I'll clean the lice from your hair."

After she sat down, he laid his head in her lap, and she began picking the lice from his beard until he fell asleep. Then she quickly took the herb and stuffed it into both ears so that he fell into a deeper sleep. Afterward she left him in the garden and rushed back into the house, took the salve, and rubbed it on the prince so that he came back to life once more. Than she ran into the other room where the dead maidens were lying, and she rubbed all of them with the salve, first her sisters, then all the other young women whom the evil Ohmy had murdered one by one. When they were all alive once again, Maruzza gave them rich gifts and sent them back to their homes. She and the prince took the rest of the treasures and traveled to the prince's realm. Just think of the joy of the king and queen as their son came home, for they had wept for many years and had thought that he was dead. Now he had returned and even brought with him a beautiful and clever maiden. So a splendid wedding was celebrated, and the prince married the beautiful Maruzza and lived with her happily and content.

In the meantime, Ohmy lay in the garden and slept and slept for many years. Eventually, however, the herb became old and rotten because of the wind and rain, and one day, it fell out so that Ohmy awoke from his sleep.

'Where am I?' he asked himself. Then he jumped up and ran into the house. When he saw nothing but empty walls, however, he became furious and yelled, "That no-good-for-nothing Maruzza! She betrayed me after I had placed so much trust in her. Just wait. I'll get my revenge on her!"

So he set out and wandered through many countries in search of Maruzza. He wandered far and wide until, one day, he finally came to the city in which Maruzza lived. When he went through the streets, he accidentally raised his eyes and saw the beautiful Maruzza standing at a window.

"Ho-ho!" he thought. "You're here, and you're living splendidly in a royal palace!? Just you wait! I'm going to get you yet!"

So he went to a shop and made a statue out of silver that was just as large as he was himself and hollow on the inside. Then he placed many instruments inside to make music, called for a young man, and said to him, "I'll give you a magnificent gift if you carry this statue on your back through the entire city and charge people money to see it. After you've done this, you're to bring it to the king and let it stay with him for some days."

The young man promised Ohmy to take care of everything, and Ohmy locked himself in the statue. The young man carried the statute through the streets of the entire city and cried out, "Hey, look at the beautiful Saint Nicholas, and listen to the beautiful music he can make!"

When the people heard the young man, many of them called him over and asked, "Let Saint Nicholas stay here for some days so that we can enjoy his music. We'll give you a beautiful gift if you do this."

So the young man brought the statue into different houses, and Ohmy played so wonderfully that everyone in the city spoke about the marvelous statue and nothing else, and everyone wanted to see and hear it. Gradually, the news spread to the king and to Maruzza, and she said, "Oh, call the young man with the statue to us one time. I'd like to keep the statue here with us for a few days."

So the king had the young man summoned to the castle and gave him a beautiful present so that he would leave Saint Nicholas with them for a few days, and he had the young man carry it into his bedroom, where he enjoyed the beautiful music with Maruzza. In the evening, however, when both of them had laid down to sleep, Maruzza suddenly heard a soft noise and cried out, "Help!"

"What's the matter?" the king asked, and all the people in the palace were terrified and gathered together.

"I heard a noise near the statue," Maruzza said. But when the servants looked through the entire room, they found nothing, and the king thought that Maruzza must have dreamed something. When everything was quiet again, the same noise could be heard again. Maruzza cried out once more. The servants came running, but they couldn't find anything, and the king said, "Maruzza, you're dreaming. If you cry out again, I don't want anyone to come."

Meanwhile, Ohmy heard that in the statue, and this was exactly what he wanted. So when the king fell back to sleep, he quietly opened the statue and came out. Maria screamed out loud, but nobody came because Ohmy quickly placed a bottle with a potion on the bed, and as soon as he did this, the king and all the people in the palace fell into a deep sleep. Nobody could wake up. Only Maruzza remained awake and saw Ohmy approach her and grab her by the arm.

"You betrayed me!" he cried. "And you thought you were safe here! Now you're in my power and won't escape your punishment."

Then he went into the kitchen, started a large fire, and placed a huge kettle with oil on top of it, and when the oil was boiling just right, he rushed back into the room, grabbed the poor Maruzza, and wanted to drag her into the kitchen to throw her into the kettle with the boiling oil. She wept and screamed, but nobody heard her because the king and everyone in the castle had been cast under a spell. As she sought to defend herself, the bottle with the potion fell off the bed and broke on the ground. All of a sudden the king awoke, and the servants came storming into the room. Maruzza cried out, "Help! Help! This vicious monster wants to murder me!"

Then the servants grabbed hold of the evil Ohmy, and the king recognized him and ordered the servants to throw him into the same kettle with boiling oil in which he had wanted to kill Maruzza. And this is what happened. The wicked Ohmy was thrown into the boiling oil and was miserably burned to death. But the king and Maruzza lived for a long time still, rich and consoled, and we have nothing as we get old.

The Cobbler and His Three Daughters (Bluebeard) (1877)[228]
Wentworth Webster

Like many others in the world, there was a cobbler who had three daughters. They were very poor. He only earned enough just to feed his children. He did not know what would become of him. He went about in his grief, walking, walking sadly on, and he meets a gentleman, who asks him where he is going melancholy like that. He answers him, "Even if I shall tell you, I shall get no relief."

"Yes, yes. Who knows? Tell it."

"I have three daughters, and I have not work enough to maintain them. I have famine in the house."

---

228. *Basque Legends* (London: Griffith and Farran, 1877).

"If it is only that, we will manage it. You will give me one of your daughters, and I will give you so much money."

The father was very grieved to make any such bargain, but at last he comes down to that. He gives him his eldest daughter. This gentleman takes her to his palace, and after having passed some time there, he said to her that he has a short journey to make—that he will leave her all the keys, that she might see everything, but that there is one key that she must not make use of—that it would bring misfortune on her.

He locks the door on the young lady. The young girl goes into all the rooms and finds them very beautiful, and she was curious to see what there was in that which was forbidden. She goes in and sees heaps of dead bodies. Imagine her fright!

With her trembling she lets the key fall to the ground. She trembles for the coming of her husband. He arrives and asks her if she has entered the forbidden chamber. She tells him "Yes." He takes her and puts her into an underground dungeon. Hardly, hardly did he give her enough to eat and that was human flesh.

The cobbler had finished his money, and he was again melancholy. The gentleman meets him again and says to him, "Your other daughter is not happy alone. You must give me another daughter. When she is happy, I will send her back, and I will give you so much money."

The father did not like it, but he was so poor that, in order to have a little money, he gives him his daughter. The gentleman takes her home with him like the other. After some days he said to her too: "I must take a short journey. I will give you all the keys of the house, but do not touch such a key of such a room."

He locks the house-door and goes off after having left the food she needed. This young girl goes into all the rooms, and, as she was curious, she went to look into the forbidden chamber. She was so terribly frightened at the sight of so many dead bodies in this room that she lets the key fall, and it gets stained. Our young girl was trembling as to what should become of her when the master should come back. He arrives, and the first thing he asks: "Have you been in that room?"

She told him "Yes."

He takes her underground like her other sister.

The cobbler had finished his money, and he was in misery. When the gentleman comes to him again and says to him, "I will give you a great deal of money if you will let your daughter come to my house for a few days. The three will be happier together, and I will send you the two back again together."

The father believes it and gives him his third daughter. The gentleman gives him the money, and he takes this young girl like the others. At the end of some days he leaves her, saying that he is going to make a short journey. He gives her all the keys of the house, saying to her: "You will go into all the rooms except this one," pointing out the key to her. He locks the outside door and goes off.

This young girl goes straight to the forbidden chamber. She opens it, and think of her horror at seeing so many dead people. She thought that he would kill her too, and, as there were all kinds of arms in this chamber, she takes a sabre with her and hides it under her dress. She goes a little further on and sees her two sisters almost dying with hunger, and a young man in the same condition. She takes care of them as well as she can till the gentleman comes home.

On his arrival he asks her: "Have you been in that room?"

She says, "Yes," and, in giving him back the keys, she lets them fall on the ground on purpose, and at the instant that this gentleman stoops to pick them up, the young lady cuts off his head with her sword. Oh how glad she was!

Quickly she runs to deliver her sisters and that young man, who was the son of a king. She sends for her father, the cobbler, and leaves him there with his two daughters, and the youngest daughter goes away with her young gentleman, after being married to him. If they lived well, they died well too.

Translated by Wentworth Webster.

Redbeard (1881)[229]

Paul Sébillot

Redbeard had been married seven times and had successively lost his wives after a short period of living together. He lived ten years on good terms with his eighth wife with whom he had two daughters and a don. But during that period Redbeard grew to hate his wife so much that he decided to get rid of her.

One Sunday, just as she returned from Mass, he said to her: "Jeanne-Marie, today is the day that I'm going to kill you."

"Allow me," his wife responded, "to put on my wedding clothes that I wore when I married you."

"All right, go up to your room and hurry because I don't have much time."

Before getting dressed, she opened the door to the house to let out her little dog and put a letter in its ear for her brothers who lived a few miles away.

In the meantime Redbeard sharpened his sword and kept repeating:

I'm sharpening, I'm sharpening my knife
And soon I'll use it to kill my wife.

"Are you ready, Jeanne-Marie?" he cried out.

"No, I haven't put on my petticoat yet."

A few moments later her husband repeated:

I'm sharpening, I'm sharpening my knife
And soon I'll use it to kill my wife.

---

229. "Barbe-Rouge," *Littérature orale de la Haute-Bretagne* (Paris: Maisonneuve, 1881).

And for the second time he asked her whether she was dressed.

"No," she said, "I'm putting on my stockings."

"Are you ready?" he repeated after a quarter of an hour.

"No, I'm combing my hair."

About a half hour later, Redbeard cried out: "My knife's well sharpened. Come down, or I'll come get you."

"Just wait a little while longer. I'm fixing my hair."

After she pinned her hair, she looked out the window and saw men on horseback riding down the road. So she signaled to them.

"Your time is over!" Redbeard cried out. "I'm coming upstairs and will do my work there."

"I only have one more pin to place, and then I'll come down."

One minute later, she said: "I'm ready."

And she began slowly to descend the stairs. As soon as she arrived downstairs, there was a knock at the door, and Redbeard hid in the hallway. But the leaders of the group of men discovered him and killed him.

Jeanne-Marie left the house with her children, and at the end of her mourning period, she married one of the soldiers who had rescued her.

Told in 1878 by Jean Bouchery of Doudain, a farmworker at Ercé.

The Story of a Turner (1881)[230]

J. Adolpho Francisco Coelho

There once lived a turner who was in the habit of going into a forest which was some distance from his cottage to cut down wood to make spoons. One day as he was sawing a venerable old chestnut tree, he noticed a deep hole in the tree, and being curious to see what was inside he unluckily penetrated within, and immediately an enchanted Moor came forward to meet him, and in angry tones at the intrusion said to him: "Since you have dared to penetrate into my palace I order you to bring me the first thing you shall meet on reaching your cottage, but take heed that you comply with my command, otherwise you will surely die within three days."

The turner now departed and went home, where he had three daughters and a little pet dog which always came to the door to meet him. That day, however, contrary to the dog's custom, as ill luck would have it, it was his eldest daughter, and not his dog, who came out to meet him. This of course so distressed him that he, weeping bitterly, told her what had happened to him and what the Moor had demanded from him. But he entreated her at the same time to go with him and give herself up to the Moor, for otherwise she and her sisters would remain without a supporter or protection.

---

230.   "O Colheareiro," *The Folk-Lore Record*, vol. 4 (1881).

The eldest daughter very unselfishly consented to go, and prepared to set out with her father; and after taking leave of her sisters she left home for the enchanted Moor's palace.

We shall now leave the turner and his two daughters and record how the Moor acted towards the eldest daughter. As soon as the girl arrived at the tree and entered the enchanted Moor's palace he gave her the keys of all the apartments, and at the same time he put round her neck a very fine gold chain with a key which belonged to a chamber into which he forbade her ever to enter under pain of death.

One day, however, the girl full of curiosity longed to enter and see for herself what was contained in that chamber, which it was so essential she should not find out. Unable to contain her curiosity she took the chain from her neck, and with the gold key opened the forbidden chamber.

Great, however, was her surprise and horror to find a number of bodies with their heads cut off. Much frightened and terror-struck at the fearful sight she immediately shut the door, and trusting not to be found out she put back the chain and key round her neck, but when the Moor returned to the palace, the first thing he did was to look at the gold key hanging from her neck, and finding a tiny mark of blood upon it, he knew what had happened, and without saying a word cut her head off that instant, and laid her down on the floor in the apartment with the other corpses.

A few days after this occurrence, the turner, in hopes of seeing or hearing some news of his daughter, and desirous to know how she was getting on with the Moor, returned to the palace and inquired of him how his daughter was, to which the Moor replied: "Go and fetch me your next daughter to be a companion to the one already here, as she feels very lonely and dull without her."

The turner went back for his second daughter and brought her to the Moor. Like the first girl she received all the keys, and the chain with the one particular key which belonged to the chamber which she was never to attempt to open; but like her sister she also was led by her curiosity to the same fate, and had her head cut off by the Moor on account of her disobedience.

The turner as before called at the Moor's palace to know how his daughters were and met with the same reply, and was ordered to bring his third daughter. This of course grieved the good honest man very much, who was loath to part with his only remaining daughter, but, fearing to disobey the Moor's commands, he brought her also to him as desired. When she arrived in the palace, the Moor gave her the same injunctions as he had given to her two sisters. But the girl did open and enter the forbidden chamber in spite of the command, and she saw her beheaded sisters, and although horrified she had sufficient courage to remain in the chamber and inspect everything in it. She touched her sisters' bodies and finding that they were still warm, she felt a great desire to bring them back to life.

In this chamber there was a cupboard in which she found a number of earthenware pots containing blood; and seeing that two of them had her sisters' names upon them, she stuck the heads of her sisters to their bodies with the blood; and when she found that they adhered and remained perfectly set, she wiped the blood off from their necks. When she had finished this operation, her sisters came to life again. She, however, enjoined upon them perfect silence, telling them that she would manage to send them home to their father again, unknown to the Moor, whilst the sisters recommend her to wipe the key very carefully from any spot of blood, that the Moor might not discover what she had been doing.

The Moor returned home, and, not seeing any spot of blood upon the gold key, he did not, of course, suspect anything, and believing her to be an obedient loving wife, he soon began to love her very much, until he idolized her to such a degree that he at last allowed himself to be domineered over by her, and she could rule him as she pleased; and thus he became a complete slave to her, and ready to do anything at her bidding.

One day she begged the Moor to take a barrel of sugar to her father, for he was very poor, and it would not come amiss to him. To this he readily agreed. She then put one of her sisters in the barrel, and desired the Moor to go quickly and return soon, as said she, it was joyless to her to be long separated from him; and that to make sure he did not stop anywhere she would go up to the watch-tower and look after him all the way. Before the Moor set out on his journey with the barrel, she told her sister to repeat the following words all the way: "I can see you, dear, oh, I can see you, dear," so that the Moor should believe that the voice came from her in the watch-tower. The girl who was hidden in the barrel obeyed her clever sister's injunction, and continued to repeat the words in sweet tender tones: "I can see you, dear, oh, I can see you still, darling," whilst the Moor, quite fascinated with his charmer, answered her most lovingly: "Magnificent eyes that can see so far; yes, I am running, dear," and he ran until he reached the turner's cottage. He left the barrel, and after a few hurried words, turned towards home, running all the way.

Some days had elapsed when she again asked the Moor to take another barrel with provisions to her father; he again consented, and she sent her second sister home in the same manner as she had done the first.

She was now the only one remaining in the enchanted palace, and to extricate herself from the Moor was a much more difficult affair; but, as she was clever and quick at inventing, what do you think she thought of? She made up a figure with straw, dressed it up with her own clothes, and placed it in the watch-tower, as if she were looking out. She now told the Moor that another barrel was ready to take to her home, and that she would go up to the turret of the tower and watch for him until his return. Then she secretly got inside the barrel, and whilst the Moor carried the barrel she went repeating the same words as her sisters had done: "Oh, I can see you, darling, yes, I can see you, quick, quick, dear," and the Moor replied: "Yes, darling, I am running, I am running as fast as I can, beautiful eyes that can see so far."

Thus did the three sisters find their way back to their father and home. When the Moor returned to his palace and did not find the girl at the threshold ready to welcome him back, he ran up quickly into the watch-tower, and on endeavoring to embrace the straw figure, which he believed to be his bride, he missed his footing and fell from the tower down to the ground and was picked up quite dead.

The venerable chestnut tree and the palace immediately disappeared, for the whole had been but the work of enchantment.

Told by Coimbra and translated by Henriqueta Monteiro.

A Tuscan Bluebeard (1905)[231]

Isabella Anderton

Once upon a time there was a woman who had three daughters. One day a sexton knocked at her door and said, "Good wife, give me a piece of bread."

The woman said to the eldest daughter: "Take the poor man a piece of bread. He looks very wretched."

But when the girl got outside the door with the bread, the sexton said: "It's you I want," and he caught her up and carried her away.

After a while they reached a field where there was a hole in the ground. In the hole the girl saw steps, and when they got to the bottom of these, she found herself in the most beautiful palace she had ever seen.

"Now," said the man, "this palace shall belong to you. I shall be away all day, but shall come back every evening. So, you need not be lonely. While I am away, you may amuse yourself as you like. Here are the keys. You can explore the whole palace except the room which this key opens. There you are never to go."

"Very well," said the girl, "I won't."

"Take this ring," continued the man, putting one on her finger. "So long as the gold remains bright, I shall know you have been obedient. When it is cloudy, I shall know you have opened the door."

For some days the girl was quite happy exploring the wonders of this underground palace, but little by little she began to want to see what was in the room which was forbidden her, and at last the desire to open that door quite overcame her dread of punishment. She put in the key, turned it, pushed open the door, and went in. She found herself in a marble courtyard opening on to a beautiful garden. In the middle of the courtyard was a pond, in which was swimming a lovely gold-red fish.

"Oh, I must catch you," said the girl, and plunged her hand into the water. But the fish bit her so sharply that she withdrew her hand immediately, and then she saw that the ring was covered with blood. She rubbed and rubbed, but the

---

231. *Tuscan Folk-Lore and Sketches: Together with Some Other Papers* (London: Arnold Fairbairns, 1905).

blood would not come off. The ring was stained and cloudy, and sadly she went out, locking the door behind her.

When the man came home that night, he found her sad and dejected.

"Ah," said he, "you have disobeyed me. Let me see the ring."

She tried to hide her hand, but it was no good. He looked at the ring, and then cut off her head, and put head and body against one of the columns in the marble courtyard. After that he went back to the girl's home, and again asked for bread.

"Go," said the mother to the second daughter, "carry the poor man something to eat."

But when the second daughter came to him, he treated her as he had done the first. He carried her off to the underground palace, gave her the keys, and a ring, and told her, too, that she might do anything she liked, except open that door. It happened to the second as it had done to the first. She got tired of wandering about the palace with nothing to do, opened the door, and went into the marble courtyard. She, too, tried to catch the fish; she, too, was bitten; her ring became cloudy, and she was beheaded and put beside her sister.

Then the man returned and carried away the youngest girl. Now the youngest is always cleverer than her elder sisters; and so it happened in this case. After she had spent some time in the palace, she, too, determined to open the forbidden door. So she took off her ring, put it in her work-basket, and went in. She tried to catch the fish, as her sisters had done, and then began to wander about. She soon saw her sisters' heads and bodies, and that made her sad. When it was near evening, she left the courtyard, put on her ring, and went to meet her husband as brightly and cheerfully as ever.

"Ah," said the man, "I can see that you have not disobeyed me. You're a dear, good little wife."

Every day, as soon as her husband was gone, the girl took her work into the garden and sat there, knitting or playing with the fish, but she was unhappy because of her sisters. One morning as she was at work, she saw a little lizard without a tail; the tail was lying on the ground beside it. She watched the creature and saw it bite a leaf off a certain plant, turn its head over its back, and touch its body and its tail with the leaf. Instantly tail and body grew together, and the lizard ran off quite merrily.

"Aha," thought the girl, "now I know what to do!"

So she picked the plant, went into the courtyard, put her sisters' heads on to their respective bodies, touched the necks with plants, and there were her sisters quite well again. Then she took them upstairs and hid them.

That evening she said to her husband, "I am afraid my mother must be very unhappy. She is old and poor, and now there is no one to work for her or take care of her. Let me go and see her."

"No," said the man, "I can't spare you."

"Well, then, let me fill a chest with clothes and money, and you shall carry it to her."

"Very well," said the man. "Have it ready by to-morrow morning."

So the girl put linen and gold into a chest. Then she made her eldest sister get in and shut down the lid.

"Now," she said to her husband, "you must not set down the chest at all. Remember, I can see you all the way. Go straight there and back again, for I want you at home."

The man put the chest on his head and set off. After a time he began to want to put down his burden for a little and said to himself: 'My wife can't possibly see me, there's this hill between me and her,' and he began to set down the chest.

"Do you think I can't see you?" a voice said. "Silly man, I can see you everywhere."

'Oh dear, oh dear,' said the man to himself, 'what a clever wife mine is! She can see me even through a hill. And how fond of me she is! She knows what I am doing wherever I am.'

So he staggered on to his mother-in-law's, threw down the box, and went home again. A little while after the second sister was sent home in the same way, and now the girl began to think how she could get away herself. One evening she said to her husband: "I want you to take some more things to my mother. I shall get everything ready to-night. Don't wake me in the morning before you go, as I shall come to bed very late. I have to make the bread."

The man went off to bed, and the girl set to work. She made a great doll of dough and put it in her bed. Then she put clothes and money into the chest, crept in herself, and pulled down the lid.

The next morning the man got up early.

"Wife, wife," he shouted, "good-bye!"

No answer.

"Ah, I forgot, she was up late making bread. She's a dear little wife and works very hard."

So he crept on tiptoe to her bedside, saw the figure under the clothes, and went out as quietly as he had gone in. Then he took the chest and started. Again he wanted to set down his burden, again the warning voice stopped him, and at last he flung down the box at his mother-in-law's door, declaring that this was the last he would bring her.

When he got home, he called, "Wife! Wife!"

Still no answer.

"What, is she still asleep? She must be tired."

And he went to shake her. Then he found that there was no wife there, but only a figure of dough, and that he was alone once more in his underground palace.

SHORT BIOGRAPHIES

Addy, Sidney Oldall (1848–1933), British solicitor and folklorist, who wrote several important books on English history and folklore. He studied at the University of Oxford and retired from his law practice in 1902 to focus on collecting tales in dialect and writing about local history in the Yorkshire/Derbyshire region. Aside from writing histories about traditions in this region, he contributed numerous articles to magazines and journals of folklore. His most important works are *Household Tales and Traditional Remains* (1895) and *The Evolution of the English House* (1898).

Afanas'ev, Alexander (1826–1871), Russian folklorist, who held positions as lawyer, historian, and journalist before embarking on a major study of Russian folklore. His most important work is *Narodyne Russkija skaski* (*Russian Folk Tales*, 1855–1867). Inspired by the Brothers Grimm, this collection was published in eight fascicles and contained 640 stories. The tales, which came from over thirty provinces, were recorded largely second-hand from records and manuscripts of other people. In his late life, after he had been punished by the Russian authorities for publishing anticlerical and vulgar tales and prohibited from doing further research on folklore, Afanas'ev managed to publish an important scholarly study, *The Poetic Interpretation of Nature by the Slavs* (1865–1869).

Anderton, Isabella (1858–1904), British writer, who lived many years in Italy. Her book *Tuscan Folk-Lore and Sketches: Together with Some Other Papers,* was edited by her brothers H. Ormond Anderton and Basil Anderton and published posthumously in 1905.

Andrews, James Bruyn (1842–1909), American lawyer, who had to give up the legal profession due to fragile health. He moved to Europe and served for a short period as the U.S. consul at Valencia, Spain. In 1871, he retired and moved to Mentone, where he became an expert on the folklore of the Alpes-Maritimes/Genoa region of France. The tales that he collected in *Contes ligures, traditions de la Rivière* were originally published in French in 1892, but he sent English translations to the Folklore Society in London, England. He was also the first person to record the Mentonnes dialect and was well known among European linguists.

Arnim, Friedmund von (1814–1883), German writer, son of the famous novelist Achim von Arnim, and son of his equally famous wife, Bettina von Armin, a prominent writer. He published an important collection of oral folk tales, *Hundert neue Mährchen im Gebirge gesammelt,* in 1844.

Asbjørnsen, Peter Christen (1812–1885), Norwegian folklorist, who worked as a private tutor and began collecting folk tales with his friend Jørgen Moe in the 1830s. Together they published three collections of tales: *Norske folkeeventyr* (*Norwegian Folk Tales*, 1841–1844). Similar to the Brothers Grimm, they sought to foster the natural language and culture of the Norwegian folk through the publication of fairy tales, legends, fables, and humorous anecdotes. After Moe was ordained as a clergyman in 1853, he stopped working on folklore, and Asbjørnsen independently produced two other volumes of tales, *Norske huldreeventyr og folkesagn* (*Norwegian Hulder Fairy Tales and Folk Legends*, 1845–1848).

Bain, Robert Nisbet (1854–1909), British folklorist, translator, and historian, who edited and translated several important collections of folk and fairy tales including *Russian Fairy Tales* (1892), *Cossack Fairy Tales and Folk Tales* (1894), *Turkish Fairy Tales and Folk Tales* (1896), *Tales from Tolstoi* (1901), and *Tales from Gorky* (1902).

Baudis, Josef (1883–1933), Czech professor of Celtic and comparative philology at the University of Bratislava. He was joint secretary of the Philological Society of London and one of the founders of the journal *Philologica*. In 1917, he translated twenty-three Czech folk tales in *The Key of Gold*.

Bladé, Jean-François (1827–1900), French magistrate and writer, who studied law at universities in Toulouse and Paris and eventually became a judge. However, he maintained a great passion for literature and wrote novels and stories while gathering folk tales in the region of Gascogne. His major work is the three-volume collection *Contes populaires de Gascogne* (1886).

Busk, Rachel (1831–1907), British pioneer folklorist, who spent a good part of her life traveling in Europe and recording folk tales. Her major publication is *The Folk-Lore of Rome, Collected by Word of Mouth from the People* (1874). Other important works are *Patrañas, or Spanish Stories, Legendary and Traditional* (1870) and *Household Tales from the Land of Hofer, or Popular Myths of Tirol* (1871).

Cadic, François (1864–1929), French priest and writer, who stemmed from a family of peasants. After studying at a seminar in Vannes, he was ordained as a priest in 1889. Several years later he became a professor of history at the Institut Catholique de Paris, where he founded the Breton Parish at Notre-Dame-des-Champs that consisted of 40,000 people and became the center of Breton culture. Devoted to Brittany, Cadic published numerous collections of Breton tales, songs, and legends. Among the most significant are *Contes et légendes de Bretagne* (1914) and *Nouveaux contes et légendes de Bretagne* (1925).

Campbell of Islay, John Francis (1822–1885), Scottish folklorist, writer, and lawyer, who studied at the universities of Oxford and Eton and later became the foremost authority on Celtic folklore and the Gaelic people. He did meticulous field research in the Scottish islands, West Scotland, Ireland, Scandinavia, London, and on the Isle of Man. The result was his prodigious *Popular Tales of the West Highlands: Orally Collected and Translated*, published in four volumes that contain folk tales, heroic poems, proverbs, songs, children's stories, myths, and essays.

Campbell, John Gegorson (1836–1890), Scottish folklorist, who studied at the University of Glasgow and practiced law until 1858 when he became a Presbyterian minister and developed an interest in Scottish folklore. He began collecting all types of folk tales in the late 1850s and 1860s, often publishing them in journals like *The Celtic Review, Transactions of the Iverness Gaelic Society*, and *The Celtic Magazine*. The majority of his collected tales, however were published posthumously in *Clan Traditions and Popular Tales of the Western Highlands and Islands* (1895), *Superstitions of the Highlands and Islands of Scotland* (1900), and *Witchcraft and Second Sight in the Highlands and Islands of Scotland* (1902).

Carey, Martha Ward (b.1837–?), American scholar and translator of French folk tales gathered in *Fairy Legends of the French Provinces* (1887).

Carnoy, Henry (1861–1930), journalist who became a teacher of French at a lycée in Paris. During the latter part of the nineteenth century he created a literary and artistic movement in the northern part of France and founded the journal *Revue du Nord de la France* (1880). Aside from writing several novels and stories based on folklore, he published two important collections of tales, *Littérature orale de la Picardie* (1883) and *Les Légendes de France* (1885).

Cenova, Florian (1817–1881), Kashubian and Polish doctor and folklorist, who was the first to publish a Kashubian dictionary. A nationalist, he participated in the 1848 Revolution and struggled for Polish independence and for the rights of the Kashubs.

Chodźko (Chodsko), Aleksander Borejko (1804–1891), Polish poet, Slavist, and Iranologist, who worked as a Russian diplomat in Iran from 1830 to 1844, and after serving in the French foreign ministry in Paris, he was appointed professor of Slavic languages at the College de France from 1857 to 1883. Aside from his poetry, his major work in folklore was *Fairy Tales of the Slav Peasants and Herdsmen* (1896).

Coelho, Adolpho Francisco (1847–1919), Portuguese writer and philologist, who became a prominent professor at the University of Lisbon. Productive in the fields of ethnography and anthropology, he was a respected intellectual and published numerous essays and books not only on Portuguese folklore, pedagogy, and philology but also on popular beliefs and customs in other European countries. He published the first systematic collection of Portuguese folk tales,

Contos Populares Portuguese (1879), partially translated by Henriqueta Monteiro in *Tales of Old Lusitania* (1885), and an important book of games and nursery rhymes, *Contos Nacionais para Crianças* (1882).

Colshorn, Carl (1812–1855), German choirmaster, who collaborated with his brother Theodor in producing *Märchen und Sagen aus Hannover*.

Colshorn, Theodor (1821–1896), German scholar and folklorist, who had a close relationship with the Brothers Grimm. Aside from publishing a popular collection of folk tales, *Märchen und Sagen aus Hannover*, with his brother Carl, he edited textbooks and anthologies. He also wrote a popular study of German myths, *Deutsche Mythologie fürs deutsche Volk* (1853).

Comparetti, Domenico (1835–1927), Italian professor of Greek classics, who taught at various universities and became one of the foremost scholars of folklore in Italy. Not only did he write on Greek culture and history, Comparetti's prolific work also covered all aspects of European literature and folklore from ancient Greece through nineteenth-century Europe. Among his important books on folklore are *Virgilio nel Medio Evo* (two volumes, 1872), *Novelline popolari italiane* (1875), and *Il Kalevala o la poesia tradizionale dei Finni* (1891).

Coronedi-Berti, Carolina (1820–1911), Italian writer and linguist, who specialized in the dialects of Bologna and published an important dictionary, *Vocabolario dialettale bolognese*, in two volumes between 1869 and 1874. In addition her book *Novelle popolari bolognesi* (1873) was the first publication of Bolognese folk tales ever published.

Cosquin, Emmanuel (1841–1919), French folklorist, who devoted most of his life to the study of European folklore and its origins. Between 1877 and 1881 he collected numerous tales from the region of Champagne that he published in the journal *Romania*. Each tale was fully annotated and demonstrated Cosquin's comprehensive knowledge of folk and fairy tales. As a result of this work, he published *Contes populaires de Lorraine* (1886), which compared the folk tales in this collection with other French and European tales.

Curtin, Jeremiah (1835–1906), American folklorist, translator, and ethnologist, who traveled to Russia after his graduation from Harvard in 1863. He remained there thirteen years and became a specialist in different Slavic languages. When he returned to America, he began publishing books about his travels, translations of Polish novels, and several anthologies of folk and fairy tales. Among his most interesting collections are *Myths and Folk-lore of Ireland* (1890), *Myths and Folk-tales of the Russians, Western Slavs, and Magyars* (1890), and *Tales of the Fairies and of the Ghost World* (1895).

Dardy, Leópold (1826–1901), French priest and folklorist, who collected various types of folk tales in the region of l'Albret. His two-volume collection

Anthologie populaire de l'Albret, sud-ouest de l'Agenais ou Gascogne landaise (1894) contains proverbs, prayers, and unusual folk tales.

Dasent, Sir George Webbe (1817–1896), English scholar, journalist, and folklorist, who studied at King's College London and Oxford University. Upon graduation he was appointed to a diplomatic post in Stockholm, Sweden, where he met Jacob Grimm, who encouraged him to learn Scandinavian languages and folklore. Dasent remained in Stockholm until 1845, when he returned to London to work for *The Times*. In 1853, he was appointed professor of English at King's College London, but his real interest was Scandinavian culture, and he published numerous essays and translations of Scandinavian folk and fairy tales. His most important translations are *Popular Tales from the Norse* (1850) by Peter Christen Asbjørnsen and Jørgen Moe, another edition of *Popular Tales from the Norse* (1888), and *East O' the Sun and West O' the Moon* (1888).

Denton, William (1815–1888), British priest and folklorist, who was active in causes to help the poor and persecuted people in eastern Europe and Turkey. Aside from writing numerous pamphlets and commentaries on the Bible, he took a great interest in Serbian folklore and edited *Serbian Folk-lore: Popular Tales* (1874).

Deulin, Charles (1827–1877), French writer, who held various jobs as secretary to a lawyer, historian, and journalist for many different magazines and journals. Though he did not collect folk tales, most of his important collections of stories such as *Contes d'un buveur de bière* (1868) and *Contes du roi Cambrinus* (1874) were based on them. One of his most important books, *Les Contes de Ma Mère l'Oye avant Perrault*, which featured tales that preceded Perrault's stories, was published soon after his death in 1877.

Dietrich, Anton (1833–1904), notable German painter who was a member of the Düsseldorf School. In 1857, he published *Russian Folk Tales* in German, one of the first collections ever published in Europe.

Dirr, Adolf (1867–1930), German philologist, linguist, and scholar of Caucasian languages, who became a curator in the Museum for Folklore in Munich in 1913. He is best known for his superb collection *Kaukasische Märchen* (1923), translated into English as *Caucasian Folk-Tales* in 1929. This work contains more than ninety-eight folk and fairy tales, fables, legends, and humorous tales in over fifteen different dialects that Dirr translated and annotated.

Erben, Karel (1811–1870), Czech, historian, writer and poet, who is best known for his book *Kytice* (*The Bouquet*), a collection of Czech ballads, songs, and poems with folkloric and fairy-tale motifs. As member of the Bohemian Society of Sciences and the Academy of Sciences in Vienna, he collected more than 2,200 Slavic fairy tales. A selection was published in 1865, titled *Vybrané báje a pověsti národní, jiných větví slovenských* (*Selected Folktales and Legends from*

Other Slavic Branches), now regarded as a standard work of Czech fairy-tale research. Inspired by this work, Erben began to write fairy tales for children, which were published posthumously.*Česk pohádky* (*Czech Folktales*, 1905/1906), illustrated by Josef Lada, is often compared with the Grimms' fairy-tale collection *Kinder- und Hausmärchen* (*Children's and Household Tales*).

Erdélyi, János (1814–1868), Hungarian poet, critic, philosopher, and folklorist, who was the editor of an important literary review in Pest and member of the Hungarian Academy of Sciences. His most important work was a collection of Hungarian national poems and folk tales, *Magyar népköltési gyűjtemény, népdalok és mondák* (*Collection of Hungarian Folklore, Folk Songs and Tales*, 1846–1847). In addition, a collection of folklore was published the year after his death with the title *A nép költészete: népdalok, népmesék és közmondások* (*Poetry of the People: Folk Songs, Tales, and Proverbs*, 1869), which includes important fairy tales.

Fleury, Jean François (1816–1894), French journalist and folklorist, who began his career in 1837 as editor of the newspaper *Journal de Cherbourg*. In 1852, he moved to Saint Petersburg, Russia, to become a professor of French at the Imperial University.

Gaster, Moses (1856–1939), British scholar and folklorist, who was born in Bucharest and studied at the University of Leipzig. After receiving his Ph.D. in 1878, he attended the Jewish Seminary in Breslau and returned to Bucharest to teach Romanian literature at the university. Expelled from Romania and accused of irredentism, he went to London and held various positions in synagogues, schools, folklore societies, and community centers while collecting and doing research on Samaritan, Hebrew, Slavic, and Arabic manuscripts. Among his more significant works are *Jewish Folk-Lore in the Middle Ages* (1887), *Rumanian Bird and Beast Stories* (1915), and *Children's Stories from Roumanian Legends and Fairy Tales* (1923).

Geldhart, Edmund Martin (1844–1885), British Unitarian minister who authored religious books for children. He was also a scholar of modern Greek and wrote several books about the Greek language. In 1882, he published *Folk-Lore of Modern Greece*, an important collection of Greek folk tales that he intended as a corrective to Johann Georg von Hahn's notable collection *Griechische und albanesische Märchen* (1864).

Glínski, Józef Antoni (1817–1866), self-educated Polish writer and journalist, who was born into a peasant family in Belorussia. He moved to Vilnius, where he edited the journal *Kurier Wilenskiego*. Aside from writing and collecting poems and fables, he published four editions of Polish folk and fairy tales under the title *Bajarz polski* in 1862.

Gonzenbach, Laura (1842–1878), storyteller and amateur collector of Sicilian folk tales, who was the daughter of a German Swiss merchant but grew up in

Messina, Sicily. In response to a request by German historian Otto Hartwig, she gathered ninety-two Sicilian tales in dialect, primarily from women peasants, and translated them into high German. The tales were published as *Sicilianische Märchen* in 1875, and this German collection was significantly the first major collection of Sicilian folk tales.

Gregor, Walter (1825–1897), Scottish clergyman and folklorist, who was a founding member of the Folklore Society and published numerous Scottish tales in *The Folk-Lore Journal*. Moreover, he was known for major works on Scottish folklore such as *The Dialect of Banffshire* (1866) and *An Echo of the Olden Times from the North of Scotland* (1874).

Grimm, Brothers (Jacob Grimm, 1785–1863, and Wilhelm Grimm, 1786–1859), German librarians and philologists, who published seven editions of their pioneer collection *Kinder- und Hausmärchen* (*Children's and Household Tales*) from 1812 to 1857. This work along with their other scholarship dealing with ancient and medieval literature profoundly influenced the development of folklore studies and collections in the nineteenth century. During the period from 1806 to 1810, when the brothers had become librarians and began writing scholarly articles about medieval literature, Jacob and Wilhelm started to systematically gather folk tales and other materials related to folklore. From 1810 to 1813, they published the results of their research on old German literature: Jacob wrote *On the Old German Meistergesang*, and Wilhelm, *Old Danish Heroic Songs*, both in 1811. Together they published a study of the *Song of Hildebrand* and the *Wessobrunner Prayer* in 1812. Their major publication at this time was the first volume of the *Kinder- und Hausmärchen* (*Children's and Household Tales*) with scholarly annotations and the second volume in 1815.

After securing the position of second librarian in the royal library of Kassel, Jacob joined Wilhelm in editing the first volume of *German Legends* in 1816. During the next thirteen years, the Grimms published the second volume of *German Legends* (1818) and *Irish Elf Tales* (1826), while Jacob wrote the first volume of *German Grammar* (1819) and *Ancient German Law* (1828) by himself, and Wilhelm produced *The German Heroic Legend* (1829). In 1829, Jacob and Wilhelm resigned their posts as librarians in Kassel and, one year later, traveled to Götttingen, where Jacob became professor of old German literature and head librarian, and Wilhelm, librarian and, eventually, professor in 1835. In addition to their teaching duties, they continued to write and publish important works: Jacob wrote the third volume of *German Grammar* (1831) and a major study entitled *German Mythology* (1835), while Wilhelm prepared the third edition of the *Kinder- und Hausmärchen*. Though their positions were secure, there was a great deal of political unrest in Germany due to the severely repressive political climate that had developed since 1819.

In 1837, King Ernst August II succeeded to the throne of Hannover and revoked the constitution of 1833 and dissolved parliament. Jacob was compelled to leave Göttingen immediately and returned to Kassel, where Wilhelm joined him a few months later. It was during this time that Jacob and Wilhelm decided to embark on writing the *German Dictionary*, one of the most ambitious lexicographical undertakings of the nineteenth century. Finally, in November 1840, Jacob and Wilhelm received offers to become professors at the University of Berlin and to do research at the Academy of Sciences. For the rest of their lives, the Grimms devoted most of their energy to teaching, research, completing the monumental *German Dictionary*, and working on the different editions of the *Kinder- und Hausmärchen*.

Grundtvig, Svend (1824–1883), Danish folklorist, ethnographer, and historian, who is regarded as the founder of Danish folklore. Influenced by the Brothers Grimm, he issued two manifestos in 1844 and 1854 urging the Danish people to collect ballads and folk tales for a national library. He himself initially focused his research largely on Danish traditional music and folk songs, but he also produced three important volumes of folk tales: *Danske Folkeæventyr* (1876–1883), some of which were translated into English at the beginning of the twentieth century; *Fairy Tales from Afar* (1900); and *Danish Fairy Tales* (1919).

Gubernatis, Angelo (1840–1913), Italian philologist, Orientalist, poet, and editor, who was one of the most prominent intellectuals in Italy during the late nineteenth and early twentieth centuries. He taught at universities in Florence and Rome and edited three different journals. As a specialist in Asian studies he was known for his books *Piccola enciclopedia indiana* (1867) and the *Fonti vediche* (1868). His most significant works in folklore were *Novelline di S. Stefano di Calcinaia (1869)* and *Zoological Mythology or The Legends of Animals* (1872).

Hahn, Johann Georg von (1811–1869), Austrian folklorist, philologist, and diplomat, who spent many years in Albania and Greece and eventually became the Austrian consul-general in Athens. He is considered the founder of Albanian studies in Europe and published essays and studies of both Albanian and Greek folklore. His most significant work is the two-volume collection *Griechische und albanesische Märchen* (1864), first published in German.

Imbriani, Vittorio (1840–1886), Italian folklorist, writer, and literary historian, who devoted much of his life to the study of folklore. His earliest collections were of folk songs in various Italian dialects, which were compiled in the two-volume *Canti popolari delle province meridionali* (*Folk Songs of the Southern Provinces*, 1871–1872). His most significant fairy-tale collections are the *Novellaja fiorentina* (*Florentine Tales*, 1871) and the *Novellaja milanese* (*Milanese Tales*, 1872).

Jacobs, Joseph (1854–1916), prominent British historian and folklorist, who was born in Australia. He was educated and resided many years in England before moving to the United States; he became an American citizen in 1900. His earliest writings were on Jewish anthropological studies that led to a general interest in folklore. From 1889 to 1900 he edited the British Folklore Society's journal *Folk-Lore*. In 1890, he began a series of retellings of folk tales for children, beginning with *English Fairy Tales* (1890), followed by *More English Fairy Tales* (1893), *Celtic Fairy Tales* (1891), *More Celtic Fairy Tales* (1894), *Indian Fairy Tales* (1892), and *Europa's Fairy Book* (1916).

Jahn, Ulrich (1861–1900), German teacher and folklorist, who specialized in the folklore of Pomerania. His major works are *Hexenwesen und Zauberei in Pommern* (1886), *Schwänke und Schnurren aus Bauernmund* (1889), and *Volksmärchen aus Pommern und Rügen* (1891).

Halliwell-Phillipps, James Orchard (1820–1899), English Shakespearean scholar who was an avid collector of nursery rhymes and fairy tales. Educated at Cambridge, he devoted himself upon graduation to collecting ancient literature and made a name for himself with the publication of *Nursery Rhymes of England* (1842) and *Nursery Rhymes and Nursery Tales*. The latter book contained the first printed version of "The Three Little Pigs." He continued his antiquarian research by collecting chapbooks and rare children's books, but turned more to the study of Shakespeare after 1850.

Kennedy, Patrick (1801–1873), Irish folklorist and bookseller, who is regarded as one of the fathers of the Irish folklore renaissance in the nineteenth century. The purpose behind most of his work was to preserve tales from the oral tradition, and he either wrote his own stories or tried to capture authentic Irish fairy tales in retellings. His most significant collections are *The Fireside Stories of Ireland* (1870) and *The Bardic Stories of Ireland* (1871).

Kropf, (Lewis) Lajos (1852–1939), Hungarian engineer and historian, who emigrated to London, where he co-edited *The Folk-Tales of the Magyars* (1889) with W. Henry Jones.

Kuhn, Adelbert (1812–1881), German philologist and folklorist, who initially began collecting and publishing folk tales from north Germany. Among his most important collections are *Märkische Sagen und Märchen* (1842), *Norddeutsche Sagen, Märchen, und Gebräuche* (1848), and *Sagen, Gebräuche und Märchen aus Westfalen* (1859). Strongly influenced by Jacob Grimm's *Deutsche Mythologie*, he founded a new school of comparative mythology and also wrote numerous books about the myths, language, and history of the Indo-Germanic peoples.

Kulda, Benes Methods (1820–1903), priest, writer, and folklorist, who studied philosophy and theology in Brno before being ordained as a priest. A strong supporter of Czech nationalism, Kulda published several collections of folk tales, rhymes, and songs as well as numerous articles, patriotic pamphlets, and sermons.

Kulish, Panteleiman (1818–1897), Ukrainian writer, historian, and folklorist, who studied at the University of Kiev, where he published an essay on Ukrainian stories and became a devoted Ukrainian nationalist. In 1857, he founded his own publishing house that promoted the works of Ukrainian writers. He wrote numerous novels and stories, and even translated the Bible into Ukrainian. In addition to his own writings, he collected and published Ukrainian and Cossack tales.

Lang, Andrew (1844–1912), Scottish folklorist, writer, historian, and journalist, who was one of the most prominent men of letters in England during the late nineteenth century. Educated at Glasgow and Oxford, Lang was a prolific writer and was influenced by the anthropological writings of Edward Burnett Tylor (1832–1917), especially his two-volume study, *Primitive Culture* (1871). This influence is clear in Lang's early historical and theoretical writings such as "Mythology and Fairy Tales" (1873), *Custom and Myth* (1884), and *Myth, Ritual, and Religion* (1887). In 1884, Lang wrote an important introduction to the first complete English translation of Jacob and Wilhelm Grimm's *Children's and Household Tales*. In addition, he wrote his own fairy tales: *The Princess Nobody* (1884), *The Gold of Fairnilee* (1888), and *Prince Riccardo* (1893). Today he is best known for his series of color fairy-tale books, which he edited from 1889 to 1910. Lang, his wife, and other collaborators translated and also adapted many well-known and unknown tales throughout the world that appealed both to children and adults.

Luzel, François-Marie (1821–1895), French folklorist, who was one of the foremost collectors of Breton folk tales. He held various positions as instructor, historian, and journalist and also wrote poetry. Early in his life he developed a great interest in folk tales and began publishing collections such as *Contes Bretons* (1870). Many of his collections consisted of tales in the Breton dialect with translations into French along with historical data. In the 1880s, he secured a position of curator in the Archives at Quimper that enabled him to do far-reaching research on Breton folk tales. As a result, he published numerous collections, such as *Veillées Bretonnes* (1879), *Légendes chrétiennes* (1882), and *Contes populaires de Basse-Bretagne* (1887). At the same time, he contributed a vast number of tales to different folklore journals in France.

Marelle, Charles (1827–n.d.), French folklorist and writer of miscellaneous works, who is known chiefly for his collection of folk stories in *Affenschwanz* (1880).

Meier, Ernst (1813–1866), German professor of Oriental studies and folklorist, who also published studies of Swabian folklore. His most important collection of Swabian tales is *Deutsche Volksmärchen aus Schwaben* (1852).

Millien, Achille (1838–1927), French writer and folklorist, who followed a career as lawyer until the death of his father when he inherited enough money to begin working as a folklorist, collecting tales and songs in the region of Nièvre. In addition, he produced numerous books of poetry. Though he collected over 2,000 songs and 1,000 tales and legends, he published only a tiny selection of them in books and journals. Most of his collections of folk tales, such as *Contes du Nivernais et du Morvan* (1953) and *Contes de Bourgogne* (2008), were published after 1945 and have been edited by leading French folklorists.

Mistral, Frédéric (1830–1914), writer and lexicographer, who was raised in Provence and studied law at Aix while writing classical poetry. In 1904, he won the Nobel Prize for his poetry. During the 1850s he took a great interest in the folklore of Provençal. In addition to writing significant poems, plays, and stories, he published a number of folk tales in the journal *Almanach*.

Moe, Jørgen (1813–1882), Norwegian clergyman, folklorist, and poet, who collaborated with Peter Christen Asbjørnsen in publishing *Norske folkeeventyr* (*Norwegian Folk Tales*, 1841–1844). Inspired by the Brothers Grimm, Moe and Asbjørnsen employed a natural colloquial style in all sorts of stories that included wonder tales, legends, humorous anecdotes, and fables. In the second edition of *Norwegian Folk Tales* (1852), Moe wrote an important introduction about the relationship of the Norwegian language to humor. After he became a clergyman in 1853, he more or less abandoned his study of folklore and gave his collection of tales and legends to Asbjørnsen, who assumed editorship of future editions of *Norwegian Folk Tales*.

Naaké, John Theophilus (1837–1906), folklorist and translator, who worked in the British Museum and translated *Slavonic Fairy Tales* (1874).

Němcová, Božena (1820–1862), Czech writer and folklorist, who some consider to be the mother of Czech prose. Němcová often traveled by herself and gathered folklore material in Bohemia and Slovakia. Her research enabled her to write many books, including collections of Czech and Slovak folk tales and fairy tales. Němcová's first published works were the patriotic poem *To the Czech Women* (1843) and the book *Folk Fairy Tales and Legends* (parts 1–7, 1845–1847). In the 1850s, she published realistic short stories and novellas about common people. In addition she collected Slovak fairy tales and published them in Czech translations in 1857–1858.

Nerucci, Gherardo (1828–1906), Italian lawyer and historian, who fostered schools in rural regions of Italy. He collaborated with Imbriani, Comparetti, and Pitrè in promoting the study of folklore in Italy. His most significant work is *Sessanta Novelle Popolari Montalesi* (1880).

Pedroso, Zófimo Consiglieri (1851–1910), Portuguese politician, ethnographer, and writer, who was one of the founders of anthropology in Portugal and fostered the study of myths, legends, and folk tales. His most important folklore work was *Portuguese Folk-Tales* (1882), which was first published without variants in English by the Folklore Society of London. Later, in 1910, Pedroso added variants to demonstrate the widespread dissemination of different tale types.

Pitrè, Giuseppe (1841–1916), Sicilian doctor, folklorist, and ethnographer, who played a major role in fostering the study of popular traditions in Italy. He developed an anthropological and historical approach in his voluminous essays and collections of Sicilian and Italian tales. In addition, he edited the influential folklore journal *Archivio per lo studio delle tradizioni popolari* (*Archive for the Study of Popular Traditions*, 1882–1909), corresponded with major folklorists throughout the world, and founded a museum of folklore in Palermo. Among Pitrè's most significant works are *Biblioteca delle tradizioni popolari siciliane* (*Library of Popular Sicilian Traditions,* (1870–1913); *Fiabe, novelle e racconti popolari siciliani* (*Fairy Tales, Novellas, and Popular Tales of Sicily,* 1875); *Novelle Popolari Toscane* (*Popular Tuscan Novellas,* 1885); and *Curiositá popolari tradizionali* (*Curiosities of Popular Traditions,* 1894).

Polevoi, Peter (1839–1902), prominent Russian historian, archeologist, and Shakespearean scholar, who adapted thirty-six of Afanas'ev's folk tales for children and published them under the title *Narodnuiya Russkiya Skazki* (*Popular Russian Fairy Tales*) in 1874.

Pröhle, Heinrich (1822–1895), teacher and folklorist, who studied at the universities of Halle and Berlin, where he was strongly influenced by Jacob Grimm, who encouraged him to collect folk tales in the region of the Harz Forest. Thanks to Grimm's encouragement, Pröhle published several important collections: *Kinder und Volksmärchen* (1853), *Harzsagen* (1853/1856), *Unterharzische Sagen* (1856), and *Rheinlands schönste Sagen und Geschichten* (1886).

Ralston, William (born William Shedden) (1828–1889), British librarian and folklorist, who worked in the British Museum most of this life and was very active in folklore circles. His major interest was in Russian culture and history. In 1868, he translated a selection of Ivan Andreevich Krylov's fables as *Krilof and His Fables.* He followed this publication with *Songs of the Russian People as Illustrative of Slavonic Mythology and Russian Social Life* (1872) and *Russian Folk Tales* (1873), a major translation of tales mainly from Alexander Anfanas'ev's collection with notes. Ralston, a brilliant scholar, also wrote articles on folk tales from other countries and collected tales for the journal of the British Folklore Society.

Rochholz, Ernst Ludwig (1809–1892), German historian and folklorist, who left Germany in 1836 due to political difficulties. Afterward he began devoting himself to the study of Swiss folklore and published important books such as *Schweizersagen aus dem Aargau* (1856) and *Aargauer Weistümer* (1876).

Schmidt, Bernhard (1837–1917), German professor of classical and modern Greek at the University of Freiburg, who was also an expert on Greek folklore. He published two important books on this topic: *Das Volksleben der Neugriechen und das hellenische Altertum* (1871) and *Griechische Märchen, Sagen und Volkslieder* (1877).

Schneller, Christian (1831–1908), Austrian professor and folklorist, who studied at the universities of Innsbruck and Vienna. He had a special interest in the folklore of south Tyrol and published a significant collection of folk tales gathered in this region, *Märchen und Sagen aus Wälschtirol: Ein Beitrag zur deutschen Sagenkunde* (1867).

Sébillot, Paul (1843–1918), French painter and folklorist, who studied law at Rennes and Paris. From 1870 to 1883, he devoted himself to painting and had a successful career. However, his interest in folklore grew, and by 1885 he was named secretary of the first French folklore society (*Société des traditions populaires*) and editor of the notable journal *Revues des traditions populaires*. He was a prodigious collector of all types of folk tales, and among his most important works are *Traditions, superstitions et légendes de la Haute-Bretagne* (1880), *Contes populaires de la Haute-Bretagne* (1882), *Contes des provinces de France* (1888), and the four-volume *Folklore de France* (1904–1907).

Strickland, Sir Walter William (1851–1938), writer, translator, and naturalist traveler who had anarchist leanings. He left England toward the end of the nineteenth century and traveled widely in Europe, the Dutch Indies, New Zealand, Mexico, and other countries, studying the language, literature, traditions, habits, and customs of the people he lived among. He studied the Slav languages for over ten years and translated Viteslav Hálek's best stories, Svatopluk Cech's classical mock epic *Hanuman,* and Karel Erben's complete folk tales with commentaries and notes. He published Erben's tales in four different volumes in the 1890s and then published all four books in *Panslavonic Folk-lore* in 1930.

Sutermeister, Otto (1832–1901), Swiss professor, writer, and folklorist, who wrote numerous books for children and taught German literature at the University of Berne. His most significant collection of folk tales is *Kinder- und Hausmärchen aus der Schweiz* (1868).

Thorpe, Benjamin (1782–1870), English folklorist and scholar of Anglo-Saxon, who studied philology from 1826 to 1830 at Copenhagen University. After returning to London, he went on to publish significant studies on Anglo-Saxon literature. In addition, he produced two important collections of folk tales, *Northern Mythology* (1851), which contained different types of stories from Scandinavia, Germany, and the Netherlands, and *Yule-Tide Stories* (1853), which included solely Scandinavian tales.

Vernaleken, Theodor (1812–1907), German writer and professor, who studied and taught in Switzerland. In 1850, he moved to Vienna and assumed different positions as a teacher and director of education. Influenced by Jacob Grimm, he began collecting folk tales in the 1850s and published several important collections that include *Alpensagen: Volksüberlieferungen aus der Schweiz, aus Vorarlberg, Kärnten, Steiermark, Salzburg, Ober- und Niederösterreich, Seidel, Wien* (1858) and *Österreichische Kinder- und Hausmärchen* (1864).

Vondrák, Václav (1859–1925), Czech professor of Slavic philology at Vienna University and Brno University, who specialized in comparative Slavistics. He published a number of studies dealing with Slavic folklore. Among his important works are *Zur Würdigung der altslovenischen Wenzelslegende und der Legende von heiligen Prokop*, Vienna (1892) and *Kremsmünsterská legenda o 10.000 rytířích* ("The Kremsmünster Legend of 10,000 Knights," 1886).

Webster, Wentworth (1828–1907), British priest and folklorist, who was educated at Oxford. He was ordained as a priest in 1861 and in 1869, was sent to the Basque region in France to become chaplain of the American Church. Assisted by the Basque folklorist Julien Vinson, he began collecting Basque folk tales, which he translated and published in 1877 as *Basque Legends*.

Wilde, Lady Jane Francesca Elgee (1821–1896), Irish poet, political activist, translator, and folklorist, who had a strong interest in Irish fairy tales as is evident in her poetry and prose. She also published a major work on Irish folklore, *Ancient Legends, Mystic Charms, and Superstitions of Ireland* (1888).

Wolf, Johann Wilhelm (1817–1855), German folklorist, who spent his early years working as a merchant and went to Belgium, where he collected Flemish folk tales and published them as *Niederländische Sagen* in 1843. Soon after he returned to Cologne, he joined his brother-in-law, the writer Wilhelm von Ploennies, and together they collected folk tales from soldiers in Oldenwald that were published as *Deutsche Hausmärchen* in 1851. Wolf was also founder of one of the first folklore journals in Germany, *Zeitschrift für Deutsche Mythologie und Sittenkunde* (1853).

Wratislaw, Albert Henry (1822–1892), English Slavonic scholar of Czech descent, who studied at Cambridge University. He held the position of headmaster at various private schools and wrote essays and books about Slavic literature and history. In 1889, he published *Sixty Folk-Tales from Exclusively Slavonic Sources*, which were based on Karel Erben's *Čítanka* (1865). Wratislaw did all the translations himself and provided the notes.

Zingerle, Ignaz (1825–1892), Austrian writer and folklorist, who became professor of German in Innsbruck. Aside from writing poetry and short stories, he published numerous collections of Tyrolean folk tales and legends. Among his most significant works are *Sagen aus Tirol* (1850), *Kinder- und Hausmärchen aus Tirol* (1852), *Kinder- und Hausmärchen aus Süddeutschland* (1854), and *Sagen, Märchen und Gebräuche aus Tirol* (1859).

Zingerle, Joseph (1831–1891), Austrian professor of biblical studies at the University of Vienna and priest, who collaborated with his brother Ignaz in publishing *Kinder- und Hausmärchen aus Süddeutschland* (1854).

BIBLIOGRAPHY

Collections

Addy, Sidney Oldall. *Household Tales with Other Traditional Remains: Collected in the Counties of York, Lincoln, Derby, and Nottingham.* London: David Nutt, 1895.

Afanas'ev, Alexander N. *Narodyne russkija skaski (Popular Russian Tales).* Moscow: Gratschew, 1855–1864; 2nd ed., 4 vols., 1873.

———. *Poeticheskie vozzreniia slavian na prirodu.* 3 vols. Moscow: Gratschew, 1865–1869.

———. *Russian Fairy Tales.* Translated by Norbert Guterman. New York: Pantheon, 1945.

———. *Narodyne russkija skaski* [1855–1863]. Edited by L. G. Barag and N. V. Novikov. 3 vols. Moscow: 1984.

Allen, H. N. *Korean Tales.* New York: G. P. Putnam's Sons, 1889.

Anderton, Isabella. *Tuscan Folklore and Sketches: Together with Some Other Papers.* London: Arnold Fairbairns, 1905.

———. *Fairy Tales from Tuscany.* London: Arnold Fairbairns, 1907.

Andrews, James Bryn. *Stories from Mentone.* London: Folk-Lore Record, 1880.

———. *Contes ligures: Traditions de la Rivière recueillis entre Menton et Gênes.* Paris: Ernst Leroux, 1892.

Arnason, Jon. *Icelandic Legends.* Translated by George Powell and Eirkr Magnusson. London: Longmans, Green, 1866.

Arndt, Ernst Moritz. *Mährchen und Jugenderinnerungen.* Berlin: Reimer, 1818.

———. *Märchen aus dem Norden.* Berlin: Reimer, 1843.

Arnim, Friedmund. *Hundert neue Mährchen im Gebirge gesammelt.* Charlottenburg: Egbert Bauer, 1844.

———. *Hundert neue Mährchen im Gebirge gesammelt.* Edited by Heinz Röllecke. Cologne: Eugen Diederichs, 1986.

Asbjørnsen, Peter Christen. *Norske huldreeventyr of folkesagn.* Christiania: C. A. Oybwad, 1848.

———. *Fairy Tales from the Far North.* Translated by H. L. Bræstad. London: D. Nutt, 1897.

Asbjørnsen, Peter Christen, and Jørgen Moe. *Norske folke-eventyr.* Christiania: J. Dahl, 1852.

———. *Popular Tales from the Norse.* Translated and Introduction by George Webbe Dasent. Edinburgh: Edmonston and Douglas, 1859.

———. *Round the Yule. Norwegian Folk and Fairy Tales:* Translated by H. L. Braekstad. London: Sampson Low, Marston, Seaarle, & Rivington, 1881.

————. *East O' the Sun and West O' the Moon*. Translated by George Webbe Dasent. Edinburgh: David Douglas, 1888.

————. *Popular Tales from the Norse*. Translated by George Webbe Dasent. Edinburgh: David Douglas, 1888.

Bain, R. Nisbet. *Russian Fairy Tales: From the Skazki of Polevoi*. London: Lawrence and Bullen, 1893.

————. *Cossack Fairy Tales and Folk-Tales*. Illustrated by E. W. Mitchell. London: Lawrence and Bullen, 1894.

————. *Turkish Fairy Tales and Folk Tales Collected by Dr. Ignácz Kúnos*. London: Lawrence and Bullen, 1896.

Balladoro, Arrigo. *Folk-Lore Veronese: Novelline*. Verona: Frateli Drucker, 1900.

Baring-Gould, Sabine. *Old English Fairy Tales*. London: Methuen, 1895.

Basile, Giambattista. *Lo cunto de li cunti overo Lo trattenemiento de peccerille*. De Gian Alessio Abbattutis. 5 vols. Naples: Ottavio Beltrano, 1634–1636.

————. *The Pentamerone of Giambattista Basile*. Translated and edited by N. M. Penzer. 2 vols. London: John Lane and the Bodley Head, 1932.

————. *The Tale of Tales, or Entertainment for Little Ones*. Translated and edited by Nancy Canepa. Illustrated by Carmelo Lettere. Detroit: Wayne State University Press, 2007.

Baudis, Joseph, ed. and trans. *Czech Folk Tales*. London: George Allen & Unwin, 1917.

Bechstein, Ludwig. *Deutsches Märchenbuch*. Leipzig: Wigand, 1845.

————. *Ludwig Bechsteins Märchenbuch*. Leipzig: Wigand, 1853.

————. *Neues Deutsches Märchenbuch*. Vienna: Hartleben, 1856.

————. *Sämtliche Märchen*. Edited by Walter Scherf. Munich: Winkler, 1968.

Beckwirth, Martha Warren. *Jamaica Anansi Stories*. With music recorded in the field by Helen Roberts. New York: George E. Stechert, 1924.

Ben-Amos, Dan, ed. *Folktales of the Jews: Tales from the Sephardic Dispersion*. Translated by Leonard J. Schramm. Philadelphia: Jewish Publication Society, 2006.

Bernoni, Domenico Giuseppe. *Fiabe popolari veneziane*. Venice: Fontana-Ottolini, 1873.

Bladé, Jean-François. *Contes populaires de la Gascogne*. 3 vols. Paris: Maisonneuve frères et Ch. Leclerc, 1886.

Bleek, Wilhelm. *Brief Account of Bushman Folk-Lore and Other Texts*. 1875.

Boas, Franz. *Kutenai Tales: Together with Texts Collected by Alexander Francis Chamberlain*. Washington, DC: Government Printing Office, 1918. (Smithsonian Institution, Bureau of American Ethnology, Bulletin 59)

————. *Chinook Texts*. 1894.

————. *Tsimshian Texts*. 1902.

————. *Bella bella Tales*. New York: George E. Stechert, 1932.

Bødker, Laurits, Christina Hole, and G. D'Aronco, eds. *European Folktales*. Hatboro, PA: Folklore Associates, 1963.

Bompas, Cecil Henry. *Folklore of the Santal Parganas*. London: David Nutt, 1909.

Boncoeur, Jean-Louis. *Contes du Berry*. Aigurande (Indre): Roger Rault, 1965.

Bradley-Birt, Francis. *Bengal Fairy Tales*. London: John Lane, 1920.

Bray, J. Christian. *Danish Fairy and Folk Tales: A Collection of Popular Stories and Fairy Tales. From the Danish of Svendt Grundtvig, E. T. Kristensen, Ingvor Bondesen, and L. Budde*. New York: Harper & Brothers, 1899.

Briggs, Katharine, and Ruth Tongue, eds. *Folktales of England*. Chicago: University of Chicago Press, 1965.

Busk, Rachel H. *Patranas; or Spanish Stories, Legendary and Traditional*. London: Griffith and Farran, 1870.

———. *Household Stories from the Land of Hofer: Or Popular Myths of Tirol*. London: Griffith and Faran, 1871.

———. *Sagas from the Far East: Or, Kalmouk and Mongolian Traditionary Tales*. London: Griffith and Farran, 1873.

———. *The Folk-Lore of Rome. Collected by Word of Mouth from the People*. London: Longmans, Green, 1874.

Cadic, François. "Georgik et Merlin." *La Paroisse Bretonne* (February 1915).

———. *Contes de Basse-Bretagne*. Illustrated by Claude Verrier. Paris: Éditions Érasme, 1955.

Callaway, Henry. *Nursery Tales, Traditions, and Histories of the Zulus*. London: Trübner, 1868.

Calvino, Italo, ed. *Fiabe*. Torino: Einaudi, 1970.

———. *Italian Folktales*. Translated by George Martin. New York: Harcourt Brace Jovanovich, 1980.

Cameron, Arnold Guyot, ed. *Tales of France from the Works of Georges d'Esparbès, Auguste Marin, Anatole Le Braz, Jules Claretie, François Coppée*. New York: American Book Company, 1904.

Camparetti, Domenico. *Novelline Popolari Italiene*. Bologna: Forni, 1875.

Campbell, John Gregorson. *Superstitions of the Highlands and Islands of Scotland*. Glasgow: James MacLehose, 1900.

———. *Witchcraft and Second Sight in the Highlands and Islands of Scotland*. Glasgow: James MacLehose, 1902.

———. *Clan Traditions and Popular Tales of the Western Highlands and Islands*. London: David Nutt, 1895.

Campbell of Islay, John Francis, ed. *Popular Tales of the West Highlands: Orally Collected*. 4 vols. Edinburgh: Edmonston and Douglas, 1860–1862.

Carey, M. *Fairy Legends of the French Provinces*. New York: Thomas Y. Crowell, 1887.

Carleton, William. *Traits and Stories of the Irish Peasantry*. Dublin: W. Curry, 1830.

Carnoy, Henry. *Littérature orale de la Picardie*. Paris: Maisonneuve, 1883.

———. *Contes Francais*. Paris: Ernest Leroux, 1885.

————. *Collection de contes et de chansons populaires*. Paris: Ernest Leroux, 1885.

————. *The Fiddler and the Elves, from the French of Henry Carnoy, and Other Stories*. Translated by Eleanor Simeon and Annie M. Westwood. Glasgow: Blackie & Son: 1937.

————. *Contes de Picardie*. Edited by Françoise Morvan. Rennes: Éditions Ouest-France, 2005.

Carter, Angela. *The Bloody Chamber and Other Stories*. London: Gollancz, 1979.

Cerquand, Jean-François. *Légendes et récits populaires du Pays basque*. Pau: Bulletin de la Socitèté, Lettres et Arts de Pau, 1877.

Cézérac-Perbosc, Suzanne. *Récits & Contes populaires de Gascogne*. Paris: Gallimard, 1979.

Chodźko, Alexander. *Slav Peasants and Herdsmen*. Translated by Emily Harding. London: George Allen, 1896.

Christiansen, Reidar, ed. *Folktales of Norway*. Chicago: University of Chicago Press, 1964.

Clouston, W. A. *Popular Tales and Fictions: Their Migrations and Transformations*. 2 vols. London: William Blackwood & Sons, 1887.

————. *The Book of Noodles: Stories of Simpletons; Or, Fools and their Follies*. London: Elliot Stock, 1888.

————. *Some Persian Tales*. Glasgow: David Bryce and Son, 1891.

Coelho, Adolpho Francisco. *Contos Populares Portugueses*. Lisbon: F. Plantier, 1879.

————. "Portuguese Stories." Translated by Henriqueta Monteiro. *The Folk-Lore Record* 4 (1881): 141–55.

————. *Contos Nacionais para Crianças*. Porto: Livraria Universal de Magalhães & Moniz, 1882.

————. *Tales of Old Lusitania, from the Folklore of Portugal*. Translated by Henriqueta Monteiro. London: Sonnenschein Ywan, 1885.

Cole, Mabel Cook. *Philippine Folk Tales*. Chicago: A. C. McClurg, 1916.

Collognat, Annie, and Marie-Charlotte Delmas. *Les Contes de Perrault dans tous leurs états*. Paris: Omnibus, 2007.

Colshorn, Carl, and Theodor Colshorn. *Märchen und Sagen aus Hannover*. Hannover: Carl Rümpler, 1854.

Comparetti, Domenico. *Novelline Popolari Italiane*. Bologna: Forni, 1875.

Corazzini, Francesco. *I Componimenti Minori della Letteratura Popolare nei Principali Dialetti*. Benevento: Gennavo, 1877.

Coronedi-Berti, Carolina. *Novelle popolari bolognesi*. Bologna: Tipi Fava e Garagnani, 1873.

————. *Favole bolognesi*. Bologna: Forni, 1883.

Cosquin, Emmanuel. *Contes populaires de Lorraine*. Paris: Vieweg, 1886.

————. *Les Contes populaires européens et leur origine*. Paris: C. Douniol, 1873.

————. "Le Taureau d'Or." *Romania, recueil trimestriel consacré à l'étude des langues et des littératures romanes*. Paris, 1877.

———. *Jean de l'Ours et autres contes populaires*. Bern: Francke, 1943.

———. *Contes populaires de Lorraine*. Edited by Nicole Belmont. Arles: Philippe Picquier, 2003.

Cox, George. *Tales of Ancient Greece*. Chicago: Jansen McClurg, 1883.

Cox, Marian Emily Roalfe. *Cinderella: Three Hundred and Forty-Five Variants of Cinderella, Catskin, and Cap o' Rushes, Abstracted and Tabulated with a Discussion of Medieval Analogues, and Notes*. Introduction by Andrew Lang. London: Folk-lore Society, 1893.

Coxwell, C. Fillingham. *Siberian and Other Folk-Tales: Primitive Literature of the Empire of the Czars*. London: C. W. Daniel, 1925.

Crane, Thomas Frederick. *Italian Popular Tales*. Boston: Houghton, Mifflin, 1885.

Croker, Thomas Croften. *Fairy Legends and Traditions of the South of Ireland*. 3 vols. London: J. Murray, 1825–1828.

Crooke, W. *The Talking Thrush; Stories of Birds and Beasts*. Retold by W. H. D. Rouse. London: J. M. Dent, 1899.

Crooke, William. *Folk-tales from Northern India*. Bombay: British India Press, 1906. (Reprinted from the Indian Antiquary, Vol. XXXV, 1906).

Cunningham, Allan. *Traditional Tales of the English and Scottish Peasantry*. London: Taylor and Hessey, 1822.

Curtin, Jeremiah. *Myths and Folklore of Ireland*. Boston: Little, Brown, 1890.

———. *Myths and Folk Tales of the Russians, Western Slavs, and Magyars*. London: Sampson Low, Marston, Searle, and Rivington, 1890.

———. *Hero Tales of Ireland*. London: Macmillan, 1894.

———. *Tales of the Fairies and of the Ghost World*. New York: Blom, 1895.

———. *Creation Myths of Primitive America in Relation to the Religious and Mental Development of Mankind*. London: Williams and Norgate, 1899.

———. *Fairy Tales of Eastern Europe*. New York: McBride, 1914.

———. *Seneca Indian Myths*. New York: Dutton, 1923.

Cushing, Frank. *Zuni Folk Tales*. New York: G. P. Putnam's Sons, 1901.

Dardy, Léopold. *Anthologie populaire de l'Albret*. Agen: Michel et Médan, 1891.

Dasent, George Webbe, ed. *Popular Tales from the Norse*. Edinburgh: David Douglas, 1888.

Day, Lal Behari. *Folk-tales of Bengal*. London: Macmillan, 1883.

Dégh, Linda. *Folktales of Hungary*. Translated by Judit Halász. Chicago: University of Chicago Press, 1965.

Deulin, Charles. *Les Contes de ma Mère l'Oye avant Perrault*. Paris: Dentu, 1878.

Delarue, Paul, ed. *The Borzoi Book of French Folk Tales*. Translated by Austin Fife. Illustrated by Warren Chappell. New York: Knopf, 1956.

———. *French Fairy Tales*. Illus. Warren Chappell. New York: Knopf, 1968.

Delarue, Paul, and Marie-Louise Tenèze. *Le Conte populaire français. Un catalogue raisonné des versions de France et des pays de langue française et d'Outre-mer*. 4 vols. Paris: Maisonneuve et Larose, 1957–1976.

Denton, William, ed. *Serbian Folk-lore: Popular Tales*. Translated by Mme Csedomille Mijatovies. London: W. Isbister, 1874.

Dietrich, Anton. *Russian Popular Tales*. Introduction by Jacob Grimm. London: Chapman and Hall, 1857.

Dirr, Adolf. *Kaukasische Märchen*. Jena: Diederichs, 1920.

———. *Caucasian Folk-Tales*. Translated by Lucy Menzies. London: Dent, 1925.

Dorsey, George A. *Traditions of the Skidi Pawnee*. Boston: Houghton Mifflin, 1904.

Dorson, Richard, ed. *Folktales Told around the World*. Chicago: University of Chicago Press, 1975.

Douglas, Sir George. *Scottish Fairy and Folk Tales*. London: W. Scott, 1894.

Dozon, Auguste. *Contes Albanais*. Paris: Ernest Leroux, 1881.

Dozon, Auguste, and Holger Pedersen. *Tricks of Women and Other Albanian Tales*. Translated by Paul Fenimore Cooper. New York: William Morrow, 1928.

Edwards, Charles L. *Bahama Songs and Stories: A Contribution to Folk-Lore*. Boston: Houghton and Mifflin, 1895.

Epstein, Morris. *Tales of Sendebar*. Philadelphia: Jewish Publication Society of America, 1967.

Erben, Karel Jaromir. *South Slavonic Folk-lore Stories*. Translated by Walter Strickland. London: Forder, 1899.

———. *Russian and Bulgarian Folk-lore Stories*. Translated and edited by Walter Strickland. London: Standring, 1907.

———. *Panslavonic Folk-lore in Four Books*. Translated by Walter Strickland. New York: Westermann, 1930.

Erdélyi, Janós. *Ungarische Sagen und Märchen*. Translated by Heinrich Christian Gottlieb Stier. Berlin: F. Dümmler, 1850.

Ey, Karl August. *Harzmärchenbuch: Oder Sagen und Märchen aus dem Oberharze*. Stade: F. Steubel, 1862.

Fabre, Daniel, and Jacques Lacroix. *Histoires et Legendes du Languedoc Mystérieux*. Paris: Georges Kogan, 1970.

Fansler, Dean S. *Filipino Popular Tales*. Lancaster: George E. Stechert, 1921.

Fauset, Arthur. *Folklore from Nova Scotia*. New York: George E. Stechert, 1931.

Fiorentino, Ser Giovanni. *Il Pecorone*. Milan: Giovanni Antonio, 1554. Reprinted and edited by Enzo Esposito. Ravena: Longo, 1974.

Fillmore, Parker. *Czechoslovak Fairy Tales*. Illustrated by Jan Matulka. New York: Harcourt, Brace and Howe, 1919.

———. *The Shoemaker's Apron: Czechoslovak Folk and Fairy Tales*. Illustrated by Jan Taulka. New York: Harcourt, Brace, 1920.

———. *Jugoslav Folk and Fairy Tales*. New York: Harcourt, Brace, 1921.

Fleeson, Katherine Neville. *Laos Folk-lore of Farther India*. Illustrated by W. A. Briggs. New York: Fleming Revell, 1899.

Fleury, Jean-François. *Littérature orale de la Basse-Normandie*. Paris: Maison-neuve, 1883.

Ford, Robert. *Thistledown: A Book of Scotch Humour, Character, Folklore Story and Anecdote*. Paisley: Alexander Gardner, 1891.

Fortier, Alcée. *Bits of Louisiana Folk-Lore*. Baltimore: American Folklore Society, 1888.

Frere, Mary. *Old Deccan Days or Fairy Legends Current in Southern India*. With notes by Sir Bartle Frere. 1868.

Fryer, Alfred Cooper. *Book of English Fairy Tales from the North-Country*. London: W. Swan Sonnenschein, 1884.

———. *Fairy Tales from the Harz Mountains*. London: David Nutt, 1908.

Gaal, György von. *Mährchen der Magyaren*. Vienna: Wallishauser, 1822.

Galland, Antoine. *Les Milles et une nuit*. 12 vols. Vols. 1–4, Paris: Florentin Delaulne, 1704; Vols. 5–7, ibid., 1706; vol. 8, ibid., 1709; vols. 9–10, ibid., 1712; vols. 11–12, Lyon: Briasson, 1717.

Garnett, Lucy. *The Women of Turkey and Their Folk-Lore*. London: David Nutt, 1888.

Gaster, Moses. *Rumanian Bird and Beast Stories*. London: Folk-Lore Society, 1915.

Geldart, Rev. Edmund Martin. *Folk-Lore of Modern Greece*. London: W. Swan Sonnenschein, 1884.

Gerber, Adolph. *Great Russian Animal Tales*. New York: Burt Franklin, 1891.

Gibb, E. J. W. *The History of the Forty Vezirs, or the Story of the Forty Morns and Eves. Written in Turkish by Sheykh-Zada*. New York: Scribner & Welford, 1887.

Glínski, Antoni Józef. *Polish Fairy Tales*. Translated by Maude Ashurst Biggs. London: John Lane, 1920.

Gonzenbach, Laura. *Sicilianische Märchen*. 2 vols. Leipzig: W. Engelmann, 1870.

———. *Beautiful Angiola: The Lost Sicilian Folk and Fairy Tales of Laura Gonzenbach*. Translated by Jack Zipes. New York: Routledge, 2006.

Green, Jesse, ed. *Zuñi: Selected Writings of Frank Hamilton Cushing*. Lincoln: University of Nebraska Press, 1979.

Gregor, Walter. "John Glaick, The Brave Tailor." *The Folk-Lore Journal* 7.2 (1889): 163–65.

Griffin, Gerald. *Tales of the Munster Festivals*. London: Saunders and Otley, 1827.

———. *Tales of the Jury Room*. Dublin: J. Duffy, 1842.

Grimm, Albert Ludwig. *Kindermährchen*. Heidelberg: Morhr und Zimmer, 1808.

———. *Lina's Mährchenbuch*. Frankfurt am Main: Wilmans, 1816.

Grimm, Jacob, and Wilhelm Grimm. *Kinder- und Haus-Märchen. Gesammelt durch die Brüder Grimm*. 2 vols. Berlin: Realschulbuchandlung, 1812/1815.

———. *Kinder- und Hausmärchen gesammelt durch die Brüder Grimm* [1812/1815, Erstausgabe]. Edited by Ulrike Marquardt and Heinz Rölleke. 2 vols. Göttingen: Vandenhoeck & Ruprecht, 1986.

———. *Kinder- und Haus-Märchen. Gesammelt durch die Brüder Grimm.* 2 vols. Berlin: G. Reimer, 1819.

———. *Kinder- und Hausmärchen gesammelt durch die Brüder Grimm* [1819, zweite Ausgabe]. Edited by Heinz Rölleke. 2 vols. Cologne: Diederichs, 1982.

———. *Kinder- und Hausmärchen gesammelt durch die Brüder Grimm.* 7th ed. 3 vols. Göttingen: Verlag der Dieterischen Buchhandlung, 1857.

———. *Kinder- und Hausmärchen gesammelt durch die Brüder Grimm letzter Hand mit Originalenanmerkungen* [1857, siebte Ausgabe]. Edited by Heinz Rölleke. 3 vols. Stuttgart: Philipp Reclam, 1980.

———. *Kinder- und Hausmärchen. Nach der Großen Ausgabe von 1857, textkritisch revidiert, kommentiert und durch Register erschlossen.* Edited by Hans-Jörg Uther. 7th ed. Darmstadt: Wissenschaftliche Buchgesellschaft, 1996.

———. *Kinder- und Hausmärchen der Brüder Grimm: Vollständige Ausgabe in der Urfassung.* Wiesbaden: Emil Vollmer, 1955.

———. *Household Stories from the Collection of the Brothers Grimm.* Translated by Lucy Crane. London: Macmillan, 1882.

———. *The Complete Fairy Tales of the Brothers Grimm* [1987]. Translated and edited by Jack Zipes. 3rd rev. and enlarged ed. New York: Bantam, 2003.

Grimm, Gebrüder, ed. *Deutsche Sagen.* 2 vols. Berlin: Nicolaische Buchhandlung, 1816/1818.

———. *The German Legends of the Brothers Grimm.* Translated and edited by Donald Ward. 2 vols. Philadelphia: Institute for the Study of Human Issues, 1981.

Grierson, George Abraham, ed. and trans. *Hatim's Tales: Kashmiri Stories and Song.* Recorded with the assistance of Pandit Govind Kaul by Aurel Stein, and with a note on the folklore of the tales by William Crooke. London: J. Murray, 1923.

Groome, Francis Hindes. *Gypsy Folk Tales.* London: Hurst and Blackett, 1899.

Grundtvig, Svendt. *Danske Folkeæventyr.* Copenhagen: Reitzels Forlag, 1876–1883.

———. *Fairy Tales from Afar.* Translated by Jane Mulley. London: Hutchison, 1900.

———. *In the Bear's Paws and the Eagle's Claws and Other Fairy Tales.* New York: McLoughlin Brothers, 1909.

———. *Danish Fairy Tales.* Translated by Gustav Hein. New York: Thomas Y. Crowell, 1914.

———. *Danish Fairy Tales.* Translated by J. Grant Cramer. London: Four Seas Company, 1919.

Gubernatis, Angelo. *Le novelline die Santo Stephano.* Turin: A. F. Nego, 1869.

———. *Zoological Mythology or the Legends of Animals.* 2 vols. London: Trübner, 1872.

Guelbenzu, José María. *Cuentos populares españoles.* Madrid: Siruela, 1996–1997. Translated into German by Susanne Lange as *Spanische Hunger und Zaubermärchen.* Frankfurt am Main: Eichborn, 2000.

Guerber, H. A. *Legends of the Rhine*. New York: A. S. Barnes, 1895.

Günther, Marie Alker. *Tales and Legends from the Tyrol*. London: Chapman and Hall, 1874.

Gwyndaf, Robin. *Welsh Folk Tales*. Cardiff: National Museums & Galleries of Wales, 1989.

Hahn, Johann Georg von. *Griechische und albanesische Märchen*. Leipzig: W. Engelmann, 1864.

Haksar, A.N.D. *Shuka Saptati: Seventy Tales of the Parrot*. New Dehli: Harper-Collins, 2000.

Hale, Horatio Emmons. *The Iroquois Book of Rites*. Philadelphia: D. G. Brinton,1883.

Halliwell-Phillipps, James Orchard. *The Nursery Rhymes of England*. London: Percy Society, 1842.

———. *Popular Rhymes & Nursery Tales of England*. London: John Russell Smith, 1849.

Haltrich, Josef. *Deutsche Volksmärchen aus dem Sachsenlande in Siebenburgen*. Berlin: Springer, 1856.

———. *Zur Volkskunde der Siebenburger Sachsen*. Vienna: Graeser, 1885.

Hardy, Philip Dixon. *Legends, Tales, and Stories of Ireland*. Dublin: John Cumming, 1837.

Hartland, Edwin Sydney. *English Fairy and Other Folk Tales*. London: Walter Scott, 1890.

Haupt, Karl. *Sagenbuch der Lausitz*. Leipzig: Wilhelm Engelmann, 1863.

Heiner, Heidi Anne, ed. *The Frog Prince and Other Frog Tales from Around the World*. Lexington: SurLaLune Press, 2010.

———. *Rapunzel and Other Maiden in the Tower Tales from Around the World*. Lexington: SurLaLune Press, 2010.

———. *Sleeping Beauties: Sleeping Beauty and Snow White Tales from Around the World*. Lexington: SurLaLune Press, 2010.

———. *Bluebeard Tales from Around the World: Fairy Tales, Myths, Legends and Other Tales about Dangerous Suitors and Husbands*. Lexington: SurLaLune-Press, 2011.

Henderson, William. *Notes on the Folk-Lore of the Northern Counties of England and the Borders*. London: Longmans, Green, 1879.

Hindes Groome, Francis. *Gypsy Folk-Tales*. London: Hurst and Brackett, 1899.

Hunt, Robert. *Popular Romances of the West of England*. 2 vols. London: John Camden Hotten, 1865.

Hynam, F. Ethel. *The Secrets of the Night and Other Ethonian Tales*. Illustrated by H. Oakes-Jones. London: Elliot Stock, 1899.

Imbriani, Vittorio. *La Novellaja fiorentina*. Livorno: F. Vigo, 1871.

———. *La Novellaja Milanese*. Livorno: F. Vigo, 1877.

Jacobs, Joseph. *English Fairy Tales*. London: David Nutt, 1890.

———. *Celtic Fairy Tales*. London: David Nutt, 1892.

———. *Indian Fairy Tales*. London: David Nutt, 1892.

———. *More Celtic Fairy Tales*. London: David Nutt, 1894.

———. *More English Fairy Tales*. London: David Nutt, 1895.

Jahn, Ulrich. *Hexenwesen und Zauberei in Pommern*. 1886.

———. *Schwänke und Schnurren aus Bauernmund*. 1889.

———. *Volksmärchen aus Pommern und Rügen*. Leipzig: Diederich Soltau's Verlag, 1891.

Jamieson, Robert. *Popular Ballads and Songs from Tradition, Manuscripts and Scarce Editions*. Edinburgh: A. Constable, 1806.

Joisten, Charles. *Contes Populaires du Dauphiné*. Vol. 1. Grenoble: Publications du Musée Dauphinois, 1971.

Jones, Christine, and Jennifer Schacker, eds. *Marvelous Transformations: An Anthology of Fairy Tales and Contemporary Critical Perspectives*. Toronto: Broadview Press, 2013.

Jones, Rev. W. Henry, and Lewis Kropf. *The Folk-Tales of the Magyars: Collected by Kriza, Erdélyi, and Others*. London: Elliot Stock, 1889. A publication of the Folk-Lore Society.

Kennedy, Patrick. *Legendary Fictions of the Irish Celts*. London: Macmillan, 1866.

———. *The Fireside Stories of Ireland*. Dublin: M'Glashan and Gill, 1870.

———. *The Bardic Stories of Ireland*. Dublin: M'Glashan and Gill, 1871.

Knust, Hermann. *Italienische Märchen* in *Jahrbuch für romanische und englische Literatur* VII (1866): 381–401.

Kosch, Marie. *Deutsche Volksmärchen aus Mären*. Kremsier: Druck und Commissionsverlag Heinrich Gusek, 1899.

Kremnitz, Mite. *Roumanian Fairy Tales*. Edited by J. M. Percival. New York: Henry Holt, 1885.

Kuhn, Adalbert, ed. *Märkische Sagen und Märchen*. 2 vols. Berlin: Reimer, 1843.

Kuhn, Adalbert, and W. Schwartz, eds. *Norddeutsche Sagen, Märchen und Gebräuche aus Mecklenburg, Pommern, der Mark, Sachsen, Thüringen, Braunschweig, Hannover, Oldeburg und Westfalen*. Leipzig: Brockhaus, 1848.

Lang, Andrew, ed. *Perrault's Popular Tales*. Oxford: Clarendon, 1888.

———. *The Blue Fairy Book*. London: Longmans, 1889.

———. *The Red Fairy Book*. London: Longmans, 1890.

———. *The Green Fairy Book*. London: Longmans, 1892.

———. *The Yellow Fairy Book*. London: Longmans, 1894.

———. *The Pink Fairy Book*. London: Longmans, 1897.

———. *The Grey Fairy Book*. London: Longmans, 1900.

———. *The Violet Fairy Book*. London: Longmans, 1901.

———. *The Crimson Fairy Book*. London: Longmans, 1903.

———. *The Brown Fairy Book*. London: Longmans, 1904.

———. *The Orange Fairy Book*. London: Longmans, 1906.

———. *The Olive Fairy Book*. London: Longmans, 1907.

————. *The Lilac Fairy Book.* London: Longmans, 1910.

Larmine, William. *West Irish Folk-Tales and Romances.* London: Stock, 1893.

Le Braz, Anatole. *Contes du soleil et de la brume. Paysages de légende; Nuits d'apparitions; Equipées de printemps.* Paris: C. Legrave, 1912.

————. *Contes Bretons.* New York: Henry Holt, 1915.

Lee, Frank Harold. *Folk Tales of All Nations.* London: G. G. Harrap, 1930.

Légot, M. "Le Petit Chaperon Rouge: Version Tourangelle." *Revue de L'Avranchin* 9 (1885): 90–91.

Legrand, Émile. *Recueil de Contes Populaires Grecs.* Paris: Libraire de la Société Asiatique de Paris, 1881.

Leland, Charles Godfrey (Hans Breitmann). *Legends of Florence. Collected from the People and Retold.* London: David Nutt, 1896.

Lemke, Elizabeth. *Volkstümliches in Ostpreussen.* 3 vols. Mohrungen: Harich, 1884–1887.

L'Héritier de Villandon, Marie-Jeanne. *Ouevres meslées.* Paris: J. Guignard, 1696.

————. *La Tour Ténebreuse et Les Jours lumineux.* Paris: Barbin, 1705.

Linderman, Frank B. *Indian Why Stories: Sparks from War Eagle's Lodge-Fire.* Illustrated by Charles M. Russell. New York: Charles Scribner's Sons, 1915.

Lover, Samuel. *Legends and Stories of Ireland.* Dublin: Wakeman, 1831.

Luzel, François-Marie. *Contes Bretons recueillis et traduits.* Quimperlé: Clairet, 1870.

————. "Koadalan, conte populaire breton." *Revue Celtique* (1870–1872): 106–31.

————. *Légendes Chrétiennes de la Basse-Breteagne.* Paris: Maisonneuve, 1881.

————. *Contes populaires de la Basse-Bretagne.* 3 vols. Paris: Maisonneuve et Leclerc, 1887.

————. "Jannac aux Deux Sous." *Mélusine* (September, 1888).

————. *Celtic Folk-Tales from Amorica.* Translated by Derek Bryce. Llanerch, Wales: Llanerch Enterprises, 1985.

————. *Contes Populaires de la Basse-Bretagne. Les Contes de Luzel.* Edited by Françoise Morvan. Rennes: Presses Universitaires de Rennes, 1996.

————. *Contes Bretons. Les Contes de Luzel.* Edited by Françoise Morvan. Rennes: Presses Universitaires de Rennes, 1994.

————. *Contes Inédits. Les Contes de Luzel.* Edited by Françoise Morvan. Vols. 1–3. Rennes: Presses Universitaires de Rennes, 1994–1996.

————. *Contes de Basse-Bretagne.* Edited by Françoise Morvan. Rennes: Éditions Ouest-France, 2007.

Ma, Y. W., and Joseph S. M. Lau. *Traditional Chinese Stories.* New York: Columbia University Press, 1978.

MacGowan, John. *Chinese Folk-Lore Tales.* London: Macmillan, 1910.

Macinnes, Donald. *Folk and Hero Tales.* London: Folk-lore Society, 1890.

Mackenzie, Donald. *Scottish Wonder Tales from Myth and Legend.* New York: Frederick A. Stokes, 1917.

MacManus, Seumas. *In Chimney Corners: Merry Tales of Irish Folk Lore*. New York: McClure, Phillips, 1904.

Magnus, Leonard. *Russian Folk-Tales*. New York: E. P. Dutton, 1916.

Marelle, Charles. *Affenschwanz. Variantes orales de contes populaires et étrangers*. Braunschweig: Westermann, 1888.

Marzocchi, Ciro. *Novelle Popolari Senesi* [1879]. Edited by Aurora Milillo. Rome: Bulzoni, 1992.

Maspero, Gaston. *Popular Stories of Ancient Egypt*. Translated from the fourth French edition by Mrs. C. H. W. Johns. New York: G. P. Putnam's Sons, 1915.

Massignon, Geneviève, ed. *Folktales of France*. Translated by Jacqueline Hyland. Chicago: University of Chicago Press, 1968.

McCulloch, William. *Bengali Household Tales*. London: Hodder and Stoughton, 1912.

McNair, John, and Thomas Barlow. *Oral Tradition from the Indus*. Brighton: Cranbourne Print, 1908.

Megas, Georgios, ed. *Folktales of Greece*. Translated by Helen Colaclides. Chicago: University of Chicago Press, 1970.

Meier, Ernst. *Deutsche Volksmärchen aus Schwaben*. Stuttgart: E. B. Scheitlin's Verlagshandlung, 1852.

Millien, Achille. "La Veillée dans les puits." *Revue des Traditions Populaires* (1886).

————. "Le Petit Chaperon Rouge: Version I de Nièvre." 3 *Mélusine* (1887): 272–73.

————. "Le Petit Chaperon Rouge: Version II de Nièvre." 3 *Mélusine* (1887): 428–29.

————. "La Cendrillon." *Cahiers de Pougues* (1889–1890).

————. "Guillaume-Sans-Peur." *Étrennes Nivernaises* (1896) and later the cycle "L'Homme sans peur." *Revue du Nivernais* (1901–1902).

————. "Il Père Roquelaure" in *Revue des Traditions Populaires* (1908).

————. *Contes de Bourgogne*. Edited by Françoise Morvan. Rennes: Éditions Ouest-France, 2008.

Millien, Achille, and Paul Delarue. *Contes du Nivernais et du Morvan*. Paris: Éditions Érasme, 1953.

Mistral, Frédéric. *Prose d'almanach*. Edited by Pierre Devoluy. Paris: Grasset, 1926.

————. *Nouvelle Prose d'almanach*. Edited by Pierre Devoluy, Paris: Grasset, 1927.

————. *Dernière Prose d'almanach*. Edited by Pierre Devoluy. Paris: Grasset, 1930.

————. *Contes de Provence*. Edited by Françoise Morvan. Rennes: Éditions Ouest-France, 2006.

Mitford, A. B. (Lord Redesdale). *Tales of Old Japan*. 1871.

Monteiro, Mariana. *Legends and Popular Tales of the Basque People.* With illustrations and photographs by Harold Copping. New York: A. C. Armstrong, 1887.

Montgomerie, Norah, and William Montgomerie, eds. *The Folk Tales of Scotland.* Glasgow: Birlinn, 2008.

Mooney, James. *Myths of the Cherokee.* Washington, DC: Government Printing Office, 1900.

Moulis, Adelin. *Contes Merveilleux des Pyrénées.* Verniolle: Éditions de l'Auteur, 1976.

Müllenhoff, Karl. *Sagen, Märchen und Lieder der Herzogtumer Schleswig, Holstein und Lauenburg.* Kiel: Schwesche Buch, 1845.

Münch, Johann Gottlieb. *Das Märhleinbuch für meine lieben Nachbarsleute.* Leipzig: 1799.

Musäus, Johann Karl August. *Volksmärchen der Deutschen.* 5 vols. Gotha, 1782–1787.

Naaké, John, ed. and trans. *Slavonic Fairy Tales.* London: Henry S. King, 1874.

Nemcová, Bozena. *Das goldene Spinnrad.* Leipzig: Gustav Kiepenheuer, 1990.

Nerucci, Gherardo. *Sessanta novella popolari montalesi.* Edited by Roberto Fedi. Milan: Rizzoli, 1977. Based on the edition *Sessanta Novelle Popolari Montalesi* (circondario di Pistoia). Florence: Successori Le Monnier, 1880.

Nino, Antonio de. *Usi e Costumi Abruzzesi: Fiabe.* Florence: Edizione Barbera, 1883.

Nov, Dov. *The Folktales of Israel.* Chicago: University of Chicago Press, 1963.

O'Hanlon, John. *Irish Folk Lore: Traditions and Superstitions of the Country, with Humorous Tales.* Glasgow: Cameron and Ferguson, 1870.

O'Sullivan, Sean, ed. *Folktales of Ireland.* Chicago: University of Chicago Press, 1966.

Ovid. *Metamorphoses.* Translated by Rolf Humphries. Bloomington: Indiana University Press, 1961.

Owen, Elias. *Welsh Folk-Lore: A Collection of Folk-Tales and Legends of North Wales.* 1896.

Ozaki, Yei Theodora. *Japanese Fairy Tales.* New York: Grosset & Dunlap, 1903.

Parker, Catherine. *Australian Legendary Tales.* London: David Nutt, 1896.

Parker, Henry. *Village Folk-Tales of Ceylon.* 3 vols. London: 1910–1914.

Parry, Edith, ed. *The Stories of the Bágh O Bahár.* London: W. H. Allen, 1890.

Parsons, Elsie Clews. *Folk-Lore from the Cape Verde Islands.* Cambridge: George E. Stechert, 1923.

———. *Folk-Lore of the Sea Islands, South Carolina.* Cambridge: George E. Stechert, 1923.

———. *Tewar Tales.* New York: George E. Stechert, 1926.

———. *Kiowa Tales.* New York: George E. Stechert, 1929.

Pedroso, Consiglieri. *Portuguese Folk-Tales.* Translated by Henriqueta Monteiro. London: Folklore Society, 1882.

Pellizzari, Pietro. *Fiabe e canzoni popolari del contado di Maglie in Terra Otranto.* Maglie: Tip. del Collegio Capace, 1881.

Perbosc, Antonin. *Contes de Gascogne.* Edited by Suzanne Cézerac. Paris: Éditions Érasme, 1954.

Percival, J. M. *Roumanian Fairy Tales.* Collected by Mité Kremnitz. New York: Holt, 1885.

Petrovitch, Woislav. *Hero Tales and Legends of the Serbians.* New York: Frederick A. Stokes, 1914.

Pitrè, Giuseppe. *Fiabe, novelle e racconti popolari siciliani.* 4 vols. Palermo: Lauriel, 1875.

———. *Novelle Popolari Toscane.* Florence: G. Babèra, 1885.

———. *The Collected Sicilian Folk and Fairy Tales of Giuseppe Pitrè.* Translated and edited by Jack Zipes and Joseph Russo. 2 vols. New York: Routledge, 2008.

———. *The Swallow Book: The Story of the Swallow Told in Legends, Fables, Folk Songs, Proverbs, Omens, and Riddles of Many Lands.* Translated by Ada Walker Camehl. New York: American Book Company, 1912.

———. ed. *The Bawdy Peasant: A Selection from the Russian Secret Tales Collected by Alexander N. Afanasyev.* Introduction by Gordon Grimley. London: Odyssey Press, 1970.

Polevoi, Peter. *Narodnuiya Russkiya Skazki.* St. Petersburg, 1874.

Pröhle, Heinrich. *Kinder- und Volksmärchen.* Leipzig: Avenarius and Mendelssohn, 1853.

———. *Märchen für die Jugend.* Halle: Verlag der Buchhandlung des Waisenhauses, 1854.

Pulci, Luigi. *Morgante: The Epic Adventures of Orlando and His Giant Friend Morgante.* Translated by Joseph Tusiani with an Introduction by Edoardo Lèbano. Bloomington: Indiana University Press, 1998.

Rak, Michele, ed. *Fiabe campane.* Milan: Mondadori, 1984.

Ralston, William R. S. *Russian Folk-Tales.* London: Smith, Elder, 1873.

Ranke, Kurt, ed. *Folktales of Germany.* Translated by Lotte Baumann. Chicago: University of Chicago Press, 1966.

Redesdale, Lord. *Tales of Old Japan.* London: Macmillan, 1908.

Ritson, Joseph. *Fairy Tales.* London: Payne and Foss, Pall-Mall, and Pickering, 1831.

Robbins, Rossell Hope. *The Hundred Tales: Les Cent Nouvelles.* New York: Crown, 1960.

Rochholz, Ernst Ludwig. *Schweizersagen aus dem Aargau.* 2 vols. Aarau: Druck und Verlag von H. R. Sauerländer, 1856.

Röllecke, Heinz, ed. *Die älteste Märchensammlung der Brüder Grimm.* Cologny-Geneva: Fondation Martin Bodmer, 1975.

———, ed. *Märchen aus dem Nachlaß der Brüder Grimm.* 3rd rev. ed. Bonn: Bouvier, 1983.

————, ed. *Die wahren Märchen der Brüder Grimm.* Frankfurt am Main: Fischer, 1995.

————, ed. *Grimms Märchen und ihre Quellen: Die literarischen Vorlagen der Grimmschen Märchen synoptisch vorgestellt und kommentiert.* Trier: Wissenschaftlicher Verlag Trier, 1998.

————, ed. *Es war einmal . . . Die wahren Märchen der Brüder Grimm und we sie ihnen erzählte.* Illustrated by Albert Schindehütte. Frankfurt am Main: Eichborn, 2011.

Sarnelli, Pompeo. *Posilicheata.* Naples, 1684

Sastri, Natesa. *Tales of Tennalirama: The Famous Court Jester of Southern India.* Madras: G. A. Natesan, 1900.

Schiefner, F. Anton, ed. *Awarische Texte.* St. Petersburg: Kaiserliche Akademie der Wissenschaften, 1873.

————. *Tibetan Tales, Derived from Indian Soures.* Translated by W. R. S. Ralston. London: Trübner, 1892.

Schmidt, Bernhard. *Griechische Märchen, Sagen und Volkslieder.* Leipzig: Teubner, 1877.

Schneller, Christian. *Märchen und Sagen aus Wälschtirol.* Innsbruck: Verlag der Wagner'schen Universitäts-Buchhandlung, 1867.

Schönwerth, Franz Xaver von, ed. *Aus der Oberpfalz—Sitten und Sagen.* Vol. 1. Augsburg: Rieger, 1857.

————. *Aus der Oberpfalz—Sitten und Sagen.* Vol. 2. Augsburg: Rieger, 1858.

————. *Aus der Oberpfalz—Sitten und Sagen.* Vol. 3. Augsburg: Rieger, 1859.

————. *Prinz Rosszwifl und andere Märchen aus der Sammlung von Franz Xaver Von Schönwerth.* Edited by Erika Eichenseer. Regensburg: Morsbach, 2010.

Schott, Arthur, and Albert Schott. *Walachische Märchen.* Stuttgart: J. G. Cotta'scher Verlag, 1845.

Sébillot, Paul, ed. *Contes populaires de la Haute-Bretagne.* Paris: Charpentier, 1880.

————. *Contes des paysans et des pêcheurs.* Vol. 2 of *Contes populaires de la Haute-Bretagne.* Paris: Charpentier, 1881.

————. *Littérature orale de la Haute-Bretagne.* Paris: Maisonneuve, 1881.

————. *Contes des Marins.* Vol. 3 of *Contes Populaires de la Haute-Bretagne.* Paris: 1882.

————. *Contes de terre et de mer.* Paris: Charpentier, 1883.

————. *Contes des provinces de France.* Paris: Léopold Cerf, 1884.

————. *Fairy Legends of the French Provinces.* Edited by J. F. Jameson. Translated by Mrs. M. Carey. New York: Thomas Y. Crowell, 1887.

————. *Littérature Orale de L'Auvergne.* Paris: Maisonneuve, 1898.

————. *Croyances, mythes et legends des pays de France.* Edited by Francis Lacassin. Paris: Omnibus, 2002.

Seignolle, Claude, ed. *Contes, récits et légendes des pays de France.* Paris: Omnibus, 1997.

Seignolle, Claude, and Marie-Charlotte Delmas, eds. *Le Grand Livre des contes populaires de France*. Paris: Omnibus, 2007.

Seiki, Keigo, ed. *Folktales of Japan*. Chicago: University of Chicago Press, 1963.

Simone, Roberto. *Fiabe Campane*. 2 vols. Turin: Einaudi, 1994.

———. *Il presepe popolare napoletano*. Turin: Einaudi, 1998.

Simonsuuri, Lauri, and Pirkko-Liisa Rausmaa, eds. *Finnische Volkserzählungen*. Berlin: Walter de Gruyter, 1968.

Skeat, Walter. *Fables and Folk-Tales from an Eastern Forest*. Illustrated by F. H. Townsend. Cambridge: Cambridge University Press, 1901.

Smithers, Leonard C. *The Transmigrations of the Mandarin Fum-Hoam* (Chinese Tales). London: H. S. Nichols, 1894. (Translation of Thomas Simon Gueulette)

Somadeva. *The Ocean of the Streams of Story: Somadeva's Katha sarit sagara*. Edited by N. M. Penzer. Translated by Charles H. Tawney. 10 vols. Delhi: Motilal Banarsidass, 1968.

Somma, Michele. *Cento Racconti* [1821]. Edited by Patricia Bianchi and Rodolfo Rubino. Naples: Istituto Grafico Editoriale Italiano, 2000.

Spence, Lewis. *Legends and Romances of Brittany*. New York: Frederick A. Stokes, n.d.

Steel, Flora Ann. *Tales of the Punjab. Told by the People*. With illustrations by J. Lockwood Kipling and notes by R. C. Temple. London: Macmillan, 1894.

Steel, Flora Ann, and R. C. Temple. *Wide-Awake Stories: A Collection of Tales Told in the Punjab and Kashmir*. Bombay: Education Society's Press, 1884.

Steere, Edward. *Swahili Tales, as Told by the Natives of Zanibar*. London: Bell and Daldy, 1870.

Stöber, August, ed. *Elsäsisches Volksbüchlein: Kinder-und Volksliedchen, Spielreime, Sprüche und Märchchen*. Straßburg: G. L. Schuler, 1842.

Stokes, Maive. *Indian Fairy Tales*. With notes by Mary Stokes and an Introduction by W. R. S. Ralston. London: 1880.

Straparola, Giovan Francesco. *Le Piacevoli Notti*. 2 vols. Venice: Comin da Trino, 1550/1553.

———. *Le Piacevoli Notti*. Edited by Pastore Stocchi. Rome-Bari: Laterza, 1979.

———. *The Facetious Nights of Straparola*. Translated by William G. Waters. Illustrated by Jules Garnier and E. R. Hughes. 4 vols. London: Lawrence and Bullen, 1894.

———. *The Pleasant Nights*. Edited by Donald Beecher. 2 vols. Toronto: University of Toronto Press, 2012.

Strickland, W. W., ed. and trans., and Karel Jaromir Erben. *Segrius Irritant, or Eight Primitive Folk-Lore Stories*. London: Forder, 1896.

———. *North-West Slav Legends and Fairy Stories: A Sequel to Segrius Irritant*. London: Forder, 1897.

———. *South Slavonic Folk-Lore Stories*. London: Forder, 1899.

———. *Russian and Bulgarian Folk-Lore Stories*. London: G. Standing, 1907.

Strickland, W. W., and Vitzlav Hálek. *Three Stories*. New York: J. Sampson, 1886.

———. *Halek's Stories and Evensongs*. New York: Westermannn, 1930.

Stroebe, Klara. *Nordische Volksmärchen*. Jena: Eugen Diederichs, 1915.

Sutermeister, Otto. *Kinder- und Hausmärchen aus der Schweiz*. Aarau: Sauerländer, 1873.

Swynnerton, Charles, ed. *Romantic Tales from the Panjab*. Westminster: Archibald Constable, 1903.

Tales of Firenzuola, Benedictine Monk of Vallambrosa XVIth Century. New York: Valhalla Books, 1964.

Taylor, Edgar, ed. and trans. *German Popular Stories, Translated from the Kinder und Haus Märchen*. London: C. Baldwin, 1823.

Teit, James. *Traditions of the Thompson River Indians of British Columbia*. Boston: Houghton Mifflin, 1898.

Teit, James, Marian K. Gould, Livingston Farrand, and Herbert Spinden. *Folk-Tales of Salishan and Sahaptin Tribes*. Lancaster: George E. Stechert, 1917.

Tenèze, Marie-Louise, and Georges Delarue. *Nannette Lévesque, conteuse et chanteuse du pays des sources de la Loire. La collecte de Victor Smith 1871–1876*. Paris: Gallimard, 2000.

Teza, E. *La Tradizione dei Sette Savi nelle novelline magiare*. Bologna: Tipi Fava e Garagnani al Progresso, 1864.

Theal, George Mcall. *Kaffir Folk-Lore*. London: Swan Sonnenschein, 1885. (African tales)

Thompson, C. J. S. *The Hand of Destiny: Everyday Folklore and Superstitions*. London: Rider, 1932.

Thorpe, Benjamin, ed. *Northern Mythology, Comprising the Principal Popular Traditions and Superstitions of Scandinavia, North Germany, and the Netherlands*. 3 vols. London: Henry Lumley, 1851.

———. *Yule-Tide Stories: A Collection of Scandinavian and North German Popular Tales and Traditions from the Swedish, German, and Danish*. London: Henry G. Bohn, 1853.

Tomkowiak, Ingrid, and Ulrich Marzolph, eds. *Grimms Märchen International*. 2 vols. Paderborn: Schöningh, 1996.

Tremearne, Arthur. *Hausa-Folk-Tales*. London: J. Bale, Sons & Danielson, 1913.

Tremearne, Marie. *Folk-Lore and Folk-Stories of Wales*. 1909.

Uther, Hans-Jörg, ed. *Märchen vor Grimm*. Munich: Eugen Diederichs Verlag, 1990.

Vernaleken, Theodor. *Alpensagen: Volksüberliefrungen aus der Schweiz, und aus Vorarlbeg, Kärnten, Steiermark, Salzburg, Ober- und Niedersterreich*. Vienna: Seidel, 1858.

———. *Kinder- und Hausmärchen in den Alpenländern*. Vienna: Braumüller, 1863.

———. *Österreichische Kinder- und Hausmärchen*. Vienna: Braumüller, 1864.

————. *In the Land of Marvels: Folktales from Austria and Bohemia*. Translated and with a Preface by Edwin Johnson. London: Swan Sonnenschein, 1884.

Villeneuve, Gabrielle-Suzanne Barbot de. *La jeune Amériquaine et Les Contes marins*. La Haye aux dépes de la Compagnie, 1740.

Visentini, Isaia. *Fiabe mantovane*. Rome: Loescher, 1879.

Webster, Rev. Wentworth. *Basque Legends: Collected Chiefly in the Labourd*. With an essay on the Basque language by M. Julien Vinson. London: Griffith and Farran, 1877.

Werner, E. T. C. *Myths and Legends of China*. London: George G. Harrap, 1922.

Westervelt, William D. *Legends of Ghosts and Ghost-Gods*. Boston: Press of George Ellis, 1915. (Hawaiian mythology)

Wheeler, Post. *Russian Wonder Tales*. New York: Century Company, 1919.

Widter-Wolf, Georg, and Adam Wolf. *Volksmärchen aus Venetien*. In *Jahrbuch für romantische und englische Literatur* VII (1866): 1–36; 121–54; 249–90.

Wilde, Lady Jane Francesca. *Ancient Legends, Mystic Charms, and Superstitions of Ireland*. Boston: Ticknor, 1888.

Wilson, Epiphanius. *Turkish Literature Comprising Fables, Belles-Lettres and Sacred Traditions*. Rev. ed. London: Colonial Press, 1901.

Winther, Mathias. *Danish Folk Tales* (1823). Translated by T. Sands and J. Massengale. Madison: WITS, 1989.

Wolf, Johann Wilhelm. *Niederländische Sagen*. Leipzig: Brockhaus, 1843.

————. *Deutsche Märchen und Sagen*. Leipzig: Brockhaus, 1845.

————. *Deutsche Hausmärchen*. Göttingen: Dieterich'sche Buchhandlung, 1851. (Republished as *Verschollene Märchen*. Nordlingen: Franz Greno, 1988.)

————. *Märchen, Sagen und Lieder aus Hessen*. Darmstadt: 1851.

————. *Hessische Sagen*. Göttingen: Dieterich, 1853.

Wratislaw, Albert Henry. *Sixty Folk-Tales from Exclusively Slavonic Sources*. Boston: Houghton, Mifflin, 1890.

Xenophontovna Kalamatiano de Blumenthal, Verra. *Folk Tales from the Russian*. Chicago: Rand, McNally, 1903.

Yeats, William. *Fairy and Folk Tales of the Irish Peasantry*. London: W. Scott, 1888.

Young, Ella. *Celtic Wonder-Tales*. Dublin: Maunsel, 1910.

Zaunert, Paul. *Deutsche Märchen aus dem Donaulande*. Jena: Diederichs, 1923.

Zingerle, Ignaz. *Sagen aus Tirol*. Innsbruck: Wagner, 1891.

Zingerle, Ignaz, and Joseph Zingerle. *Tirols Volksdichtungen und Volksgebräuche*. 2 vols. Innsbruck: Verlag der Wagner'schen Buchhandlung, 1852–1854.

————. *Kinder- und Hausmärchen aus Süddeutschland*. Regensburg: Pustet, 1854.

Zingerle, Joseph. "Die faule Katl." *Zeitschrift für Deutsche Mythologie und Sittenkunde* 2 (1855): 364–67.

Zipes, Jack, ed. *Beauties, Beasts, and Enchantment: French Classical Fairy Tales.* New York: New American Library, 1989.

———, ed. *Spells of Enchantment: The Wondrous Fairy Tales of Western Culture.* New York: Viking, 1991.

Reference Works and Criticism

Aarne, Antti. *The Types of the Folktales. A Classification and Bibliography.* Rev. and enlarged by Stith Thompson. Helsinki: Suomalainen Tiedeakatemia, 1961.

Addy, Sidney Oldall. *The Evolution of the English House.* London: Sonnenschein, 1898.

Anderson, Graham. *The Fairytale in the Ancient World.* Routledge, 2000.

Barzilai, Shuli. *Tales of Bluebeard and His Wives from Late Antiquity to Postmodern Times.* London: Routledge, 2009.

Bausinger, Hermann. "'Historisierende' Tendenzen im deutschen Märchen seit der Romantik. Requisitenverschiebung und Requisitenerstarrung." *Wirkendes Wort* 10 (1960): 279–86.

———. *Märchen, Phantasie und Wirklichkeit.* Frankfurt am Main: dipa-Verlag, 1987.

Baycroft, Timothy, and David Hopkin, eds. *Folklore and Nationalism in Europe during the Long Nineteenth Century.* Leiden: Brill, 2012.

Beckett, Sandra. *Recycling Red Riding Hood.* New York: Routledge, 2002.

———. *Red Riding Hood for All Ages: A Fairy-Tale Icon in Cross-Cultural Contexts.* Detroit: Wayne State University Press, 2008.

Bendix, Regina. *In Search of Authenticity: The Formation of Folklore Studies.* Madison: Wisconsin University Press, 1997.

Berendsohn, Walter A. *Grundformen volkstümlicher Erzählkunst in den Kinder- und Hausmärchen der Brüder Grimm.* 2nd rev. ed. Wiesbaden: Sändig, 1968.

Berlioz, Jacques, Claude Bremond, and Catherine Velay-Vallentin, eds. *Formes médiévales du conte merveilleux.* Paris: Stock, 1989.

Böhm-Korff, Regina. *Deutung und Bedeutung von "Hänsel und Gretel."* Frankfurt am Main: Peter Lang, 1991.

Bolte, Johannes, and George Polivka. *Anmerkungen zu den "Kinder- und Hausmärchen."* 5 vols. Leipzig: Dieterich, 1913–1918; reprint: Hildesheim: Georg Olms, 1963.

Bolte, Johannes, and Lutz Mackensen. *Handworterbuch des deutschen Märchens.* Berlin: W. de Gruyter, 1931.

Brednich, Rolf Wilhelm, ed. *Enzyklopädie des Märchens.* 11 vols. Berlin: Walter de Gruyter, 1977–2012.

Bürger, Christa. "Die soziale Funktion volkstümlicher Erzählformen—Sage und Märchen." *Projekt Deutschunterricht 1.* Edited by Heinz Ide. Stuttgart: Metzler, 1971. 26–56.

Calabrese, Stefano. *Gli arabeschi della fiaba dal Basile ai romantici*. Pisa: Pacini, 1984.

———. *Fiaba*. Florence: La Nuova Italia, 1997.

Calaresu, Melissa, Filippo de Vivo, and Joan-Paul Rubés, eds. *Exploring Cultural History: Essays in Honor of Peter Burke*. Farnham: Ashgate, 2010.

Campbell, Matthew, and Michael Perraudin, eds. *The Voice of the People: Writing the European Folk Revival, 1760–1914*. New York: Anthem, 2012.

Canepa, Nancy L. *From Court to Forest: Giambattista Basile's Lo cunto de li cunti and the Birth of the Literary Fairy Tale*. Detroit: Wayne State University Press, 1999.

Clodd, Edward. "The Philosophy of Rumpelstiltskin." *Folklore Journal* 7 (1889): 135–63.

———. *Tom Tit Tot: An Essay on Savage Philosophy in Folk-Tales*. London: Duckworth, 1898.

Cocchiara, Giuseppe. *Storia del folklore in Europa. Collezione di studi religiosi, etnologici e psicologici 20*. Turin: Einaudi, 1954.

———. *The History of Folklore in Europe*. Translated by John McDaniel. Philadelphia: Institute for the Study of Human Issues, 1981.

Davidson, Hilda Ellis, and Anna Chaudhri, eds. *A Companion to the Fairy Tale*. Cambridge: D. S. Brewer, 2003.

Dégh, Linda. *Folktales and Society. Storytelling in a Hungarian Peasant Community*. Translated by Emily M. Schlossberg. Bloomington: Indiana University Press, 1969.

———. "Grimm's Household Tales and Its Place in the Household: The Social Relevance of a Controversial Classic." *Western Folklore* 38 (1979): 83–103.

———. "What Did the Grimm Brothers Give to and Take from the Folk?" *The Brothers Grimm and Folktale*. Edited by James McGlathery. Urbana: University of Illinois Press, 1988. 66–90.

Delarue, Paul. "Les Contes merveilleux de Perrault et la tradition populaire." *Bulletin Folklorique d'Ile-de-France* 12 (1951): 221–28, 251–61, 283–91.

Denecke, Ludwig. *Jacob Grimm und sein Bruder Wilhelm*. Stuttgart: Metzler, 1971.

Denecke, Ludwig, ed. *Brüder Grimm Gedenken*. Vol. 2. Marburg: Elwert, 1975.

———, ed. *Brüder Grimm Gedenken*. Vol. 3. Marburg: Elwert, 1981.

———, ed. *Brüder Grimm Gedenken*. Vol. 4. Marburg: Elwert, 1984.

———, ed. *Brüder Grimm Gedenken*. Vol. 5. Marburg: Elwert, 1985.

———, ed. *Brüder Grimm Gedenken*. Vol. 6. Marburg: Elwert, 1986.

———, ed. *Brüder Grimm Gedenken*. Vol. 7. Marburg: Elwert, 1987.

Denecke, Ludwig, and Ina-Maria Greverus, eds. *Brüder Grimm Gedenken*. Vol. 1. Marburg: Elwert, 1963.

Dundes, Alan, ed. *Cinderella: A Folklore Casebook*. New York: Garland, 1982.

————. "The Psychoanalytic Study of the Grimms' Tales with Special Reference to 'The Maiden without Hands' (AT 706)." *The Germanic Review* 42 (Spring 1987): 50–65.

————, ed. *The Study of Folklore*. Englewood Cliffs: Prentice Hall, 1962.

————, ed. *Little Red Riding Hood: A Casebook*. Madison: University of Wisconsin Press, 1989.

————. *Holy Writ: The Bible as Folklore*. Lanham: Rowman & Littlefield, 1999.

Ellis, John. *One Fairy Story Too Many: The Brothers Grimm and Their Tales*. Chicago: University of Chicago Press, 1983.

Erixon, Sigurd, ed. *Papers of the International Congress of European and Western Ethnology 1951*. Stockholm: 1951.

Escarpit, Denise. *Histoire d'un conte: Le Chat Botté en France et en Angleterre*. 2 vols. Paris: Didier, 1985.

Falassi, Alessandro. *Folklore by the Fireside: Text and Context of the Tuscan Veglia*. Austin: University of Texas Press, 1980.

Falnes, Oscar. *National Romanticism in Norway*. New York: Columbia University Press, 1933.

Fehling, Detlev. *Amor und Psyche: Die Schöpfung des Apuleius und ihre Einwirkung auf das Märchen*. Wiesbaden: Steiner, 1977.

Franci, Giovanna, and Ester Zago. *La bella addormentata. Genesi e metamorfosi di una fiaba*. Bari: Dedalo, 1984.

Fränkel, Ludwig. "Wolf, Johann Wilhlem." In *Allgemeine Deutsche Biographie (ADB)* Vol. 43. Leipzig: Duncker & Humblot, 1898. 765–77.

Genardiere, Claude de la. *Encore un Conte? Le Petit Chaperon Rouge à L'Usage des Adultes*. Nancy: Presses Universitaires de Nancy, 1993.

Ginschel, Gunhild. *Der junge Jacob Grimm*. Berlin: Akademie Verlag, 1967.

Giudice, Luisa Del, and Gerald Porter, eds. *Imagined States: Nationalism, Utopia, and Longing in Oral Cultures*. Logan: Utah State University Press, 2001.

Goldberg, Christine. *The Tale of the Three Oranges*. Helsinki: Academia Scientiarum Fennica, 1997.

————. "The Donkey Skin Folktale Cycle (AT 501B)." *Journal of American Folklore* 110 (Winter 1997): 28–46.

Grätz, Manfred. *Das Märchen in der deutschen Aufklärung. Vom Feenmärchen zum Volksmärchen*. Stuttgart: Metzler, 1988.

Grimm, Jacob. *Circular wegen Aufsammlung der Volkspoesie* [1815]. Edited by Ludwig Denecke, with an Afterword by Kurt Ranke. Kassel: Brüder-Grimm Museum, 1968.

————. *Deutsche Mythologie*. Göttingen: Dieterich'sche Buchhandlung, 1835.

Groome, Francis Hindes. *Gypsy Folk Tales*. London: Hurst and Blackett, 1899.

Hamman, A.-G. *L'Epopée du Livre: La transmission des textes anciens, du scribe à l'imprimerie*. Paris: Perrin, 1985.

Haney, Jack. *An Introduction to the Russian Folktale*. Armonk: M. E. Sharpe, 1999.

Hannon, Patricia. *Fabulous Identities: Women's Fairy Tales in Seventeenth-Century France*. Amsterdam: Rodopi, 1998.

Harf-Lancner, Laurence. *Les Fées au Moyen Age: Morgane et Mélusine. La naissance des fées*. Paris: Honoré Champion, 1984.

Hartland, Edwin Sidney. *The Legend of Perseus: A Study of Tradition in Story, Custom and Belief*. 3 vols. London: David Nutt, 1894.

Hearne, Betsy Gould. *Beauty and the Beast: Visions and Revisions of an Old Tale*. Chicago: University of Chicago Press, 1989.

Hennig, Dieter, and Bernhard Lauer, eds. *Die Brüder Grimm. Dokumente ihres Lebens und Wirkens*. Kassel: Weber & Weidemeyer, 1985.

Hermansson, Casie. *Bluebeard: A Reader's Guide to the English Tradition*. Jackson: University Press of Mississippi, 2009.

Herranen, Gun. "'The Maiden without Hands' (AT 706)." *D'un Conte à l'autre: La variabilité dans la littérature orale*. Edited by Veronika Gorog-Karady. Paris: 1987. 105–15.

Hetmann, Frederik. "Die mündlichen Quellen der Grimms oder die Rolle der Geschichtenerzähler in den Kinder- und Hausmärchen." *The Germanic Review* 42 (Spring 1987): 83–89.

Hobsbawm, Eric, and Terrence Ranger, eds. *The Invention of Tradition*. Cambridge: Cambridge University Press, 1983.

Holbek, Bengt. *Interpretation of Fairy Tales: Danish Folklore in a European Perspective*. Helsinki: Academia Scientarium Fennica, 1987.

Hopkin, David. *Voices of the People in Nineteenth-Century France*. Cambridge: Cambridge University Press, 2012.

Hult, Marta Hvam. *Framing a National Narrative: The Legend Collections of Peter Christen Asbjørnsen*. Detroit: Wayne State University Press, 2003.

Jolles, André. *Einfache Formen*. Tübingen: Niemeyer, 1958.

Jones, Steven Swann. *The Fairy Tale: The Magic Mirror of Imagination*. New York: Twayne, 1995.

Kamenetsky, Christa. *The Brothers Grimm and Their Critics: Folktales and the Quest for Meaning*. Athens: Ohio University Press, 1992.

Karlinger, Felix, ed. *Wege der Märchenforschung*. Darmstadt: Wissenschaftliche Buchgesellschaft, 1973.

———. *Grundzüge einer Geschichte des Märchens im deutschen Sprachraum*. Darmstadt: Wissenschaftliche Buchgesellschaft, 1983.

Kvideland, Reimund. "The Collecting and Study of Tales in Scandinavia." In *A Companion to the Fairy Tale*. Edited by Hilda Ellis Davidson and Anna Chaudhri. Cambridge: D. S. Brewer, 2003. 159–68.

Laiblin, Wilhelm, ed. *Märchenforschung und Tiefenpsychologie*. Darmstadt: Wissenschaftliche Buchgesellschaft, 1969.

Landry, Tristan. *La mémoire du conte folklorique de l'oral à l'ecrit: Les frères Grimm et Afanas'ev*. Saint-Nicolas: Les Presses de L'Université Laval, 2005.

Lauer, Bernhard, ed. *Rapunzel: Traditionen eines euopäischen Märchenstoffes in Dichtung und Kunst*. Kassel: Brüder Grimm-Museum, 1993.

Leavy, Barbara Fass. *In Search of the Swan Maiden: A Narration on Folklore and Gender*. New York: New York University Press, 1994.

Leerssen, Jeep. *National Thought in Europe: A Cultural History*. Amsterdam: Amsterdam University Press, 2006.

Lindahl, Carl et al. *Medieval Folklore: A Guide to Myths, Legends, Tales, Beliefs, and Customs*. Oxford: Oxford University Press, 2002.

Lüthi, Max. *Das europäische Volksmärchen*. 2nd rev. ed. Bern: Francke, 1960.

———. *Volksmärchen und Volkssage*. 2nd rev. ed. Bern: Francke, 1966.

———. *Once Upon a Time. On the Nature of Fairy Tales*. Translated by Lee Chadeayne and Paul Gottwald. New York: Ungar, 1970.

———. *Das Volksmärchen als Dichtung*. Cologne: Diederichs, 1975.

———. *The European Folktale: Form and Nature*. Translated by John D. Niles. Philadelphia: Institute for the Study of Human Issues, 1982.

Mackensen, Lutz, and Johannes Bolte. *Handwörterbuch des deutschen Märchens*. Berlin: W. de Gruyter, 1930–1940.

Marin, Louis. *Food for Thought*. Translated by Mette Hjort. Baltimore: Johns Hopkins University Press, 1989.

———. "Puss-in-Boots: Power of Signs—Signs of Power." *Diacritics* 7 (Summer 1977): 54–63.

———. *La parole mangée et autres essais théologico-politiques*. Paris: Meridiens Klincksieck, 1986.

Martin, Ann. *Red Riding Hood and the Wolf in Bed: Modernism's Fairy Tales*. Toronto: University of Toronto Press, 2006.

Mazzacurati, Giancarlo. "Sui materiali in opera nelle Piacevoli Notti di Giovan Francesco Straparola" and "La Narrativa di Giovan Francesco Straparola: sociologia e structura del personaggio fiabesco." *Società e strutture narrative dal Trecento al Cinquencento*. Naples: Liguori, 1971.

Mieder, Wolfgang. "Survival Forms of 'Little Red Riding Hood' in Modern Society." *International Folklore Review: Folklore Studies from Overseas* 2 (1982): 23–40.

———. *Tradition and Innovation in Folk Literature*. Hanover: University Press of New England, 1987.

———. "Grimm Variations: From Fairy Tales to Modern Anti-Fairy Tales." *The Germanic Review* 42 (Spring 1987): 90–102.

———. *Hänsel und Gretel: Das Märchen in Kunst, Musik, Literatur, Medien und Karikaturen*. Vienna: Praesens Verlag, 2007.

Naithani, Sadhana. *In Quest of Indian Folktales: Pandit Ram Gharib Chaube and William Crooke*. Bloomington: Indiana University Press, 2006.

Ong, Walter. *Orality and Literacy*. London: Methuen, 1982.

Orenstein, *Little Red Riding Hood Uncloaked: Sex, Morality, and the Evolution of a Fairy Tale*. New York: Basic Books, 2002.

Philippson, Ernst. *Der Märchentypus von König Drosselbart*. Folklore Fellows Communications N. 50. Helsinki: Academia Scientiarum Fennica, 1923.

Propp, Vladimir. *Morphology of the Folktale*. Edited by Louis Wagner and Alan Dundes. Translated by Laurence Scott. 2nd rev. ed. Austin: University of Texas Press, 1968.

———. "Les Transformations des Contes Fantastiques." *Théorie de la littérature*. Edited by Tzvetan Todorov. Paris: Seuil, 1965. 234–62.

———. *Theory and History of Folklore*. Translated by Adriadna Y. Martin and Richard P. Martin. Edited by Anatoly Liberman. Minneapolis: University of Minnesota Press, 1984.

Ranke, Kurt. *Die zwei Brüder: Eine Studie zur vergleichenden Märchenforschung*. Helsinki: Academia Scientiarum Fennica, 1934.

———. "Der Einfluß der Grimmischen 'Kinder- und Hausmärchen' auf das volkstümliche deutsche Erzählgut." *Papers of the International Congress of Western Ethnology*. Edited by Sigurd Erixon. Stockholm: International Commission on Folk Arts and Folklore, 1951. 126–35.

———. "Betrachtungen zum Wesen und Funktion des Märchens." *Studium Generale* 11 (1958): 647–64.

———. "Der Einfluß der Grimmschen Kinder- und Hausmärchen auf das volkstümliche deutsche Erzählgut." In *Die Welt der Einfachen Formen: Studien zur Motiv-, Work- und Quellenkunde*. Edited by Kurt Ranke. Berlin: Walter de Gruyter, 1978. 79–91.

Rearick, Charles. *Beyond the Enlightenment: Historians and Folklore in Nineteenth Century France*. Bloomington: Indiana University Press, 1974.

Richter, Dieter. *Schlaraffenland. Geschichte einer populären Phantasie*. Cologne: Eugen Diederichs, 1984.

Riordan, James. "Russian Fairy Tales and Their Collectors." In *A Companion to the Fairy Tale*. Edited by Hilda Ellis Davidson and Anna Chaudhri. Cambridge: D. S. Brewer, 2003. 217–26.

Roberts, Warren E. *The Tale of the Kind and the Unkind Girls: AA-TH 480 and Related Titles*. Detroit: Wayne State University Press, 1994.

Röhrich, Lutz. *Gebärden—Metapher—Parodie*. Düsseldorf: Schwann, 1967.

———. *Märchen und Wirklichkeit*. Wiesbaden: Steiner, 1974.

———. *Sagen und Märchen. Erzählforschung heute*. Freiburg: Herder, 1976.

———. "Der Froschkönig." *Das selbstverständliche Wunder: Beiträge germanistischer Märchenforschung*. Edited by Wilhelm Solms. Marburg: Hitzeroth, 1986. 7–41.

———. *Wage es, den Frosch zu küssen: Das Grimmsche Märchen Nummer Eins in seinen Wandlungen*. Cologne: Eugen Diederichs Verlag, 1987.

————. "Dragon." In *Medieval Folklore: A Guide to Myths, Legends, Tales, Beliefs, and Customs*. Edited by Carl Lindahl et al. Oxford: Oxford University Press, 2002. 101.

Rölleke, Heinz, ed. "Texte, die beinahe 'Grimms Märchen' geworden wären." *Zeitschrift für deutsche Philologie* 102 (1983): 481–500.

————. *Die Märchen der Brüder Grimm*. Munich: Artemis, 1985.

————. "Wo das Wünschen noch geholfen hat." *Gesammelte Aufsätze zu den "Kinder- und Hausmärchen" der Brüder Grimm*. Bonn: Bouvier, 1985.

————. "Die 'Kinder- und Hausmärchen' der Brüder Grimm in neuer Sicht." *Diskussion Deutsch* 91 (October 1986): 458–64.

Rooth, Anna Birgitta. *The Cinderella Cycle*. Lund: Gleerup, 1951.

Rumpf, Marianne. *Ursprung und Entstehung von Warn- und Schreckmärchen*. Folklore Fellows' Communcations 160. Helsinki: Suomalainen Tiedeakatemia/Academia Scientificarum Fennica, 1955.

Schacker, Jennifer. *National Dreams: The Remaking of Fairy Tales in Nineteenth-Century England*. Philadelphia: University of Pennsylvania Press, 2003.

Schenda, Rudolf. *Volk ohne Buch*. Frankfurt am Main: Klostermann, 1970.

————. *Die Leserstoffe der Kleinen Leute*. Munich: Beck, 1976.

————. "Folkloristik und Sozialgeschichte." *Erzählung und Erzählforschung im 20. Jahrhundert*. Edited by Rolf Kloepfer and Gisela Janetke-Dillner. Stuttgart: Kohlhammer, 1981. 441–48.

————. "Alphabetisierung und Literasierung in Westeuropa im 18. und 19. Jahrhundert." *Sozialer und kultureller Wandel der ländlichen Welt des 18. Jahrhunderts*. Edited by Ernst Hinrichs and Günter Wiegelmann. Wolfenbüttel: Herzog August Bibliothek, 1982. 1–20.

————. "Mären von deutschen Sagen. Bemerkungen zur Produktion 'Volkserzählungen' zwischen 1850 und 1870." *Geschichte und Gesellschaft* 9 (1983): 26–48.

————. "Volkserzählung und nationale Identität: Deutsche Sagen im Vormärz." *Fabula* 25 (1984): 296–303.

————. "Volkserzählung und Sozialgeschichte." *Il Confronto Lettario* 1.2 (1984): 265–79.

————. "Orale und literarische Kommunikationsformen im Bereich von Analphabeten und Gebildeten im 17. Jahrhundert." *Literatur und Volk im 17. Jahrhundert. Probleme populärer Kultur in Deutschland*. Edited by Wolfgang Brückner, Peter Blickle, and Dieter Breuer. Wiesbaden: Harrasowitz, 1985. 447–64.

————. "Vorlesen: Zwischen Analphabetentum und Bücherwissen." *Bertelsmann Briefe* 119 (1986): 5–14.

————. "Telling Tales—Spreading Tales: Change in the Communicative Forms of a Popular Genre." *Fairy Tales and Society. Illusion, Allusion, and Paradigm*. Edited by Ruth B. Bottigheimer. Philadelphia: University of Pennsylvania Press, 1986.

————. *Folklore e Letteratura Popolare: Italia—Germania—Francia*. Rome: Istituto della Enciclopedia Italiana, 1986.

————. *Von Mund zu Ohr: Baustein zu einer Kulturgeschichte volkstümlichen Erzählens in Europa*. Göttingen: Vandenhoeck & Ruprecht, 1993.

Scherf, Walter. *Das Märchen Lexikon*. 2 vols. Munich: Beck, 1995.

Schlauch, Margaret. *Chaucer's Constance and Accused Queens*. New York: New York University Press, 1927.

Schmidt, Ernst, ed. *Briefwechsel der Brüder Grimm mit nördischen Gelehrten*. Berlin: F. Dümmlers, 1885.

Schödel, Siegfried, ed. *Märchenanalysen*. Stuttgart: Reclam, 1977.

Schoof, Wilhelm. *Zur Entstehungsgeschichte der Grimmschen Märchen*. Hamburg: Hauswedell, 1959.

Seitz, Gabriele. *Die Brüder Grimm. Leben—Werk—Zeit*. Munich: Winkler, 1984.

Seifert, Lewis C. *Fairy Tales, Sexuality, and Gender in France, 1690–1715: Nostalgic Utopias*. Cambridge: University of Cambridge Press, 1996.

Siegmund, Wolfdietrich, ed. *Antiker Mythos in unseren Märchen*. Kassel: Röth-Verlag, 1984.

Sielaff, Erich. "Zum deutschen Volksmärchen." *Der Bibliothekar* 12 (1952): 816–29.

————. "Bemerkungen zur kritischen Aneignung der deutschen Volksmärchen." *Wissenschaftliche Zeitschrift der Universität Rostock* 2 (1952/1953): 241–301.

Sokolov, Y. M. *Russian Folklore*. Translated by Catherine Ruth Smith. Hatboro: Folklore Associates, 1966.

Soriano, Marc. *Les Contes de Perrault. Culture savante et traditions populaires*. Paris: Gallimard, 1968.

Suhrbier, Hartwig. *Blaubarts Geheimnis*. Cologne: Eugen Diederichs, 1984.

Tatar, Maria M. "From Nags to Witches: Stepmothers in the Grimms' Fairy Tales." *Opening Texts: Psychoanalysis and the Culture of the Child*. Edited by Joseph H. Smith and William Kerrigan. Baltimore: Johns Hopkins University Press, 1985. 28–41.

————. *The Hard Facts of the Grimms' Fairy Tales*. Princeton: Princeton University Press, 1987.

————. *Off with Their Heads: Fairy Tales and the Culture of Childhood*. Princeton: Princeton University Press, 1992.

————. *Secrets beyond the Door: The Story of Bluebeard and His Wives*. Princeton: Princeton University Press, 2004.

Tenèze, Marie Louise, ed. *Approches de nos traditions orales*. Paris: Maisonneuve et Larose, 1970.

Thompson, Stith. *Motif Index of Folk Literature*. 6 vols. 1932–1936. Bloomington: University of Indiana Press, 1955.

———. *The Folktale*. New York: Holt Rinehart & Winston, 1946.

Velay-Vallantin, Catherine. "Le miroir des contes. Perrault dans les Bibliothèques bleues." *Les usages de l'imprimé*. Edited by Roger Chartier. Paris: Fayard, 1987. 129–85.

———. *L'histoire des contes*. Paris: Fayard, 1992.

Velten, Harry. "The Influence of Charles Perrault's Contes de ma Mère L'Oie on German Folklore." *The Germanic Review* 5 (1930): 14–18.

Verdi, Laura. *Il regno incantato: Il contesto sociale e culturale della fiaba in Europa*. Padua: Centro studi sociologia religiosa di Padova, 1980.

Verdier, Gabrielle. "Les Contes de fées." *Actes de Las Vegas: Théorie dramatique, Théophile de Viau, Les Contes de fées*. Edited by Marie-France Hilgar. Paris: Papers on French Seventeenth-Century Literature, 1991.

———. "Figures de la conteuse dans les contes de fées feminins." *XVIIe Siècle* 180 (1993): 481–99.

Verdier, Yvonne. "Grand-méres, si vous saviez: Le Petit Chaperon Rouge dans la tradition orale." *Cahiers de Littérature Orale* 4 (1978): 17–55.

Volkmann, Helga, and Ulrich Freund, eds. *Der Froschkönig . . . . und andere Erlösungsbedürftige*. Baltmannsweiler: Schneider Verlag Hohengehren, 2000.

Warner, Marina. *From the Beast to the Blonde: On Fairy Tales and Their Tellers*. London: Chatto & Windus, 1995.

———. *No Go the Bogeyman: Scaring, Lulling, and Making Mock*. London: Chatto & Windus, 1998.

Woeller, Waltraut. *Der soziale Gehalt und die soziale Funktion der deutschen Volksmärchen*. Habilitations-Schrift der Humboldt-Universität zu Berlin, 1955.

Wolfzettel, Friedrich. "La lutte contre les mères: Quelques exemples d'une valorisation émancipatrice du conte de fées au dix-huitième siècle." *Réception et identification du conte depuis le moyen âge*. Edited by Michel Zink and Xavier Ravier. Toulouse: Université de Toulouse-Le Mirail, 1987. 123–31.

Zago, Esther. "Some Medieval Versions of Sleeping Beauty: Variations on a Theme." *Studi Francesci* 69 (1979): 417–31.

———. "La Belle au Bois Dormant: Sens et Structure." *Cermeil* 2 (February, 1986): 92–96.

Zipes, Jack. *Breaking the Magic Spell: Radical Theories of Folk and Fairy Tales*. London: Heinemann, 1979.

———. *The Trials and Tribulations of Little Red Riding Hood: Versions of the Tale in Socio-Cultural Context*. South Hadley: Bergin & Garvey, 1983; 2nd rev. ed. New York: Routledge, 1993.

———. *Fairy Tales and the Art of Subversion. The Classical Genre for Children and the Process of Civilization*. London: Heinemann, 1983.

———. *The Brothers Grimm: From Enchanted Forests to the Modern World*. New York: Routledge, 1988.

————. *Fairy Tale as Myth/Myth as Fairy Tale*. Lexington: University Press of Kentucky, 1994.

————. *Happily Ever After: Fairy Tales, Children, and the Culture Industry*. New York: Routledge, 1997.

————. *When Dreams Came True: Classical Fairy Tales and Their Tradition*. New York: Routledge, 1999.

————, ed. *The Oxford Companion to Fairy Tales: The Western Fairy Tale Tradition from Medieval to Modern*. Oxford: Oxford University Press, 2000.

————. *The Irresistible Fairy Tale: The Cultural and Social History of a Genre*. Princeton: Princeton University Press, 2012.